I0831310

The Best of Times

Volume 5: The DeLaine Reynolds Journey

Cover Art: Andrea Brooke Cox

Dedicated To My Parents

Roy Rogers & Donna Rogers Lutenbacher

Thanks for the unconventional childhood,
for always loving me and making sure I knew it
and teaching me to be a good person above everything else!

Message from the author

Dear Trusted Reader,

As DeLaine's story begins to evolve and mature, so do the themes in her life. I want to take a quick moment to state, that as an author of fiction, I am constantly developing traits and aspects about characters that aren't always desirable.

I have touched on some mature themes in previous volumes and I will continue to do so in subsequent volumes as the main characters age, just as real people do when they go from childhood, into their teens and beyond. As such, this volume touches on many mature themes that I feel need to be disclosed.

Alcoholism and addiction, teen sexuality and pregnancy, as well as teen suicide are explored in this next part of DeLaine's journey. I hope that my story opens up conversations about all of these topics with my readers. Kids in the 1980's truly dealt with much the same pressures and insecurities of any generation.

Derogatory terms are used throughout to lend credence and authenticity to the characters. They do not reflect my personal beliefs or opinions.

As always, if you feel led, please remember to support your favorite indie authors, musicians and artists through social media and reviews!

~SR

The Best of Times: Prologue

If misery loves company, then it had been throwing a party for me on a daily basis!

Since moving to Oklahoma City, only three months earlier, I'd lived in two different houses, worked at my parents' restaurant almost daily, been left in a house with no food and been made fun of, shunned and left to redo my sixth-grade education as an eighth grader!

I absolutely hated my existence since being forced to leave in the middle of possibly the best school year of my entire life!

I had been devastated to leave my hometown of Wichita Falls, Texas because I had to leave the most important people in my life, my best friend, Bailey Rains and the boy I loved with my whole heart, Kevin Strong. I missed Bailey's boyfriend, Levi and I even missed my ex-boyfriend, Jax!

I didn't want to breathe some days because I longed to see all of them so much. I thought about them every day and missed each one more than I thought a person could miss anything.

Bailey had been the closest friend I'd ever had in my entire life. She was beautiful, cool and believed in me! More than that she made me believe in me!

I'd never had a friend who seemed to breathe life into me by simply being there. I wrote to her every single day and mailed my letters to her twice a week. She was doing the same.

Kevin had been my deranged, oldest, step-brother's best friend. We had such a complicated relationship, but it didn't matter to me most of the time as long as I got to be around him. That couldn't happen until my oldest, step-brother was no longer a threat. I loved Kevin with every fiber of my being, though.

I never would have had any of them in my life if it weren't for April 10, 1979 or as everyone in Wichita Falls called that day, Terrible Tuesday. A huge tornado destroyed my entire world that day, upending everything I'd ever known!

The following school year we had to go to school inside the high school. It felt as if we got to be high school students for a whole year even though we were only 13. Our school was finally completed, and we entered eighth grade in the newly constructed Milam Junior High as the first eighth grade class.

We had literally ruled the school. We felt much older than the regular eighth grade classes after spending a year at Samson High.

For the first time in my life, I felt like I was somewhat normal. That ended after Christmas, when we found out we were leaving, and moving to the God-forsaken world of Oklahoma City. We had been promised trips back to Wichita Falls on weekends to visit our friends, but by the beginning of April, I knew that was just a pipe dream. It proved true and the first possible time I would have to go to Wichita Falls would be at the end of the school year, when my oldest step-brother, Geoffrey, drove down to pick up my younger step-sister, Lisa. He was dropping me off at Bailey's. I would spend a couple weeks at her home before we both flew to Corpus Christi to see my mama.

My step-mother, Clarice could keep me away from Wichita Falls while I was under her care, but when it came time for my mama's summer visit, she had absolutely no say so. I could not wait until I was away from her beady-eyed stares and her passive-aggressive ways.

I truly wished I could be a fly on the wall when she found out, at the end of the summer, that I had a huge surprise in store for her. I wasn't coming back to Oklahoma City and there was nothing she could do about it! She would no longer have me around as a slave laborer at home or the restaurant. I would be free as a bird, living with my mama, finally.

I couldn't wait for my plan to fall in place. The first part was just getting out of Oklahoma and back to Texas, to the people I loved the most in the world!

Chapter 1

I waved heartily at my step-brother, Geoffrey, as he pulled out of my best friend's driveway. I was finally home, and I couldn't wait for the devil's spawn to leave! He had no idea why I smiled so brightly at him.

"Okay, you gonna tell me what the hell that was about?" Bailey inquired, as we stood in her driveway, in the warm, early, summer evening.

"Oh? What? You mean the wave?" I smiled sweetly at my best friend.

"Uh, do I really want to know?" Bailey asked now, even more curious.

I shrugged. Bailey looked at me expectantly. I couldn't wait to tell her that I was halfway through with an elaborate plan to finally escape. "Well…you see…I made a decision a couple of weeks ago."

I stopped and turned to begin walking towards the house. When we got to the steps of her porch, Bailey grabbed my arm before I could go inside. Her eyes were as big as silver dollars.

"Oh…my decision? Is that what you're wondering about?" I toyed with her just a little longer.

"Lala! What are you doing?" Bailey asked in a whisper, even though there was no one around to hear our conversation.

I deadpanned, "I'm NOT going back to Oklahoma City, that's for certain."

Bailey looked at me quizzically. "So what are you going to do? You can't run away. I mean, you can! I'll hide you. The Strong's might hide you for that matter, but it probably wouldn't last that long."

I started giggling, "No, Bay-bay…I'm not running away. I'm just moving again." Bailey looked perplexed still. Finally, I finished telling her my plan. "I'm not coming back from Corpus Christi."

My best friend got tears in her eyes. I felt awful! I hadn't wanted to make her cry. I realized that she was thinking like I had when I first began to think of my escape. I would never get to see her ever again. "Lala, I'll never see you!" Bailey wailed.

I wrapped my arm around her shoulder, "How many weekends did I get to come down in the last three months?"

"None," Bailey replied, confused.

"Exactly! I can guarantee that if I go back, I won't get to come back for any weekends again until either Christmas, if I'm really lucky, or next summer. No matter if I live four hours away or eight hours away, I'm not going to be able to visit, except once or twice a year. I don't want to live there. The kids in Oklahoma hate anyone from Texas. I've sat by myself at lunch too many days now."

"Daddy and Clarice are always at the restaurant. Clarice hasn't gone to the grocery store since we moved there. If Geoff gets pissed or has plans, we don't go to the restaurant. If we don't go, we don't eat. I'm tired of it, Bailey. I'm tired of being the grown-up! I wanna be a kid for a change!" I finished.

Bailey hugged me close, "It makes sense. I'm just glad we're gonna get to spend the next month together. No Clarice telling you to come home by noon, or Geoffrey constantly being around, acting like an asshole."

We walked up the steps and went into the familiar home that was a safe place to me. We walked into her room and she began to tell me about Kevin. He'd come around every couple of weeks to check on me. After that, we moved on to Bailey's boyfriend, Levi and then Jax. I was excited we were going to the skating rink.

It felt so wonderful to finally be home! I wished I could see Kevin, but I wouldn't be able to do that until the next day, when Geoffrey left. As if we were connected in some strange, telepathic way, Bailey's phone rang. She handed it to me.

It was Kevin!

He explained Geoff was in the kitchen with his mom. He told Geoff he was going to the bathroom. He was sitting in there, with the phone. I started laughing, imagining Kevin sitting on his toilet, with his telephone. He had wanted to say hi and he would come to Bailey's the next day, after Geoff left.

I felt as if my whole body was about to burst! Everyone I loved was near and could be touched finally.

That night felt like old times when we walked into Skate-whirl. Bailey's brother had driven us up there. The inside of the skating rink never looked different. We found the best booth in the snack bar and as soon as Levi and Jax walked in, Levi picked me up and swung me around. Jax gave me a tight bear hug.

I was ecstatic to be around both of them. It felt like I'd been gone on vacation for a couple of weeks and everything was the same again. Life felt right, finally.

I looked at the door often, wondering if Kevin and Geoffrey were going to come. By 10 o'clock, I felt it was a safe bet they'd either stayed at Kevin's or gone cruising on Kemplar.

In a way, I felt better that Kevin wasn't there. I knew he'd see Jax sitting with me and probably have something to say. I felt confused about both of them still! Especially with the way my last night had gone, before I moved to Oklahoma City.

My other best friend, Kelly White started screaming when she saw me. She knew I would be down, but I guess she didn't think I'd come to the skating rink my first night. We'd talked about her coming to Corpus for two weeks too during the summer! We'd spend a night or two together as well, while I was visiting Bailey.

Bailey knew how much Kelly meant to me. Her endless stream of chatter made me grin as she sat down. She could talk so fast, sometimes I had to ask her to slow down, because I didn't always understand her. She would go off into her trademark giggles when that would happen. I had missed Kelly and her happy personality that never seemed to flag.

When Kelly eventually went to skate, more of the other people I'd run around with all school year came by. So many people came to hug me and hear all about how awful Oklahoma City was. Polly Green and Crystal Box sat with me for almost an hour. Everyone seemed excited I was going to school on the last day. Milam Junior High was still in session to make up for a snow day during the year. I was happy I would get to go to the last day with Bailey.

At 11:00, the sock hop started. The first song they played was "With You I'm Born Again" by Billy Preston and Syreeta Wright. Jax and Levi had been sitting with me and Bailey for a while. When that song came on, Bailey and Levi jumped up to dance. Jax looked over at me and shyly asked if I wanted to dance too. I smiled and nodded my head. We walked out to the floor and I wrapped my wrists around his neck. Jax leaned his head down and his mouth was near my ear. "I really missed you, DeLaine,"

Pulling back, I looked into the laughing, grass-green eyes, "I've missed you too." Jax smiled, then pulled me close. I smelled the familiar scent of leather and soap. Jax managed to dance with me several times. Before the sock hop was over, the four of us went outside to wait on Jason. We sat on the tailgate of Jax's truck.

Bailey and Levi began to kiss while we sat there. After a few minutes, Jax and I hopped down and went to the cab of the truck. We didn't want to watch Levi and Bailey make out.

I naturally got in the driver's side, like I always had, and scooted as far over as my normal spot. After Jax got in, I realized I shouldn't sit so close to him. I didn't know what kind of message I was sending. I didn't understand what message was in my head. The old confusion began to descend on me. I loved Kevin, but couldn't deny that I loved Jax as well. My love for Jax felt more childish though than the feelings I felt for Kevin.

When I scooted further over, Jax looked at me funny, "I don't bite. Why'd you scoot way over there?"

"I dunno," I muttered quietly. "I guess I just figured since I'm not your girlfriend any more, I shouldn't really sit in my old spot."

"Do you have to be my girlfriend to sit by me?" Jax asked softly.

I shrugged my shoulders. "I'm not sure Jax. I don't know what to think. I don't know how this works."

Putting his hand on the outside of my right thigh, Jax pulled me back to where I normally sat, "Why do we have to know how it works? Why can't we just let whatever happens, happen?"

"I don't want you to think that I'm leading you on or anything," I replied gently.

Jax began chuckling. "DeLaine, I don't think you're leading me on. I know that you don't live here anymore. I know that we can't be together for real, but it doesn't mean that we can't see each other when you come to visit."

I knew I had to tell Jax about my plan. Once I had him sworn to secrecy, I told him I didn't intend to go back to Oklahoma City. I explained that I was horribly miserable. I told him I knew my mama would let me visit Bailey in the summers, and maybe even during Christmas or spring break.

Nodding his head, he asked, "Well, how long are you going to be here this time?"

"We fly out of Dallas on June 15th. Bailey's mom is going to drive us down there. It's on a Monday." I explained.

"Well, then we'll see each other when we can while you're here." Jax shrugged his shoulder.

"Jax, I'm not going to lie to you, I plan to see Kevin while I'm here too," I looked at my hands in my lap.

Sitting for a beat, Jax finally responded, "I figured you would. But, I'm not your boyfriend, so I can't tell you not to. I just hope you'll make a little time for me too." I nodded my head and then he surprised me by tilting my chin and kissing me soft as a butterfly's wing.

When he pulled away, he smiled at me. I smiled back, then kissed him like I used to, when he was my boyfriend. I was in love with him too. I didn't know how I could be any more alive than I was at that moment.

Jason Rains pulled up behind Jax's truck where his sister was making out with her boyfriend. He honked his horn.

Jax and I turned around, then grinned at each other sheepishly. He got out of the truck and I slid out behind him. I grabbed him around the neck and hugged him quickly, then was off with Bailey in Jason's rock and roll, thumping machine.

When we pulled onto the highway, Jason turned his music down for the first time ever while I was in his car, "Damn Bay! Makin' out with your boyfriend and DeLaine in the pickup, makin' out with hers! What are you kids doing?"

Bailey began laughing. I'd never heard Jason say my name before. Jason continued to good naturedly tease his sister. If Geoffrey had ever once teased me, like Jason and Bailey did, maybe our entire lives together could have been so much different.

It was funny listening to Jason try to sound like his mom and dad, giving Bailey grief over standing outside kissing Levi.

Chapter 2

The next afternoon Kevin called and asked if I wanted to come to his house. I told him I would, and literally walked on air, all the way down Granville. I thought briefly about kissing Jax the night before. Neither boy was my boyfriend, but I didn't want to be thought of as loose.

I'd told Jax I had every intention of seeing Kevin. He didn't seem thrilled about it, but he seemed to accept it. I wondered if I could be as honest with Kevin. I decided to wait until we were alone and gauge whether I should tell him or not.

When I got to the corner of Fairfax and Portland, Kevin was standing outside, in his driveway. He literally swung me up in the air when I hugged him. I didn't want to let him go. If Jax's hug the night before had felt good, Kevin's felt like I'd finally made it home. His muscular arms and shoulders were strong and warm. I put my face immediately into the crook of his neck and didn't want to let go ever, as I drank in his familiar, clean scent. Thoughts of Jax melted away.

We walked into his house and I made the rounds for hugs. Even Mr. Strong hugged me. I sat in the living room for a while with Kevin's parents and Donna and told them about Oklahoma City and how much I hated it.

I wanted so badly to tell them I wasn't planning on coming back, but I knew Geoff would come back the next weekend. I didn't want someone to accidentally slip, so I decided to wait until the day before I left to tell them. I tried to skim over most anything about my life in Oklahoma and wanted to listen to them and what had happened in their lives since I left.

Donna was so excited for me to be there and Mrs. Strong invited me to dinner. I called Bailey and asked if she minded and she told me to stay and have fun and be home by 10. I excitedly told them I could stay.

Once that was established, Donna decided she'd waited long enough for some attention from me! Kevin told her that we'd come and read one story in her room, but then he and I wanted to visit too. I'd come back in one more time before I left, when it was her bed time. She reluctantly agreed with a little bit of pouting, but Kevin made her laugh and her pout was quickly forgotten.

After spending time with Donna, I was again feeling as if I was going to burst when I went with Kevin to his room! We scrambled up on his bed and he piled his pillows behind his back, then held his arms out for me.

I quickly went to him and listened to his strong, steady heartbeat. I couldn't believe I was finally in his arms. I had missed him so badly. I didn't know how I would live with only seeing this boy once or twice a year, but I knew that I was making the right decision. I knew if I stayed in Oklahoma City, the flaming Goddess that lived within me would eventually escape from my belly. It would consume me in the process. I knew that I had to leave for my own sanity.

After dinner and reading to Donna again, we went back into his room and listened to music. I told him in detail about all the things that I had endured and when he heard I'd actually given Geoffrey a black eye, he roared with laughter. He was as shocked as I'd been at his response too.

I told him about some of Geoffrey's new friends that I'd met. None of them seemed as close to Geoff as Kevin had been, but they were nice enough guys. One of them had been a big, tall blonde-headed guy and when he'd first come to our house, I immediately thought of Kevin. He had spent the night only one time and he'd teased me unmercifully.

I saw him another time when I went with Geoffrey to the grocery store where he worked. That time I became aware that he liked teasing me because he actually liked me. Once I realized that, I avoided him like the plague. I didn't need a repeat of history in Oklahoma City.

Geoffrey didn't seem to hang around with him for long though. I left out the part of realizing he liked me to Kevin. I knew he could be jealous.

I wanted to tell him about moving to Corpus so bad and told him that I wanted to tell him something, but I wanted to wait until after Geoffrey came back, the following weekend with Lisa. Kevin looked at me curiously. I soothed, "It's a surprise and I don't want to put you in a bad position with Geoff."

Kevin rolled his eyes at me, "You're not going back."

I pulled my ear away from his chest and exclaimed, "How'd you know?"

Smiling, Kevin shrugged, "What else do you have to lose, right? I mean, you didn't get to come when you were supposed to and you told us how much you hated it there. Bailey told me a little bit about how you were either working at the restaurant or doing your normal stuff and then about the move to another house within two months. I figured that if you went back I'd have to seriously talk to you about it before you did."

"Why?" I asked him.

"Lainey, baby, you can't keep living like that. Nobody could. You told me yourself that your escape plan had always been to go to your mom's when it got to be too much. I think it's too much now, don't you?" Kevin asked softly.

I nodded my head and he continued, "You'll still get to visit during the summers and shit, right?" I bobbed my head again and told him I planned on talking to my mom about that. I knew that I'd have to go to Oklahoma City too because my daddy would get summers, but I somehow didn't think he'd fight too hard about making me come for the whole summer.

"Just don't tell Geoff, Kevin. I don't want them to even suspect it until I'm safely in Corpus Christi. I'm not getting any of my stuff I left there. That's how I always get sucked back. This time, I'm not going back to get it. Hopefully the few things I couldn't fit in my suitcase will still be there, but I'm not going." I revealed, adamantly.

Kevin nodded while I told him how I'd packed almost everything I owned in the large suitcase, and how Clarice asked why I was taking so much stuff to my mom's. He laughed when I told him how I smuggled almost everything out of my room. Then he surprised me when he asked, "Did you take your jewelry?"

"Yea, why?" I asked.

"Just curious if you got your necklace." Kevin replied absently.

I smiled at him and pulled the crystal, tear drop pendant out of my shirt and asked if he meant that one. He smiled his sunshine and rainbows smile and I felt my heart flip flop over. Then he leaned down and kissed me back home to him.

Later he walked me to Bailey's. We had to get up early the next day to go to school and Kevin kissed me goodnight when he dropped me off at the porch. I came back at 9:30 so I didn't bother anyone with coming in too late. Kevin told me he'd call me the next day and I smiled as I opened the storm door to go inside.

I felt like I could actually be Kevin's girlfriend for once. I wasn't hiding and trying to sneak around, terrified we'd be found out at any turn.

Chapter 3

The next day at Milam, I was welcomed back by everyone and put up part of the time in the library. I also got to go to some classes with Bailey and everyone wanted to sign my year book. I felt so excited to actually have one. I was missing from the photo of the newspaper staff and the choir, which made me sad. They were the first extra-curricular activities I'd ever been a true part of at school.

My yearbook was signed by teachers and students alike. It was insane how full it was and how many people wanted to sign it. Some people signed it that hadn't been that close to me, but I let everyone sign it who wanted to. Jax even scribbled in it, stupidly. I just rolled my eyes when I saw his chicken scratch. It reminded me of the short and not so sweet note he had given me when we'd broken up.

I had enjoyed going to choir with Levi and seeing everyone in there except Joy Oliver. I noticed at lunch she and Chrissy were still sitting on their own, away from the other girls. I had enjoyed this day much more than my other last day because I'd been a complete, crying mess that day. This time, I was happy and relaxed and felt as if I'd lost all the things that had caused me grief and fear. I was on my way to a better life with my mama

I went to my old Language Arts class and Mrs. Parnell had a gift, which surprised me. When she gave it to me, I cried. I may not have been in the year book as a member of the newspaper staff, but she'd found a way to recognize my accomplishment.

On a small piece of white marble, Mrs. Parnell had gotten a brass plate engraved with my name, and name of our school newspaper, with the school year. She told me in private that she saw great potential in me as a writer, and that I should always pursue my dreams. I hugged her and was so happy to have had her as my teacher. It meant more to me than she would ever know. I was sure I'd cherish it forever.

Jax took me to Health & Family and we had a blast in there, as we sat around talking about our first project of being a family. Jax and I had funnily enough been picked to be the parents of our family group. Polly Green and Mateo Rubio had been our kids. The teacher had fun talking about all the stuff we'd done through the year.

Jax had pulled a chair next to his chair and I'd sat beside him through class.

Then we began talking about the sex part of the class. I began to blush furiously. It had come up after mine and Jax's attempt at going all the way, and the mess it seemed to have created in our relationship. Jax smiled at me every once in a while. I tried to keep my eyes lowered.

When we walked out of class, he picked up my hand, out of habit, and began walking towards the media center, where I'd meet up with Bailey. I'd get to say goodbye to Mr. Simmons again. As I pulled my hand back, Jax looked down and grinned, then kissed me on the cheek and I went with Bailey. Of course, my best friend had a million questions in her eyes. I just laughed and shook my head.

Jax gave me and Bailey a ride home, along with Levi, after school. We were once again the inseparable foursome we'd been for the fall and winter of 8th grade. It felt good riding with the windows rolled down. The wind was blowing Bailey's long, blonde-streaked hair, as well as Levi and Jax's hair too. They both had caps on, so their hair only blew around on the bottom. My hair was still short enough that the wind just made it stick up all kinds of crazy because of my curls.

We talked about getting to go to the pool the next day for the big grand opening day. I realized I never got to do anything during the summers, while I lived in Wichita Falls, because I was always gone. I was going to get to go to the pool for the first time ever.

When we got out of the truck, Jax leaned over and kissed me on the cheek again. I grinned at him and went running up the stairs of Bailey's cement porch. We got cokes and chocolate donut holes and went to her room to giggle and talk about the last day of eighth grade. We were both looking forward to being freshman finally! I was sad I would never walk the halls of Samson, like I thought I would when Bailey and I walked out the doors, the year before.

The next few days were full of going to the swimming pool and going to Kelly's house. I interspersed time with Kevin.

Jax was working at his uncle's farm every day. I wished I could go with him and see the horses we used to ride, Buttercup and Moon Boy, but I knew he was working out there. His uncle's place was busy at this time of year with the cattle and the horses as well as breaking new horses. The first week flew by and I knew I wouldn't see Kevin until Sunday, because Geoffrey was bringing Lisa down on Saturday.

Bailey and I went to the skating rink again. It was another night of reliving my time with three of the most important people in the world to me. Jax and I danced a little again, but we went outside at 11:30. Jax was planning to take me and Bailey home that night.

We got inside the cab of his truck. The nights were already hot. We had the windows down, but I still felt like I was melting. We finally got out of the cab and sat in the bed of the truck.

We talked more it seemed, and I was glad to have him to talk with. After a while though, we began kissing. I was still thrilled when he kissed me.

I would think back to how silly I'd been in 6th grade, with my crush on him. Then I'd remember the day he asked me to be his girlfriend, before my birthday in October. I wondered if I'd never moved, would we have worked out our problems and gotten back together?

I wondered then if Kevin and I would have been able to finally be open about our relationship, once I got to Samson. I'd never know. I thought I knew how my life was going to work out the year before. Now it was as uncertain for me as taking a trip in a foreign country with no map.

I didn't know where my life was headed. I felt a little adrift in a way, but I hoped that the choice I was making would be a good thing.

Chapter 4

The next afternoon Kevin called me and asked what I was doing. When I told him nothing, he asked if I wanted to come see him. I said yes but knew something didn't sound quite right about him. He sounded weird. I asked if everything was okay. He told me it was and I asked if something had happened with Geoffrey. He told me that Geoff was fine and he'd left. I told him I'd go tell Bailey and be at his house in a few minutes.

Kevin paused, then asked, "You know where Kevin Welks lives, don't you?"

I knew exactly where he lived! He lived right down the street from Jax. I felt as if I'd gotten a shot of ice water in my veins when he asked me. I finally said I knew where he lived.

"Come to his house. I'm over here hangin' out." I told him okay, then went to find Bailey.

I told her about meeting him at Kevin Welks and Bailey looked at me seriously, "He probably found out you've been seeing Jax, too."

I nodded and felt like I should be shot. I claimed to love Kevin, but I also loved Jax. They were two totally separate loves, but I didn't know how to choose which boy to be with when I had so little time to see them.

When I got to the corner I used to feel was haunted by Kevin's memory, I touched the sign pole for Woodbane and Woolery for good luck. I felt like I was about to walk into something that wouldn't be great.

I'd never been afraid of Kevin, but I was afraid of hurting him. I would rather cut my wrists than hurt him, I thought, as I turned onto Andrew Street. I saw Jax's truck in his driveway, but kept walking, hoping and praying he wouldn't see me out his front window.

When I got to Kevin Welks' house, I walked up the driveway and knocked on the door. Some guy I didn't know opened it, and I walked in. Kevin Welks was sitting there, smoking a cigarette and drinking a beer. I was shocked to see a boy who'd just finished his freshman year of high school drinking and smoking.

Kevin Strong was standing in the doorway that led off to a kitchen. When he saw me he set down a beer can behind him. I was surprised that my Kevin was drinking too, but didn't say anything to him.

Looking at Kevin curiously, I noticed he had an angry look on his face. When I got up to him, he told Welks, "Hey man, we're goin' out back, okay?"

When he got what I thought was an affirmative response, he took my hand roughly in his, pulling me through the kitchen, out the back door, into the backyard. I saw an old travel trailer along the far fence, among other pieces of junk and Kevin pulled me into it.

When we got inside, I growled, "What the fuck is wrong with you, Kevin?" It was sweltering in the trailer and I wouldn't close the door.

Kevin began rolling out the windows on the travel trailer and mercifully there was a breeze blowing. It began to cool down immediately in the tiny, tin can.

"Close the door," Kevin barked, brusquely.

"What is wrong, Kev?" I asked, feeling like I knew. I pulled the door reluctantly closed.

Kevin stood up from the bed that was at the far end of the trailer, and pulled me over to the foam mattress. The place smelled like all old trailers; musty and acrid. I looked at him wondering if he was ever going to talk to me, but after looking at his stormy-sky colored eyes, I thought it best to be patient and wait for him to tell me what he was mad about.

Finally, after what seemed forever, Kevin shouted, "Did you fuck, Jax?"

I was shocked. I didn't even know how to answer him. I sat there with my mouth hanging open and finally squeaked, "What are you talking about?" I thought he'd heard I'd been seeing Jax too. I still wasn't certain if that was what he was talking about.

"When you were goin' with him, at Christmas time…did you fuck him?" Kevin asked me, through clenched teeth.

"Kevin you're starting to scare me a little," I whispered, as I began scooting away from him.

He looked down at his shoes and then barked, "Just answer me, DeLaine. It's a simple yes or no answer."

I began to stand up. I thought Kevin was either half drunk or all the way smashed. When I got to my feet, he pulled me back down beside him, "I guess that's a yes, huh?"

"I can't even believe you are asking me this, Kevin," I replied angrily.

"You said you'd wait for me," Kevin muttered, sounding miserable.

"Maybe you need to tell me who the fuck told you that shit!" I demanded, hotly.

Kevin began shaking his head and got a strange grin he'd never had on his face before, around me. "Well, let's see, someone saw you coming out of Garrett's storm cellar one day, when you were going with that stupid, fuckin,' shit-kicker. I figure that's where you went to fuck him." He finished bitterly.

I realized Welks had been the one to tell Kevin. I wondered how Welks had known what had happened in the storm cellar.

"First of all, unless someone besides Jax said something to you, I don't know that I'd believe everything you hear from others. I thought you knew better than that. Second of all, I was going with him! You were with Lori, Kevin. You didn't want me, remember?" I was beginning to feel really angry. "What the hell do you want from me?" I cried.

"I want you to let me be the first, dammit!" Kevin replied sullenly. "That isn't gonna happen now. Garrett already got there."

"Give me a god-damn break, Kevin! I didn't screw Jax, okay?! Do you feel better now? Maybe you should ask me, instead of listening to other guys' bullshit. Now, if Jax said he did, then I want to know, because I'll personally walk over to his house right now and kick his ass! That is not what happened when we were in that storm cellar." I sat there hurriedly thinking about it, while I was yelling at Kevin.

I honestly didn't think that what had happened between us equaled my first time, but I wasn't really sure. I know it definitely wasn't pleasant and it was over quickly.

Drunkenly, Kevin tried to pull me back onto the foam bed, in the old trailer. I started fighting him. "What are you doing?" I shrieked.

"We're going to do it! I want to be your first and we're going to do it now! I'll know I'll be the first!" Kevin growled as he started pulling at my clothes.

"Kevin, NO!" I began fighting him as his hands pulled on me. "Dammit, I mean it, quit it!" I was starting to cry. I began to fight him like a wildcat. He finally pulled me under him and was holding me down by sitting on top of me.

"Why not, DeLaine? What else do you need from me?" Kevin asked me, still surly.

"How about an I LOVE YOU! Have you ever thought that I might need to hear those words from you? God-dammit! I've been in love with you for over a year and you act like it, but you've never said it once! I don't know what I have to do to get you to tell me!" I shouted up at him as I continued pushing his hands away.

Kevin leaned over and tried to kiss me roughly, but I turned my face. "Dammit, DeLaine, I love you! Are you happy? I thought you understood that without me having to say it!"

"Well, gee, Kevin, you were able to tell Lori, but you can't tell me once? No, it wasn't understood, Babe! Sorry to inform you of that! I also don't want you to try to do this now! You're drunk, and I don't want you on me!" I began to try to buck him off of me.

He bent over me and scooted his butt down onto my thighs and grabbed my hands and held them beside my head.

"DeLaine, I love you. Baby, why don't you believe me? I only wanted to be the first for you for everything. I didn't want you with that fuckin' shit-kicker. I never thought you'd go all the way with him." He sneered, as he tried to bend over and kiss me again.

I turned my head and felt the tears sliding down the sides of my face.

"I didn't, Kevin! Go ahead, if you want to be the first!!! Go ahead!!! Break my cherry and find out for yourself!" I spat into his face as he kept trying to kiss me.

I was afraid when I saw his face change. Gone was the Kevin I loved, the Kevin who had saved me more times than he ever knew.

In his place was an angry, snarling monster that was only inches above me, "Fine, I'll find out if you're lying to me!"

No longer fighting him, I lay there as he yanked my shorts down forcefully and undid his jeans. When he put himself next to me, I closed my eyes tightly, waiting for the pain I knew would happen. As soon as the intense pain shot through me, I grabbed his hair. "Are you happy? Get off of me god-dammit!" I snarled like a rabid dog into his ear.

Pulling up and looking into my eyes he pleaded, "But, Lainey, I love you." I repeated my demand and he sat up and started zipping his pants.

I pulled my shorts up and started for the door. Somehow Kevin made the leap to the door and he grabbed it, "I'm sorry, Lainey! I shouldn't have done it like that!"

"You're damned right about that you sonofabitch!" I opened the door and began trying to find a way out of the back yard without having to walk through the house. I couldn't find one, so I opened the kitchen door and stomped through the house. When I got to the front door to yank it open, Kevin Welks and the other guys in the living room started cheering and hollering.

I turned around, looking furiously at Welks and barked, "Next time you want to tell Kevin something about me, don't, you stupid fuckin' idiot! You don't know what happened with me and Jax! Keep your mouth shut about me!"

Slamming out of Welks' house, I began stomping down the sidewalk, trying to get away as fast as I could. Kevin Strong caught up to me in no time. He was riding some kid's small bicycle.

I passed by Jax's house and wanted to bang on his door and ask him what he'd said to Welks! I didn't think it would be a good thing with Kevin, inebriated, right beside me.

While I was walking and trying to ignore Kevin, he rode the bike ahead of me a little ways and then he'd turn back around and try to get me to talk to him. I kept my face closed off to him.

I was still shocked that he had done that! I hurt like hell between my legs and just wanted to get to Bailey's.

As we finally turned onto Woodbane, he rode ahead of me. I yelled at him, "You know what Kevin, one of these days I'm gonna have a little boy and I'm going to name him Kevin and I'm gonna teach him how to treat a woman! I thought you knew, but I was seriously mistaken! I cannot believe you just did that to me! Now, you want to know what is wrong with me! I don't know if I ever want to talk to you again!"

Kevin rode the bike back to me, right before we turned onto Portland and he smiled, asking, "So what if you don't have a boy?" I couldn't believe that was his response!

"I will have a boy! I'll have a blonde haired, blue-eyed boy just so I can do exactly what I said! You wait and see! You hurt me, Kevin! I don't know if I'll ever forgive you!" I roared.

Grinning at me in his lazy, half smile way, with his eyes hooded, he shrugged his shoulders, "Sure you will. You love me. You just told me so."

"That's probably changed, Asshole!" I growled again.

Still beaming at me, Kevin responded nonchalantly, "Well, it didn't change for me. I love you, DeLaine. I always have. I thought you knew it."

I shook my head and kept walking down Portland. We were only a couple of houses from his and I was still so angry at him I couldn't see straight. It was beginning to be dusk and I wanted to get to Bailey's house. "Go home, Kevin. Don't call me for a while. I have to get over being so mad at you."

As I walked past his driveway, Kevin rode the bike in front of me, pleading, "I'm sorry, DeLaine. That's not how I wanted that to happen." I looked him evenly in the eyes, eyes that I'd loved for so long. I began to tear up again and walked around him, as I crossed the street to make my way to Granville.

I cried the whole walk up Granville.

Kevin had been my savior. He had never hurt me physically. Now I couldn't say that. All the love I'd had for him over the last year and a half was seriously injured. I was afraid it could never be fixed. I couldn't forgive him for hurting me the way he had.

I didn't even know how to tell Bailey what he did. I knew how protective she was as well. I was afraid if she knew, she would never forgive him, even if I did. I didn't want there to be bad blood between them.

When I was about five houses away from Bailey's, I stopped and wiped my eyes.

I stood there on the side walk and let the evening wind ruffle my hair and dry my face. When I felt like I could walk into Bailey's house without melting down, I continued on the way.

After I got back, she asked me what happened. I decided to give her an abbreviated version of events. I told her that Welks had told him about me and Jax and the storm cellar and that Kevin had been angry, wanting to know if it was true.

I told her we had argued about it and that I had even tried to do it with Kevin, but it hurt too much. Then I told her I didn't want to talk about him for a few days, because I was so mad at him. Bailey looked at me worriedly, then nodded her head without another word.

When I took a shower that night, I saw that there was much more blood in my underwear than there had been when Jax and I had done whatever we'd done. I figured if Jax hadn't gotten my virginity, it looked as if Kevin had at least succeeded, even though it hurt. I hoped it would never be like that again. I sighed and then cried in the shower for the next ten minutes.

The rest of the week was taken up with time at the pool and even a trip to the lake with Bailey and her parents. They all waterskied, but I was too afraid to try, so when they stopped for a while, Bailey and I swam off the side of the boat.

I noticed that my tan was becoming much deeper. I remembered briefly Mrs. Strong commenting on my tan only a few months ago, when I'd first gotten home from Corpus Christi, before 8th grade began. Then I thought about Kevin and tried to push him out of my brain as soon as possible.

By Thursday, I decided that Kevin and I would probably never speak to one another again.

Late that night there was a tap on the glass and when Bailey got up to see who it was she turned to me and announced, "It's Kevin. Do you want to talk to him?"

I sat there for a minute and then nodded my head. I might as well get this over, I thought. I went to the front door and quietly slipped out. I headed to the street light, just past Bailey's house, where Kevin was waiting on me.

"Hey," Kevin whispered, quietly. I looked at him with a pinched face and nodded my head. "Lainey, I'm so, so sorry! I don't know why I did that on Sunday."

"Because you were afraid that Jax Garrett got something that you felt was yours. Since you weren't sure, you wanted to make sure. Are you happy now?" I retorted, grimly.

Kevin hung his head down. "Lainey, I can't ever tell you I'm sorry enough."

Chuckling low in my throat, I looked at Kevin hard, "You got that right. There is no being sorry enough for what you did to me, Kevin. I didn't want to hear you tell me you loved me, as you drunkenly took my virginity. I wanted it to be a little more mutual too." I stated, just as meanly as I could.

"DeLaine…Lainey, I just felt crazy when Welks was telling me about seeing you and Garrett coming out of his storm cellar over Christmas break. I guess I just thought that you'd…well, I figured you'd decided that since I'd been with Lori that there was no reason to wait, even though I asked you to." Kevin commented softly.

I sighed, "Okay, Kevin, you apologized. Your conscious is clear. Mine isn't though. I can't figure out how to forgive you." my voice cracked.

"I don't know how to forgive myself," Kevin muttered miserably. "I just want to hold you. I just want everything to go back to how it always was."

Shaking my head. I looked up at him with the tears that had now taken over my face once more, "It can never be like it was before, Kevin. I wanted you to tell me you loved me for a year and a half. When you finally said it, it meant nothing to you. Surely you knew that I've been in love with you since my 13th birthday. All I ever wanted was to hear you say you loved me! Instead, you say it when you're drunk and force me to lose my virginity, right then and there."

Kevin's head hung lower. I hoped I was hurting him as much as he had hurt me. Finally, he asked, "Will you at least walk with me and sit down and talk. I want to get out from under this damned streetlight."

I looked at him uncertain if I wanted to go anywhere alone with him.

"I swear to God…better yet, I swear on Donna that I won't hurt you, Lainey." I looked at him warily but consented. We walked over to the elementary school and went inside the tunnel.

After several minutes, Kevin finally looked over at me. In the light, shining from the street lamp, from the parking lot of the elementary school, I could see Kevin's face just in shadow.

"DeLaine, I don't like to say I love you. I usually don't tell people I love them, except for Donna. I never knew real, unconditional love when I was little, so it's hard for me to say it. The only reason Donna is different is because she was mine from the minute my birth mom brought her home. I can't remember not loving Donna. I love my mom and dad and have maybe told them one or two times in almost 12 years."

" I don't remember really loving anyone else besides them, until I met you. I don't know why, but there was something about you. I needed someone who tamed my cocky bullshit. What did you used to call me, King Kevin?" he paused and laughed softly while shaking his head.

"I only told Lori I loved her because she said she wouldn't do it with me any other way. Geoffrey kinda pushed us together. I wanted to break up with her so when you got home we could just be together! Then Geoffrey kissed her and told me a bunch of bullshit about how I would never be a real man unless I claimed her and took her back! The only way I could do that was to prove I was a man! She'd told Geoff she thought I might be a fag since I never wanted to touch her. I felt like I had to do it!"

I snorted when he said that, and he looked over at me. "You two never had any problems on the make-out wall at Skate-whirl," I muttered.

"That's just the thing though, Lainey, I never wanted to go over there with her. I wanted to be with you. She'd pull me out there and when I'd get pissed at you, I'd try to show you that I could be with her just fine, but I really didn't want to be. When Geoffrey told me that she thought I was gay, well, I don't know, it made me a little crazy that a girl would ever think I was a faggot. I mean, I am the most, un-gay guy I know!" Kevin continued. "When Lori started that shit that she wouldn't do it with me unless I said I loved her, I told her. They were just words to me. They don't mean the same thing to me that they mean to most people. It doesn't mean that I don't feel love. I do. I feel it, but I just don't like to say the words. I feel like it takes away from the feeling for me because my birth mom would say she loved us all the time, but she didn't. She loved whatever dope-head boyfriend she had that month. She loved getting drunk and high. She certainly didn't love us though. So, I put more into showing how I feel about people.
That's why I'm so protective. I want to prove to you I love you and not just say three words that anyone can say. Does any of this make sense?"

Nodding my head, I realized that I had already forgiven Kevin. Part of me was angry for forgiving him so simply, but another part of me understood the sadness and loneliness of the little boy who'd been so horribly hurt. I realized that I was so fortunate that my parents did say they loved me. I always believed them when they did. I didn't have to have a hang up about the words. I actually needed to hear and say them.

Finally I said, "I understand Kevin, but I've always had parents who told me they loved me. Those three words aren't meaningless to me. I was afraid if I told you, you would cut and run the other way. I wanted it to be you who told me first."

"I wanted to know I was worthy of it from you. And I never wanted to have sex with you because everybody else was doing it."

"I wanted to have sex with you to show you in another way how much I loved you. I didn't want it to be a race to make sure you got it before someone else did. But you were with Lori. I'm not gonna lie and say I didn't mess around with Jax, Kev, but I'm thinking it is safe to say that you got my virginity. I didn't want it to ever happen that way though. Now I have this horrible memory of you. It makes me sad to think of you that way."

Kevin took my hands in his and kissed them tenderly. "I know, DeLaine. I can never ever say I'm sorry enough. There's nothing I can ever do to take it away. I can only tell you that if I never say it to you again, please know that I do love you. I have ever since I kissed you on the corner at Woodbane, the first time. I was so shocked when I kissed you and realized that I loved you. It was such a weird feeling to me. I'd never felt for a girl, the way I felt about you. You didn't think I was all that special. You didn't put up with my shit! You just acted like I was some dumb guy. I wasn't that golden boy that everybody always thought I was."

"Seriously, Kevin? Why do you think I used to call you King Kevin? I thought I was a lowly peasant. Hell, I didn't even know if I was a peasant as far as you were concerned. I was terrified of you in the beginning. I could barely breathe the first time I realized you and Geoff were friends and you came to the house." I was laughing then.

"Sure fooled me, because from the first time Geoffrey had you make me an egg sandwich, I knew you were something else. You gave it to me and didn't act all silly because you got to do something for me, like all the other girls I had known. I thought that you were so much more with it than the stupid, little girls at school. I had always been able to play with them and they all ate it up, but you just…I dunno."

He shrugged, "You just treated me like I was normal. Maybe I knew I was in trouble with you before I kissed you the first time. I don't really remember how it happened, I just knew by the time I kissed you the first time, I was done." His voice came to me softly, as he remembered our first encounters.

I had forgiven him completely. I still didn't like the memory he'd left for me, of our first time together intimately. I forgave him, though. I felt a kinship with not just him, but with the soul he possessed.

I had more baggage than most 14-year-olds. Kevin was 16 now and he had grown up in reverse too. I still expected him to always behave like the mini-adult that he'd been since he was little, but I had to remember biologically he was still a stupid-ass boy.

Gingerly, I scooted over to where I was sitting next to him and whispered, "Kevin, I forgive you. I can't ever forget what you did, but I can forgive you…just please…don't ever do that again."

"You need to understand this too…I cared a lot about Jax. The truth is I loved him too in a way. I am still constantly confused about how I feel about the two of you, but you're the boy I love the most. Without a doubt in my mind, I love you, but, you don't own me, Kevin. You said so yourself, I kinda have my own mind! I'm finally, for the first time ever, feeling the freedom to use it without being terrified."

Nodding at me, Kevin asked quietly, "May I kiss you, DeLaine?"

I giggled and nodded my head. He leaned over and tenderly kissed me. I tried to push away the fear I had experienced a few days before, because the Kevin I loved was back.

The drunk asshole that he'd been was gone.

Chapter 5

The next day after Bailey and I spent the day swimming with Levi at the pool, I went to Kevin's. I thought I was going for dinner, but when I got there, Kevin surprised me.

He'd gotten what every 16-year-old dreamt about; his driver's license. I was shocked. He was going to take me to dinner and wanted to take me to a movie. I giggled when he first told me.

"You mean, like a real date?" I asked.

Nodding, Kevin replied, "Yes Ma'am! Like a real date, Lainey! Something we never got to do!"

I was actually going to get to go out with him like I was a real girlfriend. He was truly in the best mood. I couldn't believe that only 48 hours earlier I didn't know if I still loved him or not or could ever forgive him! Now, here I stood in front of him, in his room, giggling and about to go on my first date with him.

We went into Donna's room before we left, and she crowed when we told her we were going to go eat and to a movie. We both looked at Donna peculiarly.

"I told you, DeLaine! I told you he loved you and that you should be his girlfriend and not that weird Jax-person!" Kevin looked at me as I began to laugh.

"I'll tell you later," I whispered, as Donna cackled.

"Well, Squirt, maybe DeLaine already is my girlfriend…at least for tonight!" Kevin said smiling at his little sister.

Donna smiled her own version of the sunshine and rainbows smile at Kevin, "But I was right, Kev, you love DeLaine! I knewed it!"

Kevin looked at Donna and stroked her hair, "But you're my best girl."

"It's okay, Kev, you can love DeLaine too. I give you permissions because I love her too!" Donna chirped.

Smiling indulgently, Kevin stated solemnly, "Well, okay, thanks for your permissions, Little One, I'll take it under advisement."

Donna looked at Kevin a bit pouty and demanded, "Kevin, you DO love DeLaine, don't you?" Kevin's gorgeous, blue, summery eyes glanced over at me and then back to Donna and he nodded with a smile.

"Don't forget to tell her then, like you do me, okay?" Donna stated, suddenly serious.

"Okay, Sissy. Now, we gotta go or else we won't be able to eat before we go to the movies."

Kevin leaned over and kissed Donna on her flaxen, silky hair. I moved in behind him and kissed Donna on the cheek and told her I was going to come over Sunday afternoon to see her one more time before I left. I had planned to tell his family then about my decision to go to Corpus Christi.

We went to tell his parents bye and to get his mom's car keys. Before we walked out, his mom called me back into the kitchen and she pulled me to her, "I'm glad you two are finally getting this chance. I wish it could be for longer, but I'm glad you're going out tonight."

I pulled back from her and smiled. I nodded. and tears came to my eyes.

"My boy's loved you a long time. I know this has been hard for both of you." The tears came out of my eyes then and I nodded once more as she pressed a tissue in my hand. I walked out with my head down, wiping my eyes to meet Kevin in the driveway.

After eating at Mama Z's Pizzeria, we went to the movie theater. We didn't see much of anything either of us wanted to watch. We went through the mall one time, then looked at some silly stuff in Spencer's while walking around holding hands.

I was happy to be on the only real date I would probably get to go on with Kevin. I realized as we walked through the mall that I probably would be only a memory in a year. I knew we wouldn't get to talk on the phone and I could write to him now, but I didn't know if he'd ever write me back. I wished there was something that I could give him to remember me by, but I had no clue what to give him. I didn't even know if he wanted something from me.

As we were heading on our way out of the mall we saw Lori and Barbie as they walked in the door. Lori saw us, then saw Kevin holding my hand. She got a vicious smile on her face. I felt Kevin's arm get tense, but he looked away after he'd registered her presence. I didn't. I wanted to see what she was going to do or say.

Barbie looked at me and smiled hesitantly and I smiled back. She'd been my best friend a million years before and I'd never forget that. I'd really cared a lot about her. We had been so much younger, and our lives had been so different. The tornado changed so much for all of us. I flicked my eyes back to Lori and she continued to grin evilly at me. I wondered what the hell she had planned. I was so glad that Kevin was away from her.

We got into the car and Kevin looked at me disappointedly, "I'm sorry our date seems to be a gigantic bust! I don't know what we should do." I smiled at him and he asked, "So, did Lori say something when we walked by?"

"Nah, she just gave me looks that could kill, but I wouldn't put it past her to try to create some kind of havoc for one of us." I replied, smiling ruefully. Kevin nodded his head.

It was so early the sun was still out. You had to love those long summer days. Kevin started the car and was about to go to his house, then he smiled at me, "I've got an idea!" I smiled at him and asked what it was and he shook his head, "We gotta go back by the house and then we are off on an adventure!" I smiled, nodding my head and told him to lead the way.

When we got to his house he told me to wait in the car. I nodded, and he ran inside. I sat there watching the sky begin to deepen and smiled just to be waiting on Kevin.

After a few minutes he came out with a big pile of stuff. I rolled the window down and he hollered, "Close your eyes! You'll ruin the surprise! And roll up the window too!"

I beamed, closed my eyes and rolled up the window.

Kevin opened the trunk and then slammed it closed and jumped back into the driver's seat, asking, "Do you trust me?"

I looked at him warily and bobbed my head slowly. "Why?" I asked.

"Because I want you to keep your eyes closed until we get there. Unless it's gonna make you car sick, that is, then keep 'em open!" He was laughing.

I loved this playful Kevin. He'd been my protector for so long that we'd never gotten to have too many carefree moments. I said, "I'll close 'em, but for how long?"

"Not long," he assured me.

I felt us turn left on Fairfax and then I felt us stop at the light at Parkway Hwy. When we didn't turn I knew we were going out straight towards Levi's house. I tried to think about what was out this way. The only thing I could think of besides houses was the lake. Inwardly I groaned.

I couldn't believe that Kevin was taking me to the lake. That was the place that made me think of Jax. That was the spot that we had spent so much time with Levi and Bailey through the winter. I thought about telling Kevin, but he seemed so excited to take me on an adventure. I would try really hard not to say anything about being out there with Jax.

It felt like we had driven a lot longer before he turned. When he did, it didn't feel like the same way we would be turning if we were going to the spot where Jax, Bailey, Levi and I all went together. I decided maybe I didn't need to worry. Maybe Kevin was actually taking me somewhere different.

The car went off of whatever road we were driving on and I could tell we were now on a bumpy terrain. I wasn't sure what it was, but I wanted to open my eyes so badly.

I kept giggling as Kevin made sounds like we were going to crash then he'd tell me silly stuff about where we were heading. I loved hearing the joy in his voice.

Finally, he brought the car to a stop and he told me to wait in the car. He warned me not to peek and I crossed my heart and swore on Donna. I figured that would become our sacred thing to swear on after his swearing on her the night before. After a few minutes he came and got me out of the car.

I kept my eyes closed as I walked to where Kevin led me. I could smell grass and hear water, so I knew we were somewhere around the lake, but I didn't have a clue where. The evening breeze made the early summer warmth bearable. When we reached the destination, Kevin put his hands over my eyes. I was excited to make a new memory with him.

Slowly, Kevin pulled his hands away. I opened my eyes timidly to protect myself from the unwanted glare after having them closed so long. When I looked out, I felt my breath catch in my throat. I couldn't believe it. We were at the lake, but at a different part than where I went with Jax and our best friends. That wasn't what caught my breath though. I turned and looked at Kevin with huge tears welling in my eyes. Then I turned around again and stared.

The place I stood was a large grassy area covered in tiny, yellow flowers that were bending delicately in the evening air. I felt flabbergasted. I looked at the water and saw the sunset being masterfully painted on top of the lake. The sky overhead held stubbornly to a tiny bit of the summer blue in it. The puffy white clouds were lit from behind by the brilliant oranges, golds, pinks and even some magentas of the sunset. When I looked at the water itself I saw it was a beautiful teal color in the deeper areas away from shore.

I looked at what Kevin had made me wait in the car for. He had spread out an old wool blanket on the ground and on top of that was a round piece of cloth that looked like it was a big tablecloth. The way it laid on top of the wool blanket created a perfect circle amid the yellow flowers. A portable radio and a candle, with a picnic basket and two cokes, in bottles, sat on the blanket.

It was probably the most romantic thing I'd ever seen in my life.

I kept looking from Kevin, to the flowers, and lake, because I had dreamt about this. I had dreamt about the grass, yellow flowers, Kevin and summer blue skies. It seemed as if my dreams were going to come true tonight. For once in my life my dreams were actually coming true.

I turned to Kevin and he was shocked to see tears streaking my cheeks. I kissed him quickly on the mouth when he asked me what was wrong.

I shook my head and said, "Nothin'…absolutely nothin'! For once in my life I think everything is perfectly perfect!" Kevin grinned and asked why. I murmured, "Come sit down with me and I'll tell you. He nodded and then he held my hand as we walked over to the little picnic area he'd set up.

"Kevin, do you believe we can dream about stuff and it comes true?" I asked him seriously. He shrugged and said he wasn't sure. "Well, would you believe me if I told you that I've dreamt of these yellow flowers almost since you first came into my life?"

He looked around and smiled, then looked into my eyes, "Well, after seeing the shocked look on your face and the tears in your eyes as soon as you looked, yea, I guess I would probably have to say I believe you."

"When I opened my eyes and saw this, it was like, well, like I was dreaming all over again," I whispered, smiling. "All my dreams are coming true about you tonight, Kevin. I can go out with you, for the first time and not be frightened. The field that I dreamed about is real. It's right here. I'm sitting in it for real. I just thought it was a field that I would dream about when I dreamt about you. It's like everything I ever wanted to make me real, like Donna's bunny, is right here tonight. I'm afraid I'll turn into a pumpkin or something at midnight," I giggled.

"If I remember the story right, it was actually the stagecoach that turned into a pumpkin, not Cinderella. But you do remind me of Cinderella with the evil, bitch step-mom! Instead of ugly step-sisters you got step-brothers, but you definitely got all the shit chores," he whispered as he leaned over and kissed my cheek making me giggle.

"It wasn't a stagecoach. That's only on *Gunsmoke*, Dork! It was a carriage!" I sniffed.

"Oh yea, what was I thinkin'?" Kevin whispered as he kissed me from my cheek on over to my mouth. I wrapped my arms around his neck and kissed him freely. Feeling so happy to be in a place where I knew I was always supposed to end up. It wasn't easy to get here. The last week alone I never thought I'd be here, but here I was.

I leaned against Kevin and we watched as the reds and magentas of the sunset deepened into the deep purples and navy blues and when the first star came out to twinkle, I told him we had to wish on it. He indulged me and we wished. I told him not to tell me his because they wouldn't come true! I felt so carefree. I felt silly and young. I felt the way I thought maybe I was supposed to feel.

Kevin grabbed the cokes and got out a bottle opener from the picnic basket. He handed me the semi-cold drink, "Oh, by the way, the candle and picnic basket was Mom's idea, so don't think I'm like super boyfriend or anything. I was just gonna grab the old blanket.

"She's the one who went rushin' through the house picking stuff up and throwin' it in the basket and telling me what I had to do and actually she's the one who reminded me about this part of the lake. We came out a few times when I was younger. Donna always liked this part because it had the yellow flowers."

"See, I knew there was a reason she and I got along so well," I laughed. "I think to be honest, I love this date much more than I would have liked sitting in a sticky, stinky movie theater."

"Yea, I think I like it to. I think as far as dates I've been able to drive on, it is probably right at the number one slot!" Kevin was laughing.

I snickered, "Gee, I'm glad, since I'm the ONLY date you've been able to drive on!"

"See, and you think I don't listen. You think I don't appreciate how brilliant you are!" Kevin kissed me on the side of my mouth.

I pulled away and asked, "Okay, truth…where exactly DOES this date rate on your date top 10?"

Kevin started laughing, "What is this *Dick Clark's Top 10 Date Billboard* or what?" I nodded and he pondered, "Okay, well, hmmm, let's see, I'd say it is definitely gonna be in the top 5!"

"What?" I squeaked.

Laughing and rolling on the blanket, Kevin exclaimed, "Oh my, Lainey, you are so funny! I would say it is probably the top one if I had to really think about it. But, let's just say, I'm enjoying this night so much and I'm so grateful we're even here. I've hated myself so much this whole week. I didn't know how I'd ever convince you how sorry I was." He looked at me suddenly serious.

I sobered too and then shook my head, "That's past now. We're not going to talk about it ever again, okay? I don't think you would ever intentionally hurt me, Kevin. I also don't think you were in your right mind. I've forgiven you and I want it to be over and done."

Kevin looked up at me in the candle light.

Finally, I stated seriously, "I don't like you when you drink. If Kevin Welks ever shows his sorry face to me again, I'll probably shove my fist into his mouth!"

Kevin smiled as he looked at me. He raised his hand up to my face and stroked my jaw line with his finger. I smiled at him and he mused, "I don't know why in the world you ever thought I was worth being there for."

Surprised I asked, "What?"

Smiling, Kevin responded, "I'll never know why in the world you thought I was worth all the trouble you went through, just to be with me."

"Are you serious, Kevin? It's the other way around. I needed you. It was you that was there for ME." I whispered, quietly.

He pulled me down with his hand, under my ear, along my neck and I found his mouth and leaned in to kiss him.

While I kissed Kevin, I realized that I was happier at that particular moment than any other that I could remember. Before long we were lying side by side on the ground with the candle glowing near our heads setting off a little ways in the grass.

I had no fire burning in my belly in rage. The only fire burning at that moment was in my heart. I lay there kissing Kevin and was happy that he was content to only kiss me. I had been so afraid of him only days earlier. I think he knew that and it was the reason he hadn't tried to be any more amorous than he was.

After a while I lay with my head on his chest and he murmured, "It has felt like a part of me was missing. I am so happy I got that piece of me back. It seems like you always eventually find your way back to me though. I hope you always do, Lainey. I can't think of never seeing you again for the rest of my life."

Smiling up at him I admitted, "I can't think of that either. I'd be so sad if it ever happens. You promise you won't forget me?" I murmured as tears smarted in the corners of my eyes.

"Are you serious? You silly, little, Lainey! Of course I'll never forget you. You're my Lainey. You'll be back either at Christmas or Spring Break or at the end of the school year. It's not like you'll be gone forever." Kevin surmised.

"It sure feels like forever to me. You're liable to have a new girlfriend next year when I finally get here," I muttered quietly.

"Nope, probably not," He stated resolutely.

"Kevin, give me a break, you aren't going to become a priest. You're sixteen for God's sake. You aren't going to give up on girls for me." I chided with my right eyebrow arched.

Deep laughter bubbled out of Kevin's chest and he shook his head, "Nope, don't plan on it, but there's always a place for you in my life no matter who else is there. I mean it, DeLaine. I don't care. You will always trump any other girl in my life. If you can live with it, then I can. I'm not going to be a priest or a monk or anything stupid, but you will always get my time when you are here. I can't say no to you. I can't turn away from you. I don't know why. I just know that I can't imagine never kissing you again, or holding you, or talking, or laughing with you. I can't imagine it and I'm not going to do it either if I have anything to say about it."

Looking at him seriously I disagreed, "What if you find someone you feel serious about though? I mean, it could happen. What if I find a boyfriend in Corpus?" I quipped, trying not to laugh because I couldn't imagine ever having another real boyfriend again.

"Lainey, I don't plan on getting serious about anyone until I'm at least 18. Until then, you are the main woman I plan to be serious about. Doesn't mean I'm not gonna date and if you find a boy you feel serious about I'll respect it when you visit. But I still want to see you when you come back home to visit," he sighed to me softly.

"Kevin, you can't say you won't get serious about a girl until you're 18!" I raised my eyebrow even higher.

Nodding his head Kevin chuckled, "Oh yeah, I really can, DeLaine. It's only two more years. I don't plan on getting serious." I insisted he couldn't know for a fact and he adamantly stated, "I know I can't say with all certainty but I don't plan on looking for it, how's that?"

I nodded my head, "You know, Kevin, I don't think there is anyone else out there who will ever care about me. I think I kinda got a fluke thing with you and well, Jax too, but I can't imagine anyone else liking me."

"DeLaine! Stop it! Right now! Do you hear me? Get Geoffrey out of your damned head! Those Corpus boys don't even know what kind of hell they are about to be in for," he smiled and then kissed me. "Lainey, you're gonna have another boyfriend. I don't know when and it will drive me nuts so you probably shouldn't tell me!"

I started giggling again, "Okay, deal. You gotta promise the same thing though!"

"I already told you, it won't matter. She'll have to either be okay with me seeing you or she's not gonna be anything other than someone I see sometimes!"

Shaking my head I declared, "I give up! But I just don't think you really are going to be unattached every time I come here." He told me to wait and see and I shook his hand playfully.

"Okay, no more talk about other boyfriends or girlfriends. I'm your boyfriend for tonight. You are my girlfriend for the night. Shh, lay down beside me and watch the stars, woman!" Kevin playfully pulled me beside him to lie on my back.

As I looked into the heavens and saw the millions of stars folded out before me on the virtual black, velvet blanket that I always dreamed about, I grinned. I was amazed at how beautiful the diamond lights looked, laying there flat on my back, near the lake.

"So what was all that shit Donna was saying about telling you I loved you and that I should be your boyfriend instead of Jax?" Kevin asked out of nowhere. Laughing I explained, "Well, I told her that I'd gone horseback riding with Jax right before he and I broke up and realized I'd never told her about having a boyfriend."

"She got all bent out of shape because she didn't understand why you weren't my boyfriend and she told me that you loved me."

" I tried to explain to her about how love was different in all types of situations and friends could love each other and you didn't have to be my boyfriend to love me, but she wasn't having any of it! You know, I just realized you and Donna are both so hard headed when it comes to trying to talk y'all into something."

"Yeah, it's a family curse thing!" Kevin was smiling. I smirked, and he leaned up and over, kissing me softly, then whispered, "You know, it's spooky how she sees stuff that others don't see."

"Yeah, it is, but that's something else that makes her special, you know, Kev?" I replied. He nodded, and I scooted my head onto his arm to finish looking at the stars. We lay there forever content to just talk and look at the sky with all of her jewels on for the night.

With all good things though, the night came to an end, and Kevin had to drive me back to Bailey's. Before we left I reached over and picked one of the yellow flowers.

"What are you going to do with that?" Kevin asked me softly when he opened the car door for me. I shrugged and got in. While he put everything in the trunk I put my nose next to the fuzzy, little, yellow bloom and smelled the earthiness of it.

Kevin pulled his mom's car up outside of Bailey's house at 12:15. I had 15 minutes to get in the door. "You know, usually girlfriends scoot over to the middle to give their boyfriends goodnight kisses," Kevin grinned devilishly.

"Is that right? Huh, well, you know, I've only ever had one real boyfriend until tonight. Now I can say I've had two real boyfriends. The other one was a shit-kicker and he drove a truck, so I wasn't sure what I was supposed to do in a sedan." I said in mock seriousness.

"A shit-kicker, huh? Damn, I took you for a girl with better taste than to date a damned shit-kicker! They smell like shit!" Kevin mocked, smirking.

"Now, wait a minute, there are some nice things about kickers that I kinda like…you know, horseback riding is a lot of fun." I insisted a little more adamantly than I figured was good, but it was true.

"Well, yeah and the girl shit-kickers, they are damned fine with those tight wranglers on!" I knew he was trying to gauge my reaction.

"Really?" I asked him playfully. "Well, we agree on one thing then about kickers, they look damned nice in those Wrangler jeans!"

"C'mere Lainey," Kevin playfully growled. I had already scooted into the middle of the seat and leaned in to kiss the boy of my dreams. Tonight had proven to me who was the boy of my dreams after all. I still felt confused as ever over both boys. I knew in my heart of hearts if I had to choose between Kevin and Jax, Kevin would always win.

Pulling away from, him I breathlessly whispered, "I just want to say this one time while you're still officially my boyfriend because I haven't turned into a pumpkin yet, okay?" Kevin smiled and nodded his head. I looked him directly in the eyes. I could just make out the sky-blue in the light from the porch light, "I love you, Kevin Strong. I will for the rest of my life. I think as your official girlfriend it is my right to tell you that," I finished with a grin.

Looking at me as if I were some rare bird, Kevin whispered huskily, "Lainey…DeLaine Marie Reynolds, I love you too. As your official boyfriend for the night, I can say that!" then the spell broke like a soap bubble popping and we moved in to kiss one more time. I started to grab the door handle and Kevin held his hand up and jumped out of the car. He ran around to open my door and then he walked me to the porch. "The spell is almost broken. Tomorrow we just go back to plain Kevin and Lainey."

"Kevin, I don't think we'll ever be just Plain Kevin or Plain Lainey! I just don't think it is in the cards for us, Darlin'. I think we're always gonna be extremely complicated but I'm willing to be complicated. If that's how it has to be, then it has to be. I'm not willing to give you up just now. Not after I finally fled the Terror Bunch!" I stated, smiling up at him.

"Is that a play on *The Brady Bunch* because you know, Lainey, you're awful good at those funny little word things." Kevin spoke quietly.

"Yeah, so I've been told," I replied wryly. "Kiss me again before you aren't my boyfriend anymore because it's like over in 2 minutes!"

"Happy to oblige, Little Lady," Kevin imitated a silly, Western drawl.

"What is with you and *Gunsmoke* tonight?"

"You noticed that, huh? I just thought I'd talk like those damned shit-kickers you like!" laughing blue eyes shone down at me in the porch light.

I playfully slapped him on the arm and said, "Shut up and kiss me you dork!" He did.

Chapter 6

The next day Bailey and I went to the mall to do a little shopping for her trip to Corpus. While we were out, I went into a small card shop that also had bibles and religious items. I had never been raised in a religious home. I'd gone to a sleep away camp when I was in elementary school and accepted Jesus. The only religion I got though was from going to church with my friends.

I'd been to church with both Bailey and Kelly White, but I didn't know much about any of it except the bare minimum kid stories I'd seen or heard while I'd gone to Sunday school with friends. I always felt I was missing something by not going to a church. It didn't mean I hadn't been raised to believe in God. My parents just had conflicting religious upbringings and for whatever reasons, of theirs, our family had never been religious. I found little stores like the one at the mall, intriguing because I so wanted to believe Someone was looking out for me.

While I was there, I found some silver necklaces with different Saints on them. I didn't know anything about them, but they each had information cards. I was struck by St. Michael, the Archangel, medal. He was supposed to be the ultimate archangel of protection. Kevin's middle name was Michael. I had wanted to get him something to remember me by, so when I saw that it was something I could afford, I bought it quickly.

I also found out that St. Christopher was the Saint to protect travelers and I found a small charm of Saint Christopher on a silver bracelet and bought it as well. I'd never been to a Catholic church, but I hoped since Saints and Angels alike worked for God, they must protect everybody, including people like me who really didn't have a religion.

I also found a sweet little bear with Angel wings on it for Donna. I knew that she would like having something to remember me by until I got to come back. I planned to write her when I got to Corpus, although it probably wouldn't be weekly, like I'd done the year before.

After I made my purchases I went back to the shop where I'd left Bailey. When she saw me with a bag she asked what I'd bought. I grinned at her and admitted, "Well, I bought a present for a couple of the people I love the most in the world."

"You bought Kevin AND Jax presents?" Bailey asked me surprised.

I started laughing, "Bay-Bay! Do you think those are the only people I love the most?" She nodded her head. I grinned, "Well, you got a lot to learn my friend! I'll show you when we get home." Bailey shrugged and began telling me about the two outfits she'd liked the most.

When we got back to her house, I called Kevin. I told him that I was going to hang out with Bailey and Levi and I'd come over Sunday afternoon to spend time with him before I left. I told him I had a surprise for him and he started giggling, "Really, that's funny, 'cause I got one for you too!" When I tried to wheedle it out of him he just laughed and told me I had to wait until the next day.

Bailey came into her room, after I hung up the phone, with drinks for us. She sat on her floor while I brought out the things I'd bought in the small shop. I showed her the St. Michael pendant I bought for Kevin and she said she thought he'd probably really like it. I was happy. It was so hard to buy a present for a guy! They were more difficult to shop for when you had only a little bit of money. As it was, I'd spent almost every dime of the spending money my daddy sent with me, but I thought what I'd gotten was good stuff.

I pulled the little Angel bear out next for Donna and Bailey agreed that she would love it. I laughed and told her I hoped she just didn't name it DeLaine too, like she'd done the dolphin I'd brought back for her the year before. Then I pulled out the other small box with the bracelet. I handed it to Bailey.

"Is this what you got for Jax?" She asked me curiously.

"Open it and tell me what you think," I replied smiling.

Bailey opened the tiny box and looked at it curiously, stating, "I don't think Jax is gonna wear a bracelet, Lala." Then she stopped and looked at it, "Wait, who is this for?"

Laughing, I crowed, "Duh, Bay! It's for you, silly!"

Looking at me curiously she looked at the bracelet and charm, "Why did you get me a St. Christopher medal?"

"He's the Patron Saint of Travelers. You're about to be traveling and I want you to be safe. Plus I figured he'd protect you no matter what while I'm gone." I smiled.

She grinned back, "But you know I'm not Catholic, right?"

"Oh my God, Bay! I know you're Church of Christ. You know, I've gone to church with you and I'm pretty sure I've read the name of the church at least a half dozen times!" I cackled.

Smiling, Bailey chirped, "Oh yea, DUH!" Then she hugged me and told me she loved it.

"I wish I was going to be around. I hope these will help y'all remember me a little," I stated, smiling. She nodded, then reached over and grabbed a tissue and wiped her eyes. "Oh Bay, don't cry!"

"I can't help it. I'm gonna miss you so much, Lala!" Bailey wailed.

"Me too Bay, but I promise on Donna I'll be back!" I reassured her.

Bailey looked at me perplexed, "Promise on Donna? What in the world does that mean?"

I explained how it seemed if Kevin said he promised on Donna, I knew he meant business. She giggled and said that was a pretty good one!

"So, do you believe me that I'm coming back?" I asked her. She smiled at me and nodded her head again. "Okay, call that boyfriend of yours and find out what we're doing since we're not going skating according to him!"

"Okay! Lala?"

"Yeah?" I replied.

"I love you," Bailey whispered softly. I smiled and told her I loved her too, and then I got up to go to the bathroom. I didn't want Bailey to see me cry for the millionth time since I'd been back home. It seemed I cried every single day about something, but at least it wasn't to the point that my eyes were swollen like I'd done before I left to go to Oklahoma. This time I had made my own decision. It was one that I felt was forced on me to make, but it was still my choice.

Chapter 7

When I went back to Bailey's room she had just gotten off the phone with Levi and asked, "Um, do you mind hanging with Levi AND Jax tonight?"

I looked at my best friend and thought about it. I was technically lying by omission to Kevin, but he'd only been my boyfriend for last night. I also had been open with Jax about seeing Kevin too. I wanted to be able to say goodbye to Jax and I'd enjoyed my time when I'd seen him. We hadn't done more than kiss a little since I'd been home, as well as dance, and I didn't plan on anything more being done with him. Kevin and I both agreed we were always going to be complicated the night before. He told me he didn't want to know if I found a new boyfriend. So, if he didn't want to know, I wouldn't tell him.

As I stood there thinking all of this through, in my head, I realized that I was making excuses for myself to be okay with seeing Jax. I started telling Bailey everything I was thinking.

"You know, DeLaine, you said it right at the beginning…you and Kevin aren't boyfriend and girlfriend. You love him, I get that, but unless he commits to you, and he already said he wasn't gonna be a priest while you're gone, then I don't know why you think you have to justify seeing Jax too. Trust me, it doesn't mean you're a bad person if you date two boys. If you start screwing both of them, then we might have to look at it, but you aren't doing that with either one. Well," she broke off, then muttered, "You know what I mean." I glanced down thinking about the Sunday before with Kevin and nodded my head. "I think you should see Jax and enjoy yourself. You aren't leading either of them on. But knowing Kevin's hot head, it probably is best if you just forget to tell him. Hopefully he won't find out either…for Jax sake!!" she was laughing.

"Yeah, it probably wouldn't end too good for me or Jax if he knew," I looked at the floor. "You know what? You said it, when you said he wasn't going to be a priest. He already said he didn't own me. So, unless he wants to marry me, I'm gonna see Jax tonight it looks like!" I shrugged my shoulders.

"Yay! I already told Levi okay!" my best friend was clapping her hands. I shook my head and began to laugh with her.

That night when Jax and Levi came to pick us up, we told her mom we were going to the skating rink. I wondered if her mom thought Jax had a hardship license, but never asked. We headed out to the lake like I knew we would.

When we got to the part of the lake that we always hung out at, I smiled as I remembered where Kevin had taken us the night before. I saw in the back that they had brought lawn chairs and an ice chest along with their own radio. Bailey and I, both, were tanned by our time at the pool, and I realized Jax and Levi were as well, even though I felt certain that Jax's probably ended at the sleeves of his shirt. It was still daylight since it was only 6 o'clock.

The boys took the lawn chairs to the shallow part of the lake and came back giggling. I asked why they set them up out there and Levi grinned and said to wait. They weren't done. I looked at Bailey and she shrugged her shoulders. She and I were wearing sandals so we took them off and waded to the chairs that were sitting at the water's edge. The water was already really warm, but it felt good to slip my toes into the silt and mud that was gluing the legs of the lawn chair into the lake.

Levi and Jax both came up and had stripped out of their jeans and boots and I was shocked to see they had on swim trunks. They both had stripped their shirts off too and I looked at Jax and realized that even though I'd felt his bare chest, I'd never seen it in the light. I was surprised when I saw that his tan didn't end at his shirt sleeves. In each of their hands they were holding fishing poles. I looked at Bailey and she started laughing.

"Are you guys serious?" I asked, with my nose wrinkled up.

"Yeah, fishin' is fun!" Jax was smiling impishly at me.

"Well, I'll bait the hook if you got worms, but other than that, I'm not much at fishin'!" I grinned back.

"Awww, stick with me, I might teach you a thing or two," Jax snickered.

Bailey was always up for an adventure it seemed because she was next to Levi, already getting their fishing poles together. Within only a few minutes, we were all four sitting in our lawn chairs holding our respective fishing poles. Jax exclaimed, "Oh shit, I forgot! Here, DeLaine, hold my pole!" and he thrust his fishing pole into my hand as he jumped up and ran to the edge of the water where they'd set the ice chest. Walking back, Jax had four beers in his hands. "I forgot! I got these from a ranch hand at my uncle's today. He bought me two six packs."

I looked at him and rolled my eyes. I was not too keen on drinking beer. After the Sunday before, when I'd walked into Welks' house and found Kevin drunk on beer, I really didn't want much to do with it.

Jax leaned over and handed Levi and Bailey beers and when he handed me one I asked, "You wouldn't happen to have a coke in there would you?"

"Uh, no, I only have beer. Don't you want one?" Jax exclaimed. I looked at the can and knew that I detested the taste of beer.

"Well…" I trailed off.

"C'mon, DeLaine, just drink one. If you don't want any more I'll run up to the little store and get you a bottle of coke," Jax coaxed sweetly. I nodded and he pulled the pull-tab ring off of the aluminum can and handed it to me.

I took a tiny sip of the beer and even though it was really cold, it was also really nasty as it hit the back of my throat. I tried not to gag and then handed Jax his fishing pole.

When Jax finished his beer, I suggested, "Hey, go ahead and drink mine," I hadn't drunk more than the first sip.

"Are you sure, DeLaine?" Jax asked me a little concerned.

"Yeah, I just can't stand how beer tastes," I insisted, with the wrinkle back in my nose and lips. Jax shrugged and took my beer and began drinking it too. After a while, I saw Levi get up and he got another beer for him and Bailey. I knew that the first six-pack was gone now and I wondered if Jax, Levi and Bailey planned on drinking the other one as well. I tried to quell my uneasiness and told myself I was being a big party-pooper. I knew that teenagers drank all the time. I also knew that technically we were high school kids now that we were out of 8th grade.

As the sun began to hang lower in the horizon, we finally caught a couple of fish. I happened to catch the first one. When I reeled it in, Jax helped me get it all the way up and asked if I wanted to take it off. The smell alone made me snarl my lip and I declared, "Hell no, take that smelly little thing off!" Jax started laughing and unhooked the small, silvery fish and threw it out into the lake again. "So, what is the point again to fishing?" I grumbled, crossly.

"To sit, relax and drink beer," Jax crowed, looking at me with his meadow green eyes.

"Well, as far as past-times go, this has to be the worst one in the world," I replied, sarcastically.

Levi began laughing, "Lala, it's fun, you just sit here and enjoy the sunshine, friends and drink a couple of cold ones!"

Shaking my head, I stated, "Well, I'm just too much of a city girl I guess, 'cause this is pretty stupid. Especially if you don't like beer!"

Jax snapped his head over, "Oh shit! I was supposed to go get you a coke! I'm sorry!"

I shook my head and he jumped up and exclaimed, "No, really, y'all hang tight! I'll be back in a few minutes!" With that statement Jax was running to his truck and started it up and took off.

Levi looked at me seriously, "Damn, DeLaine, that's the first time I've seen him run since football season!" Bailey and I both collapsed into giggles.

Jax returned within 15 minutes with a cold bottle of coke and he picked his way over the stickers and rough grass to come back to his seat.

"There you go madam!" Jax gushed with a flourish. I smiled at him and he asked, "So, why don't you like beer, DeLaine?"

I shrugged my shoulders and said, "I dunno. I just think it tastes nasty. It also makes me burp like crazy. Just not crazy about it."

"Cool, it means there's more for me and Levi!" Jax was laughing.

By the time the sun was just a distant memory in the sky, and the first stars were beginning to twinkle, the boys had put up the fishing poles and they'd each drank another beer. The sky was deepening from a dark pink into a deep purple which I knew would become the velvet black of regular night without us even realizing it until it was already over.

We had moved the chairs into the tiny grove of trees where we'd sat in the winter time and Jax had pulled the big portable radio out and turned it on the country station while we all sat there and talked about everything and nothing at the same time. I knew this would be the last time I'd spend here for probably at least a year with these three people. I wondered how many changes each of us would go through in that time. I felt like I had known this time the year before, how everything in my life was supposed to turn out! Now I saw that nothing I had planned for my life, from the previous year, would ever come to pass.

I would never walk back into Samson High School again. Bailey and I would never walk in the doors together as freshman for our first day. I wasn't going to ever live on Belfast again in my life. I would never be worried that Geoffrey would kill me because I loved Kevin Strong and I would never know what it was like to go to high school with my friends.

Right now my life was like a huge, blank page. There was no writing on the page. I thought back over my life and realized that it had happened like a book. I had chapters and even whole sections about certain things and times in my life.

Right now, my book didn't even have a diagram for the next part. It was blank as blank could be. I worried that I wouldn't know how to write on the pages of the future I was supposed to have.

I wondered who the friends would be that I would write into those blank pages. I'd thought I'd known just six months ago who all those friends would be.

I thought that my blank pages would include stories about me and Bailey, high school together, sleep overs and me pining for Kevin and going with Jax.

I thought there would be more stories of me and Jax to write, as well as stories about me and Kevin. I knew there would be stories that included Levi and Bailey together and maybe some with the other people who were in my life like Kelly White, Polly Green, Crystal Box and all the other girls from lunch. I even wondered if I would have written a chapter about Chrissy and what a pain in the ass I thought she was.

Now I looked at those empty pages and saw lots of question marks. Living in Corpus Christi was as unknown as moving to Oklahoma had been, except I wanted to live in Corpus Christi. I had never wanted to live in Oklahoma.

I didn't understand why living more than twice the amount of time from Wichita Falls than I did in Oklahoma was preferable, except that I was so miserable and lonely. I had been miserable living with Clarice and Geoffrey for a long time, but now that I didn't even have the benefit of one friend, I was so lonely I couldn't stand it. At least in Corpus Christi I'd have my mom and I was closer to her than I was to Clarice or Daddy. I also had Kelly and Robin Stubbs there. At least I had a couple of friends to talk to. They weren't Bailey, but they were still close to me.

I sighed as I looked around our little circle of four in the light of the small campfire Jax had built earlier in the evening. Jax looked at me and asked if I was okay. I smiled and nodded my head. Bailey looked at me and she leaned over and said something softly to Levi. I saw Levi nod his head and he told Jax he was gonna grab one of the blankets and he and Bailey were gonna go lay by the water and look at the stars. Jax grinned and nodded his head.

When they were gone he smiled at me and instructed, "Well, I guess we need to stay up here for a while."

I looked at him curiously and then said, "OH! Um, yeah, I guess so!" then I began to giggle. I noticed that Jax seemed pretty relaxed. I didn't think he was drunk. But he seemed pretty mellow. Both boys had drunk four beers apiece and Bailey had drunk two.

"Come on, there's another blanket in the back of the truck," Jax grinned at me. I wondered what he had in mind. I hoped it wasn't what he thought that Levi and Bailey were doing because I knew that wasn't going to happen with us. No matter how much Jax might want it to, it wasn't in any way, shape, or form going to happen with me tonight. We walked to the old Ford and he pulled out an old horse blanket. I smiled when I saw it.

We walked out away from the grove of trees we had been sitting. I didn't know where Bailey and Levi had gone.

Jax carried the blanket near the water, where we could hear it as it lapped at the shore. I sat down cross legged on the blanket with him and asked how the horses were that we used to ride. He smiled and told me that Moon Boy was almost like a drug to him since he was able to ride him every day now that he was back working for his uncle. I smiled. I told him to give Buttercup some love from me and he smiled and nodded his head.

He asked what I thought it would be like living in Corpus and I shrugged. I told him that when I lived there after the tornado for a few months, it was a lot different than Wichita had been.

I told him the schools inside of Corpus were really rough and I'd gone to a school out in one of the suburbs of Corpus. We used my mom's best friend's address and she drove me out there every day. I told him that the suburb was a lot more like Wichita, but still different. Jax teased me and asked if I was gonna start surfing. I shook my head and told him I wasn't crazy about the beach! I told him about getting stung by jellyfish and how bad they hurt.

After a while we lay on the blanket and looked at the stars like Kevin and I had done the night before. We didn't have a candle to cast a glow to light up where we were, plus I didn't lie on his chest and listen to his heartbeat like I had with Kev.

The moon would be full in a few days, so the moonlight over the water was illuminating the night enough for us to be able to see. I looked over at the lake and noticed the moon beams on the water and remembered how I had wanted to glide out on them during the winter. I started giggling softly, and Jax asked why I was laughing. I told him about the winter when we'd been out there and how I'd wanted to glide on the moon beams. He laughed and told me I was probably the weirdest girl he knew.

When he first said that, I looked at him and wondered if he meant it to be hurtful. When I didn't say anything, Jax turned his head to look at me, "I'm just teasin' DeLaine. You aren't weird. You're a dreamer is probably what my uncle would say. He says some people are workers and some are dreamers. I think you're a dreamer. Aunt Betty told me when I was little that there wasn't anything wrong with being a dreamer, when Uncle Rob first said that around me. She told me dreamers were the people who were inventors and writers and painters. So, if you're a dreamer, I say be a dreamer." He smiled at me sweetly.

"So, are you playing football next year?" I asked Jax.

"Yeah, I think I'm gonna try it, but I'm also gonna do rodeo. If I like rodeo more then I'm probably getting out of football," Jax admitted as he looked at the stars. I knew he wouldn't look at me because he knew how much I worried when he'd ridden the bull last fall.

"Well, you know, even workers have to have dreams, Jax," I murmured softly. He looked at me and smiled again.

Jax leaned up onto his elbow, "So what do you think you'll do in school next year, when you get to Corpus?"

"I dunno. I mean, I don't know what they have there. High school is new as it is. I don't even know where I'm going to go to school when I get there," I shrugged my shoulders. "I guess I'll just have to wait and see. I sure wish I was going to Samson," I sighed, quietly.

Jax looked at me seriously, "Yeah, me too. I hate you're moving even further away."

I nodded and he continued, "I'm gonna miss you again, you know right?" I felt the lump rising in my throat.

He finally leaned over and kissed me under the bright moon and stars and I let him.

When he quit kissing me he leaned up and I murmured, "I'm gonna miss you again, too. But I'll be back."

Jax nodded his head and then kissed me even deeper. I let him again.

Chapter 8

The next day after going to church with Bailey, I called Kevin and made arrangements to go to his house later in the afternoon. Bailey didn't mind because she knew that we were going to be together for two more weeks. This would be my last time to see Kevin for maybe another year. I planned to tell his family about my next move, today. It would be hard to tell them goodbye, knowing it may be another year before I got to see them, but I knew they would be supportive no matter what I chose to do.

As I was getting ready to leave, the doorbell rang and Bailey went to answer it. When she came back Kevin was standing in the doorway. I was shocked to see his tall form filling her room. I smiled when I saw him and grabbed the bag that contained the gifts I'd gotten for him and Donna.

I gave Bailey a quick hug and Kevin and I were out the door. I almost skipped down the concrete steps of her porch as Kevin and I began the walk down Granville. I wanted this last day with him to be the best one yet. I still felt conflicted about kissing Jax the night before, but then I thought of all the reasons I wasn't a bad person, like Bailey said. I felt okay with all of my decisions about Kevin and Jax. I could differentiate between the two and my feelings between each one. It just didn't make it any easier to have feelings for both. I knew that the one that I wanted more than anything was the one I was walking with right now. I felt giddy walking beside him and chattering away happily. Kevin even glanced at me a time or two and then seemed to join in with the mood I was bubbling over with!

When we got to his house we went into the living room where his mom, dad and Donna were watching TV. We talked about it on the way to his house that I would tell them my plan. I knew that they would keep my secret. The only one I truly worried about was Donna. I told her when I left for Oklahoma City that I would get to come visit her on weekends, and it never happened. Now, I would be telling her I'd only get to see her once or twice a year. That seemed like forever for me, I couldn't imagine what it would seem like for her.

Kevin was the one who initiated the talk, for which I was grateful. We sat side by side on their couch as his parents each sat in their large, cushy recliners and Donna in her special wheelchair.

"Um, DeLaine wanted to talk with us about something that is going on with her. I told her that tonight was the best time to do it," Kevin spoke softly.

Jean Strong got up and turned the TV off, "Well, DeLaine, sweetheart, please tell us. What's on your mind?"

I smiled at Kevin's mom because she'd always been the warmest and kindest woman I'd ever known. She'd loved me when I needed it. She was such a blessing to me and I missed her. I always felt safe when I received her warm embraces.

"Well, I've made a difficult decision because I've been so miserable since I left. It was a hard one to make, but I think it is best for me," I began, hesitantly. "I'm not going back to Oklahoma City at the end of the summer. I'm going to stay at my mom's, but I don't want anyone in Oklahoma City knowing until the last minute. I don't want anyone up there to make me go back."

Mrs. Strong nodded her head as she digested what I'd said and Donna began to cry. I felt like a heel. "Donna, sweetie, DeLaine isn't going away forever, she's just moving to another town like she did before. I'm sure she will come back to visit," their mom tried to soothe her daughter.

"But if you move away again, will you be able to come on weekends like you were going to before?" Donna asked me with her gorgeous, blue eyes shining with tears through her tiny, wire-framed glasses.

"Donna, Corpus Christi is further away," I began trying to keep my own tears at bay. "I know that my mama will let me come visit. It may only be once or twice a year though. I haven't been able to come down on any weekends so far, even though that's what I was promised when I left here for Oklahoma City."

"But if you move even further away you'll forget me even more," Donna cried, as she wept openly.

I looked at Kevin for some kind of help. I knew if she continued to cry I would eventually lose it, and begin my own water works.

"Sissy, DeLaine, is always gonna be a part of us. She isn't living in a nice place and if she moves to Corpus Christi to live with her mama, she'll be happier. She doesn't have any friends where she lives right now and she has to work all the time. She's sad living there. She isn't going to get to come here on weekends like she was promised. If she lives with her mama, we know we'll get to see her at least sometimes. I bet she'll even write you like she did last summer, right, DeLaine?" Kevin smiled at me. I nodded my head.

"If you promise to write me," Donna croaked, through her sniffling.

I nodded my head and crowed, "You bet! You can get your mama to write to me or Kevin even," I smiled at Kevin, hoping that it would prompt him to write to me too.

"Brother won't write. He don't like it," Donna said with a hint of a smile.

I smiled and covered her tiny hand with my own, "Well, that's okay. Maybe your mama will write sometimes."

Donna nodded her head and I explained, "I don't want to put you in a bad position but you are all so important to me and I wanted you to know." I finished as I looked at my other hand in my lap. Kevin reached over and covered it with his own warm one.

Jean Strong smiled at me brightly, "If you are that miserable and you think you will be happier with your mama, then I think you are making the right decision. If your mama will let you stay, she will won't she?" she asked me, a little worriedly.

"Yes ma'am, I'm the one who chose to live with my daddy. I tried to go live with my mama before, but when my daddy cried, when I'd come back to get my stuff, I'd stay. This time I'm not going back for my things. I packed as much of it as possible. My suitcase is so heavy I don't know how I'll get it to the car. If my mama wants to go pick up my stuff, then she can, but I won't go to Oklahoma City again unless it is because I have to for summer or Christmas," I stated.

Even Mr. Strong was nodding his head after I explained about my past in trying to escape the insanity of my home life. Their mom looked at me with the same warm smile.

She placed her hand on top of mine. "DeLaine, sweetheart, I just want you to be happy and find peace and if you've been this unhappy in such a short time, then you need to do what you feel is right. I know your mama. She's a good lady and I know how much she loves you. So, if you can only come see us once or twice a year, then I still count us blessed that you are able to come when you can. In the meantime, you keep us updated on how you are and I am going to pray for you. I'm going to pray that God's loving Hand is upon you until you come home to us again," she smiled brightly and I saw tears glinting through her glasses too.

I knew if we didn't get out soon or change the subject I was going to lose it, especially seeing his mom with tears in her eyes.

I decided this would be a good time to give Donna her present.

I remembered to thank Mrs. Strong, "Thank you for loving me and for praying for me. I don't want Geoffrey to know."

Both of Kevin's parents nodded in unison and I smiled. Then I reached into the handled bag that had my presents for Kevin and Donna,

"And Donna, I got a present for you so you can always think of me until we see each other again," I pulled out the Angel Bear and handed it to the tiny, fragile girl.

Her face lit up like a Christmas tree and she gushed, "Oh my GOSH! DeLaine, I wanted one of these! I love her!"

I smiled at her, "I'd like to think she's your Guardian Angel Bear who can sleep with Floppy and DeLaine the dolphin. I'll know there's someone around to watch out for you."

Donna nodded her head and smiled her sunshine and rainbows version of her own smile. My heart melted.

"So, what do you think you're going to name her?" I asked Donna.

"Well, I would name her DeLaine, but my dolphin is named that, so I think I'll just name her Angel Bear!" she giggled.

I grinned back at her, "I think that is the best way to go! Keep it simple, huh?" Donna nodded and I rose up and kissed her on the cheek.

Kevin finally spoke up, "Well, we're gonna go hang out in my room, so I guess just holler when it's dinner time." His mom told him she would and we walked back into his room. I still had the small present I'd gotten for Kevin.

When he closed the door to his room, I felt I was going to bubble over if I didn't give it to him! "Um, I got you a present too," I whispered, shyly.

Kevin smirked at me, "Did you? Well, I got you a present too."

Excitedly, I insisted, "Well, I have to give you yours first!" Kevin nodded and we climbed up on top of his large water bed. Sitting crossed legged from one another, I took the tiny box out of the bag that had only moments before held the Angel Bear also. I handed it to him and he looked at the box. Kevin then looked at me curiously.

Not understanding his curiosity I waited for him to open his gift. He removed the top of the box, looked inside the tissue and a big smile crossed his face. "It's a St. Michael," I began.

Kevin nodded and I continued in a rapid fire of words, "He's supposed to protect you. I got it because your middle name is Michael and I was reading that he was the biggest of the Archangels. He's a warrior and I guess that is how I see you."

"You see me as a warrior?" Kevin asked, amused at me.

"Well, yeah, you fought for me and well, I wanted to give you something that would keep you safe 'til we could see each other again. I know it's a little corny, but I just wanted to know that you were covered." I twiddled my fingers around each other in my lap.

Kevin stated, "Hang on, and let me get your present!" I nodded, and he opened the tiny drawer on his nightstand. He handed me a box. I realized it looked almost like his and it looked a lot like the one I gave Bailey.

I opened it and found the exact same St. Christopher bracelet I'd bought for Bailey. My mouth dropped open and Kevin said, "It's a St. Chr—…"

I cut him off, "Christopher. Kevin, you aren't going to believe me when I tell you this, but I bought this exact same bracelet for Bailey."

Kevin's mouth opened as he looked at me, then he began to grin, "No way! I went with my mom and we wanted to give you something before you left. She helped me pick that out. She said he is the patron saint of travelers and it might be nice for you to have one."

Nodding my head I agreed, "Yea, I know. I wanted Bailey to feel safe traveling with me."

"I can't believe we didn't see each other at the mall!" Kevin exclaimed, excitedly. I told him when we were there and he remarked, "That's crazy because we were there about an hour before you!"

I wondered how we could have been on the same wavelength again with our parting gifts. I held my arm out to him and told him to put it on me.

He did and then he grinned almost boyishly, "While we were there, I saw something else that reminded me of you. I wanted to give it to you."

"You got me two things?" I asked him. "Kevin, the one is beautiful. You didn't have to get me something else!" I beamed at him.

He looked back at me, admitting, "It isn't anything big or fancy. I'm calling for boyfriend privilege one more time for the rest of your visit tonight!" I giggled and nodded my head and he handed me an even tinier box.

I looked at him curiously and opened the small box. Nestled inside, on a tiny card, were some post earrings that were the shape of small, yellow, enamel painted flowers. I started laughing out loud! "I love them, Kev!"

"They aren't fancy, and I hope they don't turn your ears green, 'cause they weren't really expensive, but I remember you telling me about dreaming about the field of yellow flowers. I figure that for whatever reason those little yellow flowers are always going to remind me of you now!" Kevin stated quietly, as he held my fidgeting fingers.

"I don't care, I'll treasure them always and if they turn my ears green, I'll put them up and keep 'em forever just to look at, so I can remember you." I murmured.

Kevin leaned over and kissed me softly. "I guess we had the same idea. I wasn't sure how you'd take the bracelet, we've never talked about religion and I knew you guys didn't go to church. I wasn't sure how you'd feel, getting a piece of jewelry with a saint on it.

I laughed, "Oh Kevin, it could have been a rock from outside and as long as you gave it to me I'd be happy!"

"What's even funnier is Donna was looking at those Angel Bears and got mad when mom told her that she wasn't getting one! Then you walk in with it! That's just a little weird, Lainey!" Kevin was giggling.

"I know, I'm just weird like that for some reason! I don't know why, but I am," I explained.

"As my dad always says, 'Great Minds Think Alike'! I guess we got great minds, huh?"

"I think we do Mr. Strong!" I agreed, as I leaned in to kiss him again.

Since I hadn't worn any jewelry when I came over, I immediately put the little yellow flowers in my ears. Kevin had me put his St. Michael necklace on. I was happy he liked it so much.

We spent the rest of the time lying on his bed, listening to his stereo and talking about what I could probably expect from high school when I got to Corpus. I decided it was better than going back to school with those mean kids in Oklahoma City! I loved being held in his arms. I couldn't believe it would be so long before I got to do this again.

I went to Donna's room and read her a story and wanted to bottle some of her essence and take it with me. Whenever I got blue, I could open it up and have a little of her light shine onto me. I read the Velveteen Rabbit one more time and after I finished, she asked, "Did you remember your bunny from Kevin?" I nodded and she declared, "That's good! Don't lose it!" I promised her I would not lose the bunny or the book about the bunny she'd given me two Christmases back. I leaned over and kissed her goodnight because Kevin wanted to take me for one last walk. I'd have to go back to Bailey's soon, since we had to get up early so we could get to Dallas on time.

We began walking down Portland, the way you would walk to go to Jax's house. I wondered what he was going to do. As we walked slowly to Woodbane and Woolery, Kevin began to slow down. "You know, I told you that this is where I knew I was falling in love with you." Kevin began thoughtfully. I nodded and he admitted, "I lied."

I looked at him worried and he continued, "I think I fell in love with you when you made me an egg sandwich and you didn't make one for Geoff. He didn't ask, while you were making mine. I knew right then and there that you'd probably eat my nuts for breakfast!"

I started laughing and trying to make a face at the same time, but I'm sure it came out totally stupid. "No, I'm not real big on those for breakfast…lunch maybe, but I think you were pretty safe," I replied with my usual bit of sarcasm, still blushing a little.

"Seriously, Lainey…you are such a strong girl! You are so much tougher than you realize. Don't let anybody ever tell you different! Just don't forget me, okay?" Kevin looked so vulnerable in the deepening twilight. He leaned over and kissed me one more time at Woodbane and Woolery. It might be a haunted corner for my life, but I was willing to live with the ghosts that hung out here now. Especially since I knew that he loved me the first time he kissed me here.

We only kissed for a few minutes and then we began walking back towards Portland. When we finished our long walk all the way back to Bailey's, up Granville, Kevin asked what time I was leaving. I told him what time Bailey's mom had said and he nodded, "Well, if I wake up early enough I'll try to run up and tell you goodbye. But I'll say goodbye now, just in case," he grinned his lazy half-smile. The one that he had first started melting my heart with, in the first few days I knew him. I kept feeling like I should pinch myself sometimes that King Kevin loved me, and I was standing here kissing him. My heart was already aching at missing him.

Chapter 9

The next morning, Bailey and I rolled out of bed early, excited for our adventure that was about to begin! She thought it was totally cool how Kevin gave me the same bracelet as the one I bought her. We were going to try to eat at a nice place in Dallas before we had to catch our flight that afternoon. We would get there late in the evening, so we really had plenty of time, but her mom wanted to make sure, since Dallas traffic was always crazy.

After I had gathered up the very last bits of my stuff into my bulging suitcase, I set it up and was amazed at how much heavier it felt. I told Bailey she might have to help me carry it. We decided it would be the last thing we'd take out. I helped her finish gathering her stuff and we were still doing great on time.

Her mom had made me my favorite waffles for my last breakfast there. I was already missing their chocolaty goodness! We told her mom about me moving when I first got there, so she knew I wouldn't be back for a while. I was so grateful for my friends and for their parents who cared about what was happening with me.

As we were making one more sweep of Bailey's room, before we tried to strong arm the huge suitcase of mine, the doorbell rang. I ran and answered it for Bailey as she was putting some stuff up in her room. When I opened the door and saw summer, blue eyes staring back at me, with the same color behind him in the actual sky, framing his blonde hair, I smiled happily. "I hear someone in this house has a really big suitcase that is super heavy," Kevin teased, smirking at me.

I went bouncing back into Bailey's room with Kevin on my heels and told her about him coming to carry my suitcase to the car. When he picked it up, he coughed out, "Good God, Lainey! What do you have in here, those damned bricks you had to sort when I first met you?"

I couldn't believe he remembered that. As a punishment, one of the first times he came to our home, after the tornado, I'd been made to sort through a huge pile of bricks in our back yard by Clarice. That was the first time Kevin's kindness was shown to me because he brought me a pair of cheap cotton work gloves on the sly.

I smiled at the memory and he grumbled as he tried to maneuver his way out of the tiny room with two teenage girls standing in front of him and getting in his way no matter which way he stepped.

Finally, Kevin was able to carry the suitcase outside and Bailey's mom gave him the keys to her trunk.

She told me that since Kevin had helped we'd just get someone to help at the airport and the only time we'd have to worry about it was when we got to Corpus. I was glad to hear that because I didn't know how we were going to get that thing checked in and carry Bailey's stuff too.

The moment had finally come that I'd been dreading. Glenda Rains sat in her hot car and started it cooling off, with the air conditioner. It was only the middle of June and it was already near the 100-degree mark. Bailey surprised me when she hugged Kevin really quick and then she showed him her bracelet too. We held out our wrists for him to inspect the funny coincidence. I think Bailey was trying hard to drag out the goodbye as long as she could for me. Bailey finally ducked inside her mom's car and Kevin stepped over and enveloped me literally into his tall, muscular body.I wanted to die right there. I wanted to die in the comfort of his embrace and I knew that I'd die happy. The boy that I loved the most, I knew loved me too.

Finally, I knew I had to pull away. It was hurting too much to keep dragging it out. He leaned down and kissed me softly on the mouth and whispered, "Don't forget how I feel about you, okay? I probably won't ever write back. Donna was right about that, but I'll read a letter if one comes in the mail for me!" I grinned at him and nodded my head because I was afraid if I opened my mouth there would be nothing to come out except wails.

Kevin's hand came up and caressed my face and he kissed the tip of my nose and then wrapped his hand around the back of my head and brought my forehead to his lips. "Just remember, it wasn't you who needed me! Don't fall in love with a surfer, okay?"

I looked forlornly at Kevin, and finally declared, "I love you, Kevin Strong. I always will. Be safe and don't forget me!"

Kevin smiled as he whispered hoarsely, "Never, Lainey. Never." I turned away from him and climbed into the back seat of Bailey's mom's car. As we backed out of the driveway, I held my hand up as Kevin held his high, with his other hand stuck down deep in the pocket of his jeans. I knew I had no way to know when I'd see him next. I only hoped it wasn't longer than a year.

I sat in the backseat as I watched all the houses that I'd walked by daily in 7th grade stream by slowly, as we rode down Granville. Silently, I said goodbye to each house as I remembered being so jealous of the people who lived in them, after the tornado, while we lived in a government trailer. Now I watched as they slipped by me in a blur of tears and memories.

When we touched down in Corpus Christi that evening I was so excited for mine and Bailey's big adventure for the next two weeks! She would get to meet my friends here and we'd get to go to the beach and to the pool where Kelly and Robin lived.

I couldn't wait to see my mama. I hadn't seen her since the end of the previous summer, since she'd had back surgery during my Christmas break. Even though I got to talk to her on a regular basis it still wasn't the same. I knew I wasn't telling her about staying as soon as we got there, but I was excited to get to that point. For now, though I wanted to concentrate on having a blast with Bailey.

We walked down the jet way together, giggling and I looked down the ramp to see if I could see my mama. She was standing at the bottom, smiling big. I couldn't wait to hug her tight! She was standing there with her cowboy boots, jeans and a button-down blouse on. She looked like she was about to stomp out her cigarette as the first of the passengers started breaking apart around her to find their loved ones waiting on them.

I grabbed my mom in a huge hug! She smelled familiar. The only problem was one of the familiar scents wasn't one I wanted to smell. She had her signature smell of perfume and cigarettes on her, but instead of coffee too, which was a scent I loved on her the most, she had the smell of booze as well. When I pulled away from her I didn't say anything, but I already felt on guard.

My mama was a wonderful mom, but when she drank she got surly. She never seemed to mean whatever she'd say, but I usually didn't see that side of mama unless it was just me and her, or me, her and Ray, the man she lived with. I was actually embarrassed now for Bailey to be around my mom, I realized, almost immediately. I silently prayed that she wouldn't be too drunk right now. I hoped that she'd just had a drink in the bar, at the airport, while waiting on our flight. Hopefully she wasn't completely blitzed out of her mind.

Mama leaned over and hugged Bailey, and I wondered if she smelled the booze on my mom. I cautiously started talking to her, trying to gauge her level of sobriety. She seemed for the most part okay.

I told her when we got my suitcase we might need to get a cart or someone to carry it. She asked me why, and I told her I'd brought a bunch of junk, so the boys didn't get into my stuff while I was gone. She nodded her head, and we went to the baggage claim.

Once we got our bags, we got into her red Cadillac, took off for her singlewide trailer, and my future home. I had the two smaller bedrooms for my own use, because the rooms were so tiny, but I didn't mind. When we pulled out of the airport, there was a lot of road construction. I wasn't really sure which way we were going.

Bailey and I chattered away happily as we all three sat in the front, along the bench seat in her car. After a while I looked up and didn't recognize anything about where we were. I asked Mama finally if she was going a different way to her house and she told me that she was going the way she always went.

I told her I thought we might have gotten turned around in the construction and she told me she knew exactly where she was.

I looked at Bailey and she grinned at me, thinking that it was a little funny. My mama was in her funny phase of being drunk, thankfully, and hopefully she wouldn't cross into the mean phase.

So, we continued to talk about everything as she drove. She asked me how I liked Oklahoma City and I said, "I hate the damned place!"

My mom turned to me, surprised, then nodded. She asked how things were with Geoff. She knew we had tumultuous relationship, but I'd never told her anything he'd ever done to hurt me on purpose.

"He's still an asshole!" I responded, matter of factly.

Bailey was sitting on the right of me cracking up, because I was literally cussing in front of my mom. I'd never had the guts to do that before, but I figured if I was going to live with the Queen of the Cussers, I better get my feet wet around her to test and see how far she'd let me go.

Mom started laughing, "He's an asshole, huh?"

I shrugged, and I looked up at the road again, "Mom we've gone this way already."

Mom insisted, "We have not gone this way dammit, I know where I'm at."

"Yes, by God we have gone this way dammit," I blurted, a little more smart-assed than I should.

Mama looked at me, demanding, "So since when do you cuss?"

Bailey couldn't contain her glee at the whole exchange and I grumbled, "I've always cussed, I just didn't say it around you and Daddy, but I guess since I'm about to be in high school, I might as well go ahead and cuss in front of you." My mom shook her head and advised if that is what I thought, then I should, if I felt like I was a big girl enough to do it. This was the beginning of my cussing without trying to hide it from my mom.

Finally, Bailey elbowed me and looked up at the street sign. I knew we'd passed that same sign three times now, and when I told my mom, she got angry and said she knew where she was. I knew it was taking us way too long to get to her house. Finally, she told me and Bailey to look for the exit that would take us on the Crosstown to I-37.

I looked at my best friend, and through the silent way we'd started communicating at times, I knew she would be the one to keep her eyes peeled while I kept Mom talking.

Thankfully, Bailey saw the sign quickly and we finally got on the side of town that I was more familiar with. I could help guide Mom to the right exit to get us to her house. I was shocked that Mom had been so drunk she didn't know where she was going. I thought that maybe me jabbering might have thrown her off too, but I just wasn't sure.

Both my parents drank alcohol as far back as I could remember. I didn't like it, but it was the way it was. I knew Mama was drinking a lot more since I'd been gone and living with Daddy and Clarice. This was the first time I felt shame being around her. I had wanted Bailey to meet the funny and silly Mama that I loved. Instead she met the drunk, and getting close to belligerent, Mama.

When we finally got into the trailer with all of my stuff, we went into the tiny room that had a queen bed only and closed the door. I looked at Bailey, muttering, "I'm sorry Bay. She doesn't usually act like that."

Bailey looked at me curiously, "Lala, really? I've seen Clarice who is bat-shit crazy. So, your mom's a little drunk. No big! Don't worry about it! I still love you! Besides, I've seen your daddy a hell of a lot drunker!" I smiled at her wanly and thought that she was right about that. It didn't mean it made me feel any better that she'd seen both of my parents being drunks. I hoped that Mama wouldn't let the scary side of herself show while Bay was here. I wanted her to think that I was going to something better than what I was leaving.

Funny thing was I wasn't sure if I was trading one scary home for another. I sure hoped that this would be the right decision. Besides, I told myself, once Mama knew I wasn't going back, she'd cut back on the drinking since she really hadn't started drinking so heavy until I left to live with Daddy and Clarice. It was really all my fault to begin with…

Chapter 10

I sat in my room writing to Bailey while I listened to the clock radio sitting beside my bed. I was horribly homesick as I listened to the country music station in Corpus Christi, TX. Bailey was back home in Wichita Falls, TX.

My mama called me into the dining room where she was sitting, smoking and reading her paper. She asked if I'd gotten my report card from Oklahoma City since I'd been in Corpus Christi. I nodded my head, wondering why she'd asked. That had been the other part of my plan to leave Oklahoma also.

When we got to Oklahoma I had been made to take Science again, which I'd taken in 7th grade. The teacher and I had not gotten along very well. Because I had a serious attitude problem, and he did too, I had made the first "C" of my entire life on a report card. I was angry because every other class I was in I was doing 6th grade work, while being an 8th grader, but wasn't smart enough for them to put into their gifted school. When I found out what my final score in Science was going to be, I'd had the office mail my report card to my mom's, in Corpus Christi, since that's where I'd be for the summer. They'd given me an envelope and I'd addressed it to my mom's address. I'd gone to check the mail a few days before and received the cursed report card that showed the ugly 72 in a computer generated form.

When I'd gotten it, I'd tried to figure out how I was going to change the grade. Finally, after some smudging, I made the report card show a 92 instead, which wasn't unusual for me. My mama asked to see it, so I went to my room getting it from the drawer I'd hidden it in. When I showed it to her, she explained, "Well your daddy and Clarice called early this morning wanting to know if you'd gotten it. I told them I didn't know. They said that you'd gotten it sent here, instead of to them, and they were very upset about it."

I felt my breath hitch inside of me and wondered how much my mama knew. She looked at me steadily, asking, "Why did you have it sent here?"

"I figured that they wouldn't care where it came since they don't seem to care about anything except the restaurant," I remarked disdainfully.

Mama nodded her head and instructed me, "Well, you need to call them and tell them you got it." I nodded and felt my friend, the Flaming Winged Goddess deep in my belly. I had always bowed down to everyone and never let my true feelings out. She seemed to only come out when I was angry and if I was really raging she almost engulfed me. Right now, she was only stretching, but I knew that I would have to call, like my mama said. I sat at the dining room table and picked up the desk top phone that she kept in there. I dialed the number to my daddy's restaurant, after I dialed 0 for the Operator, so I could call them collect.

When Clarice answered, I felt my stomach drop even further because I figured I could sweet talk my daddy. At least I hoped so, but Clarice was a whole other matter. Even when I didn't need to pull something over on her, she found fault. "Hey Clarice," I stated, softly.

"DeLaine," she replied curtly.

"Um, Mama said to call you and let you know that my report card did come here," I started, hesitantly.

"Yes, I've already found that out. Now do you mind telling me why you had it mailed there, or should I tell you why you did it?" Clarice barked briskly.

"Well, I'm curious why you think so," I tried to sound neutral, as my mama looked on, still not understanding what I'd done.

"You know good damn and well why you had it mailed there. You thought you'd hide the fact that you made a C in Science. You know you are grounded when you get home, right?" my step-mother enunciated each word carefully.

"I kinda figured," I muttered sarcastically, while noticing my mama was still looking at me curiously. I stood, picking up the phone and walked out of the dining room to the built on sunroom. The cord was long enough, and I hoped my mama would quit looking at me like she was.

"You should have known I would find out when the boys' report cards came and yours never did! I don't know who you are trying to fool, but you haven't fooled us! Your daddy is very upset with you," Clarice continued almost to the point of becoming screechy.

"I understand," I whispered, solemnly.

"What gets me is why you thought you had the right to do that," Clarice shrieked, still in her high pitched voice.

"I guess I felt it was my right since it was my report card," I popped off, feeling braver, realizing that she'd have to drive close to 12 hours to reach me. I knew my mama would wring her neck before she'd let her do anything to me, no matter if I got a C in Science or not.

"Your daddy wants to talk to you," Clarice growled, breaking off from our conversation quickly as my daddy got the phone.

"DeLaine, why the fuck did you have your report card sent to Corpus?" He demanded, loudly.

"Because I wanted to see it before you did," I whispered softly, hearing how much my voice quavered and hating myself for not being braver.

"Were you going to try to hide the fact you got a god-damned C in Science?" my daddy asked, angrily.

"No," I hoped my voice didn't break because I could feel myself close to tears. I hated making my daddy angry, but I hated disappointing him more than anything. I knew that he was so proud that I never made anything below a B and that wasn't that often either. Not to mention the fact that I had made straight A's, except for the stupid grade in Science.

"Well, I'm sure Clarice has told you that you WILL be grounded when you get home," Daddy boomed scarily.

"Yeah, I know," I sighed, wearily. It didn't matter any way, I thought, because I wouldn't be going back! I was just sorry that they seemed so upset over a damned C in Science, when they hadn't seemed the least bit bothered that I was doing 6th grade work again and being made to repeat a class I'd taken the year before. A class which I'd passed with an 88 in 7th grade! The only reason I'd gotten a C was because I hated the teacher, and he gave a participation grade, as well as a grade on the actual work. If it hadn't been for that, I'd have passed well over the B mark.

"Let me speak to your mother," my daddy demanded, sharply.

Uh-Oh, I thought! I'd hoped I would skate by without Mama knowing what I'd done, but that wasn't going to happen now! I told him to hang on and walked back into the dining room. I knew she'd been trying to listen to my side of the conversation, so she knew what was going on, but I'd tried to keep my voice as low as possible, so she didn't.

"Daddy wants to talk to you," I muttered, with tears in my eyes. I put the phone on the table and walked into my room. I didn't know what my mama could take away from me, but Daddy might tell her I had to come home early. If that was the case, then she'd do it and then the tug of war was going to get started before I was ready.

I closed my door when I went into my room and picked up the large puppy dog and the Velveteen Rabbit that were the stuffed animals I'd gotten from Jax while in 8th grade, and Kevin in 7th grade, for Christmas presents. I sat in the corner of my bed near the wall and held both of the stuffed animals up to catch the tears I cried. They'd caught their share of salty tears from my eyes, and it looked like the amount wasn't going to quit any time soon. I reached up to my throat and felt the two necklaces I wore, that had been gifts from Bailey and Kevin.

One Kevin had slipped inside of the Velveteen Rabbit's pocket and was a crystal tear drop. It had been his secret present to me, so Geoffrey didn't know he'd given me something. It had also been his way of telling me I was loved, because the story was his little sister's favorite, and I'd read it to her countless times. When the bunny cries a tear, he becomes real which only happens when a toy is loved.

So, it was his way of saying I was loved. The other was half of a heart that said, "Best Friends" and my half had a "B" on it for Bailey while she wore the other half with a "D" on it.

Finally, after what felt like forever, my mama knocked softly on my door and came into my room with the faked report card. "Hey DeLaine, let's talk," my mama spoke softly. I sat up and nodded my head mutely but kept holding onto the puppy and the rabbit.

"Why'd you feel like you couldn't tell me the truth?" Mama asked quietly.

I shrugged my shoulders and then said with tears rapidly falling from my eyes, "I knew that you'd be disappointed. I knew Daddy and Clarice would just be mad. I hated having to take Science again! I didn't know that the stupid asshole teaching the class was giving me a participation grade either," I wiped the tears away furiously.

"I know you were bored up there, the fact that every grade except Science is a 97 or above tells me that. I just wish you'd felt like you could tell me, instead of lying to me," my mama soothed.

"I'm sorry, Mama," I wailed, as fresh tears began to pour from my eyes. She leaned over and pulled me to her. I held tightly to her, thankful that she was still sober. She still smelled like coffee, cigarettes and perfume. I knew if this had happened later in the day, that the result probably would have been a shouting and screaming match between the two of us.

Mama leaned back and explained, "Well, your daddy said I needed to ground you, and that even if I didn't, you were going to get grounded when you got home. I told him I didn't think that you always being grounded was the right way to handle this, but he told me that it is the way they believe in punishing you. I told him he could do what he wanted when you go home, and I'd do what I wanted while you were here." I still wasn't sure what to say.

"You aren't grounded Bug, just remember you can come to me any time, okay?"

My mom stood up and told me to dry my eyes, and it was all going to be okay. When she walked out, I pulled my stuffed animals up to my face and silently sobbed.

I hated Oklahoma even more now and was so angry that Clarice couldn't just talk to me and make me feel like I wasn't such an awful kid. I never felt like I could do anything right or even worthwhile.

No one up there said one thing about how high all the other grades were. They zeroed on the 72 and instead of saying, 'what's wrong with this picture' they immediately began to chastise me. I knew I was making the right decision to not return, even more.

Chapter 11

When the first of August finally rolled around, my mama came into my room while I was reading a book. She asked when I wanted to go back to Oklahoma City. I had been waiting for this talk since the plane touched down on June 15, 1981.

"I'm not going back," I responded, absently, never wavering from looking at my book, even though I wasn't reading one word in front of my eyes.

"What?" my mom asked, sharply.

"I said, I-am-not -going-back," I repeated, slowly.

Mama looked at me funny, "DeLaine, I can't go through this again. Honey, I really can't deal with you saying you want to live with me, then we get there and you change your mind."

"That's why I'm not going back," I muttered, still in the absent, almost aloof way.

"What do you mean you aren't going back?" Mama asked insistently.

"I mean, I'm NOT going back. I don't care if I get the rest of my shit from my room or not, if you want to go up there and get it, fine, leave me at Bailey's, but I'm not going to Oklahoma City again," I replied, shrugging my shoulders.

Mama sat on my bed and took the book out of my hands, "DeLaine, what do you mean you aren't going back, and I can go if I want?"

I sat up and sighed, "Didn't you find it weird that I brought so much of my personal stuff with me this summer?" Mama looked at me curiously, then she slowly nodded her head. "Well, it wasn't to keep Lisa or the boys out of my shit! It was because I didn't plan on going back. I made up my mind in May that I wasn't going back, Mama. I hate it there. They're two years behind Texas schools, and I'm bored out of my mind. I hate that creepy old house we live in, and I don't have even one friend. I'm not going to make any either because if I'm not at home cleaning the damned house, then I'm at the restaurant working. If Clarice would go grocery shopping maybe it wouldn't be so bad but she hasn't since we moved there, and if Geoff gets pissed at me and William, then we don't eat!"

"What the hell do you mean you don't eat?" my mama's ire was now getting stoked.

"I mean, we don't eat! There's nothing in the house to eat! I go to bed hungry if Geoff gets pissed at us, and I'm not gonna eat another cake mix with water mixed in it, just so my belly doesn't grumble," I could hear the sound of my voice rising.

"I'm also sick of being slave labor. I'm tired of mixing queso with my hands, because Clarice gets off on watching me do it that way! I'm NOT going back! I've already told Bailey and Kevin. I'm staying with you." I finished, resolutely.

Slowly bobbing her head, I could tell that my mama was angry. I hated getting her angry, because I knew that she could go completely unhinged angry, or just a slow burn, which sometimes was even worse. I knew that in order for her to understand why I wasn't going back, I'd have to tell her some of what happened while I was in Oklahoma. I didn't want her to know everything about my life, at the hands of Clarice or her insane oldest child, but I also wanted her to see how serious I was. I'd never tell her everything. I knew I'd told her enough, though, to make her not send me back.

"I'm sorry, Mama," I whispered.

"Why are you sorry?" She asked me, forcefully.

"Because I should have told you before now, but I didn't want you to make me go back. I thought if I told you when I got here, you'd tell Daddy what I wanted to do. I figured if he didn't know until the last minute, he wouldn't waste a lot of time on it. He's gonna be pissed off, but it will take too much work to get me back now. If he knew earlier he could work on me all summer, and I didn't want to listen to his and Clarice's bullshit lies," I looked down at my hands in my lap.

Mama gazed at me with her dark, brown eyes intently. "No, you can stay. I do want to get the rest of your stuff though, because your stereo and TV are still there, that I gave you, and I want you to have it. If you don't want to go to Oklahoma with me, then I'll take you to Bailey's and let you spend the night and pick you up the next day, I guess."

I bowed my head, "I don't want to go back up there unless it is for Christmas to visit, or something, but I don't want to stay long."

"Now, DeLaine, you have to go visit your daddy at some point. He's going to get pissed if you don't," Mama stated,

"Probably not," I muttered dismally.

"Why would you say that?" She asked.

"He'd have to notice I was gone to want me to be somewhere," I felt tears begin to leak out.

Mama grabbed me and held me to her, "DeLaine, he'll notice you're gone. He loves you."

"I know he loves me Mama, but I'm not one of his priorities right now. That stupid restaurant and his stupid wife are. Not me," I whispered, as I held tight to my mama.

"I think you are selling your daddy short, but I understand how you can feel a little lost in the shuffle," Mama soothed me. I nodded and pulled away from her and got up and went into the bathroom to blow my nose. I didn't want to talk about it anymore. I had told her. That was the important thing. All the rest she had to figure out. I didn't care where I went to school, as long as it wasn't Lee High School, in Oklahoma City, I was happy.

Chapter 12

Later that week, Mama told me she was going to call Daddy and she wanted me available to talk to him, because he was going to want to talk to me. I waited for her to call me after she got him on the phone. When she didn't call after a while, I walked out into the dining room where she normally sat, when she talked on the phone, and found she was sitting there with the phone already sitting in its cradle.

"Didn't you call Daddy yet?" I asked her perplexed. She nodded her head. "Didn't he want to talk to me?" I whispered quietly. My mama shook her head, and I sat down in one of the dining room chairs. "Why not?"

Mama looked at me intently, "He said that if you wanted to stay here, then he didn't give a shit, and he didn't have time to talk about it right now." I sat there staring at her in disbelief. I couldn't believe that my daddy didn't give a shit whether I came back or not. I felt hurt beyond words or tears. I numbly ducked my head down, and walked back into my room.

The next time I walked out, I saw my mama had already gotten well on her way to being drunk for the day. I sighed and smiled tightly at her, as I walked from the kitchen back to my room. I knew when she started playing Ray Price and Willie Nelson on her stereo, things might be getting a little ugly by dark. Instead they got there before dark when Daddy called back, to talk to her, about me not coming back.

By the time he made time to talk, Mama was well into her V.O. and water. I could hear her, even with my door closed. I still felt like once it was a done deal, Mama would back off of the V.O. and be happier to have me with her. However, right now, it was going to take a little bit of getting there. She was yelling at Daddy about not having time for me and about me going to bed hungry. I winced when I heard her yelling at him about that, then I heard the cussing start.

My mama could out-cuss a sailor and make at least a fleet of them blush tomato red. When she cussed you, it was a safe bet it was not going to end well. I decided staying in my room unless she came in, was going to be the best thing for me to do for the rest of the evening. When she got as mad as she was now, it was best to steer as far away from her as possible. I knew even Ray would end up going to bed early to avoid her.

When the phone slammed down with a loud bang and clang, I jumped. I listened for her footsteps to come stomping back to my room and when I didn't hear them, I breathed out a huge sigh of relief.

I got my stationery out and began a new letter to Bailey. I had to tell her about what was going on. I wished I could pick up the phone and just call her, but I knew it was expensive to do that. I knew my mama didn't have a lot of money. So I wrote letter after letter to my best friend. I also wrote to Levi and Kelly White. I wrote Donna and every once in a blue moon I would write Kevin too. I knew he'd never write back, and neither would Levi, but I knew that Kevin was reading my letters and he was listening to the ones I wrote to Donna as well. He'd told me he would. I missed him so much when my mama got scary drunk. I hadn't written to him about that yet.

Kevin knew everything there was to know about me, but I had been too ashamed to tell him that my mom's drinking was bad enough it scared me now. I didn't know if I knew how to explain it to him. I also didn't want to seem like all I could do was complain. I mean, he'd seen me living in some pretty toxic mental and emotional abuse, as well as Geoff's physical abuse. I didn't want to constantly whine. I just missed him. I always felt safe when he was around me.

The next morning, when I got up, Mama was sitting at the dining room table with her paper, coffee, and cigarettes. I came out and got some milk and pop-tarts.

When I sat down, Mama told me that she talked to Daddy that morning. He'd apologized for being short the day before, but he had a crisis at the restaurant. He would support whatever decision I made. She told me that we would be going up on the 21st and she'd drive on up to Oklahoma after dropping me off at Bailey's. I agreed, and then asked if Daddy knew I wasn't coming with her.

She chuckled, "Nope, and he's not going to until after I get there!" then she grinned at me conspiratorially. I smiled back and was glad it was morning. That was always the best time to be around my mama, I was beginning to learn.

She told me that she'd go up and get my stuff and then pick me up either Saturday evening or first thing Sunday morning depending on what happened in Oklahoma City. I nodded and realized that I would literally have only hours with Bailey and hopefully Kevin.

I went into my room and wrote Bailey a letter to let her know when to expect me. I put a stamp on the envelope and ran out to put it in the mailbox before the mailman got there. I wanted Bailey to get the letter as soon as possible.

When the weekend of the 21st finally got there I was excited. I knew that I would only have overnight with Bailey probably. I wanted so much to see her and Kevin one more time, before school started, to remind me why I was doing all of this. If I could just get through high school, then I could move back to Wichita Falls! We could all be together again, I thought! I was frightened, but I knew this was the only choice I had for now.

As we drove into Wichita Falls that evening, the sun was streaking the Western sky with dark orange, gold and stunning reds. I felt like I was about to burst! I wasn't sure how long I'd be there, if it would be overnight, until the next evening, or if Mama would get a motel room when she came back on Saturday night. She would call me when she got there and tell me what was happening. That meant I couldn't really leave Bailey's house for most of the day, but that was fine. The most important ones either lived there or right down the street from her, so I knew that it would be fine!

Mama didn't stay long when we got to Bailey's. She basically kissed me goodbye and told me she'd call the next day. I nodded and told her thank you. Mama squeezed me a little harder. I knew that this was the only way I would ever make it away from everything I despised about Oklahoma City. I wanted to be completely free of the insanity I lived with and I knew that unless I did it this way, I'd never be able to leave forever.

Bailey and I went bounding up the steps to her house. I was once again thrilled to find the turquoise and lime bedroom that felt like my own room, in so many ways. She told me Kevin had called three times. He said he wouldn't call any more until I called him. I looked at her, feeling bad for wanting to call him so quickly after getting there, and she smirked, "Really, Lala? Call that crazy boy before he paces a hole in his carpet!" I laughed and dialed the number I knew by heart.

"Hey Kev," I whispered, quietly, when he answered.

"Lainey?" the boy who owned my heart asked anxiously.

"Yep! In the flesh and in Wichita Falls, Texas!" I giggled.

"When'd you get here?" he asked.

"Just now! Bailey said you've been goin' nuts so I decided to call you before you started getting to the Clarice stage…I don't want you to go to her hospital after all," I was still snickering.

"Shut up," Kevin growled, good-naturedly. "So, how long are you here for?"

"I dunno, maybe just until tomorrow evening about the same time. It kinda depends on my mama and how long it takes 'em to give my mom my shit tomorrow," I replied.

"Damn, Lainey, that's not very long," Kevin whispered.

"Yea, I know," I muttered.

"I'll come over later tonight. Do you want to see me during normal visiting hours or after?" he was laughing again.

"Hang on and let me ask my hostess," I was still feeling extremely giddy. When I asked Bailey, she said if he wanted to come over after her parents went to sleep it was cool. We knew how to sneak out of her house. When I told Kevin, he said he'd come over later, but he'd call before he left.

Bailey and I hung out happily in her room, the entire evening. I was grateful her mom and dad were early birds when it came to going to bed. Kevin was knocking on the window by 10:30pm. We both actually snuck out to sit with him, on the curb. When he saw Bailey come sneaking out too, he looked at me oddly. I knew that my best friend would give us some alone time too. She just wanted to hang out with me for a little while longer.

We sat at the curb, near her driveway and talked well past midnight, when Bailey dusted off her shorts and told me to be quiet when I came in. I nodded and she went inside, leaving me alone, finally, with Kevin. I had missed him so much and even with Bailey around, he'd still been affectionate in holding my hand and stealing tiny, chaste kisses while we sat in the late summer night. It was still around 90 degrees outside, even in the dark, but at least there was a breeze that made it somewhat bearable.

After Bailey had gone inside, we decided to walk over to the elementary school playground that was behind her house, to sit inside the old, playground tunnel. It offered some privacy, as well as some place to go sit, without getting in trouble.

***

I climbed inside the dusty bottomed tunnel and noticed that most of the old, dry, crunchy leaves were gone now. I scooted over to Kevin and found my spot along the curve of his body, inside the crook of his arm. We sat there together, talking quietly. He hadn't told his little sister that I was coming because I didn't think I'd have enough time to go visit her. We had both agreed on that before we'd hung up the phone. He caught me up with how she was doing. She'd had another hard summer with pneumonia, which concerned me.

I worried about Donna whenever I heard she'd been sick. I was terrified that if anything ever happened to her, Kevin would completely fall apart. He had saved her from his birth mother's boyfriend, who had beaten them, and losing her would be like losing a part of his identity, I thought.

I prayed that she stayed well, and that Kevin would be in a better place within himself before he lost her. He would eventually lose her and before any of us were ever going to be ready for it. She was actually 6 months older than me and she loved that fact. I couldn't imagine that she'd already lived probably more than half her life already.

Shaking my head to erase the thoughts, I leaned my head against Kevin's shoulder. He asked what was wrong. I told him it must be a mosquito buzzing around my head. I didn't want to tell him about the morbid thoughts that had been swirling momentarily around my brain. I wrapped my arm around his middle and held him tightly. I couldn't believe I was actually here with him. I had wished for time to freeze so many times in the last year, but this time, I truly hoped and almost prayed it would. I wished that I never had to leave his side ever again. I wanted to hold onto him and never go to Corpus Christi either. I knew it wasn't realistic, but it was still what I wanted.

We sat in the tunnel for a long time, just murmuring to one another about nothing important, after the beginning of catching up, and kissing only occasionally. I was so happy to be able to hold Kevin and not be terrified of being beaten by my step-brother, Geoffrey for it. I asked Kevin if he'd seen much of Geoffrey and he said he hadn't seen him since the beginning of the summer when I'd still been there visiting Bailey, before leaving for Corpus. I nodded my head and realized that the promises of going to pick up Lisa had never come true, just like I had thought they wouldn't. We talked about it, and Kevin said he felt he'd see me more even living further away, than if I stayed in Oklahoma City.

I told Kevin I was worried about going to high school. Mama had already begun looking into me going back to the school district I'd gone to when I'd had to go in 6th grade, after the tornado. That meant my friend, Kelly Stubbs and I would go to the same school again, so at least I'd be starting out with ONE friend.

When I told him that, he told me I was already ahead in Corpus than I'd been in Oklahoma and I agreed. The only thing missing would be him and Bailey though, I told him, and he laughed softly. He kept telling me all of the positive things that I needed to hear.

I wanted to believe everything he told me except the part about finding another boyfriend, who would make me forget all about him. He told me he wanted me to try. I told him I would, even though I somehow doubted it very much.

By the time we finally decided to leave, it was almost 4 a.m., which seemed to be our normal time to go in from a night like tonight. We walked slowly back to Bailey's, hand in hand, and when we got to her front porch, he pulled me to him tightly and kissed me tenderly.

I didn't know if I'd see him the next day or not and told him I'd call when I knew something. He beamed his sunshine and rainbows smile that made me melt inside and kissed me on the nose. When I got back inside her bedroom, I looked outside. By the streetlight, he stood. The light created a silvery halo out of his blonde hair. He held his hand up, and I put my own on the glass. I knew he saw it when he turned, and the night claimed all trace of him.

The next day, my mama called to tell me that she would pick me up that evening. We would make the long drive back to Corpus Christi, then, because she wanted to get home. I could tell she was really agitated. It made me wonder what had happened when she got to Oklahoma City with my daddy and Clarice.

When I hung up the phone, I told Bailey I was leaving that evening. Even though we were sad that I wasn't getting to spend another night, we decided to enjoy the few hours we had left. We walked up to the pool and met Levi there and swam for a couple of hours, which was fun. I was happy to get a chance to say hi to Levi.

I called Kevin before we went to swim, and he was waiting at Bailey's when we came walking back down Granville. I felt self-conscious because I'd never been around Kevin in a bathing suit before. He grinned a little salaciously when he saw me. Bailey ran up the steps, and I told her I would be in shortly.

"Wow, Lainey, why haven't I ever seen you in a bathing suit before?" Kevin crooned, sweetly.

"I dunno, I guess because you never go swimming," I answered, as I watched Kevin walk up closer to me. I was holding my towel in front of me because I felt self-conscious in a bathing suit as it was, but I felt even more so in front of Kevin.

Kevin pulled me to him while I held the towel in front of me and murmured, "You're all wet!" I started laughing.

"Yes, I just got out of the swimming pool, you dork," I giggled.

Looking at me with his sweet smile that always seemed to make me feel all giddy Kevin asked, "Are you cold?" I shook my head and he whispered, "Move the towel, I want to look at you."

"Kevin!" I felt a little embarrassed.

"What? I think you're beautiful, Lainey. I don't know why you aren't wearing a bikini like Bailey," he replied huskily.

I rolled my eyes, "Seriously? I am way too fat to wear a bikini!"

"You have to get Clarice out of your head, Darlin'! Quit believing the bullshit she told you all these years. You are just as beautiful as any other girl out there! I think you'd look gorgeous in a bikini," Kevin whispered, seriously, as he leaned down to kiss me.

"Well, you are biased," I snickered, as I kissed him back.

"Maybe," he responded as his mouth was on mine. I giggled again and then pulled away.

"Okay, you asked for it, but after I do this, I'm running inside and putting on shorts," I stated, bravely, as I pulled the beach towel away from my stomach.

I stood in front of Kevin in my turquoise and black, one-piece, bathing suit. I saw his face light up as he looked at my body appreciatively. I realized that even though we'd touched one another, I had never really stood before him bare. Even though everything was covered I still felt like I was standing naked in front of him. "There, you got a look, now come on in and let me change!" I grabbed his hand.

Once we were inside, Bailey came walking out of her room with cut off, blue jean shorts and a tank top on. When she saw Kevin with me, she grinned and told him to come in and she'd get us all something to drink. I ran into her room and shimmied off the wet bathing suit and grabbed my own clothes to begin throwing on. I could still smell the chlorine in my hair and I grabbed a brush and tried to rake it through the fast-drying curls on my head.

Walking into the kitchen in my own cut-offs, Kevin looked at me and smiled, "You're a little sunburned."

I looked at my shoulders and noticed that he was right. I knew my face felt tight from the chlorine too and asked if my face was red. They both laughed and told me it was. I had gotten a good tan at the beginning of the summer, but since I didn't stay out all the time, the tan had already begun to fade and my normal, porcelain white skin was beginning to show. The red hopefully wasn't bad enough to peel. Maybe I'd begin school with a little bit of a tan.

After a while, Bailey went to her room to call Levi, and Kevin and I told her we were going for a walk. Because we had so little time together, I knew that there would be no chance to spend any real quality time with him. The few hours I got to share the night before had been all I would be guaranteed. I was sad about it, but I knew that this short amount of time was so much more than I'd have had if I were still in Oklahoma.

We talked a little about my mom being agitated with Clarice and my daddy while getting my stuff in Oklahoma. He chuckled saying he was hoping my mom didn't get arrested for murdering Clarice.

We both began to giggle after that because Kevin had seen my mom and Clarice in action when I'd gotten hurt in 7th grade. He and his mom were in the waiting room of the hospital while I was in surgery, having the lens from my glasses removed from my skull. It was a freak accident that almost claimed my life.

Kevin had been there to be my savior once again. There were far too many times he had literally saved me, and far too little I could ever do to repay him.

Walking to the elementary playground together, we skirted past the tunnel we normally sat in, and went to the swings. I smiled when I saw where we were headed.

I loved to swing and rarely ever did it any more, since I was now a teenager. It was the greatest feeling to me, to swing as high and as fast as I could, to feel the wind rush across my face and through my hair. The only other thing I'd ever had to compare that feeling to was when I had dated Jax, and he would take me horseback riding at his uncle's place.

Kevin sat on a swing and watched as I pushed myself back and forth faster and faster, until I no longer touched the ground under me. I was now pumping my legs in the air to gain height and speed on the swings.

I had a silly smile plastered across my face and as I began to go higher, I closed my eyes and felt the air rush across my face and through my hair. I felt so free and alive when I was high in the air. After a few minutes of pure abandonment, I slowly opened my eyes, in the 100-degree heat, and began to slow down, as I looked at Kevin, watching him smile up at me.

When my feet finally were touching the packed dirt under my swing, I asked Kevin, "Why are you looking at me like that?"

Smiling, he replied, "You looked like a little girl. I've never seen you look so free and like a little girl before. I mean, I know you were just twelve when we met, but you seemed so much older and always have. I guess I just never thought about you ever being little. I've never seen pictures of you little. My mom has pictures of me all over the house as a little kid, but I just realized I've never seen one of you."

I thought about it and shrugged, "Yeah, my mama is the picture person. I don't even know if my daddy has a picture of me in his wallet. Probably not."

"I was smiling because it was nice to see that little girl in you, I guess," Kevin responded, softly, as he looked at my sandaled feet in the dirt.

Glancing at Kevin, I realized he had on blue jeans, a t-shirt and tennis shoes in the stifling heat. I'd never seen him in shorts. I had a dark image pass across my face when I thought about it, because it made me sad that he felt so self-conscious. I knew there was a reason for it, I just didn't know if he'd ever tell me why. I thought I might know the reason, at least partially.

I decided I didn't want to spoil the fun and carefree last little bit of time we had together, with questions that would only be heartbreaking for us both. I challenged him to swing with me, to see who could get the highest. At first, he balked, but he finally told me he would, just so I'd shut up.

While we swung on the swing set, in the elementary school playground, I thought back to all the years I had gone to Bowie Elementary. I always jumped on the swings with pure abandon, as I was now. Kevin and I kept looking at one another as we swung on the pendulum of the swings. I could suddenly see the little boy he had been. I wondered briefly if he was seeing the same little girl that had lived in me. We finally stopped swinging and were both laughing as we jumped out of the swings and went running for a tree to sit under.

We sat down under the tree to catch our breath. I rested my head against Kevin's chest to hear his heartbeat one more time. He lazily and absently stroked my shoulder while we sat there and watched as little boys in pee-wee football practiced out in the field behind the elementary.

"Why aren't you practicing already for football?" I asked, suddenly realizing that Kevin should be at a practice.

"That's pee-wee leagues. They practice on Sundays if their parents let them. We're high school. We only practice on weekdays and Saturday mornings." Kevin explained.

I nodded my head thoughtfully and then asked, "You are playing this year right?"

Kevin sat there for a minute and said, "Yea, I'm gonna play J-V this year. I don't know if I'm gonna play anymore after this year though."

I sat up and looked back at him shocked. Kevin was a jock. He'd played football since he'd been in the pee-wee leagues, like the little boys who were practicing way out in the field from us. "What do you mean you don't think you're going to keep playing?"

Kevin's shoulders shrugged up, "I dunno, I'm just not having fun with it anymore. I don't think I should keep doing it if I don't like it. High school ball is a lot different than the other stuff. Everybody is all about their stats and what college they're gonna play for. I'm not going to college and it takes all the fun out of it."

"Why don't you think you'll go to college?" I asked sincerely.

"Lainey, I told you last year, I'm not smart. I'm a jock. Even being a jock doesn't mean I can go to college. I can play football all year long, but in college I have to be able to do the work. I can't do it. So, I'm not going to college," he lifted his shoulders at me again.

I didn't know what to say. I wanted to go to college with a passion. I loved school. I didn't know how I'd ever get to college, but I wanted to go so badly. I wanted to be a teacher, and I wanted to learn, and I couldn't imagine anyone not going to college if they could. "What are you going to do after high school then?" I asked softly.

"Probably try to get on out at PPG or something like that. I dunno. I just don't want to keep playing football. Can we change the subject?" he asked me, sounding a little irritated. I nodded my head.

I couldn't believe that King Kevin had doubts about his abilities. We had a conversation the year before, after his first freshman game, and he'd been completely down and out over losing that game so miserably. He had told me then that if he wasn't a jock he didn't know who he was. I worried that if he didn't stay in sports, he would lose sight of who he was to some degree and that worried me.

I leaned back against him and declared, "Well, whether you're a jock or not, you're always Kevin, and that's the person I like anyway." I smiled up at him from my position resting on his shoulder.

Kevin glanced down into my sienna colored eyes and smiled. "Well, that's good 'cause that's all I've got to give you." I wrapped my arm around his waist and squeezed tight. It was hotter than Hades, but I didn't care, as I watched the little boys throw the brown pig skin ball back and forth.

Eventually, when the heat became too oppressive, we began the walk back up Granville to Bailey's. I didn't think that Kevin would stay, but he surprised me when he came in the air-conditioned house and into Bailey's room with me. We all three hung out, talking and laughing. I was so happy to have the two people that meant the most to me, right beside me.

Too soon though, my mama came to pick me up. I was sad and wasn't sure when I'd see them. I hoped it wouldn't be another year, but I just didn't know.

Mama told us all the stories about how Clarice and Daddy had been so angry when she showed up without me. Clarice had the boys pack up all of my stuff. She said she doubted the boys actually did it, because everything was thrown into trash bags. She wasn't sure, but she thought they might have even packed trash.

I shook my head and Mama's eyes gleamed. I knew she'd already begun drinking, but I didn't say anything. I was just grateful she was still functioning, pleasant and that her bitch switch hadn't gotten flipped already by the V.O.

She seemed happy to see Kevin there and even hugged him before we left. Bailey had tears in her eyes as soon as Mama got into the driver's side of her red Cadillac. I hugged her and told her that I'd be back soon. She told me that going to Samson wasn't going to be the same without me. I tried hard to keep my eyes dry, even though I was fighting a losing battle.

When it came time for Kevin to hug me goodbye, he didn't shy away from brushing his lips against mine. I knew Mama would have a million questions about it, since she had wondered if Kevin was my boyfriend back in 7th grade. I didn't care if Mama had a billion questions though, when I wrapped my arms around Kevin's neck and held him close. I wanted to smell the clean smell that was his alone, one more time. It would have to go with me to Corpus Christi and last for at least a good ten months, before I'd probably see him, I thought.

I had looked forward to going to Samson this year with Bailey and Kevin. I had even held out hope that one day Kevin and I would be able to have a real relationship even. Now those dreams were shattered on the rocks, and I knew that they would never be.

I hugged Bailey one more time and just as I reached for the door handle on my mama's Cadillac, Kevin walked over and grabbed me to him and kissed me one more time for good measure, I thought. It wasn't anything overly passionate, but it was more than the chaste little kiss he'd first given me. He smiled down at me and barely croaked out, "Just so you remember me."

Looking into the summery eyes that I loved, I whispered, "I can't ever forget you, Kev. Haven't you figured that out yet?" He smiled back and opened the door for me. I slid into the front seat, amazed that I still had no tears coming out of my eyes for once.

As my mama backed out of the driveway and I raised my hand to my best friend, and the boy I loved the most, I felt the tears as they prickled in the corners of my eyes. I wanted once to be able to leave them without crying, or at the very least, without them seeing me cry. I wanted them to think of me as brave and strong like Kevin had told me he believed I was, before I'd left for Oklahoma City. When the Cadillac was headed down Granville Street I finally let the torrent of tears I'd been holding in, flood from my eyes. My mama said nothing but handed me a tissue from the box that was in the center part of the front seat. I smiled as I took it and held it to my eyes. I wasn't sure if I was brave and strong at all. I didn't know how I would possibly get through a new school again, and new people, except that I had at least one friend already built in. Maybe with that, I could begin again. I knew though that there would never be anyone like Bailey or Kevin in my life again. I was so terrified they would both replace me before I came home again.

Chapter 13

Because Labor Day wasn't until September 7th that year, school started the week before, which meant we got a three day weekend on our first weekend out of school. I was going to Woodway High School, with Kelly Stubbs. We still lived inside of Corpus Christi, but the school district I was in had a large gang population. My mom used her best friend's address, out in Annaville, which was the suburb that Woodway was in. It wasn't very far to drive out there, since we were close to the edge of town.

During the summer, I'd already begun hanging out with Kelly more. We were able to start going to a place called The Gameroom on the weekends. It was where all the local high school kids went to hang out. It was a small building that housed a few pool tables, foosball tables and every electronic game you could think of, as well as having a snack bar.

When I first came down for the summer, I was surprised that Kelly had started getting a little wilder than she'd been before. During 8th grade, while I'd been in Wichita Falls hanging out with cheerleaders and football players, she had started running around with the kids who liked to party. She began drinking and smoking. Even though I'd had my own experimental times with alcohol, I was hardly the party type. I actually smoked a couple of times with her during the summer, but I wasn't too big on it. I had my own share of living with people who drank, so drinking wasn't in my sights either. I didn't want to start school without any friends though, and Kelly had been such a good friend to me since 6th grade. I went along with her because I wanted to have some means of a teenaged life.

Football games were every other Friday, just like they had been in Wichita Falls, and we went to every home game. The football stadium was nothing like the one in Wichita Falls. We could walk around with people we knew, and watch the game practically on the field itself, from around a chain link fence, that cordoned it off from the bleachers.

Saturday nights, instead of skating, we went to The Gameroom and played video games and watched cute boys. I didn't think there were really very many attractive boys in our grade or even the grade above ours. Most of the good-looking boys were seniors. There were several I liked to watch.

My heart might have belonged to Kevin Strong, in Wichita Falls, but my teenage hormones were still screaming my name when I saw a cute boy.

I had hoped that my mom's drinking would slow down once I had made it clear I wasn't leaving, but I was disappointed that instead of lessening, sometimes it seemed as if she drank more. I loved my mama and we were very close when she was sober.

I could always tell when her drunk switch flipped. It didn't flip every single day, but it flipped at least three or four times a week, which always made life a little interesting to navigate.

One Thursday evening, after I had gotten home from school, Mama came in my room after she and Ray had gotten into an argument. When they argued I tried to stay inside of my room, with the door shut, because I didn't want to face down my mother's wrath. When she threw open my door, she asked me if I wanted a piece of her too. I looked up at her feeling the fear begin to well up inside of me. I had tried to avoid her entirely. Now, here she was in my room, trying to find another fight.

It felt like she hadn't gotten her fight completed with Ray, so she was going to come into my room and start one with me. Looking up into her angry face, I shook my head. I didn't want to argue with her. I actually wasn't sure at that point why I'd wanted to live with her. I'd been in school for almost a month, and it seemed as if the longer I was there, the more she drank.

I shrank back on my bed, into the corner of the wall, and Mama advanced into my room with her dark brown eyes spitting fire at me. I didn't know what to do or say. I'd thought if I stayed out of her way, she'd leave me alone. It had been working so far, at least, but this night, she seemed like she just wanted to fight for the pure pleasure of it.

"Mama, I don't want to fight with you," I muttered quietly, as I scooted further into the corner of my bed.

"Why not? Ray wanted to, I figured you'd want a piece of me too, since both of you are always so fucking ungrateful for everything I do around here," my mama snarled angrily.

"Mama, I'm grateful for everything you do, please don't start this tonight," I whispered.

My mom started making a nasty face at me as she said in a whiney voice, "Mama I'm grateful for everything! You fuckin' little liar! You're the most ungrateful little bitch there is! Why don't you go see if Kevin, who isn't your boyfriend, but you still kiss, or Bailey, who is so perfect... or even Kevin's mom who is such a saint, will do everything for you like I do!"

Shocked, I looked at her, not quite believing she'd said what she'd said. She knew how homesick I was. She knew how much my friends meant to me.

We still had never even spoken about Kevin kissing me goodbye when she picked me up. Where this particular viciousness had come from, I didn't know. Slamming out of my room, my mom continued shouting at no one, as Ray had gotten into his car and left the house, when he was sick of listening to her scream.

Sitting on my bed, I picked up my stuffed rabbit and puppy and held them close to my chest, as the salty tears streamed onto their stuffed bodies.

I felt like I'd traded one type of insanity for another. I felt so hopeless and so trapped. I didn't know how to change any of it.

I knew I could never go crawling back to Oklahoma City. I also knew that at 14 I couldn't just pack up and go live wherever I wanted to. I was stuck now with someone I both loved and feared. Someone I adored and yet loathed. I felt completely and inextricably stuck.

I pulled my photo album out that I kept beside my bed. I had put all of my photos of Bailey, Levi, Jax and Kevin in it, and opened it up. I looked at all of their pictures and felt so lost and alone.

How was I supposed to ever make it four years here, when after only a few months, I was at my wits end? My mama wasn't normally like the way she was when she drank. When she wasn't drunk she was funny and sarcastic and soft and loving.

When she drank she became mean spirited and angry. It was almost like living with Dr. Jekyll and Mr. Hyde. She got a look in her eyes when she was drinking which turned her switch on. I was beginning to realize this the longer I was there. There was no turning the switch off until she'd slept it off, but sometimes after she slept, she would get up and start all over again.

As I sat in my bed, holding my two stuffed animals to my chest, listening to her rant and rave as she slammed through our little trailer house, I wondered what I was supposed to do. I didn't know how I was supposed to go on. I was already tired. I had begun to be weary once we moved to Oklahoma City, but now I was far from weary. I was now completely worn down to the bone and didn't know where else to turn. I didn't want to keep crying. I didn't want to complain to anyone else, because I had billed moving to live with my mama as the end all to my worries.

I wanted to tell Bailey so much about what this was doing to me, but I felt ashamed to admit the truth to her. She'd seen my mom in action only a little when she'd come down.

Kelly White had been able to come down in July and she'd seen my mom's behavior too, but thankfully Mama didn't get too carried away when Kelly White had been there either.

Kelly Stubbs was beginning to see more of my mama than any of my friends, and I sometimes tried to avoid her spending the night with me, because I was terrified what my mom would say or do while she was there. I wanted so much to write Kevin and pour my heart out to him, but I knew he would feel helpless and there was nothing he could do for me either.

I had to figure my own way out of my misery, and I didn't have an answer for it.

On the one hand I could beg Daddy to let me go back to Oklahoma City, but Oklahoma was the devil I knew already, and detested more than anything.

Then there was the devil I had left to me, which was living with my mercurial mother, who never seemed to have a rhyme or reason for her anger. Sometimes it could be set off just because no one noticed she'd gotten her hair cut, or because she'd had a flat tire. Sometimes it got set off because she had been in a good mood and no one had joined in that bright mood with her.

Sighing deeply, I sat in the corner of my bed against the wall, and listened for my mom, as she stomped around and yelled for no apparent reason. She turned up the record player that she played Tammy Wynette and Willie Nelson on, while she sat in front of it with her V.O. and water, and her ashtray and cigarettes. I had to find a way out and I didn't know what it was.

Looking at my photo album, my heart literally ached for Kevin. I wanted to sneak out and go to his house, as I'd done when life seemed too much. I wanted to feel him hold me and tell me that everything was going to be alright. I thought back to how he'd been raised when he was little, and I knew that my mom wasn't a drug addict. She loved me, unlike Kevin's birth mom, but I also was tired of having nowhere else to go.

Finally, I knew what the only way I had to go was. It was a permanent solution to the pain and misery I found myself in. I'd felt nothing but pain, it seemed like, the entire year since Daddy and Clarice had announced we were leaving Wichita Falls.

I had survived Geoffrey's maniacal physical abuse, and Clarice's own brand of lunacy. I had lived through moving to Oklahoma City where all the kids hated me. I made the only decision I could, which was to move in with my mama. Now, I was out of options. There were no more choices that I could make. I was too young to make my own legal decisions. I couldn't tell my parents that I didn't want to live with either of them and move in with the Strong family.

Going into our bathroom, I closed and locked the door. I looked inside the closet that my mom kept the towels and linens, as well as all the medicines, and first aid supplies.

I began to pick up all the prescription bottles that she had in there, which were quite a few, and began to read the labels. I didn't know what any of them were. I also didn't know how many it would take, or which ones it would take, but I decided a few from each bottle should be enough. Surely combined, all of the muscle relaxers and pain medications that my mom had, from before and after her back surgery, would do what I needed them to do.

I was ready to actually go ahead and float away for real now. There was nowhere else for me to go. Sleep wasn't nearly long enough to float through, and I was no happier here than I'd been in Oklahoma City. I had friends here, but there was still so much insanity all around me, I simply couldn't function anymore the way I was.

Taking the pills that I had poured into my hand and slinking along the dark hallway back into my bedroom, praying my mom didn't see me, I was able to get back inside my tiny room unnoticed. I had put all the bottles back up in the closet in the bathroom and didn't take enough out of any one bottle for my mom to know what I'd done. I figured that if I just went to sleep and never woke up, then my mom would cry, but she'd no longer have me to worry about. If I only took a few from each bottle she wouldn't realize what I'd done, until it was too late.

I got my stationery out and wrote a letter to Bailey and one to Kevin. I addressed them and put them on my dresser. In both letters I thanked them for loving someone as unlovable as I had been. I told them they each had made more difference in my life than they would ever know, and that I was so sorry to hurt them this way. I didn't know what else to do because life was just too hard. I explained how I had left one devil only to find another in Corpus, except the demon here I loved as much as I loved them. I just didn't know how to tame this one. Because of that, I decided to take myself out of this world. I was tired of the pain.

In Kevin's letter I told him that I hoped there would be a lake with yellow flowers beside it. I wanted him to be happy in life. I forgave him for any hurt he had ever caused me, and I apologized for any that I'd ever caused him. I told him to make sure Donna knew how much I loved her.

In Bailey's letter I asked her to have Jax take her and Levi out to our place by the lake and sit and remember me with laughs and no tears. I asked her to please tell Jax that I truly had loved him, and that I was grateful to him for giving me the chance to be just a 14-year-old girl when I was with him. I told her to tell him how much I loved riding Buttercup, and that I was sorry for everything I'd ever done to hurt him with Kevin.

I also asked her to tell Levi thank you for being my best guy friend. I included a short note to Kelly White with Bailey's letter. She had been the other friend who had stuck by me, and given me so much joy, never asking for anything back.

Then I wrote a letter to my parents and told them both how sorry I was that I had ever caused them pain. I told them that I couldn't stand living any longer the way my life was. I explained that I was so tired. Also, I couldn't take either of their drinking any longer. I told my parents that I hoped that without me around they would no longer have a reason to drink and that they would find a way to forgive me for doing what I was doing

When I finished, I laid the spiral notebook that I had written the note in on top of my dresser, along with the two letters addressed to Bailey and Kevin. Then I picked up each pill and put it in my mouth, and swallowed them one at a time, with the coke I had sitting by my bed.

I opened my photo album to the page that showed all my pictures of Bailey and me, and Kevin and me along with Jax and Levi. I put both of my necklaces on that I had received from Bailey and Kevin, and the bracelets I had from Bailey and Levi and the St. Christopher one from Kevin.

Finally, I put the little yellow, flower earrings in my ears. From the small wooden jewelry box Jax gave me, I pulled the now dry, yellow flower I'd picked, the time Kevin had taken me on a real date. I held the dry flower under my nose, hoping to smell the last traces of summer earthiness from it, then I set it gently back inside the little wooden box.

After changing into a night shirt and shorts, I lay down on my bed. I pulled my Velveteen Rabbit and my floppy eared puppy from the corner and crawled under my covers. I reached up and turned the light out in my room and looked at the clock. It was only 8 p.m. I felt the tears trickle out of my eyes, and rolled down the sides of my face, into my ears and curls, and closed my eyes. I prayed that God would take my soul to Heaven. I prayed that He would forgive me for being such a coward. I prayed that dying wouldn't hurt, and then I fell asleep for what I hoped would be the last time.

***

My eyes fluttered open and I looked inside of my darkened bedroom. I lay there for a few minutes, looking at the open photo album. It was late in the day. I could tell by the light that was filtering through my bedroom window.

I glanced around my room a little confused. I glanced at my dresser and saw the spiral notebook with the two envelopes laying on top of it still. I looked at my clock and saw that it was 4:30 in the afternoon.

I looked back at the photo album on my bed and saw Jax's green eyes staring out at me.

Suddenly I felt a profound sense of euphoria engulf me, and I sat up, hugged my knees to my chest. I began to pray to God and thanked him for letting me wake up. I thanked him for letting me live through what I'd done, and I asked him to please forgive me for being so stupid. I suddenly had a huge sense of gratitude for my life.

I thought of all of the times that I could have died, and I had decided to try to end my life to escape the hardships I was facing. I felt the tears roll down my cheeks as I silently continued to thank God over and over.

I looked at my room and my body, realizing I truly was still there.

Swinging my legs over the side of my bed I quietly opened my bedroom door and walked out into the living room to find my mama sitting in there, watching a movie. "Hey Bug! Do you feel better?" she asked me.

I didn't quite know how to respond. I didn't know if she had any idea that I shouldn't even be awake. I still wasn't sure how I was awake, even now.

Smiling at my mama, I nodded my head, "Um, yeah, I feel lots better, actually!"

"When I tried to wake you for school this morning, you wouldn't hardly move. I asked you if you felt bad, and I got a grunt, so I just let you sleep," Mama was smiling at me, her anger no more a memory to her, than my grunt that morning was to me. "I think maybe you were just exhausted," Mama kept smiling at me. Then she looked at me closely, "Your eyes are a little red though. You sure you feel okay?"

I nodded my head again, "Yeah, I just had a really bad headache last night. Maybe I'm getting a head cold, even though I feel a lot better now," I lied, quietly.

"Well, you look okay, except for your eyes. I think you should stay in tonight since you didn't go to school, anyway," Mama smiled at me. I grinned back at her and nodded my head.

"I'm gonna get something to drink and go back into my room," I declared, walking towards the kitchen. I walked into the kitchen, still marveling at the fact that I was alive. I didn't understand how I could be alive. I'd taken at least 20 pills the night before, of all kinds of different things. I didn't even know what any of them did. Once I got something to drink, I smiled at my mama as I walked through the living room.

When I closed the door softly, I immediately pulled the spiral notebook to me and tore out the letter I'd written to my parents. I reread it and then I tore it into a thousand tiny pieces. I opened my letter to Bailey next and did the same with it. When I came to the letter to Kevin, I opened it and realized for the first time that I once again had tears sliding down my cheeks. I read Kevin's letter slower, then I began to rip it slowly to shreds after I finished it.

Kevin believed I was strong and brave. I had almost proved him completely and totally wrong. I was so grateful that my plan hadn't worked. I had never felt more alive than I did at that moment.

I wiped the tears staining my cheeks and took each letter and wrapped it into a sheet of paper from the spiral and squashed all three balls into the smallest paper balls I could scrunch together. I threw all three of them into the trash and decided that from that day forward, I was going to be brave and strong. I wasn't going to be afraid any longer. If I ever was afraid, I'd fight through it and keep pushing forward.

I wasn't going to back down, even for my mama. I had to claim my life. I had to live my life. I had to start living and not feeling sorry for myself.

I opened the spiral once more, and since it was a relatively new, with only a few pages missing, I began to write in it. I began writing a journal for the first time since Geoffrey had breached my privacy and read my diary. I didn't have to worry about Geoffrey finding this one, and my mama respected my privacy, so I didn't think there was anything to worry about with writing down all of my most private thoughts. My journal would be the place I would tell my fears to. It would be the place I turned to write about any heartache I encountered, but to the world, I would be fearless. I had to be. God had given me another chance at life. I didn't know why, but I knew that I shouldn't have it.

As I thought about God giving me another chance at life, I thought back to the tornado and how I probably could have died in it, back in 6th grade. Then I thought about the freak accident in 7th grade, where my heart had stopped for almost a whole minute, even though I didn't remember any of it. I realized that I had cheated death yet again, and I still wasn't certain why I'd been spared.

I wrote in my first entry of my journal about the euphoria I was feeling at just being alive. When I finished writing in it, I got out my stationery and began to write Bailey a new letter. I thought about telling her what I'd done, then decided I couldn't tell her I'd been so cowardly. Instead, I told her that I was trying to change the way I was thinking about my life and that things hadn't been exactly easy with my mama. When I finished, I addressed an envelope to my best friend.

I was actually happy to be alive, for the first time in a very long time. I wasn't sure if I fully grasped what exactly life was, until this. Now I was certain I understood it better.

Chapter 14

The following weekend, Kelly Stubbs and I went to a football game, over in Calvin High's stadium. Calvin High was the other school district, in the suburb of Annaville, and they were the staunch rivals of Woodway High. I didn't really understand why they would be so intense in their rivalry, since they were only a few miles apart.

While we were at the game, Kelly began flirting with some older boys, who were actually seniors. Before long, she came over to me and told me there was a river party not far from the stadium, and asked if I wanted to go.

I told her we shouldn't go, because my mom would be picking us up after the game was over. She assured me that we'd be back in plenty of time, so I eventually relented and went with her.

I knew the games were usually over by 10 or 10:30 and knowing my mom, she'd get there after everybody had left anyway. Kelly was spending the night, so I agreed to go. I didn't want her to leave, and then not come back, and me have to explain where she'd gone. I knew Kelly wasn't real good about paying attention to things like time, especially when there were boys around.

We climbed into a car with some different boys than the ones she'd originally been talking to, and when I asked her what we were doing, she told me that they were all going to the same place.

I climbed into the car, even though I still felt a little off about the whole thing. As we rode in the back seat with another guy who had already graduated, I was surprised to hear music like Jason Rains listened to, screaming out of the back speakers near our heads.

I didn't have a clue where we were, but I knew we were down by a river. True to the other boys' words there was a small party going on, with a keg of beer even. I'd never had beer out of a keg before. I didn't really like beer anyway, but I felt a little weird standing there not drinking anything, especially when three different boys had tried to give me a cup of beer.

I finally took one, and sipped on it. It wasn't quite as bad as the beer I'd drunk when I'd been with Jax, Bailey and Levi, but it still tasted pretty gross. It didn't tickle the back of my throat or nose as much as the canned beer had, so I managed to actually drink the whole cup.

There weren't nearly as many girls at the party as there were boys. Most of the boys I either didn't know, or else they were older than Kelly and I. I kept checking the time because I was terrified we'd be late getting back to the game, before my mom.

When it was 9:45 I told Kelly we had to find someone to take us back in case my mom got there by 10:00. Kelly was already half drunk, and flirting with the boy that had ridden in the back of the car we'd come to the party in. He was already 20 and Kelly was only 14. I had just had a birthday, so I was finally 15, but I even thought 20 was too old.

Finally, after getting pissed, Kelly got the older guy's friend to give us a ride back to the stadium. He rode back with us, and I sat in the backseat, next to them, as they made out. I hoped and prayed we got there before all of the cars were out of the parking lot. When we turned the corner to the stadium, I saw the lights were already out at the field. I couldn't believe it!

I looked at my watch and saw it was only 10 o'clock! I was shocked to see that all the cars were out of the parking lot, except for my mother's. I groaned and began slapping Kelly on the back, as I yelled, "We are so busted! Dammit!"

The guy driving the car pulled up as far away from my mama's car as he could. I pulled Kelly out by the tail of her shirt, to face my mom, who was so mad, she was literally screaming over the guy's stereo. I walked up to her car, knowing she was going to rip into me. I was in a world of trouble. I was just grateful I hadn't gotten drunk by the beer I'd had.

Mom was screaming about how long she'd been standing there waiting, and how she'd been worried sick. I hung my head and she kept hounding me about where we'd gone, and what we were doing, riding with a car full of boys.

Finally, I told her we'd just gone to a party down by the river and she began to scream even louder. By the time we walked in the house, she was still going strong. I was ready to scream back at her. We walked into my room and surprisingly, my mom followed Kelly and me. I figured she'd leave me alone once I got into the house.

Once we were in my bedroom, she continued to scream about how stupid I'd been, and how Kelly and I could have been raped and murdered. I mistakenly rolled my eyes when she said that, and found myself backhanded so hard, I literally stumbled backwards, into my closet door.

I grabbed my face, when I finally got over being stunned, and glared at my mom. Kelly was sitting on my bed with her mouth dropped open, as she stared in terrified shock.

I glanced at Kelly because I felt like she should be the one who'd gotten the slap, and not me, because she'd been the one who'd given me so much grief about wanting to go! I was the one paying for it now.

After Mama backhanded me, with her hand that held a ring on every finger, she turned around and stomped out of my room. I tasted the blood inside of my lip, where it had raked across my teeth.

Kelly began to apologize for getting me into so much trouble. I walked past her, and told her to shut up, as I slammed into the bathroom.

I heard my mom in her bedroom, as she ranted to Ray about what had happened. I felt touched when he told her to settle down. He told her I was a kid.

I spit into the sink as I listened through the paper-thin walls, next to my mom's room. I cupped my hand under the faucet to get water to swish in my mouth. I rose up to see if my lip was swollen and noticed only a tiny bit that hopefully would go down by the next day. I wet a washrag and took it with me back to my room.

Kelly was still sitting on the edge of my bed when I walked back in. "What's wrong?" I asked her brusquely.

"I'm really sorry, DeLaine," Kelly muttered quietly.

I felt so much shame, but I didn't want Kelly to know that, so I shrugged nonchalantly, "Well, you know if Rita ain't happy, then ain't nobody happy!"

"I didn't think the game would be over before 10 though," Kelly moaned, miserably.

"Well, it was, and we can't worry about it now. Don't worry. She's not gonna knock the shit outta you…just me. I thought I was done with all the slapping though." I began to chuckle darkly and looked at Kelly, "Oh wait, I am done with the slapping. Now I'm getting the backhanding." I shook my head angrily as I grabbed a nightshirt out of my dresser. Kelly got up and grabbed hers out of her bag and did the same.

"Do you think you're gonna get grounded or in more trouble tomorrow?" Kelly asked me once we were lying in my bed.

I shrugged my shoulders and told her I wasn't really sure. This was the first thing I'd really done to get in real trouble, since I'd been here. Since my mom never grounded me when I visited, I didn't know how she'd go about punishing me. I told Kelly not to worry about it. My mom had finally settled down back in her room.

I rolled over holding on to my rabbit and puppy and closed my eyes.

***

The next day, when we got up, Kelly asked if she should go out with me. I told her my mom hadn't had a problem with backhanding me in front of her, if she was still pissed, she'd probably have no problem with telling me, whether Kelly was there, or not.

When we walked into the living room I could see Mama sitting in the dining room, smoking cigarettes and reading her newspaper. I was happy to see she was still drinking coffee. Mama looked up and before we could walk into the kitchen she said, "I want to talk to you girls."

We stopped, and Mama began softly, "You two scared me to death last night! I just want you to know that if you go to a football game, I expect you to stay at it. I was terrified something had happened to you. You don't know what kind of crazy people are out there, who could rape and kill you. Did you know those boys you were riding with?"

Kelly and I both shook our heads and my mom told us that if anything like that ever happened again, she would tell Kelly's mom, and we wouldn't be able to go anywhere together again. I nodded and glanced over to see Kelly's face drain of all color. Mama told me that if we wanted to do something we needed to call her, but we were to never leave some place we were again, without first checking with her. Then she got up and began cooking sausage and biscuits and gravy for us for breakfast.

I grinned at Kelly when Mama walked out of the room. I was so grateful my mama wasn't Clarice. I knew if she had been Clarice, I'd have maybe been grounded until I turned 17.

Chapter 15

By the time November rolled around, I had begun to make more friends, even though none of them I considered really close, except Kelly. There were a few boys at school that I found myself crushing on, but none that I thought would even consider looking at me.

Kelly never seemed to have trouble finding a boy to make out with every weekend, whether we went to a game or the Gameroom. I had slowly begun to smoke a little when I was out with her, because it seemed everybody at the Gameroom did. Every once in a while, I'd drink a beer when someone would come up there with them. I didn't get drunk, but I had gotten buzzed a couple of times.

The weekend before the Thanksgiving break, Kelly was spending the night with me and we planned to go to the Gameroom. When I got home that afternoon I could tell that my mama was in a pretty crappy mood, even though her switch wasn't quite tripped yet. She and Ray were going to go out to one of the bars they hung out at, after they took Kelly and me to the Gameroom. They'd pick us up at midnight and take us back to the house. After that, they planned to go to the lake house that Ray owned.

Right before we left to pick up Kelly, my mom began her decline into her dark mood, and I was trying to keep my head down. The entire way to Kelly's house she kept trying to pick a fight with me, and finally I got angry and popped off to her. She turned around right before we got to Kelly's and told me if I didn't like living with her I could always go back to Clarice. I looked at her shocked and was even angrier when I saw the pure meanness in her face, as she sneered at me.

Once they dropped us at the Gameroom, some of the people we ran around with began talking about a big party that was going on down at the river bridge. I told Kelly that the last time we'd gone to the river, we'd gotten in serious trouble. She told me that it was so early, we'd get back in plenty of time. I looked at the clock and saw it was just a little past 7:30, so I reluctantly agreed. We began trying to find someone who was going down there, and when almost everyone was gone, we were forced to accept a ride from a big guy, Jeremy Tobias, with a pretty, sweet Camaro. He wasn't someone we normally ran with, in our crowd, but he was going down there, so we tagged along in the Camaro.

As usual, I got thrown in the backseat, next to the damned, thumping speakers. While we were heading towards the Nueces River Bridge, Kelly was up front, doing her coquettish flirting, even though she wasn't in the least bit interested in Jeremy. He wanted to cruise up and down Leonard Street, a couple of times, because his Camaro was new. He wanted to show it off.

While we were driving through the Sonic, I noticed wrapped in a sweatshirt, on the seat beside me, was a brand-new bottle of Wild Turkey. Jeremy had been bragging about it while we'd been driving around. I picked it up, as I sat in the backseat, listening to AC/DC sing about the highway to hell. I laughed when I heard that line in the song because I figured I'd been on the highway for a while.

I'd never drank Wild Turkey before and had never drank any alcohol straight. I'd always mixed it with coke. I broke the seal on the bottle and decided to taste it. I didn't figure Jeremy would notice. Besides he'd been sitting up there bragging to Kelly how he'd share it with her when we got to the river bridge. I figured since I was her best friend, he could share it with me too. When I took my first tentative swig from the bottle, I felt like I'd just swallowed fire, feeling the urge to cough and hack. I didn't want Jeremy to get mad at me before we even got out there.

After the initial swig, I decided to try it again. Something in me wanted to feel the burn as it slid down my throat one more time. I tilted the bottle back again and the second swig went down so much easier than the first one. I wondered if each swig got better, each time you took one. I didn't think I'd drink much by taking a couple more swigs. Besides, now, not only was my throat warm, but my gut was feeling the familiar burn I felt when I'd first drank back in 7th grade. I'd gone riding around with Duke Reed and his dope dealer dad in a Trans-Am.

I laughed quietly in the back, as AC/DC continued to pound through my brain. I could never tell the difference in Trans-Ams and Camaros, and here I was feeling the burn of alcohol again, except this time I didn't have damned old Duke Reed trying to get me drunk so he could take advantage of me. I was getting drunk just fine by myself.

When I got out of the backseat of Jeremy Tobias's Camaro, I handed him the Turkey bottle, with only about half of it left. I was feeling absolutely no pain, and for the first time, finally understood why my parents got drunk. It was fabulous.

I was funny and people liked me. I entertained and flirted. Even when Kelly ran off with a boy who I thought was really cute, I didn't care. The only thing I cared about was getting back to the Gameroom before midnight. I might have been drunk, but I wasn't entirely stupid of what the consequence would be if my mama showed up, and I wasn't there.

Kelly had given me her cigarettes to hold, and while I drank someone's beer, standing there with a bunch of people from Woodway, I smoked her cigarettes. I couldn't remember ever feeling as confident as I did that night. I felt confident and invincible and extremely strong and brave. I missed Kevin too, but knew he'd be so disappointed in me, as would Bailey. I'd been gone from them only a few months and I was changing so drastically. I didn't know how they'd ever forgive me for turning into a dumbass.

When we got back to the Gameroom, at 11:45, I was a happy drunk. I sat at the counter of the snack bar, while Kelly went to the bathroom. I still had her cigarettes, and lit one, knowing that I still had a few minutes before my mom got there. I was talking to a girl I had befriended in my class. Her name was Debbie Vance, and she was just as drunk as I was. We were sitting there smoking and talking when I heard a familiar and terrifying voice next to my ear say, "PUT OUT THAT GOD-DAMNED CIGARETTE AND GET YOUR ASS OUT TO THE CAR!"

I whipped around on the barstool I was sitting and saw my mother's angry face. "It's Debbie's, Mom," I managed to slur out, but my mom's back was already walking out the door.

When Kelly came out of the bathroom, I grabbed her and told her, "Be cool dammit, my mom's already here and she walked in while I had a cigarette in my hand!" Kelly's mouth dropped open, and I nodded. I didn't know how I would pull off not being drunk, because I felt like my brain was moving around, and I was walking in some weird gelatin state.

Climbing in the backseat of Ray's Lincoln, my mama threw a pack of her Winston's at me and told me if I was going to smoke, I was going to do it in front of her.

I nodded my head and took one out and lit it up. She then told me, I was going to smoke the entire pack in front of her. I told her fine. Kelly sat beside me, quaking, as she listened to my mom chew me out. Ray told my mom to cut me some slack. I was a kid and I was going to experiment.

Then they began to discuss how old they'd been when they first started smoking and the fact that I was 15 meant I waited at least four more years than my mom had, Ray kept trying to point out to her. I just kept smoking cigarettes even though my mom's didn't taste anything like the Marlboros that Kelly smoked.

Being drunk was making me feel a little cockier than I normally would have felt, but I was also taking on a whole new outlook that in order to fit in, I was going to have to do like everyone else did. I didn't think I was being too unreasonable. I wasn't drinking and driving like my mom did all the time. I wasn't out having sex with every boy who walked by, or making out with a different boy every weekend. I wasn't smokin' dope.

I felt like there were a lot worse things that I could be doing. I didn't realize that before the end of the school year, I'd be doing a few of those worse things.

Chapter 16

I didn't get in as much trouble for the drunken night at the party, under the Nueces River Bridge, except to get backhanded across my mom's bedroom. Clarice would have slapped me and probably locked me in my room. In the greater realm of things, I figured that I just needed to not get caught from now on.

We moved shortly after this happened, to Annaville, but we moved into a house in the Calvin School District. Because I was already happy at Woodway, my mom kept me in that school. I was ecstatic to be in a real house. The room I had now, was actually bigger than my old room in Wichita Falls, which was nice.

I continued to hang out with Kelly and began to smoke regularly behind my mom's back. Because she was such a heavy smoker, she never realized what I was up to. I also continued to drink every weekend. Some weekends I'd only get to the buzzed state, but there were more times than not that I was as drunk as I'd gotten at the river bridge.

I was hanging out with a lot of senior boys, and had a horrible crush on a boy named Willie Morgan. He was really tall, and a football player. He had dark hair and gorgeous hazel eyes. He was in my Typing I class and he was the class clown. Every girl in the school seemed to have a crush on him. I was too shy to ever approach him. He ran around with all the same senior boys that Kelly and I had become friends with, but he never seemed to notice me, until the typing teacher moved him from the back of the room, next to me, in the front row. Then he noticed me enough to always borrow typing paper and white out. I didn't care. He'd joke with me when he did, and I couldn't resist his silvery, braces filled smile. I'd never noticed a boy who looked good with braces, but Willie was one that did.

Senior boys weren't the only ones who ran in the group that I was now in. There were kids from other grades too. One of them was a blonde girl, named Christy Gilley, who I thought was so cool. She wasn't cool the way I thought Bailey was. This girl was a hippie spirit. She was free and all the boys liked her. She was about 5'9" and had a striking figure. For whatever reason she liked me and we'd hang out, if I wasn't busy with Kelly. She was a junior. I would go into the girls' bathroom at school and smoke with her, and a bunch of other girls, including Kelly.

I noticed that in our little group, I was still the one who acted like the mother. I was also the one who was becoming known for having a mouth on her. I would stand up to any teacher or any student. I wasn't belligerent to teachers, but I didn't back down from any of the more intimidating ones.

I continued to excel in my classes. I was finally back where I belonged in the accelerated classes and even though I hated math, I was in Algebra as a freshman which not many freshman got to do. Most were in Intro Algebra. I wasn't very good at it, but I could still bring home a solid B. I continued to keep my grades at A's and B's, so I didn't think a lot about the changes that were happening to me as a person. I didn't think that what I did on the weekends was so bad, since everybody else was doing the same thing.

I was also becoming very good at deception from my mom, which kept me safe from her wrath, most of the time, unless she and Ray got into an argument. Then she usually looked for me to get into a fight with after he'd storm out of the house.

By Christmas, I was firmly among the party crowd. I drank beer, or whatever else I could try, and had even begun to smoke pot, every now and then. I liked the numbing I felt when I would get drunk. I also liked the confidence I felt when I was drunk. I could talk to boys, like Willie Morgan, at parties if I were drunk or stoned. I wondered often how I would admit to Bailey and Kevin who I was becoming.

I never talked about what I did on the weekends in my letters to Bailey. I didn't want her to think that I was becoming a pothead like Jason. I knew she'd probably be upset because if I were at Samson, I'd be out in the smoking pit with all the other heads, since those were the types of people I was hanging out with.

I had to go to Oklahoma City for Christmas, and I was not looking forward to it. I knew I wouldn't get to go to Wichita Falls unless Geoff had to go get Lisa or take her home. At any rate, I didn't think I'd be seeing Bailey or Kevin. Bailey normally went to her grandparents for a big part of Christmas, so with my luck we'd end up going when she would not be there. She'd already sent me a letter with the dates, so I would know, just in case.

When Mama took me to the airport, I felt terrified to fly up there. I was afraid that once I got there, they would never let me leave. Mama hugged me before I walked up the ramp to the plane, and told me to try to enjoy myself. I just nodded at her.

***

Because I was now 15, I could sit anywhere I wanted on the plane, so I walked towards the back where I knew they let the smokers sit. I had my pack of Marlboro Lights in my purse. I didn't know how I was going to sneak around and smoke with Geoffrey and William around, but I hoped I could go for a walk or something, so I could at least get a couple smokes in a day.

Once we reached Oklahoma City, as the plane taxied on the runway, I wasn't sure what to expect. Because I was in the back of the plane, I would not make it off until the very end, but I wasn't in any hurry.

I didn't even know who was picking me up. I didn't know if Clarice or Daddy would take time off from the restaurant to come to the airport.

I hoped my Daddy would be the first person I'd see. I had actually missed him, even if he didn't seem to be very interested in my life.

Walking down the ramp, I was disappointed to see Geoffrey waiting for me with a big, genuine smile on his face. He looked almost foreign to me.

"Hey Sister!" Geoffrey exclaimed, as he caught me up in a big, tight hug. I pulled away quickly, and looked at him, trying to figure out who this imposter Geoffrey was.

"Um, hey Geoff," I muttered, uncertainly.

Geoffrey began to laugh and started walking towards the baggage claim area. He had grabbed my hand up in his and was talking crazy fast, and laughing the whole time. "Why do you smell like cigarette smoke?" Geoffrey asked me suddenly.

"Probably because my mom smokes like a train, not to mention I could only find a seat back towards the smoking area of the plane," I responded, testily. Thankfully Geoff just nodded and grabbed my bag when it came off the carousel.

"We gotta go to the restaurant first," he crowed, cheerily. I was still trying to figure out what was up with this new Geoff.

We jumped into his old Chevy Luv. I immediately flashed on all the times I'd ridden in it, sitting on Kevin's lap. I couldn't believe the sight of his old truck took me back so quickly. It was cold and wet outside. I had gotten used to the South Texas climate. I was glad Mama had made me take my red, down coat, even though it still hadn't been cold enough to wear it since I'd been in Corpus.

Pulling into the restaurant parking lot, I was amazed at how full it was. "Wow! It's really busy!" I exclaimed.

"Yea, it's been super busy. Your daddy is even playing music every single night now, instead of just on the weekends." He smiled over at me.

I still couldn't get used to this genuine smile. It was creeping me out a little, but I tentatively smiled back at him.

As I walked into the restaurant, I saw it was packed. There were only a couple of empty tables, and I'd seen people pulling into the parking lot. I knew those tables would be taken within a couple of minutes.

Because Christmas wasn't until Friday, I knew I'd have almost a whole week trying to pretend to be happy there, before the actual holiday. I couldn't fly home until January 2nd. This was going to be the longest two weeks of my life, I thought.

I walked in behind Geoffrey, and I saw my daddy sitting on the little bandstand, singing and playing his guitar.

I was suddenly transported to my early childhood and was reminded how I had worshipped my daddy when I was little. I suddenly felt the hardness in my heart towards him begin to melt a little. I just wanted him to quit singing and tell everybody his daughter just walked in the building, and he was going to take a break because he hadn't seen her since June.

Unfortunately, even though he saw me walk in, and even smiled at me, he didn't do that. He continued with his set. I walked on into the kitchen and said hello to the cook. He'd been there since we opened. Then I met several new workers. Geoffrey walked around the corner to go towards the office, and I followed. We found his mom in the back, working with money and reports, it looked like.

Clarice smiled at me frostily. She stood up, walked over and hugged me with little emotion. She chatted politely, but I could tell that she'd rather not spend any more time with me than was necessary. After she had fulfilled her dutiful greeting, she said she had to go back to working on the books. Geoffrey and I walked out of the office and on around to the dishwashing area.

William was back there with a rubber apron and gloves on, slinging racks with dishes and glassware around. When he saw me come around the corner his face erupted into a big, happy grin. I felt like running over and hugging him tightly, for the first time ever in my life. Because of the rubber apron and gloves, I refrained, but I could see in his face the happiness he truly felt at seeing me. We talked only briefly because he was working, but I promised we'd catch up when he got home.

Geoffrey asked if I was hungry. It was well into the dinner hour, and I realized I was starving. I'd had to rush around DFW Airport, running from one terminal to another, to get to the correct plane to get to Oklahoma City. I then had to sit for two hours on the lay-over waiting on that plane. I hadn't eaten since that morning

Walking back towards the back booth, by the bar that was used for employees I sat down. Geoffrey ran to the hostess stand and got me a new menu, since they'd changed it a lot.

I ended up getting my favorite burger that was flame grilled, and was thrilled to eat finally after such a long and harried trip. While I sat there eating, Geoffrey sat across from me and was pumping me for information about school, and how much I liked it. When I finished eating, Geoffrey grinned at me, "You've gained a little weight since you've been gone."

I grimaced at him, "So, what are you, the fat police?"

Shaking his head, he replied sincerely, "No, you look good." I stared at him shocked, because my weight had always been a digging point for him and Clarice. For him to mention my weight gain, then telling me I looked good, and actually sounding like he meant it, I kept waiting for the catty comment I knew would be next.

After a while, when it never surfaced, I felt myself relax a little bit more, and answered his questions about my school.

I wanted to ask if he'd seen Kevin, but I knew that it would only make the happy Geoffrey become the old sullen and mean one. I still didn't trust the Geoffrey that was sitting before me, but I liked him a whole lot more than the old one.

Finally, my daddy took a break and made his way to the table where we'd been sitting for almost an hour. I jumped up and hugged him and he seemed happy to see me. He asked if I'd seen the new menu and if I'd been in the back yet. I told him I had. I scooted over so he could sit down, but instead he pushed Geoff over and sat across from me to tell me all about how great the restaurant was doing. He seemed so excited, and I was happy that his dream was being realized.

I thought back to the day that Geoffrey and Kevin had finally gotten into a fist fight. Kevin had caught him choking me, until I almost passed out. I was reminded how Clarice had begged me not to tell my daddy. She said it would kill his dream of opening the restaurant. I remembered wondering why his dreams were so much more important than me or mine, but seeing his face made me happy that I'd kept it from him. I wanted him to be happy. I hoped if he was happy with the restaurant, he'd not drink as much as he had before I left. When he got the bartender to bring him a gin and 7, I felt a little tug at my heart.

Daddy stayed with me for about 15 minutes. After that, he got up and made some rounds to talk with customers, then he took the bandstand again and began to play music. I watched him with my little girl heart feeling both happy, to the bursting point, and saddened that I had only rated a quick 15-minute visit after 6 months.

I chastised myself silently as I watched him pick up his guitar. I realized he was doing what he'd been meant to do. He had a business to run. He didn't need to bow down just because I'd shown up for a visit. I was just a 15-year-old kid. There was no reason for me to rank higher than the restaurant, which was his livelihood.

Geoffrey finally brought me out of my reverie as I watched Daddy on the bandstand. He asked if I wanted to go to the house. I decided there wasn't anything else I needed to see here, and I'd gotten to eat something, which was important since there probably wasn't anything in the house. I nodded and we got up to go. I followed him into the back again, so he could tell his mom he was taking me to the house.

I still couldn't believe that Geoffrey was acting so genuinely happy. Once we got to the house, he carried my bag upstairs. We turned to go into what had been my old room. When we walked in, I was shocked to find that it had completely become a little girl's room. My old ugly furniture that they'd got for me after the tornado was gone! In its place was pretty, girly furniture. There were toys and baby dolls scattered around, and the bed itself was a little smaller than a regular twin bed. I looked at Geoffrey a little puzzled.

"Oh yea, Mom wanted to make sure Lisa felt like she had a place here, so she made this her room." Geoffrey shrugged his shoulders.

"Oh," I whispered softly. She had made a place for Lisa, to make sure she felt like she had a place, thus erasing me completely from the family, I felt like. She'd bought all the pretty furniture for Lisa, but when they'd gotten my furniture, for my room, they'd bought me plain, utilitarian furniture that was absolutely hideous.

Geoffrey smiled, "I actually got your bed with the trundle. If you want, you can sleep in my room too."

Looking at him, still trying to figure out what alien had seemed to be possessing his body, I finally nodded my head, "Sure, yea, I guess that will work. I obviously can't fit into Lisa's tiny bed."

Picking up my bag, we walked into Geoffrey's tidy room. He pulled the trundle out, and pushed it over towards the wall, to leave a tiny walk way between the two beds. I put my bag on the trundle bed and wondered what I was supposed to do with my stuff. I had assumed I'd have my room to put my clothes in the closet, but it didn't look like that was going to happen.

I looked around and asked Geoffrey if he knew what I could do with my stuff. He nodded and moved some of his clothes in his closet. "Here, you can put your hang up stuff in here, and hang on, I think I can move some stuff around in one of my drawers and you can put stuff in there."

I looked at him for the first time, with what I thought was an authentic grin. I didn't know what had happened to Geoffrey, but I was grateful for whatever it was. I noticed then that he must have also gotten my dresser too, because when we'd moved here, he didn't have a dresser. The boys only had one dresser and William had gotten it in his room. I shook my head slightly as I began to take my stuff out of the bag I had brought.

Chapter 17

Later that night, when we went to bed, I was hoping that Geoffrey would continue to be nice and not give me any grief while I was asleep. I still felt slightly wary of him. Most of our night time visiting hadn't been very pleasant, except for a short time before our house was completed, in Wichita Falls, when he had originally tried to be nice to me.

"Hey D.?" Geoffrey whispered quietly, in the dark.

"What?" I answered a little grumpy. I was tired after all the traveling.

"Why'd you leave?" he asked me softly.

I sat up on my elbow and looked over at him in the blue light of the night that was in his room. "Really, Geoff? You have to ask?" He sat up on his elbow, facing me and nodded his head. I sighed. "Why do you think?" I responded, faintly.

Looking down at the dark, inky blackness of the floor, he asked timidly, "Was it because of me?"

Laughing, I stated, "No, Geoffrey, believe it or not. You weren't the deciding factor."

Geoffrey's head snapped up, "Really?" I nodded my head. "So, why did you do it?" he persisted.

"I was miserable here, Geoffrey. I didn't have any friends. Everything I loved was in Wichita Falls. I was tired of being your mom's personal maid and then having to work at the restaurant as slave labor in another way. The schools were so far behind, and I hated it here. I didn't want to be here anymore. There wasn't any one deciding thing. There were a ton of reasons." I declared, looking steadily at him across the dark chasm of floor.

"I just wanted to make sure I didn't push you away," Geoffrey muttered, sounding almost sad. "Things are so different since you've been gone. Clarice is back to being a fuckin' nut job. Your dad's drinking so much, and he's hardly ever home. I think he's even slept at the restaurant a few times. It really sucks since you've been gone."

I was surprised to hear all of this. I wasn't surprised that Clarice was a nut again, but I was surprised that Daddy wasn't even coming home sometimes. I was even more shocked to hear Geoffrey say that things sucked since I'd been gone. I figured he'd be thrilled to be rid of me.

"I didn't know," I muttered.

"Something else you probably didn't know…I quit school." Geoffrey announced solemnly.

Shocked, I exclaimed, "You WHAT? Why? What the hell Geoff? You're a senior this year! What the hell?" I repeated. "Why didn't you finish school? Why would you quit?"

"Probably the same reason you hated school here. It wasn't nearly as good as I tried to make you all believe last year, after we moved here. I didn't fit in with these dumbass Okies. I also got another job and quit working for Mom and Russ." Geoffrey explained.

Not understanding the whole reason behind his deep confessional, I lay back down on the pillow and asked softly, "So why'd you quit working at the restaurant?"

"I needed to pay for my truck. Russ and Mom finally started paying me and William, but I found a job where I could make a lot more money. I decided I should go do it. I didn't like most of the people at school. I mean, I've finally begun making some really great friends now that I'm out of that stupid school."

Feeling a slow burn begin in my gut, I was angry to hear that I'd been unpaid labor for three months, and now they were paying William, and had been paying Geoffrey, finally.

William wasn't just in the back, washing dishes, but he was also making a pay check. When I didn't say anything after a while, Geoffrey asked if I was alright. "Yeah," I replied, tersely.

"Well, I guess I'll let you sleep," Geoffrey whispered. "Oh and D., I have to go pick up Lisa on Tuesday. You wanna ride down with me?"

Now my interest was back in the conversation. "Well, of course," I sat back up on my elbow. I was surprised to see Geoffrey's smile in the dark of the room. The only difference on this night was I wasn't afraid seeing his teeth shining in the dark.

"I figured I'd get your attention," Geoffrey was actually giggling.

"Just driving down or spending the night?" I asked, suddenly worried. I knew Bailey would already be gone to her grandparents.

"Spend the night and leave first thing in the morning with her on Wednesday," Geoff replied.

"Oh," I responded a bit dejectedly.

"Why? Can't you just spend the night with Bailey?" Geoffrey asked.

"No, she's in Abilene with her family by then. I guess I'll just have to stay here because Kelly's also going out of town too." I muttered, sadly.

"Well, you can still go. I know Mrs. Strong will let you stay at Kev's with me."

Now I felt the trap about to snap, I thought. "You don't want me to spend the night with you at Kevin's," I stated, quietly.

"D. really, I don't mind. He's your friend too. I know that. I'm okay with it now. Really. I mean it!" Geoff blurted, plaintively.

Laying there, again looking at the dark ceiling, I mumbled, "I'll think about it. I'm tired, Geoff. I'm gonna go to sleep. G'night!"

"Goodnight, DeLaine. I'm glad you're here." Geoffrey replied honestly.

Chapter 18

The afternoon before we left for Wichita Falls, Geoffrey, William and I were riding in his mom's car to do errands. After getting the oil changed, and doing a few other things, we began our trip to the restaurant, to drop William off for his shift.

While we were sitting at a red light, Geoffrey whispered to me that he needed to tell me something. I looked over at him curiously. His continued congeniality was now becoming something pleasant. I was glad that I didn't have to constantly be on guard with him.

"What?" I whispered back. I glanced over my shoulder at William, who was sitting with his head against the backseat, with his eyes closed. We had the radio on a little loud.

I didn't understand why Geoffrey was whispering to me, but I guessed he didn't want William to know whatever it was that he wanted to say.

"I want to tell you something, but it's a secret," Geoff continued, almost inaudibly. I nodded my head, wanting him to continue. Then he said even more softly, "I'm gay."

Turning my head slowly, I looked at his face in horror, then I simply started crying. I didn't know what else to do. I thought of all the times that we'd called him a fag when we'd been mad at him. I remembered how many girlfriends he'd had while we'd lived in Wichita Falls. I thought about his relationship with Kevin. I began to get a sick feeling in my stomach.

"What the hell did you do to her, Geoffrey?" William yelled from the back seat.

"Nothin' dumbass! Just shut-up! You fuckin' retard! She just told me a sad story about something that happened at her school. You know what a fuckin' crybaby she is," Geoff yelled, in the old snarky voice I was used to.

"Dammit, Geoff, you said you were going to be nice to her while she was here, and now here you are makin' her cry," William growled, hotly.

I turned around to look at William, while I sniffed and wiped the tears off of my face.

I shook my head, "Really William, it's nothing. He didn't do anything. He's right, you know what a damned crybaby I am!" I flashed a watery smile, to try and reassure him. William sat back and nodded his head.

We turned into the parking lot of the restaurant, and after William opened his door to get out, Geoffrey leaned over to plead, "Please don't say anything until I explain it to you, okay?"

"Does your mom know?" I asked, faintly.

"Yeah, but just wait till we get into my truck, then we can talk about it, okay?" Geoff begged. I nodded and walked over to his truck, since we weren't staying at the restaurant.

When we were safely in his little Chevy, I looked at Geoffrey, "So, why did you choose to tell me right then, while we were at that damned red light?"

"Because I've been trying to figure out how to tell you, since you got here. I've enjoyed getting to talk every night with you, before we go to sleep. I didn't know how you were going to take it. I just had the urge to tell you, right then, so I just did it. Sorry, I guess it was kind of a bad way to tell you something like that." Geoff muttered.

Looking at my hands in the gray daylight, I looked over at him curiously, "Are you sure? I mean you've had a ton of girlfriends Geoffrey, how can you just be gay, all of a sudden?"

He began chuckling, "I've always been gay. I was just confused about it. That's one of the reasons I quit school. I couldn't keep lying about who I was any more. I had to get out of that setting. I had so many girls that kept bugging me. I tried to make myself believe I wasn't gay, but I met a guy who helped me understand who I am. His name is Gabriel. He was my first real lover."

I felt myself blanche, "Can we not call him that? I mean, Geoffrey, you've had sex with girls, how can you possibly be gay? I still am having a hard time understanding this."

"No, D., I never had sex with a girl." Geoffrey admitted.

"Wait, what about the time it was drizzling rain, at the skating rink? I went and interrupted to get the keys, because I was tired of standing in the rain with Kevin, while we waited on you? Didn't you have sex?" I asked.

"No, you dork, I was just messin' around with that chick. I lost my virginity to Gabe." Geoffrey admitted to me, smiling.

I shivered because I'd never known anyone who was openly gay. I knew the stereotypical ideas about gay men, but I'd never known one for real. I'd never had a personal glimpse into them and their sex lives.

The thought made me a little nauseated. I didn't understand anything about being gay. I could only briefly imagine what two men having sex must look like, and in my limited 15-year-old experience, it wasn't something I was comfortable with.

"So, William doesn't know, I guess?" I asked him. Geoff shook his head. "But your mom does know?" I probed, and he nodded his head. "Does Daddy know?" I asked, with dawning horror about what my daddy would say. Geoffrey shook his head. I sat there, wondering how my daddy would take it. He always made fun of gay guys. He called them fags and I'd been raised that it was okay to say that word.

"D., I told you because I wanted you to know that, now that I know about myself, I feel a little more, I dunno. I guess I feel a little more at peace inside of me. It's been a hard thing to understand, but now I do. I told Mom and she's … well she's okay with it. We haven't talked a whole lot about it, because she hasn't completely wrapped her head around it, but I wanted her to know. You're only the second person I've come out to." He finished looking a little embarrassed and shy.

I wasn't sure what I was supposed to say. Suddenly I started thinking about all the new friends he'd made while I was still living there and wondered if they'd all been gay.

"So have all of your new friends, since we got here, been gay?" Geoffrey smiled at me and nodded his head slowly.

I looked in horror, as I asked if the big tall guy, he'd first been friends with, who I'd avoided like the plague, had been gay. He started laughing and assured me that he wasn't. He was probably the only straight guy he'd actually been friends with, in a long time.

"Wait, he's the only straight friend you've had in a long time?" I croaked. Then I flashed to the conversation I'd had with Kevin, about why he'd actually had sex with Lori. Geoff had told him that Lori thought he was gay. Kevin had sex to prove her wrong.

Sitting there, I felt as my stomach began to do a free-fall. What if Kevin had actually had a relationship with Geoffrey, like that! I couldn't even begin to grasp that one, and so tentatively I uttered Kevin's name for the first time. I had thought because Geoffrey had made out with every available teenage girl in Wichita, meant he wasn't gay, but here he was telling me he was. What if Kevin actually was too but wouldn't tell me. "And Kevin?" I finally mumbled.

Geoffrey threw his head back and roared with laughter, "Relax, DeLaine, Kev's not gay, that I know of. I was going to tell him when we go down." He finished a little more quietly.

"You mean he doesn't know?" I squeaked out.

"D. what part of you are the second person I've come out to did you not hear?" Geoffrey demanded.

I shook my head, "But you said you told your mom, I figured you weren't counting her. Do your other gay friends know?"

"Yes, dumbass, it's just the people in my life who have never known that I'm talking about." Geoffrey almost sounded like his old, condescending way. "I want you to meet Gabe, if you don't mind. I think you'll like him," Geoff was smiling again.

"Uh, okay, I guess," I was really unsure what I was supposed to say. Geoffrey grinned and cranked his truck up. I sat there wondering what Kevin would say about the whole thing.

When we got to Gabriel's house, I was surprised at how much older he looked than Geoffrey. He looked like he was in his late 20's. Geoffrey was now 18, but this guy definitely looked a lot older. He had a gorgeous old home that wasn't creepy like the one that Geoffrey lived in, with my daddy and Clarice, but I was uncomfortable with him. I didn't know how to talk to him.

I was a stupid, fifteen-year-old girl that didn't understand anything about being gay. Thankfully we only stayed a little while, and then went back to our creepy, old house.

I walked upstairs and grabbed the book I was reading for English. I went to the built-in bench-seat that was in a nook, right at the top of the stairs. The gray clouds had finally pushed out, and it was sunny. The late afternoon sun was shining just perfectly, to warm up the little corner. The whole house always felt cold, so I was glad to have this spot to read in.

Geoffrey and I had been the only two at the house, and he'd gone into his room. He left the door open, then he hollered out at me, "I have one more thing to tell you, D." I sat there thinking that he was going to tell me he was just messing with me about being gay, so I waited for him to continue.

After several minutes, when Geoffrey didn't say anything else, I encouraged, "Okay, I'm waiting." Geoffrey walked out from his room, wearing a leopard speedo looking thing that left nothing to the imagination as to what his boy parts were.

"Holy SHIT! Geoffrey! What the fuck is wrong with you?" I yelled, as I averted my eyes.

Laughing, Geoffrey crowed, "The new job I got, that I'm making a lot better money at, is this," he explained, as he moved his hand up and down his body, as if he were Vanna White on Wheel of Fortune.

"As a damned speedo model or what?" I was still agitated at him for standing there practically naked in front of me.

"D., you crack me up! No, I'm a stripper. See," he was smiling as he turned around. I could see that the speedo looking thing was showing his butt cheeks.

"Jesus, Geoffrey! Seriously, I don't want to see that! Gross! Go put some damned clothes on! Have you lost your god-damned mind?" I yelled, while I kept my eyes shut tight, and my head down.

"Oh good lord, DeLaine, don't be such a prude. I figured you'd know what a guy looks like by now!" Geoff finally sounded like his old self.

"Um, no, I don't, and I certainly don't want to see your stuff, if I did! Jesus, Geoffrey! You're my step-brother! I think you lost your damned mind, when you lost your virginity," I was trying to sound mad, but actually felt giggles beginning to bubble up.

Soon, Geoffrey stood in front of me, giggling too, but I still wouldn't raise my head. "Why in the world would gay guys strip?" I asked him, seriously.

Geoffrey began telling me that most of the guys, who worked in the ladies' strip club, he worked at, were gay. He told me that it was good because they didn't get all hot and bothered by the females. The women had no clue, and since they couldn't touch the dancers, it worked out well. I told him to go get dressed again and breathed a sigh of relief when he finally went back to his room and grabbed his jeans. He pulled them on over the leopard print G-string that he was wearing. I could still feel the flush in my cheeks.

I didn't know how to deal with how I felt about the whole business of Geoffrey being gay. I wondered heavily how Kevin would take it. He had seemed so angry when Geoff told him that Lori thought he was gay. That was the reason he proved to her he was all man. I softly snorted at the memory of Kevin telling me that, while Geoffrey was zipping his jeans up. "What was that about?" Geoff asked me.

"Nothin', just something I remembered about…it doesn't have anything to do with you," I lied smoothly. If nothing else I was learning how to lie effectively.

"Well, just remember nobody knows, so please keep my secret. I want to tell people in my own way and time." I nodded my head and then asked if my daddy knew about his new job. Geoffrey grinned and told me it was something else only he and Clarice knew about. I could hardly wait to find out what my daddy thought of everything. I just hope my daddy didn't have a stroke when he did find out all of it!

Chapter 19

The next day, on our way to Wichita Falls, Geoffrey told me all about how he finally came to terms about who he was. It was like he felt the need to unburden himself to me. I didn't know if he felt the need to explain why he'd always hated me, or if he was just trying to work up his courage to tell Kevin. I knew he was worrying about that. I was worrying about that myself.

As we pulled into the driveway on Portland, I felt thrilled. I couldn't wait to see Kevin, even if he didn't know what he was about to be bombarded with. As soon as Mrs. Strong saw me and Geoffrey at the front door, she pulled us in. She hugged Geoff briefly, and then held me tight to her chest, like a long-lost child. I stayed in her arms as long as she would hold me. I had missed her warm embrace so much.

Kevin came walking out of the hall into the hallway foyer and saw us. I burst out laughing at the look of pure shock on his face. He smiled at Geoffrey, but I saw the smile never reached all the way to his summer, sky blue eyes. When his eyes swept over to me, I saw the smile continue into the creases around his eyes. He gave Geoff a quick guy hug, and then he wrapped me up in a big bear hug. I decided that Geoffrey would just have to get over it. Kevin had kissed me goodbye, when we'd driven out of the driveway to begin our trip to Oklahoma City, back in February. If Geoff was going to get angry, he'd have to get over it. I didn't even care if he got mad enough to leave me there with nothing, but a change of clothes!

We all three trouped back to Kevin's room. I asked how Donna was as soon as the door closed. I figured that she would have heard all the commotion when we walked in, but her room had remained quiet. I thought she might be napping.

"Uh, she's in the hospital," Kevin responded, quietly.

"What?" I cried.

"Yea, um, that damned pneumonia again. It's so hard for her, because her ribs won't let her lungs work properly. Dad's sitting with her right now to give me and mom a break," Kevin muttered softly.

Looking over at Geoffrey, I declared, "We have to go see her later, Geoff!" Geoffrey nodded his head, knowing that the only person in the world that meant everything to Kevin, was his little sister.

As I looked at the two friends, who seemed a little uncomfortable around one another, I announced, "I'm gonna go visit with your mom for a few minutes. Then I'll be back."

After visiting with Jean Strong for a while, I walked quietly down the darkened hall to Kevin's room, wondering if Geoffrey was going to tell him yet. I tapped on the door, then I opened the door. They were sitting like they had a million times since Kevin had entered my life, both on the bed, with their backs against the headboard.

They didn't look as if they were deep into any kind of life altering talk, so I came all the way in, and began to climb onto Kevin's bed. I was surprised when I realized that Kevin's bed was no longer a waterbed. He still had the frame, but he had a regular mattress now.

"Wow, what happed to your wave machine?" I asked, sarcastically.

"Ah, the damned thing sprung a big leak, so my mom said she was just getting me a regular mattress. It's cool. This bed is warmer!" Kevin grinned at me.

"So, did you ask him, Geoff?" I asked my step-brother, who looked at me as if I'd lost my mind. Finally, I looked at Kevin and posed the question, "Do you think I can spend the night? Bay's out of town, and so is Kelly."

Kevin nodded his head absently, "Um, yea, I was actually going to spend the night with Donna, but you and Geoff can stay here." I felt uncomfortable now, knowing that Donna was sick.

Geoffrey suggested, "Um, well, D. if you wanna stay at the hospital with Kevin, and your mom doesn't mind, I can just stay here." I liked the sound of that idea even more. I knew I wouldn't get much sleep, but I'd be with Kevin and Donna.

"Let me go talk to Mom. Be right back!" Kevin jumped off his bed and out the door.

"Why'd you suggest that?" I asked Geoffrey, tentatively.

"Because I owe it to you," He replied, softly.

"But Kevin's your friend, Geoff. You want to see him." I was trying to make sure he didn't get angry at me for jumping at the chance to spend so much time with Kevin.

"It's cool D. We can visit and I'll even go up to the hospital for a while. After that, I'll drive back here. Really, she'll be happy to see you," Geoffrey was smiling.

Before I could say anything else, Kevin came bounding in the room. He had his sunny smile that made my heart flip-flop in my chest. "She said that's cool! Visiting hours are over at 9 so you'll be able to come back here by 10. So it's cool." I beamed at him.

"Cool," Geoffrey agreed, amiably. "Let's go get some pizza, then we'll go up there."

Kevin looked at me suspiciously. I just shrugged my shoulders, "Sure, Mama Z's or Pizza World?" I asked.

"Mama Z's, duh, D.!" Geoff declared, laughing.

On our way out the door, Geoffrey swung into the kitchen to talk to Mrs. Strong. It gave Kevin a chance to whisper in my ear, "What the hell is going on with Geoff, and by the way, I'm soooo happy to see you Lainey!" then he kissed me softly on the cheek.

"I dunno. He's been so nice since I got to Oklahoma I don't know what to think," I shrugged. I didn't want to be the one to tell him that Geoffrey's demons had finally been let out of the proverbial closet.

***

When we walked into Donna's room at the hospital, I remembered the floor well from my time there in 7th grade. I was shocked at how frail and fragile Donna looked in the huge bed. She had to wear an oxygen mask, which took up half of her face. Her little, blue glasses were lying on the tray table that was within her reach, but she was sleeping soundly when we came into the room.

I felt my breath intake change, when I saw her, as if I wanted to help her breathe. Each time I watched her tiny chest struggle to rise, it literally made my heart ache. I didn't know how Kevin or his parents could go through this so many times.

I had to fight the tears that kept threatening to creep into my eyes. Kevin grabbed my hand when we first got in there, as naturally as if we'd been holding hands in public for years. I didn't even bother to look at Geoffrey in fear, when I felt Kevin's long, graceful fingers wrap around my own. He squeezed my hand. I looked at him and he winked. He didn't smile with his wink, but I knew that it was his way to tell me he was right there beside me. I gave him a brief grin.

We all walked out into the hallway, down to the small waiting lounge, by the nurse's station, so we could talk without waking Donna. Geoffrey asked how long they thought she'd be there. Kevin told him they weren't sure. Every bout of pneumonia weakened her considerably. Since she'd been getting it at least once a year now, she was becoming weaker and frailer.

I knew that Kevin was basically telling us that Donna's time wasn't long. She might not even live to be 18 years old, I realized. I sat there, trying to imagine what the world would be without Donna Strong's sunny smile, and effortless cheer. I wondered what Kevin would do. I hoped that he wouldn't go off the deep end.

I felt like because of Jean and Steve Strong, he surely would be able to rally, even without the one person in his life that he adored.

I kept waiting for Geoffrey to finally tell Kevin his bombshell, but by the time they made Geoffrey leave, he still hadn't broken the news to Kev.

We had sat beside each other, with our hands clasped together, almost the entire time Geoffrey had been sitting there. I didn't even realize until Geoff got up to go. I had never once looked at him, worried that he'd be angry. I wondered how he would behave the next day towards me. I honestly didn't feel the least bit frightened of Geoffrey, for the first time in my life. I couldn't believe it.

Kevin and I walked back to Donna's room together. There was a cot set up, along the wall, under the window, for Kevin or his parents to sleep when they were there. The chair in the room also reclined back, but I didn't even want to think about sleeping just yet. I wanted to sit with Kevin and spend as much time with him as I possibly could. He picked the small, reclining chair up and moved it over beside the cot and he put a straight back chair beside her bed so if she woke up someone could sit close to her.

Once he got the reclining chair in place he sat on the cot and pointed to the chair, so I would sit down. We sat in the corner and whispered as softly as we could, so we wouldn't disturb Donna. As loud as the oxygen was, I didn't think she would ever be able to hear a normal speaking voice, much less a whisper.

"So, what's the deal with Geoffrey?" Kevin whispered, as he looked deep into my eyes. I shrugged my shoulders and he stated, "You didn't look at him one time when I held your hand. What's up, Lainey?"

"Nothin' Kev, he's just different. I don't know how to tell you. He's different. He quit school. Did you know that?" I questioned him.

"Are you shitting me?" Kevin seemed surprised. I shook my head. "Why did he do that? I mean, that's stupid. DeLaine, I haven't seen him since June, when he brought Lisa back. That was the last time I saw Geoff."

That last day Kevin saw Geoffrey had almost destroyed our relationship forever. It seemed as if that day had happened over a year before. I was surprised to realize it had only been six, short months.

I leaned up in the chair and wrapped my arms around Kevin's neck, "I've missed you so much, Kev! I wish I could call you sometimes. I just miss hearing you. There is so much that happens that I wonder what you'd think, if I told you," I confided, quietly, next to his ear.

Hugging me, Kevin rubbed my back, as he held me close. "I know, Lainey! I have thought about you so many times. I almost bought you a birthday card in October, just because I was missing you so much. I figured it was lame, and you probably had a boyfriend already."

"Are you serious, Kevin? Don't you think I'd tell you if I did?" I asked him as I pulled back to look into his eyes.

"No, I told you, I didn't want to know about any boyfriend shit," Kevin stated simply.

Shaking my head, I snorted, "Yeah and what did you say about if you were seeing someone when I came to visit? If I don't care, then she better not, or somethin' crazy like that," I laughed. "Kevin, even if I had a boyfriend, which I don't by the way, I haven't kissed anyone since I kissed you goodbye! Besides, he wouldn't be checking my mail, and if he says anything about you, then he'll find his ass on the curb!"

"Wow, somethin' about Corpus makes you a badass every time you come back around. What is it, little Lainey? You sound different somehow?" Kevin was chuckling softly.

I shrugged. I knew what he meant. I was different, in just a few months of going to school there. I had a pack of cigarettes in my purse. I had been managing to go into the bathroom, at the house, and open the old window that didn't have a screen on it to smoke a cigarette, a couple times a day. Since I did it when no one was upstairs, I'd been able to pull it off so far. That didn't even touch all the other stuff I had started doing, like drinking and smoking pot.

I smiled tentatively at Kevin. I felt like he'd be so disappointed in me if he knew.

"Things are a lot different in high school. Especially in Corpus Christi," I muttered.

"What? Do you have to be a bad ass, so those gang members don't beat you up, or what?" Kevin joked, grinning.

"No, I'm going to school out in the suburbs again. We even moved out there, but I'm still not in the right school district. It's working for now. There aren't any gangs out there, but the kids are just, well, I don't run around with very many people in my class, except my best friend there, Kelly Stubbs. Most everybody else is older. You know I'm not good with people my own age," I smiled, hoping he couldn't see the changes.

"Lainey, just be careful hanging out with older people. I know I'm only a sophomore, but I'm older than anybody else in my class. I just want you to be careful." Kevin murmured sweetly, as he held my face in his hands.

I nodded, thinking about all the stupid things I was doing. I was riding in cars and trucks with people I barely knew, to go to river parties. I was drinking every weekend. I felt shame when I looked at Kevin's dear face. He leaned in then and his lips brushed mine. I realized that for the first time, I was actually feeling some whiskers on his face. I pulled away from him and looked closely at him. The hair on his face was as blonde as his eyelashes, and he actually had a lot more stubble than I realized.

"What is it?" Kevin asked me, with a puzzled expression on his face.

"You've got razor stubble," I stated, surprised.

Kevin started laughing quietly, "Yeah, I've been shaving for over a year, DeLaine. You didn't know that?" I shook my head. "Well, it's been getting to where I need to shave a lot more regularly lately. Since it's blonde hair, most people don't know I have it. Which is good for school, in case I forget to shave." He then ran his hand across his rough, whiskery face. "I haven't shaved since yesterday morning. No school and just coming up here. Now if I'd known that you, my dear Lainey, were going to be showing up on my doorstep, this afternoon, I probably would have shaved this morning." Kevin leaned over and began kissing me again.

While Kevin and I were kissing tenderly, Donna began to cough. We pulled apart to look at her bed. I was surprised to see her smile trying valiantly to come across her face, as her coughs racked her tiny body. "Hey, DeLaine," Donna finally managed to croak out, after her coughing fit.

"Hey, Sweetie," I replied, quietly, as I got up to sit in the old, wooden, straight back chair. "How are you feelin'?"

"Were you and Kevin kissing?" Donna asked, as she looked at me intently with her summer, sky blue eyes. I smiled and nodded. She grinned and managed a whispered, "I thought so. It's about time!" Kevin and I both started laughing. "Kevin, can you go get a nurse?" Donna asked her big brother.

"What's wrong, Sissy?" Kevin asked, with a worried look on his face.

"I think one of my ribs is broken from coughing," Donna replied, stoically. I sat there, shocked. Kevin took off at almost a dead run. I asked Donna if she was in a lot of pain. She shook her head and said, "Promise me, you'll love Kevin for me, when I'm gone."

"What?" I asked her surprised.

"I know that I'm not going to live for as long as you will, DeLaine. Mama and Kevin try to pretend like they believe I will, but I'm not stupid. I've been in the hospital a lot. Kevin's gonna need you, so please promise you'll always love him for me." Donna pleaded with me, matter of factly.

"I promise, Donna," I whispered, breathlessly. I didn't know what else to say. I was surprised that she was talking to me, as if she understood everything there was to understand about life. Her mental abilities were supposed to be of a small girl, but here she was talking to me as if she were my equal, intellectually. "Donna, you're gonna be fine though, Honey," I insisted.

Instead of talking, she just smiled at me and nodded, "You promised. You can't break a promise, remember that, okay?"

I bobbed my head. I didn't know how I could possibly be there for Kevin, should something happen to Donna.

I could promise to love him, because I already did, but how did you promise to be there for someone who lived eight hours away from you?

The nurse came shooshing into the room, in her white, nurse shoes, and her white dress and stockings. I jumped out of her way, as she set about checking Donna, and talking cheerily to her. I was amazed at how quickly the room began to fill up with other nurses and orderlies. Within only a couple of minutes they had whisked Donna out of the room, in her bed, and Kevin and I were left standing there. I reached down and took Kevin's hand in my own, this time, and looked at him starkly, asking, "So, what just happened?"

"Because her bones are so fragile, when she coughs a lot, she breaks her ribs very easily. They worry that if it is a bad enough break, she will have a piece of rib that will puncture a lung. Anytime she feels like there's a problem, they take her down for X-rays." Kevin explained quietly.

I nodded as I saw the unmasked terror and pain in his eyes. I didn't know how to make it better for him. All I could do was sit with him, in the chairs by the nurse's station, as we waited on them to bring her back from the X-ray room.

I was uncertain if I should tell him about what Donna had said to me but decided that it was something that she wanted to tell me privately. I also didn't know what good it could do to make him even more frightened. Finally, I whispered, "So, you said she gets weaker every time she has pneumonia. Does that mean what I think it means, Kevin?"

Kevin looked down at his clasped hands, as he leaned his elbows on his thighs. He wouldn't look at me, but he slowly nodded his head. "Yes, it means that she probably won't be alive in another two years. She might not even last another two months. Each time she gets sick, it makes her weaker. Each broken bone takes more of her strength to recover from, and when she has both at the same time, it's like a double whammy to her.

I saw tears streaking down his face, and he responded, finally, "She has three broken ribs right now. She probably won't be alive by the time I graduate, Lainey."

The tears I had been able to keep at bay poured out of my eyes, unbidden. I couldn't even begin to imagine life without knowing that a tiny girl, who was a true burst of pure love and light, lived in Wichita Falls, TX, with the boy I would love for the rest of my life. It didn't seem right somehow that someone with her sweet spirit wouldn't be there always.

I stuck my arm through his and placed my hand on top of his clasped hands. I leaned my head on his broad shoulder. Who would hold him when she was gone? Who would be there for him, when he cried?

We sat there without saying another word, until they finally wheeled her bed back into her room. She was asleep again, and while some of the other nurses were getting everything set up again, another came out to tell Kevin what was happening.

"Hey, Kevin," the nurse spoke kindly. "Well, she definitely has two more broken ribs. We've made her comfortable, and done all we could, which as you know is little, but she should sleep for the rest of the night. We may have to put her under an oxygen tent, so we can administer some medications through the oxygen. We're going to see how she does tonight though, before we do anything drastic, but be sure to tell your folks when they come in tomorrow morning, okay?"

Kevin nodded his head numbly.

I was shocked that they talked to Kevin as if he were her parent or guardian. Then I chastised myself silently, because Kevin had basically grown up on this floor with her. That was why he'd been allowed to sleep in my hospital room when I was 13. The nursing staff knew him intimately. I slipped my hand inside of his and we walked back into the room.

He turned off the bright, fluorescent light and switched on the table lamp that was in the corner, away from her bed. It cast a weak yellow light into the corner of the room.

Kevin's long, lanky form walked gracefully across the room, back to Donna's bedside. He stood there as he watched her sleep, stroking her silky, flaxen hair. I saw such pain and tenderness all mixed together, in a boy and man's face. I watched as he loved his little sister, who would soon be taken from him. I wanted to comfort him and didn't know how.

Finally, I walked up behind him and slid my arms around his waist and rested my head on his back. Kevin reached down, wrapped one of his large hands around my forearm, and squeezed me reassuringly.

After a few minutes, Kevin sighed deeply, "C'mon Lainey, let's lay down."

I followed him over to the cot. I wasn't sure how we were going to both fit on there. I started to sit in the recliner instead, and Kevin assured me, "We can both fit, I promise." Smiling, I nodded, and he lay down first and scooted against the wall. I got down on my side, and he wrapped his arm around my waist.

Rising on his elbow he leaned over and whispered into my ear, "I've missed this. I miss sneaking into your room and holding you. Thank you for being here for me right now. I'm…well, I'm glad that you are with me."

"Me too," I whispered through the tears that threatened to choke me. I tried so hard to hide from him that there were tears pouring out of my eyes, as I looked up at the tiny, fragile girl who was asleep in the bed, only a few feet from us.

Kevin settled his head on the pillow, after kissing my cheek. I grabbed his hand that was resting firmly on my stomach and held on tightly. "I love you, Kev," I whispered into the quiet room.

I knew he was already asleep though. Knowing that, was the only thing that gave me the courage to tell him, in the quiet of the room, as the oxygen whooshed out of the wall, into the mask that rested on his little sister's face. I finally closed my eyes and was grateful for sleep to steal me quickly, as I lay in Kevin's arms, unafraid and without hiding finally.

Chapter 20

My eyes opened slowly, as the sun hit them the next morning. When I first woke up, I wasn't sure where I was, then I realized I was in Donna's hospital room. I felt Kevin's hand still draped on my stomach. I looked over my shoulder to find him looking down at me. Surprised to see him awake already, I grinned sleepily, and tried to stretch. I quickly realized I felt stiff from lying in the same position all night. I was happy to have slept next to Kevin, even if it was only a few hours.

"Good mornin', Sunshine!" Kevin smiled down at me.

"G'mornin'," I replied beaming up at him. "How long have you been awake?"

"Just a couple minutes. I wanted to watch you sleep for a few minutes. You know I used to do that when we'd sleep in your family room. If you fell asleep before me, or if I got up before you, like after your dad's birthday party, I would watch you sleep." He admitted to me.

"What? Why?" I asked him, suddenly shocked that he watched me sleep so many times.

Shrugging his shoulder, he finally whispered, "Because when you're asleep, you look so peaceful. You look…happy. You never looked happy most of the time, when you were living with Clarice and Geoffrey. I mean, you would laugh, and I loved hearing you laugh, but you just looked happier in your sleep. You looked like there was nothing weighing you down, like you did when you were awake."

Nodding my head, I smiled at him, asking, "Do I still look like I have stuff weighing me down?" I thought he would tell me no, now that I was finally away from Geoff and Clarice. What he said next shocked me.

"Lainey, I'm worried about you. You look like you have an even bigger burden on your shoulders and it worries me, because I don't know what it is and I don't think you're going to tell me either," he admitted candidly.

I finally sat up, and swung my legs off the side of the cot. I looked behind me, at him, as he lay there, propped on an elbow, "That's crazy, Kev. Everything is fine now, that I'm away from Clarice and Geoffrey." Kevin nodded at me slowly, still looking me in the eye. He sat up and swung his legs over the side of the bed also.

He walked over to Donna's bed and looked at his sleeping sister. I saw again the unmasked fear and pain in his face, however, before I had a chance to say anything more to him, his mom and Geoffrey walked in.

I looked at the clock on the wall, and noticed it was 7:30 a.m. I couldn't believe that Geoffrey was up that early. I knew we had to pick Lisa up at noon, so we could get back to Oklahoma City before dark.

Kevin walked over to his mom and gave her a hard hug. He began to tell her about everything that had happened the night before, and everything the nurse told him to relay to his parents. I was impressed that Kevin could tell his mom everything the nurse said. He talked so grown up, it seemed, as he talked about Donna's condition.

Geoffrey walked over to the cot where I was still sitting and sat beside me. "So, did you get any sleep?" I nodded my head. Geoffrey smirked, "Did Kevin sleep here too?"

I whipped my head around until I was looking at Geoffrey hard. I noticed that whatever my expression was must have been dark enough that Geoffrey held his hands up. He told me he had just been teasing and didn't mean to upset me. I was shocked by that as well. It seemed my morning was full of surprises. I just nodded at him and then Geoffrey asked if I wanted to go get breakfast. I shrugged my shoulders. I wanted to know what was going to happen with Donna before we left. I hadn't even needed the overnight bag I'd packed, since I'd slept in my clothes and stayed at the hospital. Geoff still had it in his truck.

Jean Strong walked out of the room briefly, to go talk to the nurses, and to find out when the doctor was making his rounds so she could know more about Donna's condition. I finally got up and walked over to where Kevin stood by the bed, watching his little sister sleep. I knew he was worried, but I didn't know how to reach him. Finally, I touched him lightly on the shoulder. He seemed to snap out of the trance he was in while he looked at Donna.

Geoffrey looked over at Kevin, "Hey man, you wanna go grab some breakfast somewhere? We're gonna have to leave after that and go pick up Lisa so we can get back in time. My treat even," Geoffrey was smiling at the boy who used to be his best friend. I somehow didn't think that the title applied any longer.

Kevin's mom walked in and heard the end of Geoffrey's proposal and suggested, "Kevin, you should go get some breakfast. Nothing is going to happen here for a little while. Go eat and visit with DeLaine and Geoff. They can bring you back and you can take my car home and get some rest while I'm here. Daddy will come up here this evening."

Looking over at his mom, Kevin finally nodded his head. He leaned over and kissed Donna's silky, blonde hair before we left. "Love you, Little One," Kevin whispered. I felt the lump rise inside of my throat. I quietly excused myself to run down the hall, to the bathroom, before the tears could come out in front of anyone.

Thankfully, they were only a few. I was able to splash water on my face to hide them, so I could go back to the room.

Geoff asked if I was ready and I nodded. We all three traipsed out of the hospital to Geoffrey's little Chevy Luv.

***

After breakfast we took Kevin back to the hospital. When we walked into the room, they had erected a huge, see-through tent over Donna's bed. I was terrified when I first saw it.

Mrs. Strong came over to explain everything about it. She told us we could climb under it, and it wouldn't hurt us, but we could only visit with her one at a time.

I noticed Kevin never took his eyes off of the huge contraption, as he looked at the ceiling and all the way around the bed to study its makeup. Kevin asked his mom if Donna had woken up and she smiled and said she had. She asked her mom if she'd dreamed that I'd actually been there.

I smiled and Jean Strong urged, "DeLaine, I think that she really wants to talk to you because when she found out it wasn't a dream, she said she had something important to tell you."

I nodded at her, remembering the promise Donna had extracted out of me, before they whisked her off for X-rays earlier.

Walking towards the huge, clear, plastic tent, I parted the material at the slit of an opening and scooted the wooden chair as close to her bed as I could, so that I was now completely enclosed in her tent with her. I could hear the loud hissing of the oxygen, and I noticed there was a slight mist that would spray in the air every once in a while.

As soon as Donna's blue eyes saw me, she smiled as best as she could. I was surprised that she was able to smile at all, with five broken ribs, but she was. "Hey, DeLaine," she croaked, shakily.

"Hey, Lil' Bit," I murmured, softly, but just loud enough so she could hear me over the hissing in the tent. "How are you this morning?" I asked her, sincerely.

"Oh, you know, I'm just sitting here under the tent, while they squirt medicine in the air every once in a while. It's supposed to help keep my lungs opened up. These doctors and nurses like to bother me with all this stuff every time I come here. It seems like it is always something new. I never had a tent before, this is kinda neat," Donna joked, with a little giggle in her throat, sounding so grown up suddenly.

I reached up and slipped my hand over her tiny, fragile one, and noticed how cold it was. Normally they were so warm. Today, they felt as if they were ice cold. "Are you cold?" I asked, concerned. Shaking her head, Donna told me she was fine.

Donna looked over at me, as I saw the familiar twinkle trying to come to her eyes. "DeLaine, do you remember the promise you made me last night?" I nodded my head, wondering where she was going with all of this. "You know that Kevin is going to have a hard time. Please make sure that he is going to be alright, for me. You promised, and a promise is a promise," she stated, with her cherubic smile finally lighting her face up.

"Donna, you know you're gonna be okay, after you get out of here and get home, and get back to where you feel best, right? You'll be back with all of your babies, and your Barbie dolls, and you'll feel better," I declared, more trying to convince myself than her.

Looking thoughtful, the tiny girl, who was six months older than me, demanded, "DeLaine, just tell me you'll do what I asked."

I looked at her startled. She'd been a perpetual little girl her entire life. She'd known so much pain in just 15 years, and yet her disposition remained sunny, funny, and happy. Now, she was worrying about her brother. Her protector and most loyal family, she knew that her death would unravel the brother she loved with as much devotion as he loved her. I realized that trying to placate her wasn't going to work this time. Slowly, I nodded my head as I looked into her blue eyes. "I'll be there for him, Donna." I reassured her solemnly.

"Don't forget to tell him you love him, okay?" she insisted, anxiously. I nodded my head and she finished, "He doesn't like to say it too much to anybody, but he knows how. He's just scared is all. So, just remember, if he doesn't tell you back, I know he does."

I smiled at her, praying that the tears I wanted to cry, would go away, because I wanted to be as strong and brave as this little girl was. I reached across her bed and picked up her Bunny named Floppy, and the silly stuffed dolphin I'd brought her from Corpus Christi a year and a half ago. I made sure she could reach them. She tucked the bunny in her arm on her right side, then she fumbled with the dolphin until it was safely tucked into her other arm.

"We're going to have to leave in a few minutes, so I'm probably just gonna tell you 'bye right now. I'll see you either in a couple of months at Spring Break, or at the first of the summer, okay? And you better be all well and ready to go shopping, because now that Kevin can drive, I'm gonna make him take us to the mall!" I smiled and winked at her.

Smiling as much of her own version of the sunshine and rainbows smile as she could muster, she gently nodded her head. As I began to walk out of the plastic that surrounded us, I felt her cold, tiny fingers as they grazed my wrist. I turned back to look at her and she whispered, "I love you, DeLaine. Can I hug you before you leave?"

I laughed and told her what a huge dork I was for not hugging her in the first place! I leaned over and felt her tiny arms snake around my neck, as she pressed her heart shaped face next to my cheek. She surprised me by kissing my cheek, which she'd never done before. Her lips were as dry as the dead leaves that were still swirling around from the fall. "Don't forget me, okay?"

"Never in a million years, Lil' Bit!" I replied with a smile that was certainly many shades brighter than I felt at this goodbye. It felt wrong for some reason to leave her. I wanted to stay and hold onto her. I wanted to climb up into the bed and let her lay in my arms until they said she could go home again. "I love you, Donna. Hope Santa finds his way to the hospital this year. I'll see you before you know it, okay?" Then I stepped out of the enclosure because I knew I had little ability to hold my tears inside.

When I stepped out, I smiled brightly, in an almost maniacal way, at Geoffrey, Kevin and Mrs. Strong and stated, "I think she wants to see you real quick, Kev. Let me go to the restroom, Geoff, and I'll be ready when you are." Geoffrey nodded as he looked at me seriously. I barely made it around the corner, outside of the door, before the floodgates opened. I stumbled back to the bathroom to splash water in my face once more. Afterwards I thought that maybe I could finally make it to her room and out, before I felt the overwhelming urge to cry again.

As I walked past the nurse's station to go back into Donna's room, I glanced at the nurse who was sitting at the station and saw her sad eyes as they looked at me. I saw something else in her eyes that told me all that I truly needed to know about Donna Strong. She gave me a tight and sympathetic look.

I wanted to go scream in her face to quit looking at me like that! I wanted to tell her that Donna was going to be fine. She was just a stupid nurse who didn't know anything!

Donna was going to be okay and go home to her pink and white bedroom, where she'd take Floppy, the bunny, and DeLaine, the dolphin, and join Angel Bear, as well as the myriad Barbie dolls, and story books that stood waiting for her, in the quiet room on Portland Street.

I didn't say any of those things, though.

Walking back into the room, I saw Kevin was already out of the plastic tent. His mom was inside of it now. As she talked, all I heard were tiny murmurs coming out, just under the sound of the ever-present hiss of the oxygen.

Geoffrey stood and asked if I was ready to go. I looked at Kevin and wanted to tell him I was just staying, but I knew my daddy would throw a fit, so I bowed my head slightly.

I didn't want to leave Kevin, though. I had made a promise to Donna. I was already running out on him. "I'll walk you two downstairs, then I'm gonna drive Mom's car home and get some rest." Kevin murmured, quietly.

"Did you get to visit her?" I suddenly asked Geoffrey, unsure if he'd even had a minute to say hi to Donna. Geoffrey smiled tightly and gave a nod of his head. We all turned then and began to make our way out of the room, and the awful hissing noise of the oxygen. It sounded like a giant, pissed off snake that never quit hissing, even to take its own breath.

Once we were by the old Chevy, Geoffrey pulled Kevin to him and they hugged like they actually were friends once more and when Kevin pulled away, I could see tear drops in his eyes. As he walked around the truck, I saw that those tears were now causing tracks on his face, as they spilled from his eyes. Geoffrey climbed in, and Kevin walked up to me. He pulled me close and held me, as if I was going away for many years, instead of just a few months. I tried to lighten the mood, and laughed as I pulled back, and told him I'd be back soon.

Kevin nodded as he looked down into the ruddy brown of my eyes, "I know, it's just gonna seem like forever. Don't worry. If mom doesn't write, I'll send you a note and let you know how she is," Kevin assured me, softly.

I wrapped my arms around his neck, in almost a death grip, so sad that we wouldn't see each other again for a while. "I'm gonna miss you, Kevin." I whispered.

Kevin looked at me and his watery eyes showed no sign of slowing down in the tear department. "Not half as much as I'll miss you, Little Lainey," he kissed me then on the forehead, as he held my head with each hand on either side of it. After kissing my forehead, Kevin kissed the tip of my nose, and then each eye, as my own tears began to flow freely.

Then holding my face between his palms, he brought his mouth down to mine and kissed me achingly. It wasn't a long kiss, or even a very passionate one. It conveyed all of his fear, hurt, anger and uncertainty into a brushing of his mouth on mine. It was not in a chaste way, but in one that spoke volumes without being overly filled with ardor. "I love you, Lainey," Kevin uttered softly, as he stared into my eyes, all the way into my soul.

I couldn't believe he'd said it so easily. I finally said through my tears, as I put my hand on the door handle, of the door, "Me too, Kevin. Let me know how she is when you can." Kevin ducked his head, and I slid into the passenger side of Geoffrey's truck. He closed the door securely, and then his long, lean, graceful form began to make its way through the parking lot, towards where his mom had parked her own car.

Wiping the errant tears off of my cheeks with the back of my hand, I sniffed deeply, since I didn't have any tissues. I slowly brought my face up to Geoffrey's. "For what it's worth D., I'm sorry I was so jealous of your relationship with Kevin. I wish so much that I could change that about our lives before." I tried to give him a better fake smile.

"Let's go get Lisa, and get this show on the road," I commanded, in my happy, spirited voice, which was as fake as it sounded. Geoffrey smiled at me compassionately, and we left the parking lot of the hospital to go to Lisa's daddy's house. Geoffrey would bring her home the Sunday before school started again. I'd leave the day before. I wondered if he would finally tell Kevin then. When we passed the city limits sign, I felt my heart grow heavy, as I knew it would be quite a while before I saw them again.

Chapter 21

My Christmas in Oklahoma wasn't exactly exciting. I babysat Lisa most of the time, and only saw Daddy for any length of time on Christmas day. I was glad that Geoffrey and I seemed to be getting along better than we ever had before. He seemed so much happier. He and William still sniped at one another quite a bit, and William was either always at the restaurant working, or he was holed up in his room. I wondered many times if he'd found new pothead friends to hang with, or if he'd quit smoking pot. With Geoffrey and me in a basically whole new dynamic, I think William felt a little left out in some ways.

One evening all three of us went to the movie, "Ghost Story" and it scared me half to death. It was what I thought of as a true, scary movie. It didn't use some dumb guy with a chainsaw, and lots of blood, it was an actual story that was creepy! Every time I jumped or squealed, both my step-brothers seemed to find true joy. I realized sadly as we sat there, giggling when I'd get scared, that we'd never all three sat down, and done anything together or enjoyed laughing with each other before. As we drove home from the theater, I felt sad about that.

Christmas morning wasn't too exciting. I noticed an extremely disproportionate amount of gifts given to Lisa, while I got three and the boys both got four. I was shocked when I saw all the high dollar toys that Lisa got while I looked at Geoffrey, William and my gifts. I wondered how Clarice could possibly think it was fair.

While I helped the boys clean up the living room, I felt like Clarice must have been reading my mind when she said to all of us, "I know it seems like Lisa got a lot compared to y'all, but she doesn't get to come up here as much and visit."

I looked at her angrily and blurted, "Me neither!"

Clarice jerked her head to glare at me, "That's was YOUR choice, not ours. Lisa has no choice in the matter.

I looked at Clarice and felt my mouth spread into a malicious grin. I hoped so badly she would try to slap it off of my face. I'd toughened up a little bit more since she'd had control. She no longer scared me now that she had no control over my life. "Yes, it was and it was the best damned decision of my life!!"

Unfortunately, my step-mother didn't understand that punishing me was no longer her job. She was standing across from me, then walked over, and smacked me across the face.

I continued to glare at her, but I also smiled, which must have unnerved her. She turned around and slammed into her bedroom, where Daddy was lying down and napping.

"Damn, D. You pissed her right the fuck off," Geoffrey whispered.

I looked at him and shrugged, then I smiled genuinely, whispering back, "That was what I intended to do when she made the comment. I can't believe she pulled that shit, buying her all that crap, then making it seem as if we were being punished or something. I don't really care if I got anything, but I think it is just wrong to give one kid that much more over the others. I mean, she should have at least gotten y'all something more. If she's pissed at me, so be it, but she doesn't have to do y'all shitty too."

"Nah," Geoff responded lazily. "She's been pretty pissed off at us too. Since we both work and before I got out of school, neither one of us had time to do all the stuff you used to do. So, she's been pissed, saying how ungrateful we are for everything she gives us, and all she does around here. I mean, I guess I knew how much you did, but I don't even know how you did so much while you lived here. You were going to school and working at the restaurant. We can't even keep the laundry up."

I looked at Geoffrey and realized that Daddy was now finally seeing the bitch he married in her true light. No wonder she was so pissed off at me. I had left and made her look guilty.

Then I remembered something Kevin had told me long before. He told me that if I ever left, Clarice would lose her hold over Daddy. I wondered if that was beginning to happen already. Times like these made me miss Kevin even more. I wanted to bounce all of this off of him and see what he thought. Then I thought about Donna and wondered if she'd gotten to come home for Christmas.

"Well boys, I can honestly say it is because I'm just that good," I popped off, sarcastically. I continued to look at all of the presents Lisa received. I picked up the box that had wrapped one of the sweaters I'd gotten, and now held two, as well as a stationery set. One of the sweaters I'd already decided to wear to the New Year's Eve Party that they were holding at the restaurant.

Daddy had suggested that I hostess that night, even though Clarice had wanted to. Daddy wanted her free to move about the restaurant, talk to customers, and take care of problems.

During the days after Christmas, Geoffrey would take me around and introduce me to a lot of his new friends. It became a running joke almost as to if I could tell who was gay and who wasn't among his new friends. I wasn't very good at it, because every single one of them were gay! Half of them I would never have known if he hadn't told me. I realized I just didn't know a lot about gay men. I knew the stereotypes, but I'd never had one in my life before, in a close way. For some reason I think that he was glad he now had mostly gay friends.

As I puzzled over this one night, as I was lying in bed, trying to go to sleep, I realized that Geoffrey had been in love with Kevin. He didn't mind me being around his friends any longer. He didn't get angry if they were flirty with me, which many were, no matter if they were gay or not. It was quite a revelation to me to realize that the first boy I'd ever loved was also the first boy that my step-brother had loved as well. That was the reason he was so volatile in his reaction to Kevin being interested in me.

I remembered what Kevin had told me about Geoffrey telling him that Lori had thought that he was gay because he wouldn't touch her, and Geoffrey kissing Lori to get Kevin to prove what kind of man he truly was. I lay there wondering if Geoffrey had secretly hoped Kevin was gay as well, and would finally confide in him the truth, but instead he'd pushed them even closer together.

No wonder he wanted Lori to approach me as soon as I'd gotten home in 8th grade, to tell me about her and Kevin. He knew how much it would hurt me, and in some strange way he was paying Kevin back for not being what he wanted him to be. I thought Geoffrey probably didn't understand what he was in the beginning, he just knew he was attracted to Kevin for some reason and they struck up a friendship. It all began to make so much more sense as I lay there, watching the huge, old, spooky branches, as they scratched at the windows.

I had always wondered why Kevin and Geoffrey had become friends. They just never seemed to be best friend material. They didn't have a lot in common, but they had gotten so close, so fast. I had thought about mine and Bailey's relationship too, many times, and how different she and I were, but I realized that we complimented each other. That's what made us so close.

No, we weren't a lot alike, but we were like the heart necklace she'd given me for Christmas, the year before. It was cut in half, and she had half, and I had half. Each half made a whole, and in my friendship with Bailey, we each complimented the other, and brought out different things in one another. Kevin and Geoffrey had never seemed to complement each other.

Suddenly, I felt an overwhelming urge to forgive Geoffrey for all the hurt he'd put me through. I forgave him for hurting me in every way he could, because I realized he was hurting too, but in so many different ways. I had thought all of his rage was coming out because of Clarice. I wondered if his sexual preference was because of her as well. The rage, however, was coming out because he was in love with someone who he could never have. Then there I was, having that person wanting to be with me. That was the reason behind the possessiveness. I shook my head as I thought about it. I had honestly never seen this one coming. Finally I rolled over and put my pillow over my head. I hated this house and the spooky trees that scraped the windows.

When New Year's finally came, Clarice had gotten one of their employee's daughter to babysit Lisa. William rode to work a lot earlier than Geoff and I did, so when we left around 5 in the afternoon, we were the last of the family to leave, except Lisa. I had taken particular care for some reason to dress up, with my new sweater and a black skirt I'd brought in case I need to dress up for something. I had gone through great pains to fix my hair and had even consented to let Geoffrey help me with it. At first I felt a little weird, then I realized he was really good at it.

The restaurant was already busy, and Clarice was manning the hostess stand when we first got there. She told us to go eat quickly, and then to come up there, and she'd show me what to do. She and I were getting along after her smacking me in the face on Christmas Day, but I felt the strain between us. I tried to help the boys out in getting some of the household chores caught up, while I was babysitting Lisa, to occupy my time when I wasn't running around with Geoffrey.

After eating a fast dinner, I went to the hostess stand, and Clarice showed me in about 5 whole seconds what to do, then she left. I felt woefully unprepared when people began to walk into the doors immediately after she rushed off. Daddy was already on the stage entertaining and living his dream. I squared my shoulders, smiled my best DeLaine Reynolds smile, and walked each group of customers to their tables and continued to do it for the next few hours.

Around 10 o'clock, a very cute guy came in. He was only a little taller than me and he had curly blond hair and a smile that would melt an icicle. I smiled as he came in, and he asked if Geoffrey was there. I nodded and then remembered that earlier in the week, Geoff had told me he wanted me to meet a new friend of his. He had already told me he was gay, so not to get my hopes up. I loved how we laughed about it now. When I asked him to tell me more about the guy, he'd just smile a mysterious smile and ignore me.

I glanced back at the guy again, as I walked towards the kitchen to get Geoff, and thought it was such a shame that this guy was gay. He was actually quite cute. He was beautiful, the way Kevin was, but his blond hair was not at all like Kevin's. He was still really cute, though.

Geoffrey grinned really big as he took off the apron he'd had on while he did prep work in the kitchen. I asked who the guy was, and he just smiled and walked out of the kitchen, past me, to go to the front of the restaurant. I was clueless why he was being so mysterious.

At 11:00 p.m. Clarice came to me at the hostess stand and told me that seating was now going to be seat yourself, so I could go in the back booth, and hang out with Geoffrey and his friend. I was glad to go sit. My feet were aching in the stupid spike heels I'd brought with me.

Daddy had a lot of important people in the restaurant all evening, from the man who was his best friend, who had helped him get the restaurant off the ground, to several other close friends who had been around for him for his entire life. I knew he didn't want any of us to act improper and embarrass him, so I had decided to lie low, and stay out of Clarice's way. During one of Daddy's breaks, he walked over to the booth where I sat, with Geoffrey and his friend, Terry. Clarice had been standing there, trying to be her falsely, funny self in front of Geoffrey's friend.

As Daddy walked up, I noticed Clarice's whole demeanor changed, which surprised me. She glared at Daddy, and he walked to the end of the bar. It was next to the booth we were sitting in. He instructed the bartender to start setting up the champagne glasses, and tray them up for the servers to begin handing out soon. Daddy turned around and looked at Clarice, as she glared daggers at him, and said, "Clarice, we are not going to discuss this here. You need to straighten your shit up, because we have important people here tonight, and I'm not getting into it with you in front of them. So if you want to be able to hold on to this place, put a fucking smile on your face, and just deal with it." Now I was extremely curious what this argument was about.

After Daddy walked off to go visit with the customers, and his special guests, Clarice turned around, and stalked off towards the kitchen. Geoffrey and I continued to sit in the booth with Terry. When I had first gotten back there, Terry had moved over in the booth, and patted the seat beside him. I had sat there happily chatting with the two guys. I wasn't worried about Geoffrey's ire, because I knew that Terry wouldn't find one thing in the world to be interested in me.

When the bartender set one of the trays of champagne flutes on the end of the bar, near us, Geoffrey dared me to get them, and put them on our table.

I refused, because I knew what Daddy would do if he caught us. I knew he'd flip his lid. Terry told me to move, and he jumped up, grabbing the six glasses off of the tray, without moving it, setting them on the table, in front of us. I was shocked, but secretly impressed. Geoff and Terry each drank one flute quickly, and then dared me to do the same. I looked at the champagne, uncertain if I could, or even would.

Terry began to tease me, flirting with me, finally convincing me to drink it. When I first put the delicate glass flute up to my mouth, the bubbles in the champagne tickled my nose, like beer from a can did, but it didn't smell like beer.

I tentatively took a little swallow, thinking that it didn't taste too bad. I wasn't sure if I could drink it down, as they had, because I tended to gag when I tried drinking anything like that. I got the small amount of champagne down, finally, and they both started cheering me on. There were plenty of revelers that no one was paying attention to the three of us. I began to feel a little light headed, within five minutes, of drinking the champagne.

Daddy started playing music again. Terry asked if I wanted to dance. It was a fairly slow song, but the only dancing I'd ever done had been at the skating rink. That wasn't really dancing, as it was swaying to the music, so you could make out with your boyfriend. I tried to decline, telling him I didn't know how, but he told me he'd show me how.

When I still wouldn't, Geoffrey began to give me a hard time, telling me to go. I finally agreed, since the song was halfway over. I walked out on the dance floor with Terry. I felt a little strange. He was so flirty, and he acted so much like a guy would, that was interested in me, I thought. I wasn't sure what to think about the whole thing. Geoffrey didn't seem upset that Terry had been so openly flirtatious, but I still felt funny about the whole thing.

When that song ended, and I tried to walk off of the dance floor, Terry pulled me back to dance to a fast song this time. I had never danced to a fast song in my life, and figured I'd look like a spazz out there trying to dance fast. I kept shaking my head no, but Terry kept holding onto my hands. Finally, he consented to going back to the table.

I was so thirsty, that I drank the next glass of champagne in almost one gulp. Terry leaned over, and pulled three more glasses off another tray that the bartender was making ready. I realized the two boys had already drank their second one too, and now we had a third one. As soon as that one was gone, I realized that I was getting buzzed, really fast. I knew I had to maintain control, so I tried really hard to slow down, but before I knew it, Geoffrey had grabbed three more.

Terry finally convinced me to dance again, but before we left, I looked at him and blurted out, "Are you really gay, or is Geoff just yankin' my chain?"

Looking over at Geoff funny, Terry nodded his head, admitting, "Yea, I just haven't come out to my family yet." I nodded as I looked at him, trying to act serious, because it felt like a statement I should have a serious face on for, but the champagne was beginning to give me the giggles. I broke down into gales of laughter. Soon both boys were laughing along with me. I let Terry grab my hand and lead me out on the dance floor.

We'd just started dancing to the slow song that had been playing, but as soon as it was done, Daddy broke out into a fast one.

This time, I stayed, when Terry tried to keep me out there. I was breathless and sweaty when we danced. I didn't know what I was doing out there, but I'd loved moving around so freely. Daddy cut the song short to begin a final countdown of the clock, to ring in 1982. I thought back to just two short years before, when I'd stayed at Kelly and Robin Stubbs house for New Year's Eve, ringing in a whole new decade. Then I remembered the year before, when we still lived in Wichita Falls, and I was dating Jax Garrett. We had argued, but finally made up at the last minute. So much seemed to have happened in one short year, I realized.

A waitress, carrying a tray full of champagne, walked beside me and Terry, as we stood on the dance floor. Terry grabbed two glasses off of the tray and handed one to me. When the countdown got to zero, Terry clinked his glass with mine and shouted, "Happy New Year!" I smiled at him and mouthed the same thing to him. I knew he'd never hear my voice over everyone else's. Suddenly, Terry leaned over and planted a big kiss, right on my mouth. It was quick, and I was surprised.

"Why'd you do that?" I asked, suddenly wary.

"Because you're supposed to kiss at midnight, and you're who I'm with." I looked at him oddly, nodding my head. I found myself fervently hoping that Geoff hadn't seen it. When I saw him looking straight at me still, with the same smile on his face, I wondered what he must be thinking.

I began to walk back to our booth, when I noticed the bartender had my daddy in a lip lock, beside the stage. It was no innocent, little, New Year's Eve kiss. I knew from watching them, that there was actually some tongue action. I felt my stomach lurch inside of me. I glanced around for Clarice, and I saw her walking out of the kitchen, straight for the bartender and my daddy. I knew there was about to be an ugly showdown, and I didn't want to be anywhere near it.

As we walked to the booth, I passed another waitress with a tray of champagne flutes. I grabbed three and kept on walking. She smiled at me dreamily, and

I wondered if she'd been smoking pot with William or something. When I got to the table, I handed a glass to each of the guys, and drank it down fast, again. I was afraid Geoff was going to be pissed at me, but he continued to laugh and tease me just like he'd been doing. I still wasn't sure what was up with Terry. He kept acting straight, but they kept telling me he was gay.

Geoffrey asked what had pissed Clarice off, and I marveled, "You didn't see it?" When he shook his head, I crowed, "The bartender had her tongue down Daddy's throat!" Then I cringed after I said that. Geoffrey started laughing, saying that the bartender had been chasing my daddy for a while.

Terry got up and went to the restroom, and while he was gone, I asked Geoffrey what the deal was with Terry. He started laughing, "Nothin', he's gay, he's my friend, he didn't have anyone to have a good new year with, and so I told him to come here tonight."

Looking at him seriously, because I really didn't want to jeopardize the way things had been between us, for some guy who was just a flirt, I commented, "Geoff are you sure he's gay, I mean, he keeps acting straight!"

Laughing, Geoffrey nodded his head. "Yes, I'm sure, DeLaine! Ask him when he comes back, he'll tell you again." I shook my head, telling him that seemed rude.

Terry walked up and exclaimed, "Okay, how come there are no cops. I just knew your mom was gonna kick that woman's ass!"

Geoffrey shook his head, then told him that Clarice was too afraid of getting hit in the face. Then he grinned, almost wickedly, at me, and declared, "So, Terry, DeLaine is confused. She wonders if you're really gay or not, because you keep flirting with her!"

I looked at Geoffrey, with my mouth hanging open. Laughing, Terry leaned over and explained, "Sorry, but I really am, but it doesn't mean I don't like flirting with girls. I like flirting with you, DeLaine. You're funny and cute." Then he winked at me. I gave him a half, sick smile. I didn't know what to think about him.

Clarice came stomping over to the booth just then, steaming hot. Daddy was following, telling her that he was sorry, and that the bartender was just drunk. He said she needed to calm down, and quit acting stupid. I sighed, as I wondered what new fresh drama was going to play out now, between them.

"Russ, I don't want to hear it. Either you fire her tomorrow, or you can find a new wife." Clarice shouted at him.

"Dammit, Clarice, it was a kiss! I didn't screw the woman! Then you could be pissed, but we didn't do anything, except kiss. Everybody's a little drunk! Hell, even the kids have been dipping into the champagne.

I couldn't believe we'd been busted for drinking champagne. "Geoffrey, I want you to take DeLaine home, because we've still got a couple more hours. You don't have to come back to clean up. Pay the babysitter and send her up here." She hurriedly told her oldest son. Nodding, we all got up. Geoff told Terry to come with him. Terry smiled, and we grabbed our coats to walk outside, into the frigid air. I couldn't believe how incredibly buzzed and happy I felt, even though I didn't have Bailey or Kevin around. We all climbed into Geoffrey's pickup, all of us were giddy from the champagne. I kept glancing at Geoffrey, because Terry was shameless in his flirting. Geoffrey still kept the smile on his face, all the way to the house.

Once we got there, Geoffrey gave the babysitter the money Clarice told him to pay her with. She had her own car, so that meant we were finally in for the night. We clomped up the wooden steps that creaked like a haunted house staircase and I walked into Geoff's bedroom, to grab some pajamas. I was glad I had at least one pair of regular pajamas, because I felt funny about wearing one of my old night shirts and sweat pants in front of Terry.

When I got in the bathroom to change, I laughed at myself. I had never felt weird around Kevin in my grungy old night clothes, and this guy was gay! I went ahead and washed my face while I was in there and brushed my teeth. I didn't know if Geoffrey was taking Terry back to the restaurant, but I was going to bed. My delicious buzz was quickly fading, and I could feel a little bit of a headache beginning. Then I remembered what Kevin had made Bailey and Geoffrey do, the year before, when we'd all snuck bourbon at my daddy's birthday party.

When I walked out of the tiny half bath, that was upstairs, I went down the creaky stairs again. I hated going back down, because everything was dark downstairs. I got to the first light switch, by the door, to light up the foyer. I walked through the dining room, and then into the old kitchen. I grabbed a big glass and filled it with ice and water, drinking half of it. I refilled it and walked back the way I came, to go into Geoffrey's room.

Opening Geoffrey's door, I was shocked to find Geoff had pushed his bed up against the wall and slid the trundle underneath. He'd pulled both twin mattresses onto the floor, and put blankets and sheets and pillows, building a pallet of sorts, with the mattresses. I looked at him and arched my right eyebrow.

He and Terry had been sitting cross legged on the two mattresses, deep in conversation. When they heard me, they turned around and both smiled warmly. I sometimes felt like I was in an episode of The Twilight Zone with Geoffrey right now, since he had become so sweet and warm.

"Hey guys, what's up? Do I need to go sleep on the couch?" I asked, hesitantly. I didn't know what Geoffrey had planned with Terry.

Geoffrey began to laugh, "No dumbass, I just made a pallet like we used to do in Wichita, when Kev used to spend the night, and we'd all sleep in the family room."

Nodding my head, I stated, "We never drug my mattresses out to sleep on."

"Duh, dumbass! Do YOU want to sleep on a hardwood floor, in winter?" Geoff asked, sarcastically.

I looked at the set up and realized he actually had a point. We'd slept on carpeting, and in the winter, the fireplace was usually still throwing out heat, so it was warm in the family room. Here in the creepy, old house, it was constantly cold. I was sure a hardwood floor would be much more uncomfortable, than a carpeted one.

"So, um, is Terry staying too, I guess?" I asked both of them. Geoffrey nodded, "Oh, okay, um, well, do you think we're all three gonna sleep there?"

"Why not?" Geoffrey asked me, mystified.

"Um, do you really think Daddy is gonna be too thrilled with me sleeping with two boys? And two boys that he thinks are straight?" I asked, seriously.

"DeLaine, really? Your daddy won't even know what planet he is on when they finally get here. He and Clarice are going to be screaming, I'm sure. I bet HE sleeps on the couch, so it's just as well that Terry stays here tonight. I'll get up and take him to his car, in the morning. Trust me, no one will even know he's here." Geoffrey replied.

"Well, I am NOT sleeping in the crack." I stated, seriously, which sent both boys into gales of laughter. I realized how it sounded and began to giggle too.

The boys had already taken off their shoes, and Terry jumped in the middle, declaring, "It's cool, I'll sleep in the crack, DeLaine. You know, I kinda like cracks," and again we all three broke into silly laughter.

I just didn't get the whole gay thing still, but it was funny, listening to them tease. It was reminiscent in so many ways of Kevin's many overnight sleepovers, only this one didn't crackle with an undercurrent of tension from me being terrified of Geoffrey.

Even if this Terry guy was a flirt, for some reason, Geoffrey seemed just fine that he flirted with me. I tried not to be too flirty back, but there was a part of me, when I got to know someone, was a natural flirt. Add some champagne on top of that, and it was even worse. Of course, I was also hopelessly sarcastic, which some guys took to be a form of flirtation, and that confused me too. Suddenly I missed Kevin so much, I ached deep inside.

"Fine, but don't you two steal all the covers, 'cause it is a cold bitch up here!" I warned, flippantly.

Terry grinned, patted one side of the makeshift bed, and waggled his eyebrows, saying, "Don't worry, Darlin'…I'll keep you warm!" I glanced at Geoffrey, hoping he was still in the celebratory mood, which thankfully, he still seemed to be.

"You know, I think maybe I should have volunteered to be in the middle," Geoff remarked, suddenly. I looked at him, feeling like it had all been trap for him to find something to be angry at me about. Then Geoffrey started laughing, "Terry's gonna stay warm being in the middle!"

Looking at Geoffrey, I understood what he was saying and drolled, "Well, too bad I didn't stick with the crack, huh?" For some reason both of them found that funny. I rolled my eyes, as I drank a little more of the ice water.

I dropped onto my knees, on the mattress closest to me, and Terry, grinned. "C'mon Geoff! Time to lie down and keep me warm on the other side!"

Suddenly, I felt a little odd about lying with them, but then chastised myself about my misgivings. I knew that even if they wanted to fool around, they wouldn't have done it with me in the same room. I noticed, thankfully, they both kept their jeans and shirts on. I was the only one with pajamas. When I got down there, I flipped onto my side, with my back to Terry. Terry flipped to where he faced my back, and he wrapped his arm around my waist. I rose up and glanced over my shoulder at him and he grinned. I looked just past him and saw Geoff lying on his side doing the same position with Terry.

I shook my head, stating, "You know, I have to say, this is probably the most bizarre thing I've ever done!"

Terry lay behind me giggling, "Oh honey, you need to visit more. We can show you some bizarre shit!" then he began to cackle with Geoffrey.

Shaking my head, while it was on my pillow, I muttered, "Um, yeah, that's cool! I'll just take your word for it!" Both boys continued snickering.

I lay there, feeling Terry's hand rest loosely around my waist. I began to feel myself relax. I realized the way he had his arm around my waist was no way the same as how Kevin would have if he'd been there with me. Kevin would have been holding me next to him, with his hand firmly holding my stomach. I also would have relaxed my arm, with my hand over his. With Terry, I curled both of my hands under the pillow, and before I knew what was happening, I was actually finding myself drifting off to sleep.

Thinking of Kevin lying behind me, with his arm around me, made me miss him even yet again. I hated that he was so strong on my mind. I wanted to hear his voice so badly.

I felt myself sigh as I physically began to relax, thinking about Kevin. Soon, I was sitting at the edge of a lake, with bright summer blue sky over me, the earthy smell of grass, and the yellow flowers all around me. The sun felt warm on my legs and stomach, which I thought was funny, since my shoulders felt like a cool breeze was blowing around. I noticed I was sitting right at the edge of the water with my toes literally dug into the muddy silt, at the edge, where the water met the dry part of the land.

I felt happy in my own special place that was my hideaway; reserved, just for me and Kevin. Soon, though, even that world began to slip away into the oblivion of sleep.

Chapter 22

The next morning, at 7 o'clock, the light came in Geoffrey's darkened room. I felt my eyes begin to squint open, as the light assaulted them. When I could finally get them opened all the way, I saw Geoffrey and Terry scrambling for shoes. I sat up watching them, wondering what they were doing. We hadn't even gone to sleep until 3:30 a.m. "What the fuck, Geoff?" I asked grumpily.

"Sorry D., I gotta take Terry to get his car! Go back to sleep!" Geoffrey whispered. I didn't know why he was whispering. No one would hear us talking.

Terry smiled over at me, "Thanks for keeping me warm, DeLaine! It was very nice to meet you! Hope to see you again!"

Returning the smile genuinely, I nodded, "Thanks for the dances, and for keeping me warm too! See ya later!" Then I lay back down and pulled the covers over my head.

Later, when Geoffrey returned, he crawled on the other side of me, and was back asleep within minutes. I woke up though and lay there for a long time, thinking about the bizarre New Year's Eve night I'd spent for 1981.

It was by far one of the most confusing and strange nights of my life, I decided. I knew that the next day, I'd be flying home to Corpus. I would be glad to go back, I realized. I didn't miss living in this family. Even with Geoffrey and I getting along so much better, I was still happy that I didn't have to live in the insanity that was my daddy's marriage to Clarice.

Corpus wasn't where I truly wanted to be, but it was better than Oklahoma City. My mama and I had our own share of issues, but I still felt like I was in more control of my life than I'd ever felt like living under the same roof as Clarice. Ideally, Mama would move back to Wichita, but I also knew that she would never go back. She was forever done with Wichita Falls, TX. Her life was in Corpus Christi.

Lying there, listening to Geoffrey's gentle breathing, I glanced over and saw him with his mouth open, drooling on his pillow. I had to stifle the giggles that came over me, as I remembered all the nights that Kevin and I had to wait for Geoffrey to look just as he did right then.

With that thought of Kevin, I couldn't help it. I felt like the ache for Kevin had swallowed me whole, then I realized that I had stupid tears dripping down the sides of my face. I felt the necklaces around my neck, and touched the one that held a crystal, blue stone, shaped like a tear drop.

Not able to stand it any longer, I quietly got up and stole down the creaky stairs as quietly as I could. I walked through the silent downstairs floor. I saw Daddy and Clarice's bedroom door closed, and on my way down, I'd noticed Lisa and William's doors still closed too. I tip-toed into the kitchen and froze when the stupid swinging door squeaked loudly. When no one came out to see what the loud, squeaky door was, I breathed a sigh of relief.

I grabbed the yellow phone that hung on the wall, right next to the swinging door. I quietly dialed long distance, pushing in Kevin's phone number. I knew it was still pretty early for New Year's Day. I wasn't certain if Kevin would even be there, but he answered on the second ring.

As soon as I heard his sleepy voice, my heart jumped up in my chest. I felt a knot come into my throat, threatening to make me cry. "Hey Kev," I whispered, hoping he could hear me. I didn't want to talk too loudly. I knew that when they got the phone bill, they'd probably be pissed, but I figured if I didn't talk but a couple of minutes, they might not even notice it.

"Lainey?" Kevin asked, sleepily. When I confirmed it was me he asked, "What's up? Are you okay?"

Chuckling softly, I whispered, "Yeah, tired. We had a big thing at the restaurant, and I've just been missing you, since last night. I wanted to call you real quick. I don't want to talk long, 'cause I'm hoping they don't even realize whose number this is, and they think each other made the call. I just really needed to hear your voice, for some reason," I finished, softly.

"Funny, I've been thinking the same thing. I miss you even more since you were here. Donna's still in the hospital. She's not doin' so good, Lainey," Kevin whispered. It sounded like he got a slight hitch in his voice as he said the last few words.

"I'm so sorry, Kev," I murmured. I truly was sorry. I was terrified that he was going to lose her. Then I wondered if he did, if I'd be able to go back up there. I felt horrible for even thinking about going up there for her funeral. I didn't want to think about that. She wasn't going to die, I tried to tell myself, but the reality of it was, I knew eventually she would. If not this time, then it would happen another time.

"Just worried," Kevin mumbled, as if he had quickly gathered himself together. "I miss you, Lainey," Kevin breathed out sadly.

"Me too. I just needed to hear your voice. Happy New Year, Kevin! Hopefully I'll be back up for spring break in March. Hang in there. I'm sorry, Babe, I have to get off. I just needed to hear your voice one more time before I go home tomorrow. I'll probably catch hell if they ever figure out it was me who made the call."

"I'm just glad you got to, even for a minute. Be safe, Lainey. I'll let you know how Donna is." Kevin assured me.

"Thank you, Kevin. I'm just saying it, because I wish you'd been here to kiss at midnight, but I love you. I'll talk more later!" We hung up quickly, and I crept back to the wall to hang up the receiver.

Slowly I padded back up the rickety sounding steps, to go back to sleep, beside the step-brother I'd been so terrified of. Now, he'd been my constant companion on this whole visit. Thankfully, Lisa got to stay up late to watch the *Dick Clark's Rockin' New Year's Eve* so she was sleeping in too. I rolled away from Geoffrey, closed my eyes, and went back to sleep, fairly quick.

***

Later that afternoon, after all of us were up, except Daddy and Clarice, we were sitting in the living room, watching TV, when we heard a loud crash in our parents' room and then shouting. Looking over at Geoffrey we both rolled our eyes as we wondered what was happening now.

I looked at William and then Lisa and thankfully he understood what I was trying to say, "Hey, Lisa, come upstairs and play Atari with me. I bet I can beat you at Pong." Lisa jumped up and started squealing because she loved to play the game on the TV. We'd gotten the Atari as a joint gift the year before and had to play it in the family room but after we moved William put it in his room with an old black and white TV that he'd found at a garage sale for $5.00.

As they were going up the stairs, Clarice threw open their bedroom door, that was just off of the living room, and glared at me and Geoffrey, as she stomped out of the room. I glanced nervously at Geoff because I didn't know what to think.

Geoff leaned over to whisper in my ear, "I think Clarice has been off her happy dope for a while. She's been acting like a real bitch lately!"

I almost let out a laugh, but caught myself, fearing Clarice might hear and come give me grief.

I couldn't believe that Geoffrey actually said his mother had been acting like a bitch. I personally thought she was a conniving, manipulating bitch, all of the time. What happened next though, proved to me that she was definitely certifiable, and needed to be locked away for good. Unfortunately, the loony bin she'd visited, two school years before, wasn't around Oklahoma City. I thought Daddy needed to find a new one.

Clarice came walking back through the living-room, with her hand held down by her side, away from me and Geoffrey. When she got to the bedroom door, my daddy was about to walk out. Clarice slowly raised her hidden hand to reveal she had a gun in it. I jumped back towards Geoffrey, uncertain what to do.

I couldn't believe she was standing there, with a gun, pointing it straight at my daddy.

"Give me the fucking gun, Clarice," my daddy demanded, through clenched teeth.

Clarice shook her head, screeching, "I told you, you son of a bitch, that if you don't fire her, I'm going to kill you. I will not tolerate someone who is fucking around on me." Clarice stated, in a calm voice.

Geoffrey and I remained firmly planted, not moving a muscle, as we watched terrified, as the scene unfolded in front of us. Each of our parents had completely tuned out the fact that we were sitting there, watching them.

"Clarice, I'm going to give you to the count of three to give me the fucking gun. You are not going to shoot me," my daddy calmly and steadily walked towards the gun barrel, pointed at him. Daddy began to count, walking towards Clarice at the same time. I was holding my breath through this whole insane scene, until Daddy reached Clarice, and jerked the gun out of her hand, at the count of three. The entire time, she screamed at him, like a wild woman.

When Daddy jerked the gun from her hand, he used his other hand to grab her by the back of the head. He slammed her against the wall and began to tell her that if she ever pointed a gun at him again she better pull the trigger because if she didn't, he'd beat the hell out of her. I sat there with my eyes nearly popping out of my head. I didn't realize that Geoffrey and I were literally holding on to one another, as we watched with growing horror.

Daddy let go of Clarice and stated in a perturbed voice, "Now, get your shit together! I'm not putting up with this anymore! I'm not firing her because you are pissed off. She's one of my best employees, so get the fuck over it. She was drunk! I was drunk, hell for that matter you were drunk too! It was a stupid, fucking kiss! Now don't you EVER pull another god-damned gun on me again, do you understand?"

Clarice nodded her head slowly as she looked at my daddy with complete contempt. "Fine, you want it your way, Russ. That is just fine. Just remember, I told you to fire the bitch!" She then pushed Daddy away from her, slipping back into the bedroom.

Daddy stood there holding the gun by the barrel. It was only then that he seemed to register Geoffrey and I were sitting on the couch, clutching one another, watching in terrified silence. "What the fuck are you two looking at?" my daddy growled. We both shook our heads and Daddy turned around and walked back into his bedroom and slammed the door.

"Come on D. Let's go upstairs," Geoffrey whispered. I nodded my head and we climbed the stairs as quietly as we could.

***

The next day, Geoffrey drove me to the airport. We didn't really talk about the fight the day before, between our parents. We just played with Lisa all day, and tried to stay upstairs, out of Russ and Clarice Reynolds' way.

I hugged my Daddy goodbye, when Geoffrey drove by the restaurant, so I could eat before my plane left. Clarice looked at me with her flat eyes. I knew Geoff was right when I looked at her closely. She was definitely back to the way she'd been before she went to her special hospital. I felt sad that there seemed such a disconnect with me and them but knew there was little I could do about it.

When we got to the airport, Geoffrey walked me all the way to the gate. He even hugged me goodbye, when it was time for me to board. I was shocked, because I actually wanted to hug Geoff goodbye. It seemed such a waste that we'd spent so much time at one another's throats, mine quite literally, when the solution had been so easy. I guessed though, coming to terms with being gay was probably not as easy for the person who had been programmed to be something they were not.

As Geoffrey was about to release me from the hug, he whispered in my ear, "I'm really sorry, DeLaine…for everything. I hope you can forgive me someday for all the horrible things I did to you."

I pulled back from him, and looked into his dark, brown eyes. I saw no more demon spawn in them. I saw a sadness instead, that confused me a little.

I flashed a small smile at him and nodded, "It's okay, Geoff. You didn't know what to do with how you felt. I forgive you." Turning away from him, I began the walk up the ramp, onto the plane. How I wished things could have been so different.

Finding my seat towards the back, where I could smoke openly, I was anxious to get into the air, light a cigarette and try to forget Oklahoma City even existed. I wondered what it would be like to spend a whole summer there. I wasn't sure I really wanted to do that. I hoped that Daddy wouldn't make me. I would just be grateful to get back home and back into my routine. I missed Kevin more with each foot of altitude the airplane climbed.

Chapter 23

In January, of 1982, I met a boy, who was one of the seniors that ran with the group of kids I'd found myself in, named Chance Cahill.

He reminded me of Jax in a lot of ways. He had the same dusty, blond hair and always wore a cap. They both were around the same height and both drove orange pickups. He was funny and always one with a laugh and a joke. His eyes weren't the color of meadow grass, but they were a bright blue. They weren't the summer sky blue of Kevin's, but still they shined with a light that made me smile. He had a sweet, round face and the brightest smile of any boy I'd ever seen, including Kevin. Kevin's smile could make my heart do a flip flop, but Chance's smile was like an ad for the reason to wear braces. His teeth were beautiful, straight and white. When he smiled, it was like his entire face began to shine from within.

I began to giggle whenever I'd see him in the halls. I'd told Kelly how much I liked him. I didn't think he had a clue who I was, even though he was usually always in the same group of people I was standing with, in the parking lot of the Gameroom. I was also one of the stupid girls who stood and watched him shoot pool or play foosball.

The second Saturday in January, of 1982 I was sitting on one of the bar stools, by the front door of the Gameroom, talking with Debbie and Kelly. Debbie found out that I had a crush on Chance. To my complete horror, she walked over to the foosball table, and asked if he knew me. I saw Chance look from the table briefly, while she asked him, and he shook his head. Just from watching their body language, I could tell Debbie was telling him that I was sitting by the door.

I saw her raise her hand and point directly at me. I dropped my face down to stare at my feet. I was so humiliated.

When Chance looked at me, he shook his head again. Debbie stood there until the game was over. After the boys finished, she began to walk over towards me and Kelly, with Chance. As soon as he was standing in front of me, with his bright, pretty smile plastered across his face, I felt completely mortified and wished the floor would open and swallow me.

"Chance, this is DeLaine. DeLaine, this is Chance," Debbie smiled sweetly.

Chance looked at me and nodded with his mouth curved up. I looked up at him, feeling myself turning a great, Chrissy Combs-worthy red. Then Debbie introduced him to Kelly, and I saw a different light come into his eyes.

I felt my heart plummet as soon as I saw the appreciative look he was giving Kelly. I had seen that look on more boys' faces since I'd moved to Corpus than I liked. Kelly was cute. She was petite and about 85 pounds with a beautiful curve to her petite frame. She had a nice flair in her hips and a tiny waist that went up into a chest that was quite obvious, since most tiny girls, in her body shape, didn't have breasts that were that big. She also was quite the flirt. I didn't understand exactly what she had that I didn't have. I knew I was taller and weighed more, but Kevin always told me that the boys here wouldn't know what hit them. I was beginning to doubt that, more and more, as the months moved swiftly past in my freshman year, with no boys seeming to find any interest in me at all.

Sitting there feeling invisible, on the barstool next to Kelly's, I watched as Chance chatted her up. When she said she needed to go to the convenience store, for cigarettes, Chance offered to give her a ride up there. It was actually within walking distance, if we really needed to go, but I noticed that in Corpus nobody really walked any place, like I'd done with Bailey and Kevin and Jax.

Kelly looked at me, "Can DeLaine come with us?" I noticed the shadow cross his face when she asked, but he quickly hid it, putting on his commercial worthy smile, saying it was fine. We walked around the back of the Gameroom, and there sitting in the shadows of the building, was his orange Chevy. It looked like a fairly new pickup. Jax's orange was a dark, reddish orange color, but Chance's was more of a soda pop orange. Kelly opened the passenger door and jumped into the truck. I looked at her a little hurt that she would jump in first, knowing that I'd had such a bad crush on him.

I slammed the passenger door shut as I got in behind her. Chance started the truck and we pulled out to go around the block, to the little store. I jumped out and walked into the bright fluorescent lights of the store and went to the counter to ask for a pack of Marlboro Lights. Kelly came up behind me, asking if I was mad. I turned and looked at her innocently, and told her no.

When we both got back in the truck, Chance asked if we wanted to go ride around a little. Kelly was always up for something that we weren't supposed to do, and she quickly agreed. I sat mutely in the passenger seat, trying not to feel negative. We went up and down Leonard Street, through the Sonic and then Chance went driving through a residential area I wasn't too familiar with.

The whole time we were riding with him, I listened as he and Kelly flirted like crazy. I wished I knew how to do that. I was a flirt, but it was not quite in the same way as Kelly.

I was a little subtler, and I could usually do it with older boys, but I also had to know them a little bit before I just started flirting like crazy. Kelly didn't have to know them at all. It was almost like she just breathed, and it happened.

Kelly began to talk about sex. Being silly, she told Chance he had the makings of a threesome. I gasped when she said that! I whipped my head around to look at her, feeling my stupid blush begin. I was grateful that it was dark in the truck. Chance grinned at her, then shook his head. I sat back in the seat and lit another cigarette, cracking the window again.

Chance told us to hang on and he turned hard to the left and began going into a brushy, wooded area, driving straight up the side of a steep hill. I was shocked because we'd only minutes earlier been in a really rich neighborhood. Now we were driving up some high embankment into a bunch of trees. I had no clue what Chance was doing. I glanced at Kelly a little nervously. Chance told us he had a cool place up there that hardly anyone even knew existed.

Once his orange Chevy came to a stop, in a densely, overgrown area, I felt a little nervous. It was just me and Kelly with Chance. I began to hear my mother's dire warnings about ax murderers. Chance asked if we wanted a beer. Kelly said sure, and he reached through the window, onto the back of the truck, and opened an ice chest with beer in it. When he couldn't reach them, Kelly told him to move and she turned around in the seat, with her butt sticking up, between me and Chance. I glanced over and just rolled my eyes. There was no way I could ever compete with that.

Kelly turned around, laughing, and handed me one of the beers, and another to Chance, as she popped the pull tab off of hers. I didn't like beer, but I'd been drinking it since I'd come to Corpus, so I did the same with mine. I began to drink it a lot quicker than I normally did. I figured I needed some kind of fortification to get through whatever was about to happen.

Chance began to flirt with Kelly again, and asked her how this threesome was supposed to work. I sat there quietly, wondering what Kelly had gotten both of us into. Kelly began to giggle. She told Chance he had to sit in the middle, so she traded spots with him. I began drinking more of the beer, as I lit another cigarette.

Chance put Kelly in complete charge of whatever this stupid charade was, so she made him hold both of our hands. Then, we each had to give one another a kiss on the cheek. Then she said he had to kiss each of us on the mouth.

I noticed his smile come back across his face, as he leaned over to kiss her first. Sitting there, waiting for him to lean over and kiss me, I noticed that he wasn't stopping with kissing Kelly. I realized that he wasn't going to be kissing me that night.

I pushed myself closer to the door, as Chance and Kelly began making out. I was worried that clothes were about to come off, but thankfully he just leaned her back. I watched as her hands wrapped around his neck. I sighed and finished the beer I was drinking. When it was empty, I picked up the beer that Chance had set on the dashboard and began to drink it. He had only taken a couple of big swigs from it, so I drank the rest of it. I also began to chain smoke, as I sat there a little uncomfortable that they weren't stopping, even with me sitting right there. I didn't really know what to do. It was really thick brush where we were parked. I didn't even know how to navigate away from where we were, because he'd gone down so many different trails getting to this point. I hadn't a clue where I was supposed to go, if I tried to walk out.

Also, I didn't want to seem like I was being a big, pouty baby, but I was really mad with Kelly. She'd known that I'd had a crush on him, and she did this anyway, right in front of me. When Chance scooted over more to continue kissing Kelly, I turned around on my knees and reached through the window to find the ice chest. I grabbed another beer out of there. Turning around, I let the cigarette dangle from my lips, as I popped the top off of the can. Now that I'd drank a couple of beers, it was easier to drink the third one. I knew the fourth would go down even easier than that. I knew also from experience that the fifth beer, I wouldn't even taste, nor would I taste any other ones after a fifth.

After I finished the third beer, I reached in the back for the fourth. Chance seemed to take notice that I was going for another beer, because he finally came up for air and complained, "Don't drink all my beer!" Looking at him, I just snorted a laugh, turned around and began to drink the beer. Chance sat up and Kelly did too, as she adjusted her shirt that had gotten in a little disarray from Chance's hands. "Did you get the last beer?" Chance asked me, not in a mean way, but concerned.

Looking at him with contempt, I responded, "No, you got one left. Guess you need to go to the store now, huh?"

"Jesus, that was my last beer and I'm broke now," Chance groaned.

"Well go to the fucking store, and I'll give you money. You can get some more since I drank so many to keep myself entertained, while you two had your fucking twosome!" I snapped off, sarcastically.

I noticed Kelly look over at me sheepishly, before she and Chance switched places. Chance started the Chevy and he huffed, "Well, if you were that bored, why didn't you just leave?"

"Gee, I guess 'cause you took me somewhere that I was completely lost, and didn't have a clue where I was?" I was still feeling snarky.

Chance looked at me and replied flippantly, "Well, if you'd sat in the bed of the truck, you could have drank all the beer." He grinned at me with his pretty teeth. I stared at him balefully.

I looked at Kelly and wondered if she was getting what he was trying to say. If I had been out of the truck, he'd probably have gotten her to go all the way. I knew that she was a virgin, even though she had made out with enough boys that it was hard to believe. I knew Kelly didn't have a clue what he was saying. I just shook my head. It seemed only minutes and we were once again under the harsh, glaring lights, of the store and parking lot.

I watched as Chance began to feel in his back pocket. He was 18 so he could legally buy beer. I'd already taken a couple of bucks out of my purse and basically flung them at Kelly and she was handing them to Chance when he began to gripe that he'd left his driver's license at home. "What kind of idiot leaves their driver's license at home?" I asked him with more sarcasm, than anger. Chance shrugged his shoulder. "Give me the fucking money!" Opening the door of the truck, I got out, taking my grandmother's wedding rings, my mom had given me when I'd first moved to Corpus, off of my right hand. I switched them to my left hand.

"What are you doing, DeLaine?" Kelly asked me breathlessly.

"I'm gonna buy this fucking cry baby some more beer!" I sniped back.

Chance began laughing, "You're a kid! What are you, 14? You can't buy beer!"

Smiling at him, I spat, "Well, actually I'm 15, and watch me!" Then I sauntered up the sidewalk and walked inside. I smiled at the store clerk, walked directly to the back, and grabbed a six pack of the same beer we'd been drinking in Chance's truck. I walked up to the counter, smiling at the clerk, and shaking my head. The clerk smiled at me as I griped, "You know I hate it when my old man doesn't tell me he wants to bring people over to drink, late at night, and we don't have anything! I'm the one who gets volunteered to go to the store, with my little sister and her boyfriend!"

The clerk was a man around 30. He smiled at me and nodded his head, "Yeah, my wife hates that shit too!" I smiled sweetly at him, as I saw him look at my wedding rings, as he rang me up.

"Try to take it easy on your old man! We guys are just dumbasses!" He joked, smiling as I waved and walked out the glass door.

I smiled sweetly at Chance and Kelly, as I walked to the pickup with the brown bag. When I opened the door, Kelly started acting stupid and asking how I did that. I growled at her, "Will you just sit back and be cool!" She sat back and looked at me as if I'd reached across the seat and slapped her, like I wanted to.

Chance looked past Kelly at me, and now his smile was all bright and blinding. I slammed the door and we pulled out of the convenience store. We were headed back to the Gameroom and Chance asked, "How the fuck did you do that?"

Smiling at him, I told him it was a secret, and I couldn't be made to tell it. Then I smiled sweetly at him, asking, "Oh, by the way, do you want one of my beers?" Looking at me a little weird when he pulled back in behind the Gameroom I growled, "Oh shit boy, relax, I'm giving you four beers. That leaves two for me. I replaced all the beer you wasted on me! Now, what you wasted on her," I nodded my head towards Kelly, "I figure you got outta her by getting to feel her up!" With that said, I jumped out of the truck, and pulled two beers out of the plastic rings, setting the other four on his seat.

Kelly jumped out behind me, explaining, "I'm sorry, DeLaine, it just happened."

"It's cool, Kelly," I bit off, hiding the deep hurt I felt. "I figure you saved me a ton of shit by goin' ahead and making out with the bastard." I popped the tab of one of the cans and slugged it back.

"Um, can I have the other beer?" Kelly asked me, timidly. "I um, gave Chance the beer I had while we were at the store."

"Yeah, go ask Chance for one," I grumbled, as I walked off from Kelly. I found a group of people that we knew and sat down on the hood of one of the guy's cars. I stuck my unopened can of beer between my legs. Chance and Kelly came walking behind me from the side of the building. Chance had a big grin on his face, completely oblivious to my feelings, or that I was even mad. Instead, he shocked me by bragging to everyone about how I bought beer, cool as a cucumber, without ever being carded. Several of the senior guys turned to me and asked how I did it. I was buzzing pretty hard, so I just grinned and shrugged my shoulders.

Then I stated sarcastically, "Probably 'cause I'm a girl and those clerks like to flirt with girls more than ugly guys like y'all!" This was met with a great big laugh from all the guys, including Chance. I shook my head as I finished the first beer. Chance was so impressed that I'd been able to manipulate the clerk that he couldn't see what a jackass he'd been, after Debbie introduced him to me, because she'd told him I liked him.

After I finished drinking the last beer, I had another guy hand me one. By the time I finished that one, I knew I was completely smashed, but it was still early enough that I wasn't too worried. It was only 10 o'clock. I knew my mama wouldn't pick me up until 12:30.

Sitting there drinking the beer, that I'd gotten from Willie Morgan, I completely ignored Kelly. Chance, I noticed, had started out leaning against the car across from me. Then, he slowly moved around the circle, until he was standing beside me. I glanced at him and was completely fine with him standing there. I wasn't even mad at him any longer. I was too busy being drunk and enjoying the fun part of it.

Chance leaned over and whispered next to my ear, "You wanna go ride around?" I looked at him as someone's car stereo blasted out Ozzy.

"What?" I asked him, wondering if I'd misunderstood him.

"You wanna go ride around some more?" he asked innocently, as he flashed his pretty, toothy smile.

Sitting there for a few seconds, thinking about it, I decided why not, and jumped down off of the car I'd been sitting on. I walked back behind the building, for the second time that night. As we pulled out, Chance crooned, "You can scoot over. I don't bite!" I thought back to hearing Jax saying that before, and I scooted over, in the middle of the long bench seat. I hadn't told Kelly where I was going, but I figured someone would tell her I'd left with Chance. I really didn't care.

I still had two and a half hours until my mom would be there, and I was angry with Kelly. I wasn't even surprised when I saw that Chance didn't really drive anywhere, except by Sonic, but not through it. Then he turned to go to the trails we'd been at earlier. I figured I knew what he was going to do. At least I thought I did. I was about to be educated by the next man in my life.

After turning the key to keep the stereo on, Chance leaned over and began to kiss me. I suddenly felt myself sober immediately. I was aware, with my brain having a field day inside of my head, as it told me how stupid I was being. I was doing this out of spite, and how this had never worked for me in the past! My hormonal fires were being stoked by someone new, for the first time in over two years. I realized that I was listening more intently than I ever had before. I wondered if it was because I was 15 now, or if it was because it was someone new. Possibly it was just the fact that I wasn't terrified. Right now, I just wanted to feel Chance's hands on me, and he happily obliged.

When he tried to take his hands down to my pants, I kept pushing them away. I might have thought I felt sober, but I knew in all reality I was still very drunk. I didn't want to have sex with Chance, no matter how much of a crush I had on him.

After making out for about 40 minutes, Chance finally said, "Blow me," breathlessly. I felt myself freeze. I had never ever done that.

I hadn't really had great experiences in the sex department as it was. How in the world could I do that, with a boy I didn't know that well?

When I didn't respond, Chance seemed to intuit my hesitation. "Have you ever blown a guy?" he finally asked, pulling away from me. He looked down at my face that was lit by the light shining from the radio, in his dash.

I felt so ashamed, but I didn't want to say I had when I knew I hadn't. I shook my head slowly, looking at his pretty teeth. Chance sat up in the seat that he had just had me laid out on, as we explored one another's mouths, extensively. I thought he was going to be angry, but instead, he unzipped his jeans whispering, "I'll teach you." I felt my eyes grow large as I looked at this cute senior boy, that I had a huge crush on. I decided I was drunk enough, I could probably do it. Slowly I sat up and then began to lean my body over towards his unzipped pants, as he instructed me in how to do what he wanted. I felt a little embarrassed when I realized I would actually be able to see all of him. I'd only ever felt a boy. I'd never actually seen a boy's entire manhood. I felt nervous, but I also wanted Chance to like me.

I wasn't sure if I did it right, but he seemed happy with the outcome. After he was done, I sat up and he zipped his fly. He started the truck and began to pull out of the dense vegetation. I felt completely sober, but even worse than feeling sober, I felt somehow wrong. I told myself to quit being a baby. I was in high school now! This is what high school boys liked. I hoped that because I'd done this, somehow it meant Chance would like me.

After we pulled into the back of the Gameroom, I went to slide out of the driver's side like I had when I rode with Jax. Before I got all the way over, Chance had closed the door. I felt my face flush as I scooted towards the passenger side and opened it, hopping down. I looked around and didn't see Chance. I was surprised, so I walked around the building, and found him already leaning against another car, putting a dip in his lip. I stood there watching him act like he had just gone to take a piss or get a drink, instead of what had just happened.

Kelly came out of the Gameroom, running up to me, asking me where I'd gone and that she'd been worried. I told her I'd tell her later and then I found a group of potheads that were going on the side of the building, to smoke a joint. I walked around with them and managed to gain just enough of a buzz, off of the pot, to make me not feel so disgusted with myself, before my mom came to pick us up.

When we got home, Kelly and I went into my room. I took great lengths to tell her how Chance came up to me and asked if I wanted to go riding around with him. I wanted to hurt her as much as she had hurt me, but when she didn't seem to really care, I just felt angry.

I began to feel the fire burn slowly in my gut, for the first time at Kelly. It surprised me a little, but I decided to try to damage her somehow, so I went ahead and told her what I'd done with Chance.

She was shocked but seemed interested in all of the details, so I told them to her, as if it weren't any big deal. I pretended it didn't mean any more to me, than it seemed to have meant to him, but Kelly knew me well enough to know that I felt hurt by him. I refused to cry over that.

The next morning when I woke up, I knew I wasn't really angry with Kelly any longer, even though I still felt a little hurt. I was just angry that I was allowing myself to feel hidden again. I was letting the old DeLame DeLaine feel like she was needed, so no one could see me.

I thought about how screwed up my life was with my parents, especially with my new fucked up home life. I didn't want anyone besides Kelly and Robin to know how I lived. They had seen it before I even knew it was there, so there was no way to hide it from them, but I could hide it from others. I decided that being a little wild and a little bit of a bitch would insure that not too many people got too close to me.

One good way to insure no one got close to me, was to make sure everyone thought I was a coldhearted bitch, who didn't give a shit how she was treated. It kept boys at arms-length, since they'd just hurt me anyway.

Chance had gotten me to go riding around with him a couple more times as January turned into February. I knew that he didn't think of me in any other way, except as a girl to mess around with. I hated the fact that I was actually beginning to have feelings for him, as we talked when we'd ride around. He acted one way around me, when it was just the two of us, and another when we were around others.

I began to think that all boys were this way. I knew one thing I'd probably never understand them in my life time. Just when I seemed to think I knew about them, they proved me so wrong.

***

In a moment of weakness, I bought a carnation that the Student Council was selling, for Valentine's Day, for Chance. I could have it delivered to his class either anonymously or sign a card. I signed it from his Secret Admirer.

When I walked into the Student Center, at lunchtime, he looked straight at me, as I walked in the door. His eyes seemed to find me. We never acted like we knew one another, so when he looked straight at me, and smiled his mega-watt smile, I was confused. He glanced at the white carnation on his shirt, then looked at me with a question in his eyes. I slightly nodded my head, and he turned on the blinding white smile once more. I felt a flush begin to creep across my cheeks.

I grinned back at him, and felt Kelly pull me towards the girls' room, so we could smoke. I was feeling so confused. The carnations went out on the Friday before Valentine's Day, since we wouldn't be at school on Sunday, when Valentine's Day fell that year. I felt certain that maybe with the acknowledgement from Chance, I might actually go somewhere with him, instead of just being some stupid little freshman he messed around with. I didn't know why he had to act like I was such a huge secret. It wasn't like everyone we ran with hadn't seen me leave with him, and usually come back, sitting beside him in the orange Chevy.

The next night when I got to the Gameroom, I was crushed to see some girl I'd never seen before, hanging all over Chance. I went outside and got drunk and stoned and sat with Christy Gilley. Chance came walking out of the Gameroom with the girl who'd been hanging on him and smiled big at Christy. He glanced at me and gave me a cursory smile. I stared daggers into him. The girl who was hanging on him looked like a cheap whore. I was surprised to see him with a girl like that.

When they drove off, Christy looked at me and demanded, "Okay, spill, what's the deal with you and Chance?" I shook my head, looked down and grabbed a cigarette out of the pack sitting beside me. I lit it, trying to avoid her questions. When she wouldn't let up, I finally told her about messing around with Chance and how he just seemed like he just wanted to mess around and not be in a relationship. I was surprised when Christy began to laugh, "Honey, give up on Chance Cahill. He's a boy whore!"

"What?" I asked curiously.

Laughing Christy stated, "He just likes to screw around with a bunch of girls. He doesn't know what having a girlfriend is about." I felt really stupid then, and uncertain what to do. When a short guy named Eli came up, with another joint, asking if we wanted to go smoke with him, Christy grinned at me and grabbed my hand. She pulled me to the side of the building and we smoked the joint with Eli.

We all three began walking back to the cars where we'd been sitting and were giggling for the rest of the night. I just wanted to forget how much I hurt.

Chapter 24

On February 17th, I came in the door, after school and Mama told me to sit down. I looked at her worried. Tears came to her eyes, "Honey, there is no easy way to tell you this."

Looking at her anxiously, I began to cry, thinking that Clarice had finally lost her damned mind completely, and murdered my daddy. What came next was just as bad. "What is it, Mama?" I asked, as the tears began to slip down my face.

"Sweetie, Donna Strong passed away this morning," my Mama's voice broke and her own tears began to course down her face.

I sat there, completely dumbfounded, at first. I'd built myself into such a state, that I was about to hear Clarice had murdered my daddy, that I'd completely forgotten my concern for Donna. I had only written to her once since I'd been home. I'd been so consumed with Chance Cahill, and trying to harden my heart. The one thing that could totally shatter me, came sneaking into the tiny crevice of my soul, and ripped my heart in two.

I knew how it happened. She'd been born with a fragile body, then she'd been abused, but she'd gotten almost 16 years of life because Jean and Steve Strong had loved her.

I kept trying to have a rational brain, but my heart was aching more than I thought capable. I had never had someone that I'd loved like Donna, pass away before. I didn't know what to do with all the pain that was pouring out of every part of my soul. I literally sat in the kitchen chair, as my mama kneeled in front of me, holding me, as sobs wracked my body. I didn't know if I could ever stop the tears from falling. Every time I thought I was beginning to come to the end of crying, fresh tears would overcome me.

I don't even know how long I let my mama hold me, in her arms, while I cried for the sweet little girl who would never play with her Barbies, or read her books, again. Who was going to tell Kevin what to do in a bossy, tiny girl voice? I would never hear her funny laughter, watch her clap her tiny hands, or feel her fragile arms around my neck to hug me, again. Then I thought about Kevin. I looked at Mama and cried, "I need to call Kevin!"

Mama nodded and said that I could call him later in the evening, when the rates went down. I wanted to go to the funeral, but I didn't know how to ask Mama. I knew it would be a huge thing, because it would cost money. Since she had quit working, we relied only on Ray's income. I knew she hated to ask for anything extra.

I decided that I'd ask anyway, because I didn't know what else to do. I so desperately wanted to go.

"Do you think we can drive up for the funeral?" I asked quietly, as my hiccups began to quiet, and my nose had been blown repeatedly.

Mama looked at me with as much sorrow as I'd ever seen in her eyes. She nodded her head and replied hoarsely, "Ray was here when Jean called. He's already left the money for me." I nodded and told her I was going to my room. I asked when I could call, and she told me after 7 o'clock, so I walked into my room, with tears still streaming down my face.

Lying on my bed, I grabbed my Velveteen Rabbit. I sat up and looked over at my desk that held the few books that I owned. I reached over and grabbed the book out that I had read over and over to Donna. I knew almost every page by heart, after reading it to her so many times. Before I lay back on my bed, I grabbed the photo of me and Kevin from my photo album. When I was finally on the bed with everything, I didn't feel like looking at any of it. Instead, I lay there and sobbed even more, until I dozed off. I held the Velveteen Rabbit up to my face, and as he'd done so many countless other times, he soaked up the salty tears that flowed out of my eyes.

I felt my swollen eyes trying to open, and I looked around the dark room. I realized that it was probably too late to call! I jumped up and looked at the clock on my nightstand. I was grateful to see that it was only 7:15. Walking out of my room, I went into the kitchen and found my mama sitting there drinking coffee. I was surprised. I figured she'd be half-way, or all the way gone by now, but she looked up at me from the manicure she was giving herself. Her eyes were straight and clear. "You okay, Baby?" my mama asked me, concerned. I nodded my head and realized I was standing there holding my Velveteen Rabbit as if I were a little girl, holding my favorite baby. I felt fresh tears begin to slide out of my swollen eyes.

"Can I call Kevin?" I asked, with my nose beginning to run. Mama nodded her head. I grabbed a paper towel as I went through the kitchen, blowing my nose on the way down the hall. I knew I wouldn't be able to talk long, but I had to talk to him. When I dialed Kevin's phone number, it rang several times. I wasn't sure why he wasn't answering. I'd let it ring enough times that if he were in the living room, he'd still hear it. I hung up and dialed his parents' number. Mrs. Strong answered quietly. I began to cry as soon as I heard her voice but managed to choke out that it was DeLaine.

Jean Strong's quiet voice didn't sound like I was used to. It wasn't strong or self-assured. It was subdued. That scared me. I managed to get myself under control and told her I'd tried to call Kevin.

She said, "I know sweetheart. I heard the phone ringing. I had a feeling it was you, when it kept ringing. Kevin won't answer the phone. He won't talk. DeLaine, honey, I don't know what to do."

For the first time since I'd met her, Jean Strong sounded beaten.

"Mrs. Strong, will you tell him it's me. Ask him if he'll talk to me," I pleaded, quietly, realizing that I had to get myself straightened out, or else I couldn't be there for the one person who had been there for me more times than I ever deserved. She told me she would and she lay the phone down on the counter. In a few minutes she came back and responded, "DeLaine, he just wanted to know if you are coming."

"Yes ma'am…tomorrow. We are coming up there," I replied quietly.

"In that case, he said to tell you he'd talk when you got here. He doesn't feel like he can talk to you right now." Mrs. Strong explained softly.

I sat there for a few seconds, knowing that I was wasting precious long distance, and finally I asked, "Will you please tell him I need him to at least answer the phone. He doesn't have to speak but tell him I need to at least tell him something, before I leave." Mrs. Strong said she'd tell him, and I told her I loved her. I realized I didn't remember if I'd ever told her before. She told me she loved me too, mingled in with her tears. I hung up the phone. I dialed Kevin's number again.

As I listened to the phone ring 6, 7, 8 times, on the 9th ring, Kevin picked up and I heard a strangled "Lainey?"

I wasn't even expecting that, so it brought a fresh assault of tears that I tried to suck back. "Kev, I'm on my way as fast as I can get there. Mama said we're leaving in the morning. Hang on for me, okay?" I heard his sobs as they came over the hundreds of miles, through my phone. Each sob I felt deep in my soul.

"Hurry," Kevin finally whispered, almost so softly I didn't catch it.

"I love you, Kevin! Don't forget that!" I said a little stronger.

"Me too," he choked out, then I heard a click on the line. I knew he was gone from the call. I hung up the phone and looked at the clock. I was grateful I hadn't talked too long.

I got up and walked to my closet and began to pick clothes out. I wasn't sure what I was going to wear to the funeral. I knew you were supposed to wear black, but I'd only gone to a couple of funerals when I was younger. I hadn't really owned black back then.

I thought about Donna and about how bright her soul was. I thought about how blue was always so pretty on her and I noticed that the new sweater I'd gotten for Christmas was a pretty, soft cream with summery, blue ribbons knitted into it. I thought it was odd that I'd never noticed the summery, blue ribbons, because as soon as I saw it, I immediately saw Kevin and Donna's eyes in my mind.

Pulling the sweater out, I looked at it and felt deep inside of me that I was supposed to wear it.

I pulled out the black skirt that I'd worn at New Year's Eve and found some wedge type heels that I could wear, that would be more comfortable than the spike heels.

I pulled my smaller bag out of my closet. I wasn't even sure how long we would be gone, but I felt certain we'd be coming back by Sunday. I grabbed a few more casual sweaters out that I still had from when I lived in Wichita Falls. It didn't get as cold in Corpus as it did in North Texas, so I didn't get to wear my sweaters often. I threw some jeans and a couple of pairs of pajamas along with some underwear and bras. I grabbed some socks and closed the bag up and carried it out into the living room.

Mama looked at me, "When do you want to leave?"

"As soon as possible, if that's okay with you," I replied softly.

Mama asked, "How about we leave by 8 in the morning?" I nodded my head and went into my room. Then I wondered where we were staying, so I walked out and asked Mama. She told me that she was staying with a friend of hers who was still in Wichita Falls. I told her I didn't know if I should call Bailey or not. I hated to invite myself. "Jean said that if we needed some place to stay, we could stay with them. I knew I could stay with Barbara, and I didn't know where you'd want to stay," Mama told me.

Nodding as she said that, I knew I didn't have to think about it, "If I can stay at the Strong's, I'd rather stay with them, if it's okay." Mama agreed, and I went back into my room.

The next morning, as Mama was finishing up her coffee, and I was putting our bags into her car, the phone rang. I was surprised since it was only 7:30, but when I came out to see who it was, Mama was talking quietly. She said to hold on and held the phone out to me stating, "It's Bailey. Apparently, she knows already."

I went into my room and picked up my extension. Once I heard the click of the kitchen phone, I said hello and was met with my best friend weeping. "DeLaine! Is it true?" Bailey asked sadly.

I had finally gone an hour without a tear drop falling from my eyes. Now, I felt them coming out of my eyes again. "Yeah, Bay, she's gone." I cried sadly.

"Oh Lala! I'm so sorry! Oh my GOD! How?" my best friend wailed. I told her I didn't know anything yet. I explained I would be there that evening but wasn't sure when. She automatically thought I'd be staying with her. When I told her that I was staying with the Strong family, she got quiet, "That makes sense. I'm sorry, Lala! I just miss you. I guessed you would always stay with me."

"Oh Bay, if it weren't any other reason, I'd stay with you, but Mrs. Strong told my mama that we could stay with them. I have to be there for him, Bay. He's shattered," I whispered at the end.

"I know Lala," my best friend whispered.

"When is the funeral?" I suddenly asked curious, since my mama hadn't known the night before.

"Glenda said the obituary, this morning, said Saturday," Bailey replied. "But they're having the family visitation tomorrow on Friday."

I sat there for a minute, trying to remember in my limited experience with funerals, and finally realized I'd never gone to something like that, "So what does that mean?"

"It's where they have time to visit with the family, at the funeral home. Sometimes they have the coffin open, so you can see them," Bailey explained.

I was horrified when I thought about seeing Donna lying in a coffin, dead. Why would I want to look at that beautiful, little angel without being able to see her summer sky eyes? "Um, do they always do an open coffin thing?" I asked hesitantly.

"No, but it just depends on what the family wants." Bailey stated.

Glancing at my clock, I said, "Bay, I need to get off of the phone, so I can get out of here. I'll call you as soon as I can from Kevin's." Bailey told me she loved me, and I said the same. I walked out to find my mama pouring coffee into a thermos. I saw that her purse and cigarettes were on the table.

"Ready, Doodle-Bug?" my mama asked me softly, using her pet name for me that she'd called me since I could remember. I nodded, and she smiled back. As we walked towards the door she placed her hand lightly on my shoulder. I was so glad that she was sober and prayed she stayed that way until this was over. I needed her strength right now. I didn't know how I was going to get through this.

Chapter 25

I didn't talk most of the way to Wichita Falls. All I could do was remember all the times I'd gone to the Strong's, over the previous two years, and played or read to Donna. I could see her flaxen hair and the sweet, little, crooked smile that would light up her face every time I walked into the room. I remembered her making me and Kevin hug when I got home, before 8th grade started, after I'd found out about him and Lori. It was almost as if she knew every time there was something going on between us. Sometimes I wondered if she was real or just an angel in a human form to touch all of our lives.

I flashed on my visit in December and realized that she knew that she wasn't going to be here much longer. That was why she made me promise to be there for Kevin. She knew that he would need someone who understood his grief, who he might let in. I thought about the last time I'd felt her little arms around my neck, to hug me, and how cold she'd felt. I looked out the window and wondered why the weather had to be gray and ugly. I realized it matched my mood.

When we reached Wichita Falls, Mama knew how to get to my old house and to Bailey's, but she'd never been to the Strong's home, so I had to give her directions. When we turned, I saw several cars sitting in front of their home. Mama ended up parking across the street. We walked up and rang the doorbell. Mrs. Strong opened the door and her warm smile was working hard to come through when she saw us. I walked into the door and she enveloped me so delicately into her embrace. As soon as I felt her warmth I couldn't help it…I began to sob. I had managed not to cry the entire day, as we traveled. I couldn't hold back any longer when Jean Strong took me into her arms and cried as well.

I didn't want to let go of her, but eventually, she pulled back and brought out a handkerchief that she had been carrying with her. She wiped her face. She reached over on a small table in the foyer and grabbed a tissue from a box that was set there.

When I had the tissue in hand, I wiped my face and moved over and watched as Jean Strong did the exact same thing to my mom. She hugged her just as warmly as she'd ever done with me. I saw the look of total awe on my mom's face as if she'd been touched by the magic that made Mrs. Strong who she was.

Mama began to tell Mrs. Strong how sorry she was. I watched as the two mothers began to talk. Finally, we were ushered towards the large family room, in the back.

Just as we got to end of the hallway that led to the bedrooms, Mrs. Strong walked up behind me and whispered in my ear. "DeLaine, Kevin is in his room. He won't come out. I think he could really use you right now."

I turned around and looked into her sad, but kind eyes, nodding my head. Instead of following my mama into the family room, I turned right and walked to the end of the hall, to the bedroom on the left. I wouldn't even look to my right when I first saw Donna's bedroom door. I didn't want to see it.

I tapped softly on the door, then turned the knob quietly, pushing the door open. I saw Kevin lying on his bed in the darkened room, with his back to the door. He was looking out the bedroom window that I had come to when I found out we were moving. There wasn't anything out that window except the side of the house next door to them. I said his name softly, and when he didn't move, I walked into the room, quietly closing the door.

I kicked my shoes off and crawled onto the bed. I got behind him, as he had done many times to me and wrapped my arm around his waist. He grabbed my hand, as it rested on his stomach, and squeezed it. We lay there for what seemed hours but was only minutes. I realized he was crying. He wasn't just crying, he was sobbing.

Kevin drew his knees up towards his stomach, and held onto my hand, for dear life, as the sobs wracked his body, over and over. I lay there with tears streaming from my eyes, but I was not going to move. I knew he needed me. I needed him, but even more, I needed him to need me right now. I didn't say anything to him. I just lay there quietly, as he sobbed.

After he finally began to quiet again, I began wiping my eyes, as best as I could, with the hand that I'd put under my head. We continued to lay together, not talking. I looked over at his clock and realized I'd been there for an hour already, with neither one of us saying a word. I knew my mama would want to be leaving soon, but I couldn't stand the thought of getting up. I just wanted to hold Kevin all night, if need be. I'd stay there and not say one word, if that is what he wanted from me.

I felt Kevin stick a tissue in my hand that I had wrapped around him, and realized he had a box on the floor, beside his bed. I smiled and pulled my hand back and wiped my face, then put the wadded-up tissue in my other hand so I could wrap my arm back around him. We only lay like that for a couple more minutes.

He finally rolled over onto his back. I moved over, so he could do it without falling off the side of the bed. I stayed on my side and lay my head on the arm he put out for me to snuggle against him.

Once my head was secure in the crook of his arm, and my face lying on his chest, he wrapped both of his arms around me and just held tightly. I finally felt right.

I was where I was supposed to be. I wrapped my right arm back around his waist as he held me close. He finally leaned over and kissed the top of my head.

When my eyes opened, I didn't realize I'd fallen asleep. I glanced around and noticed that the bathroom light was on, but that was all. It hadn't been on when I came in at 4:30. I felt a little disoriented, waking up beside Kevin, all wrapped up in him. I realized there was a blanket on us. I looked over at the clock, thinking we'd dozed off for an hour or two. When I saw it was midnight, I was shocked. I pulled away from Kevin and sat up, wondering what in the world had happened. I wondered if my mom was going to be mad at me for not coming back out. I turned and looked at Kevin. His blue eyes were looking at me.

"Hey," I murmured, softly.

"Hey," Kevin replied, just above a whisper.

"Did you sleep?" I asked. He nodded his head. "How long have you been awake?"

Kevin glanced at the clock and replied, "About 10 minutes."

"Do you think your mom is gonna be mad at me for falling asleep in here?" I asked Kevin, worried. He shook his head no. He pulled me back into the crook of his arm. This time I lay with my head against his chest. I wanted to hear his heartbeat.

"I'm glad you came, Lainey," Kevin said softly. I looked up at him, as he glanced down at me. He raised himself up, just a little, where his face could reach mine. He kissed me fully on my mouth. I was a little surprised, but I kissed him back. I briefly thought about Chance Cahill and the things he'd been teaching me, but I pushed his memory away, like a pesky fly.

Before I knew what was happening, Kevin had rolled me onto my back, as he continued to kiss me. I didn't know if it was right that we were kissing like this, with Donna having just died the day before. It was all so confusing. How was a person supposed to act when they lost someone they loved as much as I had loved Donna? Then I thought about how much Kevin had loved her. If my loss was so huge, I knew his was unbearably more so. He seemed to need this closeness, so I pushed all my thoughts out and decided to get lost inside of kissing Kevin. It had been so long since we'd been on a bed and kissed.

His kisses were tender and sad. I could feel the shattered part of his soul coming into me with every kiss. I wanted to soothe his ache. I wanted to soothe his soul. I didn't know if it would ever be better. I wasn't sure how he'd come back from this.

I knew he was strong, but I also knew that most everything he'd ever done in his life was about protecting Donna and caring for her.

When he wasn't protecting her, he had been protecting me. Who would he protect now, I wondered, as he continued to kiss me with growing passion. Then I wondered who would protect him now. He had a huge hole that was gaping. I was afraid what he would do to fill it.

Soon I felt the familiar, long, graceful fingers as they slowly unbuttoned the long-sleeved blouse I'd worn. I didn't even try to push his hand away. Once he had every button undone, he pushed it open and his hands began to caress me softly. Even his touch felt sad compared to how it normally felt before. There was a need there, but it wasn't the same passionate need that had spurred him on when we had first begun our physical relationship.

Trailing soft as a butterfly kisses, down my neck, into the crevice between my breasts, he reached around and popped the snaps on my bra with one little flick of his fingers, which surprised me. He pushed my shirt completely away. Even though the bathroom light was on, the door was pulled all the way to, so the only light in the room was coming from around and a little under the door, just enough to see his face. I sat up and let him push my blouse all the way off and then he pulled my bra away. I lay back down and felt the warmth of his hands, as they slid across my body.

I ran my hands up inside the t-shirt he had on and felt his bare skin. I wished he would take his shirt off. I knew that he was embarrassed by the scars he carried, from his life before the Strong's adopted him. I decided I was going to get him to take his shirt off. I wouldn't take no for an answer. If I trusted him to look at me, after I'd gained another 10 pounds, then he could trust me to see his scars. Slowly, I began to push his t-shirt up. He stopped touching me and leaned up to look into my face. He started to shake his head no, but I nodded mine yes. We laid there looking deep into each other's faces and I was trying to will my thoughts to him. He needed to know that he was safe with me. Finally, he let go of my hand that he had grabbed to stop me.

I got the t-shirt over his head, and he was now just as bare as I was, above the waist. The warmth of his skin, against mine felt exquisite. I just wanted to lay there wrapped against him, feeling his heartbeat against my own. He finally brought his mouth back to mine and began to kiss me with renewed passion.

I touched his chest and back, but never lingered on any area that felt a little rough, as if it were a scar. I slid my hand over his skin smoothly and felt as it glided over him. He didn't go any further than removing my blouse and kissing me.

I felt my own siren song begin to sing. She had been quiet a lot. Even when I was with Chance, she never really sang. She'd stir every once in a while, but it seemed she only sang with Kevin now. As she awoke with great vigor, I realized that I was now the one that was drawing the strength I needed from Kevin because I was lost.

I surprised both of us when I reached for the button on his jeans. He wasn't wearing a belt, so I deftly put my fingers on the button and unfastened it. I had brushed my hand against him already, so I knew that his desire was definitely there. I began to unzip his pants and he grabbed my wrist suddenly, and pulled away from me, "What are you doing?"

Smiling at him, I whispered, "What we were supposed to do, when the time was right, and not in Kevin Welks' backyard, in a nasty, little, travel trailer."

Kevin looked at me pained, because that memory, I knew, wasn't a good one for either of us. I used my other hand and pulled his face back to mine. I continued unzipping his fly. I didn't know where I was getting the guts from, to do what I was about to do, but I knew that if it was going to happen for real, then it was now, because we both needed something to soothe our ravaged hearts. I wasn't sure if sex was it, but it was the only thing I could feel at the moment. We'd cried together. Now we needed to comfort one another, in a more carnal way, a way that sometimes is awoken during times of tragedy.

Reaching around, I began to push his jeans down. I knew that no one was going to come in. They had put a blanket on us and left us to sleep through the night. They probably thought we were emotionally exhausted, which we were. But, we needed to do what we were about to do now. Finally, Kevin began to help me get his jeans down, and then all he had left on were his white underwear. I didn't look down. I'd never actually seen Kevin. He'd taken my virginity, but I hadn't actually seen all of him, as I had Chance. Again, I pushed Chance Cahill away, and concentrated on Kevin. I wondered if I should do to Kevin what Chance always wanted. I wondered if he'd want to know how I knew how to do what Chance had taught me. I made myself quit thinking and concentrated on Kevin's mouth on mine. His fingers tentatively reached for the button of my jeans.

He pulled back suddenly, with a look of complete terror and remorse, "Are you sure, Lainey? I don't want to hurt you again."

I nodded my head and reached down and unsnapped my jeans for him. How I wanted to see his mischievous smile, knowing what we were finally going to do for real, but instead, I saw the sadness across his features.

He leaned back down and began to kiss me with so much longing, it almost made me begin to cry again. Slowly he unzipped my pants, and I slid them down for him, leaving only the blue, bikini-cut panties that I'd worn that morning. Now each of us only had underwear on.

Kevin began to slowly move the panties down my legs. I helped as much as I could. Then he began to explore a place that he'd explored once before, in our old family room, almost two years ago.

I was now completely lost inside of Kevin. I nudged the siren who seemed to keep falling asleep, but now she was singing so loud, I felt nothing but a pleasant hum inside of my brain.

It was better than being drunk, which I had been a lot, since I'd moved to Corpus. Even being stoned wasn't the same feeling I was experiencing in my brain, as Kevin slowly and achingly touched me between my legs.

My hands began to glide over his body, and when I reached the waistband of the white underwear he was wearing, I began to push it down as well. Before I got it even partially down he sprang forth in the front, which was a little surprising. I reached down and held him in my hand. I wondered how I had felt two other boys before I held Kevin in my hands. I was surprised at how different he felt compared to Chance. I could really barely remember Jax.

As those thoughts flitted through my brain, I had to keep pushing thoughts of other boys out of my mind, as I continued to explore Kevin's anatomy. I didn't know why my mind kept traveling around, in so many directions, when I was lying next to the boy I loved more than any other and was about to have sex with him, for real. Not angry sex, where he took my virginity in a drunken fit because he was afraid that I'd given it to someone else. This time it would be different.

I wanted us to be together, but I hated also that it seemed the reason we were actually doing this was because of our mutual grief over losing Donna. I squeezed my eyes tight and made myself focus. Whatever he was doing between my legs began to gather my attention, and thoughts of everyone else in the world were drowned out by the sensations and the siren song.

By the time Kevin finally began to enter me, I was more than ready. I was still afraid of the pain and when he finally got inside of me, it hurt badly, but this time, I held onto him as if I were holding on for dear life.

I wasn't sure really what was supposed to be so great about sex, still. I liked everything that happened up until the actual act, and then I didn't really want to get past that point. I still didn't know why so many girls talked about how great it was. So far, all I knew was it hurt. I hoped that it would change one day, for now though, it was painful, but I didn't want to tell Kevin that.

He was trying to be so gentle with me. I knew he was afraid of hurting me, even though what we were doing this time was completely and totally different than what had happened between us before.

When we were done, Kevin kissed me slowly. Looking down at me, his eyes spoke volumes, about pain and love, sorrow and life. It was as if his eyes told every emotion that was swirling inside of him, all jumbled up at once.

I reached both of my hands up, to frame his beautiful face. I pushed his blonde hair back. I looked into the shadowed, blue eyes that shone with tears. I reached under the blonde lashes, at the bottom of one of his eyes, and wiped with the pad of my thumb, as he'd done to me on countless occasions. After wiping the tear from beneath his eye, he leaned back down and kissed me, until I felt like my toes would begin to curl. After he kissed me, he slid over onto his side, but kept one leg draped over me, as he burrowed his face into my neck. I held onto his arm, as it lay draped across my stomach.

Even though I still didn't get the great mystery of sex, I had enjoyed the before, and now was enjoying the after. I felt loved and warm, as I lay there with Kevin's face nestled in my neck. "Lainey?" Kevin whispered into the crook of my neck.

"Hmm?" I replied.

"Are you sorry?" he asked, with a slight tremor in his voice.

Turning my face so he had to move his, I smiled and asked, "No. Why would I be sorry? This is what I wanted it to be like! This is the time I'm counting. From now on, what happened at Welks' house, didn't happen in my mind. This was my first time with you. I'm not gonna lie and say I understood everything about what just happened, because I really don't, but I'm not sorry. It was always supposed to be you, Kevin. You knew it before even I did," I whispered hoarsely, as I looked at him.

Sitting up on his elbow, Kevin's long, graceful fingers brushed the curls out of my face, as he caressed my cheek. "Lainey, I wish I knew how to tell you how I feel about you. It's so much bigger than saying 'I love you'…but I don't know how to say it."

Smiling into the beautiful face of the boy who would hold my heart for longer than I could possibly know, I whispered, "You just did."

Kevin leaned down and kissed me softly. Then he pulled me over to where he was lying on his back. I was now held close to his heart, where I loved to be held. I felt the rough patches of some of the scars on his chest, as my cheek rested on him. I thought back to what he endured as a little boy. It made me sad to know that he'd ever known that kind of pain. He would never be rid of it, because the scars on his chest weren't the only scars that had been left behind.

Lying on Kevin's chest, I felt my exhausted and emotional body, as it began to relax. Feeling Kevin's skin next to mine was more exquisite than anything else we'd done that night.

I glanced at his clock and saw that it was almost 4 in the morning. I wondered when we needed to be awake. When I asked Kevin, he shrugged. There was nothing official until the evening.

I nodded and lay listening to his heartbeat. I knew I needed to get up and put something on. If his mom came in and found us both without clothes on, I knew it would cause quite a commotion.

I finally tore myself away from my spot on his chest and told him we needed to get dressed again. He looked at me unconcerned. I could see he really didn't want to, but he knew we needed to. He sat up on the side of the bed, "Hang on, don't put your clothes on except your panties." I looked at him oddly. He got up and I could see his butt shining brightly, in the darkened room. I began to giggle, and he turned and whispered, "What?"

"You have one white butt, boy! I'm just sayin' I had no clue how white you were!" I giggled.

Turning around, Kevin smiled, "Sweetheart, you glow just as brightly as I do. Your summer tan is gone, and you look like a china doll." I glanced down and realized that he was actually right. He was standing at his dresser and he threw something at me. I held it up and saw it was one of his old practice jerseys from football. I slipped it over my head and saw how big it was on me. I watched as he slipped on some gym shorts and another t-shirt and then he pulled his regular bed covers back and we climbed in between the sheets and I snuggled up beside him. "There, I think even my mom will say that we are properly clothed."

Smiling at him I countered, "That is if she doesn't see that all I have on under this jersey is a pair of blue panties!"

Kevin leaned over and for the first time since I'd gotten there, I saw an almost normal smile on his face, "And they are extremely, pretty, blue panties too, by the way!"

Then he kissed me with as much aching tenderness as he had before. The grin slipped away from both of our faces as we began to breathe life back into one another.

The kiss wasn't as long as the ones before because Kevin pulled away and looked at me, asking plaintively, "Why do you always come back to me, Lainey? I've hurt you so much and you still come back?"

I looked at him puzzled, for the first time, "I come back because I love you. I'll always love you, Kevin. No matter where life goes, you'll always be my first love. I'm always going to come back to you, as often as I can, until I can't anymore."

Looking at me intently, Kevin finally nodded his head and pulled me back to his chest. That is how we fell back asleep and how we both woke up within minutes of one another at 9 a.m. the next morning. I looked around when my eyes opened and saw the gray light pouring through the shades he had on his window.

I had hoped it wouldn't be gray and cold again, but it was still February. I knew that it would most likely stay this way, the whole time I was in Wichita Falls

I looked up at Kevin, from where I was still snuggled beside him and saw the yellow, blonde of his eyelashes, as they swept down on his cheeks.

I looked at the angular way his cheekbones were in his face and I saw the slight upturn of his nose. I was reminded of Donna's tiny, upturned nose when I looked at his. Within only a few minutes I saw his eyes begin to blink and he turned his head to look at me, "I thought maybe I'd dreamed you and you'd be gone when it got to be daylight."

Shaking my head, I hugged him to me tightly, "I'm right here, Kevin. I'm always right here. I promise." Kevin squeezed me back. We finally crawled out of the covers. I grabbed my jeans that, we'd thrown off the bed, the night before, and pulled them up. I figured I could walk out like that. Kevin grabbed a pair of his sweat pants and pulled them on over the gym shorts because the morning was a lot chillier than it had been in our cozy, warm bed.

"I'll go out first and see who all is out there. I don't even know who all has been here the last two days." Kevin stated, quietly.

"Why?" I asked curiously.

Kevin looked down at his feet, "Because I haven't left my room since we got home from the hospital, the morning she died."

I looked at him shocked. He'd been in this room for two, entire days. "Have you eaten anything in the last two days?"

Shaking his head, Kevin kept looking down. Finally, he said, "I'm gonna go see who all is out there. Don't think I'm some crazy person, Lainey. I just couldn't look at or talk to anyone. I feel like a part of me died two days ago. A part that was alive inside of me."

He continued, "I didn't know what life was even worth until you walked into my room yesterday and wrapped your arms around me. You brought me back, literally from the brink. You wouldn't believe all the crazy shit that's been in my head since we got home."

I flashed on to my own attempt to end my life, when he said, that and I admitted, "Trust me, I probably know more about the brink than you think."

Kevin nodded his head and then walked out of his room to go see who was in the house, when he came back he told me that it was just his mom and dad. I felt a little funny going out there because I felt like they could surely see in my face what had happened the night before.

Finally, I decided that they couldn't. There was too much other stuff going on to worry about me. Following Kevin out of his bedroom, he held his hand out behind him. I placed my tiny hand into his large one. I wasn't sure which one of us was the comforter and which one of us was being comforted. I just knew that I felt like I was right where I was supposed to be.

Chapter 26

That evening, I rode to the funeral home with the Strongs. My mama was going to meet us there. I had called Bailey when school got out, and she told me she was getting her mom to bring her to the funeral home.

Kevin and I didn't talk about what had happened the night before. We didn't really talk much at all through the day. We lay on his bed, and just held each other. When we did talk, it was brief, small snatches of conversation. Neither of us really knew what to say.

I had been too afraid to ask the Strong's if they were going to have Donna's casket open. I felt like it was too personal. When it was time, I put on one of the skirt and sweater outfits I'd packed. I didn't bother with makeup. I knew I'd cry it off.

We pulled up to the long brick building, and I felt myself get panicky suddenly. I began to wonder if I could walk inside, or if I would have to abandon Kevin and his parents. I was so terrified of seeing Donna dead, inside of her coffin. I finally took a deep breath, as I climbed out of the back seat, behind Kevin, and said a silent prayer for strength. I took Kevin's hand that he held out for me.

The funeral home was extremely quiet. There was no one else in the building. Suddenly, there was an older man, with gray hair, who walked out and approached the Strong's. I stood there, uncertain what was going on. I'd had so little exposure to funerals, so I wasn't sure what to think.

I listened as the man talked to Jean and Steve Strong about the family having time alone, before they would allow other friends and loved ones inside the visitation room. Kevin was still holding tightly to my hand. I felt as both of our hands began to sweat, as they were clasped together.

Walking towards a door, down a carpeted hallway, I realized that I was still walking and wasn't sure if I needed to stand outside while the family had time alone. Kevin felt my step begin to lag behind his, and turned to me. I could see the stark pain, but also the question in his eyes. "What's wrong, Lainey?" Kevin whispered.

"I guess I need to wait for you out here," I stated quietly.

Shaking his head Kevin declared, "No, you go in too."

When I protested and said that the man had said that this was alone time for the family Kevin stated firmly, "You are part of her family, Lainey. She loved you. She told me that you were her sister, even if not for real." Stunned, I looked at Kevin as my eyes filled with the first tears of the evening. I bowed my head and followed Kevin as he led me into the room behind his mom and dad.

When we walked in, I saw so many flowers around the room. I could smell the sweet fragrance of them. Then I spied the tiny, white casket, at the center of the room, towards the far wall. I saw the top was raised and knew that it meant I was going to see Donna inside. I felt Kevin's hand begin to grip mine harder than it had been. I told myself that I had to keep it together for him. I had promised Donna.

Kevin pulled me down, on a couch that was sitting to the side of the coffin. His mom and dad were up there crying and looking down at the small girl they had saved when she'd been just a baby. I tried to listen as I heard their voices murmuring by the casket, but I couldn't make out any words.

I wondered what was going on in Kevin's mind, and realized he was staring straight ahead. I wondered if he was seeing the casket, or his parents, or if he was seeing anything that was actually in front of us. Was he simply staring ahead, remembering how his sister's laugh could make his heart flip upside down. How her sweet spirit could make even the gloomiest of moods disappear, even if you only sat with her for a few minutes.

His parents went to sit on one of the sofas on the other side of the room. Kevin continued to sit there. Finally, he slowly stood up. I was uncertain what it was I needed to do. I didn't know if Kevin wanted to look at her alone, or if he wanted me with him. He held his hand out to me, answering my unasked question. I took it and stood beside him. I'd never really looked intently at someone who was dead before. I had gone to my grandpa's funeral several years before, but I'd never really known him. There was nothing like this for the family, that I'd been a part of, and the funeral hadn't had an open casket.

Slowly, Kevin and I approached the unbelievably, small coffin and I tried to remember to breathe. I was holding my breath as we stood in front of it finally, clasping one another's hands. Looking down, inside the satin lined, white box was the tiny body of the little girl who was the brightest and purest person I'd ever known in my life. She would always remain that way in my heart. She was trapped inside a body that had failed her since birth, but she'd somehow known without ever letting on that she knew, it was only a temporary state for her.

Her soul knew that it would only be here for a little while. It would bless everyone it touched with her warmth, and love, before it moved back to Heaven, where it surely must belong.

Lying inside the beautiful, satin material was Donna, dressed in a sweet eyelet, white dress, with a dark blue, satin bow. She had a matching, blue, satin bow wound over the top of her beautiful, blonde hair. The same shade as her brother's hair. I knew that under the eyelids, that would never open again, were the same color of blue eyes as her beloved brother. Her tiny hands, that used to clap when she was excited, now lay stilled upon her stomach, forever silenced. I felt as the tears began to fall from my own eyes.

I noticed wrapped within each arm was a stuffed animal. In her right arm she was holding tightly to her bunny Floppy. He had gone to every doctor and hospital visit. The bunny that she'd loved enough to make real, just as the bunny in her favorite book, The Velveteen Rabbit had done.

In her left arm, held close to her, was a little dolphin, with the words Corpus Christi stitched on it. I felt my breath hitch a little when I saw the dolphin. I'd brought it to her after the first summer when she was in my life. She'd named the dolphin, DeLaine because she wanted to be able to hug me whenever she wanted to.

Looking into the sweet face that would never smile at me again, I was happy to see that her sweet features looked as if she were sleeping peacefully. I didn't want to remember her sick. I'd been afraid that looking at her dead, would make me remember her only in the state she was now, but I realized even in death, she was still a light filled angel, to me.

Kevin reached around me and pulled me close to him. I wrapped my arms around him tightly, as I tried to comfort him. I felt as if he were again the comforter more than being comforted. I reached out tentatively, with my right hand, and stroked each stuffed animal, one last time. I wanted to touch them one more time, as if by touching them, it would imprint into the very cells of my body, the sweet little girl who would hold them for all of eternity.

I wanted to feel something of the warm, little soul, who had loved me. She'd shown me about pure, unconditional love. She'd never cared who I was, or what I could do for her. She didn't care who my family was, or what they did to me. She just knew how she felt about me. That's all that was important to her. Maybe, the one exception to that was she'd known how her brother felt, even when he and I didn't.

I knew I'd never be the same after looking at the sweet angel, who looked to be peaceful, and free of pain, at long last. I wondered if I was the only one who thought that, as they looked at her. Her parents and Kevin had loved her much longer than I had. She'd been their daughter and sister. She'd been the first person Kevin had ever loved and been loved by. She was the reason that he was finally free of the birth mother who was too sick to be a parent to them. Donna was also the reason that Kevin truly had for living. I was now so afraid for Kevin. With me gone, I knew that there would be no one for him to love or protect.

After a long time of us sitting in there with her, the funeral director came in and talked softly with the Strong's. Kevin and I turned to look in their direction. I noticed each one of their parents nodded and then walked back over beside me and Kevin. His dad whispered softly that it was almost time to begin. We had just a few more minutes, by ourselves, with her.

Jean Strong sat beside me, on the opposite side of Kevin, and said quietly, "You know, DeLaine, she loved you so much. Thank you for taking the time to be her friend, and to love her too. You've been a part of our family from the minute you first came to us. Donna's falling in love with you helped us to know and realize how important you were to all of us." I smiled weakly, as my eyes began swimming in tears. She leaned over and kissed me softly on my forehead. She got up and walked back to the sofa where she'd been sitting with her husband, leaving Kevin and I alone for the last time of that evening.

Kevin pulled me tightly to him one more time and whispered in my ear, "Thank you for being here for me, Lainey. I don't know how I'd be getting through this if you weren't here right now." I squeezed him back tightly around his middle, unsure if I could even talk without breaking into full out sobs. The boy who I loved with my entire heart, kissed me softly on my forehead, where his mom had just done the same thing. After a few minutes, the funeral director came in and opened the large, heavy, wood doors into the small sitting room, where four people sat, shattered by the loss of a little girl. She lay just a few feet from us, forever frozen in time, inside a tiny, white coffin.

Chapter 27

Bailey and my mama were the first people through the door, as soon as it was opened. They both walked up to the white casket. I saw my mama wrap her arm around Bailey's shoulders when she began crying. I was touched to see my mom do that. I knew that no matter what her problems, my mama truly was a loving person. She just had this other side to her that I didn't want anyone else to know.

They both finally came to the sofa I was sitting on beside Kevin. They sat on my side to whisper quietly with me. Mama asked if I'd slept good. I nodded while she told me about how she and Mrs. Strong had found Kevin and me sound asleep, the evening before, and decided to leave us. I smiled faintly as I remembered how we'd both woken up at midnight, and what we had done. Mama told me that it was okay for me to keep staying with the Strong family, until we left Sunday morning. I began to wonder where I would sleep tonight, at their house. I didn't think that I would be allowed to sleep with Kevin again. I couldn't imagine sleeping in Donna's sweet, little girl, pink room either. I hoped that I could sleep on the couch. If they offered me Donna's room, I'd probably fall apart.

Bailey hugged me tight after our whispered conversation with my mom. Seeing her beautiful, teal eyes red from crying, made me ache. She asked if I could come to her house the next day for a little bit. I told her it depended on when the funeral was and what was happening. I didn't know what was supposed to happen before, or after the funeral, now that I was old enough to pay attention and be involved in the mourning process. Bailey bobbed her head and told me that it was okay, because she would be at the funeral too. I watched as others began to slowly fill the room.

I sat with Kevin, my mom and Bailey, through the entire visitation. I watched as people I didn't know came wandering in and out of the visitation room. I heard some small pieces of conversation from all of them. I realized Donna had touched so many others, as she'd touched me. Many of the people were from their church and everyone who talked with the Strongs also came and spoke quietly to Kevin. Everyone knew their story about the early years of their lives, so they all knew that Kevin was hurting probably more so than even their parents were.

After a couple of hours, the last of the visitors were out of the room, except for Bailey and my mama. The gray-haired man came back in, and quietly told all of us that he could give everyone a little more time with Donna, before he needed to leave. I felt Kevin's hand creep back into mine, and I felt Bailey's hand do the same thing, on the other side.

I knew that we would have to go say goodbye one more time. I dreaded it but knew I had made a promise. After watching Jean and Steve Strong go to the tiny coffin, one last time, I watched as they walked away, with Jean crying and Steve walking strongly beside her. They stopped in front of the sofa. Mr. Strong looked down at Kevin and told him they would leave him in there as long as he liked. I watched as Kevin's blonde head bobbed, wordlessly.

My mama stood up to walk out of the room with Kevin's parents. I stood when he did, as did Bailey on my other side. We three walked up to the diminutive, white casket and I looked down at the sleeping angel that was lying within it.

I knew I would never forget Donna. She would live inside of me forever, as she would live inside of Kevin, and even Bailey. She touched every heart she met, and her spirit would live through us.

I glanced over at Kevin's face, and watched as he silently let the crystal-like tears fall from his blonde eyelashes. I wanted to reach up and wipe the tears from his face. I wanted to wipe the pain from his heart, but I knew I would never wipe this pain from his life. I felt Bailey lean over and kiss me on the cheek, on my right side, as she let go of my hand. I was able now to wrap that hand around Kevin's stomach, and rested my head on his chest, as my own tears flowed from my eyes.

I didn't know how long we stood there, looking at the sweet girl in the eyelet dress, with blue satin ribbons. Kevin finally reached his free hand up and wiped the tears from his face. Then he pulled away from me and leaned over the coffin, kissing Donna's golden hair, near the blue ribbon and whispered that he loved her. When he dropped my hand to lean over her, I was able to reach up and wipe my own tear streaked face.

After Kevin stood back up straight, he wrapped his arm around my shoulder and we turned to walk back out of the flower filled room. I didn't speak and neither did Kevin. I stopped before we got all the way to the door and Kevin looked down at me. "I need to say goodbye alone for a minute," I whispered. Kevin looked at me curiously, then nodded his head, removing his arm and walked out of the room alone.

Walking back to the casket, for the third and final time, I felt myself quaking a little on the inside. I had felt Kevin's strength flowing through me, when we had walked up to it together.

Now here I was approaching the tiny body inside, all alone. As I reached the side of the casket, I felt all the fear and quaking pass, as I peered at the angelic, heart shaped face of Kevin's little sister. I stood there for a few moments just drinking in the sight of her.

Leaning over until my face was just inches from her ear, I whispered, "I promise, I will love him always, Donna. I'll love you always too. Please keep an eye on both of us, Little One!" I felt as one of my tears dropped from my face next to her on the white satin pillow. I looked at the small wet drop as it seeped into the material and remembered how the bunny in The Velveteen Rabbit had cried a real tear at the end of the story. I smiled at the seemingly sleeping, little beauty and whispered for the last time, "I love you." I kissed her at the same place Kevin had, near the blue, satin, hair ribbon, stood up and turned to walk out of the room.

As I turned out of the room, I was surprised to find Kevin standing there, dry eyed and waiting patiently on me. When he saw me, he reached out his long, graceful fingers. I loosely put mine with his. We walked toward the exit, where we found my mama, and his mom and dad, waiting for us. Bailey was already gone. When we reached our parents, they told us we were going to dinner. Kevin and I both just bowed our heads in agreement. I wasn't really hungry, and wasn't sure about Kevin, but I knew that it was something we needed to do for his parents. Even my mom, I noticed, appeared somewhat shaken up. I was just grateful she was not drinking while we were here.

I rode back to Kevin's house, with his parents, while my mom went back to her friend's house. The funeral was the next day at 3 o'clock. I was grateful for the quiet of the ride back, because the stilted conversation in the restaurant was more draining than the silence. As we walked into the house, I wondered where I was supposed to go. I knew it would be alright for me and Kevin to spend the evening in his room, but I wondered where his parents wanted me to sleep, when it was time to go to bed.

We walked into his room quietly. I kicked off my wedge shoes and sat on Kevin's bed gingerly. I could still feel what we'd done the night before. I felt my cheeks begin to burn with a blush as I thought about it.

I told Kevin I needed to put some pants on, since I was wearing a skirt. I reached over into the small suitcase on the floor, near his bed and pulled out my jeans and a t-shirt. Once I had them, I stood up and walked into his bathroom, putting on more comfortable attire I was used to.

When I walked back into Kevin's room, I noticed he had changed out of the dress slacks and the long sleeved, dress shirt that I had been shocked to see him wear.

I had never seen him wear anything except jeans and t-shirts, as well as his football jersey. He looked more like his normal self. I smiled a small, ghost of a smile and he returned it. He shoved his pillows against the wall and flopped onto the bed, holding out his arm to me to come lay beside him. I happily slipped onto the bed beside him and cuddled into his warmth. We didn't talk for a long time.

I finally asked him where I was going to sleep. He looked down at me, asking what I meant. "I can't sleep in here again," I replied, softly.

"Why not, Lainey?" Kevin asked, sounding almost terrified.

Looking at his face, I saw the frightened little boy that he must have been, when he first entered the Strong's life. "Well, I mean, I just assumed that I would need to sleep somewhere else tonight, since they let me sleep in here last night, when we fell asleep."

Kevin shook his head vehemently, "No, you sleep with me. Unless you don't want to."

Shaking my head, I assured him, "I want to, I just didn't think it would be…I guess, I didn't think your parents would want us to sleep in the same room is all."

"DeLaine, you slept in here last night. They aren't going to make you sleep somewhere else because they are awake when we go to sleep, tonight." Kevin explained.

I didn't think my mama would be too thrilled to know I slept in here again, but I didn't want to sleep anywhere else. I listened to Kevin's heart steadily beat. How could I leave him, in less than two days, to go on without Donna? How could I leave him without staying behind for him? I sighed deeply, and realized he was absently twisting his finger in the soft, dark brown curls on my head. After a few minutes there was a soft tapping on his door and Kevin called out "Come in."

Jean Strong stuck her head into the room and smiled wearily at me and Kevin, as we continued to lay on his bed. "DeLaine, sweetheart, if you want to sleep in here, it is okay. If you don't I can make up the couch in the family room."

Before I could reply, Kevin stated, "She's staying with me, Mom." Mrs. Strong nodded her head told us she was going to bed and would see us in the morning. We told her goodnight and she was gone within a few seconds. Kevin smiled at me in the sad way he had taken to smiling, since the night before, "See, Lainey, I knew she'd be okay with you being in here with me."

I looked at him for a minute, then worried aloud, "I'm glad. I just hope she doesn't tell my mom. My mama might be alright with last night, but she'd probably be pissed if she knew I was staying in here again."

"Don't worry, Little Lainey. Mom won't say anything to your mama." Kevin assured me. I lay my head against his chest again.

"Well, if that's the case, I'm going to go put my pajamas on, and brush my teeth," I sighed, after a while. I grabbed my pajamas and went back into his bathroom to change again, for the third time that evening.

I came out to find Kevin had already gotten under the covers and had turned off the overhead light in his room. "Leave the bathroom light on," he whispered softly. "Just pull the door to." I pulled the door to, where the bathroom light was peeking out around the edges, as it had done the night before. I climbed into the bed, beside him. He raised the covers up to allow me to slip in.

Lying there, I wondered if Kevin would want to have sex again and breathed a sigh of relief when he told me he was tired and wanted to sleep. I looked up at his face that was in the shadows of the bathroom light that leaked out into his room. Kevin leaned his face down to mine and kissed me with the ache that I'd felt the night before. He pulled away much sooner though. He moved his head around on the pillows he'd pulled back down for us to lie on. It seemed no time at all, and I could feel the steady rise and fall of his chest, as he found his way into his own world of sleep.

I found I was having a lot more trouble falling to sleep. Each time I closed my eyes, all I could see was Donna lying inside of the small, white coffin, in her little white dress with blue ribbons. I felt my throat swell with unshed tears. I lay there next to a sleeping Kevin, listening to his sweet breathing and the steady beat of his heart. I wished that I could live here forever. I didn't want to go back to Corpus Christi. I wanted to stay with Kevin for good. I thought wildly about what my parents would say if I said I didn't want to leave. I wondered if I told Kevin I wanted to marry him and stay with him always, what his reaction would be. I smiled ruefully into the darkened room. I knew it was as ridiculous as it sounded, even inside of my head.

Finally, after what seemed forever, I felt my eyes as they began to grow heavy. When I found myself finally falling asleep, I was standing in the yellow flowers of my dreams. The only difference this time was, I saw Donna standing out away from me, in the yellow flowers, as they blew around her delicately in a light breeze. I was surprised to see her standing! She didn't seem to hurt any longer, as she stood straight, for the first time ever, before me.

I heard the tinkling sound of her laugh and she smiled her infectious grin at me, as she began to run through the ever-expanding field of yellow flowers. I watched, as the sunshine that was setting over my shoulder, lit her from afar and made her seem to glow. She laughed and ran like the free, little spirit she was now.

I felt an ache of sadness as she ran further away from me, but I also smiled, knowing that she was free for the first time ever.

***

The next day, I went to Bailey's for a brief time, before the funeral. We would have a car come pick us up at 2 o'clock to take us to the Strong's church, then out to the cemetery.

I was happy to go spend an hour with Bailey, away from Kevin's house, even though I felt a little guilty about that. It was so sad there, and it hurt to watch Kevin as he mourned the little sister who'd been his entire world.

When I got ready to leave, Bailey told me that she and her mom would be at the church. If she didn't talk to me afterward, she would call me the next morning, before I left. I hugged my best friend close to me and she suggested I see if my mom would let me come see her for Spring Break in March. I nodded and then I found myself at a dead run, as I went down Granville Street to Kevin's house. I wanted to run myself silly, so I wouldn't have too much time alone, to begin to think about how sad I was.

We arrived at the church at 2:20, and we sat in the front, in the first pew closest to Donna's casket. I was surprised to see it was opened again.

None of us walked down to the front though, when we got there. I watched as the church pews began to fill up. I glanced over my shoulder and wondered if Geoffrey would come, or if he even knew. I didn't know why I hadn't thought to ask Kevin about whether he was going to be there.

Once the pastor finished the funeral, I watched as everyone in the congregation began to walk, one row at a time, down to the front, to peer inside the small coffin.

Afterwards, each person came by and talked briefly to the Strong's. I felt as if I didn't belong in the front pew with Kevin and his family but decided that I was supposed to be wherever Kevin was. When the last person was out of the church, we were ushered out to the waiting black car, to carry us to the cemetery.

I was happy that the sun had decided to shine when we pulled into the cemetery. There was a large, green canopy set up with a lot of folding chairs underneath. Seeing the sun peeking through the dark tinted windows, I was reminded of my dream, seeing Donna run through the field of yellow flowers. I thought about how I'd heard her silvery laugh as it grew further away from me.

I hadn't told Kevin about my dream. He knew about the dreams I'd had before, about the field of yellow flowers. I didn't feel like I was supposed to share with him about Donna coming to me, in my dreams, the night before. It was as if she was telling me goodbye, and that she was okay finally.

When we finished, we were driven back to the Strong's home. I was grateful that family had requested some private time to mourn. I knew that there were a lot of times when people normally gathered for a meal or time to remember the one who'd passed away, but the night before had been the time for the family to say their goodbyes.

I just wanted to lie down and sleep when we entered the quiet home. The loss of one tiny girl was so much larger than it would seem to be possible.

***

That night when I put on my pajamas and climbed into Kevin's bed, I was surprised when he began to kiss me as soon as I got under the covers. It was almost as if he was trying to kiss away his pain, I thought, the longer he kissed me. I could feel an almost palpable ache between the two of us, in the way our mouths came together. I let him kiss me though. I wanted to offer him some way to find solace. I didn't know what else to do for him.

When Kevin began to undo the buttons on the front of my pajamas, I let him.

When he slipped his hands at the waist band of the pajama bottoms, I let him tug them off.

Finally, I lay under him, in the dark room, without my clothes on, for the second time within a span of 48 hours.

I wanted to feel him close to me. I wanted to offer him the warmth of my body and soul, in the only way I knew how.

I pulled at the t-shirt he had on. He pulled it over his head, without any question. I ran my hand down the muscular back that I was beginning to know intimately, in every hill and valley.

We were joined together much sooner this time than we had taken the first night. It still hurt when it happened, but I didn't care. I was willing to have physical pain, if it meant that Kevin wouldn't have physical or emotional anguish.

If I could have done anything in the world, to erase the monumental torment he was in, I would have done it gladly.

We both lay cuddled against the other, without jumping up to get dressed that night. We knew no one would be coming in to check on us. His parents were in bed. There was no one else to worry about in the house.

I loved feeling the sensation of Kevin's skin against my own. I was sad that this was the last night I'd be with Kevin, for who knew how long. I hoped that my mom would let me come see Bailey at Spring break, but I knew I wouldn't get the chance to lie with Kevin, as I was doing this time. I tried to memorize everything there was to know about his young body, even when my eyes were so heavy they were literally screaming to be closed.

Long after Kevin's eyes had taken him to his own dreams, I lay with my cheek on his chest, listening to his heartbeat. I realized that neither of us had gotten dressed yet, and I didn't want to wake Kevin up, so I lay there instead, gliding my hand up and down his body, memorizing the feel of his skin. Finally, when I could no longer keep my eyes open, I drifted off into a dreamless state too.

***

The next morning, I knew my mama would be coming to Kevin's house by 9 o'clock, to pick me up and Bailey's call at 7, was the wakeup call we both needed, to get us out of bed and throwing on our clothes, quickly. I told my best friend that I was glad I'd gotten to see her, even if it hadn't been a very long visit. She told me to write her and let her know what Mama said about getting to come see her. I told her I would, and we hung up.

Before my mama got there, Jean Strong asked me to go into Donna's room with her. I followed her hesitantly. I hadn't been inside of the pink and white bedroom. It felt completely empty and devoid of any life any longer, now that its owner no longer lived. I felt the ache in my heart grow even more when I realized there was no place I could feel Donna's presence any longer. I wondered what they would do with her room now that she was gone.

Mrs. Strong walked over to Donna's bed, leaned over and picked up the small, white, angel bear I'd given her when I'd left before. I told Donna it was an angel to watch over her, until I could be with her. She'd been so happy when I'd given it to her.

Turning to me, Jean Strong's tear-filled eyes shone as she looked at the white bear. Finally, she looked at me with such a look of sorrow, I wasn't certain I could continue to stay in the room with her. Smiling, she told me that Donna had loved that bear so much. She had told her mama to give me the bear back, so I'd have an angel to watch over me, when she was gone.

I gazed at the little white bear and felt the tears come flooding out of my eyes. I took it from Mrs. Strong's hands, and felt bereft all over again. I looked at Jean Strong and asked, "So she knew she was going?"

Mrs. Strong nodded her head, "Yes, she knew it was only a little while more to suffer and she'd be back with Jesus. She wasn't frightened. She was only sad to leave Kevin…and you. I know I thanked you before, but I wanted to talk to you alone, before you left, and tell you again how much I appreciate your loving both of my kids. I might not have given birth to either of them, but they are my children and I couldn't love either of them any more if they'd been from my own body."

I nodded silently as Jean Strong grabbed me to her, in one of her warm embraces. I found myself breaking down into sobs as Kevin's mom held me close. She shed more tears with me as well. I squeezed the white, angel bear in my hand.

When Mama got there a couple of hours later, I'd already showered and put on my clothes. I clung to Kevin as long as I could, while we waited for Mama. I was so afraid of letting go of him, once she got there, and I had to leave.

We stood beside my mama's car, holding one another for as long as was possible, until my mom told us gently that we had to leave. Kevin kissed me quickly on the forehead, and then brushed his lips softly on my own. I had quit being embarrassed, in front of my mama, about Kevin's kissing me. He turned and went into the house quickly. Mrs. Strong came over, after she told my mom goodbye, hugged me and told me she loved me once more.

I climbed into my mom's car, and sat quietly in the passenger seat, all the way to our house in Corpus Christi. I knew I'd have to go back to school the next day and I didn't want to. I wanted to be over 400 miles away from my school in another town

.

Chapter 28

When I got to school the next day, Kelly Stubbs found me before our first class, asking where I'd been. I realized I'd never let her know I was going out of town. I told her what happened and she was shocked. I had tried to keep my crying down, since we'd driven up to our house, the night before. I apologized for missing the weekend with her and Robin.

Kelly knew all about Kevin and Donna. She told me how sorry she was to hear about it. She truly seemed to be concerned about me, the entire day. I made myself go through the motions, for the day and the week.

I hadn't looked forward to a weekend like I had to that following one. I wanted to go get drunk or stoned or both. I wanted something that would take away the huge hole in the middle of me. I wanted to do it quickly.

My mom had begun drinking the very next day, after we'd gotten home. I was grateful that she'd held off on the big drunk binge, until Wednesday. I wanted an escape. I had been with Kevin the weekend before. When Saturday night rolled around, and Chance Cahill approached me to go ride around, I told him I didn't really feel that great.

Later when I saw him leaving with another girl, I felt even worse. I wanted him to care a little more than he did. I began to realize that I didn't mean anything to him, even though I wanted to. I wanted him to act like Kevin and be protective. Instead, he just acted like he could trade me out with any other girl.

By the time I went home that night, I was grateful to be so drunk that the ache in my heart was finally a lot duller. Of course, the hurt I felt at feeling used by Chance also played on the highly, emotional roller coaster I was cruising as well. I just wanted all the hurt from everyone and everything to go away.

Thankfully, my mama had agreed to the trip up for Spring Break. I was ecstatic. I would catch a bus at 6 a.m. Saturday morning, after we got out and wouldn't get into Wichita Falls until around midnight.

Then I would have to leave the next weekend the same way, so I really wasn't getting a chance to have a real weekend, but I'd have all the rest of the week with Bailey, which I was still ecstatic about.

The night I got to Wichita Falls, for our Spring Break of 1982, I was literally chomping on the bit to know how Kevin was and to see my best friend. I still felt a little guilty that I was doing so many things in my new home town that I'd never have done if I were going to Samson High.

I was going to finally confess all to Bailey, and maybe even Kevin. I knew for sure I wanted to talk to Bailey. I knew she'd be more forgiving of something like this.

Kevin sometimes held me to a much higher standard than other girls, even though I didn't know why. I would wait to see how he was before I made any confessions to him.

Bailey was waiting anxiously for me. As soon as I got off the bus, I ran up and grabbed her in a tight hug. I was surprised to see Jason had come to the bus station to pick me up. I figured that he'd have the music so high, we couldn't talk. Thankfully, for the first time ever, he didn't turn his stereo up! Bailey and I talked non-stop, the whole ride home, even though we didn't talk about any of the important stuff. I knew we'd talk about it more when we got to her room.

Once we unloaded my bag, gotten drinks and chocolate donut holes, we were safely ensconced in her room. I was ready to know what all was happening, that she hadn't written to me. I had noticed that she never once mentioned Kevin, in any letters, for almost a month. It made me wonder, the last couple of weeks, what was going on with him. Bailey knew that he never wrote to me, and if she didn't tell me anything about him, then I'd never know.

"So, tell me what is going on with Kevin," I asked quietly, once we were sitting on her floor.

Bailey looked at me woefully, "Lala, I didn't want to write to you about Kevin. I think you need to go see him tomorrow, as soon as possible."

Startled that she would say that, I looked at her intently, "What is it Bay? Is he okay?"

Shaking her head, Bailey responded, "I don't know what to tell you. He was out of school for a week after you left. When he came back, he quit football and got into regular P.E. and then started hanging out in the smoking pit, at lunch."

I gazed at Bailey, wondering if my mouth was literally hanging open! Kevin had been so anti-drug, anti-weed, anti-smoking. "Is he smoking?" I asked, incredulously.

"No, but he's just been hanging out with a whole different crowd of people. It's just been so drastic," Bailey murmured softly, not even looking at me.

Now I truly was worried. It was one thing for me to be doing all the bad things. I was smoking cigarettes, pot and drinking myself stupid, almost every weekend. I had attempted suicide since I'd been gone. I was having some kind of twisted relationship with a boy, who had no problem making out with me, but didn't seem to want to make it public. I hated myself for everything that I was doing. I'd been so angry when I'd left.

When I went to Corpus, I had lost any hope of ever being with anyone like I cared for Kevin, but I didn't want to be all alone. I also hated the person my mom was, when she got drunk, which was at least 75% of the time. Getting drunk or stoned made me forget about all of it, even if for just a little while.

Kevin though wasn't the kind of person to quit doing the right things. He'd always been athletic, and into sports. He'd always taken care of his body. Even though he'd been drunk a few times, I didn't think he'd ever smoke pot. I knew that Donna's death would rock him to his core, but I found it hard to believe it would affect him this badly.

"So, is he smoking pot?" I finally stammered, looking intently as Bailey continued to keep her eyes from mine.

"Lala, I don't know for sure," Bailey whispered.

"Bay, your brother sells pot, surely you know if he is or isn't smoking it!" I spoke a little harshly.

Bailey looked at me with an incredibly pained expression and admitted, "Okay, yeah, he is. I didn't want to be the one to tell you!"

I sat there and looked at my hands. I rubbed the fibers of her carpet, back and forth, trying to soothe myself. Bailey had told me what I wanted to know. How could I be angry at him for doing something I was doing? I wanted to come clean with Bailey, right then, about everything I'd been doing. I was afraid she'd be so angry at me, that she'd tell me she didn't want me to stay. Finally, I whispered, "I'll go see him tomorrow." Bailey nodded her head. "Bay?" I asked suddenly.

"What?" she answered.

"I really want to talk to you about some stuff, but I'm worried you'll be angry at me," I spoke in a hushed voice.

"Lala, I love you. You can tell me anything, you know that," Bailey was looking at me intently.

Nodding my head, I whispered, "I know. Just not tonight. I'm tired, and I really want to go to bed." Bailey took a beat and then told me we could talk the next day. I got up and pulled out some shorts and a night shirt. I went into the hall bathroom to change my clothes. I wanted to believe that Bailey wouldn't be angry at me, but it seemed so much had changed, in just a little over a year.

My head swam when I thought about all the monumental changes, since we'd pulled out of the driveway of our house, the year before and left Wichita Falls. I felt frightened at the thought of losing one of the saner constants of my life, when I thought about Bailey abandoning me, for my behavior since I'd moved to Corpus Christi.

When I walked back into Bailey's bedroom, she had changed as well. I suddenly thought about Jax.

I hadn't seen him since the summer before. Bailey had told me a couple of times how he was, but it wasn't anything major. I wondered if I'd see him while I was in town too.

"So, what's Jax up to?" I asked quietly.

Bailey looked at me curiously, "Eh, I don't know. I mean, he still hangs out with Levi a little, but now that we're in Samson, he's got a lot more kicker friends from Bob White. He's gone with a couple of different girls, but he's not with anybody right now."

I felt a little weird when I thought about him dating different girls. I shrugged my shoulder. "Does he know I'm going to be here?" I asked.

"Actually, yea, 'cause Levi told him. Levi told me yesterday to tell you that Jax said he'd try to come over sometime this week. He's going to try to work for his uncle a few days but he's really trying to get ready for the rodeo that's this weekend." Bailey offered.

"There's a rodeo this weekend?" I asked.

Bailey looked at me and said, "Yea, it starts Wednesday night and it goes on through Saturday night. I thought maybe we could go one night, since it will be going on during the week too."

I thought about it, "Yeah, I think that sounds like a good idea!" Grinning at her, I wondered aloud if Jax was planning on riding in the rodeo this spring. Bailey bobbed her head and I felt a huge knot form in my stomach. I couldn't believe the thought of him riding those bulls still bothered me the way they did. "Well, first I'll go see Kevin tomorrow, and see what I can find out," I finally stated quietly, as I was climbing into Bailey's bed. She bowed her head, sorrowfully. Just the look on her face made me worry all the more about Kevin.

***

The next day, when we got home from church, Bailey and I changed into jeans and ate a quick lunch. She knew I was anxious to get to Kevin's, so she told me she was going to work on a book report she had so she didn't have to worry with anything else all week. I told her I'd be back later.

While walking down Granville, towards Fairfax, I noticed that there were a lot of signs of spring already. I saw some robins hopping in the front lawns of the homes I walked by. Some people had planted flowers in their beds with some coming up and even blooming. It was still a little cool, but not too badly. The sun was out and made it seem warmer than it actually was. I felt sad as I got closer to Fairfax.

I thought about all the times I'd walked this way in 7th grade and walked with Kevin or Bailey. I thought about how when I crossed Fairfax, I would take a right, instead of a left, to get to my house.

Then I corrected myself mentally.

It wasn't my house any longer. I wonder who slept in my room now. I wondered if the family used the fireplace, and if there was anyone who'd sat in front of it, and made out with a boyfriend since me, the year before, when I'd been going steady with Jax Garrett.

I wondered if the family that lived there now, was a happy family, like the Strong's and Rains' families. Sighing, I crossed Fairfax and turned left instead, to go to Kevin's home. I knew he'd be surprised probably to see me. I had thought about calling, but for some reason I wanted to surprise him.

When I rang the doorbell, Mrs. Strong opened it. When she saw me standing on her front porch, she smiled warmly. I could still see an air of sadness in the way she stood, that hadn't always been there, but her warm smile was beginning to make its way back into her features.

I stepped into the foyer and she pulled me into her tight embrace, and started laughing. "Oh sweet, DeLaine! I'm so happy to see you!" I stepped back and told her how happy I was to be there. "Does Kevin know you're home?" she asked me, suddenly, in a curious voice.

"Um, no, I rode a bus yesterday, for 18 hours, and got in last night at midnight. I wanted to surprise him," I told her, feeling a little foolish for just thinking I could show up, with no warning.

Mrs. Strong admitted, "Oh, he didn't say anything to me, so I was curious. He's in his room. You know the way, right?" She smiled at me lovingly. I smiled back at her and began to walk towards his room.

When I got to his bedroom door, I suddenly felt nervous. I knew what Bailey had told me. Now I was worried that he'd be angry at me for showing up out of the blue.

I knocked on his door a little hesitantly, then waited to hear him respond. When he didn't say anything, I knocked again and then heard him holler to come in. I slowly pushed the door open and there sprawled on his bed was the boy who could make my heart flip flop with just a certain smile…the boy I loved.

Kevin looked at me first, with a bit of a cross look, and then it began to change. I watched as a myriad of emotions flickered across his face. It went from joy to sorrow to shock and finally maybe not quite joy, but he looked a little happier than when I first pushed the door open, "Hey," I greeted him, softly.

"Lainey?!" Kevin questioned, in a breathless whisper.

"Whatcha doin'?" I asked, as if I had just walked over from Belfast, where I'd lived before I left Wichita Falls.

"What do you mean what am I doin'? What are YOU doing here?" Kevin was surprised.

I walked into the room smiling, "Well, I figured I'd come surprise you!"

"Jesus, Lainey, you shocked me!" Kevin stood from his bed and came walking across his room to sweep me up in his strong arms.

Taking in his clean scent, I felt at home, but still felt something was not right. I'd never felt the feeling I had at that moment, with Kevin. We'd always had an easy and natural rapport, but for some reason, it felt a little off. I thought it was just the surprise of seeing me, but I knew it was beyond that. After he hugged and kissed me lightly, he pulled me onto his bed. We lay across from one another on our sides, just drinking in the sight of each of us.

While I was looking at him, I noticed his smile looked a little strange. It wasn't his normal half smile that came easily, or even his hooded smile, which he wore in public. It was a little like a smile and a grimace combined. I kept staring at him, trying to pinpoint what exactly was wrong with him. He began to ask how long I'd be there and I told him. He told me how happy he was to see me.

Finally, I couldn't stand it any longer, "So, what's up with you, Kev?" Shaking his head, I gazed at him thoroughly.

"You sure you're okay?" I asked, tentatively.

"Yeah, why?" he asked me, frowning a little.

"Bailey said you quit football," I spoke quietly, holding one of his pillows under my arm, to cushion the one I was leaning on.

Nodding his head, he admitted, "Yeah, I figured she'd be telling you everything."

"So, why'd you quit?" I asked earnestly.

"I told you, I was thinking about quitting," he replied, defensively. "I just didn't see any point doing something I didn't like anymore. I quit liking football my freshman year. It wasn't any better this year. After losing Donna, I dunno, it just seemed a little stupid to do something I didn't like," he shrugged his shoulders.

I nodded my head, "What about the smoking pit?"

"Fuck! Why can't Bailey mind her own fucking business," Kevin spat, almost in a growl.

Alarmed, I looked at Kevin. He'd never said anything mean about Bailey, ever. "She told me because she knew I'd find out, and then she'd look bad for not telling me. She knows that you won't write to me, so I don't know what's happening, unless she tells me," I was quieter than I wanted to be.

"Yeah, but she needs to stay out of this shit," Kevin grumbled.

"Why because you're smoking pot now? Or because you've dumped all the people you were hanging out with, and started hanging out with potheads?" I demanded a little more heatedly.

Kevin looked at me defensively. I finally figured out what was wrong with the way he looked. His eyes were glassy. I thought he was at least a little stoned, even now. He looked down at the long graceful hand that was supporting him on the bed, and shrugged his shoulder up, as if he didn't want to talk about what I'd asked.

When he continued to sit there and not look up, I spoke his name quietly. Finally, he admitted, "Look, I'm just sick of all the bullshit, DeLaine! I thought I knew who my friends were. When Donna died nobody wanted anything to do with me. Then Geoffrey came down, the weekend after you left. I learned something about him that freaked me out and decided if Geoff could pull some kind of shit with me, then so could all those other assholes, who claim to be my friends, so fuck 'em all. I decided to change who I hung out with. At least with a pothead you know what they are. They can't hide their bullshit from you!"

I knew exactly what he was referring to. I guessed Geoffrey had finally come clean to him about being gay. Since he hadn't told Kevin until the weekend after Donna's funeral, I didn't know if I should act shocked, or if I should just own up to the fact that I'd known and hadn't told him. I finally decided that I didn't want to act like I didn't know, in case Geoff said something about coming out to me. Finally, I asked, "So, did Geoff tell you what's goin' on with him?"

Kevin looked at me wickedly. I didn't like the redness in his eyes, or the slight, maniacal grin that was spreading across his face. It wasn't a grin that I liked. It scared me. I wasn't used to that look on his beautiful features.

"Oh, what…that he's a faggot?" Kevin remarked, in, a hushed tone. I nodded my head and Kevin chuckled deep in his throat, "Oh yeah, he told me! Fucking Fag! I told him to leave and never come back!"

"WOW!" I let tumble out, without any thought.

"Yea, WOW! So what's his deal? Do you think he was in love with me, or some crazy shit? Is that why he was always so jealous of you?" Kevin asked me, still sounding angry.

I shrugged my shoulders. I suspected that was why Geoffrey was jealous of me. I thought that Kevin was right about it. "You didn't really tell him to never come back did you?"

Nodding his head Kevin declared, "Damn right I did! I told him to get the fuck out of my room! I'm not a fag, DeLaine! I don't want that sick bastard anywhere around me!"

I honestly felt a little shocked by his vehemence. I wondered what Geoffrey thought about that. He surely knew that Kevin's reaction wouldn't be well received. Especially not after losing the person he loved the most in the world. I felt so sad that Kevin seemed to have been hurting so much more than I realized.

"Kevin, I'm worried about you," I whispered.

Shaking his head, he sat up suddenly on his bed, "Don't, DeLaine! Just quit! I'm no good for anyone any longer. I'm just a pothead, piece of shit now!"

"Shut up, Kevin! Dammit! Don't talk about yourself like that!" I insisted, harshly.

"It's true," Kevin grumbled.

"No, it isn't dammit! You wanna know who is a piece of shit, Kevin? ME! That's who! I haven't been honest with you or Bailey! I started smoking and drinking after I moved to Corpus! I even smoke pot now too. I didn't want to tell you! I was afraid of what you'd think about me," I admitted, with an errant tear sliding down my right cheek.

Now sitting forward, closer to me, Kevin cried, "Oh Lainey! NO! Please, Darlin' tell me you're just messin' with me! Don't do this shit! You are so much better than that!"

I started laughing, almost maniacally myself, and shook my head, as I sat up across from him, "No, Kevin. I'm NOT better than that! My mom is a drunk! She knocks the shit out of me, and I don't want anyone to know. She's fine one minute, and then she isn't. I don't know who I am going to get each day after school! I'm not better. You are though. What the hell are you doing?" I finished, a little more quietly as I neared the end of my outburst.

We both sat upright, looking at one another, without saying a word. Finally, Kevin declared, "Lainey, I want you to quit! I also want you to find someone else down there. Forget about me. I'm not worth a shit for you, or anyone else anymore!"

I started laughing, "Are you serious, Kevin? You're telling me to get over you just like that and go find someone new?"

Kevin nodded his head.

I divulged, "Well, listen sweetheart, I haven't exactly been an angel in that department either! I've been messing around with a senior, for a couple of months, and I didn't tell you before, because I didn't want you to be upset any more than you already were!"

Kevin looked at me hard. I was worried. He'd never looked at me quite the way he was now, except when he'd gotten angry at Kevin Welks' house, when he'd taken my virginity. "What the fuck are you talking about, DeLaine?"

I was pissed at Kevin. He was letting Donna's death destroy him. I knew she'd be so upset with him. I wanted to get his attention. I thought that just admitting all the crap with the partying and my mom was enough, but now I had to bring up Chance Cahill.

"Jesus, Kevin. You told me you didn't want to know about any other guys in my life, so I kept my mouth shut. But you know what? I'm tired of you thinking I'm some kind of great person. Haven't you figured out how fucked up I am?"

When he didn't say anything, I told him, "His name is Chance Cahill."

"Have you slept with him?" Kevin asked, in a calm, quiet tone.

I jerked my gaze back to him after I let it drop to my hands. "What?"

"Have you fucked him?" he demanded.

"Are you kidding me, Kevin? Is everything about whether I've had sex with someone else?" I asked, somewhat indignantly.

"Well, yeah, I guess so, DeLaine! I didn't think you'd be with someone else like that, so quickly," Kevin had a slight edge to his voice.

"No, Kevin, I haven't fucked him! Does that make you feel better about all of it?" I was now feeling like this whole conversation was spinning wildly, and madly out of control. I didn't know how to jerk it back. I had been so excited to see him and now I sat across from him, trying to figure out who he was.

Kevin sat there for a few seconds before he looked at me and demanded, "Just leave, DeLaine! Just forget about me, okay?"

Standing up, I slipped my shoes back on. I got all the way to his bedroom door before I turned back to him and admitted, "First of all, Kevin, the only thing I've done with Chance is learn how to give a blow job! Second, you can't tell me how to feel or what to do about you or anyone else! Quit acting like you have some kind of control over me, and how I feel about you! I hope you snap yourself out of this shit you've gotten into. Just remember, you are still the same guy your little sister loved, but if you keep this up, you won't be. Think about how sad she'd be if she knew about that."

I glanced over at him for his reaction to my first revelation. I knew I'd struck a nerve by what I said, when I saw his features turn even stormier than they had gotten before I jumped off the bed. Then I watched him lower his gaze back to the bed. I wondered if he was going to say anything, or just let me walk out, maybe forever. I felt my heart aching, because this had all gone so horribly wrong.

Finally, Kevin ordered me quietly, "Just leave, DeLaine. Forget about me. And …don't ever use my sister like that again, to try to make me do what you want. Don't ever pull that shit on me again, do you understand?"

Gaping at him, dumbfounded, I turned the doorknob and cried, quietly, "I wasn't using your little sister, Kevin. I was speaking the truth. The only reason it pisses you off, that I brought up Donna in this whole argument, is because you know I'm right."

"I shouldn't have told you about Chance. I just wanted to hurt you with that. I'm sorry. But everything else I told you is the truth. I'm sorry I'm not the perfect DeLaine you thought I was. You have so much more than I do, Kevin. Don't screw that up because you hurt right now. I'll be at Bailey's until early Saturday morning. Then I won't be back until June or July. I don't want you to disappear from my life, Kevin. I never want you to go away from my life. But I can't pretend to be someone I'm not." I walked back out of the open door and slipped down the dark hallway. When I got to the end, I saw that Mrs. Strong wasn't out in the family room, or the kitchen. I wasn't sure where she was. I felt bad, but I slipped on out the front door, without waiting to see if she would come back out, so I could say goodbye. I wanted to leave as fast as I could.

After I got back to Bailey's, I knew she'd want to know what had happened. I just couldn't stand the thought of talking about all of it but knew that I needed to tell her about what I was now. I wasn't worthy of Kevin, or to have Bailey as my best friend, either. I was turning into a pothead myself. I just didn't want to feel anything anymore.

When I walked back into her room, Bailey looked at me curiously. When she saw my tear streaked face, she closed the notebook she'd been writing in, and put her stuff on the floor, beside her bed. She knew that it must have been bad because she jumped up and pulled me to her. I began to cry in great big sobs.

Finally, when I was no longer sobbing, and my air was coming out in small hiccups, Bailey sat on the floor and pulled me down beside her. She had me tell her what had happened.

I took a deep breath and finally admitted. "Bay, I have to tell you about some stuff first. Then you can make the decision about whether you even care about what happened or not."

She smiled at me reassuringly, and I began to tell her about all the bad things that had been going on with my mom, and then about the drinking and smoking. I figured that she'd be horrified about that. When she never seemed to blink, I decided to go ahead and tell her everything, so I told her about Chance Cahill. When she still didn't respond the way I thought she would, I wondered why she was not even the least bit upset with me.

"Lala, we're in high school now. I've been drinking a lot more and I tried pot when I was in 6th grade, the first time. Jason thought I wouldn't do it, and you know me, I had to prove to him I was bad-assed! I've even smoked it a couple times this year, but only because Levi wanted to try it, so I told him I'd try it too. I didn't tell him I tried it in 6th grade, though. Honestly, I think almost everybody has been trying stuff since we got to Samson. I mean, there's a couple who haven't, but you know, we're all gonna be doing different stuff," Bailey admitted, softly.

I couldn't believe my best friend was telling me this. I didn't think that Levi, of all people, would ever smoke pot. I was dumbfounded. Looking at Bailey I cried, "Yeah, but you aren't doing it every weekend, like me, Bay!"

Bailey smiled gently at me, "DeLaine, it doesn't matter how often you do it, what I'm trying to tell you is that it doesn't mean you're a bad person, because you try stuff. As far as this Chance, the asshole goes, well, Lala, I'm just saying that you've already been hidden by one guy, for a long time. Don't let another one hide you, especially since he doesn't have a reason to, like it will piss Geoffrey off!"

Looking at Bailey's grin begin to widen, I realized she was right. I was letting a boy hide me, one more time, even though I'd insisted on it with Kevin. Chance was totally different, yet I thought that maybe I could care about him. We had fun when we were together. He was cute and funny, but he did tend to make me feel like crap when he swapped me out for someone else, like it didn't matter what girl he messed around with, as long as he was with someone!

Shaking my head, I sniffled, "Bay, I think everything is over with me and Kevin. I haven't even told you about what happened when I was here for Donna's funeral last month." I looked down at my hands and felt the tears come spilling out again.

"What do you mean, Lala?" Bailey asked me gently.

"Kevin and I did it when I was here…twice." I added the last in a whisper.

"Okay," Bailey replied evenly.

I couldn't understand how Bailey never acted too shocked about anything I ever revealed to her. "Aren't you shocked?"

Shaking her head, Bailey smiled wryly, "No, should I be?"

Thinking about it, I realized that she had been having sex with Levi for over a year. I had almost had sex with Jax, then Kevin had actually taken my virginity, during an argument. Now I just confessed to giving a boy a blow job, and I was worried if she found the fact that Kevin and I had finally had a more mutual, sex experience shocking. I thought I sounded slutty. I finally just shrugged my shoulders quickly, but I couldn't find my way to look at my friend's beautiful eyes.

"Lala, listen, you and Kevin have been complicated from the beginning. I know you love him, but I also know that you aren't going to live here again, until at least after we graduate." Bailey began. "But…I'm never going to judge you for anything that happens with you and Kevin. I'm also not going to judge you for anything you do in Corpus. You can't go back to your daddy and Clarice. I know that. Things aren't good with your mom."

Bailey continued, "I love you and you're my best friend. It doesn't matter. I don't know what else to tell you other than I'm always here for you."

I looked back at her again and felt the tears spill from my eyes. I reached over and hugged her to me tightly. "Bay, I don't know what I ever did to deserve you, but I'm sure glad you're in my life!"

Bailey hugged me back, "Me too, Lala!"

Chapter 29

Levi and Jax came over late in the afternoon the next day. I smiled when I saw my best friend's boyfriend. I ran up to him when he stepped out of the truck, and he swung me around in a big hug while I giggled and squealed. I looked into his icy blue eyes, and saw the glint of laughter lurking just beneath.

"Lala!" Levi Parker yelled, when he swung me around! "How the hell have you been??"

"I'd be doin' better, if a certain guy best friend would write me back sometimes!" I was giggling as I playfully punched his arm.

"Yeah, you know I don't like to write! I did write you once!" Levi replied, defensively.

"For my birthday! That was like six months ago!" I exclaimed, with a mock pout. I grabbed Levi's neck fiercely, "It's okay. I'll let you slide for now! Just 'cause I'm so excited to see you!"

I looked over at my ex-boyfriend, Jax Garrett and noticed how dirty and sweaty he appeared, as he grinned at me, a little shyly. Finally, I walked over and grabbed him around his neck. He smelled like horses, hay, sweat and sunshine. I felt my nose wrinkle a bit, but only because I hadn't expected to smell so many of the smells that he introduced to me, over a year before.

"Hey, Jax," I whispered into his ear.

"Hey, DeLaine," I heard back in mine. I pulled away and smiled at the other boy who had stolen my heart, in another lifetime. Kevin had won my heart completely, but I always felt a slight tug where Jax was concerned too.

"You guys comin' in?" Bailey asked, as the sunlight began to wane.

"Uh, no, I'm really nasty," Jax stated, with a grin.

Bailey walked a little closer then, and I thought I'd been the only one to smell him, until I saw her nose curl a little, "Jeez, Jax, you smell like horse-shit!"

Jax let out a loud laugh, and nodded his head, "Yes ma'am. That would be me! I've been working since 7 this mornin'!"

"Yeah, okay, I think we need to sit out here," Bailey declared, as she grinned at the three of us.

Jax walked over to his truck, and dropped the tailgate, so Bailey and I could sit on it while we talked, in the last of the day's sunshine.

"Hey, you guys wanna go do somethin' tomorrow night?" Jax asked, a little abruptly. I looked at him and then at Bailey. I was her guest. I didn't know what she had planned.

Bailey looked over at me and shrugged, "Yeah, sure. What do you wanna do?"

Jax kicked the asphalt, "I dunno. Let's see how late it is when I get off and get cleaned up. Then we can decide." Bailey, Levi and I all agreed. We sat outside with the boys until the sky was deepening into a dark purple. It was fun to sit there and just enjoy our old camaraderie.

Finally, Jax told Levi he had to go get cleaned up because he felt disgusting. After a few jokes about how gross he really was, my best friend and I jumped off of his tailgate. Both boys laughed when we wiped the dirt and hay off of our butts at the same time. I hugged Levi and Jax goodbye and we stood on Bailey's front yard, as they pulled away from the curb. I laughed as we walked up her porch steps and I could smell the barnyard smell on my own clothes, from hugging Jax.

***

The next evening, Levi called Bailey and told her that he and Jax would be over and thankfully he'd given us enough time to get somewhat ready. I felt a little weird about going out with Jax, but I'd done it before. I thought about Kevin, then I felt a small stab in my heart, as I remembered what had happened with us the day after I'd gotten to Wichita Falls this time around.

I was glad when my best friend came in, wanting to know which blouse I thought looked better on her. I didn't want to sit in her turquoise blue and lime green room dwelling on what had happened between me and Kevin. I knew that unless I kept my brain busy, it would inevitably slide back to Kevin.

After Jax and Levi came to pick us up, I wasn't surprised when Jax drove out to our spot by the lake. I felt like my spot was again secure as I slid into it, through the driver's door, next to Jax. I was happy that tonight he smelled like his normal leather and soap smell. There was no mistaking my old boyfriend for a cowboy.

When we got out to our spot, I was happy to see Jax backing up to the edge. I knew he'd put the tailgate down so we would all sit out there and talk.

As I climbed out behind him, on the driver's side, I was again reminded about how different it was when I rode around with Chance. His truck might have been in the same hue as Jax's, but he treated me so much differently. Jax always waited on me to climb in or out, on the driver's side.

It was something I'd done forever. Just like with Kevin, being around Jax was a sure sign to me that I was home.

The nights were still fairly cool, so I was happy to see Jax had thrown some old horse blankets in the back. We looked out over the water, and I was glad to see that the moon was full. With a full moon it made the place look like a silver blue dreamscape. I'd looked at the moon over the water, and marveled at the color, size and shape so many times in the last eighteen months.

Levi and Bailey eventually grabbed a blanket and made their way through some of the denser, brushy areas to go be together, without me and Jax. They usually did and it was a natural way for me and Jax to end up kissing, at some point, even when we weren't going together. Now I didn't have Kevin to worry about at all. He was through with me. He told me he didn't want me around him any longer. I felt the corners of my mouth begin to droop when I thought about it, and Jax noticed.

"What's up, DeLaine?" Jax asked, concerned.

I looked at him curiously, then caught the feel of my mouth and realized I'd been frowning. Shaking my head, I smiled quickly, "Nothin' Jax. Just thinking about how much I miss living here."

Jax nodded his head, "Yeah, I wish you were still here too. I'm glad I got to see you this time. I heard about Strong's little sister last month. I'm really sorry. I know how much you liked her."

I remembered that Jax's mom drove the bus for the special needs program that Donna had been involved with, at their church. I wondered if their mom was still as involved as she'd been, then chastised myself for thinking so stupidly, since she'd been gone just a little under a month. It felt like at least a year had gone by since I'd been safely in Wichita Falls, during Donna's funeral. Looking over at the other boy who'd made my heart, body and soul sing at one time, I smiled sadly. "Thanks," I whispered.

"I've really missed you, DeLaine," Jax stated, sweetly, as he moved in closer to me. "Are you seeing Strong while you're down?"

I shook my head sadly, "Uh, no. I went by and said hi to him and his mom the day after I got in, and you know, they're all still pretty torn up over losing her." I had forgotten for a minute that Jax knew about me seeing Kevin the same time as him the summer before, even though Kevin hadn't known about Jax.

I knew that Kevin's jealousy was more than Jax's. I enjoyed being around Jax too, and I knew that Kevin would only feel threatened, because he didn't like Jax. He had been so angry about me going with him during 8th grade, even though he had a girlfriend while I'd been Jax's girlfriend. To say that my relationship with Kevin was complicated, was an understatement. Then there was the twisted quality of my relationship with Jax.

I noticed that Jax was putting his hands on the tailgate, on either side of me, as he held himself up, with his arms locked straight out. I felt the quiet thrum of my heart that I'd been noticing since 6th grade, around Jax. I smiled at him and he asked, "Well, do you mind if I kiss you?" I shook my head and felt the sweetness of Jax's kiss on my sad mouth.

Even though I enjoyed Jax kissing me, I realized that I didn't feel the same way kissing him as I had the year before. I was too sad to feel much of anything. Jax noticed that I wasn't as into kissing him as I'd always been before. He pulled away from me and asked, "You okay?" I shook my head and looked down at his hand that was resting next to my hip. "What's wrong, DeLaine?" Jax asked me concerned.

"I'm just, well, I just get sad when I think about Donna," I admitted. It wasn't a lie. He'd been the one to bring her up and I was truly and desperately sad when I thought about her. That was one of the reasons I didn't want to think or feel every weekend. Now though, I was also sad thinking about Kevin too. I didn't want to admit that to Jax though.

Resting his forehead against mine, Jax smiled his own sad smile, "I'm sorry, DeLaine, I shouldn't have brought her up."

I shook my head no, "It's not you, Jax. I'm just sad when I think about her. I haven't been the same since she died. I'm the one who is sorry to be such a huge downer," I whispered. I was happy when he walked up next to the tailgate and pulled me against his chest and wrapped his arms around me. I reached inside of his jacket and wrapped my arms around him. I loved how he smelled, as much as I loved Kevin's clean scent, I realized. I'd never met anyone who smelled quite like Jax or Kevin.

I don't know how long we were like that, but finally Jax suggested, "Let's go sit inside the truck. It's getting kinda cold out here." I jumped down off of the tailgate, then hopped into his truck and leaned my head on his chest once we were sitting warmly inside. Except for kissing me a few more times, Jax held me for the rest of the time we sat there. We'd never been this quiet, for this long, the entire time we'd dated in 8th grade. Finally, after a while, Bailey and Levi came running up to the truck and jumped in, after throwing the horse blanket in the back of the truck.

Once we were on the way back to Bailey's, Levi leaned over and asked, "So, did Jax tell you about the rodeo on Thursday?"

I glanced at Jax and shook my head, as I looked at Levi sitting on the other side of Bailey. "Uh, no, we really didn't talk a lot."

"Oh, I see," Levi said wiggling his eyebrows at me. I told him he was wrong, and he giggled. "Well, you girls need to try to come to the rodeo on Thursday night. Jax is going to ride a bull again. This is what, like the third or fourth time now, Jax?" Levi asked curiously.

I whipped my head over to Jax, who pretended to ignore me. I knew he was pretending to ignore me, because I saw him swallow. "Really?" I asked sarcastically. "Gee, Levi, Jax forgot to tell me he'd ridden again since we went to the rodeo in 8th grade."

Levi laughed, "Oh God yeah, he rode once or twice this fall, and then there was last year during the spring rodeo too." I noticed as Jax jerked his head over to Levi. I'd been really angry at Jax about riding bulls in 8th grade. I noticed that Bailey had never said anything either. I knew Levi had probably just forgotten, because he never seemed to notice how some things affected me. Once Jax glared at him though, Levi began to try to back-peddle. "Um, well, you know, um, I think I'm gonna just shut up now,"

"So, tell me about this, Jax," I crooned, sweetly.

"I told you I was thinking about doing rodeo this year. I had to try out last year during the spring. I just forgot to tell you last summer. I rode two more times during the fall. Thursday, I ride again for Samson's rodeo team." Jax explained, as he drove us back.

I shook my head, "Well, cool, I guess. I just hope you'll be careful." Jax glanced at me a little warily at first, then I noticed him barely nod his head. I knew that being in the rodeo was who Jax was. He was a cowboy, in the truest sense of the word. It didn't really matter what I thought about it at all, I knew. What mattered was that he was careful.

"Thanks," was all Jax could mumble, as he pulled up in front of Bailey's house.

"So, you think we can go, Bay?" I asked quietly.

Bailey looked at me cautiously and told Jax he needed to take us, if he could. He grinned and told her he would, but we'd have to go out early with him. She told him we would, and he announced there was a dance after the rodeo too. She grinned, "Yay! Glenda will let us stay out 'til one then!"

I looked at Bailey, so she explained, "Oh yea, if it is a rodeo dance, she lets me stay out until one now." I was impressed. I was doing good getting to stay at the game room until 12:30, on weekends.

Sliding out behind Jax, I was grateful that he'd been so sweet with me all night. I still felt horrible about the way things had ended with Kevin, but, at the same time, I realized I was still extremely sad about Donna too. When I was standing beside Jax, after he slammed the truck door, I was happy he had decided to kiss me as soon as he closed it. I wound my wrists behind his neck, as he bent over to pull me closer to him. I knew Bailey and Levi were kissing on the other side of the truck. I felt myself smile on the inside, at the picture of the four of us all kissing our goodnights, just like we'd done so many times before.

Chapter 30

On Thursday, Bailey and I went to the mall with her mom. During lunch I was surprised when her mom asked, "So, DeLaine, are you going to go to California with us, this summer?" I looked at her oddly.

Bailey jumped in and announced, "Oh yeah, Jason's not going on vacation. I was gonna ask if you thought you might be able to go with us. Mom's already paid for everything, and since Jason's not going, they said I could ask you."

"Really?" I was surprised.

"Yeah!" my best friend smiled through her glittery braces. "I mean, if you think your daddy and Clarice will let you."

"I'll have to find out, but if I can, yeah, I'd like that a lot. I've always wanted to go to California. It's one of the states I've never been to," I smiled at Glenda Rains.

"Good, it's settled then!" Bailey's mom smiled at me sweetly. "You just let Bailey know." I nodded and could hardly wait to find out if I could go.

"When are you all going?" I suddenly thought.

"We'll be leaving towards the end of July and coming back August 22nd." Glenda said.

I couldn't believe they'd be gone almost a month! I'd never heard of anyone going on vacation that long. When they saw the look on my face, they began to laugh. "We're driving," Bailey giggled.

"Oh…I see," I replied, with light dawning in my eyes.

"Yes, we're driving. We're going to go through New Mexico to get to Arizona, to see the Grand Canyon first," Glenda explained. Then she told me how they were going to drive to Los Angeles and up to San Francisco to her cousin's house. Then they'd drive back down the coastline of California, to San Diego, then back through Las Vegas to Texas.

I was shocked they were planning to drive all those places, but I vaguely remembered some of my early childhood traveling with my parents, when they had their band. I hoped my daddy and Clarice wouldn't be pissed about letting me go. If Clarice knew it would upset me, she would do whatever she could to block it.

Since I lived with my mom now, most of my communication was done directly with just my daddy, or between my daddy and my mama.

In all honesty, I couldn't really remember the last time I'd talked to my daddy, since I'd been home from Christmas. I knew I'd talked to him at least once, but I couldn't even remember when, or how long ago.

That afternoon, we were ready when Jax told us to be. Bailey was letting me borrow her old cowboy boots. I'd brought a pair of jeans, but not my boots. I didn't even think about us going to a rodeo. I suppose if I'd known Jax was riding again, I'd have maybe thought about it. Then again, I'd been so focused on Kevin, that I honestly wasn't sure I'd have thought about getting to see Jax. Especially after what had happened between me and Kevin the month before.

Once we reached the rodeo grounds, Jax dropped us off at the gates, then he drove around to where the contestants could enter. He kissed me lightly when we got out, and I told him to be careful in case I didn't get to see him before he rode. He grinned at me and told me he was always careful. He'd been practicing for a while now, on a mechanical bull.

This rodeo was much busier than the one I'd gone to back in 8th grade. I guessed it was because it was the spring. Bailey and I couldn't even go over to where the contestants were waiting. We climbed into the stands and watched the rodeo along with everyone else. We'd have to see almost the entire rodeo before they got to the bulls, which Jax would be in the middle part of the contestants. They always let the contestants who were in the fourteen-year-old category ride first, and then after that, the high school kids took off. Since he was riding for Samson High School this time, he would be competing against not just his age group, but also the different schools with rodeo groups. It made the placement a little different.

While we watched, I had peppered Bailey with questions about all the other rides Jax had done. She told me that he had done okay, but he hadn't won another silver belt buckle since the one he'd won while we were going together. I flashed on the silver belt buckle, and I felt my cheeks flush as I remembered feeling Jax under that silver buckle, a time or two, during our make-out sessions.

Finally, Jax was up! I could feel myself getting more nervous the longer each second seemed to take, to open the chute. As soon as he was released, I held my breath! I knew eight seconds could feel like eight hours when someone you cared about was on the back of a bull.

As the bull came bellowing and bucking wildly, into the middle of the arena, I watched with a mixture of fear and fascination.

Jax looked so awesome in his leather chaps and his cowboy hat. He had his back bowed just right, and his hand was waving over his head.

When the buzzer sounded, after eight seconds, I felt myself grabbing Bailey! Both of us were screaming madly!

I was so excited that he had made the buzzer again! I knew it would put him into a class of possibilities to win another silver belt buckle. We both ran to the end of the stands and rushed down to get to the gate where the contestants came out after their event. I was so glad he'd made a clean drop off of the wildly thrashing beast and didn't get hurt!

When the gate came opening up, and Jax stepped through, I ran to him and he grabbed me in a tight hug. I was squealing with excitement, as he was babbling about how his standing was in the competition. The difference with being a fourteen-year-old and a high school student meant that he would not receive his buckle until the end of the rodeo. I thought he might even have to ride again, but I was happy I'd seen him ride this time!

"I'm so excited!" I giggled, as Jax swung me around a second time.

"I know! Me too!" Jax exclaimed loudly as he kissed me hard on the mouth. I felt giddy with the excitement. I couldn't believe I'd been so sad just a couple of days before, and now I was ecstatic.

A little while later, we were dancing in the huge, open arena area. I laughed as Jax tried to teach me how to two-step. He told me we couldn't just sway like we'd done at the skating rink, because the people at these dances actually were older, and knew how to dance for real. I was hopelessly left-footed, but I had fun being held by Jax. I loved smelling the combination of his leather and soap smell, along with the smell of his horse, Moon Boy, who he had ridden at the beginning, and the end of the rodeo. During the dance, I also got to say hi to his aunt and uncle, who were heavily involved with the rodeo community.

Around 11 o'clock, Levi came dancing over to the small corner where Jax was trying to teach me to dance. He asked if we were ready to leave. Jax smiled and nodded his head. We left the dance a good two hours before we had to be home. We all laughed and talked as we walked to the dark orange Ford in the gravel and dirt parking lot.

Once we got to the truck, Levi, Bailey and Jax all got a funny grin on their faces. Levi walked to the truck bed. He leaned over and turned around, handing an ice-cold beer to me, and Bailey, then he tossed one towards Jax, across the truck bed. I heard all three of them pop their pull tabs off before I even really registered exactly what I was holding. I could drink it without a problem now. I'd gotten used to drinking beer in Corpus, even though I honestly detested it. I was just surprised that Jax had the beer out at the rodeo.

I slowly pulled the tab off the can and took in a deep pull from the beer can. I still grimaced with the first can every time I took a drink, and usually got drunk quickly, because I tended to drink the first one as fast as I possibly could stand to, so I didn't taste it for long.

We all got into the pick-up truck and took off into the night, to go to our favorite spot at the lake. Even though I was the last one to get my beer, I was the first one to finish, by the time we got to the lake. All three were surprised, since I couldn't drink beer with them the year before, because it tickled my nose and I didn't like it.

"Holy shit, DeLaine," Jax exclaimed, surprised when we got to the lake. I went around and threw my can into the back of his truck and opened the ice chest to grab another one. I grinned at him and he said, "Wow, you sure got a taste for beer in Corpus, huh?" I shrugged my shoulder up and nodded as I pulled the tab off my second can of beer.

"Wow, Bay! You didn't say our good buddy could drink like that now!" Levi was laughing. I noticed Bailey gave him a dirty look, and then I started laughing and whooping. I guessed it was time for them to see who DeLaine Reynolds was now.

The three of them looked at me, then all started copying me. Soon we were laughing, and I could feel myself getting buzzed by the time I was a little more than half-way into my second can of beer. It would still take a little more to get me drunk, but depending on how fast I drank, I could either get drunk fast, or really shit-faced over a longer period. We didn't have very long, so I decided to go for the fast drunk. By the time I was on my third can, the others were only on their second beers.

Jax had to get us home, but we'd been talking about sneaking out, and meeting the boys in the playground, behind Bailey's house. I was drunk, but I could still function. I was developing a bit of a tolerance, I had noticed, but I thought that it might have to do with the fact that my parents could drink so much as well. I knew that I would need to drink at least three or four more beers before I was stupidly drunk, and Jax didn't have enough for that.

Once we got home, we went into Bailey's room, and took off our boots. We slipped our sneakers on, so we wouldn't make noise as we walked through the house, to go to the back door, to slip out through the back fence. I noticed Bailey seemed fairly secure in her knowledge of how to sneak out of her house, even from the back side. When we were outside, near the back fence, and away from the house, I asked if she'd snuck out that way before.

She grinned at me in the silver glow of moonlight and nodded her head. We slunk through the back gate, without opening it very far. We were in the grassy area, where the elementary school's playground and park-like area met up to the back end of Samson High. It was a grassy knoll that went up to the track and practice fields for football and baseball, as well as the tennis courts.

We walked to the large tunnel that I'd gone inside of with Jax and Kevin. I started laughing at the absurdity but was happy the others thought I was laughing because I was drunk. Jax had grabbed eight beers and we drank them all. By then, I'd drank almost a six pack for the night. I was hopelessly drunk, but still functioning. I noticed that the others were just as drunk as me and had had less beer. I felt a little proud of my tolerance since I'd not even been able to stand the taste of it, just the summer before.

Bailey and Levi drunkenly lurched out of the tunnel and left me and Jax alone inside. I knew that they were going to go somewhere and make out. It took Jax less than a minute to lean over and begin kissing me. I gladly kissed him and felt my old friend, the siren that ruled my body when I was alone with Jax or Kevin too long, begin to wake up her creaky pipes. She then started screaming exceptionally loud. I was surprised, because I never felt her that loudly when I was with Chance. He'd been the only one I'd ever been with while being drunk. I thought maybe she just didn't like me when I got drunk, but if I was going by my reaction to Jax's frantic and rushed kissing, then I was wrong.

With each deep kiss, the siren of sex, who lived deep within my groin, screamed her harpy song. I felt myself tumbling back inside of it, more deeply than I had in a long time. For once, I wasn't even thinking about how conflicted I felt about Kevin either. It was like I was finally free of him, and his hold. Even though we hadn't been together when I was going with Jax, I'd always felt so conflicted over him. This time I could completely let go and enjoy Jax.

Jax began to lay me back, on the crunchy leaves and dirt, and I let him. I was only thinking about his touch and his kiss. I didn't care about what might get into my hair or on my clothes. It was chilly outside, but inside the tunnel, it was much warmer. As I kissed Jax, I found myself feeling very toasty in there. When his hand slid down to the buttons of the top I was wearing, I didn't push them away, or even feel the least bit self-conscious, or guilty.

After getting my shirt untucked, he finished unbuttoning it. Once it was open, I was immediately cold, as the spring, night air hit my exposed skin. I pulled away and sucked in my breath. "What's wrong?" Jax asked a bit irritably.

"It's fucking cold, Jax!" I replied, as I looked at him surprised that he sounded irritated.

"Well, c'mere and I'll get you warmed back up," he growled as his mouth covered mine again. He wasn't wrong. The more his calloused hand stroked the tender skin of my abdomen, it began to warm up, not to mention the tunnel didn't give us room for both of us to be completely side by side. Instead, he was lying partially on my side.

While we kissed a while longer, I felt as his jeans began to harden against my thigh. It seemed the harder his pants got, the more fevered the pitch was between us. I was still extremely drunk, but I knew everything I was doing. I felt as my hands stroked the top of his jeans and his stroked me on top of my bra. When he began to nuzzle on my neck, I leaned my face back and elongated my throat for him even more. His mouth greedily kissed me all the way from my neck, until he was trailing down my throat and to the top part of my chest, until it reached the swell of my bra. I heard my breathing speed up, and Jax reached for the button on my jeans.

I pushed his hand away, and he kept going back to my button. I finally pulled away from him and told him to stop. He stopped what he was doing and looked up from his position just above the top of my bra, asking, "Really?" I nodded. I heard Jax sigh deeply and felt troubled by his reaction. He'd always been the one to take things slow between us, in the past. The only time I'd ever been really irritated with him was during our one attempt at going all the way. I wasn't even sure if he thought we'd actually done anything. Even with the tiny little drop of blood in my panties, I knew that Jax hadn't really been the one to take my virginity completely. That honor had gone to Kevin, and after he had taken my virginity, I knew for sure Jax hadn't actually done it. The blood from Kevin could attest to what had happened.

Finally, Jax came back up to my mouth, and began to kiss me again. As I was beginning to feel better about his initial response, I was shocked when he tried again to undo my jeans button. "Dammit, Jax, stop!" I finally demanded, a little more irritably.

"Fine, then give me a blow job," Jax finally whispered, just as perturbed as I had been.

"What?" I exclaimed, shocked.

"Give me a damned blow job if you aren't going to let me do anything else," Jax stated, as he looked at me seriously.

I looked at his face and knew he was extremely serious. I was angry, but I decided if he was going to be such an ass, then I'd show him what else I'd learned how to do, more than just how to be a successful drunk, since I moved to Corpus. I pushed him up and it took only a second for us to flip positions to where he was lying beneath me.

I began to button up my blouse and Jax began to protest. "Do you want me to do this?" I asked him.

Jax nodded his head, and I growled, "Then shut up. I'm cold up here!"

Then I undid the silver belt buckle he'd won the year before, I did everything that Chance Cahill had taught me how to do, with him. Once I finished, I got out of the tunnel and left Jax lying there with his pants undone still.

As I began to stomp back towards Bailey's, I heard Jax call out in a whispered hiss to stop. I heard him trying to do his pants and buckle back again. I ignored him, and heard him cuss under his breath, as he jangled until everything was done and he caught up to me. I was closing in on the back fence to Bailey's house. I figured I could sit there and wait for her and Levi to come back from wherever they were. I was feeling much more sober. I wasn't even sure how long we'd been outside, since getting home.

Before I got back to the wood and cinderblock fence, Jax caught up and grabbed my arm. I pulled away from him and continued to stomp across the grass. "Dammit, DeLaine! Why do you always have to pull this shit?" Jax asked me angrily.

"What, Jax? Get pissed off because you treat me like a fucking whore?" I accused, as I whipped around and glared at him.

"I've never treated you like a whore!" Jax declared, then he added, "Even when you were seeing both me and Strong last summer, I never treated you like a whore!"

I gasped at him. I had told him because he'd thought I was cheating on him with Kevin, when he broke up with me. When we had made up later, after I'd left, he'd apologized, even though he had been the one to act like an ass. I told him I was going to be seeing Kevin, because I didn't want him to accuse me of stringing him along. I didn't think Jax would ever throw it into my face. I was beginning to realize that I was screwing everything up with every boy I cared about, all because I was so stupid.

"Fuck you, Jax," I finally hissed, as I turned around and continued stomping towards Bailey's.

Grabbing me more tightly, Jax apologized, "I'm sorry, DeLaine, I shouldn't have said that."

I let him turn me towards him, and I exclaimed furiously, "You're damned right you shouldn't have said that! Dammit, Jax! I only told you because I didn't want there to be anything that was a secret. I didn't even tell Kevin I was seeing you!" I realized that I'd probably screwed up by telling him that, but Kevin didn't want me any longer either, so I decided I had little to lose with each boy.

"Oh, so you told me, but you didn't bother telling Kevin? That's fucked up, DeLaine!" Jax spit at me.

"I figured it kept you alive, you dumbass!" I replied, indignantly.

"Besides, who taught you how to do that?" Jax suddenly veered off topic, "Was it Strong?"

"Wha-?" I began and then realized that Jax would naturally assume that. Shaking my head, I huffed, "For your information, no, he didn't!"

"And you want to know why I'm treating you like a whore?" Jax fumed quietly.

"You asshole!" I snarled, through my clenched teeth.

"I'm sorry, DeLaine, dammit, I'm still drunk! I'm sorry. I don't know why I'm saying this shit to you, except you drive me fucking nuts sometimes!" Jax groaned, as he ran his hand over his face, from his forehead down to his chin.

"Jax, just leave me alone, okay?" I replied, as I tried again to walk away.

Jax grabbed me again by the arm, and this time, when he grabbed me, I felt a bit of the crushing force Geoffrey had used on me, in the past. "DeLaine, I mean it, I'm sorry!" I didn't jerk my arm away because I knew from experience, that he'd leave a mark on my arm. As I stood in front of him, he tried to explain himself, "Dammit, I shouldn't have said that shit about Kevin, but shit, how do you think I feel, knowing you're seeing me and Kevin at the same time? How was I supposed to know you'd been seeing someone in Corpus?"

Quietly, I looked at him, and tried to calm myself before I responded. Finally, I stated, in a quieter voice, "I dunno Jax, I guess if you ever wrote and asked me, or even if you asked Bailey how I was sometimes, I might think you gave a shit. Since you haven't done either one…anyway, you've been seeing other girls. Why wouldn't I be seeing someone else, in Corpus?"

Jax shrugged his shoulder, "I dunno. I don't really think about what you're doing when you aren't here. I guess I just think about what you are doing when you are here. I'm sorry. There's so much goin' on since you've been gone. I just know that when you're here, I get to see you, but I guess I never think about what you do when you aren't here. I mean I think about you, but…shit, I dunno!"

"Gee, thanks, man that makes me feel really good now. At least you aren't calling me a whore anymore," I mumbled, feeling a bit dejected now. I didn't know why I was feeling dejected, but I thought about Kevin, Jax, Bailey and Levi all the time. I wondered what was going on with them all the time! I had hoped they thought about me every once in a while.

I watched as Jax shrugged his shoulder again and realized that even though I had been crazy about him, I wasn't so sure if I should still be that way.

"DeLaine, that's not what I meant!" Jax finally murmured, quietly.

"Yeah," I replied just as quietly. Thankfully, Bailey and Levi came running up behind us and were both still happy, either from being drunk, or being together. They had no clue that Jax and I were arguing, until they were both standing next to us.

"Goodnight, Jax. Be careful if you have to ride again," I offered, as I turned away from the three of them. I slipped into the wooden gate and left Bailey and Levi standing beside Jax.

I walked away from the gate and went up to the back door and sat on the steps to wait for Bailey. I could hear the hushed conversation but wasn't sure what was being said.

Bailey finally slipped into the backyard and came up to me on the back steps. She didn't say anything, and neither did I. I simply followed her inside of the house and into her room. We changed into our night clothes, went into the bathroom, to brush our teeth, and go to bed.

Once we were lying under the covers, of her bed, Bailey finally asked me what had happened. "You mean Jax didn't tell you and Levi?" I asked quietly.

"No," Bailey replied.

"Well everything was fine until he kept trying to get into my pants and I told him to quit. Then he told me to give him a BJ and so I did. Then when I got done…or rather when he was done, I got out of the tunnel and started coming up here because I was pissed off at him. Then we argued, he told me I was acting like a whore, and we argued about Kevin, then y'all showed up," I finished a little abruptly.

"Are you shitting me?" Bailey asked me, in a hiss.

Sighing, I assured her that I wasn't and told her everything that had been said. Then I told her that he was right. I'd been going back and forth between him and Kevin, and he was the only one who knew. I knew that I hadn't told Kevin, not just for me, but also because I knew Kevin's temper. I knew he'd lose it, at Jax, and get in trouble. I didn't think the few kisses I'd shared with Jax were worth either of them getting hurt, or in trouble, as would be the case for Kevin. I knew that Jax could hold his own with a crazed bull, but I didn't think he'd fare as well with the Taurus bull that was Kevin.

Bailey told me that I wasn't going with, or married to either of them. She told me all the things a best friend is supposed to tell the other, when they doubt themselves, but I knew that what I'd said was true.

I deserved to be treated like shit. I'd played both boys and it was because I couldn't make a decision. I loved both of them, although I was beginning to wonder if I really loved Jax, or had just been so infatuated with him, for so long, that I thought I did. He'd been the only other boy I'd had a really physical relationship with in Wichita Falls, and I didn't want to seem like a slut, by being physical with two boys. Yet, I'd still done it. I thought if I loved both of them, then it made it somehow better, but I was beginning to think it wasn't necessarily so.

Of course all of that had been before. It had been before I was dragged out of the only town I'd ever known as home. It had been before I'd moved to Corpus, to live with my mom, and found her to be unpredictable, at best.

It had also been before I'd begun to drink and smoke pot all the time. Finally, it had been before I'd met Chance Cahill, and let him talk me into doing things I hadn't really wanted to do. I'd been so hopelessly lonely for something from home, that I'd found someone that reminded me of Jax. I jumped at the chance to fill the huge hole, inside of my soul.

Chapter 31

The next night was my last night in Wichita Falls. I would be leaving the next morning at 6:30 and wouldn't get home until 11 that night. I was grateful that I'd be back in Corpus before midnight, so I wouldn't have nearly as long a layover in Houston. It was still going to be an awfully long ride from North Texas to South Texas.

When Bailey and I went to bed, after making sure all of my stuff was together, I hoped and prayed that Kevin would come and knock on her window during the night. When her alarm clock went off at 4:45 a.m., I realized sadly, that Kevin hadn't woken us up, knocking on the window. I found myself feeling more depressed than I could ever remember being over Kevin. I couldn't believe he hadn't shown up, at the last minute, like he'd done in the past. This time I thought that maybe he really did mean it, when he told me to leave. I felt like a huge piece of me had died as soon as I woke up.

At the bus station, I hugged Bailey, and then her mom, Glenda goodbye. When I climbed up on the bus, I went straight to the back of the bus, where it was okay to smoke. I knew I needed to smoke freely, which I hadn't been able to do while I'd been at Bailey's. I wanted a cigarette in the worst way. I lit my cigarette and felt the tiny pendant on my necklace.

I held the tiny, tear drop shaped, blue crystal, and felt my own tears fill my eyes. I wondered what Kevin had done while I'd been in town all week. I felt bad for not going back to at least visit Mrs. Strong, but I just didn't think I could separate the two right now. Maybe I could see her during the summer. I looked over my shoulder, out the tinted windows of the bus, and saw Bailey still standing on the cement, beside the bus. I took my hand away from my necklace and placed it on the window and wondered if Bailey could see it. I didn't know how my life had begun to unravel and spin violently out of control, but I was really tired of all of it. I sighed deeply and put my head against the seat. I closed my hand back around the blue crystal that was supposed to symbolize a teardrop.

When I got home that night, inside of my bedroom, I was so happy to be where I had all of my personal things. I walked to my mirror to look at the photo of me, with Kevin. I touched the Polaroid that was the only picture I had of Kevin and wiped the outside corners of my eyes.

I was glad I could rest all the next day before I had to go back to school on Monday.

The next morning, when I came stumbling out of my room, I was happy to see my mama. I looked at her and noticed she had an odd look on her face. "What's up?" I asked her, a little apprehensively.

Mama looked at me, over the cup of coffee she was drinking, "I need to talk to you, DeLaine. Your daddy called me this morning. I have some really important news to tell you." I looked at her as if to say, 'tell me more.' Finally, she blurted, "Your daddy left Clarice."

I couldn't believe my mom had just said the four words I'd dreamt about hearing for literally years. "What do you mean he left her?" I whispered, hesitantly. I couldn't believe I was hearing this.

My mom told me that Daddy had called her to tell her that Clarice had embezzled the restaurant, and he'd lost everything. I couldn't believe it. I knew that they had their issues, but she had been the one to tell me not to tell my daddy about Geoffrey's last violent episode, because it would destroy his dream! Then she ended up embezzling from it. I asked my mom exactly what it meant, and she told me that she had been taking all of the cash instead of depositing it. Daddy had started bouncing checks for everything, everywhere. I didn't really understand what it all meant, "So, what does this mean for the restaurant?"

Mama patiently told me, "DeLaine, it means he's lost it all…the restaurant, and their house. There is nothing left."

Mama explained that because of the expenses, Daddy had sold out his share of the restaurant to his friend, who had been invested in it. He had spent the last month taking care of closing the restaurant. He walked away from the creepy, Victorian house that he and Clarice had been living in. The bank was going to take it back and resell it. Then she told me even Geoffrey had been affected. Instead of paying the loan that Daddy had signed on his truck, Clarice had taken that cash as well. Geoff's little Chevy Luv, that I'd ridden in with Kevin, and William, was now gone.

I began to think about all the stuff that Lisa had gotten for Christmas. I felt certain Clarice had begun taking money before Christmas. I knew that Clarice wasn't a stupid woman, by any means, and I knew also that she was cunning and manipulative. I just couldn't figure out why she would completely destroy all of them. I wondered what would happen to Geoffrey and William. I knew that Geoffrey could get out on his own, if he needed to, but William was still in school.

When I asked my mama, what happened to the boys, she shrugged her shoulders. She hadn't asked my daddy. I couldn't believe that the witch was basically gone. She had been guilty of throwing the water on herself though and had melted her own life.

Not sure how I was supposed to respond to the news, I finally went back to my room. Sitting in the middle of my bed, I thought about how my whole life had been destroyed, by the decision to open a restaurant that Clarice would use to destroy my daddy. Not only had it destroyed the life that I was finally living, but it would be hard for my daddy to come back from losing something so big.

I wondered what my daddy would do now. I didn't understand everything about the business end, and embezzling, but what I'd gotten from the conversation was my daddy was living in a tiny apartment, and about to begin working as a bartender. I knew my daddy had an amazing work ethic, but it broke my heart to know that he had given up everything he'd worked hard to achieve, to work in a bar. He was truly living his dream-life, being able to play his music, and have a means to support a large family. I'd hated it, but I didn't want to see my daddy hurt.

My daddy may have been an absent parent, most of the time, but I didn't want Clarice to hurt him or for him to lose everything. I felt sad knowing that not only had Clarice destroyed me, and my daddy, but she'd also hurt both of her boys. I sighed as I flopped back onto my pillows. I turned my head to look over at the pictures of Bailey and Kevin. So much had been ripped away from me, and now it seemed like Clarice was getting away with literally killing everything all by herself. She wouldn't ever really pay for any of her transgressions. Mama told me Daddy had sold his part of the restaurant, so his friend wouldn't have her arrested. I felt disgusted.

I realized I didn't know what exactly I was supposed to feel. Was I supposed to be thrilled that the bitch was finally gone from my life? Was I supposed to feel bad for my daddy, who'd lost everything? Was I supposed to be angry because I had lost so much by the whole move? Was I supposed to be grieving for Kevin and Jax? I felt so conflicted. There were just too many feelings to think about, and I didn't want to feel any of them. Eventually, I rolled over, closed my eyes and went to sleep. It was the only way I knew to escape from all of it.

***

The next day when I went to school, I told Kelly about my daddy and Clarice. She was just as shocked as I'd been. Kelly was the truest friend I had in Corpus. I told her about Kevin, and Jax too.

During lunch, Kelly and I went behind the school auditorium with some kids that we hung out with that smoked pot. I didn't feel like standing around the girls' bathroom. One of the guys, David Jeffries, told Kelly during their typing class, that he had a joint and was going to smoke it at lunch. We'd never smoked pot at school before. Kelly was worried we would get caught. I felt so emotionally void, that I wanted something to make me feel anything, even fear was better than the wasteland that was my heart.

David Jeffries was a really cute boy in our class, who was funny and sweet. He also happened to love smoking pot. He listened to rock and roll and had long, brown hair and happy, blue eyes. David had most girls in school swooning over him or his brother.

His brother was Harvey Jakes and he was two years older than we were. I liked David more than Harvey, even though most of the girls almost panted when Harvey would walk by. David was more approachable. Harvey was arrogant and completely untouchable. Their mom and my mama actually worked together, when my mom worked in the bars, in town.

When we got out for lunch, Kelly and I both began to walk towards the auditorium. I could see David standing there grinning his silly smile at us. There was another guy there, named Nick Vance who was Debbie Vance's brother. He had a twin brother named Noah. They were a year ahead of us, but David and Nick were best friends. As we walked up to them, I noticed Nick was cute, in a surfer boy way. He and his brother were both tall and thin. David was my height, and slim.

The four of us got behind the school, and David lit the joint. I made sure to stand beside him, because I wanted to smoke it worse than anything I'd ever wanted before. I wanted to not feel. I knew I couldn't get as stoned as I did on the weekends, because I had to maintain my appearance in class, but for just a few minutes, I wanted to feel nothing. There were so many conflicting emotions happening. Kelly and I also lit cigarettes, as well as David, so when we had the joint, we would have to hold our cigarettes in the opposite hand, as we took hits off of it.

After a few tokes on the joint, I thanked David for sharing it with us, and walked back around to get to the snack bar before it closed. I knew I didn't have time for a real lunch and it didn't matter much. I tried not to eat much, but I was already feeling the gnawing in my gut, from the little bit of pot I'd smoked. Kelly finally caught up with me, and we sat on one of the concrete benches, in the outside student common area. I'd never gone to a school where you could hang outside during lunch.

Samson had been regimented and there were no outside areas, except the smoking pit. Even that was enclosed. I didn't know if it was because it was a coastal town or not, but it was nice to be able to sit outside during our breaks and lunch. I shared my powdered donuts with Kelly and she giggled like a crazy little girl.

When the bell rang, I was glad. I realized as I walked to typing that my buzz from the pot was already burning off. I wondered how Kelly could still be so giggly. I must just have a higher tolerance to stuff that made the mind fuzzy, I guessed.

Sighing, I was glad to see Willie Morgan's ridiculously bright, silvery smile. I might not have a crush on him anymore, now that Chance was around, but I still enjoyed looking at Willie. "Hey, do you have some typing paper I can borrow," he asked, as I sat at my electric typewriter.

"Yeah, but you know, Willie, you really don't have to give it back to me," I chuckled, through my half-grin that I liked to think I'd learned from Kevin. As soon as I thought that through, I felt a slight stab to my heart. I wondered how long it would take to get anything that had to do with Kevin to finally go to sleep, and never wake up again.

After school, I was glad that my mama wasn't drunk all the way! We'd get home in time for me to go to my room, and work on my homework, with daylight still streaming through my windows. As soon as I sat on my bed, I looked at the pictures of Kevin and me, and Bailey and me. I picked them up. I wanted to throw away the picture of Kevin, but I knew I'd regret it. Instead, I picked up my photo album and slipped both Polaroid photos inside the magnetic cling page. I wanted to forget Kevin, and yet, I couldn't bear the thought of losing him forever, either.

I'd written to Bailey the night before to tell her about Daddy and Clarice. I knew she'd find the whole thing shocking. I hoped she'd feel as indignant as I did about all the hell we'd been through, only to have Clarice destroy everything for all of us. I wanted to ask her if she'd talked to Kevin but restrained myself. I knew she was still irritated with him anyway, so it was probably just as well I not bring him up. Once I was done writing to her, I addressed the envelope and set it on my desk. Finally, I picked up one of my text books and dove into doing my homework.

By the end of the week, I was happy that all the strange emotions I had running through me had begun to settle down. I was looking forward to going over to Kelly's house, and hanging out at the game room. I hoped that Chance would want to go riding around, because I decided that I wanted to try to establish something more than the strange relationship we seemed to have.

***

Before lunch, I was called down to the front office. I wondered if I was in trouble. I never got called to the office for anything. When I walked into the door I saw my mama standing in the middle of it. I felt my heart jump into my chest. I knew that now would be when I would find out that my daddy was dead, and Clarice had killed him.

"Hey, honey," my mama spoke a little too brightly.

I nodded my head and asked her why she was there. Laughing my mama explained, "You forgot you had a dentist appointment too? I totally forgot about it, so I came down to get you." I didn't know what she was telling me. We didn't have insurance, and she hadn't said anything to me about going to the dentist at any point. I waited until we were outside. Finally, I couldn't stand the weird, chipper way she was talking, so once we were out of the school, I asked what had happened. She simply shook her head and told me we could talk about it as soon as we left the school.

I noticed that my mama had been scanning the parking lot, the entire time we walked from the front of the school, out to her car. She was acting a little strange, even for her, I decided. When we turned off the street the school sat on, she put the car in park and asked me if I'd talked to or noticed anyone new around the school. I shook my head. My mama told me that Clarice had called and was making death threats against us. I knew that she'd just royally screwed up! When someone threatened my mama idly, she didn't take it with a grain of salt. She usually came out with the ferocity of a bear, and the over protective nature that lived within her.

I looked at her curiously. Why in the world would Clarice be doing this crazy stuff, I wondered? Then I remembered that she was a certifiable, nut job! She didn't have to make sense. I also knew that she was just unbalanced enough that she would and could do stuff she threatened. She had a brother who rode in a motorcycle gang, and Mama began to ask me about him. I told her I didn't know him that well. My mom told me that Clarice had said she knew some tough people who rode with her brother, and she knew some who would kill for money, and she had plenty.

I tried not to laugh but couldn't help it.

Mama looked over at me and asked what was so funny.

I told her, "Mom, Clarice is so full of shit. Yeah, she's got a brother who is a biker, but they don't even talk to each other. Most of her family is a nut, like her, but she doesn't have any pull with her brother, Jimmy."

My mom looked at each car that was passing by us, as we drove home. "Well, she stole enough money from the restaurant that your daddy is taking the threat seriously and has called the police in Oklahoma City."

"Mom, I'm just telling you, she's not gonna do anything. She is a nut. I'll give you that, but she isn't stupid. Trust me. She might act like it, but she's manipulating you and Daddy. Y'all are falling for her shit!" I replied, still with a smile playing around my lips. I was hiding how I really felt though.

I knew that Clarice was nuts enough to do something this stupid. She might even carry it out, but if my mom knew I was afraid, it would make her act stupid. That was the reality here. If she got drunk, she was liable to drive to Oklahoma City, track down Clarice, and kill her. Then I'd be made to go back to Oklahoma, to live with my daddy, and I didn't want to do that. I loved him, but I could never go back to the most hideous place on Earth, in my opinion. Plus, all of this had been going on now for over a month. Daddy had just told my mom less than a week before.

I was actually angry with him for not calling before. It was almost like he decided that anything important in his life wasn't important to me.

When we got to our house, I went in my room and thought about how creepy it would be if there was someone seriously following me, and my mom. I wondered where they would hide, if they were on our street.

We lived down a gentle slope, in a brick house now, on almost a whole acre of land, in an older subdivision of Calvin school district. There were huge trees all around our house, in the back, and in the front. I thought about the logistics of the neighbors, where people parked, and thought about how a car sitting on the street would stick out like a sore thumb. Someone would think some strange guy walking down the block was odd too.

I looked out the curtains at the street outside. There was no one out there, but I couldn't shake the fact that I was quite afraid. I knew telling my mom would result in her doing something extremely stupid, so I had to act like Clarice was not scaring me, in the least.

I walked out to the dining room, off of the kitchen, and asked my mom if I would still be able to go to out with Kelly and Robin. "I think you should call and see if they can come spend the night with you, instead. I'd rather you stayed home this weekend, until we can get this all straightened out, about Clarice. Your daddy is supposed to call me and tell me if I need to get a restraining order on her, or not." My mom explained to me. Nodding my head, I shuffled back to my room. I knew Kelly and Robin's parents would probably say no, since they'd gotten to spend the night with me, last time, before spring break.

Because I'd gone home early, it seemed like forever before I could call them to see if they could spend the night with me. I lay on my bed and watched as the sun came through the drapes, casting lights and shapes on my wall.

I saw the shadows of the tree branches as they blew gently in the spring wind. I began to wonder what Kevin was doing. I wondered if he had been upset by my leaving, and not coming back. Or, had he done what he wanted to do, in pushing me away. I couldn't believe he hadn't come to Bailey's window by the time I left. I still felt the ache deep in my heart, knowing how far we'd come and gone, in only a month.

Then I began to think about Jax and our entire relationship. He'd been so sweet while we'd been boyfriend and girlfriend. Even though we'd broken up and hadn't really been on good terms when I left, we'd gotten back to being in a good place with each other, while I'd been up last summer. I thought about the night before I left, and how nice it had started out, with Jax, Bailey and Levi. Then I flashed forward to how we'd left each other. How angry I'd been with him. I didn't know that we could ever come back from that either. I wasn't entirely sure I wanted to, in all honesty.

I looked over at my photo album. I thought about getting out my pictures and looking at everyone again. I hated that my heart, and even my soul, seemed to still be stuck in the year before. I hated that I wasn't fully invested in being in Corpus yet.

Even though I'd made some friends, and was acting like a stupid teenager, or at least like how I thought one was supposed to act, I still felt like I was a big fraud. I'd felt that way almost my entire life. I didn't think I'd still feel that way at fifteen. Taking a deep sigh, I rolled over and looked out the window, where our house was in the shadows of the afternoon. It was darker on that side of the house and was completely covered with trees. I watched as the shadows flitted around on the backside of the curtains. I felt like that was how my mind looked on the inside…dark and twisted.

After I got off the phone with Kelly and Robin, I went into the dining room, where my mom was idly sipping on her V.O. and water. She wasn't drunk, which I was happy to see, but she was still drinking. I knew the threat of it could still happen. Mama asked if Robin and Kelly were going to come over, and I shook my head. "No, their mom said that they couldn't because they spent the night here the last time, so I guess I'm just stuck here all weekend."

My mama looked at me sadly, "I'm so sorry, honey, but I want to know that you are safe." I got up and shook my head, as I made my way to my room. It was going to be a long weekend.

Chapter 32

By the next Monday, my daddy had finally called Mama and told her not to bother with a restraining order. I'd been so depressed, the entire weekend that I hadn't done much more than sleep. I'd managed to do my homework, but that was all.

During lunch, Kelly told me that one of the girls that smoked with us in the girls' room, knew someone who had speed. I knew what speed was, and Kelly asked if I wanted to try it. I decided that if I only took one, surely it wouldn't hurt me. We went out to the student parking lot, and met up with the girl and her boyfriend, who was selling the pills for $5 each. It would take up half of my weekly lunch allowance, but I also got my regular allowance, and since I hadn't gone to the game room, I still had all of it. We each looked at the little black pill, and drank our cokes, as we swallowed the tiny capsule.

I was hoping that speed would make me happy. I knew they were called uppers, and I knew my mood needed uplifting. I hoped it would create some kind of euphoric feeling, so the dread and sadness that seemed to be my constant companions would finally fly away, for a while. When I got drunk, I was able to get rid of it, for a bit, but the next day, I always felt like such a hypocrite. I hated my parents' drinking, but I was doing the exact same thing. Just as the lunch period was coming to an end, I felt myself getting jittery. It was more of a hyper feeling than a happy one, but it was okay, I decided.

I walked into typing class and felt like my mind and body were racing around. When we started working on our typing drills, I was amazed at how fast I was typing. I felt like I was flying! I felt certain I had made a ton of mistakes, as fast as I had been going. The teacher picked up our drills and gave us our assignment. After she was done grading them, toward the end of the class, she got up to begin handing them back to us.

Bending over to whisper in my ear, my typing teacher asked me if I played piano. I looked at her surprised, because no one had ever asked me that. I shook my head, and she smiled warmly at me, stating, "I'm only asking because I've watched you, and you type extremely fast. Today you were exceptionally fast. Your "words per minute" was the highest in the class. Usually those are my students who have taken piano."

I looked at her sincere face and smiled squeamishly. I accepted my typing drill from her and saw that my average words per minute that day had jumped from 60 to 75. I was thoroughly surprised.

I wondered if I would have been able to do that if I wasn't speeding from the stupid, black pill I'd taken. I wouldn't know until the next day though. I wondered if she'd know that I was actually on speed because I couldn't repeat the same words per minute, the next day. I decided it didn't really matter. By the end of class, I felt the hyper feeling beginning to leave my body. By the end of the day, I was back to my normal self, even though Kelly was acting silly and happy. I decided I was a screw up even with speed. How would I ever figure out how to be happy, I wondered?

After no more news about my daddy and Clarice, I figured that all the worry was done. I continued with my life the way it had been going, before my mom had gotten me out of school early the week before. I spent the night with Kelly and Robin and went to the game room. I'd even gone riding around with Chance Cahill. I was briefly reminded of Jax, while I had been out parking with Chance. I squeezed my eyes tightly when Jax's face loomed over me, instead of Chance's, but thankfully it was replaced quickly with the right boy's smiling eyes and mouth.

March turned into April, and life was going along fine. Bailey had written me a few times since I'd been up there for spring break. We were both really excited about going to California, since my mom had agreed to it, after we found out that Daddy and Clarice were separated. I probably wouldn't be going to Oklahoma at all for the summer.

Daddy had talked to my mama and told her that he didn't have a place for me to stay. He would come down in May to see me, since I couldn't come up there. I'd just listened vaguely when my mama told me that. I hoped that he'd actually see me this time, since he normally didn't seem to see me unless it was to gripe at me. If he came down to Corpus, there was little to take his mind away from me, so I wanted to feel excited.

I had gotten angry with him after first learning about him and Clarice. I felt like he never told me anything important. I'd removed all his photos from my room and put them inside my closet. I'd also packed away my photo album with Kevin, Bailey and Levi's photos in it, so I could work on making myself happy in Corpus. I knew that as long as I hung on to my old life, it would never happen. The only photo I'd taken out was the one of me and Bailey together, that Kevin had snapped the summer after 7th grade. I'd slipped it into the mirror, on my dresser, and looked at it at least a few times a day.

In April, Kelly went for a ride with Willie Morgan. When she came back, she was no longer a virgin. I was shocked when Chance got into a fight with Willie. I didn't understand it at first, but then I realized it was all because Chance had some kind of thing for her still.

When I thought about the first time I'd ever gone riding around with him, I remembered the long kiss they'd shared. I looked at Kelly, who was drunk, and sitting on the tailgate of someone's pickup, in the parking lot. I stalked over to the pickup, after I helped to pull Willie and Chance apart, and asked Kelly what she'd been doing with both of them.

Kelly looked at me and was giggling. I got so angry at her. I also felt like I'd been stabbed in the heart by her as well.

"Dammit Kelly, have you been messing around with Chance," I asked her quietly.

"No," she grinned at me drunkenly. Then she began to tell me in full detail about what had happened between her and Willie. I realized that I had been the one with the crush on Willie first too. I sat there and half-way listened, as she recounted every gory detail, in full, and wondered if she'd been messing around with Chance, when I wasn't up at the game room with her.

I didn't want to think like that. Kelly was my best friend in Corpus. I was suddenly missing Bailey so badly.

***

Soon May was pushing April out of the way. I was getting more excited, because I knew it wouldn't be long, and I'd be back in Wichita Falls. I couldn't wait to be back where I knew the streets and all the people. I felt a little heartsick about not knowing anything about Kevin, since I'd been at Bailey's, in March. I'd wanted to ask Bailey, but I never had. I also hadn't asked her any questions about Jax either. She hadn't volunteered anything. I felt like if he'd been hurt at the rodeo, she'd have told me. She and Levi were still going together. I'd at least get to see them.

I knew though, that I'd also get to see Kelly White too, as well as a lot of the others I'd gone to school with, when we went to the pool. I was going to get to spend over a month with Bailey! I couldn't wait. I was going up the Saturday after the 4th of July, on the 10th, and wouldn't come back until August 25th.

My daddy came down finally, on May 7th. He was sitting at our kitchen table when I came home from school. I walked over to him for a hug. I saw that he and mama were both drinking. I knew that the combination of them drinking, and being around one another, was a volatile one.

I hoped that they could at least maintain a little bit of peacefulness, while I was around. I was used to them constantly fighting and arguing, any time they got around each other. When I realized they were both actually very happy and relaxed, I felt my own shoulders begin to ease.

Ray told mama that he was going to the lake house, while my daddy was in town, so he could stay with us, in the guest room. I was worried when I first found out he was staying with us, but after seeing how easy they were around each other, I was happy that I was mistaken that they couldn't be nice to each other. I was planning on staying home that night, to visit with Daddy. I didn't know what would happen the next night.

Daddy told me and mama about Clarice. He explained everything she'd done as far as stealing from the club, and what all they'd lost because of it. I was blown away by the sheer insanity of it all. He said that Clarice was following him all over Oklahoma City. She was causing him grief on his job and had even gone so far as to get a job at the same restaurant he was bartending at. He had changed jobs to a very exclusive supper club that was for rich people, and he liked it better than the place he'd been at.

I was completely dumbfounded when he told me that she had gotten a hostess job at the same place. He told us stories about how she and Geoffrey had both been following him around and were calling and threatening him. He explained everything to me about the weekend that I'd had to stay home, because she'd made death threats. I listened and realized that she had fallen off the deep end again. I asked daddy if she'd quit taking her medicine. Daddy looked at me funny and asked what medicine.

"Daddy, I know that she was on some kind of medicine that she got in the loony bin," I responded, quietly.

My daddy nodded his head and said she hadn't been on it since we'd left Wichita Falls. I couldn't believe she'd quit taking it back then. I began to think quickly over how she had changed and started acting like her old self again. Then I thought about how agitated she seemed all the time by Christmas. He had known she wasn't taking her medicine, yet he hadn't done anything about it. Finally, I couldn't stand it any longer. I asked him why he didn't insist she get back on her medicine.

"Hell, Sis, she didn't need that shit," Daddy was grinning at me. I couldn't believe he was saying this after everything she'd put him through.

"Hmm," I mused, thoughtfully. "Seems like maybe she did! From the sounds of it, she still does. I mean, she is acting pretty damned crazy in my book! The whole gun thing at Christmas was pretty crazy too."

Daddy glanced at me with a bit of a hard look in his hazel eyes. Then I saw his sad look begin to creep its way into his face. I hoped he wasn't going to cry in front of me. Any time I saw him do that, it totally undid me in a bad way! My mama picked up on the gun issue, and went to town with it, questioning my daddy.

I knew that Daddy wasn't exactly happy at me for sharing that small nugget, but it took only a few minutes to calm my mama down, which shocked me all over again.

She was behaving like I'd not seen her behave, since I was a lot younger, around my daddy. She was funny, laughing and talking sweetly.

I didn't know what time warp I'd fallen into, but it was nice to have them getting along with one another, for a change.

I learned that my mama's wedding ring from Daddy had fallen victim to Clarice's madness as well. My mom had given it to me, but my dad thought I was too young to take care of it, so he put it up. Clarice told him he must have lost it when he was moving his stuff out, and he searched the front lawn, on his hands and knees, in the dark, with a flashlight, searching for it. A few weeks later a friend of his who owned a pawn shop had come to the club and told him he had some jewelry that Daddy might be interested in.

When Daddy went down to the pawn shop, he found Clarice had pawned that ring and a signet ring, he had worn for as long as I could remember. Daddy had to buy both rings back. He told Mama about the ring being lost, but she hadn't told me, which surprised me. I glanced at her and she griped, "I'm glad you were able to get it back, because I was ready to go up there, and beat that bitch's ass just for that!"

Daddy shook his head as he stood up, and walked into the kitchen, to mix himself another drink. I couldn't believe that Clarice had been so stupid. I realized that she wasn't just stupid, but insane. She knew my mama's temper, still she stole the ring that my daddy had given to her.

While Daddy was mixing his drink, my mom got up and went into the kitchen with him, to begin mixing her own. I sat there, watching them when the phone rang. I jumped when the loud trilling began, and raced over to the phone, mounted on the wall, next to the refrigerator.

"Hello?" I answered.

"Hey, Sister," I heard Geoffrey say amiably.

I felt myself stiffen, as I recalled what Daddy had just told us about Geoffrey and Clarice following him all over Oklahoma City.

I had let Geoffrey take me in, during Christmas, with his words about changing, and his coming out to me. I'd learned that he was back to his crazy ways, with his equally crazy mom.

"Uh, hey, Geoff," I remarked, uncertainly. I saw Mama and Daddy both turn towards me, as I stood there, holding the phone receiver up to my ear. Mama started making a motion for me to hang up the phone. I ignored her, because I wanted to know what Geoffrey wanted. I shook my head and turned my back towards my parents.

Daddy walked up behind me, and in my other ear he snarled, "Hang the fucking phone up, DeLaine! He's trying to find out if I'm here."

Turning I looked at my daddy curiously. Daddy stood away from me and whispered for me not to tell Geoffrey he was here.

I felt confused why Daddy wouldn't tell them where he was. Then I remembered we were talking about two unstable people. Quickly, I stammered, "Uh, Geoff, I can't really talk right now. I'm about to leave to go out with my friend Kelly. Maybe we can talk another time?"

Geoffrey told me that was fine, but I could tell he had a bit of a sarcastic humor underlying his words. Once I hung up, I looked at Daddy. He knew that I wanted him to explain, so he said, "Come sit down again, Sis. I know that your mama told you about the death threats. We've talked several times since then," I was shocked to hear my daddy admit that he and my mama were talking regularly on the phone, since I never got to talk on a regular basis with him. "We decided not to tell you that she keeps making threats against me, you and your mom. We knew how much it bothered you the first time. Since your mom hasn't seen anyone suspicious around, we both think that Clarice is making idle threats. But, I didn't let anyone up there know where I was going this weekend. I didn't want her to try to follow me here and find out exactly where you and your mom are living now."

I questioned my daddy, "So, why didn't you think that she'd carry out on it?"

"She just likes to create drama, DeLaine. She and her brother aren't close. You know that. She likes to think that she is some kind of badass, but face it, Sis, she's just a crazy bitch. She and that oldest kid of hers, who turned out to be a fag, are both fuckin' crazy!" Daddy finished. I tried to keep my face neutral when Daddy admitted that he finally knew about Geoffrey's being gay.

I couldn't believe that I felt a strange bit of protectiveness towards Geoff. He'd been my tormentor much longer than he'd been an actual brother, or friend, yet I felt bad for him. I knew that he'd had a horrible childhood. He'd been abandoned over and over by Clarice.

I was the person who was there for him to take it out on. He'd tried, in the limited ways he knew how, at different times, to be friendly with me. For whatever reason, his rage would inevitably win out, and I'd become his punching bag again. After our Christmas together, I'd hoped that all of our differences were finally buried. Now I realized that no matter what, we were never going to be a true brother and sister. I'd hoped to have a true sibling for once.

"What do you mean?" I asked Daddy, innocently.

"You didn't know that Geoffrey's a faggot?" Daddy asked me curiously.

I shook my head, hoping that my face didn't tell on me for being a liar. Daddy nodded his head and told me how he had found out that Geoffrey was gay, and working at a female strip club on top of everything else! Plus, he'd quit school.

I realized that everything Geoff had admitted to me had been cleverly kept from Daddy, until the end of his relationship with Clarice. I thought about how closed-minded Daddy was about Geoffrey, and chided myself for mentally taking up for Geoff. If the shoes were reversed, he wouldn't have done the same for me.

Daddy told us he'd found out about all of that when they were finally apart, and how mad he'd been about it all. I realized my daddy disliked gay men, which I found interesting. He had talked about knowing some before and had never used the vehemence he was showing towards Geoffrey. I didn't understand why I felt bad for Geoffrey. Especially after Daddy told us about things Clarice had done to him, using Geoffrey in some instances, to do bad things to my daddy, his van and his apartment. She also threatened anyone who was around him.

By the time it was dark, I thought all the surprises were out, until the phone rang again. Out of habit, I jumped up and answered it, before it had a chance to ring more than once. I was honestly hoping for a reprieve from my parents, and all the talk of Clarice and Geoffrey. When the voice first came across the phone line, I felt myself get a little lightheaded.

"Hello, DeLaine," Clarice purred into my ear. I stood there with what must have been a terrified look, because I saw Mama and Daddy both look over at me intently.

"Uh, hey, Clarice," I replied uncertainly.

"Is your daddy down there by chance?" Clarice asked me silkily.

"No, why?" I responded crossly. I thought that maybe I could finally talk to her the way I wanted to for so long.

"You know, DeLaine, I can always tell when you are lying. Did you know that?" Clarice was still using the quiet, but deadly sounding voice she used.

"Whatever, Clarice. What the hell do you want?" I demanded, with a little more bravado.

"I'm just trying to find your daddy, Honey. He's left Oklahoma City, and I don't have a clue how to get in touch with him. I thought that you might have an idea how to find him," she continued.

"Why don't you just leave him alone, Clarice? He finally figured out who you are. Of course, you didn't help yourself by stealing everything, but since you were the one who stole his dream, instead of me, you really only have yourself to blame," I used just as deadly a tone as she did.

I could feel my blood begin rising into my cheeks. I had never really talked disrespectfully to her, in front of my daddy, and I didn't normally cuss in front of him either. My cursing had become another way of speech around my mama, so I didn't think she really noticed any longer.

Clarice began to chuckle low, "Well, I'm glad to know I've finally found him. Why don't you tell him I'll have someone there tomorrow, to make sure I'm left a widow, instead of him divorcing me. I think I'll make sure whoever it is likes teenaged girls too, so I can have you taken care of for a change. Oh, and don't worry, I'm going to make sure your bitch mother gets what's coming to her too, for the way she always tried to undermine my authority. Of course, whoever I get will have to like chubby girls, since you've put on some weight, but most of those bikers don't mind, as long as they can get ahold of a young virgin. Of course, knowing you, you've probably already given it up, now that you aren't around me to make sure you keep yourself from being soiled by a stupid boy. So, just hang on because there will be a big guy there tomorrow, to take care of all of you."

I guessed Daddy could tell that Clarice was saying something awful to get my attention. He stood up, walked over to the phone and pushed the metal cradle down, cutting off Clarice. When he let go of the cradle, I was surprised to hear Clarice's hateful voice, now spewing horrible, disgusting things through the receiver. When she heard the click of the receiver, she started laughing, "I'm not hanging up, DeLaine, so you can hang up all you want, but I'm not releasing this line! If I have to sit on your phone all weekend, I will!" This time, I was the one to slam the receiver into the cradle! I walked over to the table and told my parents what she said.

My mama got angry and wanted to pick up the phone to cuss Clarice. My daddy finally convinced her that it was exactly what she wanted. We decided none of us would pick up the phone, until the next day, and see if Clarice finally got tired of sitting there, with a phone to her head.

I had finally had enough. I told Mama and Daddy I was going to bed. I felt sick about all the vile threats that Clarice had made to me. I wondered if she would really have someone nearby that would come in to kill my parents and me. When I thought about some big, scary man coming in and raping and killing me, I felt myself get cold chills up and down my spine.

***

The next morning, when I got up, I picked up the phone. I was shocked to find Clarice still on there. When she heard the receiver pick up, she began to say my daddy's name over and over. I sat there on the side of my bed holding the phone receiver to my ear, and away from my mouth. Sensing somehow that it was me, Clarice began to spew her hate filled tirade again. I quickly hung up the phone.

I walked out into the kitchen to find my parents sitting there, drinking coffee and talking. "Clarice is still on the phone," I remarked, sullenly. My parents told me they knew, and I sat down. "So, what am I supposed to do? I can't call Kelly and Robin later to let them know if I'm going out."

Daddy smiled at me, asking where I was going. I told him about the game room. He hadn't really asked me anything about my life in Corpus, when I was in Oklahoma City, at Christmas. I felt a little bit sad and a little bit bitter at the same time.

"Why don't I just take you up there?" Daddy asked me, smiling. I shrugged indifferently at him and he offered to even drive over to Robin and Kelly's house. I got excited about that. He didn't show much interest in any of my friends, or what I did, normally. I was excited to have him tag along for a bit.

Later that evening, we drove over to the trailer park that Kelly and Robin called home. He met them and their parents. Afterwards, he took all three of us out to Pizza Hut, then drove us over to the game room. It was still light outside, which meant not many people were there. I thought it was a good thing, so Daddy didn't act all tough around anyone like Chance Cahill or Willie Morgan. I still wanted to fit in. I figured if my daddy being up there getting tough didn't start people talking, I didn't know what would

Just as Chance got there, Kelly pointed him out to my daddy. Daddy walked over to him and asked him to a game of pool. I was so embarrassed, but Chance good naturedly accepted. They weren't supposed to play for money, but everyone did. Daddy soundly beat Chance at all three games. I sat over to the side, a little mortified and proud, both.

When Chance found out he was my dad, his whole demeanor changed. I could see the respectful side of him come out.

I sat there giggling with Kelly, as we watched Chance talk to my daddy like he was picking me up for prom, or something; the way he 'yes sir and no sir'ed' him.

Later on, once it was dark out, my daddy told us he was going to leave. He asked Chance if he minded taking me home. I was mortified at first, and then I decided maybe this would finally get Chance going in the right direction, to actually becoming my boyfriend. Chance agreed to it, when he found out that Daddy wouldn't make him pay up on the pool, if he just gave me a ride home.

Daddy came over and kissed me goodbye, and then he was gone. Of course, he'd been his charming and cool self, and all the teenagers who'd met him liked him immediately. I realized that Daddy had never really acted like that with any of my friends in Wichita. Then I realized that most of the kids in the game room were older.

When it got to be a little more than an hour until my curfew, Chance walked over to where I was sitting, playing Pac-man and asked if I was ready to go home. I looked at the Coke clock, and back at him curiously. "I thought maybe we could go spend some time together, if we left a little early," Chance smiled sweetly.

I grinned back at him, and felt my heart do a little leap. Maybe it was a good thing for him to meet my daddy, I thought. I found Kelly and Robin and told them that Chance wanted to take me home now.

Kelly grinned at me, because she kept telling me I needed to do more than what I'd been doing with Chance. I'd argued that it seemed to keep him happy, but since her ride with Willie Morgan, she'd been even pushier about me going all the way with Chance. I laughed at her as I walked out the glass door, to go out to Chance's truck.

Once we were inside his truck, he was asking me all about my dad. I told him more about my family and my life before Corpus, than all the times we'd ridden around rolled together. He told me he liked my daddy. I felt warm and happy sitting there beside him. I hoped that there was finally some kind of spark of mutual interest. He'd always been sweet, but he'd never acted like he wanted more than to just skulk around with me. I wanted an actual boyfriend! I felt the pang in my chest when I thought about how I'd wanted that with Kevin. Now, that would never happen.

When Chance got me home, right on time, he kissed me goodbye in my driveway. I hoped this was the dawning of a new era for us. I knew he was graduating soon, but it wasn't unusual for girls in high school to have older boyfriends. I climbed out of the Sunkist orange truck, turned and waved, while smiling brightly at Chance. I felt my heart do a little leap when he smiled just as broadly back at me.

After I got inside the house, I was surprised to see all of the lights out already. I knew it was 12:30 and Mama was usually in bed, but I thought with Daddy there they'd still be up drinking and talking. I shrugged as I locked the door, and walked towards the kitchen, to get something to drink.

After turning off the kitchen light, I began making my way down the dark hallway, to my room, on the end, to the right. Mama's room was on the left. The guest room was the first bedroom on the right. I realized that it was in the same spot as Donna's room had been in their house. I'd never thought about how our bedrooms were arranged similarly to the Strong family's bedrooms.

I passed by the guest room, and just as I got to my bedroom door, I turned around and walked back to the doorway of the bedroom that my daddy was sleeping in.

He wasn't in there. The door was open and even though the room was pitch black, I could make out the bed that was still made, and a suitcase sitting on top of it. I glanced towards the end of the hall, to my mama's room. I stood there for a few minutes, trying to make sense out of what I already knew.

Turning away from the open doorway, I walked back to my room and stopped briefly outside of my mom's bedroom.

Pushing the door to my room open, I slipped inside quietly, hoping that no one heard me come in. I felt the blush begin to flame out across my face. I knew where my daddy was, and I couldn't believe that they were actually in the same bedroom. A small piece of my heart lifted in childish hope, but the jaded side won over when I realized that it was silly to think that my parents could or would get back together.

After getting out of my clothes, I picked up my spiral journal and began to write in it. I was shocked that my parents were sleeping together. I thought about all the messing around I'd done in the last year with boys. I realized I never really thought about my parents in a sexual way. Except for the time I walked in to find Daddy and Clarice having sex, I'd been spared from seeing it either. I wondered if they'd even admit to it. I decided not to say anything and see if they told me. I didn't know how they could possibly think they'd keep it away from me, since the guest room had been left wide open.

I didn't understand why they'd left that room open. If they'd closed the door, I'd have never been any wiser.

I looked at the yellow desk phone that was sitting on my night stand. I reached over to see if Clarice had finally gotten tired. When I still heard the line open, I shook my head and quietly replaced the receiver. I wondered if all adults acted so insane, or stupid, or both, when they reached a certain age.

I didn't understand them any better than I understood most of the kids I knew. Maybe it was just a people thing, I tried to explain to myself. Then I felt depressed all over again. If that was the case, it meant I would never understand anyone. I already felt like a weird outsider as a kid, and now a teenager. If it was just a human condition, then I knew there was no hope for me to understand a soul.

***

My daddy's visit ended on Sunday, and by that night, the phone line was finally clear. I figured Daddy had paid Clarice a visit, when he got back to Oklahoma City. One way or another, he'd gotten her to hang up the phone. I realized I was glad that Daddy was gone and back up there, so he could deal with her. Hopefully, she wouldn't send any crazy men to rape and kill my mom and me. I did bring out my photographs of my daddy though and put them back in my room.

The next weekend after getting buzzed on beer, Chance came over and asked if I wanted to go riding around. I was happy because he'd actually been a little friendlier at school after meeting my daddy. I nodded and jumped off the car I'd been sitting on and walked over to his orange pickup. Kelly saw me walking away and grinned at me. We didn't even bother with a pretense of riding around any longer. It was now May. I'd been 'riding around' with him since January.

It was a pretty safe bet, if I went somewhere with him, where it was going to end up. When he turned to the edge of the trails and his truck began the steep climb, I put my hand on his right thigh.

Once he put the parking brake on and turned the ignition key so the radio stayed on, he leaned over and began to kiss me immediately. The beer I'd already drunk made me completely open to him. This time when his hands strayed to the buttons of my Levi's, I didn't push him away.

The song, "Open Arms" by Journey began to play on the radio. I opened my eyes and looked at his face, as it loomed over mine, and realized that I wanted to feel loved more than anything. I knew that Chance wasn't Kevin, but he was the closest I was going to have maybe for the rest of my life. I doubted Kevin would ever want to speak to me again. If he did, once he found out I'd been with someone else, he'd be completely finished with me.

When Chance finally obtained the elusive prize, he'd been after since January, he never lost eye contact with me. He never kissed me while we did it, and I thought that it was a little odd.

I think he was afraid I was a virgin, and he'd hurt me. I grimaced at first because I'd only had real sex twice. The third time still wasn't a charm, and I still didn't understand what the big deal was about it. As soon as my face screwed up in pain, Chance sweetly asked me if I was okay. I nodded and kept my eyes on his. After he was done, he leaned down and kissed me tenderly. I lay there feeling his weight on me and felt as a tear slid out of each eye, and down either side of my face, into my hair. I wanted to cry and sob, but I managed to keep from doing more than the two tiny tears, that slipped out unnoticed, by Chance.

Kelly was excited later that night when I admitted to her that I'd let Chance go all the way.

I hadn't told her about Kevin, so she thought that Chance was my first. I decided to let her believe that. In many ways he was, because the DeLaine that had been with Kevin, no longer existed. I'd left her in Wichita Falls, in February, when I left Kevin's after Donna's funeral. The DeLaine I had become, was no longer anyone I knew. I wasn't sure how you could completely lose sight of who you were, but I had. I was now the thing I had been so afraid of becoming, I realized, after I let Chance go all the way. I was now just a slut. There was no way anyone would want anything else from me, I was certain.

There wasn't enough beer or pot to make me ever feel good enough. I went to a lot of different graduation parties, before the graduation of the class of 1982, which was most of the boys that ran around in the circle of my friends. I was able to stop a bunch of boys from taking advantage of a seriously drunk and stoned Kelly, at one pool party, but still didn't feel any better about myself, since I'd gone into a bathroom and messed around with Chance, during the same party.

Kelly, Christy Gilley and I went to the graduation and afterwards, we all went to a party that was at the main weed supplier's house. Kelly, Christy, David Jeffries and Nick Vance all went over to a corner of the back yard, and I followed. When we got back there, we smoked two joints. I was sitting on the hood of an old 1970's Monte Carlo, with David. We were laughing and joking around. I realized that I was seriously stoned when I couldn't even walk. I sat on the car with David for almost an hour. He sat with me while everyone else eventually wandered away.

David was eleven days older than me, and so funny. Kelly had told me about him during the summer, before I began our freshman year. He was also one of the people I smoked pot with, because he usually had some, and never made me pay for it.

We both sat there, jamming to the music blasting from the garage. It was intermittently a mixture of music from the local rock station, and a bunch of people who were jamming live. I was glad that David had stuck by me, after I realized I'd gotten too stoned to walk.

I could see myself liking him, but I could never see him liking me. He had a girlfriend who went to Calvin, who was a couple of years older than us. She didn't seem to like any of us from Woodway, but I didn't have to run around with her, so it didn't bother me one way or another.

The song, "Dream On" by Aerosmith began to blare from the stereo out in the garage. I turned to smile at David. I was surprised when he leaned over and began to kiss me. I couldn't believe that he was actually kissing me for real. It wasn't a sweet, friendly peck. It was a full-on French kiss and his left arm reached around my shoulders.

I felt my body get the giddy, shaky feeling it did when someone new kissed me. I wondered if David still had his girlfriend. He didn't always hang out with her, and he hadn't said anything about breaking up either. I only let the thought of her flit through my mind briefly, then I concentrated on kissing him. I was shocked and couldn't understand why he chose to kiss me. We'd been talking about music and other people and then out of nowhere he'd leaned in for the kiss.

After what felt like forever, but was probably less than a minute, we pulled apart and David grinned at me. I smiled back, a little shyly. We'd always been good friends, and I'd never felt shy with him before. As soon as we pulled apart, Nick and Kelly came up. I wondered if they'd seen us.

Kelly stood on her tiptoes and whispered in my ear, "I saw that! You just kissed David Jeffries!" I grinned at her and nodded my head, then I hopped off the hood of the car and told her I had to go find a bathroom. We walked off towards the house and went into a bathroom that was off of the garage.

"So, what's goin' on, DeLaine? Does he kiss good?" Kelly asked me, giggling. I nodded and then found myself snickering too.

"You lucky dog!" Kelly exclaimed, in a bit of a pout.

"Oh, give me a break, Kel! You've been with Willie Morgan! Shut up! You've kissed way more of the cute boys in our school than me. I've just kissed Chance, and now David! So, don't give me any crap about one kiss, with one cute boy!" I rolled my eyes and then giggled some more.

We walked out of the bathroom and grabbed beers out of the ice chests in the garage.

"Yeah, but c'mon! David Jeffries!!!!! He's like the hottest guy in our class!" Kelly stated, with just a hint of jealousy. I shook my head and kept smirking. I didn't know what to think about it.

Walking out towards the back, where we'd been hanging out with Nick and David, I saw David's older girlfriend was now standing there. I felt the excitement of his kiss fly away, just as quickly as it had flown onto my face. Kelly glanced at me worriedly.

I shrugged one shoulder up and fixed my face behind one of the new masks I was learning to place on myself, in order to hide what I truly felt or thought.

Chapter 33

A couple weeks before I left for Wichita Falls, I went to another house party, with Kelly, down the street from the Gameroom. I was shocked when Chance asked me to dance. There was a dance floor set up in a gazebo that was in the backyard of the house. Country music was blaring from the stereo all night. I wondered if Chance was beginning to actually like me enough to want to be seen with me, but I wasn't sure. He still held me at arms-length in public, as far as letting others know that we even messed around. I knew most everyone we knew realized I was crazy about him.

Chance was exceptionally drunk. When I asked him what was wrong, he kept laughing and telling me nothing was bothering him. Kelly was already drunk and had left with Keith Holmes. I'd actually decided not to drink as much.

While Kelly was gone, Christy and I walked down the road to the Gameroom to use the bathroom. While we were in there, Christy told me she was happy to see that Chance and I were together, even after what he'd found out about Carla. I looked sharply at Christy, while she washed her hands at the sink.

"What do you mean?" I asked her with dread, slowly creeping into my stomach like a hard, cold fist.

"You know, about her being preggers," Christy explained, innocently.

"What?" I yelped.

Christy looked at me, "Shit, I just assumed you knew, since y'all were slow dancing, and Carla's been sitting outside all night."

"You better start talkin'," I demanded, darkly. While Christy told me that Chance had gotten Carla Feldman pregnant, I felt my blood run cold. I knew I wasn't the only girl Chance had been with, but I had hoped that the reason he was dancing with me had to do with how he felt about me and not him trying to avoid another girl. I didn't know what to think.

Carla Feldman was a girl in my class. She was the one who knew everything about everyone. I didn't know anyone that she didn't know something about. I liked her well enough, and she was always in the same circle of people I was.

We walked back down the street to the house party. I saw Carla sitting outside with Debbie Vance, crying. I walked up to Carla and demanded, "So what the fuck is this I hear that you're pregnant, Carla? Is it really Chance's?"

Carla looked at me, stunned, then began to nod her head. She asked where I'd heard it and I told her it didn't matter. Then I asked her if she was sure it was Chance's. "Yes, I'm sure! He took my virginity! I think I'd know if I'd been fucking anybody else!" Carla answered, hotly.

I wasn't really sure what to do with this information. I felt my heart crumble up like an old, dry, autumn leaf. I turned around and looked over at the gazebo, where Chance was standing up, with a beer can. I wanted to go claw his eyes out. I looked over at Carla. I knew that no matter what, Chance was the dog here. I could be angry at Carla, but it wasn't really her fault. She'd been a stupid, little, freshman girl, just like me. She had a ton more friends than I did, because she'd gone to school at Woodway since kindergarten, but she was still just a dumb girl like me, that got overly infatuated with a senior boy.

I turned away from her, walked up to the gazebo, and grabbed a beer from the ice chest that was sitting on the steps. I pulled the tab off the can and turned the light beer up, and drank it down in about 5 swallows. I chunked it into the large wastebasket that was sitting next to the rail, then grabbed another beer. After the first few swigs, I walked over to Chance, and smiled sweetly at him. Kenny Rogers was singing about decorating someone's life. Chance grabbed me around the waist with his free hand while he drank the beer he was holding in the other hand. I followed suit with holding his waist with my free hand and drinking beer with my other hand. He still didn't know that I knew.

Chance smiled down at me with his gorgeous, straight teeth. I wanted to slap him across the face, but I managed to keep my calm. I still wasn't sure how I was going to let him know that I knew what was going on with Carla. He wasn't really dancing a true two-step, but he managed a couple of real dance steps every once in a while. I looked past his shoulder. I wouldn't return his direct gaze after the first time. I was feeling a slight buzz, because I'd finished the second beer before the end of the song. I wanted another one, and when the song finally ended, I began to walk away from Chance, to go back to the ice chest. I was surprised when he grabbed my wrist lightly and asked where I was going. I shook the empty beer can and smiled. He nodded his head, shook his, and held up two fingers, asking if I'd get him one also. I nodded and grabbed two ice cold beers and walked back towards him. He opened one and handed it to me, then took the second beer and popped its top too.

Surprisingly he again reached for me by the waist and began dancing again. I tipped the can back and took three large swigs. I was getting to the point that if I tried to drink it too fast, I would vomit, but I had finally managed a pleasant buzz, even though it wasn't a happy one. It was more of a numb feeling, which is what I wanted.

Finally, I reached my hands up around his neck. Chance looked at me surprised. Up until then, I'd followed his unspoken rule of showing little physical acknowledgement between us, but by this point, I really didn't give a shit. I was hurt and angry.

I suddenly pulled his face down to my own, and our lips met for the first time in public. I felt his resistance in the beginning, but then he went with it. I kissed him well enough to make his toes curl, I hoped. I must have accomplished my task, because when he pulled away, he whispered in my ear, asking if I wanted to go riding around. I leaned back and smiled warmly at him. I wanted this to be real and yet I knew that it wasn't. I didn't mean any more to him now, than I had before.

"You wanna go riding around, Chance?" I asked innocently. He nodded his head as his straight toothed smile began to broaden. "What do you want to do if I go with you?" I asked him seductively. Chance leaned over me and kissed me deeply. I began to feel myself waffle a little, as I let myself get swept up in his kiss. Then Carla's tear streaked face flashed in front of me. I pulled away from him and smirked. "You sure?" I whispered, a little more raggedly.

Chance took my hand in his and began to lead me out of the gazebo. I followed him down the steps and looked over to the place in the dark yard, where Carla Feldman had been sitting with Debbie Vance. I knew we would walk that direction, to go back to the game room, where his pickup was parked. Thankfully, Carla and Debbie were still sitting there. It was too late for Chance when he finally realized who was sitting in our path. I felt him pull up short, as if he wanted to turn and head into another direction, but I continued in the path we were going in.

Coming to a complete and abrupt halt, Chance turned to look at me. I could see the confused look on his face, as he realized I wasn't stopping or turning with him. "No, I think we're going in the right direction," I cooed, sweetly.

"Yeah, I wanna grab another beer first," Chance stated, innocently.

"It's okay. We can go to the little store and get some," I smiled at him. He had nothing else to get himself out of the direction we were traveling in, so I saw the resigned slope of his shoulders.

As we got close enough to Carla, I finally taunted, "Oh, Chance, you know Carla right?" He nodded his head, trying to avert his eyes from both of us.

I kept a death grip on his hand that he had only moments earlier been leading me away from the gazebo with.

"I think I'm just gonna go home," Chance spoke quietly.

I grinned at him with what I hoped was a predatory smile, that hopefully was every bit as terrifying as Lori Kirk's used to seem to me, when she and Kevin had been going together. I must have succeeded, because Chance's face took on a faintly, terrified expression.

"What's wrong, Chance? Are you afraid that Carla and I are going to compare notes and find out which one of us you were fucking each weekend?" I asked, as venom dripped from each syllable. "What are you planning on doing now that Carla's pregnant?"

"What the fuck? Did you plan this?" Chance sputtered, a little indignantly. I smiled at him with every bit of the false cheer I could. "You know what? Fuck both of you stupid, little, freshmen bitches!" Chance finally shouted, as he shook his hand out of mine.

"Chance, that's not very nice to say to two of your weekend girls. I mean, I'm assuming you only have a couple of us. I mean, I'm sure you have extras during the week. No matter, you never wanted anyone to know you were taking me out and fucking me in the trails, every weekend. If I didn't go, you'd go with Carla or whoever else would let you, huh?" I ranted, sarcastically.

He stood with Carla on one side, with tears running down her face, and me standing in front of him, on the other side. I was angry. I was more than angry. I was angry and hurt. I'd hoped that Chance would end up being at the least another Jax, if he couldn't be a Kevin, for me in Corpus. He was fun, but I wanted Kevin more than anything. Now I felt like a complete and total fool. "I didn't think you could be this cold blooded, DeLaine," Chance huffed, indignantly. I smiled the deep, feline smile at him. I wished I had fangs to show him, because it was how I felt.

Shaking my head, I finally spouted off, "You got that wrong, Chance. I'm more cold blooded than you will ever know. You aren't going to rip my heart to shreds, you sonofabitch! I can't speak for Carla, but I hope she tells you to go screw yourself too! I can tell you this, I don't need your shit. You aren't going to use me again, Chance. If we're ever together again, it will be because I'm going to use your sorry ass." I took a big swig of the beer I still had in my hand, and swallowed it, then I tilted the can up and finished it. Once I was done, I squeezed the thin aluminum in my hand. Once I had squashed the can, I chunked it at Chance. "Fuck off, Chance Cahill!" I spat at him. I walked around him, went back to grab a beer and go back to the Gameroom, to wait for Kelly. I couldn't believe she had no clue about what was happening.

I noticed as I walked away from the house, where Carla, Debbie and Chance were all still in the dark recesses of the yard, that Chance was stalking towards Christy Gilley. When I saw that, I realized that Chance had been the one to tell her. He knew she had been hanging around with me.

I wondered what he was about to say to her. I hated that I had tears streaming down my cheeks, as I walked in the humid night, back to the lights of the parking lot at the Gameroom. Before I got all the way there, I rubbed my palms across both cheeks.

***

The rest of the summer that I was in Corpus Christi was spent with Kelly and Robin. Chance avoided me, and Carla had gone to her grandmother's house. I didn't know what she was going to do. It didn't really matter. I couldn't imagine her and Chance married and having a baby. It actually made me want to cry when I thought about it. I didn't love Chance, but I had hoped that there might be something with him.

I saw David Jeffries one more time before I left, and smoked part of joint with him and a couple other guys. We never mentioned the kiss at the graduation party. I decided to chalk it up to a drunken and stoned thing. I wasn't even sure if he remembered it. I knew that no matter how drunk and stoned I'd been, I'd always remember the kiss. I didn't want to screw up my friendship with him though, so I never reminded him about it. Besides, he had a girlfriend. I didn't need to have some girl after me. In Wichita Falls I had more back up when Lori wanted to beat me up, but in Corpus, I had little support.

When I got on the bus to Wichita Falls, I was extremely happy to escape from all of the insanity that my life was becoming once again. I had to deal with my mama's drinking. I had the memory and knowledge of her and my daddy sleeping together while he was down visiting. Chance had gotten Carla Feldman pregnant, and she was gone. I was drunk or stoned or both every weekend now. Even the weekends where I wanted to stay sober, to prove I didn't have a problem, like both of my parents, I still managed to find a reason to get there. Add on top of all of that the fact that my step-mother kept threatening to have me raped and murdered, and I was ready to be away from Corpus Christi. I didn't really want to ever come back.

Chapter 34

I wanted the peace that normally accompanied me to Wichita Falls, but the last time I'd been there, Kevin had basically kicked me away, and told me he didn't want me any longer. Jax had shown me what a true ass he was, as well. I wondered if all boys turned into flaming assholes once they got to high school. I thought they must. I was glad I would be on a long ride through the desert, then back and forth through California for a month, with Bailey. I had nowhere to turn for peace of mind, and a soothing of my broken heart and spirit, any longer. Even my safe haven of Wichita Falls was no longer a guarantee, now that Kevin had fallen apart and pushed me away, and Jax had become just another jackass like Chance Cahill.

The whole ride to Wichita Falls, I thought about the three boys who had played huge roles in my life for the last year. Two of them were boys who were, and most likely always would be, a part of my heart and soul. The third boy had just been in my life for a little over six months, but he'd hurt me just as badly and deeply as if he had been around as long as Kevin and Jax. I found myself looking out the window as the miles slipped under the bus, and thinking about Kevin the most.

I wondered if he was still smoking pot or if he'd gotten himself back together after a little while of unraveling, since losing Donna. I wanted to go see his mom, but was worried that I'd see him as well. I didn't want him to think I was using his mom as an excuse to see him. I felt so torn about him. He had been the boy I'd loved the most. Now, he was just as lost to me as Jax and Chance.

I had lost all three boys due to different circumstances, but they were all three lost, nonetheless. I began to think about the loss of Donna too. I felt the unwelcome tears as they silently slid down my cheeks. I looked into the dim reflection of my face, in the bus window, as the scenery blurred past me.

I leaned my forehead against the coolness of the glass and wondered what was going to happen when I got there. I wondered if Kevin even knew I was coming. I wondered if he'd even bothered to ask Bailey. I wanted to know that he actually had, more than anything, but there was no way to be certain. Bailey had said nothing to me in any of her letters about either Kevin, or Jax.

When the bus pulled into the station, I was so happy to get off of it, and stumble out to Bailey and Jason Rains. It was 11 p.m. and thankfully the trip this time, had been a tiny bit shorter. It was still an awfully long one, by myself.

Bailey grabbed me tightly and I held onto her even more desperately than I normally did. She pulled away from me and I knew she could tell without me voicing it that I was in trouble emotionally. She simply gave me her warm smile. I watched as her teal eyes lit from within and caressed my troubled soul. She pulled me by the hand, and we waited for Jason to come back to his car with my suitcase.

After we got to her house, we never once spoke Kevin or Jax's name. I'd written her already to tell her about Chance and Carla, so I was grateful she didn't ask anything about that either. We talked about extremely benign things. I was thankful my best friend understood how fragile I was inside, even if on the outside I was showing a much stronger side than I really had.

She understood that I had the need to disguise myself, behind my wall, and she was patient for the real DeLaine to finally work up her courage to peek out.

The next morning when I woke up, I was thrilled to smell the divine scent of chocolate waffles wafting through the air. Bailey opened her eyes and smiled at me from under her turquoise pillowcase. I grinned back at her. Glenda Rains' chocolate waffles were a scent of safety for me. I was so happy she fixed them for my first morning back! I wasn't sure if Bailey understood how extremely blessed she was.

I knew she didn't always get along with her mom, but I would have given almost anything to have felt safe and secure like she did. She had parents who were steady and normal. They weren't ruled by alcohol or fueled by anger either. They provided a stable and loving home-life. She thought they were horribly boring, but I would have traded with her in a heartbeat, if all I had to complain about my parents was that they were boring. How I wished my parents were completely and irrevocably boring.

Instead, I always felt like a piece of scenery when I was around them. They were both larger than life, and there was never enough room for me to shine when one of them was around. They shone too brightly for my own light to show through.

Bailey and I went swimming that first afternoon and met up with Levi. We still hadn't spoken Jax or Kevin's name.

I saw several of my friends from Milam Junior High. They all wanted to know what it was like to live in Corpus Christi.

Everybody thought that it was surfers and beaches all day and night. They seemed disappointed when they found out that I'd only been to the beach a couple of times in the last year.

I found out who was going with who and when someone mentioned Jax's name, I noticed my ears perked up even more. I felt so stupid for it, since I'd left so angry at him.

When Bailey and I broke away, and spread our beach towels on the grass, to begin working on our tans before our trip to California, I finally asked her what had happened with Jax, since I left.

"He's really been involved with the rodeo kids a lot more. He and Levi hang out some, but he doesn't talk to me very much, since you were down last time," Bailey responded, evenly.

"Does he have a new girlfriend?" I asked, angry at myself that I even cared.

Bailey looked thoughtful, and I was grateful she was honest with me, "Well, he was going with a girl that does barrel racing, in the rodeo club, but they broke up the last day of school."

I didn't know what that meant as far as me. I wasn't sure if I really wanted to see him. Once again, the cowboy with dusty blonde hair and laughing, meadow green eyes was causing conflict in my soul. Then, of course, my mind wandered to Kevin. I didn't know how two boys could possibly cause me so much turmoil. Especially since the last time I'd seen both of them, I'd been so angry.

While we lay out in the sun all afternoon, I thought over and over about seeing Jax and Kevin. By the time we left that afternoon, I had made up my mind that I didn't care what Kevin said, I was going to his house after I got dressed. At least I could go see his mom. If he was there, then I'd just see what happened between us, but his mom was extremely important to me too. I wasn't going to let him take that away from me too. He might be able to take himself away, but I needed the warmth and security of his mom in my life too. She was the only adult, besides Bailey's parents, who seemed to care about me and what was happening with me. I didn't feel as close to Bailey's mom and dad, as I did Jean Strong, but it was only because I had limited contact with them, so far.

Jean Strong had been a literal lifesaver and I felt a deep connection to her. She had held me up when I needed it, and had provided me sanctuary, from my insane home-life, when I was younger, and needed a responsible adult in it.

After we got dressed, I told Bailey I wanted to go see Mrs. Strong. My best friend looked at me with deep concern. "You haven't mentioned Kevin at all, so I'm assuming that things haven't changed with him," I spoke quietly. Bailey shook her head and I insisted, "Well, if he's there, I don't care. I need to go see his mama." I finished resolutely.

Thankfully my best friend smiled at me and told me she understood. Bailey surprised me by hugging me around the neck, as I left. I smiled gratefully at her. I still wondered sometimes why Bailey had become my best friend. It seemed I had drama going on no matter which way I turned.

When I crossed Fairfax, and got to the corner of Portland, I saw the Strong's home immediately. It was a brown brick home and the trim was a deep, rust-brown color. Mrs. Strong's blue sedan was parked in the driveway. I smiled when I saw her car and remembered the one real date Kevin and I had gone on. I remembered how cherished I'd felt that night. I walked up the familiar driveway and knocked on the door more confidently than I felt.

Jean Strong opened the door. I saw her bright smile, as it crossed her features. She seemed older and sadder in some ways, but she still smiled and held me close to her, as soon as she ushered me inside their foyer. I loved when she hugged me. She was a tall and strong woman and she made me feel as safe as her son always had. She oozed warmth and kindness in everything she did.

"Oh, my dear DeLaine! What a wonderful surprise. I wondered if you'd be able to come see us this summer! I'm so happy you are here!" Mrs. Strong gushed, smiling deeply at me.

"I should have written. I'm so sorry. Life's been so hectic it seems like," I finished lamely. I felt self-conscious that I had not written to her since Donna had died and had only seen her briefly during the March spring break.

Nodding her head, Mrs. Strong replied heartily, "Oh honey, you need to be enjoying everything you can right now. Don't ever apologize for being a teenager! I'm just thrilled you came by to see us." I smiled at her. I wondered if she would say anything about Kevin. As if sensing I was in the house, I saw movement from the corner of my eyes, and glanced at the hallway to find Kevin standing there in all of his blonde glory. I felt bad that the first thing I looked at were his eyes, and felt relief when I realized they weren't red. "Kev, look who has made her way to our door, finally!" Mrs. Strong sang, smiling. I wondered if she knew how I'd left things with Kevin.

"Hey, Lainey," Kevin whispered, softly.

I felt my face betray me, when my mouth began to curl up, and replied, "Hey, Kev. You look good."

Kevin nodded at me and his mom instructed, "Well, you kids get caught up and then you come in the kitchen, if you have time, and we can finish up these cookies I'm baking for the Sunday schools."

I smiled at Jean Strong. I remembered how the first time I met her, she had put me to work making cookies, in order to help me when my daddy and Clarice had gotten crossways one evening.

Looking at Kevin, I was waiting for him to tell his mom he was busy or something, in order to get out of having to see me alone, but he didn't. Instead, he gave me a small smile and turned back towards his room.

I squeezed Jean Strong one more time, and followed behind Kevin, down the familiar hallway to his room. When I walked through the door to his room, I saw it was basically the same as it had always been. I didn't even try to glance at Donna's empty room. I wondered if it was still painted little girl pink and held all of her things in it. I felt weird asking, so I kept that thought to myself.

"Sit down, Lainey," Kevin whispered sweetly, as he threw his pillows on the bed and propped himself up against the wall.

Sitting gingerly on the edge of the bed, I felt uncomfortable with Kevin for the first time that I could ever remember, after we'd began our relationship. "How have you been?" I whispered, and found I had to clear my throat a couple of times to get it out all the way.

Shrugging one shoulder up, Kevin began to look a little more relaxed and like his old self. Finally, he admitted, "Listen Lainey, I'm sorry. I was an asshole last time you were here. I just feel a little lost. Well, I actually have felt really lost, since February."

I nodded as I thought about how things had left off the last time I'd sat in his room. He'd been stoned. We'd argued about him being involved with all the pot heads at school. He told me to leave and forget him, but I hated to think that I had tried to hurt him by telling him about my own partying, and then had told him about Chance. I had tried to hate him away, by being with Jax and then Chance.

"I'm sorry, Kevin," I whispered softly. I glanced up at him and saw his sad smile. I wondered if he'd ever give me the sunshine and rainbow smile again. Even the sad smile reminded me how much I would always care for him.

"You wanna go walkin'?" Kevin asked, quietly. I surprised myself by nodding my head, without even thinking about it.

We got to the end of the hall, and he told his mom we were going for a walk. She smiled what seemed to be her ordinary smile, but something told me she didn't smile that way very often since Donna died. I smiled back and felt my heart ache for her.

I knew that she was worried about losing Kevin too, even without her telling me. I followed Kevin out the glass, storm door, into the late afternoon sun.

I still felt the tightness of the pool's chlorine on my skin, and could still smell it a little in my curly hair, as we got outside in the dry heat.

Kevin turned immediately to the left, after we got to the end of his driveway. There were no words said between us for several blocks. When I saw Woodbane and Woolery, I smiled a little, remembering the first kiss he'd given me. Then I thought about the kiss he'd given me, later, on my 13th birthday, on the same corner.

Kevin stopped when we got to the corner, and he turned to look into my eyes.

"I'm really sorry, Lainey. I wanted to tell you that after you were here last time. I wasn't sure if I'd ever see you again," he muttered, quietly, as he dropped his gaze to his white sneakers.

My heart completely melted when he said that. I stepped closer to him and touched his cheek. "Oh Kevin, it's okay. I'm so sorry I tried to hurt you back," I whispered, hoarsely.

"Lainey, thinking about you being with another guy just kills me. I haven't been with another girl since you were here for the funeral. I don't want anyone else. I know that you're gonna be with other guys, but out of everything you said to me, the part about that asshole is what pissed me off the most. I know it's stupid. I just…I don't know what to say except it just kills me." He whispered.

I dipped my knees until I was looking up into his downcast face. "Kevin, I'm sorry I hurt you. I was hurt and I wanted to hurt you back."

"I can't think straight, since Donna…well, since she's not here anymore. She's been my whole life since I can remember, and now I feel like there is nothing for me. I feel like there's not much point in anything. You're gone and now Donna is too. I'm not sure what it is I'm supposed to do." Kevin finished, sadly.

I felt my heart breaking as he spoke. I knew that Donna's death would undo him to some degree, but I was never sure what it would be. I reached up, wrapped my wrists around his neck, and stood up straight, forcing him to stand up straighter.

When we were standing up, all the way, I pulled him to me. I heard his sobs and immediately found tears pouring from my own eyes. We were like two shipwreck survivors, who just found one another, after the storm that wrecked the boat. I held tightly to him as he kept his arms wrapped around my waist.

We stood like that on the corner, that I now considered ours. I had no clue how long we stood there, holding one another, but I knew there was nowhere else in the world I wanted to be at that moment, except in Kevin's embrace.

After a long time, he had finally cried himself out. I held him close to me, as he hid his face in the curve of my neck. Finally, he pulled his head up and looked away from me, as he wiped his face on the back of his wrist and hand. He kept his grip on my waist with his other arm.

I stood there quietly, waiting for him to get under control. I knew that he hated for me to see him cry. During the funeral it had been one thing, but I knew that he thought he should have everything under control. He never seemed to mind that I was constantly bawling about something, but he felt weak, I knew, by showing me his tears.

Sniffling, but with the tears wiped dry on his face, Kevin looked at me and gave me a lop-sided version of his half smile, that I'd missed so dearly. "Sorry, Lainey, I just, well I'm just a total fucked up mess, I guess," Kevin smiled as a tiny chuckle came out of the back of his throat. I smiled at him and shook my head, then pulled him back to me. I hugged him as tightly as I could.

When I finally loosened my death grip on him, Kevin pulled away from me, "I really am sorry for everything."

"Shut up, Kev! I'm sorry too. I'm worried about you also. I don't want you to lose yourself."

"Lainey, I'm already lost. I just don't understand why you want to hold onto me." He muttered softly.

"Because you are important to me. I don't want to ever lose you, Kev. I don't care if you are with someone new or not. Isn't that what you told me last summer? It doesn't matter if you're with someone or not, she's gotta understand I come first? Well, guess what dumbass, I feel the same way. So shut the hell up and know that it doesn't matter, Kevin. You can be a jock, or pothead, or whatever you feel you need to be, but it doesn't change who you are to me, okay?" I admitted, seriously, as I looked up into his eyes. They made me think of free falling up into the sky.

Finally, he nodded his head and suggested, "Let's go back to the house. I just feel cooped up in there sometimes, and it's hard." I felt happy when he wrapped his arm around my shoulder, as we walked back to his house. "You smell like the pool," he stated, conversationally as we walked.

I grinned, "Yeah, I went swimming with Bailey today. I'm going to California with her in a week."

"Yeah, Jason told me last week." Kevin replied, absently.

"Jason Rains?" I asked him.

Kevin nodded his head. He knew now that I knew he'd been keeping tabs on me, even though I had thought he hadn't been.

It might not have been as good as getting information from Bailey, but I was certain Bailey had given him the evil eye quite a bit after I was there last time.

"So, my daddy and Clarice split up." I stated solemnly.

"Yeah, Geoff told me when he came down and told me he was a fag!" Kevin replied, with a mean sounding chuckle.

"Wait, you knew in February?" I stopped walking and Kevin dropped his arm around my shoulder, as he nodded his head! "Are you fuckin' kidding me???" I exclaimed loudly.

"What?" Kevin asked, alarmed.

I stood there and let out a low scream of frustration. Kevin stepped back and asked if I was okay. He looked terrified now. I felt the hot scorching tears as they slipped down my red cheeks. I was so mad. I was angry. Hell, I was FURIOUS!

"DeLaine! What the hell is wrong?" Kevin asked me, anxiously.

Shaking my head, I finally looked at him and swiped at my own tear streaked face. "Oh, nothin' Kevin, you just knew about them splitting up before I did!" Kevin looked at me in shock and I admitted, "Oh yeah, I didn't know they'd split up until after I got home from Spring Break, in March. It sucks that you knew something about my parents before I did!" I thought about the last sentence and then said, "Well about my PARENT, because Clarice is no longer one of my parents, thank-fucking-goodness!" I spat out angrily.

"That's fucked up, DeLaine," Kevin quietly shook his head. I pursed my lips in a grimace and agreed. I finally just shrugged my shoulders and began walking towards Kevin's house again. I felt so angry and betrayed that someone else knew about what was happening in my daddy's life, before me, when it was something so important. I felt like I didn't matter when it was something important. I felt such a rage pushing at my chest. I still felt like screaming again, but I stuffed it down as far as I could. After about a block, Kevin gingerly put his arm around my shoulder again. I finally felt myself begin to breathe a little more calmly.

Just as we got to Portland Street, I looked at Kevin and apologized. "Awww, Lainey, we already know they are fucked up. Don't sweat it, Kid." He knew I hated it when he called me kid and when I was about to go off on him, I looked up at his face to find the sunshine and rainbows smile, that I'd wondered if I'd see again in my lifetime.

I playfully smacked him on his stomach. I was happy to see that it still remained muscular, which meant that he was still working out. I felt like if he was still taking care of himself physically, then maybe the pot smoking would fade quickly.

I thought dismally to my own behavior and wondered if I could say the same for me. I'd gained some more weight and was now wearing a size 12. I was heavier than I'd ever been, and I felt even more self-conscious about my size. I remembered when I had been a size 7, and thought I was a cow because Geoffrey and Clarice had always told me I was.

Now I was twice that size and felt even more so. Kevin hadn't said anything to me about how much bigger I was, but I knew that he could see it. I realized that my mind had traveled from smoking pot to how big I was and grinned at myself. I decided what I was doing was a temporary thing, for sure.

I didn't want to be like my parents, but I didn't know anything else to do. Drinking and smoking pot were my escape from my drunk mother. It was a way to deal with my loneliness and the awfully empty pit I felt inside of myself, being 500 miles away from where I thought of as home.

After I went back into Kevin's house, and visited with his mom, I called Bailey and told her I was going to stay for dinner. She sounded surprised but told me it was fine. I told her I'd be home by 8:30. I enjoyed eating with Kevin and his mom and dad. I was happy to see his dad, Steve, was still his old jokester self. I knew without anyone telling me, that he did it to try to mend his family's broken heart. I was glad he could do that though. Jean Strong seemed to brighten up even more when he came into the house. It made me smile to see someone's parents who seemed to love and care for one another.

At 8 o'clock, as the evening sky was beginning to turn into its nightly, painted masterpiece, Kevin and I walked out of the front door. I promised Mrs. Strong to come back for a visit. We crossed Fairfax and went to Granville and began the trek to Bailey's. He grabbed my hand as soon as we got on Granville and we walked in silence that was comfortable, for a change, instead of feeling sad or angry.

As we got to the little side street that led to the elementary park, behind Bailey's house, Kevin turned. I realized that he wanted to go to the park before we got to Bailey's. I didn't want to sit inside of the tunnel now. Somehow it seemed tainted with a horrible memory. It had the makings to be a happy memory, but Jax had been drunk and pushy. I didn't want to creep inside of its dirt floor and sit inside the circle of the giant pipe.

I was grateful that Kevin didn't sense my hesitation, because we had been having such a nice time, after my tantrum about him knowing about Clarice and my daddy. I didn't want to bring up Jax. I knew it would only create more animosity with us.

Instead of walking to the tunnel though, I was thrilled when he walked to the swings, "I've wanted to swing with you again, since I saw you swing last summer." I smiled at him gratefully and hopped into the rubber seat of the swing.

Pumping my legs back and forth, after pushing off on the packed dirt, under the swing, I was thrilled to feel my stomach leap up the higher I got in the air. Soon, I felt as the wind blew through my chlorine smelling curls. I closed my eyes, as I leaned back, holding onto the large chains and felt the flip flop of my guts.

I began to smile and feel as if all of my cares and troubles could be gone, just by living on the swing forever. I felt happier than I could remember feeling in a long time. It seemed as if I hadn't been happy in over a year.

When I thought about that, I felt a brief falling of my light-heartedness, but then I shook my head and felt the wind ruffle the dark curls. I found the smile coming back across my face. I felt exhilarated as I went higher on the swing. I hadn't opened my eyes in several minutes and was lost inside of the squeaking chains, as they carried me up and down, and back and forth on the swing set.

I felt the wind caress every part of me, as I pushed through the air, I thought that what I was feeling must be close to how a bird feels, when it flies with the air whooshing up and over every part of your body. I wished I could be a bird and fly away sometimes. After what felt like hours, I remembered I'd said I was going to be back to Bailey's by 8:30. I thought we'd been gone for at least an hour, which would make it 9 o'clock. My eyes flew open. I saw that it was definitely getting darker, but what surprised me was Kevin had moved from the swing next to me, to standing in front of the swing set, watching me intently.

I felt suddenly embarrassed by my carefree abandon at swinging without a thought in the world. I stuck my feet down to begin slowing myself and felt my face begin to blush. I'd gotten a little bit of a sunburn at the pool that day, so I wasn't sure if Kevin could see the blush or not. Because of the burn, I could definitely feel it more. When I'd finally stopped myself, I jumped off the U-shaped swing and half ran to Kevin.

"What?" I whispered up at Kevin, as I noticed him never taking his eyes off of me once, after I'd opened mine.

Shaking his head, Kevin whispered, "You just look so free when you swing. You look at peace. You look like a kid. You don't look like one very often, but when you swing, I don't know, you just have this light that is all over your face. I can't describe it. But you look beautiful when you swing. I wish you always could look that happy, Lainey."

I was a little dumbstruck by his statement. He told me I looked beautiful and happy when I was on the swing. I smiled shyly at him and murmured that I felt free when I was on the swing. He leaned over and kissed me on the forehead, as he held my head in both of his large, long fingered hands. Gently, he tilted my face up. I felt myself holding my breath, as his mouth came down onto my own. I wrapped my arms around him and felt his warm embrace, as he kissed me tenderly. I wanted to feel this way forever. Free from the swing and now warm and loved by Kevin's embrace. I didn't think life could ever be this good again.

When Kevin pulled away from me, he smiled and cupped my cheek with one of his hands. "I've missed you so much, Lainey." I smiled at him and tucked my face into his palm, then turned my mouth to kiss the inside of his hand.

"Me too," I managed, in a tiny whisper.

We stood there for a few more minutes, without speaking, then Kevin took his hand back and we turned to walk the rest of the way to Bailey's. I just knew I was going to be really late, but when I walked inside the house, after kissing Kevin quickly goodbye, I was happy to see it was only 8:45.

"I'm so sorry I'm late," I said quickly, when I walked into the family room where Bailey was watching TV with her parents.

"Are you late?" Bailey asked me.

I nodded my head. "Yeah, I said I'd be home by 8:30 and it's 8:45."

Bailey snorted and teased, "Oh no, 15 whole minutes, Mom you need to ground her, I guess!" I looked at Bailey and realized she thought it was funny, but she also didn't realize that it was no laughing matter for either household I lived in if you were late. I would have been automatically grounded if I was still living on Belfast with Clarice and my daddy. I was too terrified of my mom's drunken rages to even dare be late. Finally, I smiled and shrugged my shoulders. Bailey jumped out of the chair that she'd been laying in sideways, and we walked to her room. She had a big smile on her face, as we walked through the house.

"So, tell me, Lala!" Bailey demanded, grinning.

"Tell you what?" I asked her innocently.

"LALA!" Bailey was exasperated. I began to giggle. Then I told her every detail about what had happened and what was said. When I finished, Bailey smiled at me and admitted, "I knew that something good must be going on since you called to say you were staying for dinner."

I smiled and surprised both of us when I reached over and hugged her tight. I felt like I was going to burst I was so happy. I was with my best friend, and Kevin and I were back on track, I thought.

I thought about Chance Cahill and wanted to say out loud, "Chance Who?" but figured even Bailey might think I was cracking up if I did that, so I just pulled away from her and squealed, "I'm so excited! I'm here and we're going to California!"

Bailey giggled with me and we began talking about what we were doing the next day. She wanted to go shopping for California. I'd done a little while I'd been in Corpus Christi. I had some spending money for the whole trip, but I was trying to be frugal. I was excited to be going with her anywhere, even if it was just to the mall the next day.

I was just happy to finally feel at home. It had been too long coming.

I knew that it had only been a couple of months since I'd been there, but it seemed like every day in Corpus was a battle. I was either battling with Mama and her demons, or I was battling with my own demons. I couldn't find any peace, no matter how hard I tried. I wanted to feel safe and happy, but I never did.

I hoped that drinking or smoking pot would offer me the relief from the worry and care, but it never seemed to. It only added more guilt and shame on me. It seemed like no matter what I did, even when I decided I wasn't going to do it, I still managed to end the night intoxicated and miserable. I was hoping to make a new start when I got back to Corpus, after this trip to Wichita Falls.

I was feeling optimistic that if Kevin and I could make up, then I could turn myself around. I was still smoking cigarettes, but Bailey wasn't upset with me. She had even smoked one when we walked up to the swimming pool. I was glad to be away from Corpus and the drama of Mama's drunk fueled rages and Chance Cahill.

I was right where I always wanted to be no matter what.

Chapter 35

The few days we were in Wichita Falls, before leaving for California, were packed with getting ready for a 3-week vacation. I was excited about going to places I remembered seeing when I was really little. It was going to be a real vacation, like a normal family does. I wasn't traveling because my parents had a gig, in some officer's club, on a military base, or a club in the mountains of Colorado.

This trip I would be an actual tourist, taking pictures, and going on tours of places I'd never seen before. I couldn't believe that the Rains were including me in this trip. I knew how extremely lucky I was to have this chance. I didn't think that Bailey realized what a true treat a trip like this was to me. She was used to going on family vacations every year, but I wasn't. When I traveled, it was because my parents were making their living, playing music. When that ended, all my travel became about going between each of my parents.

I had seen Kevin only one more time before we left, and it had been a short visit. We'd felt like our normal selves again, and I was grateful for that. We didn't do anything except hang out in his room for a little while. I wanted to ask him about how he was feeling since Donna was gone, but I didn't want to bring the saddest topic up between us, so I kept quiet about the little girl we both missed.

The day we left on our cross-country trip, we left Bailey's house at 6 in the morning. Neither of us was very excited about leaving so early. Once we got into the back seat, of her parents' car, we crashed out and slept most of the morning. I had grown up sleeping in vehicles, so I had little trouble getting comfortable, and staying asleep for a long time. We woke up as her dad was driving through the desert part of Texas. I felt the excitement begin building all over again.

We played car games and ate junk food in the back seat. We gossiped about everybody and everything. I couldn't believe her parents stopped at lots of little history markers, and tourist spots, to take pictures and look around. When I was little, we sped past everything like this, on our way to the next gig. It was a treat to get out and look at everything. Bailey seemed bored with it, but I was thrilled to see things I'd missed as a kid, when we traveled.

On our trip west, we stopped in New Mexico and saw part of the mountains. Then we went to Arizona, where we spent the night in a cabin at the Grand Canyon. We took lots of pictures of the Canyon and watched some daring souls ride donkeys to the bottom.

It was one of the most beautiful things I'd ever seen. I remembered seeing it when I was little. Daddy had actually stopped to let us look at it, when we'd been near it a few times in our travels. Seeing it with my 15-year-old eyes though, was different. Now, I could truly appreciate the magnificence of all the colors it showed, and the sheer enormity of it. I could now appreciate that it was something only God could have made. It was truly extraordinary to me.

When we finally got to California, I was shocked to see how much traffic there was. I was glad Bailey's dad had a calm demeanor and didn't get too ruffled by all the horns and cars. We went to Universal Studios and took a long tour of the place. We saw how they made bridges explode, and how they could make it rain, on a street that was built just to shoot movies on. As we rode over a small body of water, they explained how they shot the movie Jaws and how they could make the small area of water look like the vast ocean. As the tour guide talked, I almost jumped out of the open train car we were riding in! The actual mechanical shark came out of the water, on the side of the cart that I was riding in. There was a woman in front of me that went into such hysterics, it caused Bailey and me to convulse in wild giggles.

The train drove through a large row of sound stages. We learned many shows that were popular, were filmed in them, as well as upcoming movies. There was a new movie called *Fast Times at Ridgemont High* that was being filmed there. Bailey and I hoped to see someone famous, but we were disappointed when we didn't see anyone we knew. We vowed to go see the movie that was being filmed, when it came out.

While we were at Universal Studios, we took a ton of pictures. We went to an indoor show as well, where the Incredible Hulk came out into the audience. I didn't know if it was the real actor who was on the TV series or not, but it was fun seeing a big, green, muscular man running through the audience growling at everyone.

Our next stop was to drive up the coast to San Francisco and visit Mrs. Rains' cousin and her family. They lived right outside of San Francisco. Her cousin and her husband were going to take us to San Francisco though while we visited, and we were going to go to Fisherman's Wharf and sightsee there as well. We were stumped as we drove across the desert of Arizona when Bailey's mom asked if we'd brought jackets.

We laughed at her and told her it was the middle of the summer and we were going to California, which was considered a sunshine state.

Once we got to San Francisco, with Glenda Rains' cousin and her family, Bailey and I both understood the importance of a jacket. We were wearing shorts, sandals and tank tops!

When we got out at Fisherman's Wharf, we ran quickly into a gift shop and both emerged with oversized sweatshirts. We were still cold on our legs though. Much of the time, if we sat down, we tucked our legs up inside the sweatshirt to warm them up.

After a tour of the Wharf, I was shocked when we began our way to a loading dock to get on board a boat headed to Alcatraz Island. We were going to visit the infamous prison and go on a tour there as well. I'd seen movies about Alcatraz but had no clue we were going to go there also.

The inside of the prison gave me a creepy feeling as soon as we walked inside of it. I didn't know if it was because of all the lost souls who had been there, or if it was just the run-down state, but I was glad when we left there. It was interesting in a historical way, and I loved history, but I was happy to get back on the boat.

The Golden Gate Bridge was covered in a thick shroud of fog. Even after driving over it and back, we never saw it through the soup of clouds covering it. I enjoyed our guided tour with Glenda's cousin's husband, but her cousin rubbed me the wrong way. I was extremely polite to her, because that was how I was raised, but I really wasn't sure about her. At the end of our day, we ate at a restaurant called Spago's.

By the time we left their cousin's, I was itching to get back on the road. We went back down the coastline to San Diego, where Bailey and I played on the beach for an entire day. I was shocked at how cool the breeze was, yet how warm the sand felt. It was such a contradiction in temperatures. We rented boogie boards and even though we didn't know what we were doing, we got into the freezing water and rode the waves in as best as we could. I was impressed at how much larger the waves were, than the small waves I was used to seeing in the Gulf of Mexico. I was surprised at the huge difference in the temperature of the ocean and the Gulf too.

Both of us left San Diego severely sunburned. With the cool Pacific breezes, we ended up staying outside much longer than we should. We traveled back to Texas through Las Vegas. We only spent one night, but still managed to tour the Hoover Dam. By the time our vacation ended, I felt even closer to Bailey. It was the most intense time we'd ever spent together. There was little outside distraction from others for three weeks. We talked about Levi, Kevin and even Jax.

The day after we got back to Wichita Falls, Levi came over and didn't come alone. He showed up with Jax, who brought him over. I was surprised because Bailey told me she told Levi everything that happened with me and Jax, the last time I'd been home visiting.

Jax walked into Bailey's turquoise and lime green room, like he'd done a million times. I felt my back stiffen when I first saw him, but he acted extremely polite to both Bailey and me. As always, I felt confused by him.

Bailey and I were still on a post-trip high from everything we'd done. Eventually, I just accepted Jax being there. Soon, it seemed like the four of us were once again our normal foursome. We even snapped pictures with our cameras, to finish up the film in order to get our vacation photos developed. The boys didn't stay very long. I could tell Levi really wanted all of us to go do something together, but I was still a little angry at Jax. I also wanted to spend my time with Kevin, if I wasn't going to be with Bailey.

Once the boys were gone, I told Bailey I was going to Kevin's and I'd be back later. I practically skipped down Granville to Fairfax Blvd. I was excited about seeing Kevin, after 3 weeks on the road. I wanted to tell him all about the trip and everything I'd seen. Knocking on the door, I couldn't wait to see the summer sky blue eyes that I still dreamed about. When his mom answered the door, she gave me her customary warm hug and greeting. She commented on the deep tan I'd gotten, after the sunburn had peeled from San Diego.

Closing the door behind us, she listened to a couple of my vacation stories, then nodded towards Kevin's room, "He's down there in his room. I wish I could say he's been expecting you, but I think he forgot what day you were getting back."

I looked at her oddly and bent my head slightly, as I turned down the hallway to go to Kevin's room. I knocked briefly on his door, and when I didn't hear an immediate greeting, I knocked again. Instead of hollering at me to come in, the door suddenly jerked open, pulling away from my hand that I grasped the door knob with.

I gasped because I was startled and Kevin looked down at me with a strange gleam in his eyes. Smiling, he stepped back for me to come in. I saw his windows were opened all the way, and I was confused why he had them open. It was over 100 degrees outside and the air conditioner was running.

I walked into the room and immediately recognized the reek that the open window was supposed to be airing out. I also noticed a skinny guy, who was sitting cross legged on the floor, by one of the windows. I didn't know him, but he seemed to know me. When Kevin closed the door the skinny guy chirped, "Hey, DeLaine! About time I met you, I guess!"

"Do I know you?" I asked him a little stiffly.

"Nah, but I used to know your step-brother. My name's Freddie." He declared, grinning at me.

I noticed his teeth were really crooked, and he had a sick, sallow look about him. He was so pale, he seemed translucent. He had brown hair and really red lips. I wondered if his lips looked so red because the rest of him was so colorless. He was odd looking but looked fairly harmless.

I glanced at Kevin and knew that his eyes would be red and glassy. I wasn't wrong as soon as I looked up into the blue eyes I loved. He looked a little ashamed, but he covered it with his cocky grin and his hooded look. I rolled my eyes and looked over at the thin kid, named Freddie.

"Hey Kid, c'mon in and pull up a piece of bed," Kevin grinned like a loon.

I sat down on the edge of the bed. I hated acting like a prude. I did exactly what they had done, all the time when I was in Corpus, but I'd never dream about doing it in my room, where my mom might catch me. I looked over at Kevin and I wanted to shake him. If anyone deserved to act like a jackass, around their mom, it was me, but I still respected her enough, that I would never smoke dope in the house. I also valued my life. I knew it would warrant a swift smack across the face, if she ever found out I smoked it once, much less doing it in our home. I knew Kevin's mom knew what was happening in his room. That was the reason for the look that crossed her face, when she nodded down the hallway.

Freddie and Kevin began talking and giggling, like stoned people do. I watched them both and wondered if I acted as stupid as they were acting. I wanted to smoke a cigarette more than anything. Kevin looked at me and asked, "So how was your trip, Kid?"

"It was great, but the trip you are about to take isn't gonna be so great," I spoke grimly. Kevin looked at me surprised. Finally, realizing he didn't have a clue what he was doing, I sniped, "You call me Kid one more time, Sparky, and we are going to have a fucking problem!"

Freddie began to bark laughter, as he coughed deeply. "Damn, Dude! She's a tough, little woman! I wouldn't fuck with her, if I was you dude!"

I watched as Kevin turned his summery blue eyes towards his friend. His lips turned up into a smile, but I saw it wasn't in Kevin's eyes. "Yeah, dude, she'll probably beat the shit outta me if I ain't careful," Kevin began snickering.

I stood up, disgusted, and hit Kevin hard in his upper arm. "Fuck you, Kevin!" I stomped to the door. Before I could open it though, Kevin had jumped up, taking two long strides to reach the door and hold it closed.

"C'mon, Lainey! I'm sorry! I didn't know you were getting home today! I don't even know what day it is!" This statement caused both of them to break down into giggles again. I stood there fuming at Kevin. I wasn't in the least bit amused with either of them.

"So, I guess if you remembered I was coming home, then you'd have held off on getting stoned, until I was gone, or you knew I wasn't coming around, is that what you're saying?" I asked him in a low whisper.

Kevin smiled down at me, "Well, yeah, I'd have held off and not gotten stoned right before you got here. I know you get pissed about it."

I stood there gaping at him. He didn't really understand what made me the angriest, I realized. Finally, I demanded, "Go to your bathroom with me, please!" Kevin and Freddie looked at each other and both broke into a grin. I rolled my eyes as I stomped over to the small bathroom, in the corner of his room. Kevin followed behind me, obediently, and I closed the door. Once the door was closed, Kevin grabbed me and began kissing my neck, rubbing his hands up my sides and trying to slide them inside my tank top. I stepped back, smacking his hands. When he still continued trying to grope me, I got both of my hands on his throat and shoved him, growling, "Get the fuck off of me, Kevin!"

He stood there unsteadily, smirking at me, "Lainey, I just want to be with you! I know you only got a couple days left. I miss you so much!"

"Are you fucking serious?" I hissed between my teeth.

"What's wrong, babe?" Kevin asked me earnestly.

"Jesus, Kevin, first of all, I don't want you groping me as soon as the door is closed. If you think we're doing something in your bathroom, with some weird druggie in your room, and your mom in the kitchen, you're delusional! How could you do this to your mama, Kev?" I demanded.

Kevin stood up and his whole demeanor changed, as he looked soberly at me. "What, DeLaine? How can I do what to my mom?"

"Smoke that shit in her house! If you're gonna be a pothead, that's one thing, but at least respect your parents enough not to do that shit in their house! That's just so wrong, Kevin! What the fuck is wrong with you?" I asked, sadly.

"God-dammit, DeLaine, what the fuck is your trip? You act like you've never done any of this shit! From what you told me before, you've been partying like a rock star since you got to Corpus!" Kevin growled, more menacingly.

"You're right, Kev, but I don't do this shit in my mama's house. First of all, she'd beat the shit out of me! Secondly, I respect her, even as a fucking drunk, too much to do this kind of shit under her roof!" I explained, softly.

"Well, I forgot what a fucking saint you are, now didn't I, DeLaine?" Kevin drawled, sarcastically.

His remark stung. He was acting like my mom, when she had a completely different personality. I sighed, "No, Kevin, I'm the furthest thing from a saint. I am just disappointed you're doin' this shit around her. Don't you think she's having a hard enough time, without having to worry about what you are doing right now?"

"Fuck you, DeLaine! Don't you dare say Donna's name!" Kevin snarled, ferociously.

I looked at his face, as two bright red spots began to show high in his cheeks. "Kevin, I never once said her name. You did. I just said your mom has enough on her mind and doesn't need this added to worry about. So, don't get pissed at me for saying something like the truth. If you can't handle it, then I won't come back anymore, but just know, if I walk out this time…I'm not ever coming back." I declared a little more bravely than I actually felt.

Kevin immediately grabbed my hand, and his face got a haunted look. "Lainey, please, don't ever leave me again! I'm sorry! I'll quit smoking pot at home, if you think it is really upsetting my mom, but don't walk out and never come back."

"Kevin, tell that weird guy to leave," I whispered. Kevin nodded and then he opened the door and told Freddie to get lost. I was surprised that he amiably got up and left. Once he was gone, we walked out into his bedroom. "Kevin, I know you hurt, but you have to remember your mama is hurting too. Watching you destroy yourself, over your pain, is hurting her even more. Just think about that before you keep getting fucked up! Your getting wasted is tearing her up. Trust me. I know." I admitted, softly.

Kevin looked down, nodding his head. "I'm sorry, Lainey. You're right. I need to straighten my shit up around my folks. They've done everything right and don't deserve a fuck-up for a son. Donna was the best one of the two of us. I should have been the one to die." He trailed off.

I inhaled sharply. "Kevin, NEITHER of you should have died. She was a beautiful soul; however, she was never going to live a long life. We both knew that. I know you are hurting, but don't ever wish it was you who died. Don't you realize how important you are to so many people?"

Soberly, I pled, "Donna couldn't help she was born sick, any more than I could help being born with curly hair. You can't ever compare which one of you was more worthy of living. Please, don't ever do that again,"

Finally, Kevin's red eyes looked in my direction. He pulled me to him, and I pressed my ear to his chest. I listened as the pounding of his heartbeat finally began to slow down. I squeezed him tightly. "Kevin, promise me you won't ever do anything stupid, okay?" He agreed, then leaned down and kissed the tip of my nose.

"I promise I won't do anything stupid. I promise I won't act like a jackass again when you are around. When you aren't around, I can't promise anything, because I pretty much act like a jackass most of the time! When you are here, I'll behave!" He smirked at me.

"And no more 'kid' shit, do you understand Mister Strong? If you call me "KID" one more time, I'm going to punch you right in the mouth!" I finished, huffily.

Kevin giggled and nodded. I smiled back at him, "Good, glad I got that point across, Sparky!"

We walked over to his bed and climbed on it. I lay against his chest as I told him about all of my adventures with Bailey. When Kevin fell sound asleep, I smiled, as I kept my head resting on him. I knew that after watching Kevin get stupid smoking pot, I had little right to get angry with him. I just hated seeing him destroy himself.

It was different. He had a great family. He still had great parents who loved him so much. He had so much potential.

I on the other hand, didn't have it so grand. Both my parents were alcoholics. I hardly ever knew what was happening with my daddy. I was already heading down the same path as my parents, and I wasn't even 16. I sighed deeply and felt myself begin to doze, as I rested on Kevin's chest.

Chapter 36

I went with Bailey, Levi and Jax to the lake, fishing, a few days later. When Jax broke out the beer, I declined. Jax and Levi talked about how I had drunk the beer like a champ at Spring Break. Now, I was turning it down. I reminded them, "Yeah, well, if you'll remember, I also acted like a moron," I turned my head to look at Jax, "If you'll recall, things didn't end so great with us, either!"

Jax looked grimly at me and agreed. Bailey declined a beer too, so the boys were the only ones who drank while we sat at our spot with fishing poles. We talked about what to expect in the next year as sophomores. I wished I was going to be walking through the doors of Samson with them. I was supposed to graduate from Samson High School and not Woodway High in Corpus Christi, but that was never going to happen.

After almost two hours in the folding lawn chairs, in the shallow water, with the fishing poles, Bailey and Levi took off for a walk through the wooded area. I had hoped that they wouldn't leave me and Jax alone together. We hadn't been alone since the whole incident at Spring Break, but now here I was, right where I had hoped I wouldn't be.

Finally, about 15 minutes after our best friends left, Jax looked over at me, "I'm sorry, DeLaine. I shouldn't have acted like an asshole when you were here last time."

I thought about what he'd said. It seemed like every time I came back home, I was either apologizing to Jax or Kevin, or they were apologizing to me. I couldn't understand how we always ended up right back to where we were right now. It seemed like every time it was about something different. I was so tired of all the miles tearing us apart.

I looked over at Jax and finally warned, "Just don't do it again, okay, Jax?" I saw those green, laughing eyes crinkle, as he smiled at me.

This boy had been making my heart act crazy even longer than Kevin. I felt the familiar conflict hit my soul. I reminded myself that Jax and I were just sitting here fishing, and nothing more. If I had anything to say about it, that is how it was going to stay. I had to draw a line between Jax and Kevin. I couldn't keep bouncing between them. If something happened with Kevin, I couldn't run back to Jax again, and vice versa. I had to quit using one or the other for a crutch.

Thankfully, Jax never tried to do anything more than be my friend, while we sat at the lake. Soon, our easy and playful banter began again. I was grateful for that. If anything, we'd always been great friends. I wanted to always be his friend.

I didn't see Jax or Levi any more, after the day we all went fishing, before I left to go back home. I talked to both of them on the phone and was shocked when Jax called just to tell me goodbye, the night before I left. I was glad we were leaving things on a better note than they'd been left at Spring Break. I didn't know if I'd ever spend any real time with Jax again.

The only person I wanted to be with from now on when I was in Wichita Falls, besides Bailey, was Kevin. I hoped that he could find some peace from the pain he still felt over the loss of the little sister.

Kevin came over or I'd gone to his house each day I had left in Wichita. The night before I left, I went to his house and we had sex again. I kept hoping that I would eventually understand the great mystery of it, but each time I came away just disappointed by the whole thing. I loved everything before the actual act. I enjoyed lying together afterwards, but the act itself was still painful to me. I didn't know what was so great about it.

For the first time ever, I actually thought about birth control. When we'd been together in February, we had been together out of our mutual grief over the loss of Donna. Neither of us had really been in our right minds. When I had done it with Chance Cahill, which I still had not told Kevin about, I hadn't really thought about it then either. After leaving Corpus Christi with the knowledge that Chance had gotten a girl pregnant, it suddenly flitted through my mind. I would be 16 in a couple of months, but I knew that 16 was not the best age to get pregnant and have a baby.

I thought briefly about what it would mean for me and Kevin. I knew Kevin would marry me, without a second's hesitation, and maybe I would finally be where I was supposed to be. We would live with his mom and dad, and I could go to Samson again, with Bailey.

Then I thought about it and realized that I was deluding myself. If I got pregnant at 16, I'd probably marry Kevin, but going to Samson would never happen. I wouldn't be allowed to go to school pregnant. When I had the baby, there was no way I'd ever be able to go back to school.

As I lay in the semi-darkened room, I prayed fervently that I hadn't just gotten pregnant. I clung to Kevin as if he were a life raft in a vast sea of sadness and despair. I wondered what kind of life we would have if I did become pregnant.

I didn't even realize that I had tears leaking out of my eyes, until Kevin tilted my face up to his. I felt the salty puddle on Kevin's chest, where my cheek had been resting on. "What's wrong, Lainey?" Kevin asked, quietly.

I shook my head. I couldn't tell him that I was terrified that I'd get pregnant with his baby. I wanted nothing more than to marry Kevin and have his babies someday. I wanted us to both graduate high school before that happened.

I hoped I might actually get the chance to go to college. I wasn't sure how that could ever happen. I didn't know the first thing about going to college, but I loved school and I wanted to be a teacher. As all the thoughts whirled around in my head about school, college, and marriage and babies, I forgot Kevin was waiting for me to answer him.

Finally, I smiled up at him and whispered hoarsely, "It's nothin', Kev. Just thinkin' about how much I hate this part. The leaving part sucks!"

The sky-blue eyes that could melt my heart looked down, and even though I couldn't see their true color, in the shadowy darkness, I knew the color and light of them by memory. "Oh Lainey, Baby, I hate the leaving part too, but you'll be back. You always come back. I'm gonna be here every single time too," Kevin beamed at me. I hoped that it was true, but I didn't know how he could be so certain of that. It seemed so much had changed in just a few short years. Each year brought even more changes.

Kevin leaned down and kissed me tenderly on my mouth. I wanted time to freeze once again, just as I always wanted, when it was getting down to just a few more hours of precious time with him. I pulled him close to me and held him tightly. I didn't want to let go, but knew I had to in order to get dressed. I still had to walk back to Bailey's house in the late summer night.

The next day, when I sat on the bus as it sped through the highways of Texas, I replayed our last moments together over and over. I missed him when he kissed me goodbye. I missed him before we even walked out of the front door of his house.

My mind drifted through time and space. I thought about all the nights I'd spent with Kevin. I thought of all the times he snuck in my window when we lived on Belfast. I thought about all the nights I snuck out of Bailey's just to spend some time with him. I was shocked most of the trip, I'd basically ridden the bus without being aware of anything or anyone around me.

I wrapped myself into a thick cloak of sweet memories of a blonde headed boy, with faded, denim blue eyes and a sunshine and rainbow smile that always made my heart do a flip-flop.

I felt the smile tug on my mouth, as I watched the endless miles of blacktop speed under the window of the bus.

This road would find its way to South Texas, my other life and the other DeLaine who lived there. I felt sad to bid farewell to the DeLaine I always left in Wichita Falls. I wasn't sure I liked the DeLaine that lived in Corpus Christi. She was harder than the one from North Texas.

It made me sad to know both were still me, just with a different exterior.

When I got home, I noticed my mama had been acting strange, but it was late. I just chalked it up to her being half drunk. I wanted to get to my room and go to bed.

I told her I'd tell her all about my trip the next morning. She smiled and kissed me goodnight, as I walked into my room. I opened my suitcase and pulled out my stuffed rabbit and puppy. They went everywhere with me. I felt silly for still carrying the presents that Kevin and Jax had given me, but they'd mopped up a lot of tears in the last couple of years. I walked over to my desk to pull out my photo album. I wanted to get my picture of me and Kevin out, so I could look at it before I closed my eyes.

When I pulled it out of the drawer, I noticed a couple of my notebooks looked messed up, but I figured I hadn't put them back neatly. My rummaging around, trying to pull out my photo album, had probably dislodged some of them.

I found the Polaroid photo of me and Kevin. I smiled when I thought back to that day the summer after 7th grade, when Kevin and I had just begun our relationship. I still didn't understand exactly what it was I had with Kevin then, but I knew he was someone special. I fell asleep with the square photograph clutched loosely in my fingers. I smiled as I remembered that only a mere 24 hours prior, I'd been lying in Kevin's room, wrapped around him. I couldn't believe how just one small day could mean such a difference in one's life.

Chapter 37

I got up around noon the next day. I could see my mom was already well into pulling a hell of a drunk. I groaned inwardly, as I cussed her inside my brain. I wished she could have at least given me a day or two before she pulled her drunk bullshit. Sadly, it didn't work on my schedule and it never had.

I grabbed a bowl and some Lucky Charms, along with the milk jug, and sat down at the table. I wanted to eat some cereal in peace, then go unpack all my stuff. I felt my mom's eyes on me while I ate, but I never once looked up at her, for fear of provoking an attack, just by looking her in the eyes. When I was done eating, I carried my bowl to the sink, and put the milk and cereal back where they belonged. I sat back down in the chair. I knew if I tried to sneak off to my room, it might provoke the evil beast that lurked under the surface of my mom's demeanor when she began drinking this heavily in a day.

I sat there for about fifteen minutes. When she never said anything, I finally got up and began to walk to my room. I knew the only way to get her to say something was if I pretended to not notice that she had something on her chest.

Just as I reached the furthest exit, from the kitchen, towards the hallway, my mom stated, "DeLaine, I want to talk to you about some stuff before you begin unpacking."

I stood there for a beat trying to collect my patience and turned around with a smile that might have seemed just a little too bright.

"Sure, Mom, what's up?" I smiled cheerfully, even though I felt far from the way I responded.

"Have you been smoking pot?" my mama asked me, suddenly.

Stunned, I began to make my way to the kitchen table, unsure how I should answer. Finally, I asked suspiciously, "Who told you that?"

"Never mind who told me, just answer me," my mama demanded sharply.

I knew to admit it, was to sign my own death warrant, but I also knew if she caught me in a lie, it might be even worse. I decided to go with a lie, because I couldn't know how she might possibly have a clue about any of it. "That's just stupid, Mom. No, I'm not smoking pot!" I replied, evenly.

The next thing my mama asked me totally floored me. Looking me dead in the eyes, my mama asked me, "Were you pregnant with Chance Cahill's baby?"

"WHAT?" I managed to sputter, trying not to choke on my own spit. "Why in the hell would you think that?" I finally spat out, roughly. I knew something was definitely wrong with my mom asking me such insane questions.

"Just answer me, DeLaine," my mama threatened, quietly.

"God NO, Mom! Geez, really? Of course not! I wasn't pregnant by Chance Cahill!" I sputtered hotly. I saw my mama nod her head, thoughtfully. "Mom, why are you asking me all these stupid questions?" I demanded, annoyed.

"It doesn't matter. I found out about Carla Feldman and well, someone called me while you were gone and told me that you were smoking pot every weekend, partying and that you had left because you were pregnant with Chance Cahill's baby. I thought maybe there might be some truth to it, so I went and looked for your diary." Mama admitted softly.

"You WHAT?" I roared, incredulously.

"I read some of your journal, you keep in your desk," my mama responded.

"How could you, Mom?" I screamed at her. I didn't care what she said to me, I wasn't about to let her invade my privacy like that. I'd had to endure it from Clarice and Geoffrey, but I couldn't believe my own mama would actually treat me like the evil She-devil and her demon-spawn!

"I was worried about you, DeLaine!" My mama shot back at me. I got up and stomped back into my room. Now it made sense to me why the papers and notepads were all messed up in my tiny desk top. I pulled open the drawer of my desk and jerked all the spiral notebooks out. I found the one I had made into my journal. I slung it across my bedroom and then began to do the same with the others from the drawer also.

My mom walked into the doorway of my room, "You need to calm down, DeLaine!"

"Why? Because that's what a good girl is supposed to do, Mom? I'm supposed to mind you and let you invade my privacy, like Geoffrey, and that bitch Clarice used to do?" I snapped the last sentence off crisply. I knew I'd hit my mark when I saw my mom wince.

"Don't you dare compare me to that fuckin' lunatic!" my mother's eyes flashed the familiar fire they had, when she was on the verge of flipping the switch of her dual personality.

"Don't act like the crazy bitch, and I won't compare you to her, or her demon spawn!" I spit out, just as viciously. "I can't believe you'd go snooping in my shit because some idiot called and told you a bunch of bullshit!" I yelled, as tears slipped down my cheeks.

I was so angry. I wanted to know who had called my mom! "Who the fuck called you anyway?" I practically screamed at her.

"She said her name was Tara," Mama finally told me. I stood there with my mouth hanging open.

Tara O'Neal was a tall, blonde girl that I thought was a phony, two-faced bitch, but I didn't really run around with her. She'd been trying to get close to Kelly Stubbs, the last couple of months of school. I didn't like her. I avoided her as much as possible. She liked to get her nose stuck in everyone's business. Why she felt it necessary to call my mother and start this shit storm in my life was beyond me.

Grabbing the small desk drawer all the way out, I dumped the contents onto my bedroom floor and screamed at my mother, "There! If you want to go through my shit, go ahead! It's all there for you to dig through! And if you want to know something just ask me! But let me tell you this about Tara O'Neal, she is a two-faced bitch and doesn't hardly know me from Adam, so I wouldn't believe a fuckin' word that comes out of that lying whore's mouth!"

I walked around my mom and grabbed some clothes out of my open suitcase that was lying on the floor. I stomped into the bathroom and got dressed. When I came out, I found my mom sitting at the kitchen table again. When she saw me, she asked where I was going. I picked up the keys to the car and told her I had to get out of the house for a while. I had never told my mom anything. I'd always asked, but I was beyond asking for anything from her. I felt betrayed enough by her drunkenness, I would be damned if I'd let her take away everything else.

"I didn't say you could go anywhere, young lady," my mom began to admonish me.

Whirling around I said through my gritted teeth, "It doesn't matter what you say, Mom! Either you let me go now, to calm down, or I will fucking walk, but I'm getting out of this house!"

For one of the only times I could ever remember, my mom simply stared at me. Even though she didn't say it was okay or not okay, I still picked up the keys to the car, and threw my purse strap over my shoulder. I was going to find Tara! She would learn quickly that she was never going to call and talk to my mom, about any shit, ever again. I would make sure of that.

I peeled out of the long driveway and was at the Gameroom within only a few minutes.

It was a Sunday afternoon, so there weren't too many people around. I felt I could find Tara and once I picked up a possible place she might be, I began to track her down. I stayed away from my house the entire afternoon and when it began to get dark, I had driven all over Annaville, several times, in order to find her.

When I found out that she was with Kelly Stubbs, of all people, I drove as fast as I could to the trailer park that she and Robin lived in.

After getting to Kelly's house, I found that I had missed them by about 15 minutes. I turned back to the Gameroom. Even though it was a Sunday evening, it was still summer time, so there were quite a few people hanging out, even though they wouldn't be up there until 2 a.m. like on Friday and Saturday nights.

I turned into the parking lot, and immediately spied Tara's creamy Pontiac. When she saw me, the color in her face drained out, immediately. I saw her trying to act innocent toward Kelly. She was trying to make her way to the back of the building, but before she made a clean get away, I made it to the back of the building, where the small hallway was that led to the bathrooms and the back office.

Just as Tara got to the entrance of the hallway, I managed to somehow jump over a bar stool that was blocking the walkway. I slid into the tiled hall with my arm outstretched to block the doorway. Tara smiled innocently at me, "Hey, DeLaine! It's good to see you back from your vacation. Did you have a good time?"

I stared at her, dumbfounded. How could she act like she hadn't created one of the biggest messes I had to deal with, in my already fucked up existence of a home life! Now, she was standing there, acting as if she were as pure as the driven snow.

"You got a lot of fuckin' nerve, you bitch!" I snarled wickedly.

Kelly made it back there, when she saw me running towards Tara. She grabbed my arm, asking me what my problem was. I turned to Kelly and spat, "Well, Kel, it seems your new best friend here took it on herself to call my fucking mother to tell her I was smoking pot and partying every weekend!"

Tara began to sputter and tried to make up some lame story about how she hadn't said that exactly, and she wasn't responsible if my mom thought that. I cut her off, as I continued, "And then she decided to tell her I was pregnant with Chance Cahill's kid, and that is why I left to go to Wichita Falls so I could get an abortion!" The last sentence wasn't said very quietly.

I was vaguely aware that Chance was actually in the building playing pool. By now, I had the attention of the entire game room. Several people began to walk up to where I was standing in front of Tara.

I felt like one of the crazed bulls Jax rode at the rodeos, stamping and snorting. I wanted to have horns just so I could gore Tara O'Neal! I'd never wanted to hurt anyone more than Clarice and Geoffrey, than I did this stupid girl! She had no clue what she had created for me by her stupid phone calls.

Kelly looked at Tara asking, "Did you really do that, Tara?"

Tara shook her head, and before she could answer, I was surprised to hear Chance demand, "I'd like to know the answer to that one myself, Kelly. What the fuck, Tara? Did you really call DeLaine's mom and tell her that shit?"

Standing there with her mouth moving, but no sound coming out, Tara began to cry. I had had it with her by then. I slammed the palm of my hand on the wood paneling to the side of Tara's head. "The next time it is gonna be your fuckin' face, you stupid bitch! Now you better start talkin' and I mean, don't make up a fuckin' story either! You better tell the truth and trust me bitch, I will know if you are lying!" I snarled at her, like a feral dog.

"You know DeLaine, I think your mom was drinking the day I called. She might have misunderstood me," Tara tried to weasel out.

"Yeah, Tara, she probably was drunk, that is beside the point. Now, tell me what the hell possessed you to even bother with calling my fucking mother! I've never done a fucking thing to you! Before you go run your head about shit, you should know if you have the facts right. Then you really shouldn't get involved unless you're a part of it, which you aren't a part of anything regarding my life! So, listen to me right now because I will NOT tell you again, don't you ever call my house again! You forget my fuckin' phone number! If you don't, I promise you, you will wish you had listened to this one-time warning. I'm ready to beat your ass right now. I'm fairly certain I have plenty of people who would back me up on this one. You better walk on the opposite side of the street any time you see me walking the other way, do you understand me? As far as you are concerned, I'm your God now! If I say jump, by God, Bitch, you better jump, because if you don't, I will whip your ass up and down Leonard Street!! You had NO RIGHT to call and talk to my mom about anything!"

Tara began trying to say she would call my mom and tell her she was misinformed. I smacked the paneling again, beside her head, and growled through clinched teeth, "Did you NOT just get what I said? You FORGET MY PHONE NUMBER! YOU FORGET YOU HAVE EVER HEARD MY MOTHER'S VOICE and if you EVER call my house again, even to try to make it better, just know I am not threatening you, I AM PROMISING YOU, I will beat your ass!"

By the end of my threat, Tara had pulled herself off of the wall. Before I walked off, I slammed her back into the wall, with one hard shove, and demanded as menacingly as I could, "Do you understand me, Bitch?"

I turned to walk away from her, and found Chance was practically standing on top of my back. When he saw me, he tried to offer a half-hearted grin. I just pushed past him. I was still angry at him and I still didn't know what had happened with Carla while I'd been gone.

I stalked out of the game room to a lot of cheers and whistles. Tara wasn't a very popular girl, as she'd stabbed just about everyone, from Calvin, in the back, and had begun trying to befriend people from Woodway now. She'd already found herself at the receiving end of more threats than the ones I'd just made to her.

By the time I got outside, to my giant Ford, Chance was chasing me out the door. "Hey, DeLaine! Wait up!"

I kept walking. When I got to the car and began fiddling with the keys, Chance made it to my side in plenty of time. Sighing, I looked at him and huffed, "What do you want, Chance?"

"Hey, I didn't know that crazy bitch pulled that shit while you were gone, or else I'd have talked to your mom. I mean, she likes me, and I don't want to screw that up!" Chance flashed his gorgeous, straight teeth.

I rolled my eyes and opened the heavy door to climb in. Now I would have to face the music when I got home. I honestly didn't feel like dealing with Chance Cahill.

"Chance, it wouldn't have mattered. Tara told my mom more shit than me supposedly being pregnant! She told her about Carla too, and about me smoking pot, and partying. She took it on herself to be a one-person, wrecking ball of my life. I hardly know the stupid bitch! I don't even understand why she felt like it was her place to call my mom anyway," I shook my head.

"Probably because she was hitting on me, and I told her to get lost," Chance replied, softly.

"What? You actually told a girl to get lost? I'm surprised you didn't try to get into her pants too, Chance! Speaking of Carla, when's the wedding?" I asked, with a snarky grin.

Chance looked at me perplexed. "Are you going to marry her, since she's pregnant, dumbass?" I sighed, exasperated that he didn't have a clue what I was trying to say.

"Oh, um, no…she's not pregnant," Chance responded quietly, looking at the ground.

"What? What happened?" I asked.

Shrugging his shoulders Chance explained, "I dunno. She came back from her grandma's in Poteet last week and told me that I didn't have to worry. She made me worry all fuckin' summer though!" he fumed a little, until he looked at my uncaring face. "Any way, she just said not to worry about it that she wasn't pregnant. When I asked her what happened, she just said she wasn't pregnant and that was it, so I dunno." Chance shrugged his shoulders again. "I guess it was a false alarm."

I shook my head and turned the key in the ignition, "Well, good, you don't have to get married and have a kid yet. Good for you! Now, back off and if you see that bitch, Tara, still around here, you let me know if you hear that she's even mentioned my name! So help me, I will beat that bitch to a pulp if she even breathes in my direction again!" I jerked the heavy door out of his hands and slammed it behind me.

On the way to my house, in the dark, hot, summer night, I wondered if we were about to have World War III erupt once I walked into the house. I knew my mom would be mad as hell at me, for taking off, and talking to her the way I had. I was so pissed at Tara O'Neal, I couldn't find it in my mind or body to care anymore. I didn't know when life became so difficult, but sometimes I wondered if it was truly worth it still.

I thought briefly back to my attempt to end my life the year before. I felt guilty, because I knew that if Donna had the choice to still be alive, she would gladly take it. Here I was thinking again about ending my own existence. Everything in my life was once again completely chaotic, just a different kind…

When I pulled up to the house, I was surprised to see all of the lights out in the house. I was happy to see that hopefully there would be no more drama from my mom, at least for the night. After pulling into the driveway, I turned off the engine and realized I was suddenly exhausted. I leaned my forehead onto the large steering wheel and sighed deeply. I was more than tired, I was literally weary.

Chapter 38

The next morning, I got up and went out into the kitchen, fully prepared to face my mother's wrath. When she didn't explode at the sight of me, I wondered why she was being so quiet. I went ahead and poured a bowl of cereal, even though I already had knots in my stomach, afraid what might happen.

I sat down across the table from where my mom was drinking her coffee and smoking her cigarette, while she read the newspaper. I ate my cereal with my head hung low. I felt almost hung over from being so adrenaline charged the night before. I still couldn't believe that Tara O'Neal had actually called my mother. It just pissed me off even more as I thought about it.

I must have had a look on my face because my mama finally asked, "What are you looking so pissed off about? You know, I'm the one who should be pissed off. Don't you ever storm out of here like that again, do I make myself clear?"

I finally drug my eyes up from the bowl of milk and cereal and looked at her. I wasn't just angry at Tara, I was angry that my mother had violated my privacy. I had always felt safe that my private things were private and that my mom didn't snoop around in my stuff. To know that she had read my private thoughts, about everything, made me sick to my stomach. It reminded me of Geoffrey doing the same when we still lived in Wichita Falls, and my secrets about Kevin were exposed to the light.

The debacle with Geoffrey and my diary had taught me one thing though, and that was to use a code for certain things. Especially as they pertained to sex or any feelings I had about boys. Most of my journal writing had been little more than recounting my days, except for right after Donna died and after spring break, when I'd found out that my daddy and Clarice had broken up.

I knew that to expose myself totally, in any written form, was leaving myself vulnerable. There were many times I wanted to write, because I needed someone to talk to about my mom and her drinking, but I didn't feel safe even writing about it. In the back of my mind, I'd worried that what happened with my mom reading my private thoughts could really happen, and it did!

As I looked at my mother, I had a million smart-assed thoughts that passed through my mind, but instead of saying them, I decided I didn't want to start this day off as rotten as the day before, so I finally said, "I'm sorry Mama, I shouldn't have stormed out of here, but I guarantee you that Tara O'Neal is NEVER going to call you again."

My mama looked at me and a slightly alarmed look flickered in her eyes before she asked, "DeLaine, what did you do?"

I shook my head, "Nothing. I didn't hurt her or anything like that but trust me she's not ever going to call here again. Plus, Chance Cahill knows what she did, and he wasn't very happy either."

"So, what about him and Carla Feldman?" Mama asked me, still in a hushed tone.

"Carla's not pregnant. I dunno what happened. SHE is the one who left here, and now she isn't pregnant. It's none of my business," I shrugged my shoulders belying the true concern I felt in the matter.

I might not have wanted Chance Cahill anymore, but I had hoped there could be something with him. He'd hurt me badly by using me, and then knowing that he'd used Carla Feldman, just like me ticked me off more. I wondered how many other girls he'd used, just like us.

Mama looked at me and then finally nodded her head, "Well, I hate knowing that Chance might have gotten a girl pregnant. I hope that if you think about having sex, you'll come to me first, so we can talk about putting you on birth control. Things are different now than they were when I was a kid. My mama never told me anything about sex. I don't want you to feel like you can't come to me."

My gaze flicked back to my cereal, because I knew I could give away things with my expressions. I didn't want my mom to see that the time for talking about sex, before it happened, was long gone. A part of me wanted to tell her that I needed to talk to her now, but there was the still, small voice in the back of my mind that screamed, "Do and die dummy!" I chose to listen to the voice.

After a bit, I brought my gaze back to hers and nodded dutifully.

"DeLaine, I'm sorry I went through your stuff, but when this girl called and told me all of this…I just couldn't believe that you'd been keeping secrets from me." My mama spoke conversationally.

I realized that she was ready to close the subject. I needed to accept her apology and move on, or else it could get bad, quickly.

Finally, I acquiesced, "It's okay Mom, just next time ask me before you believe some stupid girl who calls you. I mean, these girls in high school are crazy bitches!"

My mama looked at me and grinned. I knew that we were done with the topic, unless she chose to throw it into my face when she got drunk, sometime.

We talked about my vacation then. I felt my shoulders finally relax, for the first time since I'd gotten home.

She asked if I'd seen Kevin. I nodded and couldn't help myself when the huge grin spread across my face. My mama returned the smile, and I told her about how the Strong family was doing.

I told her that Kevin was having some problems coping with Donna's death, but I didn't tell her what he was doing. I knew that she wouldn't understand and if she knew that Kevin was getting stoned to deal with it, she'd just call him a damned dopehead, then we'd be pissy with one another all over again. The rest of the day went along smoothly while I unpacked and gave mama her souvenir that I'd gotten while I'd been in California. Thankfully she didn't flip the drunk switch that day.

***

The small bit of summer that was left, wasn't that full of anything more than the usual weekend activities that I'd done since I'd moved to Corpus. I was missing Kevin again, even more than I had before. This time we left on good terms. I felt bound to him by the invisible cord that I'd felt tied with, at other times, to him. I ignored Chance even though we still hung out with the same people. I was surprised to see him actually talking more to me in public, but I still managed to give him the cold shoulder without being rude.

When the first day of my sophomore year started, I was surprised at how unremarkable it truly was. So many of the boys that we ran around with had graduated the year before. There were so many of them who weren't going to college, but getting jobs in the refineries, in Corpus Christi, or working in the oil field. School seemed a little more sedate without all of them horsing around. The boys we knew from the class of 1983 weren't nearly as loud and crazy, as the ones from the senior class, the year before.

The weekends rocked along with me still getting drunk or stoned, either because it had been a good week or a crappy one. There was always an excuse to find, to get wasted. Kelly, Robin and I were all three still running around together. They were my close circle of people, who I trusted the most. I still hung out with Christy Gilley, but she was a senior, so she did a lot more stuff with seniors. I was just a lowly sophomore.

Towards the end of September, I got sick and missed two weeks of school. I had bronchitis and went to the doctor and even to the ER. After missing two solid weeks of school, I was so happy when I was well enough to get back to a normal routine.

School was just as much an escape to me, as running around and getting intoxicated every weekend. Thankfully, my mom had been so worried about me being so sick, that she'd managed to just stay comfortably numb, instead of getting mean when she drank.

When I went back to school, I was surprised when I was called down to the office, by the assistant principal. She was new, and no one liked her. She walked around the school like a prison matron and seemed to constantly be after everyone in the school. She had almost shut down the open-air campus as much as she could.

I think even the teachers didn't like her, as she had begun stationing them around the campus during break and lunch. There was no more going around the auditorium to sneak a joint, or going out to the parking lot, before or during school. She had even stationed teachers to stand outside all the bathrooms, so there was no more smoking in the girls' room either. Thankfully, my mama had signed a permission slip that gave me access to the smoking pit. She knew that Christy Gilley smoked. I told her that Christy usually went outside, and unless I had permission I couldn't get out there to hang out with her.

I walked into the office and wondered why I was being called down there. Then I began to worry that either Clarice's stupidity had begun again, or maybe even something had happened to my mom. When I didn't see my mother, I felt myself relax a bit. I was told to sit down, and the assistant principal would be with me shortly.

Now I was really perplexed, because I hadn't done anything to get into trouble. I didn't know why Mrs. Gonzalez would have me pulled out of class to come see her. Thankfully, she didn't make me sit in the lobby of the front office too long.

Mrs. Gonzalez came to her office door and called me in. I looked at her warily because she'd established herself as a tough as nails bitch to everyone. I usually could sweet talk my way with most teachers and adults, but when she didn't respond to my politeness, I wondered what I was in for.

She wasn't very tall, and she wore dark polyester business suits, with skirts and jackets. They created a severe, almost manly appearance, on her heavy frame. She wore extremely red lipstick and lots of gold jewelry, which seemed to contradict the message she wanted to convey with the manly look.

I didn't like her, but not because of her authority status. I just didn't like her. She seemed to want to punish everyone, and it didn't matter who they were.

"DeLaine, I'm sure you are wondering why I've called you down here," Mrs. Gonzalez stated, with the same predatory grin I had seen on Geoffrey's face numerous times.

I looked at her evenly. I decided when I couldn't win her over with good manners, it might be necessary to watch her closely. She was acting like Clarice did when she toyed with me. I felt a little like fresh meat being dangled before a hungry lion.

I finally nodded my head and she continued, "Well, you know, you've missed an awful lot of school, and if you miss more than ten days, then your mother has to go before the school board and explain why, or else you can either flunk the semester, or go into in school suspension."

"What?" I asked her alarmed. "I came back with doctor's notes, why am I getting in trouble for being sick?"

Mrs. Gonzalez steepled her fingers and tapped her chin with them. "DeLaine, you aren't in trouble for being sick, but it's been brought to my attention that you don't live in this school district."

I looked at her and was beginning to feel angry. I didn't know what this woman wanted or what she was trying to do, but I knew she didn't have any proof I didn't live in the district. I left school every day and walked to my mom's, best friend's house and Mama picked me up. I didn't know who would tell her I didn't live in district, because most everyone thought I did live in district.

"I don't know why you would think that, but I live over on Garden Street, two blocks from here."

"DeLaine, let's be honest here, okay?" Mrs. Gonzalez spoke in a sickly, sweet tone. "You and your mother don't actually live on Garden Street, do you?"

I continued looking at her and decided for once to let my expression say whatever it wanted to. I didn't think I'd keep from being expelled, if I actually opened my mouth. Mrs. Gonzalez told me that there would be further investigation into my home address, and she would get back with me. She dismissed me from her office. I walked back to class, wondering what had caused all of this to come raining down so suddenly.

While I was in choir, I was called out of class again. I walked into the office this time, to find Mrs. Gonzalez waiting on me. She ushered me into her office and declared, "DeLaine, you've been checked out of Woodway High School. You need to clean out your locker and come back to the office."

My eyes opened up widely, "What are you talking about? Did my mom check me out? I don't understand."

"DeLaine, until you can prove that you live on Garden Street, you will not be allowed to come back to school."

"Wait, you checked me out of school, already? Where's my mom?" I asked angrily.

"We are still attempting to contact your mother. Once she's contacted, she can come pick you up." She smiled with her fake, red lips stretching out, showing that she had a strip of gold along the top part of one of her teeth.

"I'm just gonna walk home if you've checked me out," I spoke snidely.

"No, you will clean out your locker, then come back to the office." Mrs. Gonzalez commanded, as if I were an errant child who didn't understand simple instruction. Before I could respond, the bell rang for lunch. I turned to walk to my locker. I met Kelly and told her what had happened. She was one of the few who knew where I actually lived. She was shocked that Mrs. Gonzalez had checked me out without getting in touch with my mom first.

I knew my mom was going to be angry when she got there. I just didn't know to what extent. I walked out into the open courtyard. I figured if I was checked out of the school, then Mrs. Gonzalez couldn't very well get me for walking to lunch with Kelly, before cleaning out my locker. I still didn't understand how all of this could possibly have happened. As I stood there talking to Kelly, a teacher walked up to me that I didn't know. She asked if I was DeLaine Reynolds. I nodded my head and wondered what was going on now.

"Mrs. Gonzalez asked me to tell you to go finish cleaning out your locker. She doesn't want you to fraternize with any of the students," the young teacher explained, almost apologetically.

"Man, this is bull," I vented angrily. "Can I just walk home?" I asked hoping that if the teacher said it was alright, then I could just leave after getting my personal stuff out of my locker.

The young teacher looked over her shoulder, towards the front door, by the office. I followed her gaze and saw Mrs. Gonzalez standing there watching us. I rolled my eyes, and told Kelly I'd call her later, then told the teacher to never mind. I turned around, slamming back into the door on the other side, away from the offices, to walk to the hallway with my locker. I pulled everything out of my locker, including all of my textbooks. Once I was weighed down with every textbook, and all of my folders, I walked away, and left the locker standing wide open, out of defiance.

I walked into the office, and basically threw all of the textbooks on the front counter. I asked the secretary if I needed to go to each teacher and turn in my books. Before she could answer, Mrs. Gonzalez walked in the office door, and answered for her. "No, we will check them in here. You need to get your personal belongings out and sit over in those chairs, until your mother gets here."

"This is stupid, why can't I just walk home. If you don't believe I live there, where do you think I'm going?" I popped off.

"Have a seat, DeLaine, we finally got in touch with your mother and she should be here shortly."

I sat down in a huff and wondered which mom they got in touch with. If it was the mom who wasn't drunk and mad, then I might have a shot at getting this changed. If they got the mom who was drunk and mad, I could guarantee I wouldn't get a reprieve from Mrs. Gonzalez's decision to kick me out of school.

While I sat there doodling on a piece of notebook paper, one of the big pothead guys was brought into the office. He was a hardcore pothead and his hair was so long, it reminded me of Ted Nugent's. He was barefoot and was wearing Levi 501 jeans and an OP t-shirt. He sat in the chair next to mine and asked, "Hey dude, what did you do? Aren't you like one of those smart chicks or somethin'? Jesus, man, if that big, fat bitch is bustin' you, then I'm sure she's gonna expel my ass for goin' barefoot!"

I looked at him and grinned, but before I could respond, I felt the air whoosh out as the heavy, glass door was jerked open hard. I looked up to see my mom come storming into the school, with her eyes blazing.

Well, this is great, I was thinking, they managed to get the sober mom and make her into the raging monster without being drunk. I didn't think this was going to end well.

"What the hell is going on in this fucking school?" my mom screamed as she got into the office. I cringed and wished the floor would open up and swallow me.

The pothead guy, Kerry Page laughed, "Wow, dude that is one pissed off mom! Whoa, this is gonna be fuckin' righteous!"

I gave him a sick grin and he asked, "Oh man, is that your mom? Shit, either you're in a shitload of trouble, or that fat Gonzo Gonzalez is in for it. I wonder if your old lady will kick her ass."

I rolled my eyes. I could just see Mrs. Gonzalez having the cops called if my mom got too crazy.

I watched as the assistant principal opened her office door and stepped out, "Are you Mrs. Reynolds?"

Mama's eyes flashed over at her and she yelled, "You bet I am, and I'm pissed as hell! What the hell is this shit my daughter's been checked out of school, until I can prove I live at our house?"

"Mrs. Reynolds, if you'll come into my office, we can discuss this privately." Mrs. Gonzalez crooned smoothly. I cringed when I saw my mama hike her purse higher on her shoulder. She began to stomp towards the assistant principal. I hoped that things would settle down once Mama got behind the door. I had little belief that it would happen. I sighed as I heard my mother's voice begin to get louder, and louder.

Kerry Page looked at me, grinning really big. "Damn dude, your mom is getting all in her shit! Way to go, Mrs. Reynolds!" He pumped his fist in the air, as he finished yelling the last sentence. I seriously wanted the floor to open up and swallow me!

I heard my mama call Mrs. Gonzalez, 'Godzilla' and cringed. I could just see the stupid vice-principal calling the cops to arrest my mom, if we didn't get out of there soon. Not to mention she was causing an already excited Kerry Page to hop up in the gold chair, in his bare feet, as he began to chant 'God-zi-lla' over and over. I lowered my head and stared at the doodles I'd been sitting there drawing, praying that we'd leave quickly.

Suddenly, my mom jerked open the glass door to Mrs. Gonzalez's office, and ordered me, "Go get in the car, DeLaine!" I nodded and jumped up, hurrying out the door.

Mrs. Gonzalez walked to the door after my mom, and as my mom got to the door of the office, she turned around and looked at Mrs. Gonzalez one more time, "You know Bitch, you are going to regret ever meeting me!"

Mrs. Gonzalez smiled that smile that I equated with a hungry panther. I called my mom from the exit door. Thankfully, she didn't say anything else.

I heard Mrs. Gonzalez yell at Kerry Page to shut up and come into her office! He laughed and said, "Yes ma'am, Mrs. Godzilla, er, I mean, Gonzalez!" That brought a slim smile to my face, as I watched my sneakers cross the cement sidewalk, to my mom's car.

Mama got in and we turned out of the parking lot to go to her best friend, Margaret's house. I wondered why we were going there. When we got out and were inside of the brick house, I understood it was because my mama needed a drink, and someone to vent her pent-up anger at.

I was shocked when Margaret told Mama that Mrs. Gonzalez had actually come to her house that morning, and walked inside, unannounced.

Margaret had the front door open as she carried groceries in, and apparently Mrs. Gonzalez got there while she was busy going back and forth, from the car.

Seeing the open door, the vice-principal walked into the house, without so much as a knock, or a yelled out greeting. My mom's friend was even fuming about the woman.

After a while of listening to Margaret and my mom complain and talk about contacting the school board, I got bored and went into the other room, turning on the TV. It was the early afternoon. I wished that we would just go home, but I figured with my mom so thoroughly pissed, we might be there until late, and I'd end up driving us home. I was just grateful we didn't live too far away, now that we lived in Annaville. I wondered if I was going to have to start going to Calvin the next day, or if my mom was going to fight the assistant principal's decision.

Sighing, I pulled out one of my folders that had notebook paper and began a letter to Bailey, to tell her about what happened.

I hated the idea of going to another school. I didn't do new schools very well. I'd figured that out after my miserable year as a 6th grader, in a new school.

I went to another new school after the tornado, when I'd gone to Woodway Middle School. Then when school started all over again, it was at Samson high, in 7th grade. That wasn't anywhere as awful as having to move to Oklahoma City, and go to school there. Starting my freshman year at Woodway High hadn't been nearly as bad, because I had Kelly Stubbs as my friend and there were actually a few people who remembered me from 6th grade too.

Going to Calvin though, was a little frightening, because they were the big rival school. I hated thinking about going to school with Tara O'Neal too. She was a senior this year, at Calvin. I was afraid I'd end up getting in trouble if I had to see her too much.

I did know the girl who lived across the street from me. She went to Calvin. Her name was Tina Murphy. She was a junior, but we'd met at the Gameroom after I'd moved to our house. We'd sit out in her driveway, smoking cigarettes sometimes, so I knew her. I just hated the thought of starting over, one more time. I didn't think I could do it again.

By the time we left that night, I'd written Bailey a letter, as well as Kevin. I normally didn't write him too often, but I was missing him so much since I'd come back. I wondered how he was. Bailey had been good about keeping me updated a little more, since we'd parted on better terms. I was certain there was some stuff she didn't tell me. I knew he'd never write me back, but at least he'd know how I'd been doing, I thought.

Just as I thought, I was the one who drove us home that night. When we got to our house, Mama told me that I didn't have to worry about school the next day, until she could figure out what to do with the school board at Woodway. I nodded as I walked into my room. I was thrilled to find a letter sitting on my desk. My mom had been too angry to remember to tell me I had a letter from my best friend. I threw the folders on the floor by my bed, and slid off my sneakers, as I jumped onto my bed with the letter.

Bailey and I had this uncanny way of writing, just when one of us needed to hear from the other. I was so happy to find a little ray of sanity to the end of a crazy day. I slipped my finger under the glued flap of the envelope, eager to read about all the gossip from home. What I read shocked me. I read the letter totally and then began to reread it slowly, to see if I had misunderstood something.

I was sick to my stomach, as I read the words that my friend had written, as her own eyes had flowed with tears. She told me that she and Levi had broken up after almost 2 and a half years of going steady. I was shocked. I'd noticed that they'd been a little more short with each other, while I'd been up there, but figured it was because of all the time we were gone during the summer.

I felt tears making tiny, wet tracks down my cheeks as I thought about my best friend and Levi Parker breaking up. They seemed so perfect for each other. He'd given her a promise ring at Christmas. I just assumed they'd be together forever. How did this happen, I wondered? How did you love someone so fiercely, and then let it all go? I'd never had many conventional relationships. I had envied Bailey that she'd had those conventional relationships that seemed to elude me. She'd gone steady with Jamie Reynolds, until he moved in 7th grade. Then she had met Levi during the summer, before 8th grade, and they'd been so totally in sync with one another.

The only real boyfriend I'd ever had was Jax. He and I didn't manage to hold it all together. We'd had a lot of other things at play in our demise, like the fact that I loved someone else, besides him, and then that pesky business of me moving. Kevin and I had never been a real couple, even though we did things that real couples did. We just never had an official title to what we were.

I grabbed one of the folders and began a reply to Bailey. The letter I'd written earlier, at Margaret's, was now completely forgotten, not to mention it was totally irrelevant compared to the heartbreak my best friend was going through.

I was already three days behind, as it took two to three days for a letter to get from Wichita Falls to Corpus Christi. That meant that she would be broken up with Levi a whole week before she even got my letter back.

I didn't care. I had to write to her and I knew that writing was the only way for me to communicate. Before long, it was after midnight, and I was finally finished with my second letter to Bailey. I decided to send both, since I didn't want to completely rewrite the first one. I made notations on the first one, so she knew that I'd written that letter before I knew I had a letter already waiting on me. I wished long distance wasn't so expensive. I needed to talk to my best friend so badly.

Frustrated, I finally put my notebook down, threw on a nightshirt, and crawled into my bed. I didn't understand why there had to be so much constant change all the time! It seemed just when things seemed great, something else changed. It was so frustrating to me. It made no sense, why things couldn't just stay the way they were, before something drastic happened again.

Sighing, I turned out the light by my bed. As I snuggled down under my covers, I pulled my rabbit that Kevin had given to me and wrapped my arms around it tightly. I wished for the millionth time that it was actually Kevin, but I knew it couldn't be, so I tried to tell myself that holding the rabbit was just as good. I knew I was full of it, but it seemed to help enough for me to go to sleep, somewhat peacefully.

As I began to sink into my pillows, and my mind began to wander, as it did right before sleep claimed me, I saw the lake where I'd gone with Levi, Bailey and Jax so many times. I saw Levi standing near the water. When I walked up beside him, I was alarmed to see his eyes looking so sad. My heart broke for him too. I thought I heard someone call my name. I turned to see if Bailey was behind me. When I didn't see her, I turned back and the water and Levi were gone. Before me lay a small patch of grass, with little yellow flowers, that swayed gently in a summer breeze. I didn't understand why I'd begun to dream about Levi, only to have the field of flowers appear out of nowhere. I caught a slight movement out of the corner of my eye, but when I turned to look, it was gone. Soon, the grass began to gray, then grow darker, as sleep finally took over for me for the rest of the night.

Chapter 39

By the end of the week, I was enrolled in Calvin High School and miserable. The only saving grace, for me, was their smoking area was open. There was no need for a permission slip, so I could go out there during break and lunch, without having to dream up an excuse to my mom. She thought I wasn't smoking any more, after my earlier experimentation.

During the first break, I hung out with Tina Murphy in the smoking area. I was thrilled when I found a boy that was a former Woodway High student, I knew. We hadn't been very close, but he had always been really nice to me. His name was Buddy Tompkins and he had originally hung out with some of the potheads at Woodway, but he wasn't too hardcore like some of the others I knew there. He was tall and had black hair that he wore a little long. He seemed happy to see me there and told me that Calvin wasn't too bad.

I felt better after seeing someone I'd known at another school.I momentarily flashed on mine and Jax Garrett's first encounter at Milam Junior High, in 6th grade, after having gone to school together in elementary.

Buddy had actually gotten kicked out of Woodway, by Mrs. Gonzalez too, for living just outside of the district. He'd always been able to skate by with living just on the other side of the road, of the dividing line, but with her cracking down on everyone, he had ended up going to Calvin before the end of the second week of school. I remembered then that I'd vaguely noticed he wasn't in the halls any longer, but since he didn't really hang in the circle of kids I did, I just chalked it up to us having conflicting schedules.

There were a lot of Calvin kids who took the school rivalry a little overboard. When they'd find out I was from Woodway, they would snub me. By the end of the first full week though, I noticed there were several of them who found out I was smart, so they'd cheat off of me on quizzes and tests. I let some of them, just because I wanted to feel accepted, even though I wasn't sure where I fit in anywhere, just like I'd felt before in Wichita Falls.

I didn't like the fact that I had to take a test to get into accelerated English. Because they only gave those tests at the end of the year, I was put into a regular English class.

Thankfully, the teacher they gave me, was a former English professor. She was every bit as tough as any accelerated teacher I'd ever had. I would have a chance at the end of the year to test for the accelerated program.

I noticed there were a lot more hardcore, surfer boys in my class at Calvin. They made me laugh. They were also some of the cutest boys, but they didn't seem too interested in me, except to think I was a tough chick. On the opposite end of the spectrum, there was a huge population of kickers in the entire school. Sometimes I would miss Levi and Jax, when I'd see them, and wonder how they were doing.

I wrote Levi a letter after I heard back from Bailey and told him that I would always consider him one of my best friends, whether he and Bailey were together or not. Bailey knew how extremely close Levi and I had become.

When she wrote me back, she told me that she didn't expect me to quit being friends with him. I was glad to hear that, because I didn't know how to turn off caring about people. I hated the thought of ignoring Levi, after all the fun times and endlessly long talks we'd had over the years. He'd been there for me for so much more than just Jax. I was even more shocked when he wrote me back.

When I got home by the end of my second week at Calvin, there was a small envelope on my desk with what appeared to be a boy's handwriting. When I glanced at the return address I was shocked to see it was from Levi. I had hoped that Kevin might write to me eventually, but he still had never even sent me a tiny note.

Levi told me he was happy that we were still friends and that he was heartbroken over the breakup too, but it just wasn't working out any more with Bailey.

As I read the short letter, I realized that both of my friends were truly heartbroken and had loved one another very much. They were outgrowing each another. I felt so sad that they couldn't work through all of the problems they had, but I was happy they both felt like I was trustworthy enough, that they weren't threatened by me being friends with each of them. Levi told me that Jax said hi, and he was doing really good. He had won 3 more silver belt buckles at rodeos. I smiled when I read that, knowing that being a rodeo cowboy was exactly what Jax had been made to be.

The letter ended much too quickly, but I felt much better after reading it. I knew I'd probably never get another letter from him, but I would be able to at least talk to him on the phone, and maybe see him sometimes, when I was in Wichita Falls.

The weather began to turn cooler, and I was still hanging out with Kelly and Robin, even though I only got to see them on the weekends. We still talked on the phone every day, and they'd tell me about what happened at Woodway. I missed the routine at Woodway but tried to be as happy as I could be at Calvin. I was grateful for having Tina and Buddy there. I hung out a little bit with Tina's friends, when she wasn't there.

She was a year older than me, so Buddy was the only person in my grade that I felt like I was really friends with. The bad thing was, we never had any classes together.

Daddy and Clarice's drama had finally leveled out, as far as I knew. I wasn't as worried any longer about Clarice sending someone to rape and murder me. Daddy had begun only calling once a month. Sometimes, a couple of months would go by before I heard from him again. I missed him.

Geoffrey tried to call me a couple of times, but after the first stilted conversation with him, I told him the second time to not call anymore. It felt like I wasn't being loyal to my daddy. I was surprised to hear a hurt tone come to his voice. It seemed so ironic to me that we finally became more or less friends, at the end of our parents' relationship.

Since Daddy didn't really have much of a place in Oklahoma, for me to visit him, I ended up staying home for Thanksgiving. I would be at home through the Christmas break as well.

Mom took Christmas as a new excuse to drink differently and started drinking spiked eggnog as soon as she finished her coffee in the morning. She wasn't a lot of fun to be around almost the entire month. I tried to stay out of the way as much as possible. I continued to drink on the weekends, to be numb. I didn't want to spend any more time in the real world than necessary.

Carla Feldman and I actually began to talk on the phone and soon I was hanging out with her too. She still saw Chance, off and on, but by then, she knew they weren't going to do more than what they'd been doing. Chance would still act super sweet to me, all the time, but I usually just blew him off. I didn't know what else to do.

I managed to kiss a few more boys through the fall and the beginning of winter, but it was usually during a drunken haze. It never consisted of more than a little making out in the parking lot, of the game room.

Each time a new boy would kiss me, I wondered if they thought they'd get to take me somewhere and have sex, so I was hyper-vigilant about not going anywhere with anyone.

I already felt bad enough, but I also knew that my teenage hormones were screaming, and boys were boys. I loved and missed Kevin terribly, but I also knew that he wasn't being an angel either, whether he told me or not.

On Christmas Day, Mama gave me permission to call Kevin and Bailey. I was ecstatic to get to talk to each of them for 10 minutes. I knew that it was an expensive gift, but I was so grateful she did that for me. I was disappointed when Bailey never answered, then remembered that she was probably in Abilene at her grandparents.

Thankfully, Kevin was home when I called. Just hearing the velvet purr of his voice, through the phone line, made me smile in a way no one else could ever do. Since Bailey didn't answer, Mama told me I could talk to Kevin for 15 minutes.

I watched the clock like a hawk, so I wouldn't screw up any chance of ever talking to him again, since it was long distance.

I knew that this Christmas was harder for him and his family, since it was the first one after Donna died. He told me that the headstone for Donna's grave was finally in place. His mom was happy that it was there. It had an angel on it, which made me smile. I reached over to touch the angel bear I'd originally given to her.

Our fifteen minutes ended much too soon, but before we got off, Kevin asked, "So, you still seeing that asshole, Chance?"

I laughed softly, "No, Kev, I told you about him getting that other girl pregnant before the end of the school year!"

"Yea, but I just wondered if you would start seeing him again, when you got back. Lainey, you deserve someone so much better!" Kevin sighed, quietly.

I sat there for a beat and listened to his breath, "Yeah, I deserve to be in Wichita Falls with you."

Quietly, Kevin admonished, "Oh Darlin', don't hang everything on that. Live life. I still don't understand why you haven't completely given up and forgotten me yet."

"What? Why would you say that?" I asked, a little more forcefully than I intended.

"Lainey, it's not that I don't want the same, but unless your mama plans to move back, which we know she isn't going to do, you need to move forward. Quit holding on so tight and live your life." He replied.

"Kevin, I am living my life, but part of my life is being up there for a while, in the summers. I'm perfectly fine with waiting, until I'm there, to be with anyone." I explained patiently.

"Baby, you're 16 now. It's time to let go of me. I can't be what you need right now."

I sat there, very still before I answered, trying to mask the tears that were threatening to choke off my voice. Finally, I croaked, "Kevin, I'm living my life while I'm here, but when I'm there, I'm yours. That's just the way it will always be. I don't know what's going to happen, but you have to know that I'm not done being a part of your life, no matter how small it can be."

Kevin whispered hoarsely, "Well, just remember that if you ever do get serious about someone, I understand."

I wondered what he was trying to tell me so cryptically, and finally I stated, "Well, I'm living my life here, but when I'm in Wichita, I'm always gonna be your Lainey! You can't change that, Kevin. Unless you are going with a girl you can't bear to be without, but as long as I'm living right now, you are forever and always part of me. So, quit trying to run me off, unless you really want to be done with me. Until then, just remember you are stuck with me."

I heard the deep chuckle in the back of his throat. He finally said he wasn't trying to run me off, but simply trying to tell me that he didn't want me to feel bound to him, being so far away. "Kevin, I'm bound to you forever, no matter what," I whispered.

Kevin grew quiet on his end of the line, then said, "Oh Lainey, if you only knew…" I wasn't sure what he meant by that, but it was closing in on my 15 minutes with him. I knew I had to wrap up the call.

"I do know, Kev," I whispered thickly. "I know that no matter what, you will always be a part of me, and I will always be a part of you. That's never gonna change. So, let's just leave it at that, for now. I gotta get off of here or else my mom will kill me when she gets the phone bill!"

"Okay, Little Lainey. Take care of yourself, Kid." Kevin stated, with his King Kevin voice, on the last sentence.

"I will, Sparky!" I joked back, sarcastically. "You take care too and tell your mom and dad I said hi! And Kev, I'll be coming back soon. I don't know if it will be Spring Break or summer, but I'm gonna be back there. Don't forget me before then, okay?"

"You silly kid, I'll never forget you. Isn't that what we just said?" Kevin chuckled and I could hear the grin in his voice.

I felt silly, but still replied, "Yes, I know, but sometimes I get afraid that you will somehow forget me. Love you, gotta go! Bye!" I said quickly when I realized I'd already gone a minute over. I hung up as I heard Kevin's soft voice almost whisper the word 'bye. I missed him even more now and was miserable. I didn't understand why growing up had to be so hard.

Chapter 40

When 1983 finally dawned, I was fully ensconced at Calvin High School. I didn't eat lunch, so I would go out to the smoking area, with Buddy and Tina. I felt more alone though, than I had ever felt, since moving to Corpus. It made no sense really, but I didn't want anyone getting too close. I was afraid they'd find out how insane my life was, between my drunk mom, my insane soon to be EX-stepmother, and my absent daddy.

I did get to see Kelly and Robin Stubbs on the weekends, at the Gameroom, and that helped. Carla and I also began to get closer. I thought it was a little strange that the only thing we really had in common, was the fact that Chance Cahill had used each of us for sex. We'd both been willing participants too. Carla still hung out with him, and went riding around, but I'd been more stand-offish, even though he'd been nothing but nice to me since the mess with Tara O'Neal. I missed Kevin. I felt the need to be faithful to him, with my body, even though I would kiss other boys if I got drunk enough. But I never went riding around with them.

Towards the end of the month, on a Saturday, my daddy sent a small package in the mail. When I got it, I was curious what he could have possibly sent to me. When I opened it, a small jewelry box was inside. When I opened it, I found a beautiful gold ring, set with a small marquis diamond and 6 tiny diamond chips. I looked at Mama surprised, and she smiled. I opened the small note enclosed and read:

Dear DeLaine,

I know this is a little late for your sweet 16 birthday, but I had a friend of mine make this ring for you. I hope you like it.

It's made from your mama's and my wedding rings. I want you to take good care of this ring and don't lose it. It is an expensive ring for a 16-year-old girl to have, but I think you can be responsible enough to take good care of it now.

Happy Late Birthday Baby Girl~

Love,

Daddy

"Did you know about this?" I asked Mama quietly. She nodded her head and beamed at me. "Why didn't you tell me?" I asked, still a bit subdued.

"He wanted it to be a surprise!" Mama explained, looking a little perplexed.

Finally, after a few seconds, I looked at Mama and muttered, "I'm gonna go call Daddy collect and tell him thank you, I guess." My mom smiled encouragingly at me. I wasn't sure what I was supposed to feel.

On one hand I was thrilled to have such a beautiful ring. It meant so much to me to own a ring that had been made from my parents' wedding rings. It was a gorgeous, free-form, abstract ring and I'd never owned a diamond that large in my life.

Then there was the other hand. It was what bothered me. I had only talked briefly to Daddy on Christmas and hadn't heard anything else from him in a long time. He'd called me dutifully on my 16th birthday, but there hadn't been any big, sweet 16 birthday bash for me. Instead I'd gone out and gotten drunk at the Game Room, after my birthday, to celebrate.

I never knew quite how important I was to my daddy. I knew he loved me, but I felt like he didn't have a clue who I was. He knew who the little kid DeLaine had been, but it seemed like since we moved onto Belfast, he quit knowing anything real about me. Then when I chose not to come back from Corpus, he withdrew even more.

I didn't know if it was because he was still dealing with Clarice or not.

I didn't have a clue what he was doing with her. It bothered me that he didn't tell me anything! Her mental and emotional abuse had been directed straight at me, even though he and my mama never knew it. I had been the one to endure her for the years he had been with her. I'm sure she did her own crap to my daddy too, but I was the one who had been her personal slave, taking care of her kids every day and weekend, even when she was around.

I sighed as I dropped onto my bed and took the tiny black box out. I opened the velvet square and pulled the yellow gold and diamond ring out to try it on. It was large enough I could wear it on my index finger.

Once I slipped it on, it shone like all new jewelry does. I sat there for a few minutes, drinking in the sight of all the sparkling facets of the marquis diamond.

I smiled and picked up my phone. I actually caught my daddy at his apartment. I thanked him for the ring. Sometimes when I talked to my daddy, I would ache because I missed him. I wished I could just be a little girl again.

When I got off of the phone, Mama came to my room and asked if I wanted to go with her across town to some friends of hers.

I knew she was going to get drunk, but the friends we were going to see were much older, so they were almost like surrogate grandparents. I decided to go with her. I could play pool while I was there, and if she got too drunk, I could drive her home, I thought.

Ray was going to meet us over there, when he finished some business he was working on. I figured it was better than just sitting at the house by myself, waiting to go out. This way I wouldn't sit around and mope, or think about Wichita Falls all day, and how much I missed everyone.

I played game after game of pool, while my mom sat with her friends, at the bar they had in their rec room. I tried to ignore how loud my mama was getting, the more she drank.

I breathed a little sigh of relief when Ray walked in. He wasn't drunk yet, but he was a quiet man who didn't say a lot whether he was drunk or sober. I continued to lose myself in playing pool, knocking the different colored balls around on the green felt.

As the afternoon wore on, I realized we weren't going to be leaving any time soon. That meant I wasn't going to get to go out. I knew better than to ask my mom if we were leaving, just so I could go out. I borrowed the phone and called Kelly. I told her I wouldn't be out, but I'd call her the next day. Thankfully, she understood, because she had been around my mom enough. I sat alone in the living room as I listened to the adults getting drunker by the minute.

Around 9 o'clock, Ray came in the living room where I was sitting, watching some stupid TV program, and told me I needed to take Mama home. I nodded and stood up. Sometimes I never knew what I was going to encounter. Mama was still in a pretty good mood and hadn't dissolved into the Ms. Hyde persona yet. I was grateful, but she refused to let me drive. She kept telling everyone that I didn't have my license and she didn't want me to drive on that side of town. She didn't think I had enough experience.

I tried not to laugh, because she let me go out every weekend, and it was usually with the 1966 Ford, that she promised I could have when I got my driver's license. Her Cadillac had died. Ray gave us the old Ford to replace it.

Mama thought that because it was basically a tank on wheels, I would be safe in it. She sometimes didn't think through all of her reasons for letting me drive, or not. Ray and I both could tell she was in no mood to start pointing out inconsistency. We had both been on the receiving end of her foul mood, when she was drunk.

As we drove along the dark expressway, to the Northwest part of town where we lived, I could tell Mama shouldn't be driving. I asked her if she wanted me to drive. She snapped that she'd already told me I didn't know how to drive on a highway, and it was different than driving up and down Leonard Street in Annaville.

I shut up but felt myself tense up every time she swerved off of the road. I began to feel a little worried, then frightened. "Mom, let me drive," I began again, a little more sternly, when she ran completely off of the road into a large grassy median.

"DeLaine, I know what I'm doing," my mama slurred. I noticed she put her hand up over her left eye. At first I wasn't sure what she was doing, then it dawned on me! She was seeing double, literally, and she thought holding her hand up would make her see only one road way.

Just as I was about to demand she let me drive, she drove off of the road again, towards the grassy middle section of the split four lane highway.

"Dammit, Mom," I began, but instead of jerking the wheel back onto the asphalt, the car continued to go into the grass.

Suddenly I could say nothing else because with a sickening racket, I heard the car as it flipped through the grass. A part of my brain rationally counted the times my head hit the roof of the car. I felt as if I were a person whose mind was literally split in two. There was the part of my mind that was freaking out, but there was a more detached part of me that knew exactly what was happening. I smelled the grass and dirt when we first began to roll. I felt like I was watching in slow motion as my body was flung through the car.

We weren't wearing seat belts, so I felt my body fly through the air and felt my forehead smash into the windshield. My bottom lip slammed into the dashboard. I tasted the metallic, penny taste of the blood that immediately flooded into my mouth. I wondered where my mother was, even as I felt my body fly through time and space, inside of the car. I wondered why I could only hear my own screams. I was amazed that I continued to keep count of the number of times my head slammed either into the ceiling of the car, or the dashboard.

After I counted to the number seven, the car landed back onto its wheels. I pulled myself up off the floor board. I could hear the engine still roaring, as the car struggled to gain purchase up the steep side of the median, where traffic was traveling in the opposite direction. I glanced around and could make out my mom, slumped down into the floor board, of the driver's side. I realized in a flash that her body weight was inadvertently pushing onto the gas pedal.

Even though the car was mangled, I wasn't certain if it would or even could get up the side of the median we had landed in. All I could see when I finally pulled myself up, was the headlights of the oncoming traffic. Turning to try to ram the gearshift up, I realized that my right arm wasn't working. I didn't understand why it was dangling beside me. I twisted around from the position I was smashed into. I tried to do it with my left hand, but felt a sharp pain run through my left wrist. I was terrified that my wrist was broken again, since I'd broken it before.

Twisting around, I finally managed to get my right arm up enough with the help of my left hand, which screamed as I did so, to grab the key out of the ignition. I heard the roar of the engine finally die away.

When the engine quit, I let out a sigh and realized I smelled smoke. I looked around, wondering where the fire was. I frantically looked at the passenger door and pulled myself back into the seat. I realized the roof of the car was smashed down. I felt again, as if there was a detached version of myself, watching the entire wreck and aftermath. It watched as the actual me began trying vainly to open the door.

I realized sitting inside of the darkened car, there would be no exiting from the driver's side. It was completely flattened to the steering wheel. My mom was completely down in the floorboard, of the driver's side, passed out.

I saw a light catch the corner of my vision and glanced to the back of the car. Sparks were shooting out, I could see, through the cracked and caved in back windshield. I began pushing on the passenger door with an even greater sense of urgency.

I didn't know a lot about cars, but I knew that the gas went into the car at the back of it. If there was something that was sparking back there, it would only take one spark to catch the grass and then the car on fire. I could actually smell gas then. I started screaming and crying as I brought my right hand up to bang on the window.

My right arm still felt detached somehow, but I could maneuver my hand better than the left one. "Mom! WAKE UP! DAMMIT MOTHER! WAKE UP!" I began to scream.

I saw the headlights of cars going by on either side of the highway. I wondered why no one was stopping. Hadn't someone seen us go off of the road? It was an extremely dark area of the freeway, but still, someone had to have seen us.

Just when I began to see flames licking the trunk, I felt the last tiny edge of sanity I had left, ebb away. I began to scream uncontrollably!

Suddenly, there was a dark shape in front of me, on the other side of the passenger side window.

"Help me! HELP ME! PLEASE!!!" I screamed from my raspy throat? It was raw from the uncontrolled screaming and the smoke that was beginning to leak into the car.

A deafening roar of grinding metal and glass threatened to burst my ear drums as the shadowed man pulled the bent door open. I scrambled out of the car and took off running through the tall grass. I wasn't even sure how far I had run when I stopped dead in my tracks. I realized I needed to go back for my mama.

I turned around and began running back to the car and was shocked to see that there was no huge burning inferno engulfing it. I saw several men standing around with flashlights as they were trying to maneuver my mom out of the car. I ran up to them and yelled at them to be careful because she'd had back surgery. Where the thought to yell that came from, I wasn't sure, but I felt like they needed to know before they began to pull her out of the car.

Once I saw flashing red lights approaching, I turned and began running through the tall, brown grasses again. I wanted away from the car. I didn't see sparks any more, but there was a lingering odor of burned grass.

I ran crying and cussing. I was so angry at my mom. If she'd just let me drive, we wouldn't be out in the median in 40-degree weather.

I ran back to the group of people, just as two ambulance attendants were strapping my mom onto a board. Once I was satisfied that they'd gotten her out safely, I turned to run off again. I heard a man say, "There's the girl who we saw running through the grass. If we hadn't seen her, we would never have known they were down here."

I turned around to look for the girl they were talking about, then it dawned on me that they were talking about me. Where was the man who had managed to pull the door open? I looked at the car and saw the door had been cut off and was lying in the tall grass.

I watched like a scared rabbit, as the group of people carried my mom on a stretcher, out of the grass. They left the car lurking deep in the dark, looking like a dead monster in the murky shadows.

Turning away from the throng of people, I began to hop through the tall foliage, like a small jackrabbit, uncertain why I was acting so skittish and frightened. There was still the detached feeling that I was watching myself, and the part of me that was living the moments.

I couldn't understand why I felt afraid to go up to the side of the road, where they had my mom on the asphalt. I saw a couple of men pointing in the darkness in different directions.

I noticed a woman with dark hair, styled in an old-fashioned beehive, looking across the grass. Her finger pointed straight at me like a spotlight. I again felt the wildness of a trapped animal. Before I could run further away from the scene of flashing lights I had two men coming at me from opposite directions.

"Hey sweetie, is that your mom?" one of the men asked sweetly. I nodded my head mutely. "Why don't you come up here with me, so those guys from the ambulance can take a look at you, to make sure you're okay," he continued in a soothing tone of voice.

I glanced over and saw the other man walking slowly up beside me, as if he was flanking me, to prevent me from running away. I was suddenly so tired. The first guy who had talked to me was edging up closer. He was younger. He wasn't much older than me, but he continued talking to me soothingly.

Before the second guy could get close enough to touch me, the first guy was beside me in one graceful stride. He reached to take my left hand. When he brushed my wrist, I jerked back, protectively.

He smiled at me and drew his hand back holding it in the air, "I'm sorry. I didn't realize you were hurt." I looked at him still feeling a little frantic. "C'mon, sweetie, c'mon up here so they can look at your hand, okay?"

"Wrist," I mumbled.

"What?" The first guy, who wasn't much older than me asked.

"It's my wrist. I think it's broke," I mumbled softly.

"Oh, well, then let's go up where there are lights and have them look at you okay?"

I suddenly thought of something that hadn't crossed my mind before. "Is she dead?"

"What?" the guy asked me, confused again.

"My mom…is she dead?" I repeated with little expression.

"Oh, um, no, I mean, she was okay when I came out here to get you to come back," he replied. I looked at him intently. He had long, blonde hair, like so many boys did. It was tousled looking, like Leif Garrett's, and I suddenly giggled. I figured the guy wouldn't have a clue who Leif Garrett was. He probably listened to Black Sabbath, or Thin Lizzy, and Ted Nugent, definitely not some bubble gum pop star.

I walked back towards where all the lights were and noticed for the first time, the traffic was down to one lane, on the side that we'd gone off. There were all kinds of police cars and an ambulance.

Just as I began to walk up the side of the grassy median, where they were working on my mom, I felt both my legs give out. I was lying in the grass. The guy who had talked me into coming back up there knelt down beside me and asked if I was okay. I held my left wrist up to my chest, as I lay on my side. I looked at the black sky and wondered where the big guy, who had opened the door, was again.

"Hey, is something wrong with your legs?" the tousled topped guy asked me anxiously.

"I dunno. My legs started hurting really bad, and then I fell," I whispered, in a weird hazy voice.

The guy told me to stay there and he was going to get one of the ambulance guys to come look at me. I nodded and watched as he ran up to the shoulder of the highway. I wondered what had happened to the other guy who had come out into the grass to help the blonde guy 'catch' me. It seemed as if he had melted into the mass of people who were gathered in the middle of the headlights.

I heard the grass moving and the blonde guy and one of the ambulance attendants came over. I noticed the ambulance guy had a board like thing in his hand.

"Hey there, my name is Kevin and I'm gonna get you up there where my partner and I can take a look at you. Then we'll take you and your mom to the hospital. I hear your legs are hurting though, so I'm gonna get you to roll over while I slide this board under you. Then I'm going to carry you over to the road, next to your mom, okay?" he tried to soothe me.

I looked at Kevin who was carrying the board. I thought it was a little funny, but I also thought it was a little bit of a sign too. I wanted my own Kevin right now, but he was almost 500 miles away.

This Kevin had dark brown hair, cut like a military cut and deep brown eyes like my own. He had a sweet face. I looked at him still feeling as if a runaway rabbit soul had invaded my body. I felt so anxious and afraid of everything and everyone, except for the blonde headed guy, who I noticed was kneeling beside the ambulance attendant named Kevin.

Once they rolled me onto the solid wooden board, I realized I had stickers all over my back. One of the police officers had come down to help carry me, strapped to the board, to the side of the road. I started crying because the stickers were really hurting the skin on my back. When they got me to the road the other ambulance attendant took a pair of scissors and began to cut the front of my jeans straight up.

"What the fuck are you doing?" I howled, as I realized he'd just ruined one of the legs of my favorite 501's.

"Honey, just let us work, we need to assess your legs to see if you've broken them!" the guy barked, gruffly.

I started yelling again as he quickly cut the other leg of my jeans up to my hips and pulled everything back to where my legs were exposed to the cool night air. I could feel the skin around my panties being exposed. I began cussing and telling the guy that my legs couldn't be broken if I'd been out running around on them. Ignoring me, he assessed my legs, then asked why I was crying.

"I've got stickers all over my back, and you put me on this hard board! They are getting embedded into my back, that's why!" I yelled belligerently.

The gruff ambulance guy, who hadn't told me his name, griped, "Well, I can't take you off of this board once you're on it, so you're going to have to hang on 'til we get you to the hospital!"

I lay there on the side of the road and cried until I heard a familiar, soothing voice. I opened my eyes and saw the tousled, blonde headed guy. "Hey, there…what's goin' on?"

I gazed up into his eyes and realized he looked a little like someone I knew, but I wasn't sure who. "I've got stickers all over my back and they won't get me off this damned board and get them out of my back." I replied angrily, as the salty tears flowed down the sides of my face.

I felt the tears going inside of my ears.

"Here, let me see if I can at least get some of them," the guy said in his melodic voice. I thanked him as he gently lifted my neck up, which hurt I realized, as I tried to help. He was able to get most of the stickers out of my hair and neck, and some of the more painful ones out of my shoulders.

"What's your name?" I suddenly asked him quietly.

"Thomas…or Tom," he answered, smiling.

"Tom what?" I asked.

"Well, you're gonna laugh, but my last name is Collins," he replied with a grin.

I looked at him funny and then I realized the reason his name sounded familiar. "Isn't that like a mixed drink?"

Shaking his head Tom quipped, "Yep! It sure is. My mom didn't realize that when she named me, and everyone has a good time with it." I smiled at him. "So, what's your name?" Tom asked me.

"DeLaine," I offered, quietly, as the tears began to dry on my face.

"That's a cool name," Tom smiled down, gently. "Where do you go to school, DeLaine?"

"Woodway. Oh no, wait, I don't go there anymore. I go to Calvin now," I replied, feeling silly.

"No shit? My kid brother goes to Woodway!" Tom told me his brother's name and I immediately recognized it. His brother was in my P.E. class my freshman year. Then I understood why he looked familiar. They resembled each other.

"How old are you, Tom?" I asked, suddenly curious. I knew he wasn't much older than me, but he was definitely out of high school.

"Me? I'm 26," he admitted. He was ten years older than me, I realized. It was a little strange that I thought he was only about 20, and he was even older than I thought. I smiled weakly at him as he finished with the stickers he could reach.

I heard my mom just as he finished, begin yelling my name. I was furious with her. She'd almost killed us, because she was too damned drunk to be driving! Tom looked at me and I must have had a dark expression cross my face. He questioned if I was okay. I nodded my head wearily. "Are they gonna make me ride in an ambulance with her?" I asked Tom softly.

"I think so," he answered.

"Fuck!" I breathed vehemently.

I noticed he gave me a lop-sided grin that reminded me of my Kevin for a brief moment. "It's okay. She didn't mean to wreck," he assured me.

"Yeah, but she should have let me drive!" I growled fiercely. "I'm at least sober!"

Again, Tom gave me the lop-sided grin, and told me sometimes parents screwed up too. I slightly nodded my head.

The nice ambulance attendant, Kevin, came over after I saw them load Mom into the ambulance. He told me they were getting a stretcher out and would take us both in the same ambulance. I looked at him and asked if I could ride in a different ambulance. I didn't want to be anywhere near my mom at that moment. I was so angry at her, I couldn't see straight, and I didn't want her talking to me. I wasn't sure how big an ambulance was, but it seemed to me it would be awfully cramped with two stretchers.

"I'm sorry hon, but all that got to the scene is me and my partner, Gabe, so you're stuck with riding with us tonight," Kevin, the ambulance attendant said. I nodded my head again and felt the familiar twinge in my neck. I told him that my neck was hurting. He jumped up and came back with a big wrap looking thing. Suddenly, he was nudging Tom out of the way to put it around my neck.

"Why'd you do that?" I asked crossly.

"To protect your neck, in case you have a fracture in there. It's a big possibility with as smashed as that car is." Kevin explained. "Did you open that door all by yourself?" he asked me curiously.

"No, some guy came up and opened it for me. But I don't know where he went. He was really big, but I didn't see him after I came back to the car the first time. I've been looking at all the people around me and none of them look like him." I admitted, quietly.

The ambulance attendant looked at me and then at Tom Collins and shrugged his shoulders, oddly. When he walked off to get his partner to come help lift me, Tom smiled at me, "Well, looks like it is time for me to split now. I didn't know my ride home from the beach was going to be this exciting!"

"Thanks," I whispered to the one man whose voice had soothed me enough to quiet my fears and got me to come back.

"You're welcome! I hope you aren't hurt too badly! Just remember, she's your only mom. She fucked up, but she's human. Try not to be too hard on her," he suggested, softly. I knew he was right, but still felt my anger as it boiled away. I felt him lightly stroke my forehead, then he was up and gone as the two ambulance attendants walked up to take his place. I felt the wind blow across me, as Gabe and Kevin pulled the stretcher up, so it would roll across the bumpy asphalt.

I heard my mom in the ambulance, calling my name, before we got all the way to the back of the vehicle. I tried to remember what Tom told me. She was my only mom. She messed up and I needed to remember I'd wanted her to forgive me when I'd screwed up before. Then I realized the things I'd wanted her to forgive me for hadn't endangered her life either.

The lights inside of the ambulance were blinding after being outside in the pitch black. The only light I'd had to see by had been the headlights. While they were bright, they still allowed a lot of the darkness to cloud my eyesight. The bright lights of the ambulance didn't allow that at all. I realized as soon as the light hit my eyes, my head was splitting; it was hurting so badly. It hadn't been too bad until the light hit my eyes. Now I wanted to cry from the pain.

"DeLaine!" My mom called out, as she saw the stretcher being pushed up beside hers. The ambulance attendant, with the same name as the boy I loved, climbed in as his partner, Gabe climbed in the front. I heard him talking on a radio to someone at the hospital. I felt my mom's hand reach for mine and I jerked away from her, roughly. The jerky movement made my head, neck, wrist, and just about every other part of my body scream out in pain. "Are you okay, honey?" My mama was still trying to talk to me.

"Just leave me the fuck alone," I growled.

The sweet ambulance attendant, with the brown hair, leaned over by my ear, and whispered, "Cut her a break kid. She didn't do it on purpose."

I lay there on the hard stretcher, with my eyes closed, and wondered why it seemed everyone was so willing to forgive her, when she'd almost killed me. Couldn't they tell she was drunk? Couldn't they smell the booze that was all over her? Didn't they find the bottle in the car? Why did I have to be forgiving of her, when I could easily be in a body bag being taken to the morgue of a hospital, instead of to the emergency room of one?

While these dark thoughts ran through my brain, I heard Tom Collins' voice in my ear, saying that she didn't mean to wreck, and that she was my only mom. I thought about everything that had changed for me in the last couple of years. Soon, Tom's voice was beginning to sound more like Kevin Strong's or maybe I was just wishing it had been Kevin Strong there on that dark road, getting the stickers out of my shirt.

Thinking of Kevin made me also think about Donna Strong and losing her almost a year now. I couldn't believe that she'd been gone almost a year. I felt as the tears slid out from under my closed eyelids and slipped down my face. They felt like scalding lava coming out. I wished I were still in 8th grade. I wished that I still lived in Wichita Falls. I wished that Donna hadn't died.

Before I realized it, as I thought about all the things I'd lost and would never have again, we came to a sudden stop. The back doors opened up. I realized while I'd been lying with my eyes closed, I'd allowed my mom to hold my hand, finally.

When she had to let go, when they wheeled me out, I suddenly felt alone and vulnerable. I couldn't believe I'd been so angry at her. What if something had happened to her? I'd have to go back to Daddy in Oklahoma. At least Clarice wasn't still around, but I didn't even know where he was frankly. I knew he had an apartment. That was about all I knew.

As the stretcher's wheels made contact with the hard tile floors of the emergency room, I was aware that most of the lights were out in the small hospital's hallways, which I was grateful for. Every third fluorescent light fixture was lit up and when it would shine on the back of my eyelids, I winced in pain. It made my head feel like someone was driving a steel spike through it. I heard the stretcher that had mom on it, get pushed into another exam room.

As the team who had me began asking questions and talking to the ambulance attendant, Kevin, who had thankfully stuck by me more closely than his more surly, counter-part, Gabe.

I was glad that they'd given me the one with the "K" name. I listened as he rattled off a bunch of numbers and strange words as the nurses asked him questions.

Once the people who were working on me were happy with his answers, he left the room and after asking the attendant twice about why my pants were cut, they then questioned me three different times and ways about why my pants were cut.

The third time, I couldn't help myself, because I decided if they couldn't understand it four times, in the span of a few minutes, they deserved my sarcastic response. "Oh, I guess they just decided to see if they could make a pair of 501's into a long denim skirt."

"What?" the nurse with the mousey brown hair stuttered, after I said that.

I rolled my head towards her voice as I was trying to keep my eyes closed against the harsh glare of the lights and repeated, "The guy from the ambulance told you twice and now this is the third time you've asked me. My legs are fine. I fell and the other stupid guy decided to cut up my good pair of 501's and now I'm pissed!"

"There's no need to get snippy with me, I have to ask these questions," she huffed.

"Well, write down the answers. I was the one in a wreck. What if I were unconscious? Would you still be running around squawking about my pants?" I sniped.

"Christina, you need to finish doing the intake with the daughter. I'm going to go assess the mother," the mousey, brown haired nurse huffed, exasperated.

I opened my eyes a tiny slit to find a girl who was in her mid-20's trying to maintain a straight face, as the older nurse walked out.

When she saw me looking at her curiously, she turned her back to me, as she rattled off a few more questions.

Finally I asked, "So are you going to ask me why my pants are all cut up too?"

"No, I got it the first time, but she likes to ask the same question over a few times before it sticks in her brain. Usually she's got someone else doing all of this. Since there were two of you, she has to oversee both intakes and we heard that the teenager was hurt worse. That's why she came in here first." Christina explained, with a hint of a giggle still under her breath.

I was surprised to hear that they considered me hurt worse. "So, is my mom okay then?" I asked, cautiously.

"Yeah, they're gonna do some x-rays and make sure everything is okay, but you have more visible wounds. They feel like you most likely have a broken wrist too. We're gonna do a lot of x-rays of you too, though, so if you can think of anything in particular that we haven't discussed, let me know." Christina smiled sweetly.

"It is broken." I stated matter of factly. "My left wrist was broken a few years ago. It's broken again. It hurts like hell. The pain feels like it did when I broke it the first time."

"Do you remember how old you were, when you broke it before?" the young nurse asked.

"Yep, it's been almost exactly three years, which would have made me 13." I remembered feeling that sharp pain the first time I broke my wrist, when Geoffrey shoved me at William, when they were fighting. Geoffrey didn't realize that Kevin was going to grab William, so I ended up sailing off of my bed, onto the floor and landed on my left wrist…then my face. I also ended up with the lens from my glasses implanted in my skull too and had been asleep for two weeks.

After recounting that, the nurse looked at me and remarked, "Wow! I bet that was pretty scary, huh?"

I chuckled, "Yeah, it was really scary. I think it was scarier for everyone else around me though." I suddenly flashed on waking up seeing Kevin, slumped in the chair beside my bed. How I wished he was going to come walking through the door of the emergency room.

"Well, I'll make a note in your chart about the previous head injury. They may want to run some other tests on you since you had that. Does your head hurt now?"

"God, yes," I admitted anxiously, as quietly as I could.

"Okay, well you hang tight. I'll go talk to the doctor and find out what he wants to do," Christina instructed, as I heard her nurse shoes go shoosh-shoosh on the smooth, cold tiles.

I lay there and dozed for a while. Then, more people came into the room and pushed me down the halls to begin the x-raying of everything. They decided to scan my head too, because of the previous injury to my brain.

I was so exhausted by the time they finished, all I wanted to do was sleep. I felt like they x-rayed me for hours, and then I had to endure the brain scans too. I didn't really know what they did when they did that.
I just knew I had to lay on that cold, hard table forever it seemed. Thankfully, they gave me a little bit of medicine that made me relax, and I slept through it.

After what felt like a whole day, my eyes started to flutter open. I noticed they had half of the lights out in the room. I was grateful since my head still hurt horribly. The pain over my left eye was intense. It wasn't as bad as the pain I'd felt after I woke up when I was 13, but it was getting close to it.

I kept my eyes opened only a tiny bit and looked around the room. When I turned towards the door, I realized there was someone standing next to me. It was the young nurse who had been helping me before the x-rays. "Hey," she spoke quietly.

"Hi," I responded. "What are you doing?" I saw her opening up a tray with some instruments on it.

"I need to pull the glass out of your belly button," she giggled a little when she said it. I smiled at her and got the giggles too.

"I have glass in my belly button?" I asked her. She nodded and then I remembered the stickers. "They had me lying on a bunch of stickers and they got all in my shirt. There was a guy out there who tried to help pull most of them out around my neck and shoulders, but I can still feel them."

"I'll take a look after we do the glass, okay?" she assured me.

I was curious what the tests had shown and what they were doing to do to me. As if she were reading my mind, the young nurse told me, "You definitely have a broken wrist. You were right. You don't have any fractures in the vertebras in your neck or back, but you do have a bad whiplash. You also don't have any broken bones in your legs either, but we kinda knew that one too, huh?" she smiled at me.

I tried to nod, but it only made my neck and head hurt worse. "So, is that why they have this stupid neck thing on me?" I asked a little crossly.

The nurse smiled and bobbed her head. She also told me that we still didn't know what the outcome of the head scans was going to tell us, so I just had to be patient.

I heard the door to the room open and I turned towards it. I realized that another thing wrong was my glasses were missing. I couldn't see clearly. Everything was a blur. I didn't know what I was going to do about that.

I began to fret a little and when I told the nurse what was wrong she told me she'd look at any personal effects they may have brought from the wreck site. I nodded and was grateful that I didn't need glasses to know whose voice was jokingly saying, "Hey Pooter, you should have driven! You're mom's a shitty driver on a sober, sunny day. She's definitely a shittier driver in the dark after some V.O.!" Ray's deep voice chuckled.

"I tried," I moaned, defensively.

"Aw, it's okay kid. The main thing is you two aren't hurt too bad. I can replace a car. So don't sweat it!" Ray snickered, good-naturedly.

"She broke my fucking wrist, Ray! Not to mention this piece of shit collar thing they are making me wear! We're waiting on the reports about my damned head!" I fumed back at him.

"Hold on, calm down, Pooter!" Ray soothed me sweetly, in a voice I'd never heard before. "She didn't mean to hurt you, you know that, right?"

I looked at him angrily, but knew he was right. I could hear the young guy's voice who stuck by me telling me I needed to cut her some slack, since even parents screwed up too. Finally, I felt my face begin to melt. I felt the tears begin to flow. "Ray, I was so scared! The car caught on fire, and I couldn't get out! I couldn't open the door, and some guy finally showed up and got it open. I didn't know what to do, so I just started running!" I blurted out in one long breath!

I felt his hand actually smooth my curls around my forehead. I realized Ray never touched me affectionately like most dads did. I liked it. My daddy hugged me when I saw him, but I hadn't seen him in so long. I realized that I was actually missing him when Ray touched my curls.

"I know, sweetheart," Ray crooned to me. I had never heard him speak so lovingly before. He wasn't mean or gruff, but he was a man of few words. He wasn't much of one to show affection in his action or words, but through what he provided. My own daddy was much more demonstrative when it came to affection and even talking.

I didn't think that Ray liked me for the first few years that he was with my mama. I finally figured him out the summer before I decided to come and stay. He wasn't crazy about kids, but he liked me. It seemed most people who weren't crazy about kids liked me though, but it was probably because I didn't act like most kids.

I felt bad that I was lying there with a sweet nurse picking out shards of glass from my belly button, and the man I considered my step-dad was consoling me. I couldn't continue to be strong enough to be pissed at my mom. "I just wish she had let me drive," I finished feebly.

"Well, you know, she does now too. She wants to come in here, but they are making her stay on that bed until they are done looking her over. She's okay though. Just some bumps and bruises. It looks like you got the raw end of this deal, Poot!" Ray had the underlying chuckle he seemed to always have underneath almost everything he ever said to me.

I scrunched my mouth up on one side. I always seemed to be the one who got the worst end of any deal. Ray handed me his handkerchief. I was surprised.

"It's clean! Hold onto it and wipe those tears. It's gonna be fine, Pooter. I'm gonna go check on your mama. She wants to know how you are," Ray said.

"Just peachy!" I muttered, sarcastically. "You can tell her we're just waiting on my head tests. Looks like I'll be getting a cast to go on my left wrist, too." Ray smiled and patted my hand as he walked towards the door.

"It's gonna be okay, Pooter! Trust me, okay?" Ray consoled, as he walked out the door.

"So is that your dad?" the nurse asked me.

I shook my head, "Nah, it's my step-dad."

"He seems really nice," Christina said thoughtfully.

"Yeah, he's pretty cool. He's much better than the bitch, um, excuse me, I mean the witch my daddy married though!" I grumbled bitterly.

Christina laughed out loud after I caught myself about to let out with a blue, cussing streak on Clarice. "Pretty bad, huh?" she asked me, as if she really were interested. I agreed, then told her that my daddy had finally figured out what she was too. "Well, looks like you're with the better parents then, huh?"

I looked at her funny because I figured they had to know that mom was bombed out of her mind. I actually was wondering why there weren't cops swarming the place, ready to haul her off to jail for a DWI. Finally, I agreed, and decided it was best not to start bitching about how my mom had been driving drunk.

Just as Christina finished the arduous process picking each tiny piece of glass out of my belly button, she helped me to stand, while she went over my back and pulled as many of the stickers out as possible before having me remove the shirt and then trying to pick out what was stuck in my flesh.

My back was horribly itchy, but I knew from the past experience I'd had after the tornado, and my skin was blown through with insulation, that it eventually gets better. It wouldn't be right away.

I protected my left hand and wrist the entire time I stood. When she finally finished, she had me slip a hospital gown on, so I wouldn't have to replace the t-shirt and get more tiny barbs poking me.

"Okay, I'm going to leave, but someone should be in here soon. We'll get you casted up and see what the doctor wants to do with you too. Of course, that all depends with what those tests show about your head!" Christina explained, as she went through the heavy door that led to the hallway and the nurse's station.

I looked at the counters full of jars with cotton balls and swabs. All the normal stuff that littered doctor's counters was on them, along with a few other things that I wasn't too sure of their purpose. I hoped they weren't going to be using anything weird on me, while I was here. I closed my eyes after a while because I was so tired. I noticed on the wall clock that it was already 2:30 a.m.

When I felt someone touch me on the shoulder, I jerked and realized I'd actually dozed off again. I turned my head and found my mom standing beside me, with Ray leaning in the doorframe. "Are you okay, Bug?" my mama asked me with tears coming to her eyes. My eyes were hard, but when I saw her eyes glimmering with tears I heard Thomas Collins say, "Even parents screw up!" Finally, I could feel the hardness in my eyes soften. "I'm so, so sorry, honey! I should have let you drive! I won't ever do that again! I swear!"

I sighed. I was tired and just wanted to be done in this emergency room and go home. "It's okay, Mama. When are they going to let us go?"

"Soon. They told me they'll be in here in about 10 minutes to put a cast on your wrist and the doctor should be coming back by in a little while too. After that, they said we'll be released." I looked at the clock on the wall and was amazed that is was only 2:45.

Just as I glanced over at Ray, Christina was trying to get around him in the doorway, along with another girl who didn't look much older than me. They were carrying a bunch of stuff. I watched curiously as they pulled a rolling table over to the gurney. They told Mama and Ray they needed to wait in the hallway.

They gently took my left wrist that had been splinted since they'd x-rayed it and began to unwrap the splint, so they could put the cast on. I watched with great interest. The cast I had when I was 13 was put on while I was unconscious. Thankfully, they'd given me a shot for pain before they began to work on my wrist.

I felt pretty good. I realized that it was almost like being stoned, but it was a better high than any pot I'd ever smoked. I was really enjoying the sense of euphoria the shot had given me.

When they finished putting the cast on, I noticed they both grinned at me. I'd been jabbering about all kinds of things the entire time they'd worked on me. I felt a little sheepish, but I just couldn't muster enough care to actually feel truly bad. I giggled and closed my eyes.

It seemed only a few seconds passed when my mom gently shook me, and my eyes fluttered open. When they did, I could feel the throb in my left wrist. I moaned involuntarily and looked at my mom with gritty eyes.

"The doctor just came by and your scans are all clean on your head. He said he was shocked that with your previous brain injury, you didn't suffer another one. You do have a slight concussion. He said it wasn't anything to be too concerned with, but you will have a headache for a while. He is going to release both of us. So, I thought you might want to wake up." My mama explained all of this as I looked at her and felt like I had come crashing back to Earth after being drunk and stoned.

I was coming back with a huge thud. I wasn't sure if I really liked whatever medicine they'd given me for pain after all. The waking up part from it really sucked!

My mom helped me up, and I sat on the side of the gurney. I thought about putting on my shirt that was full of the tiny needles from the huge sticker burs that were embedded inside of the material. "Hey, Mom, do you think they'll let me wear this hospital thing home. I don't want to wear that shirt. Besides they cut my pants up too and my panties are showing when I stand up."

Mom looked at me and said, "Let me go ask." When she walked out of the room I gingerly slipped off the gurney and picked up my OP t-shirt and wondered if I'd ever get the stickers out. My mama came back into the room and told me that I was free to take the ugly hospital gown with me, since my other clothes weren't wearable.

I glanced at the clock and was shocked to see it was already 4:30 in the morning. I had been asleep for a while. Thankfully it didn't take very long for the nurse to come in and give mom all the instructions about my care. They told us to follow up with our family doctor and then after Mom signed a couple of papers, we were walking down the dimly lit hallway to where Ray sat in his car waiting for us.

I just wanted to fall into my own bed. I was beyond tired.

Chapter 41

The next morning when I woke up, I hurt so badly I couldn't move. It seemed as if every muscle in my body had been crushed. I was terrified. I began to yell for my mom and she hobbled to my room. "What's wrong, DeLaine?" she asked me a little crossly.

"Mom, I can't move!! Everything hurts so bad I can't move. It's all in my muscles. Not my wrist or neck, even though they hurt like hell too, but everything else! I didn't hurt anything else! What's wrong with me?" I asked frantically.

My mom came hobbling into my room and gingerly sat on the side of my bed. She struggled to raise her hands to try to soothe me. "It's because of the wreck. The doctor told me we'd be sore. He just didn't tell me how much! He prescribed some pain pills and said for you to take them for a few days."

"I don't want any damned pain pills! I just want to quit hurting! Besides if they're like that stuff they gave me in the hospital, that shit is awful to wake up from. I didn't like it at all!" I groused, petulantly.

"They gave you a shot last night, and it was the good shit," my mama replied, with a slight laugh. Finally, she convinced me that taking one pain pill would help. When she went to the kitchen to get me something to drink, I turned my screaming neck to look out the window. It was another gray day. It was Sunday and I had no clue how I was going back to school.

"So, how am I supposed to go to school like this?" I asked my mom, as she walked in with a glass full of ice and coke.

"Well, you aren't going to school this week," Mama replied, quietly.

"WHAT?" I exclaimed.

"DeLaine, you cannot go to school in this condition! Depending on how you do this week you may not be able to go the next week either, but let's just get through this week. I've already called Dr. Peters and we have an appointment on Wednesday"

"Mom, I can't get kicked out of this school! There's no place else for me to go!" I worried, with an edge in my voice.

"DeLaine, they can't kick you out of this one. You are going to be okay. Maybe Tina across the street can get your school work and you can work on it, so you don't get too far behind. I refused to look at her and nodded my head as much as the neck brace allowed.

Picking up a small bottle on the nightstand, my mom shook out two of the pink pills inside of it, and handed them to me, along with the coke. I looked at them, wondering how they would make me feel. I realized I'd given up on caring about anything the night before. I put the pills in my mouth and took a huge gulp of the fizzy coke. "Try to go back to sleep, honey. You had a long night and those pain pills should make you drowsy. Try to rest and call me if you need me." I smiled at my mom even though the smile never reached my eyes.

By that afternoon, Kelly and Robin knew about the wreck and then Tina. I realized by the evening everyone in Annaville seemed to know about it. I had people call that normally never called me. I was surprised. Carla Feldman called and just minutes later Chance Cahill actually called too.

When my mom came to tell me there was a boy on the phone, I hoped that it was Kevin. I didn't know how he would possibly know what had happened, but I hoped the invisible tether had tugged at him to call me. Instead when I picked up my phone, I found Chance there, asking if I was okay. I'd told my story so many times that I just didn't have it in me to repeat it one more time. Of course, I was absolutely stunned that he'd even bothered to call. Then I wondered how he'd gotten my phone number; who had given it to him.

"You know DeLaine, I'm really sorry that things worked out the way they did," Chance said sincerely.

I sat there for a beat before answering him. "Yeah, I know, Chance. It's cool. I'm sorry I've been such a bitch too."

"I deserved a hell of a lot worse than your being a bitch," he laughed. I hated that my heart actually leapt a little when I heard his laugh.

"Well, I guess I'm gonna get off of here. I've been on the phone a lot and it kinda hurts. I mean, I have a cast on one wrist, my shoulders strained or bruised or something, so they have a sling on it, not to mention the lovely neck brace," I laughed.

"Jesus, it sounds like you really got hurt," Chance exclaimed.

"Oh, I didn't include the stitches in my lip or the black eyes!" I laughed even harder as I told him how extremely hideous I was. I wondered if he'd freak out if he could see me with my lip swollen three times its normal size, not to mention the other bruises and cuts.

"Damn, DeLaine, I'm really sorry you got so hurt. If you need something just call me, okay?" Chance insisted, sweetly. I felt myself getting madder for falling for his sweetness even though he truly sounded sincere.

"Um, okay, thanks, I guess," I mumbled, quietly.

"Maybe I can come by and see you sometime this week," Chance suggested, with a little bit of hopefulness in his statement.

I didn't know what his game was, but I was wise to him. I felt myself immediately tense up. He actually knew how to screw with my emotions. I loved Kevin, but I was so lonely without him here. Chance had been the boy I'd been the craziest about since I moved here.

"Uh, yeah, okay. I gotta go, Chance. Talk to you later!" I rushed to get off of the phone.

"Yeah, sure. Hope you feel better!" Chance replied. "Take care. Bye."

"Yeah…uh, huh, Bye!" I stammered and hung up the phone.

I felt myself feeling weird stuff about Chance and I didn't understand it. I wished Bailey were here, so I could talk to her about everything. I wanted to tell someone how damned mad I was at my mom for not letting me drive and wrecking. I wanted to tell someone how afraid I'd been that I'd cheated death once again.

Now here was Chance adding another weird knot into my twisted story. He'd been so sweet while we talked on the phone. He'd been sweet to me every time I was around him. He actually was sweeter now that I chose to ignore him, than when all I could do was moon over him. I just didn't understand any of it.

Bailey always had a way of helping me to balance out all the screwed-up thoughts that flew through my brain at exceedingly high speed.

I sighed as I struggled to put the phone back onto the table. It sucked having both arms and hands out of commission. I could still use my fingers on my left hand, and I could use my right hand, just not the arm. It helped that I liked to read, because I read a lot during my time out of school.

Tina had been great about getting my homework. Mom had gone up to the school to talk to the principal about my absences. Thankfully she went up there sober, so she didn't call anyone Godzilla like she'd done Mrs. Gonzalez, at Woodway. The principal assured my mom that I wouldn't be penalized for the time out, and if I needed two weeks, then I needed that much time out.

I was surprised at how accommodating they were. Since I was keeping up with the classwork, except the tests, the teachers were happy with me.

I usually finished the homework quickly. I usually had a headache by the time I was done with it, and the pain pills helped, but they also made me sleep.

By the end of the week, I was able to lose the sling, which I was thrilled with. I still had to keep the neck brace on. I hated it worse than the sling. My wrist was still hurting a lot, but I tried to be tough about it as long as I could. I hated how hard the pain pills hit me.

Kelly and Robin were coming over to spend the night with me since I couldn't go out. I was so excited to have some company, and to get caught up on all the gossip from Woodway. Kelly always came with good gossip about everyone.

Saturday afternoon, while I was lying in my room, just waiting for it to be 6 o'clock so Kelly and Robin would be there, I was startled when the phone rang, as I was dozing off. I didn't want to answer it for once and figured it would be for my mom anyway.

Mama came to my door with a big smile on her face. She'd been good all week and I noticed wasn't drinking much at all. I hoped the wreck had scared her enough to quit. "Bug, phone." She announced.

I rolled over and looked at her. "Who is it?" I asked.

"Just answer it!" she smiled at me.

I went to grab the phone with my casted hand and remembered as soon as I felt the weight of it that only the fingers were open. I sat up frustrated and picked up the receiver with my now good right one. "Hello?" I answered the phone. I half expected to hear my daddy's voice, but I'd already heard from him on Monday. I couldn't imagine him calling again.

"Lala! I just got your letter today! Are you okay?" I heard Bailey exclaim on the other end.

"Bay! I'm fine!" I reassured my terrified, best friend, who was sitting in her turquoise and lime green bedroom 500 miles away.

"What happened? Is your arm still in a sling? Do you still have a neck brace? What about your wrist? It's bad if you re-break something I've heard!" Bailey spoke in a rush.

"Slow down, Sister Sue! I got rid of that damned sling yesterday. I still have this stupid neck brace and of course the cast. The black eyes are going away and my lip isn't as swollen. I get the stitches out next week," I responded hurriedly, trying to remember all of her questions.

"Oh, shit, there's someone else who wants to talk to you. I'm gonna get on here though after, so don't hang up, you hear?" Bailey grumbled, irritably. I wondered who was there with her and wondered if she and Levi had gotten together again. I hoped so. I knew how much they loved one another.

"Lainey?" I heard the familiar voice whisper into the phone. Why was Kevin at Bailey's house? I couldn't understand it.

"Kev?" I whispered, not sure if I was really hearing his voice. The voice I'd missed and wanted to hear more than anything the week before.

"Are you okay, Lainey?" he continued in his soft tone.

"Yeah, I'm fine. I have a broken wrist again. The left one broke again. My shoulder was all messed up and I have whip lash really bad, and a slight concussion. Um, I also had a small part of my lip torn on the bottom, close to the corner. I have stitches there. It's probably gonna look awful," I lamented.

Kevin started chuckling. "Darlin' I think it's safe to say I've seen you at your worst. A couple stitches in your lip doesn't bother me. I was terrified when Bay called this mornin' and told me. When I heard the concussion, it scared me like crazy. I'm happy to hear your voice."

I felt stupid, but I worried about the scar that my lip would have. The scars from my other accident were healed and had been so expertly done that there was only the faintest of lines in my eyelid crease that couldn't be seen, unless I showed you. I had been terrified about them in the beginning, but I'd had Kevin there to reassure me that it didn't matter what I looked like.

"I know, it's stupid, I just don't want anyone to think I look like a freak. My lip's still swollen, but it is a lot better!" I admitted softly.

"Lainey, I knew something was wrong." Kevin admitted, quietly, surprising me.

"What?"

"Saturday night…I knew something was wrong with you. While I was asleep, I dreamed about Donna. She looked sad and when I woke up, I was thinking about you. I should have called then," I knew he was blaming himself about not following his gut instinct, even though he knew he could do nothing to help me.

"Oh Kev, don't be upset. You couldn't have known! I'm fine and honestly the day after I was on so many pain pills I was loopy for the first few days. But I'm fine. I'm gonna be fine about these stupid stitches in my mouth too. I promise. I'm really okay." I mumbled softly, trying to soothe the impotence he felt at being so far away to protect me. I knew that was his natural instinct towards me. He'd been that way forever.

Kevin sat there for a beat before saying, "I'm glad you're okay, Lainey! I was so worried about you. Do you think that you are gonna get to come for Spring Break?"

I knew that the wreck had set us back financially. I didn't want to really ask Mom for the money to ride a bus like I'd done the year before.

I felt certain she'd let me go in the summer, but with the wreck being a couple of months before Spring Break, I was pretty sure it would be a no. She'd been in such a better frame of mind that asking for money felt like something that could set her off on a binge.

"I dunno, Kev. Mama's been getting a lot of doctor bills already from the wreck, plus now Ray's gotta get us a new car. I'll let Bay know the closer it gets. For sure summer, but I just don't know about Spring Break." I admitted sadly.

The boy, who was now a young man that I loved so much, sat there quietly, and then he stated, "I'll be checking with Bailey. I'm glad you're okay, little Lainey. Feel better. Bailey's starting to punch my arm because she wants the phone back. I miss you, Kid," he whispered, and then I heard Bailey ask if I was still there.

I couldn't believe he was gone so quick. He hadn't given me a chance to say goodbye. My heart ached when I realized he wasn't magically in my ear any longer. I listened to my best friend as she asked me question after question about the wreck, even though I'd written in great detail, quite painstakingly too, with just my left fingers. I answered her amiably though, just because I was so happy to hear her sweet voice, almost as much as I had enjoyed hearing Kevin. He had walked out and waved goodbye to Bailey as soon as he got off the phone with me. Bailey thought it was a little odd, but she was too impatient to hear all the details from my own voice.

Before we got off the phone, after almost 30 minutes, (I hoped her mom didn't get too upset when she got the phone bill!) I asked Bailey, "So, you called Kevin?"

Bailey responded sarcastically, "Really LALA! Do you think I wouldn't call him about something like this? I mean c'mon! I even told Levi and Jax! You might not be here but we all still care about you, even when you are in Corpus."

I knew their lives went on, just as my own did when I was gone from them, but I still found it amazing that they continued to care about me as much as they did, while I was away. I thought about all of them, even Levi and Jax, all the time too. I looked at their photos every day, sometimes several times a day, but I never understood how they could think about me too.

"I know that, Bay-Bay!" I replied, a bit defensively. "I was just surprised to hear his voice in your room!"

Bailey assure me, "It's cool, Lala, I don't hate Kevin. Things are a lot different this year than even in freshman year. When you come you'll probably be shocked at how much has changed. Everything is fine, though. Don't worry about that."

"It's just that things are different. Everybody seems different these days. Kevin is one of the only things that doesn't ever seem to change to me. I know that sounds weird. You'll see when you get here." Bailey explained.

"Um, okay. As long as everything is okay, I'll just have to wait 'til summer to see what you're talking about. Thanks for calling him though. Hearing both of you is just the shot I needed of feel goodness!" I joked, with a chuckle in my throat.

"I'm glad you sound okay. I was so scared!!! Then Kevin mentioned how bad it was to have a concussion and I was about to go nuts 'til he got here, so I could call you." My friend cried, so sincerely, that it made my heart literally ache to be with her and Kevin. I closed my eyes and pictured them in the bedroom I was currently in. I smiled as I listened to Bailey chatter about how worried she'd been. I closed my eyes to help with the visualization of seeing the people I loved right here with me. I smiled when in my mind I could see Kevin leaning his long, graceful form inside the open door of my closet, and Bailey sitting on the other side of my bed, talking away.

When we got off of the phone, I got up and walked to my open closet and touched the door frame where I imagined Kevin's shoulder rested. The glossy white paint was as cold as usual. I had hoped to feel his warmth and felt a pang of sadness when I felt its normal temperature.

Chapter 42

I was so happy when I got to go back to school. I still felt freakish, but the stitches had come out of my lip. It still looked raw and scabby, but it was better than the Frankenstein look I'd been sporting. Everyone was so helpful. I even had someone assigned to help me with my books, since I was still under strict instructions not to lift anything heavy. Add to that the cast on my left wrist and hand, and it made carrying books a challenge. I almost felt a little like a celebrity.

My mama had continued to lay off the booze a lot, for several weeks. I was happy to see it. She was much easier to get along with, but I could also see there was a look about her that was off somehow. She seemed so unhappy. Even though we'd survived, and come out relatively okay, she still seemed restless and irritable some days.

The first weekend I got to go to the Gameroom was the first day we got our new car. It was a blue Ford that was only about 5 years old. It was still pretty big, but it had power locks and windows. Mama let me drive up to the game room. I was so ecstatic to be anywhere by myself for a change that I left super early.

When I walked into the building, I was happy to smell the familiar smell of cigarettes and dirty feet. I never knew exactly why it smelled like gym socks, but it did. Sometimes they tried to get something that smelled good in there, but it eventually evaporated and the smell came back. I thought it was probably because we spilled drinks all over the indoor/outdoor carpet and everyone also put out cigarettes on the floor.

I noticed Chance was one of the only people in there, as I walked in. When he saw me, his face lit up, which surprised me. He had that beautiful smile that could sell any dental product on the market. It was like a lit up Christmas tree when he shined that lovely grin directly on you, as he was doing to me now. I felt myself weaken a little in my stance on him for the first time since the whole Carla Feldman thing the summer before. I watched as he sunk the eight ball on purpose and was equally surprised when he put his pool cue on the table and told the guy he'd been playing that he was done for a while.

Chance walked directly up to me. I wondered what had happened that he actually didn't mind being seen with me for a change.

"Hey, DeLaine," Chance smiled again. I felt my knees shake just a little, as they felt weak.

Mentally chastising myself, I smiled at him and winced when I felt the pull of the newly scarred area of my mouth. "Hey, Chance," I replied through my grimace.

"Damn, girl, that looks like it hurts! Are you sure you're okay?" Chance asked sweetly. I nodded my head. I looked around and noticed that there weren't too many others in there and thought Chance might be talking to me just because there was no one else in there.

Smiling at him, I admitted, "Damn straight it hurts! It hurts like a mother!"

"Damn! I'm glad you're okay. So, your car's history, huh?" he was still maintaining his sugary tone. He was acting like we were long, lost friends. I felt a little weird about it all. I wanted to make him pay for hurting me so badly the spring before, when I'd found out about him and Carla, but I couldn't really stay mad at him. He had such an endearing quality about him, when he wanted to.

"Yep, I just got my new car," I grinned slowly, remembering to use the other side of my mouth more for the smile than I had done previously.

"Way cool! What did you get?" Chance asked sincerely.

I motioned for him to come out into the darkening evening, to the parking lot where my blue, Ford LTD was sitting silently, beside his orange pick up. I pointed, and he let out a low whistle. "Wow! That's a nice car! It looks expensive!" Chance was admiring the more modern car, than the old tank I'd been driving.

"Yeah, it even has power locks and windows! Can you believe it?" I mentioned excitedly, forgetting my anger with him for a moment.

Again, a low whistle between his teeth. "Damn, DeLaine! How'd you get so lucky?" Chance asked me, looking at all the angles of the big Ford.

"My step-dad wholesales used cars," I told him, shrugging my shoulders. I didn't really think the car was that great, but I did like the electric windows and locks. It also had a heater and air conditioner which I was thrilled about. The other old car didn't have an a/c. Trying to look good was out of the question in the South Texas heat, when you had to ride around with the windows rolled down, in the summer time. Of course, the summer time in Corpus was a lot longer than in the rest of the state. It seemed to be tropical in Corpus Christi from around the first part of March to September.

"You'll have to take me for a ride some time," Chance suggested, quietly.

"Uh, okay," I was suddenly a little uncertain.

"Whenever you want, of course," Chance offered amiably. I wasn't sure what he really wanted, but it was so much easier than being mean to him all the time, to just agree.

While we stood beside the car, Chance's arms had slid down on either side of me, from where he'd been standing inside of the open door, checking out the interior. "I'm really sorry you were hurt," he whispered, staring into my eyes. I bowed my head. I wasn't really sure what he was doing, but he didn't take long to show me when he leaned over and began to kiss me lightly on the mouth.

I pulled away at first, almost angrily, but when I saw the sincerity in his face, I realized that I didn't really want to quit kissing him. I enjoyed it. My heart might be in Wichita Falls, but I was becoming increasingly aware that my body was in Corpus Christi. Kissing Chance was something I enjoyed. I also realized that I was kissing him sober, for probably the first time. It was an odd realization.

In Wichita Falls, the only time I'd really been shit-face drunk, was the night of the rodeo, when Jax and I had been together, the last time. When I kissed Jax or Kevin, I was normally sober, but in Corpus, I suddenly realized I was always drunk. I tried to remember kissing a boy one time sober, while I kissed Chance, and realized I couldn't really come up with one time, which made me feel lousy.

I was enjoying kissing Chance, and the parking lot was still empty, except for us. I wrapped my arms around his waist because my right arm was still a little weak, and the cast on my left wrist was heavy. I felt so uncoordinated. After what felt like a really long time, Chance pulled away from me and smiled down, as his blue eyes looked into my brown ones.

"Wow, I was wondering how long you were going to take to let me kiss you again," Chance murmured.

I looked down and felt my cheeks flush with color. Then I shrugged my shoulders, unsure what to say. He leaned back in and began to kiss me again and I continued to let him. After a while, he pulled back and grinned. "You know this is the first time I've ever kissed you where one or both of us hasn't been drinking?" I mentioned, quietly.

Chance leaned away from me a bit, then cocked his head and mused, "You know, you're right. Well, let me say you've always been a great kisser, but doing it sober is quite a treat!" I giggled and felt angry with myself for succumbing to his sweet talk and kissing.

"Yeah, um, you too," I replied, feeling stupid doing it. "Listen Chance, about all the stuff with Carla," I began, but he cut me off.

"Forget it, DeLaine! It was a fucked up mess. Everything is a lot different for me now," Chance explained. I just nodded, knowing that no matter what, Chance Cahill was never going to be just mine.

"Hey, why don't you give me a ride in this nice, big, ol' car?" He smiled so sweetly and sincerely, that I felt my willpower cave in.

"Okay, sure," I whispered, feeling my stomach get all fluttery. I was angry at my body for being so excited while my head was screaming about what a rotten bastard Chance Cahill was!

Chance ran around to the passenger side, and I pulled the keys out of my right jeans pocket, sliding inside. I started it and began to back out of the parking space. I was still shocked at how few people were out right now, but it was only 5 p.m. I'd left home by 4:20 because I was so excited to get out finally on my own.

When I got on Leonard Street, I looked over at Chance and asked him where he wanted to ride to. "Go to the little store! I need some dip!" I turned into the store, which was only a few yards from the Gameroom parking lot.

When Chance came back out, he had a bag with a six pack of beer. I smiled at him and realized that for the first time since moving to Corpus, and beginning my social life here, I didn't want to drink. I didn't want to be out of control. The wreck was still lingering with me. I had felt completely out of control during the whole thing. I had no one to help me or be there for me, because the person who was supposed to be taking care of me, was too drunk to drive. I felt suddenly weird about drinking so much. I knew I did it to be numb from the pain and misery I felt living with my mom.

Chance slid in my new to me car and smiled his gorgeous, blinding smile, and offered me one of the beers. I shook my head no and he asked, "Oh you probably have to take pain pills huh?"

"No, not anymore, I just don't wanna drink tonight." I responded softly, as I began backing out. "So, where you wanna go?"

"Go down Viking Road, like you're going to the trails," he instructed, smiling.

"Um, Chance, this car won't go up in the trails. It's too low," I was trying to keep from going to just make out. I wasn't sure why I even agreed to us riding around. I knew he'd want to go park somewhere and probably have sex, but I didn't really want to.

Chance gave me his best Cheshire cat grin, "Oh, I know! There's a bunch of places down there that nobody knows about!"

I looked at him curiously. I knew that The Rivers housing development was out there, but I didn't know many of the streets. I'd been to a party at one of the houses, but I'd ridden with someone else.

It was a huge housing addition that had large two- and three-story homes that were like mansions to me. Rich people lived in those houses. I didn't run around with any rich kids. They were usually the popular kids and the elite jocks at school, just like they had been everywhere else I'd gone to school.

Finally, I shrugged my shoulders and drove down Viking Road, towards The Rivers. Chance kept the talking going, which was a little unusual for him. I remained quiet while he directed me through the winding roads that wound through the neighborhoods. All of the gorgeous brick homes made the brick home I lived in look like a little shack. Just when we got to the last road, I noticed a new road that jutted off to the side.

"Turn there," Chance declared suddenly, as he pointed to the road off to the side. I turned and was amazed to find several streets that had been made, but there were no houses, only sidewalks and roads.

"Wow," I exclaimed, as I looked down the slope of the road and out over the streets that stood alone without houses adorning each of them. "I never knew this was back here!" I breathed out in a whisper.

"Pretty cool, huh?" Chance asked me, grinning.

"Uh, yea," I admitted as I looked at the neighborhood that still wasn't built yet.

There were some streets that were going to be cul-de-sacs, but the grasses had grown up all around the circles. Chance directed me to one of those little turn circles, and I parked the car. I left the key turned back so we could listen to the radio. Chance sat there just talking for a while. I was surprised that he still wanted to be friendly. Usually he was on me as soon as he parked and barely had the key turned. I liked this new version of Chance a lot. I wasn't quite sure why he was being so nice and friendly to me.

After Chance had talked about all kinds of things for about fifteen minutes, I finally decided I needed to find out what he really wanted. "So, um, is there a reason we're sitting here talking?"

He looked at me curiously, "Well, I guess because we never really seem to talk when we go riding around. When I heard about you bein' in that wreck, and how bad it was, I realized that I've actually been a real asshole. I mean, I really think you are funny, and I like you, DeLaine. I just hated thinking that if you'd died, I wouldn't have ever told you that. There's a ton of a shit I've never talked with you about. I mean, I want us to be friends. I know that all that shit with Carla last year sucked. I was just being a stupid assed senior. Now that I graduated, I realize that there is a lot more out there than just gettin' drunk and acting stupid with every girl I see."

I looked at him and felt my familiar arch in my eyebrow begin to rise. I wasn't sure how much of this 'speech' was him being truthful, and how much was a bunch of bullshit because he realized I wasn't going to be easily swayed like I'd been in the past.

Finally, I stated, "Well, Chance, you're right, you were an asshole! You know I'm kinda friends with Carla now, right?"

"Yeah, I know. I mean, it's cool between me and Carla. She's a nice girl. I just wasn't prepared for her to come up pregnant. She still won't tell me what happened. I don't know if she lost it, or if she got an abortion, or if it was really a false alarm…I dunno. I feel weird sometimes about it, but I also know that either way, it was the best thing to happen, whatever it was. I mean, it's not like we were in love or anything like that. We were just having fun." Chance explained, with a little grin.

I looked at his face in the darkening evening, and realized, that no matter what, he was still a shit! He was a shit I found attractive. He was also a shit who I felt comfortable with too. I had such a hard time ever feeling truly comfortable with many people my age. He wasn't Kevin. He could never be Kevin. He also wasn't Jax, even though he reminded me more of Jax than anybody. I didn't want to be 'in love' with him either. I was already conflicted for too long between Kevin and Jax. I couldn't possibly throw in Chance Cahill too. He wasn't looking for a commitment from me. I enjoyed making out with him. I wasn't thrilled with the sex, but I wasn't thrilled with sex with Kevin either. I still hadn't figured out what the big deal was yet. I also wasn't sure I wanted to have sex with anyone else, except Kevin, because I didn't want to feel too slutty. I loved Kevin. I only liked Chance. I felt like there was a difference. Then again, when you're sixteen and hormonal, sometimes stopping in time just isn't easy.

"So, what is it that you want from me?" I finally asked him.

Chance looked at me startled, since I normally was never very direct with him. Except for the night I found out that Carla was pregnant. I normally just did whatever he wanted and walked around moon eyed over him. This was a side of me he'd never known, the more direct DeLaine. I was tired of just being the 'go to girl' for whenever there was no one else to be with.

"Uh, I dunno, DeLaine. I mean, I like you a lot and I like hangin' out with you. I really love your blow-jobs," he grinned salaciously at me.

I felt myself begin to blush from the roots of my hair to my toes. I'd never had a boy say that. Then again, I hadn't done it to anyone else except Jax.

"DeLaine, look, I want to go ride around with you, but I'm not looking for a commitment. I want us to be friends, but I also want to go ride around with you too, if you know what I mean." Chance was beginning to sound a little uncomfortable.

I giggled watching him squirm. Finally, I said, "You mean, you want to go ride around and mess around too, right?"

Chance actually seemed to blush a little I noticed, as the light was draining out of the sky quickly. He finally nodded as he tried to look a little sheepish.

"So, what are you saying?" I asked him, already knowing the answer to my question was, but wanted to hear it from his mouth.

"I want us to be friends. Okay, I want us to be good friends. I just don't want there to be any misunderstandings about what is going to happen between us, okay?" Chance was trying to muster his courage back up, after he had been put on the spot.

I looked at him seriously, as I thought about what he was saying. He wanted to hang out and mess around. He wasn't looking for anything else from me. I felt a little sad because I wondered if it was because he didn't think I was good enough to be a real girlfriend or if it was just who he was. I also realized that I didn't want any commitment from him either, because I still had Kevin. He was the one I loved. He was seeing other people I knew, even if he never told me. He had encouraged me to see other people. He actually wished I didn't care about him as much as I did, but he had no more control over how I felt than I really did.

Finally, I nodded my head and agreed, "You know what, I'm okay with that. I just don't want you to make me feel used, do you understand? That means I don't want you to mess around with me and then leave with someone else. I want you to keep treating me like you have been doing, around others. I don't want you to stick your tongue down my throat in front of others, but I don't want to feel like I'm skulking around, hiding that we're with each other sometimes, either." I was still in my quiet and calm demeanor.

Chance started laughing. "I don't think I've ever heard anyone I know use the word 'skulk' in my life!"

"Well, now you have," I answered a bit snidely. "I'm actually quite smart, but you don't know that about me. If you truly are going to be my friend, I want us to get to know more about each other than what color underwear we are wearing on a Friday or Saturday night!"

"That's crazy! What other color would I wear?" Chance asked me sincerely.

"You goofball, it's a figure of speech. I just meant, I want you to know who I am. I don't want to be another one of those stupid girls who thinks you're so cute and then you shit all over me. From now on, you treat me decent when you want me to go ride around with you. Tell me about your life too. There's a lot of things we don't know about each other. Maybe it would be nice if we tried that sometimes."

I finally saw the beginning of his smile. "I think I can handle that. I just don't like you being mad and ignoring me all the time. I mean it, DeLaine. I wanted so much to make it up to you after that night at the party, but I didn't have a clue what I was supposed to do to make it better between us."

I looked at him and then surprised myself when I said, "Well, why don't you try showing me how sorry you really are?"

"What?" Chance asked blankly. Then I saw the dawning in his eyes as he leaned across the front seat of my new, used car. "You sure?" I heard him ask me huskily.

I turned my head and closed my eyes as our lips found the other in the now dark evening. It felt good kissing Chance sober. I realized that he could be tender when he was kissing me that night. Because I was still healing from the wreck, there were several spots on my body that were still bruised and sore. If he brushed one of them and I instinctively withdrew, he pulled back, making sure I was okay. For the first time I felt special to him. I liked that feeling. I knew he would never be Kevin, but he was who was here, right now. He wasn't asking for a commitment, and I wasn't upset about it.

If I truly examined my feelings, maybe I might have liked it if he'd have wanted it, and I shot it down, but that wasn't what happened. What did happen was I began a new kind of relationship with Chance that night.

It was physical in nature, because I was sixteen, and my body was screaming every time I saw a cute boy, but the relationship finally became a friendship too, which was even nicer. We didn't spend hours of our time connected on the phone, but it was nice to go to the Gameroom on Friday and Saturday nights, or to dances in Robstown, and see Chance and know that he was going to come over and be friendly to me.

We didn't have to hang on each other, but if the night was right, or the timing was, we could go ride around Annaville and mess around, without there being any kind of resentment on my part, that he wasn't wanting more than he was able to give.

Eventually, I knew that Chance cared. He just didn't want to be tied to any one person. Since I was in love with Kevin, I didn't want that either.

Chance told me more about himself and his family, and while I didn't tell him everything about my own home life, I knew that he had part of it figured out, without ever saying anything.

I was usually his staunch ally, and if there was a girl who was bugging him that he couldn't shake, he usually talked to me about it. I would have a nice, friendly chat with whoever it was, and that girl usually left him alone. I didn't like scaring girls, but most of the ones who tried to grab onto Chance and hold on weren't girls I wanted him to get twisted up with anyway. From a friend point of view, I knew that they were either bad news or just plain trash.

Chance had a few relationships that I frowned on seriously, but they were always short lived, and I generally watched them crumble within a week or two. He always seemed to come to me when he needed someone to just listen to him, or to tell him the honest truth about girls.

I realized that we didn't have a conventional relationship, but I also knew that I never stood a chance at that with this boy. Of course, I had a little bit of a jealous streak about him, and wasn't happy when I caught Kelly messing around with him one night. I seemed okay with some of his other conquests but knowing that I cared for him in my own way and catching my best friend in Corpus with him bothered me.

***

The car wreck changed a lot for me. I began to want to stay sober on the weekends. I didn't always make it, and when I gave in and got drunk or stoned, I usually beat myself up so badly mentally, that I would vow to do better the next time I went out. I didn't want to become what my parents were. I wanted control over my thoughts and actions. When I drank or got stoned, I didn't have control over myself in any capacity.

It made for some interesting predicaments for me to get out of at parties sometimes, and when that began to happen, I really wanted to change it. I realized that when I was stoned, I was actually a lot more amorous. That is when I got into more trouble with guys, if Chance wasn't around.

It wasn't that I wanted to be a slut, even though half the time I thought I surely must be, because 'good girls' didn't get stoned and then make out hot and heavy with a guy, just because he happened to be there and showed interest. A 'good girl' didn't profess to love one boy, who lived 500 miles away, and still carry on with anyone else who caught her eye.

I was beginning to think that I probably was doomed to never be a 'good girl' anyway. That thinking usually got me drunk when I didn't want to be.

Of course, I also had to deal with my mom and her drinking. I despised it when she was drunk, which was 85% of the time, it seemed. She had slowed down a lot after the wreck, but she eventually got back to where she was by the end of the school year. I had learned how to avoid her most of the time, if I had to.

I couldn't wait to go to Wichita Falls. I was missing Bailey and Kevin and wanted to feel carefree and young again. I didn't get to feel that way a lot in Corpus Christi. I was either trying to clean up after my mom, when she was drunk, or I was trying to hide my own drinking from her.

In Wichita Falls, I actually got to feel like a kid. I went to the swimming pool and hung out with people who had known me all my life it seemed.

I didn't have to hide behind a beer can or a joint, in order to avoid feeling shame or resentment.

I could stay sober and enjoy just walking down the street to Kevin's or going to the park with him and going for a swing on the swing set.

In Corpus, I was usually the adult. When my mom got drunk, I cleaned up after her. If she got sick, I cleaned up after that too. When she and Ray got physical and beat each other up, I cleaned up my mom, while Ray left for a week or two. I endured all of my mom's irrational fears of being left alone with me, to struggle to pay the bills when things got to that point, and she would go back to tending bar for a while.

Ray always came back. I never knew if I was angry with him or not. Sometimes he hit Mama out of sheer self-defense. Other times he'd get so angry if he had been drinking too, that he'd beat her because he'd had enough of her constant Jekyll and Hyde personality shifts.

I found myself on the floor sometimes, begging her to just shut her mouth. She never seemed to know when to shut up and would constantly mouth off and entice even more brutality.

I tried to stay out of the way when they would get physical, but sometimes I would be in the middle of the room when something started. I didn't think anyone else I knew could possibly be living the life I was.

By the end of the school year, I was usually sober more often on the weekends than I had been in the past. I was finding that being in control of myself at least gave me some kind of control in my life, which I didn't seem to have anywhere else. My home life was chaotic most of the time, just in never knowing what I was going to come home to.

My social life was chaotic when I drank or got stoned. My school life was pretty much the same. I still had few friends, but at least I now knew a few more people. I still never felt like I fit in anywhere though.

I had decided that the next year I was going to take some classes that would get me involved in a more things than I had my freshman and sophomore years. I had basically skated by without being too involved with any club or group.

While I didn't think that anyone in any club or group would possibly want to be close to me, but even more importantly I didn't want to be close to them, I wanted some reason to be away from home more during the week. If it were school related, then my mama didn't seem to mind if I was out of the house.

Before I could go to Wichita Falls that summer, I had to take Driver's Ed. I was really angry about having to take the actual class since I'd been driving since I was 14, but I couldn't seem to pass the driving portion of the driver's license test without it.

The lawmakers were trying to change the law to make all drivers take a state mandated driver's education class, so they were making it harder for kids to get hardship licenses or even for a 16-year-old to get a license unless they'd taken a driver's ed. class.

I had taken the stupid driving test three times by the end of my sophomore year. Only one time did the trooper tell me what I had done wrong. The first two times the troopers couldn't get out of the car fast enough. Neither time did those troopers tell me what exactly I'd done to flunk.

Once I'd taken driver's education, it was amazing that I passed the test immediately and got my driver's license right before I left. I was so excited to finally have a real license and be legal to drive. I'd never been too worried about it before, since I'd been driving for so long, but now I was legal to drive anywhere I wanted!

I was happy about that.

It also insured that if we ever went to my mom's friends' house again, and she had too much to drink, I could legally get us home, without any excuse from her. Hopefully that meant no more wrecks. I still hated for her to ride with me, because she was constantly telling me to look out for cars and usually they were a mile ahead of us.

My daddy's life had stabilized too and for the first time I was going to visit him during the summer, since he and Clarice had divorced. He had re-met a woman at his high school reunion who he'd had a crush on since he was young. She was now divorced also. They began dating and soon they were living together.

I was leery about going up to meet her but knew that my daddy wanted me to visit. Since their apartment was a tiny, one-bedroom duplex, I was only going to visit for 10 days. He was going to pick me up in Wichita Falls, and then take me back where I'd catch a bus. I didn't mind because it gave me an opportunity to go back to Wichita, even if it was only for a couple more days.

When the summer started, I also decided to try to lose some of the weight I'd gained over the last couple of years. I felt so horribly fat. I hated the way I looked and felt. I was excited to see the pounds dropping after just a couple of weeks. Mama was supportive by fixing me a baked chicken breast every night for dinner, along with a salad, no matter what they were eating. I also had to give up my beloved cokes, which was harder than anything.

By the time I left for Wichita Falls, I was almost back down to where I had been when I'd left for Oklahoma City in 8th grade. I was really excited for Kevin to see me. I knew I must be looking good because even Chance had commented on how much weight I'd lost.

I went riding around with Chance the Saturday before I left for Wichita Falls. I had managed to put him off of going all the way when we went parking all the times previous. This time though, I had actually drunk a couple of beers, and while I wasn't drunk, I felt good. I also felt sexy for the first time.

The warm, humid night, and my hormones were just right for me to listen to the damned harpy that I thought I'd figured out how to wrangle the year before. Sex wasn't as painful as it had been in the past, but it still wasn't all that I thought it was supposed to be.

I decided that there must be something wrong with me physically. I figured that it would make sense, since everything else in my life was so screwed up, physical pleasure from actual intercourse would be elusive too. When Kelly talked about sex, she always talked about how great it was. I tried not to say much one way or another.

Afterwards, when we were putting our clothes back on, I felt horrible because I'd felt like as long as I wasn't having sex, I wasn't really cheating on Kevin. I was really quiet, and Chance looked over at me a little alarmed. "Hey, DeLaine? Are you okay? I didn't hurt you, did I?"

"What?" I asked him sharply, as I looked over at him in the green light from the dashboard. "Um, no, you didn't do anything. I'm fine." I replied distractedly.

"It's just…you look a little depressed or sad. I hope you aren't mad." Chance was still a little concerned. I couldn't believe he actually cared that much, but he did these days it seemed.

"Really, Chance, I'm fine! Just have a lot on my mind. I'm leaving in a couple of days and just got a lot on my mind," I repeated absently.

"How long are you going to be gone?" Chance asked me, after he seemed satisfied that I wasn't pissed at him.

I smirked, and felt my playfulness coming back, even though I still felt a deep sense of guilt in my stomach. "Why, you gonna miss me, Chance?" I teased him.

Chance looked seriously at me, "Yeah, I am."

I sat there for a minute and looked into the blue eyes that were always laughing, like Jax's green ones, and wondered what he meant by that exactly. If he had said it back in the same light-hearted tone I'd used, I probably wouldn't have given it a second thought, but instead he had said it while looking into my eyes with a serious expression on his face.

"I, uh, I'm gonna spend a couple of weeks with my best friend and then my daddy's comin' to pick me up. I go stay with him for 10 days and then he takes me back to Wichita Falls. I stay a couple more days and then I come back. I guess almost a month," I shrugged my shoulders, trying to dispel the seriousness that I felt Chance's reaction had brought into the conversation.

After a few minutes he smiled, "Hey, tell your dad I said hi! Man, he whipped my ass on that pool table and he did it one handed! That just blows my mind!" With that, the serious tone he'd interjected was completely gone. I felt myself relax a little.

I grinned at him and when we rode back up to the game room, I listened as he talked about his new job at the refinery. He also had just gotten his first apartment. He was really excited about that too. He stopped at a stop sign before he turned onto the side street by the game room. It surprised me, because at night, no one ever stopped at that sign. He leaned over and kissed me one more time. He had also never done that before. He always waited to kiss me until we were alone, and away from public eyes.

I pulled away after the kiss and looked into his eyes that were once again illuminated only by the dashboard lights. I wondered what mystery lay behind them. "What was that for?" I finally whispered in the darkened cab of the truck.

"Just a kiss to remember me by," he replied, sarcastically.

I shook my head, "Shit, Cahill, just when I thought you were gonna get all sappy on me! I think you need to rethink that one because I think you need a kiss to remember me by!"

I twisted beside him and wrapped my arms around his neck and kissed him deeply.

When I was done, I pulled away and began to laugh when I noticed the expression on Chance's face.

"Damn girl! When you want to mean business, you can sure make a man's toes curl, you know that, right?" Chance was chuckling.

I smiled and nodded faintly. "Well, I do aim to please," I whispered in the dark.

"Well, you do," Chance admitted, as he turned to go the half a block to the Gameroom parking lot.

Before I left that night, I was getting hugs from some of my friends who knew I was going out of town. I was surprised when Chance jumped in front of Willie Morgan and declared, "Get back, Will! You go hug Kelly or somethin'! It's my turn to hug her goodbye!" I started laughing and Chance pulled me close. It was loud out in the parking lot, with the music blaring out of someone's T-Tops (Ozzy Osbourne) and all the people laughing, talking and drinking, along with the traffic noise from Leonard Street. I heard Chance as he whispered in my ear and was surprised when he said, "Be careful and come back home soon!"

When I pulled away from him, he smiled and winked and kissed me on the cheek. I stood, stunned momentarily, and was shaken out of my reverie quickly, when I had a few others coming up before I left. I knew that Chance Cahill was one of the most confusing boys I'd ever known, just like Jax used to be. I never really knew where I stood half the time.

I knew though that with Kevin, no matter what, he loved me. He might not say it very often, but I knew without a shadow of a doubt that he loved me. I couldn't wait to see him. I was hoping that within 48-72 hours I would be holding Kevin tight to me in a hug and feeling as safe as he always seemed to make me feel.

This year would be a little different because Bailey was now working in an orthodontist office a couple of days of the week, but since I had my driver's license now, I could borrow the car she'd gotten for her birthday in February, while she was working. I was excited to be able to drive around Wichita Falls! It would be the first time I'd ever been able to do that as well.

We could now go drag Kemplar, like I'd done on the night that I'd French kissed Duke Reed and gotten drunk the first time. It seemed like I'd lived at least three lifetimes since that ill-fated night.

Chapter 50

When the bus pulled into the station at 10 o'clock the following Monday night I was exhausted from the trip. The layover wasn't as long, thankfully, in Houston, but just sitting on the bus wore me out. Then there were the people who sat next to you, who always wanted to talk! I usually liked to read or watch the miles slip under the wheels as we went down the highway. It gave me time to think and time to change back into the DeLaine I used to be.

I noticed more people thought I was already grown. I'd had two different women ask me if I was going to Wichita Falls to see my husband at the Air Force Base. The first lady I'd been honest with and said I was going to spend a couple of weeks with my friend since school was out. I decided to let her decide if I meant high school or college. The second one though I decided to have fun with.

Just as entertainment, I told her I was meeting my husband and made up this huge story about how we'd been married for a year and I couldn't wait to see him.

Part of me felt a little bad for being such a liar, but I knew I'd never see the woman again, and it was fun to be someone I wasn't, even for a few hours. She was sweet and told me about her husband and how he'd been in the service too when they had first married.

By just feeding her a couple of lines, I got to the point where I mainly listened. I didn't have to make up too much to keep my ruse with her. I always wanted to be someone other than who I was anyway, so at least for a few hours I honestly could be Samantha Sims. The lady beside me had no clue that I was just a sixteen-year-old, high school kid.

When the bus pulled inside the terminal and the greenish cast of the fluorescent lights shone on the concrete slips that the buses pulled into. I looked around to see if I could find Bailey and Jason Rains waiting on me.

I didn't see Jason's crappy car anywhere. I didn't see Bailey either! I felt my stomach do a flip flop and then I saw her sitting on a high cement ledge, with a guy I couldn't see very well. When I spotted her, she saw me at the same time! We began to squeal. She jumped off the cement ledge and came racing through the bus terminal to me!

We hugged hard. I was so happy to see my Bailey.

We pulled apart and I saw the guy she'd been hanging with as he walked up to us. His name was Donny Harkness.

He was in the same class as Kevin and had actually been our paper boy at one time. I looked into Bay's teal colored eyes questioningly. She began to giggle. I knew just through the way I looked at her and the way she looked back, without a word being spoken between us, that this was her new boyfriend. I was actually a little shocked.

Donny Harkness wasn't a bad guy, but he was definitely a level or two below Bailey. He was a scrapper and he had gotten into a lot of trouble when he'd been in junior high. We'd talked a time or two when he came to collect for the newspaper, but he wasn't someone I ever liked in a boyfriend way. Of course, even if I had, I was so enamored with Kevin, and then Jax, during junior high, that few boys really caught my eye.

I knew Donny was also known to be a big drinker and he dipped and chewed tobacco. He was only a little taller than me and Bailey which put him at maybe 5'9" and he was very slight in build. He was a kicker and he had really fair skin with some acne on his face and dark brown hair that was a little longer than most of Jax's real kicker friends wore their hair.

"Hey DeLaine! You used to live on Belfast!" Donny said by way of greeting as he walked up behind Bailey and put his hands on her shoulders. For some reason I didn't like seeing his hands on her shoulders. It upset me more than I could understand but I squelched my feeling as just fatigue from the long trip.

Smiling at him, I said, "Well, yeah, but if you know I'm Bay's best friend, then I'm assuming she could have told you that." Of course, my sarcasm didn't seem to stay in Corpus and was as evident as ever.

Laughing, Donny smiled, showing me teeth that looked like they might have had braces at one time, but were already becoming discolored from tobacco. "Yeah, you got me there! Honestly though, I did know who you were when we first started dating, didn't I, Babe?" Donny smiled at Bailey. Bailey nodded her head in agreement and smiled at me.

I knew that Bailey wanted my approval for dating Donny, but I was having a hard time with it for some reason. I knew that part of it was probably because it stung me as Levi's friend to see her with someone else. But, I also didn't think that Donny Harkness was worthy of Bailey. I hated to be judgmental after all the judging that had been done to me through the years, but somehow Donny gave me a vibe that I didn't trust.

I decided to just smile at his last statement along with the word of endearment he'd used for Bailey and just swallow my opinion for now. I knew that I didn't need to start anything in the bus station by telling Donny I thought he looked more like a weasel and that he really had no business calling my best friend "Babe" or anything else along those lines.

Leaning over, Donny won some points by picking up my bag. I decided to take a wait and see approach before I said a whole lot to Bailey about him. He could be really nice and I was letting my preconceived notions work at me. Something in my gut just felt off around him, and I couldn't quite put my hand on it.

We walked outside to an old brown and beige Chevy pickup and Donny threw my bag into the bed of the truck. The windows were already rolled down so I was right to assume that he didn't have an air conditioner. When we got in I mentioned it and they both laughed and shook their heads. I was glad it was night. I couldn't imagine what it must be like riding in this truck in 100+ degrees during the day with no air.

Thankfully the drive to Bailey's house wasn't too far and Donny didn't hang out too long after we got to her house. I think he realized I was tired, and we wanted to talk. Boy did I want to hear the story about how in the world she started going with Donny Harkness. I wondered what Levi thought about it. I wondered if Levi would even talk to me while I was there. I knew if I was going to see him I'd either have to meet him somewhere or go while I borrowed her car during the days. She wasn't going to want him in her house since they weren't together any longer which made me sad.

After Donny left I could tell that Bailey wanted to talk to me about him. She wanted to know what I thought about him, and I didn't really want to share the concerns I had about him so quickly. I told her that I wanted to go change into my night clothes and after I got into the small bathroom I looked into the mirror that I'd looked into many times since I was 13. I knew that the 13-year-old girl was not the same girl who looked out at me now. She was long gone. The fearful little girl I used to be had been replaced with someone who seemed more jaded. I wasn't sure if I liked the 16-year-old who looked out at me.

When I got out of the bathroom and back into the familiar turquoise and green room, I smiled at my best friend. I didn't understand why I didn't feel my normal sense of relief being somewhere that felt safer than anywhere else in the world. Bailey and Kevin's homes were the places in the world that I felt the safest. I felt like I could completely let go and there was nothing I did that would get me in trouble. I didn't have to be the adult in either household. The only thing that was ever expected of me was to be the teenager that I was.

The relief that I was having trouble feeling was most likely because of the change in dynamics with Bailey and Levi not being together.

I knew what our routine was when we got home when she was going with Levi. We usually talked to him and sometimes Jax too if he was over there for a little while on the phone and then we'd get off the phone and stay up talking about everything else.

I wasn't sure what to think about how we'd close the night now that Levi was no longer there to talk to before we went to bed.

"You okay, Lala?" Bailey asked me with her beautiful ocean colored eyes round with alarm.

"Yeah, Bay. Why wouldn't I be?" I asked her as I turned to busy myself with putting my clothes on the top of my other stuff in my suitcase. I didn't want to look at my best friend as I lied to her. Everything wasn't okay. Life was changing once again. My best friend wasn't still going steady with my other best friend. It just felt wrong that I wasn't going to see Levi all the time while I was in Wichita Falls. I felt like crying. I also didn't understand why in the world Bailey would be going with Donny Harkness. He wasn't like anybody else she'd been with. "I'm just tired," I said shrugging my shoulders as I turned back to face Bailey's gorgeous face.

My best friend looked at me hard and I guess I'd learned how to change my mask for my face that now, the one girl who knew me better than anyone else on the planet couldn't tell when I wasn't being honest with her. I hated myself for not telling her how I was feeling. She was the one person who I had always been honest with and trusted the most, besides Kevin, in my life. Finally, Bailey nodded her head and grabbed her night shirt, telling me she'd be back in a minute. I gave her a half smile that never reached my eyes. I was learning how to smile that way more than I liked. Most everyone thought that I was fine because I was smiling.

After Bailey came back, we climbed under the familiar turquoise sheets, and the thick, white, and lime green flowered, quilted bedspread. "You sure you're okay, Lala?" Bailey whispered in the dark.

I lay there for just a few seconds, looking up at the darkened ceiling and finally said, "It just seems like so much shit is changing, Bay. I'm afraid," I whispered.

Bailey rose up on her elbow and looked at me in the now shadowed room. My eyes had adjusted to the dark, and I could make out most of her facial features now. Her eyes looked like dark liquid pools of ink in the darkness. "Everything is the same with us though, Lala! Okay? No matter what, we're always gonna be best friends! Forever, right?"

I nodded my head, hearing my curls as they rubbed on the cool, cotton pillowcase.

Bailey said, "Things change when we get older. That's all. But we are always going to be best friends do you hear me? So, no matter what else changes, that stays the same."

I looked over at her again and wondered if she could see I was crying. I nodded my head again and she bent over me and hugged me quickly before lying back on her own pillow.

"It's just been such a weird year, Bay. I don't know what's wrong with me except I'm tired and everything is so weird and different. I've just missed you so much. I guess I was a little surprised when you showed up with Donny, too." I figured I needed to at least be somewhat honest so when I did talk to her about it the next day it wouldn't seem to come out of left field for her.

"You know, I know you probably think he's a bad guy, but he's really not, Lala. He's a lot different than he was in junior high. I dunno, I just like him. He makes me feel special." She said sounding almost like she needed to convince herself more than me.

I wasn't sure what to say to that, and I didn't want to get into this conversation in the middle of the night, in the dark. I wanted to look her in the eyes when I told her how concerned I was. She deserved someone who was great. She was beautiful. She was one of the girls who had been voted as a "Beauty" which was an honor at Samson. She'd been voted as part of the Homecoming Queen's court in eighth grade. She deserved someone who would put her on a pedestal, someone who was going to go to college and who was just as handsome as she was pretty. She didn't deserve some guy who'd end up being a factory worker or a construction worker or even an oilfield hand. I wasn't sure there was much of an oilfield in Wichita Falls as there was in Corpus Christi. She deserved the Sun, the Moon and the stars.

I realized I hoped that I'd at least get a blue-collar guy because I was beginning to worry that Kevin and I weren't going to make it until after I graduated. After seeing the drastic change Bailey made with being Donny Harkness's girlfriend, it made me realize that there was a lot of changing going on up here too. I didn't think that I deserved Kevin either. He didn't think he'd be more than a factory worker, but I saw so much greatness in him and in his heart! I couldn't imagine him doing something that wasn't absolutely astounding.

I finally realized that she was waiting on me to respond, so I said quietly, "I'm sure he's fine, Bay. I'm just tired. Let's talk about everything in the morning, okay?" My best friend reached down on top of the covers and grabbed my hand in her own smooth, soft one. She squeezed it once tightly and then loosened it just enough to where we fell asleep with our hands lightly clasped together.

My last thought as I lay there listening for Bailey's even breathing to begin was that it was a freak tragedy that brought us together to become this close. I wondered what would have happened if the tornado had never happened.

I wondered if we'd still be living in the house on Belfast, with Clarice and Geoffrey terrorizing my every waking moment. I wondered if Geoffrey and Kevin would have eventually still become friends or if he would have gone on with his life, just two streets over, without ever knowing him. I didn't understand the randomness it seemed that the Universe seemed to have sometimes in my life.

I sighed deeply and closed my eyes. I wanted to fall asleep smiling, because I would surely see Kevin the next day, but instead, I felt as a tear escaped from one of my eyes and slipped down the side of my face, to find itself absorbed by the pillow I was lying on. Instead, I just wiped the wet streak and turned my head away from Bailey's, but I kept my hand clasped in hers. We were getting too old to hold hands, when we fell asleep, too many more times. I wanted to savor and remember this, because it might be the last time it ever happened. I began to be afraid that this might be my last visit to Wichita Falls in all actuality.

Again, I sighed deeply, and then I felt myself gently roll out into the dark ocean that I saw sometimes as I fell asleep. I felt as the waves carried me further from the shore of wakefulness and reality and let myself be carried into the churning waters of my dreams.

I dreamed of yellow flowers and a blonde-haired little girl with sky blue eyes and a heart shaped face. I was glad she looked a little happy this time that I saw her. I missed Donna Strong so much but didn't realize exactly how much until I dreamed about her. I walked towards her in the high grasses and yellow flowers. Just as I got up to her I looked down and held out my hand for her to take. I saw her tiny little hand slip inside of mine and I was gone from this world until the next day when the morning light shone through the floral curtains that covered Bailey's windows.

CHAPTER 51

Bailey's mom's famous chocolate waffles woke me up the next morning, as their sweet aroma filled the air. My best friend and I opened our eyes at the same time and turned our heads on the pillows to look at one another. Her beautiful blue green eyes lit up. Smiling at one another, we both hurried out of her bed, to scramble into the kitchen, and sit at the breakfast bar for the delicious waffles, while they were still hot, with melting chocolate chips, and cold whipped cream topping.

I hadn't eaten breakfast with my best friend in a year and I always enjoyed this time with her. We always laughed and teased each other and had her mom teasing us. I hadn't felt joyful at breakfast with my own parents since I was really little. The only time I ever felt this carefree was when I was at the Rains' household. Thankfully all thought of Donny Harkness never once intruded into our conversation during breakfast.

After we finished our gooey chocolate waffles and were sitting there drinking milk, Bailey got up to run to the bathroom. While she was gone Glenda Rains looked at me conspiratorially and asked, "Do you know her new boyfriend?" I nodded my head curious what her mom was about to say. She wanted to talk to me I could tell, and she'd purposely waited on Bailey to leave the room.

The next thing she said shocked me because Bailey's mom seemed to love everyone and was so sweet and soft spoken. "I can't stand him, DeLaine! He's bad news for her and not good enough for her either! Try to talk some sense into her while you are here, okay?"

I sat there looking at her mom, thunderstruck. Her mom felt the same way as me. So, I wasn't the only one who didn't think that Bailey's new boyfriend was the right one for her. I heard the bathroom door open and before my best friend walked back into the kitchen I just nodded my head and grinned back at her mom.

"So, what are you two talking about?" Bailey asked with a touch of irritation in her voice that I'd never heard before.

Glenda smiled brightly at her and replied, "Nothing really, just about how her last school year went, since she had to change schools." I looked over at Glenda and tried not to appear shocked that she actually knew that I had changed schools.

I had no clue she knew so much about my life in Corpus. I didn't know that Bailey talked to her mom about me. I looked at Bailey a little too brightly and nodded my head a touch too eagerly as well.

"I figured you were telling her how much you hate Donny," Bailey declared, grumpily, as she sat back in her chair.

Her mom looked at her stricken. I was surprised that Bailey was talking so harshly to her mom. She'd always done her fair amount of grousing about her parents, like all teenagers did, I assumed. She'd never sounded so mean to her mom before. I glanced at my best friend and noticed that she had a look across her beautiful face I'd never seen either. It was hard and angry.

Glenda Rains shook her head and began clearing our breakfast dishes to the sink. I could tell by looking at her face that she was hurt by her daughter being so sharp with her. I felt like I needed to step in and try to make things better, so I said, "No, Bay, we were talking about me changing schools again. She never even brought up Donny. That's just crazy!" I rolled my eyes and blew air out of my mouth, trying to act like Bailey was just being silly. In all honesty, I just wanted to smooth things out with her and her mom. I had such a tumultuous relationship with my own mom, I wanted to believe that my best friend's home life was much better than my own.

Bailey stood up suddenly and began stomping out of the kitchen. I glanced over to her mama. Glenda held up her hands, and I could see the unshed tears in her eyes. I wasn't sure what to do. I cocked my lip into a half frown. Glenda held her hands up in the air and then smacked them back down onto her thighs. I shrugged my shoulders bringing my own hands up in the air. I wasn't sure what to say

I stood and whispered, "I'll try to talk to her, while I'm here. I promise." Glenda Rains just nodded her head as she turned back to the sink and began washing our breakfast dishes. I walked back towards Bailey's room, curious what I was going to walk into when I got there. I'd never seen her like that, so I was truly confused.

When I pushed open the door, I was surprised to see that she was already dressed in cut off shorts and a yellow tank top. She was making the bed as I came around the door. "Bay, what the hell?" I whispered concerned.

Bailey jerked the bedspread up hard, throwing the pillows up at the top, and turned, looking at me with a look that I'd never seen before, again. It was a cross between disgust and fury. "If you want to stay in the kitchen with Glenda and talk about Donny, just go back in there!"

I jerked back surprised by the ferocity of my best friend's statements.

"What?" I responded, a little more forcefully and louder.

Bailey and I had never gotten into a real argument that I could remember. We might have gotten irritated a time or two, but we'd never actually gotten truly mad at one another.

I could feel myself warming up though, to the familiar emotion, which was anger. I'd never been angry at her before, which felt strange!

"I know she was in there telling you how much she hates Donny!" Bailey almost spat the words at me.

I walked over to my suitcase and began to grab shorts and a tank top out. Shaking my head, as I did so, I demanded, "Did you actually HEAR her say that?"

I could feel my heart begin to flutter because I was afraid that she would admit she'd been listening to us. I had out and out lied to her when I said that I'd been talking to her mom about my changing schools.

Turning around to face Bailey, whose lovely eyes were literally sparking with fury, I grabbed my clothes up and repeated my question. After a brief beat Bailey shook her head.

"Before you go flyin' off the damned handle why don't you come in and ask nicely. What the hell is wrong with you, Bay? Jesus!" I began walking towards the door to go to the bathroom.

"I'm sorry, Lala, it's just she always bitches about Donny. She hates him, so of course Rob hates him too! Do you know what it's like to have your parents hate your boyfriend?" Bailey asked, heatedly.

I looked at her coldly and said with just a trace of sarcasm, "No, Bailey, neither one of my parents are invested in my life enough to give a shit about any boyfriends I might have. My daddy hates every single boy I might like, and my mom's too fucking drunk to care! So, no, I'm sorry if I don't get why you are upset if your parents give a shit about who you date!"

I brushed past her and stormed into the bathroom. I closed the door just in time for the tears to come streaking from my face. I stood with my back leaned against the bathroom door. I didn't want her to see me cry.

She had no clue how much better her life was than mine. What I wouldn't have given to have my mom and dad even wonder if I had an actual boyfriend!

Mama only knew that there was some sort of relationship with Kevin, but she never really questioned me a lot about it. She knew a little bit about Chance Cahill, but nothing important. She knew that I liked him, but she had no clue that I messed around with him regularly.

Since my experience in the dating department was limited, both of my parents were pretty much clueless as far as what happened with me and boys, most of the time.

They both knew about Jax and Mama knew I sometimes saw him when I was up here, but I think because of her confusion about Kevin, she never bothered to question me about what I was doing bouncing between Jax and Kevin.

I wiped my face roughly, angry at myself for getting mad at Bailey. It was so silly. So, her parents didn't like Donny! It wasn't like she was planning on marrying him. We were only 16 after all. I hurriedly did my business in the bathroom, and finally came back into Bailey's room.

My best friend was sitting on the bright lime green carpet, in her room. She had her knees drawn up and her head was resting on them quietly. I walked over to my suitcase and put my night clothes back inside it. Quietly Bailey apologized, "I'm sorry Lala. She's always bitching about him and how he's a bad influence. She thinks he isn't good enough for me," Bailey explained, with a small sneer crossing her beautiful face.

I stood up from my suitcase and stated, quietly, "She's right, you know?"

Bailey looked at me surprised, "What? What are you talking about, DeLaine?"

"I'm talking about how shocked I was that you were dating him. Why didn't you tell me in any letters? Don't tell me that it is something new. Did you think that I'd be pissed off? Is that why you never said anything in your last couple of letters?" I asked her sharply, as I looked directly into her angry gaze.

"Great, now she's even got you thinking he's a loser!" Bailey griped, rolling her eyes.

"I'm not on anybody's side, you dumbass!" I replied, angrily. "But if I was, I'm on YOUR SIDE!" I declared, a little more forcefully than I meant to.

Bailey gazed at me with the new look that I wasn't used to in the tide pools of her eyes. She suddenly stood up and stormed out of the room. I heard as the front door opened and slammed shut. I stood there completely dumbstruck by my friend's behavior. I didn't understand it. Bailey was always happy and in control. She seemed like she was coming apart at the seams. I hadn't noticed anything different by her letters. I'd noticed that we weren't writing quite as frequently, but I figured it was because we both had more stuff going on with school.

I was at a complete loss as to what to do. I came walking out of her room slowly and when I got to the entrance of the front living room, I glanced towards the kitchen to see if I saw Glenda Rains still in there. She was, and she came walking slowly into the entrance from the kitchen and looked at me questioningly.

I shook my head and stated, "I don't know what's going on with her."

Bailey's mom looked at me as the unshed tears continued to shine in her eyes. She nodded her head. I think she was afraid if she talked she would cry.

I felt uncomfortable. I didn't know what I was in the middle of, but it was something different than I'd ever seen before at Bailey's home.

I looked at the floor after a beat and tried to figure out what I should do. I wasn't sure if I should chase after Bailey or not. I was actually mad at her for acting so stupid.

Finally, after a few minutes of us both staring at the front door Bailey had slammed, I asked, quietly, "Do you mind if I go down to the Strong's?"

Glenda smiled at me and nodded her head. "I don't know how long she's going to be gone. She storms out a lot lately. Sometimes she stays gone for a while." I nodded my head sadly.

I had begun learning that I couldn't be held hostage by someone else's temper tantrums. My mama threw many drunken tantrums, and as long as we weren't actively arguing, I tried to leave during them so she had time to calm down and cool off. Bailey wasn't drunk, but I thought that she needed some time to cool off, no matter how long she stayed gone.

Glenda Rains tried to keep her smile on her face that she'd had during breakfast and that I could go to the Strong's home. When Bailey got back, she'd tell her where I was. I smiled at her and went to Bailey's room and grabbed my sandals. I decided that I wasn't going to worry with makeup. I had a decent tan started by all my time at Kelly and Robin's pool, and laying out in our backyard with my mom. I came out and waved at Glenda as I walked through the front room to the door.

Walking in the 100+ degree heat down the sidewalk that I had walked more times than I could remember, I thought about how much was changing everywhere. I was struck by the changes in Bailey the hardest though. She'd always been the one thing that I could count on. She was my life raft in a world filled with rough seas. She'd been the one person in the world, besides Kevin, who had showed me that I was worth something since 7th grade.

I still felt that I wasn't worth a lot, but when I came to Wichita Falls, I felt much more confident. In Corpus Christi my confidence was all an act. I acted tough and mean because I didn't want others to know the true me. If they did they'd all know what a phony, faker I was. People would know that I was really a big ball of fear and sadness.

Then they'd all laugh at me and I'd be viewed as one of those pathetic girls who no one wanted to hang out with, unless they had something the others could use me for.

When I came around the house on the corner of Portland Street, I saw the familiar, rust colored trim on the Strong's home. I felt myself glance at the window that a little girl named Donna used to gaze out of for years, at the world that she would leave too soon.

I felt a knot forming in my throat at the thought of Donna. It seemed as if her passing had changed so much in all of us. I rubbed the corner of my eye with my index finger to clear the moisture that had inadvertently come into it, at the thought of the little girl. I couldn't wait to see Kevin as well as looking forward to the safe and warm hug his mom would give me as soon as she opened the door!

I pushed the doorbell and listened to the chime through the door. I didn't know if Kevin knew I was coming or not. I saw movement through the small square in the center of the door and when I was met with Kevin instead of his mom I was a little surprised.

Kevin's face slowly began to go into his sunshine and rainbows smile which had gotten to me since I was 12 years old. I felt as my own face broke into a large grin too. He quickly pushed open the glass storm door and stepped out onto the porch. I was a little confused when he didn't just open the door wider to have me walk in. Kevin walked up to me and wrapped his strong arms around me in a huge bear hug. I wrapped my arms around his now familiar form and held him tight trying to feel every available inch of him!

Pulling away from me, Kevin looked down at me and said, "Lainey!"

Grinning at him, I replied, "Didn't you know I was coming in this week?"

Kevin smiled ruefully and shook his head and admitted, "I dunno. Man, it's been a little crazy this summer. I've been working as a shop hand, at a garage. I'm only off today because the boss's dad passed away and he closed the gas station."

"I'm sorry to hear that," I whispered, quietly, but I couldn't make the stupid grin leave my face. "I'm awfully glad you were home, though," I finished.

"Me too!" Kevin said with a laugh, as we stood on his covered porch that kept the smooth cement cool.

I looked at him and realized he was acting a little strange. "So, you gonna let me in?"

Kevin looked at me uneasily and explained, "Uh, I've got some company right now. Let me get rid of them and I'll come to Bay's and hang out with you."

Looking at him oddly, I nodded my head, not quite understanding why he wouldn't let me come in if he was just hanging out with some of his buddies. Slowly realization hit me. I realized he had a girl in there. I felt as if someone literally stabbed me in my heart. Finally, I said, "Oh, um, okay. That's cool!"

Kevin gave me the smile that could make me feel like a silly, junior high girl all over again. Unfortunately, it wasn't having the normal effect it usually had on me. I felt horribly awkward with Kevin. We'd never been in this situation since he broke up with his psycho girlfriend, Lori.

Finally, I nodded my head again, and stepped off the cool cement of the front porch. "Yeah, sure, I'm uh, gonna just go back to Bay's, I guess." I tried hard to smile at him without seeming pathetic and heartbroken. After all, I messed around when I was in Corpus, and he was here. I guess I'd never really understood the ramifications of us leading separate lives, with me in Corpus, and him in Wichita.

Smiling weakly at him, I stated quickly, "Okay, well, I'll be at Bay's! See you whenever you can."

Kevin's smile began to fade as he sensed that I was feeling a wave of despair. "Lainey, I'll be down there in a little while, I promise. I'm sorry! If I'd known you were going to be in town this wouldn't have happened."

I nodded my head, assuring him, "Really, Kev, I understand, it's cool! I'll see you later!" I turned and began to walk towards Fairfax Blvd. to cross over to Granville Avenue, to Bailey's house. I wanted to run away, and bawl like a baby, but I knew that Kevin was watching me. I decided to walk normally and wait until I was out of his sight before I let the tears flow. As I walked, I could feel his blue eyes following me.

Once I knew I was out of sight though, I didn't cry. I had had tears in my eyes as I crossed Fairfax, but by the time I was going up Granville, I realized that Kevin was doing nothing that I hadn't known he'd do.

I knew he'd see others just like I did, when I was in Corpus. He'd never said anything about any of them. He got it out of me that I'd been seeing someone, but I didn't ever ask him about any girls he might see when I was away.

I thought of Chance Cahill. Suddenly, I realized that it wasn't any different than if Kevin came to Corpus, and I was out riding around with Chance, and didn't know he was coming into town.

I took a few deep breaths, as I walked determinedly up Granville, as it began to slope upward. My heart felt heavy, even if I understood what was going on. I'd had to be hidden for a long time with Kevin, in the early days of our relationship. I felt like I was being hidden again. The rational brain in my head understood what was happening, but the emotional side of my brain was hurting after my strange morning with Bailey, then the odd reunion with Kevin.

So far, my trip 'home' wasn't shaping up to be too great.

After seeing both Jax and Kevin for a while, I couldn't believe that I still felt like Kevin had to be a monk for me.

The way he talked to me and made me feel when we were together, I just felt like he would wait on me forever. The rational brain was rattling again as I got in sight of Bailey's front yard. It was telling me that I was being irrational. It also told me that I deserved the pain I felt, after the way I had bounced between Jax and Kevin and never being honest with Kevin about it. I also had sex with Chance Cahill and hadn't told Kevin.

Why did I think he owed me to stay faithful? I shook my head as I continued up the sidewalk. I never deserved someone like Kevin in the first place. Why I thought that I could make something this strange work was beyond me. Everybody changed all the time. How could I expect my best friend to remain the same sunny relief she'd always been? How could I possibly expect Kevin to wait around on me, too? I wasn't waiting on him for anything. I also didn't deserve to have a person like Bailey to want to continue being friends with someone who wasn't even worthy of her friendship in the first place.

When my foot hit the lush carpet grass in Bailey's front yard, I walked towards the steps to make my way into the house. I didn't know if Bailey was back or not.

I sighed and just as I got to the cement walkway to the steps I was snapped out of my reverie when I heard, "Lala?!" whispered softly.

I jerked my head up and saw Bailey's red rimmed eyes and immediately felt the overwhelming urge to hug her and protect her from any bad feelings.

I'd only ever known Bailey to be happy, centered and the coolest girl I'd ever known. I was unsure what to say, but I stopped just short of the shade from her front porch and looked my best friend straight in the eyes.

"Hey," I whispered back.

"I'm really sorry," Bailey murmured, with a little hitch in her voice.

"It's cool," I replied, quietly. It really wasn't cool with me. I didn't understand the change in Bailey's personality, and it was confusing to me.

Bailey looked at me intently trying to read my face. Finally, she stated, "So my mom said you were at Kevin's. Why are you back already?"

I couldn't believe she could cut straight to the heart of my pain immediately. Here I was trying to understand both Bailey's meltdown this morning and had added my conflicting emotions about knowing that Kevin had a girl in his house. I wasn't sure what to feel or say. I felt tears right at the corners of my eyes and my throat felt like it was completely closed off by the knot I felt in the very center of it. I didn't want to cry though. I didn't DESERVE to cry over Kevin. Finally, I shrugged my shoulder when I felt the knot begin to loosen in my throat. When I knew I could speak without bursting into tears, I muttered, "He had company. He said he'd come by later."

"Company?" Bailey asked me, curiously.

I nodded my head, knowing that she wasn't understanding what kind of company, just as I hadn't in the beginning. I didn't want to say he had a girl there. I was afraid if I did then I truly would cry. Bailey continued to look at me curiously. I realized she wasn't getting what kind of company he had, so I barked, gruffly, "He had a girl there, okay?"

My best friend looked at me sadly. She knew that it was hard on me and she knew that I was a ball of conflicting emotions. I shrugged my shoulder up again and then skirted around Bailey to go up the cement steps. As I stepped on the first one, Bailey grabbed my hand. "You okay, Lala?"

I cleared my throat unconsciously. I turned to look at her and admitted, "No, not really. My best friend threw a temper tantrum first thing this morning, and I go to Kevin's, and he's got a fucking girl there. I'm not okay, Bay! I'm confused and upset. I just don't know what to think about any of this. I'm wondering if I should just pack my suitcase back up and go home now."

"Lala! I'm so sorry! Don't leave! I don't know why I've been blowing up like that lately! I'm sorry I did that and I'm so, so sorry that Kevin wasn't expecting you."

I looked at Bailey's tear-filled eyes and didn't really understand who this girl was that was my best friend. I loved her more than I'd ever loved any friend in my life. She was my greatest cheerleader and held me up through my incredibly, insane life so far. Now she was just as unsure as all the other teenage girls I knew.

She'd always been so poised and in control of herself and now she stood before me looking conflicted and unsure about everything. I was realizing that I couldn't rely on someone else to be the positive feelings in my life. I had to start working on it by myself. Bailey wasn't always going to be there. I thought that it was because of her that I was always able to be a little positive, because her letters were always filled with praise and goodness. I came to her in order to get a booster shot of her positivity and hopefully make it through the next school year.

I realized that Bailey was beginning to have issues, even though she still had her cool demeanor, for the most part.

She was becoming real though, which I never quite let her be, in my mind. She was always so much more in my mind.

Bailey Rains was the epitome of a cool chick to me. All the girls wanted to *be* her, and all the boys wanted to date her.

For me, though, she was an angel in disguise. She'd literally found me as a sad, little, drowned kitten and transformed me into a regal and strong feline, one that could rival any jungle cat.

"I'm not gonna leave, Bay," I sighed, sadly, after a few seconds.

I couldn't believe that I'd never really thought about Bailey as a real human before. I'd always thought that she was too cool to ever have any problems.

I always thought that she was so together, and she already had everything figured out, as far as boys and relationships. She seemed to have everything I didn't. I thought that if she had so much, she was ahead of me in knowing how to deal with real life.

Sadly, I realized that what I thought of as Bailey's perfect life wasn't as perfect as I thought. She had her own issues, even if they weren't exactly like mine.

Bailey looked up at me, from the steps on her porch and smiled timidly at me. I realized that Bailey was afraid that I would truly leave her.

For the first time ever, Bailey seemed to be the one who needed ME, and it was a shock and surprise. I felt I'd been the one who always needed her to help prop me up. I had nothing to give her, except my loyalty.

For the first time, I was seeing that maybe, just maybe, there was actually a part of me I was already giving to her and didn't know. Finally, she nodded her head slowly, and let go of my hand, so I could continue up the stairs.

When we got to the storm door, I turned to her and stated, "Bailey, you need to apologize to your mama!"

Just as she was about to protest, I held my palm up and said quietly, "I mean it Bay! She didn't deserve you talking to her that way this morning. You have so much, and you don't realize it. You have a mom who cares about you and your life. Try harder with her. I know you don't understand her. Just try. She's your mom!" I finished softly, looking down.

"I will Lala! I promise!" Bailey replied, quietly. I nodded my head and opened the front door. I walked into her air-conditioned house and breathed a huge sigh of relief as I saw that her mom wasn't still sitting in the kitchen, drying tears from the corners of her eyes.

Bailey eventually apologized to her mom. Then later, that evening, Kevin came over. I was surprised he'd even bothered, since he had said he'd be right over and that had been before lunch. Bailey and I had discussed him having a girl there. It didn't take the sting out of it any more, though. I just expected Kevin to always be there for me, just as I'd always expected Bailey to always be cool, and put together, forever.

That's the way my relationships with them had always been. Now that we were getting older, I was becoming more aware about emotions I wasn't really sure I understood.

Since we'd already had dinner, I went for a walk with Kevin when he came by. He acted almost shy around Bailey, which kinda surprised me. He held the storm door open for me as we walked outside into the hot evening.

The sun was already behind the houses on Granville, which meant we still had a good half hour of true sunlight, before it became twilight. We started walking up Granville, which was a different route than we normally went. Usually, we would walk back down, towards his house, and the small side street that went to the elementary school playground. This time, we walked towards Samson High School, where I had first met Kevin when I was in 7th grade, after the tornado.

I smiled at the memories of our first encounters, as we walked silently up the sidewalk. I was watching the cement under my feet as I had many mornings, and afternoons, walking home from Samson, when we lived on Belfast. That seemed like several lifetimes ago to me when I thought about those days. I realized that those were those sweet days that I was supposed to be having right now.

I was supposed to be falling in love for the first time and making memories like the ones I had about Kevin, right now. I was supposed to be making those memories in Corpus Christi. I couldn't let go of Wichita Falls enough to do it.

I had memories of Chance Cahill, but I realized they weren't the bittersweet or tender ones I had about Kevin. Some were nice memories, but nothing could compare to the memories I had of Kevin. Even my memories of Jax were good. I had loved two boys by the time I was 14, and I had never loved anyone else since then.

I realized I was 16 and was making no memories for myself in high school, except the countless times I hung out at the Gameroom, getting drunk and stoned. What kind of memories were those, I wondered?

"You're thinking awfully hard," Kevin's whisper intruded into my thoughts. "You're really much prettier with a smile instead of a frown on your face, Lainey."

I looked over at Kevin after shaking my head. I realized he was right, I did have a frown on my face. I shook my head again slightly, as if to shake the frown away. Then, I looked up into those beautiful, summer sky eyes that I loved to get lost in. As soon as I looked deeply into them, I found myself tearing up. I was mortified that instead of the smile I was prepared to go for, I immediately began to cry. I covered my face with my hands and stuck both of my index fingers into the corner of my eyes as if that would staunch the flow of tears that had appeared from nowhere.

"Lainey, are you okay?" Kevin asked me anxiously, as he stopped and leaned down to gently pull my hands away from my face.

The next thing I did surprised me just as much as the tears had. I began to laugh. Now the tears flowing from my eyes were tears because I was laughing so hard.

Kevin looked at me oddly and asked me if I was messing with him. I let him continue to hold my hands until I got control of myself.

Finally, even though my mouth felt thick from all the tears, I finally managed to suck as much of the tear and snot combination as I could, back into my nose, and took one of my hands out of Kevin's and used the hem of my shirt to wipe my face. There was no being a lady about it, since I'd basically had a good snot slinging cry, along with a complete and total laugh attack.

"I'm sorry," I said, once I had wiped up the mess that my face had become so quickly.

"S'ok, Lainey, I'm just worried about you," Kevin admitted, shrugging his shoulder up, but never taking the faded, denim blue eyes off of my face.

I took a deep breath and looked levelly at Kevin, nodding my head. "Really, Kev, I am okay now. I'm sorry. I just had some weird attack I guess!" I chuckled, with a slight smirk threatening on my face to begin the cascade of giggles again. I breathed in deeply again to try to gain control.

"What was that all about?" Kevin asked, as he let go of my hand.

I shook my hand, "I've just been doing a ton of thinking today. Actually, for a while now, and I dunno, today a lot of stuff just became clearer to me about shit. I dunno." I finished lamely, shrugging my shoulders.

Kevin looked down at me, seriously. I hated when he gave me the serious look. Finally, he stated, "Look, I know it was a little weird with having Jackie there, when you came over, but I woulda told her to not call or come over for a while if I'd known that you were coming home."

"Kevin, it really wasn't about that," I began, then I stopped short. "Look, okay, it was about that a little, but honestly, so much less than you think, I promise! There's just a ton of shit going on in my life, lately. School, changes I'm making in my own life and just a bunch of crap that's been running through my head. I've just been a stupid, little girl about a lot of stuff, Kevin. I guess today some things became clearer to me, that's all."

Kevin turned and began walking again, until we got to the parking lot of Samson high school. We walked in silence until we got to the track.

The bleachers were empty, and the late evening sun glinted off the metal, blindingly. I was surprised at how much sun was still out once we were on top of the hill, out from the front of the houses on Granville Street. I looked out across the wide expanse of grassy field that ran between Samson, and the elementary school behind Bailey's house.

The sun's rays literally lit everything in a beautiful, gold color. It was the epitome of a summer evening to me, the colors, the smell of fresh cut grass, the heat, all the way down to the sweat that was trickling down my neck, to my spine, between my shoulder blades. The way everything looked was how I felt about Kevin.

He was the summer to me. It wasn't just the color of his eyes that made me think that either. He was the sun that I had revolved around for so long. His large personality, and the way he completely lit up within himself, as well as the way I lit up, when he was close by. His physical appearance always reminded me of summer too. His blonde hair and blue eyes spoke of sunny beaches and blue skies, forever. There wasn't anything about Kevin that I didn't love.

We walked over to the bleachers and climbed up to the second set of risers and sat down. The metal was warm on my thighs. Kevin, as usual, had on jeans. I almost began my crazy chuckle again, as I thought about how I had just made an analogy, in my head, about him being like summer, yet, he never wore summer clothes. I kept my laugh in and instead felt a silly grin come over my face as we climbed the risers. Once we were sitting down, I noticed Kevin looking out over the vast, green field that separated the two schools, and the playground.

"So, you've been a silly, little girl, huh?" Kevin said more as a statement than a true question.

I looked down and felt the warm sun as it glinted through the sides of my eyes. "Kevin, I've held on to Wichita Falls for so long. I thought I was giving myself a chance to have a life in Corpus, but really, all I've been doing is biding my time, until I can come back here, after I graduate. In reality, I don't know how I'll come back home, even though I want to. Unless I get a scholarship, at Midwestern, for college, I'm going to have a hard time ever getting back this way for good. I've been living half in Wichita Falls and half in Corpus Christi," I finished, quietly.

After several beats, Kevin finally turned his head and looked at me deeply. He looked at my eyes intently, "I know that, Lainey. I'm never moving to Corpus. I've kept hoping that maybe your dad would move back, and you'd come back and live with him. I know that isn't going to happen, but I like to hope for it, sometimes."

I looked at him surprised, that he really thought that much about me, at all. I knew that was silly. I knew he cared about me. I knew that in his own way he loved me, too. I knew he'd probably never tell me again. I also knew that with Donna dying, he was terrified of really staying attached to me, for fear that I would be gone from him too.

I knew that he kept me at arms-length, emotionally, because he was afraid constantly something could happen to me. After the car wreck and hearing the unadulterated fear in his voice when he finally got to talk to me, I realized it even more. Part of me thought that he probably did know that I was coming this week.

Finally, I spoke quietly, "I'm not going to give up on ever coming back. Wichita is my home. It's where I belong, but I'm trying to hold onto something, while I'm trying to figure out how to start something else. I'm not getting anything done in either place."

I sighed, deeply. "Kevin, I still love you. That's not ever going to change. I still want to see you while I'm here. But, when I go back this year, I've got to invest myself more into my life there. I'm at a new school, and I'm not really partying as much."

"What does that mean?" Kevin asked me, with an edge to his voice.

Looking down at my feet on the metal rung of the bleachers I finally looked back up admitting, "Kevin, I've been partying a lot. Like I mean, a WHOLE LOT, since I moved to Corpus." I felt the hot flush as it crept up my face and burned.

"Like how much?" Kevin asked quietly.

"A LOT!" I declared, a little louder than I meant to.

"Don't yell at me, DeLaine! I was just asking!" Kevin snapped, darkly.

I heaved a huge sigh, "I'm sorry, Kev, I wasn't trying to be a bitch. I've been partying a lot. I've been doing some really, stupid shit. I mean, I told you about a little of it before, but I didn't tell you that I'm usually drunk or stoned or both, every single weekend. I have to do it to deal with the nightmare of everything my life has become!" I was trying to convince myself, as much as Kevin, that there was a legitimate reason for my partying like a maniac. "I even smoke regularly, now." I murmured, softly.

Kevin's head twisted quickly, and he looked at me angrily, "I thought you said you just did that sometimes!"

"Well, you know, I didn't want you to be mad. I've tried to quit, and I can't Kevin. It keeps me sane and from wanting to kill my mom some days!"

"Dammit, DeLaine! QUIT SMOKING!!!!" Kevin roared at me. I was shocked he yelled so loudly, and that his face became so red.

Feeling the hackles on the back of my neck begin to rise, I looked at him furiously, "Kevin, you can't tell me to do a damned thing!"

Kevin settled back, and let out a sigh, as he put both elbows on the seat behind him. Looking down at his stomach, he finally nodded his head, "Yeah, you're right, Lainey. I can't. I never have been able to. I want to. I want to save you, and protect you, all the time. The only other person I ever wanted to do that with was Donna, but I can't protect you or save you, not even from yourself." He looked back up at me and smirked. What he said next shocked me. "I started smoking last year sometimes too."

"WHAT?" I roared, loudly.

Kevin grinned and nodded his head. "Yeah, I know, but I don't do it all the time, like it sounds like you're doing." He tried to defend himself.

I smiled at him slowly and shook my head, "Doesn't matter! You can't bitch at me for something if you do it too!"

Looking up as he leaned back he stated, "Your eyes look almost deep green with the sun hitting them like that."

I blinked a couple of times and asked, "What?"

"Your eyes, they look like Christmas green. It's not like regular green eyes, it's just a weird color, but it's really pretty. They usually only look that way when you cry, but the sun hitting them the way it is makes them glow green." Kevin mused, as he looked deeply into my eyes.

I grinned at him and shook my head. "You aren't getting out of this conversation like that, Mr. Strong!"

Kevin smiled his sunshine and rainbows smile finally, just as the last of the fiery, orange sun slipped down into the horizon.

"I wasn't trying to Ms. Reynolds. Just telling you a fact about your eyes, that's all." He grinned and pulled his right arm off of the bleacher he was leaning on. He extended it until his right hand was cupping my cheek and neck. I leaned into his hand, knowing that these moments were almost done. I wanted to cry. I wanted time to stop. I wanted to stay with Kevin, like this, for the rest of eternity. I knew that it wouldn't happen. I didn't want tears to ruin one of the beautiful moments, of my memories of Kevin, so I fought through the tears, even though I felt my eyes water just a bit.

Gently, I felt the pull of his hand as he steered me to meet his waiting kiss. I silently slid my own palm up to match on his face and felt the blonde stubble scratch my palm. It was even more than the last time I'd felt his whiskers. We sat in the bleachers, just kissing until the sky wasn't even purple any longer, but a deep, dark, black velvet with diamonds winking in it. When Kevin helped me off of the bleachers, the security lights were lit with June bugs and moths frantically flying around it. I could still smell the scent of cut grass. We walked quietly, hand in hand back, down Granville Street to Bailey's house. I knew it was probably about 9 o'clock.

Before we got all the way to her house, I wound my arm inside his and leaned my head on the outside of his shoulder, as we walked. I felt the soft feel of his t-shirt, under my cheek, and could smell the clean smell that was him. It was the smell I associated with him and had never smelled on anyone else in my entire lifetime. I wondered how many more times I would smell it. I felt him lean over and kiss me, on top of my curls. I smiled as I turned my forehead more into his arm. I didn't want to let him go. I knew I would eventually and when we got to the porch, I finally broke contact with him.

"Lainey, I want to see you a little bit while you're here, but I'm working too, so I'll have to call you and we figure out some way to spend some time together, okay?" Kevin whispered, sweetly. He acted like we were going to continue the charade that we did every time I was in town. I smiled up at him and decided that I wasn't ready to quit just yet either.

Nodding my head, I affirmed, "Okay, just call me tomorrow, I guess."

"I think I can manage that," then Kevin surprised me, by grabbing me hard, and kissing me so passionately, that when he pulled away, my eyes were still closed and I was trying to catch my breath. "Goodnight, Lainey!"

'Night," I murmured, as I walked up the cement steps. I turned before I opened the door, and smiled at him.

How I loved this boy. I didn't think there would ever be anyone else in the world that I could possibly love more, in my entire lifetime. My heart was forever in this beautiful boy's hands.

***

Bailey and I went swimming the first couple of days of my time with her. It was nice, and she didn't have any more melt downs. I saw Levi while we were at the pool, the first day. I was glad to see he and Bailey were friendly with one another, even though I could tell that there was a lot of hurt between them. I saw how Levi looked at her, and my heart ached for him. Bailey basically tried to appear aloof when he came over, and sat with us, on our beach towels, when we got out of the pool.

As usual, I had a lot of people come over and visit with me. I noticed that there weren't as many of the cheerleaders that we'd hung out with come over to see us. I could see that a lot of them weren't even at the pool. There were a couple of them who didn't walk over to the towels but said hello to me when I was in the pool or went to the concession stand for a coke. I thought it was a little odd, but I figured everybody was just growing up.

The second day we went to the pool, I asked Bailey if Donny would come to the pool with us some day too. She shook her head. "Why not?" I asked curious.

"Well, he's got a job first off, and secondly he doesn't ever go. You know he's kinda skinny and pale and he is a kicker. How many times have you seen Jax out there?"

"Jax works every year, for his uncle. That's why he's never out there, but he's always really tan," I countered.

"True," Bailey replied, thoughtfully. Finally, she shrugged, "I dunno. I just know he never goes to the pool." I nodded and grabbed my towel as we headed out the door.

"So, where does Donny work?" I asked, casually. I guessed I needed to try to get to know Bailey's new boyfriend somewhat better, even though I really didn't want to.

"At a gas station over on Keller," Bailey stated, distractedly.

"That's funny, Kevin told me he's working at a station this summer, as a shop hand," I said, with a laugh.

Bailey looked at me curiously, "Um, yeah, Lala, they work together."

I stopped in my tracks and gripped the hump in the Dr. Scholl's slide on sandals I loved, with my toes. I turned my head slowly and looked at Bailey's golden, tanned face. "You mean that you knew the whole time they worked together?"

Bailey nodded her head, looking at me strangely.

"Why didn't you tell me that when I went to Kevin's and found that Jackie girl there? Why didn't you even tell me about that girl in the first place?" I asked, beginning to feel a little agitated.

Bailey looked at her pretty, pink, painted toenails and mumbled, "I figured he'd tell her to get lost since you were coming to town. He never asked me, but I told Donny to tell him. I didn't want you to feel hurt, Lala. Honest! I just thought she'd be gone by the time you went over there. That morning everything got so screwed up. I kinda thought I'd have time to tell you that they worked together. Then, well, I guess I just forgot."

I glared at my best friend. I felt somehow betrayed that she'd kept all that information from me. Not only did her boyfriend work with Kevin, she'd told that boyfriend to tell Kevin about my visit. Add insult to injury, I find out that she also knew about the mysterious Jackie girl!

"You just forgot, huh?" I quipped quietly, but with a tinge of sarcasm dripping from the last word.

Bailey nodded her head and I gripped my sandals tightly with my toes again, as I began to walk up the sidewalk to the pool. "Hope there isn't any other unpleasant surprises for me to find out about, while I'm here," I muttered, but knew it was loud enough for Bailey to hear.

She stood there for a few minutes as I walked ahead of her. Finally, she began to hurry to catch up with me. I could tell by the look on her face that she felt bad for not telling me anything.

When we got inside, I just dropped all my stuff on the ground next to where Bailey was setting up our towels and suntan oil. I went to the pool that had the deep end and just stepped off the side of it and let my body go straight down like a bullet.

I just wanted to be somewhere that I couldn't hear, see or feel anything, except the cool water that touched every inch of me. I felt so confused.

If Kevin worked with Donny, then why hadn't he told him I was going to be there, like Bailey told him to do? If Donny DID tell Kevin, then why did he have that Jackie chick over, the day after I got in, knowing that I always came to his house the following day of getting into town? I couldn't understand any of it.

I still hadn't gone back to Kevin's yet, to say hi to his mom, so I wasn't sure if she even knew I was in town.

I finally kicked off the gritty bottom of the pool, and gulped huge amounts of air into my lungs, when I broke the surface. Levi came swimming up to me. I could tell he was grinning broadly, even without my glasses on.

"Hey, Lala! Whatcha doin' down there so long?" Levi asked me, in the easy way that we had from being so close, for so many years.

I smiled at Levi. "Just trying to clear my head, I guess," I admitted, quietly, as I wiped the chlorinated water out of my eyes.

"Did it clear out, and everything float away in the water, or you still got a couple of brain cells left?" Levi asked me, giggling.

I smiled at him, "No, unfortunately, it's all in there still, it's just soggy now! Which I think makes it a little worse! Life just sucks sometimes, Levi! I just don't get people. It seems the older I get, the more confusing they get. It used to be so much easier to understand stuff."

"I agree with that, for sure," Levi replied, then laughed his goofy, big laugh! He swam over to me, where I was holding on to the side of the cement wall. He put his own large hand on the cement beside mine and cajoled me, "Hang in there, Lala! Everybody's changing. We're all growing up, and it isn't easy." I smiled at him. Levi was smarter than a lot of people gave him credit for, me included!

I didn't talk a lot to Bailey, while we were at the pool. I wasn't really sure what to say to her. I just felt like there was a lot of stuff going on that nobody was telling me. I intended to get to the bottom of it.

While we were walking home, a few hours later, I asked Bailey quietly if she knew whether Donny had actually told Kevin about me coming in. She nodded her head and told me that Kevin had said for me to come by, when I could.

I kept walking with my head hung low. I looked at her and asked, "Why would he have that chick come over, the day after I was coming in, then? It doesn't make sense." I shook my head and continued walking back, stoically.

Bailey didn't answer. I don't think she knew what to say. I think she was just worried about pissing me off even more. It felt so strange to be around Bailey and feel so confused about my feelings towards her.

I sighed deeply, just as we got to her house. She looked at me quizzically, with her beautiful, oceanic blue eyes. "Are we okay, Lala?" Bailey finally asked me, softly.

I looked over at her slowly. This was my best friend. This was the girl who had literally saved my life, in more ways than one, when I was just 13 years old. She knew each and every one of my secrets. She knew all of my insecurities. She knew me better than any other individual on the planet, even Kevin.

I loved her so much, and yet I was so angry at her, at the moment. I didn't understand how to deal with my anger and my love. I didn't know that it was okay to be angry at someone you loved, without it damaging the relationship.

The times I'd felt angry at others, it had altered my relationship with them, in some way or other. I had felt such burning anger at Clarice and Geoffrey. They had been my tormenters for so many years. When they weren't my tormenters, I found that my anger burned brightly at my mom. I felt differently about my mom now, I realized, than I had when I first moved to Corpus. I still loved her, but I was always mad at her too. When I thought about that, I realized that my relationship with my own mother was confusing. It was as confusing as the feelings I had at that moment with my best friend.

Finally, after what felt like a really long time, but was only a few seconds, I looked deeply into Bailey's eyes, and nodded my head. I knew that just like my mom, I still loved Bailey.

I also knew that our friendship was beginning to change and it scared me. Sighing again, I admitted, "Bailey, I love you. I always have, since you became my best friend. I most likely always will, unless you try to go out with Kevin, or somethin'." I joked the last part, with a grin.

Bailey's face fell when I said that though. I felt my stomach drop. I couldn't believe that my very, best friend, in the entire world, had gone after the boy I loved, more than anything. I began to feel my stomach knot up, because I wasn't sure I could forgive her for that.

"You…um, you haven't gone out with Kev, have you, Bay?" I asked her, as my mouth immediately began to feel as if I had sand in it. I felt my throat begin to feel as if someone had sandblasted it.

My best friend looked at me and shook her head. I saw her eyes begin to fill with tears.

Softly, she began to talk. It was so soft that I was having a hard time hearing her. Finally, I told her I couldn't hear her, and she stopped talking. She gazed down at her pink toenails and stated, a little louder, "I didn't go out with Kevin. It doesn't have to do with Kevin. I dated Jax for about a week, last year, though."

I felt my heart drop into the pit of my stomach. It was a really strange feeling, almost like I was on an elevator, but I was standing on the hot sidewalk, with the sun beating down on my exposed skin. I couldn't believe that my best friend was telling me that she'd kept something as important as this.

I had loved Jax also, at one time, and she knew that. Finally, I asked, "You guys were dating, or you just went out as friends?"

Bailey would not raise her face to mine. I repeated it louder, and when I did, Bailey flinched visibly. Finally, she looked up and admitted, "I went to a rodeo last year. It was after Levi and I had broken up. Levi was already seeing some other girl. Jax could see that I was upset, at the dance, after the rodeo. I got really drunk and well I started dancing with Jax. Later we went to his truck because he was going to take me home. We were sitting out there drinking beer, and talking, and I dunno, somehow we started kissing."

"Okay," I growled, tersely, wanting her to continue because she'd gotten quiet after admitting that she and Jax had made out. I felt my heart hammering in my chest. I think it had begun to hammer because it had to get ready to shatter. It had cracks throughout it, as I listened to Bailey. I knew by the time she told me everything, my heart would be in pieces, because the cracks were deep and they hurt terribly.

"Lala, I felt so bad the next day. Jax came over and we talked about it. He told me he really liked me. I told him I felt bad because I didn't want to hurt you. He told me that we should just see what happened, and if we thought it was going to go somewhere, then we'd both tell you, but if it didn't, then you never had to know. He didn't want to hurt you either, it's just something that happened. You were already completely over Jax, and with Kevin. I knew you didn't want Jax anymore, so I tried to tell myself that it was okay. That you might be upset, but since you were done with Jax, maybe if it worked out, then it would be okay, because y'all are still friends." Bailey explained.

I looked at her with my eyes flat. I couldn't believe that my best friend had done this. I couldn't believe she was standing there, trying to justify to me why they did it.

"So, what happened? Obviously it didn't work," I uttered each word, dripping with venom and sarcasm.

"Um, well, we talked to each other on the phone a lot that week and we held hands at school. He took me out the next weekend, and we cruised Kemplar. Levi got really pissed at both of us. We were sitting in one of the parking lots on Kemplar, when Levi came up in his truck. He got out and came up to us and told us what sorry pieces of shit we were. He stood up for you, Lala!" Bay said. "He told us that we weren't just screwing him by being together, but we were screwing you, and that was even worse, because you weren't here to even have a say about it. He and Jax got a little physical and pushed each other a little bit. Levi finally left and Jax and I didn't stay very long. We went out to our place at the lake and well, we kissed a little bit, but the whole time, all I could think about was what Levi had said about him and you. By the time I got home, I knew I couldn't keep seeing Jax."

"The next day he came over, and I told him it just wasn't gonna work. We were hurting two people who cared about both of us, and we cared for too. Jax agreed and we decided to just stay friends. He went over to Levi's house when he left me, and apologized and they're fine now. We don't really hang out a lot, especially since I started goin' with Donny. But we realized it was just too weird." Bailey finished.

I turned around and took a deep breath because the flaming, winged Goddess was trying valiantly to flap her wings within me. I could feel the burn of the rage that was building in my body. I didn't want her to come out, because I knew that if she ever did, I would say things I'd never be able to unsay to Bailey. Finally, I stated, quietly, "I wish you'd told me before now."

"I just didn't know how to bring it up. I was afraid you'd never forgive me." Bailey hung her head.

I sighed again, deeply, "I forgive you, Bailey. I'm hurt, but I forgive you." She raised her eyes to mine and looked deep into them.

"You sure?" she asked, softly. I nodded and then made my way into her house. I didn't want to talk about it anymore!

I felt so conflicted over everything and it was emotions I'd never felt before. Now, I was conflicted over being angry at my best friend and Kevin, and now also Jax. Levi seemed to be the only one who hadn't hurt me. I didn't know what to say or how to feel about any of them.

Chapter 53

The rest of the day, Bailey and I were a little distant. I borrowed her car to go visit Levi. It was a little, blue Pontiac Sunbird. It was cute and sporty like I wished I had. Bailey would have died if she'd had to drive a 1973 Thunderbird. Her car was only a couple of years old. It had the gear shift in the middle, but it was an automatic transmission. I didn't know how to drive a manual transmission, but I had an idea how they worked since Geoff's little Chevy Luv had been a stick shift.

Bailey was going over to Donny's, so I borrowed her car around 7:00 and drove to Levi's house. It felt so strange to be driving in Wichita Falls. I'd always ridden in a car everywhere my entire life, until I was fourteen. Then every time I came to visit, I rode still. When I backed out of Bailey's driveway, I said a quick, silent prayer that I didn't wreck her car. Even though I'd been driving for over two years, without a license, and finally got my license before coming to Wichita Falls, I would be mortified if anything happened to her car while I was driving it.

At the corner of Fairfax and Granville, I looked towards the left, which is the direction I would turn if I were driving to Kevin's house. I thought about driving over there and asking him just what the hell kind of game he was playing with me, since I now knew he had known when I was coming to town. I sat there undecided in the fading sunshine, looking over towards Portland. I could just make out the edge of his driveway from where I sat, but I turned right instead, and went to the stop light at Parkway Highway, to go to Levi's house. He was waiting on me. It felt strange going to his house without Bailey, or Jax. When I thought about them, my heart suddenly felt a stab of pain, as I imagined my best friend kissing Jax, in his dark orange pickup that I'd ridden in so many times I'd lost count.

When I pulled up to the stop light, I realized I had tears streaking down my face. I didn't want Levi to see me crying, so I pulled into the parking lot of the grocery store, on Levi's side of Fairfax and wiped my face, as I turned the air conditioner vents on high, so they could blow my face dry. I sat there for a few minutes looking around.

I was completely alone in a car for the first time, in my entire life, in Wichita Falls. I couldn't believe it when I thought about it at first. I felt like I was going to get in trouble, just for having Bailey's car. I laughed at myself and shook my head.

I wiped the back of my hand one more time across my cheeks and pulled out to finish the short drive to Levi's house.

Levi answered the door when I knocked and grinned really big when he saw me. We had hung out before by ourselves, when he'd been dating Bailey, and it had never been weird. We listened to music or talked about Jax mainly. I grinned as I followed him to his room, remembering that our usual topic of conversation was something neither of us probably wanted to talk about.

After we got in his room, he closed the door, and sat on his weight bench. I could tell that he'd been working out. Levi was an Adonis. He had well sculpted shoulders and his stomach was so rippled with muscles, I wondered if I touched him, if he would feel soft, like a normal human. It looked hard as a rock. I wondered if Levi felt as awkward as I suddenly felt. I didn't like that I felt so weird around him all of a sudden. He'd been one of the main reasons I'd survived 8th grade at Milam Junior High.

I never, in a million years, would have thought I'd have said that, even up until 7th grade, because Levi was an 'untouchable' to me. I still thought of him that way, not just because of Bailey, but because he was so beautiful, too. He was beautiful like Kevin, only with different coloring. He reminded me of a young John Travolta. He had brown hair and icy blue eyes. His chin was dimpled, and he had a big goofy smile.

After a few stilted attempts at a conversation, I finally decided to talk to him about what I'd learned that day about his best friend and my best friend seeing each other, even if it was only for a brief while. I knew that Levi would never say anything to me. He would want Bailey to tell me, for certain, and he'd hope that Jax would tell me too, if Bailey didn't. I realized I didn't even know if I'd see Jax this summer. I felt sad about it, but I had so many mixed emotions about everybody. I didn't like this new reality that was creeping into my visit.

Levi asked if I'd spot him, while he lifted some weights. I wasn't really sure what he wanted, but once he showed me, I was terrified I'd screw it up and he would get hurt. After he did a few reps with the heavy, weighted barbell, I realized that he really had it, he just wanted to give me a job to keep me somehow involved in what he was doing.

When he'd finished his first set of repetitions, I said quietly, "Bailey told me today, Levi." I gazed directly down into his cool blue eyes as he looked up at me. I saw them widen just slightly but he finished working out before he said anything. He nodded at me to show he'd heard me.

Once he put the bar back on the bench he lay there briefly, looking up into my eyes, as I gazed down into his upside-down face.

Finally, after a few seconds, he pulled himself up and sat forward, with his head in his hands. He brought his face up and looked at me intently. "What did she tell you?" Levi hedged.

I smiled at him, affirming, "You know exactly what she told me. Don't pretend like you don't know what I'm talking about. She told me about her and Jax," I finished, feeling my stomach roll when I said their names in a sentence together.

Levi sat there for a few seconds, then he stood up and walked around the work bench, pulling me close to him. He held me as I cried. I felt so stupid. I was over Jax. I didn't want him anymore. I loved Kevin. I wanted to spend my time with him, not Jax. But when I thought about the one person I trusted the most in the world, besides Kevin, had actually tried to have a relationship with someone who she knew was very dear to my heart, it just broke me. I would never, ever have thought about trying to go out with Levi.

I finally got my tears in check, and Levi pulled away, and looked at me worriedly. "Are you okay, Lala?" he asked me, using the same name that Bailey called me. He was the only other person in the world I would stand for calling me that name. It was a pet name. It was a name of love, and I loved hearing both of them say it. I nodded my head. He leaned over and plucked a Kleenex out of a box that sat on his night stand. I mopped up the tears on my face and realized how close our faces were to one another. I had a brief crazy thought that I should try to kiss him, just for pay back, but as if he could read my thoughts, Levi suddenly pulled further away from me. I quickly looked down at my shoes, feeling mortified, and ashamed. Levi smiled curiously at me. I pulled completely away from him.

"I'm okay. I'm sorry, Levi. I guess I'm still a little shocked about the whole Jax and Bailey thing," I apologized, quickly.

Stepping back from me an extra step, Levi looked at me and nodded his head. Finally, he admitted, "Lala, look, it really wasn't a big deal. They got drunk at a dance. They kissed a little. They thought they liked each other and walked down the hall holding hands some. I found out and got pissed off. I found them on Kemplar the next weekend and acted like a jackass. I really loved Bay. I still love Bay, but we aren't good for each other. I can't keep her happy. I don't understand what the hell she sees in that little prick, Donny, but more power to her if that's her speed now."

I looked at Levi and realized that he had just told me exactly what Bailey had told me. I knew she hadn't told him anything, so either she and Jax really synchronized their stories, or that is what truly happened.

Finally, I nodded my head and muttered, "Me neither, Levi. Me neither! I don't like her dating Donny, but I can't really tell her to stop. I did tell her I didn't think he was good enough for her…" I trailed off.

Levi smiled at me and I smiled back. Our moment of awkwardness was gone, but I knew that our close friendship was also never going to be the same again, without Bailey. We would always be friends, but I knew that the days of us just hanging out and being around one another were over now.

After a few more minutes of just sitting in his room talking, we walked outside to Bailey's little, blue Sunbird. I smoked a cigarette before I got back inside the car. Levi watched me smoke it, and finally he admitted, "Lala, I hope you quit smoking. I hate that you smoke now!"

Smiling at him, I nodded my head, "Yeah, most guys do, but it's hard. There's so much shit I live with every single day, Levi. I can't imagine not smoking, right now." He looked at me worriedly and finally just nodded his head. Once I finished the cigarette, I knew it was time to leave, even though I'd only been there an hour. I hugged my best friend's ex-boyfriend one last time. I didn't know if it would be the last time I ever hugged him again, or not, but I felt certain I wouldn't come to his house and hang out ever again. "I love you, Levi." I whispered, softly, when we pulled apart.

"I know, Lala!" Levi grinned his goofy grin. I couldn't help but smile. I unlocked the door to get in. I wasn't sure where I was going next, since it was only a little after 8, but my time with Levi was done. I couldn't stand dragging it out any longer. After I reached inside the car and started it, to get the air conditioner running, I turned to say goodbye to Levi, and was surprised to see him standing right behind me. He placed his large hands on my shoulders, and held me tightly in front of him, as he looked into my eyes.

Finally, he declared, "DeLaine, I love you too. You've been the bestest, girl, best friend I think I'll ever have. I just want you to know that. I'm always going to be your friend, no matter what happens with me and Bay. I think you became my girl best friend almost as soon as I met you, on the first day of 8th grade."

I glanced down at my feet, as I felt my face begin to blush. I remembered feeling so overwhelmed when I found out that Bailey was Levi Parker's girlfriend, that day. I had gone from being a complete and total 'nobody' the first day of 7th grade, to walking down the hall with Levi Parker and Jax Garrett, the first day of 8th grade. I was never sure how exactly that had all worked out, but Levi was there for me in more ways than one. I always marveled at the fact that he liked me and wanted to be friends with me. Finally, I looked back up into the arctic, blue eyes.

I whispered, "Thank you Levi, for being my friend. It has meant more to me than you can ever know!"

Levi pulled me close to him, one last time, in a tight hug, and whispered, "Everything is changing fast, Lala, but how I feel about you never will. I miss how things used to be. But I'm always here for you. Take care of yourself, okay?" I nodded and smiled at him.

I slid inside the little, blue car, behind the wheel, and grinned up at Levi one last time. I was surprised when he leaned inside and kissed me chastely on the cheek. "Take care, okay, Lala?"

I nodded my head again and Levi backed out of the way, closing the driver's side door. I waved at him through the glass and smiled one more time. I pulled away from the curb, where I had parked Bailey's car.

I looked back in the rearview mirror and saw as Levi watched me drive off and towards the setting sun. I felt like there were more endings happening in this trip than ever before. I didn't understand it at all. I sat at the corner, at the stop sign, and wondered what to do next. Finally, I drove over to Kevin's house. I knew somehow that it was where I would go.

As I stood on the porch, waiting on Mrs. Strong to open the door, I looked at the familiar cement porch. I remembered many of the times I'd stood on the exact spot that I waited on. I glanced at Donna's bedroom window, and wondered if behind that glass, the little girl, pink bedroom sat quietly, waiting on a little girl to come back home, who never would.

As I remembered every nook and cranny of the room, I'd spent many hours in, the front door opened, and Jean Strong stood there smiling broadly at me. She opened the door and ushered me in, with a hearty laugh and a smile like the ones she used to give, before Donna died. When she pulled me into her tight and warm embrace, I felt like all was right within the world one more time!

Mrs. Strong pulled away and looked at me intently. "Well, you have got a gorgeous suntan this summer, don't you?" I smiled and nodded and Mrs. Strong chuckled, "You turn brown as a berry! You are so fair, I would never have guessed that you could tan so deeply, but you look radiant!" I felt myself blush and she quickly ushered me further into the house. Once we were further inside, I smelled something delicious cooking. I was reminded of all the meals I had eaten with the Strong family. Within seconds the first time I'd eaten there, the night before I turned 13, flashed through my memories. It was one of my favorite memories in my lifetime.

"Kevin's in his room," Jean Strong said sweetly as we got to the entrance of the hallway.

"Oh, um, okay. I'd love to visit with you first, though," I replied, quietly. Kevin's mom smiled at me and nodded her head and walked into the kitchen, where the aromas were wafting from.

"Well, c'mon in the kitchen then darlin' and grab an apron. I'm cooking a lot of stuff for a big bake sale at the church this Saturday. You know me, I start almost a week ahead! But I really enjoy it and it keeps me busy now," the last few words trailed off.

I knew she meant since Donna had died. I smiled at her sympathetically, but she didn't finish the thought, even though she didn't say what I knew she was thinking. As quick as her face began to fall, she seemed to shake almost invisibly, and her smile brightened back to the way it used to.

Within seconds Mrs. Strong began to tell me what to get and amazingly, I remembered where everything was. If she was surprised that I didn't want to let Kevin know I was there, she never showed it.

As I was busy sifting flour, which was soothing to me, and for some reason Mrs. Strong knew that, I thought about Kevin, and why I wasn't bolting down the hall as soon as I walked in the door. There were so many thoughts that were flitting through my mind. I was thinking about learning about Bailey and Jax. I was thinking about the fact that Donny and Kevin worked together, and that Donny had actually told him I was coming to town, and still Jackie was here the day after I got to town. I also thought about my brief visit with Levi, and how it felt like it was the last time I'd ever see him again.

Mrs. Strong kept up a steady stream of chatter about the ladies at her church, and even though I barely heard much, she didn't seem to mind. Sometimes it seemed she knew when I needed to be kept busy, because I had lots to think about.

Before I knew it, I'd been in the kitchen with her for almost thirty minutes. She and I had mixed up two batches of homemade cake batter. I basked in her warmth, and wondered why she gave so much to me, when I gave her so little. While I was thinking that, I heard Kevin exclaim as he walked into the kitchen, "Lainey! When'd you get here?"

I jerked around and saw him standing in the door way of the kitchen. "Oh, I've been here a little while," I replied, absently.

"Why didn't you come to my room?" he asked me, sounding a bit hurt.

I shrugged my shoulders and told him I wanted to spend some time with his mom, because I hadn't seen her since I'd been there. I wasn't sure how to tell him that I was a little mad at him. Not to mention I was feeling completely overwhelmed with emotions since I'd found out about my best friend kissing one of the two boys I'd been in love with.

I knew Kevin could tell that I was bugged. He seemed to have some sort of magical power that intuited when something was wrong, whether I let on or not. He went over where the aprons hung inside of a long pantry cabinet and slid one over his head. He asked his mom what he could do to help. She began giving him instructions. Before long, we all had our rhythm. I marveled as I watched Kevin and his mom use their own shorthand that had been developed between them, over the years of doing things together, in the kitchen.

We worked another hour, and then Jean Strong shooed us out of the kitchen. She knew that I had to be back at Bailey's by midnight and I'd been there for almost two hours and it was quickly approaching 10 o'clock. We had laughed and chatted the entire hour.

For the first time in the last few days, I felt happier. I had let all the hurt and worry fall away from me magically, just like I always did any time I worked in the kitchen with Mrs. Strong. As I hung up my apron, I realized that all those feelings were coming back to me like a heavy coat made of lead. I knew that I would have to talk to Kevin now, and we wouldn't be using the same playful banter we had used while we were in the kitchen, with his mom.

I walked into the familiar bedroom where I had actually slept with Kevin during the days of Donna's funeral. We made love for the first time in this room. At least the time I counted as the first time. I felt like I knew this room almost as intimately as I knew my own. It was a place I had been vulnerable in, and one that Kevin had shown me his own vulnerabilities. Walking in here though, just made the sad feeling I had, more pronounced.

Kevin walked over to the window that was standing open and closed it. I knew that if his window was open it meant he'd been in there smoking pot. I sighed quietly, as he had his back to me. I don't know why it bothered me that he smoked pot.

It wasn't like I'd exactly been a perfect, little angel since living in Corpus. I thought of Kevin so much more highly it seemed. I held him up to a higher standard than I did myself. I thought that Kevin had so much more chance than I did to have everything he could want. He had the parents I could only dream about, and the home life that I longed for. His life didn't start out charmed, but it was now. I thought that if he didn't quit smoking pot, he would throw away everything he'd been so blessed to have, when the Strong's adopted him and Donna.

By the time he turned back around, I was sitting on the bed with my shoes off and my bare feet curled up under my thighs as I sat Indian style, near his pillows. "What's troublin' you, Little Lainey?" Kevin whispered, huskily.

I looked down at my hands lying on his bedspread and shrugged. I felt Kevin's weight come across from the side of the bed near the window he just closed. He stretched out like a giant panther on his side and propped his head on his hand that was pushed up by his elbow. His face ended up looking directly up at me, so ducking my face down had only made it impossible to look away from his azure eyes. Kevin asked again, and finally I stated, quietly, "You knew I was coming to town."

Kevin didn't say anything right away, but he never looked away from me. Finally, he admitted, quietly, "Yeah, I did."

"Why did you have that girl here, if you knew I was in town, then, Kevin?" I asked him, earnestly.

Kevin looked down now, and I sat there patiently.

Finally, he looked up at me, "There isn't any good reason, except maybe I thought if she was here and you showed up, you'd get pissed off enough that you'd never want to see me again."

I looked at him searchingly, "Why did you do that, Kevin? If you don't want to see me, then all you have to do is tell me." I was angry at the tears that threatened to drop out of my eyes.

We sat on his bed for a few minutes, before Kevin finally explained, "I already knew what you've been doing the last two years, Lainey. You told me the other night, when we walked up to Samson. You've only been living half in Corpus and half here. I figured if you got angry enough that you decided not to see me again, then maybe you'd be able to be happier down there. You have to find a life there now, Lainey. I don't like it, and I don't want it, but it's true. You know it, and I know it. I've thought about it so much…a lot more than you would think. I've laid right there, where you are sitting right now, thinking about it. Jackie is just a chick I see sometimes. She's not anybody important. She's a cool chick, but I just don't want to commit to anybody right now, Lainey."

"I still feel…lost. I thought it would get better after a while, after Donna died, but it just keeps looming over me like some kind of black cloud. No matter what I do to get out from under it, the damned thing is still there. It follows me everywhere," Kevin continued. "Letting you go is not something I really want to do. I have to do it though, Lainey. I have to…I dunno, I have to be a man about it, I guess, and let you move on. As long as I hold onto you, I know you'll never let go, and have everything you deserve down there. You deserve so much, Honey! You've had a shitty enough life so far! It's time to start reaching for more. The way you've been living isn't what you need to be doing!"

I closed my eyes tightly. I didn't want to hear him say any of this. I knew everything he said was true. I knew I had to let go of him too, but it was so hard.

I didn't know how to stop loving someone who had literally saved my life. I didn't know how to stop loving Kevin Michael Strong. I didn't know if I ever would.

Finally, I got up, and slid my feet into my sandals. I kept my back to Kevin as I blinked the tears out of my eyes. I didn't want to leave crying. It seemed I was always leaving crying.

"DeLaine, don't leave right now! Wait! I don't want you to leave upset. I don't want you driving upset."

I whirled around and looked at him and I felt the ugly sneer begin to creep across my face. "Why not, Kevin? You afraid if I wreck between here and Bailey's that you won't be able to live with that or what? Give me a fucking break! I drive much further than that shit faced drunk!"

I felt my voice rising. I reeled it back in and lowered it.

"These tears will be dried up by the time I get to Bailey's," I said. "I don't even know why I keep coming to you. I don't understand it any more than you do. But come back is exactly what I do, which pisses me off! I want to be able to tell you to get lost, or go get fucked, or something else, but I can't seem to make myself say anything like that and stick to it!"

"Lainey, don't do it this way. I don't want you to leave upset or mad. I just think that we've got to let go of each other. You've got two more years of school and so much to happen in that time! You're so smart, you're gonna go to college and you're gonna forget all about that dumb-ass jock in Wichita Falls. Trust me! You'll get into a college, get some fancy job, and get married and have kids. It's gonna be someone else who's going to be so damned lucky to have you love him. I just know that I'm not any good for you. I never have been!" Kevin seemed to be begging me, as he described the life he thought I would have.

"I doubt that," I muttered, as my anger that had tried to build earlier died silently, in my mouth. I didn't want to be angry. I was sad, and being angry, on top of being sad, was so much more to deal with emotionally.

Every muscle in my body ached and my head hurt also. "Kevin haven't you figured out that it's me who never deserved you? You weren't supposed to ever know I existed. I'm a nobody. I always have been, and always will be. Nobody sees me. I don't want anyone to see me, especially now. It isn't like I can bring a boy home and let him meet my drunk mom! So, it doesn't matter if you're in my life or not. I'm never going to be anyone! I'm never going to have someone love me again. I'm no good for anyone, who is any good! You've got so much right here, under this roof, than I'll ever have, no matter how old I get."

Kevin jumped off the bed and came around on the other side to stand in front of me. Grabbing my face roughly in both of his large hands he looked deep in my eyes. "Don't ever say that again DeLaine and don't you DARE EVER BELIEVE IT EITHER!"

I looked up at him, unsure what I was supposed to say. It seemed we always had the same issues, no matter what. He didn't feel he was good enough for me and I didn't feel I was good enough for him. He pushed me away, and I pulled him back. Or, I was the one pushing and he was the one pulling. It was like we constantly did this dance, like a moth to a candle. Each of us knowing that the light would burn but being helpless to quit.

Before I even knew how to respond to him, he pulled my face up to his and kissed me roughly. He hadn't been rough with me since the time we'd been behind Kevin Welks' house in the old, crappy, travel trailer.

At first, I resisted him kissing me so roughly, but within only a few seconds, the roughness faded, and I felt myself melt into the kiss.

I didn't want to quit kissing him. I never wanted to quit kissing him.

We were constantly doing this and it was so hard on me. I just couldn't quit loving him, or leave him alone if I was in Wichita Falls. I knew it was insanity, but it was an insanity that I seemed destined to continue, because I couldn't stand the thought of never having him any longer.

I put my hands on either side of his face after a while, and held his face to mine, as we kissed. I felt the scratchiness of the blonde stubble on his face and I slowly slid my hands up into his blonde hair. I felt my breath growing ragged and just as suddenly as he began kissing me, I quit kissing him, and pulled away. Kevin looked at me confused at first, and then he realized that even though he was telling me to leave forever, his actions were telling me to stay forever. He realized his total contradiction. Even though I was trying to pull away from him, he held me tightly, as his fingers traced the lines of my face.

"I know what I tell you, Lainey, then I do something that goes against everything I say. I don't know how to stop doing that. I want to be able to let you go, but I don't know how. Please, forgive me." Kevin whispered, huskily, as he continued to hold my face in his hands. I couldn't say anything to him. I felt completely overwhelmed for the sheer weight of the feelings I had because of this young man. Finally, after looking deeply into his eyes, until I felt I was actually looking into his soul, I realized he was doing the exact same thing.

"I should go," I whispered, as I broke away from him. Kevin looked at me sadly. He nodded his head though, and stepped back, so I could open the door to his room. I slipped down the dark hallway. Just before I got to the end of it, I stopped in front of the door that led into Donna's room.

I stared at the door, wondering if I could be so bold to just open it, and no one know I was going in there. I could hear Mrs. Strong in the kitchen, washing the dishes, humming. I knew that Mr. Strong had gone to bed earlier when we were working in the kitchen. I'd just left Kevin in his room. Finally, I decided that I had to go inside the room. I'd only been inside of it once, since Donna died, and that was right after her funeral and her mom brought me in to give me the angel bear I'd given to her. I felt my heart hammering inside of my chest and my breath was coming out in light shallow breaths. I put my hand on the door knob and listened again for Mrs. Strong, one more time. I turned the brass door knob quietly and pushed the door open.

As I stood inside the darkened doorway, I knew exactly where everything was in this room. I looked around and knew that even without turning the lights on, the walls were still painted little girl pink and her furniture was all still placed exactly as she'd left it. I even saw her books, as I peered into the murky darkness.

I felt a complete wave of grief wash over me, as I backed out of the room, and silently closed the door.

I walked the rest of the way to the end of the hall, and walked to the entrance of the kitchen and told Mrs. Strong goodnight as cheery as I could make myself sound. She had her hands immersed in a sink of sudsy dishes thankfully, so I was able to skirt out of coming all the way into the light and hugging her. I waved quickly and hurried down the entry hallway and got to Bailey's car before the tears completely obscured my vision. I wiped at them, hurriedly, and managed to get the key into the door lock to get inside and start the car. I could feel the sobs building up in my chest and my mouth began to thicken with the onslaught of tears and snot that I knew was about to happen.

I managed to get away from Kevin's house, and zig-zagged on Fairfax Blvd. to Granville. When I got to the intersection to go to the elementary school and playground, I turned, instead of staying straight, to Bailey's house. I pulled up into the small parking area that was for the teachers, near the playground, and got out in the hot night air. I walked over to the swings. My body knew where it was going, and my brain was just along for the ride. I sat in one of the U-shaped rubber swings and grabbed the heavy chain that connected it to the frame.

I pushed off the hard-packed ground, with my feet and felt as the night air began to move over my body. I'd been sweating inside the car, even with the air conditioner on, when I felt the breeze from swinging begin to cool me in each of the places my body had been sweating.

The air ruffled the curls around my head, and the hair that had been sticking to my face and neck began to flap in the breeze I created by kicking my feet along the hard-packed dirt, under the swings. I closed my eyes, and began to climb higher and higher, the more I swung.

I leaned back and straightened out my body as much as possible, as it sailed through the air on the playground swing. I closed my eyes and felt the moonlight as it kissed my eyelids. I let my mind go completely blank, as I swung back and forth, back and forth. The wind whistled as it whooshed past my ears. I felt my breathing begin to even out.

I knew that Kevin and I had to let go of one another. I knew that I'd never have a life in Corpus Christi no matter what, if I didn't let him go. I just hated to let him go. I loved him so much. As my body climbed higher and higher in the swing, and the night air caressed my skin, I let the tears slide from my closed eyes. I wished I knew how to make all the pain I felt on a daily basis go away.

I knew that drinking didn't make it go away for good. I knew that no matter how drunk or even how stoned I got, the pain in the depths of my soul was never far away. I knew that it was not going to go anywhere, anytime soon, and even though Kevin seemed to ease that pain, he also added to it some ways as well. I wasn't certain how to go on living if I didn't have Kevin here in Wichita Falls, waiting on me, every summer.

After what seemed a really long time, I let myself begin to slow on the swings. I wasn't even sure what time it was. I hoped that I wasn't late. As I finally dragged my feet through the slight, sandy part of the packed dirt, I felt as the dirt slipped under my toes, into my sandals. I sighed and spun myself inside of the swing like I remembered doing when I was little, in elementary school. I twisted around and around until the chains wouldn't let me twist them any longer, then I held my gritty feet up and felt the dizzying spin as the chains unwound. I felt the crazy and dizzying tickle in my head and stomach. When I finally came to a stop, I was grinning like a crazy kid. Even with the tears slipping silently down my face still, I felt a silly smile playing across my mouth. When all the movement was out of the swing, I got up and began walking back to Bailey's car.

I was kicking my feet as I walked to the small, asphalt, parking area, trying to get some of the sand out of my shoes. I hoped I wasn't too late and just as I got to the edge of the parking lot, I heard someone say, "Hey."

Jumping and feeling my heart hammering in my chest, I looked up and saw Kevin leaning against Bailey's car. "Dammit, Kevin! Why'd you scare the shit out of me?" I hissed, quietly.

"Do you know what time it is, DeLaine?" Kevin asked me in a whispered voice. I shook my head, and he said, "Lainey, it's 12:35. You were supposed to be at Bailey's at midnight. You left my house at like 11:30! She called me at 12:15 freaking out!"

"SHIT!" I said, still in my hissing tone.

"It's cool! Her mom and dad are in bed and you can probably sneak in. I jumped in my car and drove to her house not having any idea where you were!" Kevin admitted, quietly.

"Wait, you have a car, now?" I asked him, totally ignoring the fact that he had once again come running to my rescue, even though it had been Bailey's call that made him come running.

"Yeah, didn't you notice it when you came over tonight?" Kevin asked, grinning. I shook my head again, feeling like a stupid child. I looked around the parking lot and didn't see another car besides Bailey's Sunbird.

"So, if you drove to Bay's, where's your car?" I asked a little crossly.

Smiling at me Kevin confided, "I left it parked in front of her house. When I got there, we sat outside, and she told me she'd called Levi and Jax both, to see if you were over at their houses. When she knew you weren't at my house, or either of theirs, she was frantic. I told her I had an idea, so I ran down here. I just thought that maybe this is where you came."

"Yeah, I guess I'm predictable if I'm anything," I groused, sarcastically. I looked at Kevin wanting to feel touched that he had been worried and had known where to look. I was surprised that I was actually irritated. "Well, you found me. C'mon, I'll give you a ride back to Bay's, to your car. I'm fine."

Nodding his head, Kevin walked over to the passenger side and got inside. I started it up and saw the digital clock light up, showing it was now 12:45 a.m. I felt awful for making Bailey worry. I backed out and we were sitting in Bailey's driveway by 12:48.

I got out of the car before Kevin could say anything else to me. I didn't want to talk anymore. I was talked out. I was tired of talking. I was tired of everything! Kevin climbed his long frame out of the small, blue car and walked towards me. I stopped and shook my head.

"Go home, Kev. I'm tired. I'm sorry you were worried. I need to go inside so Bay doesn't wake her folks, thinking I'm dead!" I murmured, softly.

Kevin nodded his head and turned to walk to the car parked at the curb, behind Jason Rains' old car. I was shocked when I saw a gorgeous, black Camaro. He noticed my reaction as he was walking to his car and he grinned at me.

"Pretty, huh?" he whispered in the still darkness. I couldn't help myself, I grinned and nodded my head. I turned around though and walked quickly up the cement steps to go inside my best friend's house.

I didn't turn around to look back.

Chapter 54

After explaining to Bailey that I lost track of time, while I was swinging, we went to bed. I lay in the darkness thinking about my time on the swing. I had completely and totally lost myself, and all track of time. I thought the excuse sounded a little lame, honestly, but Bay just hugged me and told me she was glad I was okay.

I wanted to move forward, but I felt stuck in a sticky mire of quicksand. Even though it wasn't the real stuff, I felt like my entire life was a giant circle just spinning faster and faster. I was in danger of getting spun out of the circle, and fast! I sighed and just before the sun came up, I finally slipped under the blanket of sleep.

When I woke up, it was 11 in the morning. Bailey was gone to work. I was alone at her house. I wasn't sure what to do with myself. After getting up, eating and watching a little bit of a game show, I got dressed and sat in her room, reading a little bit of a book. I wanted to call Kevin and talk, but I remembered he was at work too. I wondered around her house, and finally laid back down and fell asleep around 3 in the afternoon. I was woken up when Bailey came in and shook my shoulder.

"Hey, are you okay?" Bailey asked me, with deep concern wrinkling her forehead.

Struggling to open my eyes, I finally nodded my head and sat up. "What time is it?" I asked, sleepily. Bailey told me it was 5:30 and then asked if I was getting sick. I shook my head. "Nope, unless you count being sick of my life," I replied, with a wry grin.

"I was being serious, Dippy-doo! What did you do today?" Bailey asked me, grinning as she stood up and began to move through her room to get some clothes to change from her work scrubs. I thought it was cool that she got to wear scrubs, like the doctor's normally wore, when they were in the hospital! Bailey told me that almost all the medical and dental offices were beginning to change their attire, to let all the workers in an office dress in them. "Hang on a sec, let me go change and I'll be back in here," Bailey announced, with a smile on her face.

I looked around the room and couldn't believe I'd slept so much during the day. When Bailey came back to her room, she asked if I wanted to talk.

Looking at her for a while, I finally nodded. "Look, Bay, I don't know what is so off about this summer," I began. I sat there trying to think about what exactly I wanted to say. Finally, I admitted, "I know I haven't given Donny a real chance, and I'm sorry. Let's all hang out this weekend and let me start over a little, okay?"

Bailey looked at me oddly and began to nod her head. "I figured you wanted to tell me that you wanted to leave this weekend," Bailey replied, a little sadly.

"Well, since I have to wait and go to Oklahoma City to spend 10 days with Big Russ, I guess that would be a little hard," I chuckled, quietly.

I watched as Bailey's hopeful look drooped and she looked at the ground. "I understand," she whispered.

"Bay, really? C'mon! I'm not just staying because I have to go spend time with my daddy!" I was giggling softly.

Bailey looked at me surprised. "What? Are you shitting me? Why'd you say that, you big doo-doo head?"

I started laughing when she called me a silly, little kid name. There was my dear Bailey. I leaned over and hugged her tightly. "Bay, I'm not going to say I haven't been sad about some stuff since I've been here, but when I said I was your best friend, I meant it. That isn't going to change, but let me just be clear, no matter what happens with me and Kevin, he is off limits!" I smiled at my best friend.

Thinking that Bailey would grin back at me, I was surprised when she looked stricken by what I'd said. "Lala, I can't say how sorry I am about the whole Jax thing. I don't know what the hell got into us," Bailey cried, as tears filled her eyes.

Grabbing her again, around the neck, I hugged her fiercely, "Bay! Honey, it's okay! I'm not even mad about it anymore! I promise! I just thought I better put that out there about Kevin, though," I repeated again, with a wry smile. I wondered how much of it I meant in a joking manner, though. I didn't know if I could be as forgiving with my best friend or Kevin over a transgression like she and Jax had done.

Bailey smiled, and I saw a bottomless, blue ocean light up inside of her eyes. I loved this girl so much. I didn't understand why I loved her and Kevin so much. I never felt I was worthy of either of them. "Lala, I can't ever apologize enough."

"Stop!" I commanded. "From now on, Jax is just water under the bridge! I'm not even going to talk about him, and as far as him and you, I'm not even thinking about it!"

Laughing, Bailey asked, "You aren't going to talk about Jax? Okay, who are you, and what have you done with my best friend? You know, her name is DeLaine Reynolds…"

I began to laugh with her. "Look, Sister Sue, there are a few things I know about you and one is that you love Kevin Strong. No matter what he does or how far down he goes, you aren't ever gonna stop. Another thing I know about you is, you are absolutely the bestest friend I ever had. I also know that is there is a little part of you that is ALWAYS gonna want to talk about Jax Garrett, at least a little bit!"

I smiled at Bailey. I felt like our footing was getting back on track. "Yeah, you're right! No matter what, he was my first REAL boyfriend and well, damn, he's just such a hot cowboy!" Bailey laughed, and we began to talk about the night before and what had happened between me and Kevin.

"So, Lala, what are you going to do?" Bailey asked me a little while later, after I told her all I'd been thinking about, with Kevin and me and our relationship.

Shrugging my shoulders, I admitted, "I dunno Bay. I don't know how to let him go. I want to so badly. It's killing me. I have to make a big change this year. I'm half-way through high school and the only thing I have to show for it is the ability to drink a bunch of guys under the table. I'm also able to lie really good to my mom. Oh yeah, and an almost a pack a day cigarette habit!" I was grimacing, even though I knew I wasn't in any hurry to quit smoking.

"What are you talking about?" Bailey asked me quietly.

I looked into her eyes and marveled again at the color of them. I had seen these eyes angry, sad, ecstatic, scared, worried, excited and silly. I had watched them look at me in sadness and empathy. I don't think she ever pitied me. "Well, for starters I have to quit thinking about Kevin all the time! I have to look at maybe dating someone for real and not just messing around with Chance Cahill!

"What else?" Bailey asked me.

"Get involved at school. I'm at a different school, and I still don't really know anyone that well. I know people, but it's like I'm a ghost walking through the halls. I have to do something to get me out of the house and away from my mom." I admitted the last part, feeling so ashamed for even admitting it.

"Are you planning not to come back, after graduation?" Bailey asked me, sadly.

I shrugged my shoulders. "I dunno, Bay. Things are changing so much. I don't even know how I'm going to be able to come up here. I mean, it will take money to move up here. I don't even know if I can afford to go to Midwestern. I want to, I just don't know how it's gonna work." Nodding her head, Bailey leaned over and hugged me again. "What was that for?" I asked, surprised.

"Just because I love you. I know that if you are supposed to be back in Wichita then you'll figure out a way. Look how you figured out how to get away from that bitch, Clarice, after all!" Bailey smiled at me.

"Yeah, I guess you're right," I admitted.

"And you're right, you need to start doing some stuff in school, because I heard colleges want you to be involved with something, besides just being smart!" she smiled.

I told her I had signed up for theater arts and she grinned and told me she thought I'd be awesome at that. She was aware at how well I slipped into different personas just for survival. We talked about all the classes we were looking forward to in our junior year of high school.

"So, what are you going to do about Kevin right now?" Bailey asked me, concerned. I shrugged my shoulders. "Maybe you should just try not to call him for the rest of the time you are here," Bailey suggested.

"Yeah, but I want to go see his mom one more time at least," I murmured.

Bailey grimaced as she thought. Her grimace produced a deep furrow of her eyebrows and then she looked at me and raised her shoulders. "That's a tough one, Lala."

"Yeah, I know," I agreed.

Before we could continue our conversation, Glenda Rains called us in for dinner. I figured it was just as well. I still had to think about what exactly I was going to do about Kevin. I didn't want to just completely ignore him, then leave without telling him goodbye. Wasn't that the whole point in letting him go, though? I still felt so confused about him, even though I should be better at it, since I'd had enough years of worrying about our relationship.

In the end, I called Kevin on Sunday. I couldn't believe I went that many days without talking to him, while I was in Wichita Falls. He called on Bailey's phone on Saturday, but she told him I wasn't there. I wondered where I was supposed to tell him I had been. Neither Bailey, nor I had thought about that. When I called Kevin on Sunday, I told him to meet me at Samson, at the bleachers we had gone to, the second night I'd been there. We were supposed to meet up there at 6:30. I was nervous and not sure what I was going to say to him.

I had actually seen him cruising on Kemplar when we'd gone out with Donny, on Saturday night. He had Freddie Black with him. I worried about him all night and that was one of the reasons I finally decided to talk to him, on Sunday. I knew it was silly, because he probably wasn't doing anything different than he did all the time, when I was in Corpus. After all, he'd probably be a worry wart if he was in Corpus on a weekend, watching me too.

Getting ready to go up to Samson, I felt as nervous as if I was going out on a real date with Kevin. I laughed as I carefully picked out a pastel, striped, button down blouse and lavender shorts. I wished I knew if I should try to fix my hair or just leave it alone. It still looked somewhat okay from when I had hot rolled it that morning, before church. Bailey watched me as I carefully put on some eye makeup. My tan was deep enough, I didn't need much more than a little eyeliner and lip gloss.

I looked up at Bailey, as I sat on the floor, in front of her full-length mirror, on her closet door. "What?" I asked her curiously.

"Do you know what you're going to say?" Bailey wondered out loud. I shook my head and then began rimming my eyes once again with the deep green eyeliner. "Whatever you do, just know that I'm here for you, Lala. I'll be waiting to find out everything, so don't go swing all night and leave me here worrying about you." I smiled at my best friend. We'd had a bit of a bumpy summer, which was different for us, but we seemed to be getting along a lot better.

I'd even had fun with her and Donny, on Saturday night, when we went draggin' on Kemplar. I was surprised, but I guess Bailey told him that I was having a problem with him or something. He only got smart-assed with one person and thankfully it was someone who was an even bigger jerk than he was… Duke Reed.

If it hadn't been for me and Bailey visiting with Kelly White, on Kemplar, Donny and Duke probably never would have almost gotten into it. Thankfully, Bailey and Kelly were able to stem the fight, although I felt guilty for secretly wishing they'd go ahead and beat the crap out of each other! Mainly, because I couldn't beat up both of them. I honestly didn't like either of them, even though I was trying desperately to like Donny. It was right after that episode that Kevin had almost seen me on Kemplar, with Bailey and Donny. Since he didn't slow down and look at me, I felt certain he hadn't noticed me, which I was grateful for.

I hugged Bailey a little after 6 and walked up to Samson. I would be early, but it would give me a few minutes by myself. I had to think about what it was I wanted to say.

What did I really want from Kevin? I still felt just as conflicted as ever over him. He had been the only boy I'd ever felt this way about.

I had loved Jax, in my own way. He'd been the first boy I could call my boyfriend, but even though I'd never been able to call Kevin my boyfriend, I loved him just as much as if I had called him that for years.

When I reached the bleachers at 6:15, it was still hot outside. I felt like I was melting and cursed myself for being so vain to wear any makeup.

I had only put a little on my eyes but as much as I was sweating, my eyes were burning just from the makeup and sweat mixed. I blew out of my mouth upwards, hoping to make them quit burning.

The metal bleachers were really hot, but after a little while, the extreme sting went away. I looked out over the track at the semi-green and brown field of grass that was the backdrop. I smiled as I realized that I could smell cut grass again.

Biting my lip, I glanced at the small watch on my wrist and realized I'd only been there about five minutes. I was nervous.

I took a deep breath and looked up at the sky. It still held a lot of the blue in it from the day, but it was beginning to fade at the lower points, towards the horizon line. The sun was just beginning to show some gold streaks at that point, but up high, the clouds were beginning to find their colors of the impending sunset.

While I was looking at the sky, I silently began to talk to God. I wasn't really big on praying, or religion, but sometimes I liked to talk to God. I even believed that He was okay with me just talking to Him in my head. I didn't know how to really pray. I hadn't been raised in a church. I wasn't sure if God even listened unless you said "Thee" & "Thou," but I hoped He did, because I didn't know how to talk like that.

I didn't even know what to talk to God about in regard to Kevin. In my head I admitted that, and then thought what a loser I was that I couldn't even talk to God about what was in my heart. I didn't know what I was supposed to ask for. I closed my eyes after a few minutes and smiled when I felt the breeze blow my hair off of my forehead. I hoped that was God's sign that He was going to help me out here tonight.

"You know that even when you smile with your eyes closed it makes me happy, right?" I heard Kevin say softly, right beside my ear. I jumped, and my eyes flew open. Staring at me intently was the boy I had just told God how much I loved and asked for help in knowing what it was I was supposed to do.

Normally, I would have gotten irritated at Kevin for making me jump, but instead, I smiled up at him. Judging by his reaction, I didn't think that he had expected that for my response. "Hey," I whispered to the boy who I loved so much it was literally hurting me.

"You were far away, huh?" Kevin asked me, quietly, as he gracefully swung himself up onto the bleachers. He reclined back with such ease, it appeared. Sometimes I thought of a large panther when I watched him move. He had such a muscular body, and when he made certain movements, he did it with the grace of a large cat. I nodded my head slowly. "So, my little Lainey, what were you so far away, thinking about?"

"You," I replied, quietly.

"I see. And did you find any answers out there in the great beyond?" Kevin asked me, seriously, as if he knew I was literally praying about what I was supposed to do about him.

Tilting my head just a little, I flashed a small, sad smile. "No, not really. I mean, not anything concrete anyway. Just a lot more questions really, but I'm trying," I replied, ruefully.

Kevin smiled at me. I noticed instead of his normal sunshine and rainbows smile, it was a small, sad smile like my own.

"Lainey, what can I do to help you? I will do whatever you tell me to do. I admit I've fucked up a lot this summer, in how I handled everything. I just don't want to hurt you, even without meaning to. I want you to have a good life. I want you to move on with your life, in Corpus, but I'm selfish too. I don't want to let you go completely. I just don't know what to do to help you, Sweetheart."

I sighed and nodded my head, as if I knew exactly what he was saying. I believed that he wanted to make things easier for me, but I didn't know what to tell him, so he could do that. I leaned back against the bleachers behind me, in imitation of him, but I couldn't quite pull off the exact same pose. I was shorter in not just height, but also in the length of my arms too. After a few unsuccessful attempts at appearing cool in leaning back, on the bleachers, I finally exclaimed, "Oh, screw it!" I stood up and moved to the bleacher directly under Kevin and leaned against his legs. This brought about a little laugh from both of us.

Once I was leaned against his shins, I sighed contentedly. We sat that way for a long time, watching the colors deepen, as the sunset began to unfold majestically before us. I knew that there would still be some more daylight, but the sunset would take a while to complete itself. It always did in the summer time. Finally, I explained, "Kevin, I don't know what to do now, any more than I did a week ago. I know that I have to go to Oklahoma City, to my daddy's for 10 days, then I'll be back for two more nights before I have to go home. That is the only thing I know for sure."

"You know that this has to stop, right, DeLaine?" Kevin asked me quietly. I hated when he used my whole name. He always called me Lainey. When he called me by my whole name, it was usually because he was upset with me, or frightened, or wanted to get my attention. I decided he was trying to get my attention in this case. Finally, I nodded my head, just a tiny fraction.

"So, do you just want to not ever see me again or what?" I asked in a whisper, feeling my throat closing off on the last word.

Kevin snorted, "No, Lainey, that isn't what I want! That would kill me! I don't want to ever quit seeing you. I have to think of you though and not be selfish," Kevin replied.

"I don't think I can do this," I whispered, as the stupid waterworks began to leak out of my eyes. I knew I shouldn't have worn any makeup.

We sat there for a little while longer, then Kevin declared, "Okay, this is stupid, why are we putting ourselves through so much misery right now?"

I turned around and looked up into the blue eyes that told of summer days on sandy beaches. "What do you mean, Kevin?" I asked a little afraid of his response.

"I mean, why are we making this such a big fucking deal? Why are we being so stupid? Why are we acting like this is the end of the world?" Kevin asked, grinning. I shrugged my shoulder unsure what to say.

"Look Lainey, you know that you can't keep holding on, right?" I nodded my head in agreement. "Okay, then listen, you have to go back to Corpus and begin living down there! Don't write me at all. Don't call me at all. Trust me, it will hurt me worse than you, because even though I never write back, when I come home to find a note from you, I feel like some chick or somethin'! I act all stupid reading it at least a dozen times, just in the first sitting. I smell the envelope to see if it smells like you. I mean, I'm just a spazz, believe it or not." Kevin admitted, with a chuckle.

I looked at Kevin in amazement. I couldn't picture him doing those things. I broke out into a big grin. "I don't want to forget you, Kev," I respond, quietly.

"You silly girl, you won't," Kevin admonished, with a smile on his face. I thought that he was probably appearing a lot more positive and cheerful than he really felt. "You already remembered me for the rest of forever, remember?" Again, he surprised me by remembering the lame thing I'd said to him the first time he ever kissed me, for real.

Trying to laugh, but coming out with little more than a squeak, I nodded my head, as I looked at him. Kevin sat forward on the steel bleacher and bent his head over me, as I looked up at him. "I'm afraid you'll forget me…" I broke off as the sob escaped my throat without me expecting it.

"Oh, Little Lainey! Honey, didn't you realize that I remembered you for the rest of forever too? Remember, I even said it on the corner of Woodbane and Woolery," Kevin reminded me, as he wiped the tears that were streaking down my face. "Baby, I won't ever forget you. You always say I saved you, but you don't understand that it was really you who saved me. I'm not about to forget you!"

Nodding my head, and looking down, I wiped my face once again with the heel of my palm. "I don't know if I can go a whole year without talking to you," I admitted, softly.

"Sure, you can, Lainey! You will because you are going to have the best year yet of high school! You're gonna go back to Corpus and you are going to get involved at school. I don't know what the hell you'll do, but you're gonna do something. You're gonna start making friends at school. You're gonna start living for more than drinking and getting stoned, do you understand?"

I smiled at him, feeling a little shamed. My head bobbed up and down slightly. I sniffled, and Kevin leaned over and kissed the tip of my wet nose.

Then he jumped up and slid down to the bleacher I was sitting on. He pulled me to him and continued telling me how we were going to work out the next year.

I wasn't sure I could do everything he told me to do, but I knew that he'd put some thought into what he was telling me, so I agreed to it. I decided I only had to do it for a year and if things weren't any better by the end of the school year, I could always stick it out until October of my senior year, and if my mama wouldn't let me move up here, then I could move up here on my own by then. I'd be 18 in October of my senior year. By then, Kevin would have graduated and hopefully he'd have an idea what he was going to do. I hoped he'd at least try to go to college for a little while.

When I shared what I'd been thinking about, Kevin got quiet, "Lainey, don't go into it thinking like that, because you won't give it a real chance! I mean it! I want you to really try this year at school. I want you to make some friends who aren't all about getting fucked up and start trying to do some good at school."

As I began to protest, Kevin held up his hands, "Look, I mean besides being a brainiac, and being so damned smart, and all that shit that you already are! I mean, get involved doing something. Stuff that doesn't include getting fucked up! When you come back next summer, you tell me how you are feeling, okay?"

Unwillingly I finally agreed. "What about the rest of the time I'm here?" I asked him meekly.

Kevin seemed to think about that for a long time, then he grinned, "Well, come by and see my mom at least one more time while you're here. If you wanna go see her during the week, while I'm at work, I know it would mean a lot." I agreed again. "I'll try to get with you before you leave for OKC, but if I don't I PROMISE I will come see you before you leave when you come back for those two nights, okay?"

I didn't really like the way he was trying to get out of seeing me, like it wasn't a big deal, even though we both knew that it was a big deal. I knew he was doing it for my benefit though. I tried to remember that he was trying to think of me, so it wouldn't be any harder than it already was before I went back to the Sparkling City by the Sea. I didn't know how in the world I was going to do this. I had promised him I would try. I wouldn't make a promise to Kevin unless I was willing to keep it. I didn't want to keep it, but I knew that this was what he wanted.

We sat there next to each other, on the bleachers, for a few more minutes, as the remainder of the day began to slip down the side of the Earth, leaving us with brilliant streaks of orange, gold, fuchsia and purple. When the deeper purples began to show themselves, Kevin reached out for me. I fell into the curve of his side, where it seemed I fit comfortably.

Glancing up at him, and catching him smiling sweetly down at my face, as the last of the fire in the sun died in the sky, I felt safe and cared for. While our faces were only inches apart, I could see every intimate detail of his face. I noticed the tiny scar by his mouth. I wondered if he could see the scars from my car wreck. I almost laughed at myself, remembering the horrible injuries he'd witnessed when I had the lens from my glasses stuck into my skull. I didn't know why it mattered if he could see the newer scar by my mouth.

While we were almost nose to nose, I realized that Kevin's face was bending down to meet mine. I realized sadly that this might be the last kiss I ever gave him. I hoped not, but I wanted to remember everything about it. I felt the prickly, blond stubble of the beard he hated to shave, as it poked the delicate, soft skin of my tan face. I liked kissing like this, with intent and purpose. I liked being aware of each feeling in it and every nuance. I doubted that Kevin was paying as close attention to it as I was, but I was probably only being silly in the first place. At least this way though, I would have it in my memory banks forever, in excruciating detail.

Kevin's mouth wasn't too soft and squishy, which I liked. It was firm, with just the right amount of softness. I wondered if there would ever be anyone else who could kiss me this way and make me feel like I was the most special woman on the planet. I doubted it, but I had promised him to try this year, so I was going to try, even though I thought it was probably silly to even think about it. I had let my mind wander while I was supposed to be paying attention to every nuance of this kiss.

I wrapped my wrists behind Kevin's neck and let myself fall into him, as if I fell up into the summer sky, instead of down into it. We kissed until the sky was black as velvet once again. I didn't regret any of my time spent with him.

When he walked me back down to Bailey's house, I saw that he'd driven his car up to her house, but when he found out I'd walked up there, he parked his car at the curb and walked the rest of the way up. I guessed this way he could sneak up better on me, to startle me. It made me giggle just thinking about it.

"Sweet dreams, my little Lainey," Kevin whispered, as he held me tightly to him, when he kissed me goodnight."

"'Night, Kev," I replied softly.

"I'll call in the next day or two," Kevin assured me. I hoped he wasn't just saying that.

As I began climbing the steps up to the front door, I turned and stated, "I love you, Kevin. In case something happens, and I don't see you again, I just wanted to tell you that." The boy with the hair made of gold, and eyes that were full of summer skies, and moonlight, smiled at me and nodded his head as he climbed into the black Camaro.

"Back atcha Kid," Kevin responded, in his best "King Kevin" voice. I wanted to growl in frustration. I wished he'd just say it back, but I guessed it was better than him laughing at me. He said it that way because he knew it would irritate me more I guessed. I let myself into Bailey's house grateful that I wasn't exactly sneaking in since it was barely 9:30.

Chapter 55

Bailey had to work more the last week I spent in Wichita Falls. When she wasn't working, we were going to the swimming pool, during the days. Sometimes we spent time with Donny either at her house or his. I only went one time when they went to his house. After that one time, I wiggled out of going again.

It irritated me that she spent every single evening with him, even with me in town. When she had been going with Levi, she never seemed to need to be with him every waking moment. Donny though seemed to demand her attention. Sometimes, I didn't think she really wanted to spend time with him, but she seemed almost afraid to say that to him. She mentioned one evening that she wanted to stay home with just me, and Donny got a stormy look on his face. I wasn't sure exactly what it meant, until Bailey retracted what she said, and changed her mind. Once she did that, his face smoothed back out.

I felt a deep sense of fear for my best friend. I didn't know how to talk to her about it, though. I remembered her temper tantrum the first morning I'd been there, when she just thought that her mom and I were talking about Donny. What would she do if I pointed out to her the control Donny seemed to exert over her?

I went to the Strong's house on Tuesday, while Bailey was at work, and again on Thursday. When I went on Thursday, I talked to Mrs. Strong about my fears about Bailey's relationship with Donny. I felt a little weird at first, because even though she'd always been my personal port in a storm, and had helped me in so many ways, I'd never really just sat down and talked one on one with Jean Strong.

It wasn't that I didn't feel comfortable with her, because I felt loved and cherished every time she saw me. It seemed that all the other times I'd been with her, there was always someone else there also, or I was dealing with some trauma or another. In some ways I felt like we were getting to know one another, for the very first time.

When I finally felt comfortable enough to bring up my best friend and her boyfriend, I was amazed at how easy it was to talk to Kevin's mom. We were as usual in the kitchen, baking. I wondered sometimes why Jean Strong didn't own a bakery. I'd lost 20 pounds before I came to Wichita Falls, and had been so excited by the weight loss. I was worried with all the sweets I was eating at Kevin's house, I would go back to Corpus at least with that 20 pounds back, along with a couple extra as well.

Mrs. Strong asked if I thought that Bailey was being hurt. I stopped sifting flour for a moment to think about that.

I remembered how she'd retracted her statement about wanting to spend time alone with me, when Donny seemed to not like it. In all honesty, I couldn't really say if I thought she was being hurt or not. "I think that she is probably in a bad relationship, DeLaine, but as her friend, sometimes you have to step back and let her make the mistakes she needs to make in life. I know you want to protect her, but you have to remember that you want her to come to you if she needs to, once she's figured it all out."

I looked at Kevin's mom and smiled. It made perfect sense after all. When Bailey thought I was conspiring with her mom, she got so mad. If I insisted Donny was a creep, she wouldn't want to believe it! When she figured it out for herself, if we'd argued about it, she might not feel like she could come to me, if she was upset with me. I didn't know why I didn't think about it myself. I smiled at Jean Strong. She seemed so wise. I felt so warm just being in the kitchen with her. I wished I knew how to thank her for everything she'd ever given to me.

Mrs. Strong seemed to sense that I had other things on my mind besides my best friend. She expertly steered the conversation to my life in Corpus Christi, which I was too embarrassed to tell her about everything that was happening.

I had told her before I moved that it was going to be so much better for me. To say it was just a whole new kind of hell was not something I wanted to admit to her. It wasn't necessarily worse than living with Clarice, because that had been its own brand of hell, as well. It was just different. I felt so lonely since I didn't have Bailey or Kevin there.

Without telling her a lot about my mom's drinking, I was able to tell her enough that she picked up that everything wasn't as great as I had hoped it would be. We worked in silence for a while, then Jean Strong surprised me when she admitted, "DeLaine, you know how much you mean to me, don't you?"

I glanced over at Kevin's mom. I wasn't sure what I should say. She smiled at me and dusted her hands off on her apron. She walked over to the sink, washed them with soap and water, and then dried them as she walked over to the side of the kitchen where I stood mixing dry ingredients into a large bowl. Her warm hand came down softly on my own.

I quit stirring the flour and baking powder and salt that I had been commissioned to mix. I looked at the woman who had adopted Kevin and Donna, when they were two broken little children. She knew what it meant to take two little broken souls and love them back to life. Maybe that is what I felt from her, the ability to mend a broken soul.

"Sweetheart, I want you to know that you have meant so much to me. I love you, much like a daughter. I can't explain why, but since you first came to me, the night that Clarice and your daddy had that big fight, before Clarice ended up in the hospital, I have always felt a strange protectiveness of you. You took the time to love my sweet angel, Donna. She didn't know what it was like to have a best friend. She never got to have a normal life. I knew that she wouldn't when Steve and I adopted her, and Kevin. We knew Kevin would stand a better chance of living normally, if he could overcome his emotional and mental scars, but we knew that we would only have Donna a little while. We took them on knowing that. When you came into our home, and you loved Donna without ever thinking twice about it, well, it made me know that you had an extremely sweet spirit." Mrs. Strong stated all of this, as if she'd rehearsed it. I wondered if she'd wanted to say this to me for a long time.

I bowed my head, because I didn't know what to say. Finally, I choked out, "I loved Donna."

Mrs. Strong smiled at me compassionately, and continued, "Yes, honey, I know you did and I'm so glad you did. You gave my sweet angel girl something that no one was ever able to give to her in her short life. You gave her a sister and a best friend. She always knew that, believe me when I say that. She adored you so much." She continued to smile at me. "Just as much as Donna adored you, is how much her brother adores you still."

I looked at Jean Strong, feeling a little flustered. She continued, "Kevin doesn't give himself to others easily. He doesn't love easily, and I know that he loves you, sweetheart. I know he worries about you, so much. He was always terrified that something bad would happen to you, when you still lived here. He kept Geoffrey close in order to make sure that he didn't hurt you, you know." I couldn't help it when I felt my mouth open, and knew I was openly gaping at her.

"DeLaine, I've never seen my son so twisted up over any other girl like you. I was so glad when he and that awful Lori girl broke up. She wasn't what I wanted for my boy, but I knew that there was something else at play there. I just never knew exactly what it was, and I still don't really. I do have a point in this crazy meandering I'm doing," she began to laugh, a little nervously.

Mrs. Strong went on, "I'm going to just cut to the chase, I guess. I know how much you care about Kevin as well, and it hurts me to see that you two haven't had an easy time of it as far as being able to have a normal relationship. I don't know what the future holds for the both of you, but I know this much…you sometimes have to give up something, in order to find it again. I know that doesn't mean a lot to you right now, because you are young, but I don't want you to live your entire teen years without enjoying them."

"You haven't had much of a childhood, or teen years either. My poor Kevin was never a child. I suppose that is why I turn my head to a lot of his behavior that he's been doing lately. I know he is doing what he feels he needs to, in order to deal with Donna's loss, as well as the loss of you. He feels helpless in not being there for you the way he was able to be, while you lived here. I shouldn't give him so much freedom, I suppose, but last May he turned 18 and I don't have a lot of say-so any longer."

I looked at the woman who Kevin called Mom. I was still trying to figure out what she wanted to tell me.

Finally, she explained, "Sweetie, I want you to go back to Corpus Christi and I want you to try to forget about Kevin for the next school year. I want you to go back and begin life there and get involved with others. Let go for a while and see what happens. If you are meant to be here with us again, you will find your way back. I believe that. I'm not sure when, but you will make it back. So, give yourself the chance to be a kid a little…at least as much as you can. Enjoy yourself. You're going to be 17, in October. That means I've been in love with you for almost four years. As long as my Kevin, and I want you to enjoy these last few years, because you will never get them back. When you are an old woman like me, you realize that those years are so fleeting. It doesn't seem like it when you are living through it, but I promise, you will have many more years being a grown up and worrying about grown up stuff than you will be a kid."

I didn't realize I was looking up at Jean Strong, with my brown eyes wide, and sad as well, as my mouth curved down, until she pulled me to her in the warm hug that made me feel safe.

"Oh honey, I'm not saying quit loving him. You will always love him just as he will always love you, but give yourself this chance, just for this school year. See what happens. You'll be back during the spring, or at the latest next summer. See where you are then. But do this for me. I'm asking because my own baby girl never had the opportunity that you are getting, to be a real teenaged girl. Go to a dance at school. Go to your prom, quit living here and there, and not really living anywhere."

She reached up and I felt her warm hand as it cupped my face. Her thumb wiped some of the tears that had leaked down my cheeks. "I want you to do this for yourself and if you feel you need to do it for anyone else besides you, then do it for Donna. She would want you to only be happy. I know you will remember your way here next summer. Okay?"

Smiling at her with a watery, weak grin, I didn't trust myself to say anything. Jean Strong patted my hand warmly and leaned over to kiss me on my cheek.

"Now with all of that stuff being said, I want you to come over tonight for dinner, if you don't have any other plans. I want you to come and enjoy dinner with us one more time before you have to take off for the summer. I know that Kevin won't ask you because he said that he's trying to let you move on, but I know that you aren't really going to do that until you are gone, so if you can come over, then I'd love to have you. If you have to say you are coming over to keep me happy, then so be it. If you get to spend an evening with Kevin in the process, well, all the better. You need time to say goodbye, I think."

I nodded and she turned and walked to the sink giving me a chance to wipe my cheeks a little more.

As she washed out the bowls that were in the sink she said quietly, "We'll have supper around 6:45 if you can be here by then."

"Okay," I replied softly.

"Do you think you'll be able to come over?"

I smiled at her back, "Yeah, I think it's doable."

"Okay, well, why don't you go ahead and go back to Bailey's right now and come back around 6:30. Kevin will probably be home around 6 o'clock." I nodded my head and took off my apron. I wasn't really sure what it was I was supposed to do. I knew that she was basically dismissing me, but I wasn't upset. I was actually a little curious, not to mention that I was touched by her love. She had said so much to me that I needed to think about and mull over. She kept her back to me as I finished up and left the kitchen with a promise to come back. I didn't notice the tears in her eyes as I left...

As I walked up Granville in the late afternoon heat, I thought about all that Jean Strong had said to me, that afternoon. It was almost as if she'd been inside of our relationship, without me ever realizing it. I wondered how much Kevin had told her. I wondered if he'd told her anything. I wondered if he'd asked her to invite me to dinner. I wondered a lot but didn't have a lot of answers.

***

When I knocked on the door to the Strong's house that evening, Kevin seemed genuinely surprised to see me standing on his front porch. "Hey, Lainey," he said, with a small smile playing at the corners of his mouth.

"Hi," I replied demurely. He ushered me inside and followed me as I walked towards the kitchen and family room.

"Hello, DeLaine!" Kevin's mom hailed, happily.

"Hi," I replied to her as well.

"Kevin, we're going to eat in the dining room tonight," Jean Strong said to her son. I noticed that Kevin looked at his mom oddly. I noticed that Mr. Strong, who was sitting in his big, overstuffed recliner did the same. I wondered why the Strong men were giving her such strange looks, but I didn't have much time to contemplate it. In a whirlwind, we began to get plates and silverware out and Kevin and I were in charge of setting their formal dining room table.

I smiled as I remembered eating my 13th birthday dinner in here, when I began my relationship with Kevin in earnest. It was also the night that they gave me the red, down-filled coat that was still in my closet in Corpus Christi. I didn't have a lot of use for it in South Texas, except maybe one or two days out of the year, but I didn't think I'd ever get rid of it.

During dinner, we all laughed and joked. I looked down at the end of the table, where Donna's wheelchair had sat, during my birthday dinner, so many years ago. It seemed empty down there, but I tried not to look over too often. The laughter though was still there, just as it had been that autumn night, almost four years earlier. I smiled when I looked around the table and realized that I'd been in love with this entire family that long. It was a long time to me to have people in my life.

When we finished dinner, I wasn't shocked when Mrs. Strong shooed me and Kevin out of the house and told us to go take a walk. It was finally beginning to cool off, which was good. The sun had set already, but it was still light outside for a while longer.

I walked in happy silence with Kevin, as we walked down Portland, in the direction we would take to get to the corner of Woodbane and Woolery. I wasn't surprised. I was actually happy to go back to the corner I had been convinced was cursed and haunted because of Kevin.

I smiled as I remembered the first kiss Kevin had ever given me there. It had been so unexpected, and so chaste. He had kissed me there, for real, the night before I turned 13, when we walked over to the corner, while I wore my new red coat, trying it out.

Somehow, I thought it was appropriate that we visit our beginning, if this was to be our end. I found myself getting sad when I thought of it that way. Then I remembered his mom's words from that afternoon; 'you sometimes have to give up something, in order to find it again.' I was able to find my smile once more. Instead of being sad because it felt like everything was drawing to a close, I tried to make myself grateful it had ever happened at all.

I just hoped that by letting go of Kevin, I would have a good year and it wouldn't all be in vain. I didn't want to hold on to the thought of next summer and seeing him again.It was always in the back of my mind, though

. I didn't know how I would go a whole year without writing to him, or calling him. I didn't get to talk to him often during the school year, but it had been enough, the last two school years, to keep the flame burning bright, in order to keep one foot in my life here, instead of putting both feet into a life in Corpus. I hoped that his mom was right. I hoped that I found him again. The thought of losing him forever made my heart literally ache. It wasn't even a stabbing pain, but a deep soul wrenching ache.

While I had been thinking all of that, I didn't realize that we were already upon the corner of Woodbane and Woolery, until Kevin squeezed my hand. He'd caught it in his own without me noticing that either. I looked up, startled, and smiled when I saw the street sign where I'd been standing the first time I'd ever felt Kevin's lips brush mine. It was a great deal colder then, but the fire within me burned even brighter now, than I realized it would ever build up to.

I looked up at the tall, blonde headed boy, who I couldn't imagine not loving for the rest of my life. I basked in his gaze, as he looked at me, memorizing ever angle, line, shadow and curve of my face. He reached up and I felt the very tips of his fingers as they began to trace my cheek over to my lips.

"It was right here, Lainey that I realized I was in a lot of trouble with you," Kevin whispered hoarsely. I smiled up at him. I'd known I was in trouble with him probably before that, but I never thought I stood even a remote chance with him. I'd been such a nobody at that time, in the hierarchy of the junior high social caste system. Kevin had been a ruler in it and I'd been the lowliest of the lowly peasants.

His fingertips tickled and burned both, as he traced each dip and valley of my face, and throat, that they caressed. It was as if they were the wings of a butterfly. Finally, I couldn't stand it any longer. I stood up on my tiptoes, as I reached to claim his mouth, for my own.

I didn't care who saw us. I prayed it was the right choice, and judging by the reaction of Kevin, I'd made the right choice. He responded passionately. I was swept up in the sweet, 18-year-old boy who kissed me.

I remembered what Mrs. Strong said about this time going a lot faster than I could think of it ever going. I realized she was right. I would be a grown up a lot longer than I'd ever be a kid. I tried to remember her advice as I kissed Kevin. I tried to live in that moment, not in the next summer and wondering where either of us might be by then.

When we parted, I stepped back down, flat footed and smiled at him. "I leave on Saturday to go see my daddy. I'll be up there for 10 days. Then he's bringing me back, but I only get to stay here for two more days, and I have to go home, to Corpus."

My thoughts and anxieties spilled from my mouth… "We have to start school before Labor Day this year, which is so stupid since we'll go to school for a week and then we'll have a three day weekend, but whatever. So, it's like the last chance I have to go see him, before school starts. I was kinda hopin' to get out of it, because he just has a little one bedroom apartment. I don't know anything about this new woman he lives with, but he said he wanted to see me, so I'm gonna go."

Kevin smiled thoughtfully, "Well, you know he is your dad, Lainey. He loves you. I know you think he doesn't, because he was with that crazy bitch, but he probably didn't know all the bullshit she was doing to you. I just can't believe he knew everything she was doing. Your dad's a cool guy. I don't think he'd have let her do that shit, to be honest with you."

I looked at Kevin. I wasn't so certain. After all, Clarice told me all the time that she had told my daddy every time she was hitting me with the belt, or grounding me. She even told me that Daddy told her to do it sometimes, and that she had told him that maybe they should make the punishment different. Standing there thinking about it, looking in Kevin's face, it was like I was seeing a light flash in my face. "Do you really think he didn't know?" I asked, softly.

"DeLaine, did you tell him about Geoffrey hitting you?" Kevin asked me. I shook my head and Kevin tilted his, "Well darlin' that should answer your question. No, if you didn't tell him stuff, what makes you think that fuckin' bitch was telling you the truth either?"

"Oh my God, Kevin, I've been so mad at my daddy, for so long!" I breathed out loud.

He pulled me to him and whispered, "I know darlin'… maybe you should give him a little bit of a chance. See what he says while you're visiting him. Talk to him a little. See if he knew about it. You don't have to tell him everything, but ask him about a couple of things. You might be surprised." I nodded my head, as I let him hold me.

I thought about how much I had blamed my own daddy for so much of my heartache at the hands of his second wife. After standing there a few more minutes, Kevin pulled back and assured me, "I'll come see you before you leave, one of those days when you come back, okay?" I nodded my head.

"Kevin, I'm going to tell you goodbye tonight, though," I responded seriously.

He cocked his head to the side, thoughtfully. "What do you mean?"

"I mean...well…I mean, shit, how do I say this?" I stuttered, feeling myself blush and then feeling flustered.

Kevin grinned at me devilishly, "Um, I dunno, I guess you just spit it out, Darlin'! Unless it is somethin' sucky, in which case you don't have to say it at all, 'cause then it will just be a big bummer, and I won't wanna hear it!"

I glanced up at him and grinned, because he had the whole air of his King Kevin smart ass in one simple statement. "I mean, I told Bailey's parents I was spending the night with Kelly White. I can stay out all night. I want to stay out with you all night. It's my last night to stay out with you, for as late as you want. I mean, I'm sure your mom won't let me spend the night, but I'll hang out as late as you think she'll be okay with."

I was surprised when he began to chuckle. I looked at him curiously. He pulled me to him. I loved listening to his chest when he laughed. It was deep, and happy sounding, and vibrated against my cheek and ear. Finally, he pulled me away from him by my shoulders and snickered, "Oh my, little Lainey, darlin' haven't you figured it out yet?" I looked at him and wrinkled my nose and eyebrows up, shaking my head. "My mom would let you live with us, if I asked her! She isn't going to say anything if I tell her you are spending the night!"

"You can't tell her I'm spending the night!" I yelped!

"Why?" Kevin was still giggling.

"Because Kev, I don't want her to know what we're….well, that we might be…well, you know…" I was blushing furiously.

Kevin wrapped his arm around my neck, and pulled me to him, whispering in my ear, "What, Baby? You don't want her to know we're in my room 'doin' it'?"

I swatted his chest feeling embarrassed. Kevin kissed me on my forehead. "Why, Miss Reynolds, you mean to tell me you are going to let me have sex with you?" Kevin mock whispered, as we turned from our corner to begin the walk home.

"I don't know now, Mr. Strong! After you made fun of me like that! I think I might just go back to Bailey's and tell her parents I screwed up on the sleep over, or something!" I teased back.

Kevin growled in my ear, "Fat chance, Lainey! Don't you dare!" I laughed and looked up into his smiling face. He leaned over and kissed me sweetly on my nose. I didn't know how I would be able to let him go for a whole year.

Just before we got to his house, I pulled away from his arm around my shoulders and asked, "Why did you and your dad look so strange when your mom said we were eating in the dining room?"

I saw a shadow flicker across his soft, blue eyes. "We haven't eaten in the dining room since Donna's funeral. We either eat at the breakfast bar, or on TV trays, but we haven't eaten in the dining room at all. Mom won't even clean out her room. She says when it is time, she'll know. She still keeps it dusted and clean, but she won't pack it up. It's hard in a way. I've gone in there a couple of times and it looks like she's at the doctor's office, or at her sleep away camp, or at church, and will be right back. All of her books are still there. All the babies are still there, except for Floppy and DeLaine the Dolphin, of course. I pick up The Velveteen Rabbit sometimes just to hold it, but I can't open it."

His voice became thick with the unshed tears that overcame him as he thought of the book he'd read to his little sister more times than either of us could ever remember.I reached around his waist and hugged him tightly. "I'm sorry, Kev!"

We stopped on the sidewalk, just down the block from his house. He hugged me back. I saw him reach his hand up and swipe at his eyes with his finger quickly, as he shook his head. "It's cool. Really, it's okay, Lainey! She's okay. Donna's okay now. She doesn't hurt anymore. I really believe that. She's finally the angel she was always meant to be. I just miss her a lot. It's hard not having her there to take care of still...but she's...it's cool, really," Kevin squeezed me, and I squeezed back. I wasn't sure what to say so I just let my embrace say what my words couldn't.

That night when we went to bed, I was only mildly embarrassed when Kevin went into the family room, to tell his mom that I was spending the night. I made him wait until his dad had gone to bed, and I wouldn't go out there with him. He laughed at me for being such a chicken.

When he came back in afterwards, he told me that his mom smiled and told him to tell me that she was completely fine with me staying anytime I wanted to. I hid my face behind a pillow and he opened a drawer and pulled out one of his old jerseys and threw it at me. "Here, you might want to put this on for a night shirt. I mean after all, you wouldn't want her to think there was anything inappropriate going on in here!" He broke into a vicious fit of giggles after that.

I threw a pillow at him and got off his bed, walking into the bathroom. I took my clothes off, leaving only my panties on and slipped his old football jersey on.

I was happy to see that it was a lot looser on me than it had been when I'd worn it before. I realized that Kevin still hadn't said one word about the weight I'd lost yet. I wondered if he just hadn't noticed, or if I just hadn't lost as much as I'd thought.

When I walked out, I was surprised to find that Kevin already had the lights off in his room. I looked at the clock and saw that it was only 10:15. "You getting old, Grandpa?" I asked, giggling.

"Some of us have to work for a living, you know?" Kevin yawned, sleepily. I looked a little guilty at him when I realized he had to get up early. It was a weekday after all. Bailey would be going to work the next day, for half of a day too, since it was Friday.

"I'm so sorry, I wasn't even thinking," I replied, guiltily.

Kevin jumped up and grabbed me around the waist and pulled me onto the bed growling, as I squealed! I remembered his dad was already in bed, so I tried to squelch the squeal as much as possible. "Silly girl! I'm a teenage male! I can go on little sleep, remember? I just figured if I have a teenaged girl in my room all night, then I should take advantage of that fact, as much as I possibly can, for as long as I possibly can!" I began to giggle as Kevin kissed me.

I didn't giggle for long. It wasn't very long before Kevin's kisses began burning a fire within my young body, that wasn't the flaming winged Goddess of anger and rage, but the familiar, singing harpy of desire. The fires of desire though burned even hotter than my fires of rage. Before I could even try to tamp them down, I was carried out quickly with the tide of my desire for Kevin. When we had sex this time, the world still didn't shatter, but it didn't hurt any more either. I wondered if I was still just defective even though I still enjoyed everything else about being with a boy, except the actual intercourse part of sex.

I decided that if I had to just endure that part to enjoy the rest of it, then it was a trade-off I was willing to do, for now. I wished I understood why so many others talked about how great it was.

When we were done, we lay together on top of the sheets, as the air conditioner blew cold air to cool the sweat off of our bodies. I was still self-conscious of my body, even though it was Kevin. I wondered if I would ever feel comfortable with my body. I was almost back to my former weight I was, when he met me, of 122 pounds. I still felt horribly fat.

I had put on a lot of weight though, and Kevin had never said anything, so I was surprised when he hadn't said anything about the weight loss either. As we lay there, I finally had to ask. "So, did you notice anything different about me?"

Kevin lay on his back, while I had my head resting on his chest. He stroked my back absently, with his fingertips. I listened to his heartbeat. I heard him grunt, so I asked him the question again. Finally, I could hear the boom of his voice as he asked, "Was I supposed to?" I sighed loudly. I listened as he chuckled. It sounded like a loud boom, deep in his chest, where my ear was listening. Finally, he pulled back a bit and looked down at me. It forced me to look up at him. He continued to stroke my back with his fingers. "Lainey, if you mean did I notice you lost weight since you were here last time, yes, I noticed, but I don't care what you weigh. I don't care what you look like. You're my Lainey. That's enough for me."

I snorted and he looked at me in shock. "If I gained a hundred pounds you wouldn't be saying that!"

"Well, you didn't gain a hundred pounds, did you?" Kevin replied.

"No, but what if I did?" I insisted.

Kevin sighed. "Lainey, you didn't, so what does it matter?"

"It matters! What if I had?" I persisted.

"You'd still be DeLaine, so it wouldn't be a big deal. Would you still love me if I lost all my teeth?" Kevin asked me, looking into my eyes.

I looked back at him, only able to see him in the shadows of the light from the bathroom, in the darkened room. "Well, yeah, of course I would. I love you for you. Not your teeth!"

"Then, I guess I'd love you for you and not for you being fat! So if you were fat then I'd just have extra to love, huh?" He said in his smart-assed tone.

"But I have been fat," I whispered, a little fearfully.

"Oh Jesus, DeLaine! You have NOT been fat! Give me a break, Darlin'! What the hell are you talkin' about?" Kevin asked me.

"Well you noticed I'd gained weight. So, I obviously was heavier," I reasoned.

Kevin ran his hand through his blond hair. "Oh my God! Are all chicks crazy?"

I sat up on my elbow. "I'm not crazy! I'm just, well, I've been working really hard this summer to lose the extra weight I gained. You never said anything, so I was just wondering why you never said anything," I replied, petulantly.

"Honey, of course I noticed you'd put on a little more weight, but it didn't matter to me. I didn't give a shit! You can put it back on if you want. I don't care. If you don't feel good with it though, then don't do it. You have to feel good. If you feel bad, then you need to lose it. You look good to me both ways. Of course, I noticed it, both ways!" Kevin explained, exasperated.

He leaned over and kissed me sweetly on the mouth and then commanded, "Get Clarice out of your head. That skinny bitch had no shape! Quit listening to that crazy bitch! Get her out of your head and remember that she doesn't have anything to do with you anymore. You are beautiful, DeLaine. You always have been. It is time for you to believe it."

I glanced down from Kevin's gaze, after his last sentence. How was I supposed to believe these things, without him to remind me? I sighed. I pulled myself up along his long lean form, until my face was up beside his. He leaned over and began to kiss me softly. I returned his kisses a bit more ardently, after only a few minutes, until I was the aggressor in our next round of intimacy, which was a change for us.

After a long time of kissing each other deeply, I began to trail kisses along his jawline. I pulled myself up and threw my leg over him until I was straddling him and placed my hands on either side of his head on the pillow his head was resting on. I kept kissing the stubbly jaws, and then after I was over him I was able to angle myself into a better position to kiss him just under his jaw line in the tender, sweet area between his neck and his jaw. Kevin gasped when I placed my mouth there, in the beginning.

I wasn't really sure what I was doing, but I decided to do everything I'd ever learned from anyone else, and whatever else my body told me to do. This would be my goodbye to Kevin. I may never really have another chance to be with him again. He said he would come see me, while I was here the last two days, but who knew if he would or what that might mean.

I continued down the side of his neck until I was rounding the front of his throat. He reached up and clasped my hands in his, while I sat on top of him. I leaned against his hands as I kissed him softly, tasting his skin with each kiss. When I got to the sweet spot of his clavicle bone, I heard him breathe in sharply. I could feel as he began to respond to my kisses. He pushed me up, using his hands that were clasping mine. I looked down into his face longingly. For the first time in my life, I felt sexy and desirable. I also felt this undeniable urge that I couldn't explain in every square inch of my body. I wanted and needed to be touched and tasted, as well to touch and taste too.

Whispering in the dark, Kevin breathed, raggedly, "C'mere Lainey," and I leaned my face down to his. We kissed with a heat and passion that I didn't recognize. It felt somehow new and different. We'd been intimate with each other. We'd had sex, but for some reason this felt adult in its passion. It wasn't two kids trying to figure it out. This was more about knowing one another's bodies. I felt like I was right on the edge of knowing what sex was finally all about.

Kevin's mouth felt as if it was going to consume me hungrily. I was meeting it with the same hunger as well. We continued to clasp one another's hands. I felt as our grip intensified as well. Suddenly, he let go of my hands, and grabbed my hips, sliding me down until I was sitting on top of all of him. I wasn't sure how this worked, because I'd never done anything except with me on the bottom.

I didn't have to worry. Kevin reached between us and before I knew what was happening I felt him move his hand between us and suddenly I felt him place himself gently in me. I knew he wasn't all the way inside of me and I wasn't sure what I was supposed to do. Once he had me positioned, he gently pulled me down on top of him. When he did that, I let out a gasp. I could feel every bit of him inside of me. I could also watch his face, but it also gave me a lot more control as far as how much, how far, and how fast. I was surprised at all of it. He smiled at me.

I must have looked completely freaked out because he reached up and traced the outline of my cheek and reassured me, "It's okay, Lainey. If it hurts, we can stop." I shook my head and we continued. He showed me what to do and as we continued, I began to feel a strange feeling deep inside of me.

As Kevin moved my hips up and down, gently along him, and I began to figure out how to do the job more myself, I began to feel a mounting pressure deep inside of me. At first I wasn't really sure what it was. I thought I had to pee really bad, which made no sense since I was right in the middle of having sex!

I'd never had that feeling before, then before I knew it, I realized it wasn't the need to pee, but something even bigger. Something that I'd never felt before. It was a feeling that made me think that my head was going to completely pop off of my shoulders. I remembered what it felt like the first time Kevin had ever felt me, when we were in the living room of our house on Belfast. The exquisite feelings I'd had as his fingers had explored the folds of my deepest places that he was discovering again, only in a different way this time.

Soon, I was managing the speed of the movement I made on top of Kevin. The more I controlled it, the more I could feel the difference in what I felt. It seemed the slower I went, the more I felt it. It also seemed the more it drove him crazy too, which made me smile too. He was holding my hands again, because I'd figured out how to manage it by myself, without his help. I would lean over and kiss him every once in a while, but there were a lot of times I would just look at his face. A lot of the time he kept his eyes closed, which was a good way for me to watch him privately.

Kevin's breathing began to sound a little labored and ragged, "DeLaine, you're killin' me babe, you gotta finish this!" I looked at him uncertain what he meant. I felt like such an idiot.

He looked at me and smiled. Reaching out he placed his hands on my hips again and began to move me steadily, a little faster until the warm feeling inside of me intensified. Just as I thought I couldn't stand it anymore, and my head truly was going to pop off, I felt a huge release between my legs. It wasn't anything I had ever felt before. I felt myself suddenly growing even more slick between my legs. I felt embarrassed, because I was convinced I must have surely peed myself, like I thought I was going to do earlier. I felt myself let out a surprised "OH!" and a huge intake of air, as I grabbed the pillow case with both hands, on either side of Kevin's head. I could feel my eyes roll up in my head. I threw my head back briefly, as my body suddenly stiffened, unintentionally.

Suddenly, I collapsed on top of Kevin, and was breathing as if I had just run a marathon. I lay there wondering what in the world had just happened. I felt myself shuddering throughout my entire body. My head was turned to the side and I was taking in huge, gulping, gasping, mouthfuls of air. I felt Kevin's arms encircle my body. After a few minutes, when I felt my body quiet down, Kevin asked "Are you okay?"

I nodded my head, because I wasn't really sure if I could answer him, or not. Kevin didn't say anything for a while and then he asked, "Lainey, was that your first…did you just…um, well, have you ever had a…" Kevin trailed off.

I wasn't really sure what he was trying to ask me. I was too freaked out from what my body had just done to really answer him. Finally, quietly, after taking a deep breath Kevin asked, "DeLaine, did you just have your first orgasm?"

I sat up quickly and exclaimed, "What?"

Laughing, Kevin inquired, "Did you just come?"

I felt so embarrassed, I didn't even know how to respond. I knew what it was for a boy to do it, but I never really understood what it was for a girl to do it. I had heard about it, but I felt like such a dumbass. I was too embarrassed to admit that I didn't have a clue. No wonder I hadn't understood what the big deal was about sex. Finally, I started giggling, looking at Kevin and nodded my head. He grinned at me, "Really? I was your first?" I looked at him and cocked my head to the side.

"Really, Sparky?" I demanded, sarcastically.

Kevin started laughing, "Okay, okay! You got me!" He reached up and placed his hands on my face and pulled me down to kiss me soundly on the mouth. "Well, what did you think about it, Lainey?"

"WOW!" I was smiling big. "I guess I can say, I get it now!" I began to giggle, quietly.

Kevin remarked. "Well, it explains why you never seemed too enthusiastic when we did it before. I just thought I sucked!"

"I couldn't figure out what all the fuss was about!" I admitted, a bit sheepishly.

"So is it worth all the fuss?" Kevin asked me, with a wolfish grin.

Laughing I said, "Hell yes!"

"Ready again?" Kevin asked.

Shaking my head I admitted, "Um, Yeah, that would be a big NO! But…wow! Did I saw WOW? I mean because that was definitely a BIG, HUGE WOW!"

Kevin laughed and kissed me again. After a few minutes, Kevin eased me on to his bed and suggested, quietly, "Not to be gross, but you'll probably want to go into the bathroom and clean up." I looked at him a little perplexed. "Trust me on this one." I shrugged and got up, barely making it into his bathroom before I understood what he was telling me. Once I came out, he got up and made his way into his bathroom. I assumed he cleaned up too. I wasn't too sure what it meant for a boy to clean up, but now that I knew what it was to have an orgasm, I was a pretty happy camper. I couldn't believe how exhausted I suddenly felt. I was excited to crawl into bed and curl up beside Kevin, dressed in his football jersey, and fall fast asleep.

Chapter 56

The next morning, just as dawn was making its way across the sky, the weak, gray light, of the morning, began to brighten Kevin's room. I opened my eyes and was surprised to find myself wide awake. I lay there for a few minutes, just looking at the wall and the windows that looked out onto the side yard, and the next-door neighbor's home. I listened for Kevin's breathing. When I heard the steady sound of air coming in and out of his nose, I listened as if I was trying to memorize everything about him. I wasn't certain why I woke up, since it was so early, and we hadn't gone to sleep until really late the night before.

I didn't want to wake him up, but I wanted to look at him. His arm was draped around my arm and chest. Finally, I slowly began to shift in the bed. I kept his arm across me, as I gently rolled onto my back and then to my right side. He had his left hand cupping his face on his pillow and his face was the most peaceful I'd ever seen before. I'd watched him sleep before. We'd slept beside one another several times before. He had slept beside me at my house, countless times, with Geoffrey right there. Then I'd slept here, with him, during Donna's funeral. Watching him this time, though, felt different. I wasn't sure why, but I wanted to drink in every tiny nuance of him, that I could.

His hair was messy and all over the place. Lying here looking at him in the gray, blue light of the dawn, it looked more like spun, gold thread. I was reminded of the first time I'd ever seen him asleep, on the couch, at our house, when he'd spent the night at our government trailer we had to live in after the tornado. I had to go out to sort bricks, as a punishment, by my step-mother. As I was going outside, I had turned for some reason, that I could no longer remember, but I still remembered how Kevin looked, with the morning sun trying to break through the metal slats of the venetian blinds.

A couple of rays of sun had broken through, and it looked like beams of sunlight created a gilded halo, of gold silk thread, on his head. I remember thinking when I saw him that morning how beautiful he was. I couldn't understand why he was best friends with my step-brother. They were so different. Of course, Kevin was so different back then too. He was "King Kevin" and I was just Duh-Lame DeLaine.

Here I was, almost four years later, looking at the same boy who was actually now a young man. He'd gotten a little taller, which was crazy, because he'd been tall back then. His shoulders were broader. He had already lived a lot more than most people his age.

We were so much the same, and yet we were lifetimes different too. I smiled as I looked at this beautiful boy, who I'd probably fallen in love with when I'd seen him in the morning sunlight, on that crappy couch, in that tiny, tin can trailer.

I couldn't imagine adoring anyone else as much as I adored him. I drank in his face, from the curls of his blonde hair, to the almost invisible, blonde eyelashes. I looked at the sharp cheekbones and the slight upturn of his nose. His mouth was almost a bow as he slept. I grinned as I thought about that. If I described to him what I saw when he slept, he'd take great offense, I was sure. As if he were reading my thoughts, in his sleep, I noticed his beautiful blue eyes begin to flutter open. I wondered quickly if I should pretend to be asleep, but I thought that was pretty stupid. I wanted every possible second I could get with him. Our time together was almost to a close. I couldn't believe I was going to go through with this, but I was the one who had decided it in the first place.

After a couple of false starts at opening, Kevin's eyes finally fluttered open for good. When they were focused, he looked over to me, finding my brown eyes looking intently at him. Even just waking up, he could turn on his sunshine and rainbow smile, which could melt my heart. I smiled back. "G'mornin' Sweet Lainey," Kevin groaned, sleepily.

"Wow, what a sweet good morning that was," I whispered back to him. I hoped I didn't have horrible breath. I thought about that as soon as I spoke to him. Then I decided that it was Kevin. He didn't care about how fat I was, I was sure he didn't care if I needed to brush my teeth either.

"What time is it?" Kevin asked me. I rose up and looked at the digital clock on his night stand. When I told him it was 6 in the morning he rolled his eyes, and told me he still had another hour to sleep.

"So, go back to sleep," I whispered, quietly.

Kevin looked at me and then he arched one of his blonde eyebrows. "Really, Lainey? You'll just watch me for an hour." I grinned at him.

"I've got a better idea," Kevin said pulling me a little closer to him. The bed was warm under the covers and his firm, young body felt good beside me. I wrapped my arms tighter around his middle, pulling myself to him. I realized he was more than a little interested in something else than sleeping. I felt him begin to nuzzle my neck and before I knew what was happening Kevin began to kiss me with as much passion as he had the night before.

Gone were any worries about morning breath, because I was too caught up with my own singing urges of my body.

When he entered me that morning I was once again on the bottom, but this time felt different. It seemed as if I knew what it was my body was supposed to do to achieve, or at least to try to achieve what it had the night before.

It was like my hips had figured out what it was they were supposed to do and just before Kevin was done, I felt my own eyes roll up in my head and my body stiffened again. I held my breath for what seemed forever. When we lay there quietly, afterwards, basking in the morning, and the changing of the light as the sun began to rise in the sky, I didn't know if I could ever feel happier in my entire life.

I was shocked when Kevin urged me, "Come take a shower with me."

"What?" I was surprised.

"C'mon Lainey! I need to get ready for work. You need to take a shower. I mean we got a little hot and sweaty!" Kevin was chuckling.

I wasn't sure. I knew that Kevin didn't care what I looked like, but I was still uncertain about letting him see me completely in broad daylight. It was one thing in shadowed light, as opposed to the morning light, with the lights on, in the shower, where he could see every tiny bit of my body. He'd be able to see every tiny bit of fat on me. I knew my belly was soft, not hard and taut, like all the skinny girls. Then there was my thighs and butt. After all, Clarice had taken me to a women's gym and there was a lady there who told her I already had something called cellulite which was something that only fat people had apparently, and it was all over my thighs and butt. What would Kevin think when he saw all of that. He'd probably think I was disgusting.

"I dunno, Kev, I mean, you probably need to get ready for work, and I'm just gonna get in the way, probably. You probably should just take a shower and get ready for work and I'll take one after you." I replied weakly.

Kevin looked at me as if he knew exactly why I wouldn't go in the shower with him. Suddenly, he pulled the covers off of us. I was lying beside him, completely exposed. Not only was I suddenly cold, but I felt horribly embarrassed by being so exposed, in the daylight. "DeLaine! Look at your body!"

I looked at him, feeling a cross between anger and mortification. Finally, I looked down quickly, then I looked back at him.

"No, I mean it, look, dammit! You know why?"

I shook my head.

"Because I want you to see what I see. I want you to see the beautiful, soft skin that is like porcelain. I know you have a tan right now, but you don't keep a tan very long. I know you hate your skin because you think you're so white, but I think it is beautiful and looks like some of those pretty dolls Donna has in her room in those doll cases. Those expensive ones that are so pretty. I see a cute, little, inny belly button, and this beautiful body that turns me on so much. I don't see anything at all wrong with it. I wish you could see yourself the way I do," he said.

"Kevin, how can you not see the fat and the cellulite?" I asked, timidly.

Rolling his eyes, Kevin admitted, "Oh shit, I'm not even sure if I know what the hell cellulite is, but trust me, if you have it, I don't see it or notice it." Kevin ran his hand along my stomach and made me shiver. "This is a beautiful stomach. I love this stomach. It's smooth. The skin is soft and smooth, and shit, it feels good under my hands." Then he ran his hands down my legs from the top of my thighs to my knees, "These legs, these thighs, oh my lord, DeLaine, do you know what thinking about them does to me? They are so sexy and beautiful. Especially when I see them walking down Granville in shorts. And let's not even discuss the calves under those thighs. Sweetie, you have to know how pretty you are. If you don't, I can't make you, all I can do is tell you. The rest is up to you to realize."

I looked at the blue eyes that I loved so much and trusted my life with. Slowly I stood up, "Let's take a shower." I loved the smile that crossed Kevin's features as he jumped up. We hurried into the bathroom to shower and clean up after our morning of pleasing each other, reveling in our young bodies.

After our shower, Kevin put on blue jeans and the gray and black, button down, service station attendant shirt he wore at the garage he worked at. Watching him made me wonder what his plans were for after school. "So, are you still dead set against going to college?" I asked with a smile.

Kevin didn't look up at me. He fiddled with the buttons on his shirt. I wasn't sure why he wouldn't talk to me. I repeated it, wondering if he just hadn't heard me, but he continued to fiddle with buttons that were obviously done up. "What the hell is wrong with you?" I asked him, testily.

"I quit school, DeLaine," Kevin said matter of factly.

"YOU WHAT?" I was shocked. "WHEN?"

"At the end of the school year. I wasn't doing that great. If I didn't go to summer school, I was going to have to do a few of the junior classes again. I'm already gonna be 19 when I graduate, since I got held back a grade. I don't wanna be 20 years old and graduating high school! I'll go get my damned GED! Besides, I need to start working. I'm not cut out for school. You know that! I'm not playing football anymore, so there's not any reason to keep messin' with that shit." Kevin explained, quietly.

I looked at him feeling completely flabbergasted. "Kevin why didn't you tell me, when I got here?" I finally asked him.

Shaking his head, he explained, "Jesus, Lainey, it isn't like we exactly got off to the best of starts, when you got here, did we? I mean, I dunno, why. It just didn't come up until now. I didn't want you to think that I was going back to school. I'm 18 now. It's time to start living and get going with life. I'm not into all that senior class bullshit."

I wasn't sure what I was supposed to say. "So, should I just quit school when I turn 18, so I can move back up here?"

"Jesus Christ, DeLaine! Don't be stupid! You have a fucking future! I don't! What about that are you not getting? You are smart! You have a fucking brain! You are going to go to college, get a real job, and get married and have kids! Dammit!" Kevin turned around and began to shake his head.

I sat on his bed, looking at him, feeling stricken. I couldn't figure out what had happened to our blissfully beautiful morning. "I'm sorry," I muttered, softly.

"No, Lainey, I'm sorry! I just want you to understand that there is a huge difference in me quitting school, and you quitting. YOU should graduate! I'm not going to be anything except some grease monkey, or factory guy. You have a shot at being something or somebody! You're smart, honey! I don't want you to throw that away! Stay in school, please!" Kevin pleaded.

I looked at him sadly and nodded my head. I wanted Kevin to be so much more. I believed in him, that he could be, but he didn't believe it. I realized for someone who could help others see their potential, he had a hard time seeing his own. I felt sad for him.

"I'll stay in school, don't worry. I love school too much to quit, Kev. I really want to be a teacher." I finished quietly.

"See, there you go. You'll have to go to college to do that, Lainey. So, you have to finish school! I believe you'll do it too!" Kevin was smiling, finally, at me. "I'm sorry. I guess I should have said something before now, there wasn't ever a time or place to say something.

He said, "Every time I thought about it, you were already gone. I didn't even know how to tell you. I asked Mom not to tell you, so don't be upset with her either."

I had never thought about being upset with his mom. "I'm not. I guess I'm just shocked, that's all. I had hoped you'd graduate from high school. I also wish you could see yourself the way I see you. You are so much more than a grease monkey!"

Kevin grinned at me, "So, the student becomes the teacher. You have done well, young Grasshopper!" I threw a pillow at him! He walked over to the bed and sat down beside me.

"Seriously, I know you believe there is more to me but I don't think there is, Darlin'. At least not as far as a job goes. I'm pretty much what you see is what you get. Speakin' of, I gotta get goin' or I'm gonna be late for work. I really am glad you spent the night, Lainey. It meant so much to me. I hate to rush off, and say bye, but that's the way it seems this is coming down to," Kevin said.

"I'll come by and see you before you get on the bus back to Corpus Christi though, I promise! I gotta go. Thanks for….thanks for letting me be the first for something else in your life." Kevin chuckled, with a devilish grin on his face. I smiled back.

There was so much I wanted to say and yet I'd already said it all before. How was I supposed to leave and start a life and forget all about him and pretend he didn't exist? "I'm gonna miss you, Kev!"

Kevin smiled at me, as he lightly traced the curve of my face with his fingertips. "Shhh, you'll be back next summer. Go do something while you're a junior, and find a boyfriend, for Chrissakes. And make some friends and quit partying so damned much! And be careful, Lainey. Study hard and just remember that you are beautiful. You are sexy, funny and beautiful. Do whatever you would do if I didn't exist. Live in Corpus this year, and forget about Wichita, at least for one school year, and see what happens. You might be surprised. If not, well, you can always come back after you graduate and try to get a scholarship to MSU. 'Til then…just try, okay?" I nodded my head and tried hard to keep from crying. I didn't want our last few minutes to be me crying.

Reaching over I pulled Kevin to me and hugged him tightly. I squeezed my eyes tightly to keep the tears inside and swallowed hard to keep myself in check. Finally, I assured him, softly, "I promise, I'm going to try, this year, Kev! I'm not sure how, but I'm going to try. I can't ever forget you, though. You are too much a part of who I am, you know. You were my first for too much."

I knew that the damned tears were slipping out already. I grinned weakly at him, trying to reassure him that I was going to be strong, but no matter what he said, he was always going to be a part of me.

"I know, Lainey. I know." Kevin whispered softly, as he caressed my cheek and wiped the tears off each one. "Gotta go, darlin'. Be safe." He leaned over and kissed me softly on the lips, jumped up, grabbed his car keys off his dresser and was gone before I knew what had really happened.

"I love you…" I whispered as the door closed. I wished he would tell me first, just once. He'd said it a few times before, but not in a really long time. He told me he loved my body. He would say things like he would love me if I gained 100 pounds, but he wouldn't just say the three words I craved from him. It was as if those three words were something that terrified him. I sighed.

I wondered if his mom was awake. I wondered if she'd be waiting on me to come out. I decided that I better go and find out.

I had changed into my clothes, after we'd showered, so I was ready to go when he left. I closed the door quietly.

I noticed the whole house seemed to be darkened still, and when I got to the end of the hall, I saw that the kitchen and family room were both dark. I just had to slip out of the front door and walk to Bailey's.

Just as I put my foot onto the tile in the hall that led to the front door something pushed me to turn around. I looked at Donna's closed door. I wondered if I could go in there, without getting caught. I didn't want to pry, but after hearing Kevin tell me about how it was frozen in time, I was curious. I turned around and promised myself, I would just go in quickly, then slip out. Hopefully I could do it without getting caught by Jean Strong.

I quietly turned the brass door knob. I hoped the door didn't creak and breathed a sigh of relief when it didn't. I didn't need to open it all the way, but just enough to slip inside. Seeing the room in the daylight was even more of a shock, than seeing it in the dark, as I'd done before. Just like Kevin had said, it looked like she was at the doctor's office or at church.

I smiled when I saw the sweet, little girl, pink paint on the walls. The spines of the books that I'd read countless times were all visible in the light. I walked over to the bookcase and touched The Velveteen Rabbit. I felt a silent sob escape when I did. I was surprised by it. It felt like someone had punched me in the throat. I grabbed my neck with my other hand, but never lost contact with the book on the bookshelf, that had been Donna's favorite.

I looked at the doll cases that sat on the top of the bookshelf. Inside them were two porcelain dolls that I didn't remember her having before. I was surprised, but figured I must have just missed them, for some reason. Maybe she'd gotten them while I'd been gone and I didn't know it. She had one that was fair in coloring and had long, wavy, dark brown hair. She had gorgeous blue eyes that shone brightly and almost lifelike. She was one of the prettiest porcelain dolls I'd ever seen. I marveled at how beautiful her gauzy dress was. She seemed almost ethereal. I wondered if Kevin and I had a daughter if she'd be as beautiful as that doll. I smiled when I thought about that.

I knew that if we had a child, my ugly brown eyes would probably be the more dominant coloring, but I hoped that his blue eyes would kick my brown eyes' butt when it came to procreating our kids! I giggled a little, when I thought about it.

While thinking about our kids, I looked at the other doll and was surprised at how much it actually reminded me of Donna. It had a heart shaped face and the same color of blue eyes that she and Kevin had. Its hair was long, wavy and looked like spun gold. I shook my head. I decided I'd stayed in the room long enough, and really needed to leave.

I felt like an intruder in someone's grief. This was Jean Strong's private place, right now, to come and remember the little girl who she'd adored for many years.

I missed Donna and grieved for her, too but… this wasn't my place to grieve for her.

I slipped back through into the hallway, and pulled the door closed. I hurried on out of the house undetected. I breathed a huge sigh of relief once I was on Granville. I thought about Donna's room and wondered why I'd felt the urge to go inside. I chalked it up to Kevin mentioning my skin looking like the porcelain dolls in the book case, and not remembering them. I thought that subconsciously I must have wanted to see them.

I walked in the early morning sunshine, up the street that I'd walked to school in 7th grade with Kevin and Bailey. I thought of all the mornings I'd walked with him.

I remembered all the insane and bad mornings (which there seemed to have been a ton of them) but I was also remembering all the really funny mornings too. I smiled at those memories. I knew that there was a part of me and my life that was actually ending.

I didn't feel like forever was happening for some reason. I had lived so much of my life afraid of forever, and all the ramifications of it, that I just couldn't think like that about this.

I knew without a doubt that Kevin would always be a part of my life. How could he not? I couldn't imagine my life where Kevin wasn't a part of it, ever. He felt like he'd been in it forever already, and that he would remain in it always.

This would seem like a crazy bump in the road, just like 8th grade, when I had dated Jax Garrett. I never cheated on Jax, even though I'd let Kevin in my room, a few times in the middle of the night, but I'd never done anything with him. It wasn't until Jax and I broke up that we had gone back to messing around. Jax thought that we had a thing going on. That's why we broke up before we had to, since we were moving to Oklahoma City. It had given me the chance to fall even more in love with Kevin. I shook my head as I remembered how broken hearted I'd been when Jax had broken up with me. It was amazing how life changed so much since those days, in 8th grade. I smiled as I thought of them, thinking how they'd been some of the best days of my life.

The sun was already beating out hot and it was barely 8:30. I was glad we were going to the pool one more day. I giggled as I walked, because I had a lot to share with my best friend. I wondered if she understood what the big deal was about sex.

I laughed even harder because I knew she must. She'd been active much longer than me. She was the one who had to explain some of it to me. I shook my head as I thought about some of the crazy conversations I'd drug poor Bailey into. Her house came into view. I smiled as I hurried up the sidewalk, towards the red brick house with the aqua, blue trim. I was amazed at how much energy I actually had, but I was happy to have it, no matter what the reason for it was.

Chapter 57

I left that Saturday with my Daddy to go to his small, one-bedroom duplex that he shared with the woman he was seeing now. They actually had gotten together a few months before, after their high school reunion. When they met again, at the reunion, they were both divorced, and things just seemed to click for them. He told me that he thought I'd really like her, but then again he thought that I loved Clarice, too. I tried to be hopeful on the drive to Oklahoma City, but I wasn't so certain about it all.

When we got to his place, I was shocked when Lena Ball came walking out the door. She looked so much like my mom, I had to do a little bit of a double take. She was short and petite, although her butt was a little bigger than my mom's, but they both had short black hair and olive skin tones. I climbed out of my daddy's van. She walked up to me, carrying a tiny, tan Chihuahua and I almost burst out laughing. Mama had once owned a Chihuahua that Daddy had given her as a gift. I managed to stifle the giggle and smiled at her genuinely. Lena came up and wrapped her free arm around my neck, taking me by surprise, "Hi sweetheart! I hug, so you'll probably have to get used to that, but I've been so excited to meet you!"

I pulled away from her embrace, smiling and was a little surprised, but happy that she seemed warm and genuine. There was a little part of my brain screaming that Clarice had seemed wonderful too, when I first met her, but I shut it down quickly. I reasoned that I'd just been a little kid and so sad about my parents' divorce. Clarice had known just the right things to say. I was now almost 17 years old and had lived through quite a bit. I figured I was a much better judge of character now, than I'd been as a little kid.

Daddy was busy getting my suitcase out of the back of the van. He passed by us and smiled at me. He knew this was hard for me. He knew a little bit about the things that I'd put up with Clarice, but by no means did he know the majority of it. I for some reason didn't want him to. I felt the need to shield him from the horrors I'd lived with, while he'd been married to her. I felt both angry at him, thinking he knew about most of them, and at the same time I wanted to shield him from them, if he didn't. Lena was chatting happily with me and introducing me to her little Chihuahua, Josie.

Honestly, I was trying not to laugh at the fact that Lena had Josie in the first place, because Daddy detested animals. Along with kids, animals figured pretty low on his list of favorite things. The fact that he gave my mom a Chihuahua, when they were dating, told me how much he loved her.

They had that dog my entire life until my mom had to have her put to sleep, soon after taking me back to Wichita Falls before I turned 13. Her name had been Tandy and I'd loved her like crazy. Seeing this little dog made me remember ours, and also made me look at Lena again. It was a little weird how much she looked like my mom. I wondered if my daddy realized it.

Lena showed me where to put my stuff. Even though I had a suitcase, it actually was Bailey's, because I didn't want to lug my huge suitcase that I normally used to go back and forth to Corpus and Wichita Falls. I left a lot of my stuff at Bailey's, so I wouldn't have to move everything back and forth. I was going to have to sleep on the couch, which I knew, since they only had a one bedroom.

In a whirlwind, Daddy rushed Lena and me, so he could take us out on the town, to show me where he was working. Also we were getting something to eat for dinner. He'd gotten to Bailey's around lunch time, but he didn't stop for us to eat. I was actually starving. He drove us to a small club that he was the manager of, and on weekend nights he played music there also. He took me in and showed me the whole place. I walked around trying to appear interested, but it looked like all the millions of bars I'd been in during my lifetime. It held little interest to me.

I tried to stifle the smile that came as I thought about how many other 16-year olds I knew, who probably dreamed about getting to go inside of a bar. It was so old to me, that it actually bored me to tears, if truth be told. I'd been in bars as my parents had traveled as musicians and then both of them being bartenders later on, just made it harder for me to get too excited when I walked into one. I knew that Daddy's true passion lay in the bandstand and the instruments and music he was playing. I wished I understood the excitement he had over music. Since I was so completely lacking in any type of musical abilities, it was just a foreign concept to me. I didn't understand the passion he had for it, but wished I did.

One of the guys in his band came in while we were there, and he introduced me. He was a big, bearded dude, who wore shades and Fedora hat, made of straw. He had a lot of long curly hair and Daddy said his name was "Animal".

I laughed and then Animal told me his real name. For some reason, I never remembered it.

The nickname that my daddy gave him, stuck in my head. They talked about rehearsal times and then we left to go eat.

Most of my time during my stay with my daddy was spent this way. Lena had to work during the weekdays, and Daddy slept late, since he didn't get home from the bar until about 4 a.m.

The first night I was there, we'd gone and listened to Daddy play music, with his band. I loved hearing my daddy play. He was a true entertainer and he truly loved doing it. I knew that he must have missed it very much when he'd been with Clarice and was trying to have a normal family life, even if it meant working a job where he was always traveling.

I felt a little sad thinking about it. I knew that if he'd been playing music, he'd have been gone a lot too, so it didn't really matter what he'd been doing during that time. I realized it wasn't my fault he had quit playing music for those years. I felt sad though, that he had tried to do something for someone else, only to have it all explode. I found myself close to tears while listening to him play "Summertime."

I found I liked Lena, a lot. She had a quirky sense of humor, and she listened to me. She wasn't trying to get me to like her, by trying too hard, which I liked.

Josie the dog seemed to like me, even though she was an older dog. She would sit on the couch beside me, during the day, when Daddy was asleep and I read my book. They didn't have a TV in the living room, which made it a little boring during the hours I had to occupy my time by myself. I was happy I'd brought one book. When I finished it, I was thankful Daddy and Lena both liked to read, because I read two of their books also. I also went for walks in the mornings, so I could smoke while Daddy slept. Thankfully, Lena smoked, too so if there was smoke smell on my clothes, no one noticed, unlike at Bailey's. I'd been mortified to learn that Bailey's mom had told her she knew I was smoking! Of course, Jason smoked too, so she couldn't say for sure, but she'd voiced her concerns and suspicions.

Lena came home every day at 4:30. We would all eat dinner together before Daddy left to go to the club. He never had a real day off, unless he took one. He spent a little bit of time with me each day, but it wasn't like I was a little kid, and he needed to take me to Disney World, or anything. There weren't going to ever be any visits to the Zoo, or a pool, but we did go see a movie one afternoon, which was nice. For the most part, my visit with my daddy was fairly inconsequential.

I had worried about seeing Clarice. When I mentioned it, Daddy said that she had moved back to Wichita Falls. That set me off into a whole new worry about her harassing me, when I was in Wichita Falls.

Daddy told me that everything was over. She wasn't going to bother me or my mom again. He told me that I'd never have to see her again.

I asked him about Geoffrey and William. He told me he didn't know, but he thought they'd left with her too.

I thought briefly about Lisa. She'd been an innocent in all of it. She'd never been anything except a little sister. I'd thought of her as a bratty, little kid, but now that I was 16, I realized that she wasn't exactly bratty.

She'd been a toddler when my Daddy and Clarice had gotten together and was a normal little kid. I was the person she attached herself to. I was her big sister, so she bugged me the most. I felt an inexplicable tug when I thought about her. I wished I knew how to contact her daddy. I thought about it briefly as Daddy and I talked about Clarice being back in Wichita Falls. Now that I could drive, I could always borrow Bailey's car and go see Lisa.

I thought about that really hard later that day, after I was lying down reading. I could possibly find Lisa's daddy. I would like to see her and thought about all the ways I could go about doing it. I elaborately planned it all out. After several different ways of working out a reunion with Lisa, I realized that I was only going to have barely a day and a half when I got back to Wichita. I also thought about how confusing it would be for her if I showed up to say hi, after she probably heard that Daddy and I were devils, or whatever bullshit Clarice had told her.

I felt a wave of sadness when I thought about that. I felt so stupid feeling sad about it, but I remembered all the mornings Lisa would crawl in bed with me, still warm from sleep, and snuggle under my covers, as she woke up. I reached up and realized I had tears rolling down my cheeks, as I was remembering her climbing on top of Kevin when he'd spend the night, and we'd all sleep in the family room. Of course, there were the memories of her and Jax too. I smiled ruefully as I wiped the silent tears away. I got up and went in search of a paper towel in the kitchen to blow my nose.

The day Daddy took me back to Wichita Falls, Lena had taken the morning off, so she could see us off. I was touched by that. I realized that I really liked her. Lena talked about me coming down for a little longer the next summer, and I agreed. I'd had a lot of fun with her. I almost wished I'd had a little more time to spend with them but knew that Daddy and I were beginning to irritate each other, a little, so it was probably just as well that this time was shorter. After all, it was a little cramped in such a tiny apartment too, with three people.

I hugged Lena extra hard. I was really happy Daddy was with someone like her. I thought she seemed a lot more stable than that crazy bitch he'd been married to.

When we got back to Wichita Falls, and I hugged my daddy goodbye. I suddenly felt like a little girl and was very sad to say goodbye to him. I'd been chafing for days to get away from him, and suddenly I didn't want to let him go. He noticed I was crying after we hugged and he started chuckling, "Baby girl, it's not the last time you're ever gonna see me."

"I know, Daddy, it just seems like I never see you now. I dunno, I guess I just miss you sometimes," I sniffled.

"Just sometimes?" Daddy asked, good naturedly.

Catching onto the tone he was using, I looked at him and admitted, sarcastically, "Yeah, just sometimes!"

Daddy laughed and hugged me again, "Quit crying! Go have fun with your girlfriend. I'll see you in a few months, okay?"

I looked at Daddy and asked, "A few months?"

Daddy smiled, "Well, yeah, I mean, I don't know exactly when, but I'm assuming it will be a few months!" Then he chuckled. I felt my little girl heart drop. I had hoped he meant he wanted me to come see him at Thanksgiving or Christmas. He'd just been saying it in general. I nodded my head and knew that our moment was over. I hugged him one more time, for good measure, and waved as he pulled out of the driveway.

I was surprised when I got to the door and found that no one was home. She knew I was coming back that day. Thankfully, I knew where the spare key was, so I let myself into the air-conditioned house. I was grateful for the cool air, after standing just a few minutes in the 100+ degrees outside, telling my daddy goodbye. I was a little curious where everybody was. Bailey's car had been outside, so I assumed she was at least home. I carried the small suitcase into her room. I was met with a huge mess and surprise.

Bailey's room looked like her closet had thrown up all over it. There were clothes flung all over the place and my stuff, which had been set up for almost a month, in one spot, was all put away and closed up. My large suitcase was sitting in a corner with everything I owned packed inside of it, I hoped. I walked into the trashed, teenaged girl's room, and moved the three pairs of shorts, and tank top off the top of my closed suitcase, that normally sat opened.

I threw the garments on the bed, with the other discarded clothes, and set my large suitcase down. I opened it and saw that all of my personal stuff was neatly packed inside, along with all the clothes I'd left that had been in the dirty clothes hamper.

I wasn't sure what this was saying, and I was feeling a little discarded by my best friend too.

I took all of my stuff out of Bailey's smaller suitcase, and set it inside my larger one, making sure I had everything ready in case I needed to leave and go wait out my next day and a half somewhere else. I figured if Bailey wasn't going to let me stay, I'd go down to Kevin's. I took out the book that Lena let me have and went into the front room to read until Bailey, or her mom, or Jason got there to let me know what exactly had happened while I'd been gone. Thankfully, I didn't have to wait more than an hour.

The front door banged open, pulling me out of the deep trance I was in while I was reading. I jumped as I heard Bailey coming in, talking animatedly. I looked up, curious who in the world she was talking so fast with. I hardly ever heard her talk to anybody like that, except me.

When Bailey got inside, with the other person, and the door was closed, I felt my mouth flop open. Of all people in the world to walk in the door, Zoey McGee came walking in with Bailey!

Bailey and Zoey had been best friends in 7th grade, while we were at Samson. I had gone to Bowie Elementary with Zoey and didn't like her at all. I tolerated her, as Bailey and I were getting close. Thankfully she left during 7th grade, and I tried to be a good friend to Bailey as she talked about how much she would miss Zoey. She hadn't said her name since 7th grade that I could remember, so I was completely taken by surprise when I saw her come into the room.

"OH!" Bailey exclaimed when she saw me. "DeLaine! Hey, when'd you get here?"

"About an hour and a half ago, or so," I said coolly, as I eyed Zoey. Zoey had the good grace to smile at me. I hadn't heard Bailey say my entire name, in so long, that it stung as she said it.

"You remember Zoey, right?" Bailey asked me, as she began to get reanimated. I nodded my head.

"Hey, DeLaine! How are you! Crazy we are both here at the same time, huh?" Zoey stated in her loud, annoying, fast way of talking. I smiled and nodded my head.

I didn't understand why I felt so pissed about seeing Zoey. I felt possessive about Bailey. I was surprised by my reaction to seeing her with her old, best friend. I felt like Zoey was probably the person Bailey should have been best friends with, in the first place, and not me. I felt like a lame duck, sitting there, in one of the small, gold, velvet rockers, in the front living room of Bailey's house.

I suddenly felt like I didn't fit in here, and wished I could just disappear, immediately. Any small amount of self-esteem I may have gained over the years, since 7th grade, disappeared. I didn't understand why I couldn't do the same. Instead of disappearing though, I smiled a tight, edgy smile at Zoey, and felt my back begin to bristle. If I wasn't mistaken, Zoey was doing the same thing. I don't think Bailey was even aware that both of us seemed to immediately want to claw each other's eyes out. I wanted to claw out Zoey's, so I naturally assumed she felt the same way, especially after reading her body language.

"We just went to the pool. I'm sorry, I guess I wasn't paying attention to the time. I honestly forgot you were coming back today. For some reason I was thinking it was tomorrow," Bailey spoke, still in her happy tone.

"Nope. Today. I was supposed to be back today around lunchtime. That was the day I said the entire time." I said in short, choppy sentences.

Bailey glanced at me. I could tell her happy air was quickly leaving her. She was finally picking up on the tension in the room between me and Zoey, I thought. "Um, I'm sorry, Lala."

I shook my head slightly and smiled. "It's okay, Bailey. Uh, I noticed my suitcase is all packed up. Since Zoey is here, do I need to see if I can stay at Kevin's or something?" I asked, icily.

"What?" Bailey replied, loudly. I glanced at Zoey and could swear I saw an evil, little smile working around the corners of her mouth. "NO! What the hell, DeLaine? There's plenty of room for all of us!" Bailey stated, a little agitatedly.

"I was just wondering since all my stuff was packed," I spoke quietly.

"I just put it all up when I found out that Zoey was coming, so we wouldn't accidentally get any of your stuff mixed in with her stuff," Bailey explained softly.

I looked at my best friend, feeling like a total ass. I knew that she wasn't trying to get rid of me. I just wondered how long she'd known that Zoey was coming and why she hadn't said anything to me. "So, when'd you get here Zoey?" I asked, trying to sound amiable.

Zoey grinned at me. "Oh, I've been here about a week. I called Bailey and told her I was going to get to come see her. I didn't really expect it, but I guess my mom wanted to get rid of me for a week, so she sent me down here!" Zoey laughed, as she finished. I smiled my tight smile again.

"I knew you were going to be here for two more nights and Zoey's leaving tomorrow. I figured we could all make it for one night," Bailey explained, a little defensively. I nodded.

"Sorry about the room. None of those clothes are yours are they?" Zoey asked me, coquettishly.

"No, Bailey packed all my stuff, remember?" I replied, trying to appear nonchalant.

"Oh good!" Zoey smiled. "Well, I'm gonna get dressed, c'mon Bee-Bee!"

Bailey quietly responded, "Okay Zee-Zee." I snapped my head at Bailey. I felt a little bit of a stab in my heart when I realized that she and Zoey had nicknames for each other too. I sat in the chair that I'd been sitting, when they came in. Bailey looked at me as she got to her doorway. "You comin'?"

"Um, I think I'll stay out here while you two get dressed 'Bee-Bee'." I snapped, snidely. Bailey looked at me stricken.

I felt bad, but for some reason I felt like she was being unfaithful to me, in some odd way, with Zoey. I berated myself when the bedroom door closed.

I was angry. I was taking it out on one of the people dearest to me, in the world. I didn't understand why I felt so angry at my best friend, for having another friend. I felt this incredible urge to explode deep in the pit of my stomach. If I wasn't mistaken, I thought I might even be on the verge of feeling the winged Goddess of rage, deep within me, stretching those wicked, flaming wings. I let out a huge unsteady breath. I gulped in air as I swallowed the angry tears that had come to my eyes, when the door closed to Bailey's room.

I wished I could get up and walk down to Kevin's. Even if he wasn't there, I could at least spend the day with Mrs. Strong. I didn't want to spend some of my last hours with Zoey McGee. I thought seriously about getting my suitcase and stomping down Granville to the house on Portland. I realized that was childish. Besides, the suitcase was heavy empty, much less with all my junk in it. I took another great gulping breath of air, into my lungs, and felt myself beginning to get back under control.

While waiting on Bailey and Zoey to come out, Glenda Rains came into the house with some grocery bags. She smiled when she saw me. I jumped up to go to her car and begin carrying in groceries. As I was walking up the cement steps, with the two, brown, paper bags, full of groceries, Zoey and Bailey came out on the porch.

I walked by them, hiding my face behind the paper sacks. The two other girls were able to get the final three bags, so there were no more to go after. Now I would have to face them. I really didn't want to.

"Let's go in my room, okay, Lala?" Bailey suggested, brightly. I looked at her mom, who smiled at me, unknowing what tension had been filling the living room before she got home. I nodded my head and followed her and Zoey into her now cleaned up bedroom.

We sat on the lime green carpet and listened as Zoey talked faster than anyone else that I knew. I still felt incredibly uncomfortable and was hoping that I could put up with her until after 5:00. I would call Kevin then, and try to go see him, to get away from Zoey. Maybe I'd just spend the night with him again. I smiled as I remembered how the night had gone when I'd spent it with him. As Zoey and Bailey talked, I lost myself inside of my head, while trying to appear interested, as I remembered every stroke, caress and kiss of that night. I wanted to remember running my fingers through the hair that looked like spun gold, in the sunlight, as his mouth covered my own.

Finally at 5:30, I asked Bailey if I could borrow her phone. She suggested I go in Jason's room, since he was gone, and it was quieter. I smiled, gratefully, that she understood how extremely loud her friend was. I went inside the dark, cave-like room of Jason Rains and smelled the unmistakable aroma of pot and cigarettes.

I looked at the windows and noticed he had something covering them, to make the room darker. Listening to the dull trilling noise of Kevin's phone, as it rang, I could feel myself getting more excited at the thought of seeing him before I left. I knew I'd promised to get on with living my life in Corpus and not halfway in both places, I now thought of as home. I didn't want to think about this promise though. I just wanted to see Kevin.

Just as I was about to give up on Kevin answering, I heard a gruff "Hello!"

"Kev?" I asked, hesitantly.

"Uh, no, this is Freddie."

"Freddie?" I asked confused. "Freddie Black?"

I heard Freddie begin to laugh, "Yeah, that's right."

"Oh, um, is Kevin there?" I asked, uncertainly.

I could hear suppressed giggles and the phone was being moved around against something, but I didn't know what. Finally, I heard Kevin grunt, "Yeah?"

"Kevin?" I asked, a little taken aback.

"Yeah?"

"Um, I'm back," I was uncertain what I should say to this gruff version of Kevin. I had just been sitting there remembering all the sweet things that we'd shared the last night we'd spent together. This Kevin, and that Kevin, seemed like two different people, entirely.

"Okay," Kevin barked, shortly. I heard more suppressed giggles in the background, and the phone moving around.

"Well, I just thought I'd let you know," I declared, a bit more irritably.

"Okay," again the short answer from Kevin.

"Whatever!! If you want to see me before I leave, like you said, I'll be here until day after tomorrow." I hung up, feeling broken hearted.

All the sweetness I'd left Wichita Falls feeling for Kevin was wiped out in just a minute. I sat on the side of Jason Rains' bed, smelling the deep smells of old pot, cigarette smoke and something that smelled a little like incense. I flopped back on his bed. I just wanted to go to sleep. It was the only way I could escape how I felt right now. I just didn't know what to do. I didn't want to go face Zoey, in Bailey's room, and listen to their stupid 'Zee-Zee & Bee-Bee' bullshit. I couldn't go to Kevin, which is where I would have run to, in order to escape. Finally, after sighing deeply, I drug myself off of Jason's bed and walked back to Bailey's bedroom.

When I walked in, she and Zoey had decided that we needed to go drag Kemplar and eat at Sonic, instead of eating what Bailey's mom was cooking.

I smiled what I hoped was a bright smile and grabbed my purse. I sure hoped that Bailey stopped somewhere quickly, so I could step out of her cute little Sunbird and smoke. I needed a cigarette in a bad way.

As we began to get into the car, Zoey and I both looked at one another, sizing the other up, as far as who would get to sit in the front, and who'd have to crawl behind the seat, to reach the back. When Zoey offered to ride in the back, I felt like she was trying to make me look like a bitch, insisting on sitting in front, so I told her that was fine, because I couldn't smoke in the car unless the window was rolled all the way down. We were going slowly, and since we wouldn't be doing that for a while, it didn't matter if I sat in the front or not.

Zoey looked at me and griped, "You smoke? Oh my God! You remember when we used to sneak Jason's cigs, in 7th grade, Bee-Bee? Well, if you're going to smoke, you can't do it while I'm in the car! I can't stand cigarettes." Zoey grumbled, wrinkling her nose.

I began to say something snide, when Bailey stated, "Zoey, if Lala wants to smoke, when we're sitting at Sonic, she can. She doesn't have to get out. Besides, I still smoke sometimes too, when I'm out partying!"

Zoey began to whine that if her clothes smelled like cigarette smoke, she'd get in so much trouble, because her mom would think she was smoking. I looked at her and couldn't help it, "But if you hate them so much, why in the world would she think that? Couldn't you just tell her you were at Mama Z's or something and there were people smoking next to us?"

"Um, well, one time I tried smoking again, and she smelled it, and I got in trouble," Zoey explained. I had my head down and rolled my eyes. I popped the seat up, and went ahead and crawled into the back. I figured it was better this way, so if I needed to roll my eyes, as Zoey talked, she wouldn't catch me and my expressive face. I wished she would disappear. I wished she'd go already. I wished it was already tomorrow, then I stopped myself. Tomorrow would be my last day. What if Kevin didn't come see me before tomorrow night, I wondered? As I sat in the backseat, I was lost in thought, as we drove the streets I'd grown up walking up and down, all hours of the day and night.

By 11 p.m. we were safely back in Bailey's turquoise and lime green room. She and Zoey were still just jabbering away. I was trying hard to appear interested, but I couldn't help it. My mind wasn't even in this room.

When I looked at the clock, and saw it said 12:30, I began to yawn and leaned my head on my arm, on the edge of Bailey's bed, that I was leaning against. I felt that there was no point in hoping to see Kevin tonight. I wondered if he would make me wait until the next night. Each time I thought about it, I felt myself get a little more anxious.

My eyes were getting heavy as I listened to Zoey's mouth moving 90 miles an hour. Just as I closed them, because I couldn't keep them open any longer, I thought I heard a popping noise behind me, at Bailey's window. I opened my eyes and looked at Bailey and Zoey. Zoey squatted down and looked terrified. I looked at Bailey and she and I both began to grin. "Geez, Zoey! Somebody's at the window! What's wrong with you?" Bailey asked, rolling her eyes now. If I wasn't mistaken I heard a little bit of an edge in my best friend's voice.

Bailey shut off her lights, so she could see out the window. I hoped it was Kevin, but was worried it might be Donny too. I hadn't seen him since I'd been back. Bailey and Zoey had talked about how the couple had gotten into a big fight, the night before. I felt my heart leap when Bailey stated, "Lala! We've got company!"

Turning to look at her I was confused. "We've got company?"

"Uh-huh! There are two of them out there!" Bailey was grinning.

I looked at Bailey uncertain who could be out there. One time I would have put money on Levi and Jax, but I hadn't seen Jax all summer. I couldn't believe that Kevin and Donny were both out there. Then I thought about it, because they did work at the same garage. Finally, Bailey just waved both Zoey and me out of her room. We all three snuck out of the front door. I wondered briefly if Zoey knew how to sneak out of the front door as adeptly as Bailey and I did.

The streetlight that sat at the opposite edge of the house next door, added just enough light, but they had changed it from a bright, white light, to a new peachy colored light. Everyone looked a weird orange color in the dark. I knew Kevin's form immediately, but the guy with him didn't look like he could be Donny. We all walked out there, and Kevin and the other guy sat down on the curb. I felt a little angry, and sad, because I'd hoped that if Kevin was coming, he'd come by himself, so we could spend some time together before I had to leave for a whole year, and forget him.

Bailey and Zoey sat out away from the curb, on the blacktop of the street. I was curious why they did that. I stood for a while, uncertain if I should sit down beside them or not. When we were all circled together, I could see then that the guy with Kevin was Freddie Black.

"Man, do any of you have a cigarette?" Freddie asked, breaking the silence. Before I could say a word, Bailey and Zoey both looked at me. I wasn't going to offer a cigarette, since Kevin was there. I hadn't smoked around him. Freddie looked up at me in shock and said, "You smoke, DeLaine?"

I nodded my head. I gave both girls a dirty look that I hoped they could see in the eerie glow of the peach toned light. Kevin looked up at me with a strange look, "Why don't you go get your smokes, Kid?"

Growling, I turned around and began to stomp up to the porch. He knew how much I hated him calling me that! Listening to him and Freddie giggle just incensed me more. I had to remember to be quiet and I managed to get inside and grab my cigarettes. When I got back to the curb, I had already pulled my own cigarette out and chunked the pack at Freddie. While he was digging his own out, I lit mine and inhaled deeply, glaring at Kevin. "Go ahead, Sparky! Get you one! I mean, if you want one that is." He looked at me and I wasn't surprised to see a storm cloud swirling on his beautiful face.

"Nah, kid, I'm not drunk, just stoned. I only smoke when I'm drinkin'!" Kevin explained with a shit-eating grin crossing his face.

I was almost to a livid stage, just because he was acting like a jackass. This was maybe the last time I'd get to see him.

"Well, you do other shit when you're drunk too, but it isn't anything I wanna talk about, in mixed company," I remarked, with a snarky glare. Kevin's eyes snapped up at me. I chose to sit on the asphalt, on the other side of Bailey. I was shocked at how much heat was still in the blacktop, as my thighs touched it.

Looking at Freddie, I decided I couldn't quit making mean digs at Kevin, "So, you guys are stoned?" Freddie started giggling and nodded his head. "Well what the hell? You get stoned and then come over? Why didn't you bring anything over to share?" I said the last word and looked at Kevin. I knew I was pushing his buttons, but he knew he'd pushed mine by coming over stoned, with Freddie.

Freddie started giggling and volunteered, "Well darlin' I got another doobie right here! Let's spark this bitch up!"

"NO!" Kevin spoke, forcefully.

"What the hell, dude?" Freddie asked and began giggling.

"We don't need to get these girls stoned, dude! We can get into some serious shit! We're both 18!" Kevin stated.

I rolled my eyes. "Oh please! Who the fuck is gonna ask where we got the weed from and who the fuck is gonna care?" Bailey and Zoey were both watching the verbal match occurring between me and Kevin. Poor Freddie was too stoned to really be following much of anything. He slipped the joint back into the chest pocket of his black t-shirt.

After a few minutes of Kevin and me going back and forth with snide remarks, that we continued to veil, he finally said, "DeLaine, come over here with me!" and he pointed to the side of Bailey's house.

I just glared at him and Bailey spoke quietly, "Just be quiet over there! That's right by my parents' bedroom!"

"Don't worry. We aren't going to argue," I assured her, hoping I was right. I knew that we would go over there and Kevin would begin to bitch at me and we'd get into a war of words with each other.

I reluctantly got up and followed Kevin to the side of Bailey's house, to the side yard.

When I got around to where Kevin was waiting for me to follow, I was shocked at how completely black it was in the small nook of the yard. I could see that the house next door had no windows on that side, because they had a garage there. I looked at the Rains' home and was surprised that Bailey's parents' room had no windows either. I reached out in the dark, feeling suddenly a little nervous. I hadn't expected it to be so dark in this corner of the yard. I could tell the grass was really thick, and most likely carpet grass, but other than that, I didn't know anything else. Suddenly I felt a hand reach out and grab my forearm. Just as I began to yell, I felt another hand clamp around my mouth.

I felt Kevin, rather than saw him. He was close and his mouth was right next to mine. "Don't scream, Lainey, it's just me. I know it's dark, but your eyes will get used to it. I can see you. That's all that matters! You're safe!" I felt extremely confused now. I thought I was coming over here so Kevin and I could argue. We'd started with the whole 'Kid' and 'Sparky' routine, which usually led to an argument of some sort.

As I was trying to process all of the conflicting emotions, I suddenly felt Kevin's warm mouth cover mine. I pushed against him, trying to break away from his embrace and kiss. I was angry with him and he was acting like it was no big deal that he'd come over acting like a jackass. "What the hell, Kevin?" I hissed, when I was finally able to pull away.

"DeLaine, c'mere, I'm going to miss you, baby," Kevin said in a weird, voice that sounded like some 'come on' voice, that maybe he used on other girls, but he'd never used on me before.

"Fuck you, Kevin," I snarled, still in a hushed tone. I could feel my heart beating wildly from the fear when I first got into the murky darkness, to the unexpected kiss, to the anger I was feeling at Kevin for acting so weird.

While I stood there, feeling my heart drum out a hard tattoo in my chest, I could hear every once in a while Zoey's quiet laugh, but I couldn't hear Freddie or Bailey, which made me know I was right that Zoey was a loudmouth! I shook my head, as if trying to clear it, and get back to the situation at hand. Kevin had been right. My eyes were adjusting somewhat to the dark, but I still couldn't make out real features. I could feel him, still standing close to me. He hadn't stepped back, but he wasn't touching me. I couldn't figure out what he wanted.

"What do you want?" I finally whispered.

"You, Lainey. One more time." Kevin responded, quietly.

I felt my heart speed up after he said that. I didn't want to leave angry at him. By the time I came back next summer, he might have completely forgotten me. I was so afraid without getting a note every once in a while, he'd quit caring. "Oh Kevin," I whispered, forlornly. "I don't want you to forget me this coming year."

"Baby, I'll never forget you. I want you one more time, so I'll always remember you," Kevin murmured. His voice sounded strange. Slightly off, I thought, and maybe with just a hint of that stupid come on tone, but then he pleaded, "Please, Lainey," and he took my hand in his. I stepped up and knew that it would bring me to a point of our bodies touching. I tilted my head up, not sure how he would ever find my waiting mouth, but somehow he knew exactly where it was, because as soon as I tilted my head up, his lips found mine.

I wasn't certain how he did it, but somehow he gently laid me back in the carpet grass that we stood on. We kissed over and over, and I was getting lost in him, like I always did. I bumped my arm into the brick of the house and was brought back to reality of lying in the grass, beside my best friend's house, while the boy I loved, undid the zipper of his jeans. He pulled my shorts down, and only off of one leg. He entered me without any of the usual tenderness he normally displayed, and held himself over me, with his arms extended the entire time. I could now see the murky, faint light that was shining towards the back of his head now that I was lying down. I could vaguely see the features of his face. I noticed he looked almost sad. He leaned down finally and began to kiss me, but not in his usual slow and sensual way. Instead, in some quick and hurried fashion he'd never done before. Suddenly he stopped, and he was zipped up and pulling me up from the grass. I was still a little shocked at the brevity of all of it.

"Kevin?" I spoke cautiously.

"What?" he answered, sounding a little cross.

"What happened just now?" I asked, quietly.

"If you gotta ask, I musta sucked," he said with the King Kevin, smart assed remarks that I'd remembered him for, in the beginning.

"Just forget it," I groused, as I went to walk around him.

Kevin grabbed my wrist, "Lainey, I'm sorry. I'm stoned. I'm sorry." He brought his face up to mine and tenderly kissed me one more time. I could have wept when he kissed me.

We walked out from around Bailey's house, and back down the slope of her front yard. Bailey was sitting on the curb, with Freddie Black, and their heads were together.

Zoey McGee was sitting on the asphalt still. When we walked up, I saw Freddie and Bailey begin acting weird and moving around quickly.

As we reached them, I knew exactly what was happening, because I'd done the exact same behavior before. When Kevin saw finally that Freddie was trying to stub out the joint he and Bailey had been sharing, I thought he was going to get pissed. Instead, he motioned for Freddie to pass the joint to him. I stood there and wondered what in the hell this night was supposed to mean. I was feeling lost and unsure on everything.

I looked at Zoey and asked, "So, why aren't you getting stoned too?"

"I don't smoke pot," Zoey replied, with a bit of a haughty air. I nodded my head and walked over to Kevin. I motioned for him to hand me the joint. He gave me a glaring look. I was going to get mad if he didn't give it to me, but he did, after more than a moment's hesitation.

"Just this once," he stated, quietly. I smiled sweetly and winked at him. If I was going to be confused, I may as well be good and confused, I figured.

Freddie began giving Kevin a hard time about our time on the side of Bailey's house. Kevin told him to shut up. Bailey looked at me and her eyebrows shot up. I shot my own up at her as well. I wasn't sure what I should say. Zoey continued to stand apart from the four of us. I was surprised to realize I was getting stoned with my best friend for the first time. I wondered why I was forever being two different people, when I was here and then in Corpus. I was surprised when Kevin finally wrapped his arm around my shoulders. Bailey and Zoey went inside, eventually, and got all of us cokes. The four of us who had been smoking pot had dry mouths, from getting stoned.

I could tell Zoey was acting different towards Bailey. I was just hoping she'd mouth off to her, because I was always standing up for everybody, except Bailey. I wanted to protect her and prove my loyalty. No one had to stick up for anyone though in the end. We ended up staying outside until well after 4 a.m. and when the boys finally left, I hoped that Kevin would at least kiss me goodbye.

Instead, Kevin acted as if he was going to kiss me, and then he stopped suddenly, saying, "Come down to my house. I'm off tomorrow!" I looked at him strangely and he smiled at me. "Night night, Lainey! Sweet dreams!" then the love of my life pulled away from me and was walking back down the road.

I watched as the darkness swallowed him and the weird, skinny, ghostly looking Freddie Black. I still felt a vast amount of confusion about the physical interaction we'd had on the side of Bailey's house. He'd started out as if he was going to argue with me, and then he had turned his sweet and loving Kevin on. Just as quickly he became this callous jackass worse than Chance Cahill. I shook my head unsure what I was supposed to do with this whole night.

Chapter 58

The next afternoon, while Bailey was spending some last minute time with Zoey, I walked down Granville to tell Kevin goodbye. I hoped that he would show up in the middle of the night, even though I had to leave early to get on a bus. I could sleep on the bus. At least I could ask him to come see me tonight. I needed to tell his mama goodbye, too.

When I got to his house, Kevin was outside in his black Camaro, with Freddie, messing with his stereo. He acted like King Kevin around Freddie. I just ignored it, as I talked to the sallow looking guy, who looked like he needed to eat. Freddie started griping at Kevin about taking him to a convenience store to buy a pack of cigarettes.

Freddie and I had been talking about how we were angry that cigarettes were now $1.00, and they were talking about making them $1.25. We both said if it happened, we would just quit than to spend that much on cigarettes. Freddie was talking about a place that was still selling them for $0.75 and I said, "Shit, I'm goin' with you guys! I'm gonna buy a few packs, if I can get 'em for that little!"

Kevin slammed whatever component he'd been messing with and yelled, "Load up then! Let's go! Get the fuck in the back, Freddie! I ain't ridin' with a dude in the front, if I got a hot chick in the car!" I started smiling at the compliment. Kevin turned his stereo up almost as loud as Jason Rains would've had his. As soon as he turned the key in the ignition, Styx kicked off talking about tonight being the night someone was gonna make history. When they sang about these being the best of times I felt a strange tug. Everything about the song made me think about what I was leaving.

Once we were all in the car, Kevin squealed away from the curb, in front of his house. I was shocked. He'd been such a conscientious driver when I'd ridden with him before. Since my wreck with my mom, I was not exactly a good passenger. The way Kevin was driving was scaring me, but I didn't want to look uncool, so I grabbed the door handle in a death grip. I was grateful the store we went to was less than a mile down Fairfax, back towards Keller. I didn't think about it, but I hadn't brought my purse, so I could only safely smuggle three full packs under my shirt when I got to Bailey's, but that was still a good buy.

When we left, we zoomed back down Fairfax, like we were going to Kevin's, but he cut off on another street that I hadn't gone on before. He swerved in and out, and before I knew it, we were on Andrew Street, which was Jax's street. I suddenly felt a little uneasy.

I wasn't sure what Kevin was doing, but he screeched to a stop in front of Kevin Welks' house. I began to get mad. Just seeing the house made me angry as I remembered what had happened there. Kevin popped his seat and leaned up, as Freddie climbed out of the back. I looked over to the opposite side and Freddie called out, "Well, see ya, DeLaine! You're a pretty cool chick! Much cooler than your faggy step-brother!"

"Uh, thanks, I think, but he isn't even my step-brother anymore," I was unsure how I was supposed to respond. "You goin' to Welks' house?" I asked.

Freddie shook his head, "Nah, I live across the street! See ya 'Kid'!"

"Hey," I barked, sternly. Freddie looked at me a little concerned. "Only Kevin gets away with that, and even then, he really doesn't!" Freddie broke into a grin. I noticed how crooked and yellow his teeth looked.

"Gotcha K-...DeLaine! Have a good trip back!" Freddie was grinning again. I nodded and couldn't help myself, I began to smile back at him.

"Later, dude," Kevin called, and he peeled out in the middle of the street. I was back to gripping the door handle for dear life. Suddenly, he came to an abrupt halt. I wondered what was wrong. When I looked at Kevin, he smiled at me sweetly, "Just thought I'd stop here, one time for you, in a car, since you've never seen our corner from car level!" I began laughing and his long graceful hand covered mine. He drove slower to his house.

I went into his house when we got back and told his mom goodbye. I hadn't planned on the trip to the store, or that Freddie would have been there taking up valuable time, so before I was really ready, it was time for me to go back to Bailey's. I didn't want to appear rude and not spend the time I could with her. I did come to see her too, and not just Kevin. I was certain Zoey was gone too, so I wasn't too upset about going back this time.

After receiving my warm hug from Jean Strong, I let go reluctantly. She pulled me tight one more time and whispered, "Remember, just a year, darling girl! Give it a chance, honey! You have to for yourself. Kevin will still be here." I felt the tears sting my eyes. I closed my eyes tightly.

Kevin was standing in the doorway to the kitchen and he called quietly, "C'mon Lainey, I'll give you a ride, okay?"

I turned around and smiled at him and nodded. I turned to Mrs. Strong and told her I loved her. She seemed a little surprised and said, "Why, I know that, darlin'! I love you too!" She squeezed my hands and just like that, I was out the door and once again sitting in the passenger seat of Kevin's black Camaro.

He always seemed to know when I needed his tenderness. "It's just a year, Lainey. You know we're not going anywhere." I nodded, as a quiet sob escaped me. I looked at my hands as I held them in my lap. Kevin reached over and pulled me to him. I felt so stupid for once again getting one of his t-shirts wet with tears.

After just a few moments, I pulled away hard, "This is silly, Kevin! I'm being so stupid! I'm sorry!"

"You aren't stupid, Lainey! It's okay. I know you'll miss Mom."

I looked at Kevin wondering if he knew what he just said. "I'm gonna miss YOU, Kev! You have no clue how much I'm going to miss YOU! Yes, I'm gonna miss your mama but I'm gonna miss you! I don't know what I'm going to do!"

Kevin sat there for a brief moment, "You're going to go back to Corpus and you're going to have a life, DeLaine! You are going to quit living in two places because you can't do that. I want you to be happy, baby! You promised! You have a real boyfriend this year! Quit fuckin' around with that damned Cahill loser!"

I looked at him wondering how he knew I'd begun to see Chance again. He smiled and without saying a word, he tilted his head at me, as if to say he'd known all along. I ducked my head down and shook it. "I promise." I sighed, shakily. Kevin pulled the Camaro out gently this time.

I didn't want our time to end and said just as we pulled in front of Bailey's house, "Will you come over, later tonight?"

Kevin sat there for a few seconds and then said, "Okay. I'll be over. Go Little Lainey! I'll see you later!" He leaned over and tenderly kissed me and I jumped out. I had already forgotten his strange behavior the night before and how he had acted when Freddie was around. My Kevin was back and that was all I cared about.

Bailey and I talked the rest of the evening about her and Donny. She admitted she didn't think they were actually going to make it. I told her that she needed to remember that he wasn't the only boy in the world and she looked at me funny. I started laughing because I knew we were both thinking about me and Kevin.

I was happy to have my old friend back. I had felt like I'd lost her for a big part of the summer. I felt like I was constantly walking on eggshells and felt so relieved to hear her say she was having doubts about Donny.

We talked about my promise to Kevin and his mom, to have a life in Corpus this year, and she told me that she thought that it was for the best. She felt that no matter what, I would come back after graduation, and we'd get an apartment and go to Midwestern.

I loved it when we dreamed about what life would be like when we graduated from high school. I couldn't wait to get away from my mom and all the insanity of her alcoholism. I no longer had Clarice to fear, or Geoffrey, so the only enemy I had left, once I took out my mom's drinking, would be time until graduation. It wouldn't hurt me to go ahead and have a life, just for a little bit, so I'd know what it was about, without Kevin.

My bus left the next morning at 7, and by midnight we both decided we had better go ahead and try to sleep for a little while, since we had to get up at 5. I was trying to hide my sadness from Bailey that Kevin hadn't shown up to see me, and still held out hope that he would show up any minute.

When we were lying in bed talking, and Bailey began to talk more and more softly, I knew that she would be sound asleep shortly. After her breathing became soft and regular, I lay there listening to every slight noise, hoping against hope that Kevin would be tapping on the window. I felt my own eyes begin to grow heavy after a while.

Before I knew it, Bailey's digital alarm clock was buzzing and she was shaking me awake. My eyes felt like they had been sandblasted. I also felt extremely sad. I knew that Kevin wouldn't see me anymore before I left. I felt hurt and angry. He had come over the only time he could spend time with me, and acted like a jackass. I had hoped he would make up for it by coming over, by himself, so we could go back to being Lainey and Kevin, like always. He had told me he would, then he didn't. I didn't think it was because he couldn't. I thought it was because he didn't want to. He wanted me to leave and move on.

I hugged Bailey at the bus station, and climbed on board, sad to leave, just as I always was when I left Wichita Falls. I felt tears rolling down my cheeks as the bus pulled out of the concrete terminal. I wondered what all would change in the next year. I didn't even pretend that I'd come back before next summer. I knew that Christmas or Spring Break would never happen. I'd just been fortunate my freshman year in some ways. I wondered how I was supposed to change who I was in one year's time.

I'd lost weight this year that was true. I still felt horribly ugly though. I just wanted to be invisible. I didn't want anyone to be my friend, because if they ever knew what I lived with, they'd drop me like a hot potato. It was easier to not care, or have anyone around, than to get attached and then be heartbroken. I was happy that Kelly and Robin Stubbs had been around so long that they knew everything, so I wasn't completely alone.

I had signed up for a few different things this year, since I was allowed more electives. I was excited about Theater Arts. I wasn't sure if I'd be any good, even though I thought I might be. I could pretend to be outgoing, but deep inside I was so insecure. I was afraid that just like all the other things I'd attempted in the Arts, I'd suck at it too, but hoped I might be wrong.

The bus drove across the Nueces Bridge, and I looked out the window at the bridge where I went to river parties. I sighed and leaned my head back in the air conditioning of the bus and closed my eyes. My real vacation was almost done. I wouldn't have to go back to school but my real life was about to begin again. I knew everything was about to rear its ugly head, and I truly dreaded it. I wanted life to be like it was when I was with Kevin, at his house.

Sighing, I felt myself drift off, as I remembered the beautiful night I'd spent with Kevin. I wished I had left well enough alone and let that be my last memory of him. Instead, I had the confusing night with him and Freddie Black showing up, while Zoey McGee was at Bailey's. The night when Kevin had been a jackass one minute, and then took me around the side of Bailey's house and was his normal loving self. Then he turned on some weird, creepy, come on lines that he must have thought would work. I thought that was stupid, since he knew me better than just about anyone. My mind kept drifting back to the tender night we spent together, and the exquisite feelings he had awakened deep inside of me. He didn't get even close to that on the side of Bailey's house, which confused me.

As usual I felt greatly befuddled by Kevin Strong. I also knew that he was so far away from me now, not just in the social caste of school, especially since he wasn't even in school anymore, but in miles. I'd never felt further from him until now. It was as if the promise I'd made to him about not contacting him until the next summer somehow closed some magical doorway that had previously been opened between us, no matter how many miles separated us. I felt as if the invisible tether that I'd likened us having, had been irrevocably damaged. I had thought it was cut away when I'd come home before 8th grade started and found out he and Lori had sex during the summer. It had reappeared though, in time, and I'd never felt the tear of it again, until now.

This time though, it didn't feel cut or torn. It felt completely gone. I felt as if I were going out all alone and it scared me. I didn't want anyone to know how afraid I was. I didn't have him as my back up, in my head right now. For some reason I felt as if he had hypnotized me and wasn't even going to be a thought or care to me, at all, any longer. I felt such great sadness, but I didn't know how to ignore it.

We pulled into the terminal in downtown Corpus Christi. I saw my mom standing on the side, waiting for my bus. I smiled, despite myself, when I saw her familiar face. I climbed out of the bus and when I felt the familiar muggy, sea air blowing into the diesel stench of the bus terminal, I tried to be positive.

I walked over to my mama and hugged her tight. I suddenly wanted to be a little girl again. I wanted my mama to be who she was when I was little and not to be the alcoholic she was now. I wanted to never feel confused about Kevin again. I just wanted to feel safe. It seemed now there was no place that was safe for me.

Walking to our car I couldn't help but think about the Styx song that Kevin blared in his Camaro the day before, singing about memories of yesterday lasting a lifetime.

I prayed my memories from this summer weren't all I'd have for the rest of my life. Sighing, I climbed into the Thunderbird and prayed I could get through the next school year without losing Kevin forever.

www.ingramcontent.com/pod-product-compliance
Lightning Source LLC
Chambersburg PA
CBHW030826310726
48980CB00006B/662/J
9780578474243